# SSSSSS

Asleep, princess Ya[...] window by which Jorian [...] Silently, he searched the bedroom for the cache of ancient spells known as the Kist of Avlen. The candle in the room had burnt·down and gone out, but enough light came through the doorway for his purpose.

Jorian found that none of the chests ranged around the walls was that which he sought. Nor did there seem to be any secret compartments in the walls. At last he discovered the Kist in the most obvious place: under Yargali's bed. It was a battered little chest with brass clasps.

Moving as if treading on razors, Jorian knelt beside the bed. Slowly he pulled the Kist towards himself by one of the brass handles. Grasping the two handles, he stood up and stepped back.

Then, to his utter horror, the princess Yargali muttered in her sleep and rolled over. Her eyes opened. "Ssso!" she said.

For an instant, Jorian was rooted to the spot. In that instant, Yargali changed. Her body elongated; her limbs shrank. The dark-brown skin changed to olive-green scales. Her face bulged out and became a long, scaly muzzle.

She was a serpent—but such a serpent as Jorian had never heard of outside myths and legends. The head, as large as that of a horse, reared up from the pile of coils. A forked tongue flicked out from the jaws. In the middle, the serpent's body was as big around as Jorian's waist.

Jorian thought with lightning speed. If he tried to run around the bed to get to the window and his rope, he would come within easy lunging distance of the head. If he tried to get out of the other room's windows, he would fall and break a leg or his neck.

The serpent poured off the creaking bed and came for him . . .

# BAEN BOOKS by L. SPRAGUE DE CAMP

*The Fallible Fiend*
*Rivers of Time*

**With Catherine Crook de Camp**
*The Incorporated Knight*

**With David Drake**
*The Undesired Princess and The Enchanted Bunny*
*Lest Darkness Fall and To Bring the Light*

**With Fletcher Pratt**
*The Complete Compleat Enchanter*

**With Christopher Stasheff**
*The Enchanter Reborn*
*The Exotic Enchanter*

# THE RELUCTANT KING

## L. SPRAGUE de CAMP

# THE RELUCTANT KING

This is a work of fiction. All the characters and events portrayed in this book are fictional, and any resemblance to real people or incidents is purely coincidental.

Previously published in three volumes as *The Goblin Tower,* copyright © 1968, *The Clocks of Iraz,* copyright © 1971 and *The Unbeheaded King,* copyright © 1983, all by L. Sprague de Camp.

A Baen Book

Baen Publishing Enterprises
P.O. Box 1403
Riverdale, N.Y. 10471

ISBN: 0-671-87746-1

Cover art by Ken Tunnell

First printing, October 1996

Distributed by Simon & Schuster
1230 Avenue of the Americas
New York, N.Y. 10020

Printed in the United States of America

# Author's Note

While the reader may, naturally, pronounce the names in this tale as he pleases, for Penembic names I had the following scheme in mind: *ue* and *oe* as in German; *ui* (obscured) as in "biscuit"; other vowels more or less as in Spanish and consonants as in English. Hence Ayuir rhymes with "fire"; Chaluish, with "demolish"; Chuivir, with "severe." The *h* in Sahmet, Fahramak is sounded: "sah-h'm-met," etc. The scheme is based upon the phonetics of Turkish.

# Part I

# The Goblin Tower

*To my fellow swashbuckler-in-phantasy,*
*Lin Carter*

# CONTENTS

# CONTENTS

# I

# A Length of Rope

"A curious custom," said the barbarian, "to cut off your king's head every five years. I wonder your throne finds any takers!"

On the scaffold, the headsman brushed a whetstone along the gleaming edge of his ax, dropped the stone into his pouch, squinted along the blade, and touched it here and there with his thumb. Those in the crowd below could not see his satisfied smile because of the black hood, which—save for the eye holes—covered his head. The ax was neither a woodcutter's tool nor a warrior's weapon. Whereas its helve, carven of good brown oak, was that of a normal ax, its blue steel head was unwontedly broad, like a butcher's cleaver.

The scaffold rose in the midst of the drill ground, outside of the walls of Xylar City near the South Gate. Here, nearly all the folk of the city were gathered, as well as hundreds from outlying towns and villages. Around the base of the scaffold, a battalion of pikemen in black meshmail over scarlet coats was ranked four deep, to make sure that no unauthorized person reached the scaffold during the ceremony, and likewise that the victim did not escape. The two outer ranks faced outward and the two inner, inward.

Around the three sides of the scaffold, the notables of Xylar, in crimson and emerald and gold and white, sat on benches. Another rank of soldiers sundered the quality from the commonality. The latter, in brown and buff and black, stood in an expectant, amorphous mass, which filled the greater part of the field.

5

On the western side of the platform, this multitude surged against the inner ranks of soldiery. Here the throng consisted mainly of young men. Besides the hundreds of mechanics from the city and peasants from the farms, it included a sprinkling of the younger gentry. Hucksters wormed their way through this throng, selling cakes, sausages, fruits, sardines, wine, beer, cider, parasols, and goodluck charms. Outside the crowd of spectators, armored horsemen, with the scarlet hourglass of Xylar on their white surcoats, patrolled the edge of the field.

Overhead, a white sun blazed in a cloudless sky. A puffy little wind ruffled the leaves of the oaks and poplars and gums that fenced the field. It fluttered the red-and-white pennants that streamed from the tops of the flagpoles at the corners of the scaffold. A few of the leaves of the gums had already turned from green to scarlet.

Seated among the notables, Chancellor Turonus answered the barbarian's question: "We have never had trouble in finding candidates, Prince Vilimir. Behold how they throng about the western side of the scaffold!"

"Will the head be thrown yonder?" asked Prince Vilimir around his forefinger, wherewith he was trying to pry loose a piece of roast from between his teeth. Although he was clean-shaven, Vilimir's long, light, gray-streaked hair, fur cap, fur jacket, and horsehide boots with the hair on gave him a shaggy look. His many massive ornaments of gold and silver tinkled when he moved. He had led the losing faction in an intertribal quarrel over who should be the next cham of the Gendings and hence was in exile. His rival, who was also his uncle, now ruled that fierce nomadic horde.

Turonus nodded. "Aye, and the catcher shall be our new king." He was stout and middle-aged, swathed in a voluminous azure cloak against the chill of the first

cool day of autumn. "The Chief Justice will cast the
thing yonder. It is a rule that the king must let his hair
grow long, to give the judge something to grasp. Once
a king had his whole head shaven the night before the
ceremony, and the executioner had to pierce the ears
for a cord. Most embarrassing."

"By Greipnek's beard, an ungrateful wight!" said Vilimir, a wolfish grin splitting his lean, scarred face. "As
if a lustrum of royal luxe were not enough . . . Be that
not King Jorian now?" The Shvenish prince spoke Novarian with fair fluency, but with a northern accent that
made "Jorian" into "Zhorian."

"Aye," said the Chancellor, as a little procession
marched slowly through the lane kept open by soldiers
between the South Gate and the scaffold.

"He took me hunting last month," said Vilimir. "He
struck me as a man of spirit—for a sessor, that is." He
used a word peculiar to the nomads of Shven, meaning
a non-nomad or sedentary person. Among nomads, the
word was a term of contempt, but the Chancellor saw
fit to ignore this. The exile continued: "I also found
him a great talker—too much so for his own good,
methinks, but amusing to listen to."

The Chancellor nodded absently, for the procession
had now come close enough to recognize faces. First
came the royal band, playing a dirge. Then paced the
white-bearded Chief Justice of Xylar in a long, black
robe, with a golden chain about his neck. Four halberdiers, in the midst of whom towered the king, followed.
All those near the lane through which the party proceeded, and many in other parts of the field, sank to
one knee as the king passed them.

King Jorian was a tall, powerful young man with a
ruddy skin, deep-set black eyes, and coarse black hair
that hung to his shoulders. His face, otherwise shaven,
bore a fierce mustache that swept out like the horns
of a buffalo. A prominent scar crossed his nose—which
had a small kink in it—and continued diagonally down

across his left cheek. He was stripped to his slippers and a pair of short, silken breeches, and his wrists were bound behind his back. A crown—a slender band of gold with a dozen short, blunt, erect spikes—was secured to his head by a chin strap.

Prince Vilimir murmured: "I have never seen a crown with a—how do you say it—a strap of the chin."

"It is needed, to keep crown and head together during the casting of the Lot of Imbal," explained Turonus. "Once, years ago, the crown came off as the head was thrown. One man caught the crown, another the head, and each claimed the throne. A sanguinary civil war ensued."

After the soldiers came a small, lean, dark-brown man in a coarse brown robe, with a bulbous white turban on his head. His long, silky, white hair and beard blew about. A rope was wound around his waist, and he bore a kind of satchel by a strap over his shoulder.

"The king's spiritual adviser," said Chancellor Turonus. "It seems hardly meet that the king of Xylar be sent off by a heathen from Mulvan, rather than by one of our own holy priests. But Jorian insisted, and it seemed but just to grant his last request."

"Who—how did the king come to know the fellow?" asked Vilimir.

Turonus shrugged. "For the past year, he has entertained all sorts of queer persons at the palace. This mountebank—your pardon, the Holy Father Karadur—drifted in, doubtless having fled in disgrace from his own land after having been caught in some vile goëtic witchery."

Then came four beautiful young women, the king's wives. A fifth had given birth the day before and was judged not strong enough to attend the ceremony. The four present were gorgeous in silks and jewels and gold. After the wives came the shaven-headed, purple-robed high priest of Zevatas, the chief god of the Novarian pantheon; then a score of palace officials, and the ladies-in-waiting. Last of all came Kaeres the joiner, Xylar's leading director of funerals, and six cronies of the king carrying one of Kaeres' new coffins on their shoulders.

As the procession reached the foot of the scaffold, the band fell silent. After a low-voiced consultation, the Chief Justice mounted the steps of the scaffold, followed by two of the four halberdiers.

King Jorian kissed his four wives goodbye. They clung round his neck, weeping and covering his broad, heavy-featured face with kisses.

"Na, na," said Jorian in a heavy bass voice, with a rustic Kortolian accent. "Weep not, ma pretty lassies.

"The gods, who from their puerile pipes a billion
     bubbles blow,
Have blown us here. We waft and wobble, iridesce
     and glow,
Then burst; but from these pipes a billion bubbles
     more shall flow.

"Within the year, ye'll all have better husbands than I ever was to you."

"We do not wish other husbands! We love only you!" they wailed.

"But the weans needs must have stepfathers," he reminded them. "Now get along back to the palace, so as not to see your lord's blood flow. You, too, Estrildis."

"Nay!" cried the wife addressed—though pretty, the least beautiful of the four, stocky and blue-eyed. "I will watch you to the end!"

"You shall do as I say," said Jorian gently but firmly. "You shall go on your own feet, or I will have you carried. Which shall it be?"

The two soldiers who had remained on the ground laid gentle hands on the woman's arms, and she broke away to run, weeping, after the others. Jorian called: "Farewell!" and turned back to the scaffold.

As the king mounted the stairs, his gaze roved hither and yon. He smiled and nodded as his eye caught those of acquaintances in the crowd. To many, he seemed altogether too cheerful for a man about to lose his head.

As, with a steady step, Jorian reached the platform of the scaffold, the two halberdiers who had preceded him snapped to attention and brought their right fists up to their chests, over their hearts, in salute. Behind him came the Mulvanian holy man and the high priest of Zevatas.

On the far, western side of the platform, a few feet from the edge, rose the block, freshly carved and shining with new red paint. Between the flagpoles on the western side, a length of netting, a yard high, was stretched to make sure that the head should not roll off the platform.

Leaning on his ax, the headsman stood beside the block. Like Jorian, he was stripped to breeks and shoes. Although not so tall as the king, the executioner was longer of arm and even more massive of torso. Despite the hood, Jorian knew that his slayer was Uthar the butcher, who kept a stall near the South Gate. Since Xylar was too small and orderly a city-state to support a full-time executioner, it hired Uthar from time to time for the task. Jorian had personally consulted the man before approving the choice.

"The great trick, Sire," Uthar had said, "be to let the weight of the ax do the work. Press not; give your whole attention to guiding the blade in its fall. A green headsman thinks he needs must help the blade; so he presses, and the stroke goes awry. The blade be heavy enough to sever any man's neck—even so mighty a one as Your Majesty's—if suffered to fall at its natural speed. I promise Your Majesty shan't feel a thing. Your soul will find itself in its next incarnation before you wite what has happened."

Jorian now approached the headsman with a grin on

his face. "Hail, Master Uthar!" he cried in a hearty voice. "A lovely day, is it not? By Astis' ivory teats, if one must have one's head cut off, I can imagine no fairer day whereon to have the deed performed."

Uthar dropped to one knee. "You—Your Majesty—'tis a fine day, surely—Your Majesty will forgive me for any pain or inconvenience I cause him in the discharge of my duties?"

"Think nothing of it, old man! We all have our duties, and we all come to our destined ends. My pardon is yours, so long as your edge be keen and your arm be true. You promised that I should not feel a thing, remember? I shouldn't like you to have to strike twice, like a new recruit hacking at a pell."

Jorian turned to the Chief Justice. "Most eminent Judge Grallon, are you ready with your speech? Take a hint and make it not too long. Long speeches bore the hearer, be the speaker never so eloquent."

The Chief Justice looked uncertainly at Jorian, who indicated by a jerk of his head that he was to proceed. The magistrate pulled a scroll from his girdle and unrolled it. Holding the stick of the scroll in one hand and a reading glass in the other, he began to read. The wind whipped the dangling end of the scroll this way and that, hindering his task. Nevertheless, being familiar with the contents, he droned on.

Justice Grallon began with a résumé of Xylarian history. Imbal the lion god had established this polis many centuries before; he had also bestowed upon it its unique method of choosing a ruler. The magistrate spoke of famous kings of Xylar: of Pellitus the Wise, and Kadvan the Strong, and Rhuys the Ugly.

At last, Judge Grallon came down to the reign of Jorian. He praised Jorian's bravery. He narrated the battle of Dol, when Jorian had destroyed the horde of robbers that had infested the southern marches of the kingdom and had acquired the scar on his face.

". . . and so," he concluded, "this glorious reign has

now come to the end appointed for it by the gods. Today the crown of Xylar shall pass, by the Lot of Imbal, into those hands destined by the gods to receive it. And we have been a true and virtuous folk, these hands will be strong, just, and merciful; if not—not. The king will now receive his final consolation from his holy man."

Old Doctor Karadur had been unwrapping the rope from around his waist and coiling it in the center of the platform. From his satchel he produced a little folding brass stand, which he set down beside the rope. Out of the bag came a brazen dish, which he placed upon the stand. Out, too, came a compartmented pouch, whence he sprinkled various powders into the dish. He put away the pouch, took out flint and steel, and struck sparks into the dish.

There was a green flash and a puff of smoke, which the breeze whipped away. A many-hued little flame danced over the dish, sending up streamers of vapor. The high priest of Zevatas looked sourly on.

Karadur intoned a lengthy prayer of incantation—those listening could not tell which, since the holy man spoke Mulvani. On and on he went, until some of the spectators grew restless. True, they did not wish the ceremony over too soon, since it was the biggest event in their calendar. On the other hand, when it came to hearing the unintelligible chant of a scrawny old fakir and watching him bow his forehead to the platform, a little went a long way.

Then Karadur rose and embraced Jorian, who towered over him. The fire in the brazen dish blazed up and sent out a cloud of smoke, which made those on the platform cough and wipe their eyes. Thus they failed to see Karadur, at the moment when his arms were around Jorian's huge torso, slip a small knife into the hands of the king, which were bound behind him. Karadur whispered:

"How is your courage, my son?"

"Oozing away with every heartbeat. In sooth, I'm frightened witless."

"Face it down, boy! In boldness lies your only safety."

Next, the band played a hymn to Zevatas. The high priest, a gaunt, imposing figure in his purple robe, led the throng in singing the hymn, beating time with his staff of office.

Then the priest bowed his head and prayed that the lot of Jorian's successor should fall upon one worthy of the office. He prayed to the gods to look with favor upon Xylar; he prayed that, in smiting sinners, they would take care not to harm the far more numerous virtuous citizens. His prayer was as long as Karadur's. The head of the cult of the king of the gods could not let a foreign wizard go him one better.

At last the high priest finished. The Chief Justice read a proclamation that whereas, in accordance with Xylar's ancient customs, Jorian's reign had now come to an end, he willingly offered his head as the means whereby the next king should be chosen. Judge Grallon finished with a sweeping gesture towards the block, indicating that Jorian should now lay his head upon it.

"Will Your Majesty have a blindfold?" he asked.

"Nay," said Jorian, stepping towards the block, "I will face this with my eyes open, as I did the foes of Xylar."

"One moment, your honor," said Karadur in his nasal Mulvanian accent. "I must—ah—it was agreed that I should cast a final spell, to speed King Jorian's soul to the afterworld, without danger of its being trapped in another incarnation in this one."

"Well, get on with it," said the Chief Justice.

Karadur brought a little brass bell out of his satchel. "When I sound this, smite!" He poured more powders into his dish, which flamed and bubbled.

"Kneel, my royal son," said Karadur. "Fear nought."

The crowd surged forward expectantly. Fathers hoisted small children to their shoulders.

Jorian cast a thoughtful look at the old Mulvani. Then he knelt before the block and bowed his head until his throat rested across the narrow, flat place on top. His chin lay comfortably in the hollow that had been cut in the west side of the block. His eyes, swiveling sideways, kept Uthar the butcher in the periphery of his vision. Uthar, bending over him, brushed Jorian's long, black hair forward to bare his nape.

Karadur uttered another incantation, gesturing with his skinny brown arms. This continued until Jorian's knees began to hurt from kneeling on the hard boards. Stepping back from the block, Uthar took a firm grip on the helve of the ax.

At last the Mulvani tinkled his bell. Jorian, straining to keep the headsman in sight without seeming to do so, felt rather than saw the ax swing up to the vertical. Then the bell tinkled again, meaning that the ax had started down.

Jorian's next action required exquisite timing, and he was not at all sure of success—even though Karadur and he had rehearsed for hours in his private gymnasium, with the old wizard wielding a broom instead of an ax. For one thing, Jorian was a little tired because four of his wives had insisted, the night before, on proof of his love for them.

As the ax descended, Jorian cast off the thongs that bound him, which throughout the ceremony he had been discreetly sawing through with the little knife. Simultaneously, he hurled his body to the left, falling on his side. Since the heavy ax had already begun its downward course, the burly headsman was neither quick enough of apprehension nor strong enough of arm to stop it in midcareer. It thudded into the block, sinking deeply into the red-painted wood.

In one swift movement, Jorian rolled to his feet and put the little knife between his teeth. Karadur cast something more into the dish, which flamed and smoked like a little volcano, sending up a swelling column of green smoke shot with red and purple. The wizard uttered a loud cry, flinging out his arms. Thereupon the coiled rope before him sprang erect, like some monstrous serpent. Its end shot up twenty feet or more, and the upper end disappeared into a kind of haze, as if it had pierced a hole in the sky. A tremendous cloud of smoke arose from the dish, obscuring the vision of those on the platform and hiding them from the spectators below. Some, supposing the king's head to have fallen already, set up a cry of "Red and white! Red and white!"

One long stride brought Jorian to the executioner. With the ax in his hands, Uthar the butcher would have been a formidable foe. But, despite his desperate tugs, the head of the ax remained firmly fixed in the block.

Jorian brought his left fist up in a long, swinging, ox-felling blow against the headsman's jaw. Uthar reeled back against the net and fell off the platform.

A cry from Karadur warned Jorian to turn. One of the mailed halberdiers was lunging towards him, thrusting with his weapon. With the leopard-quick timing that had once already saved his gore, Jorian caught the halberd below the head, just before the spearhead reached his skin. As he jerked the head of the weapon violently to the left, the soldier's lunge drove it past his body.

Seizing the haft with both hands and turning his back on the trooper, Jorian put the shaft on his shoulder and then bent his back, pulling the head of the halberd down. The halberdier, clinging to the shaft, found himself hoisted over Jorian's broad back and hurled head over heels off the platform, to fall with a clash of mail to the ground below.

Clutching the halberd, Jorian span to face the remaining soldier, who stood coughing smoke. The Chief Justice and the high priest of Zevatas scrambled down the stair in such haste that the latter lost his footing and plunged to earth head-first, gravely injuring himself.

Whether for fear or for love of his former lord, the soldier hesitated, holding his halberd at port and neither swinging the ax head nor thrusting with the spear point. Having nothing personal against the man, Jorian reversed his weapon and jabbed the butt against the soldier's armored ribs. A ferocious push sent the trooper tumbling off the scaffold after his comrade.

Thus, twelve seconds after the headsman's blow, Jorian and Karadur found themselves the only persons on the platform. A vast murmur ran through the throng. The events on the scaffold had taken place so quickly and had been so obscured by smoke that nobody on the ground yet really grasped what had happened. It was plain, however, that the execution had not gone as planned. People jostled and shouted questions; the murmur rose to a roar. A sharp command rang out, and a squad of pikemen rushed towards the foot of the stair.

Jorian dropped his halberd and sprang to the rope. Not for nothing had he spent months practising climbing a rope hand over hand, until the muscles of his arms and hands were like steel. As he went up, the rope swayed gently but remained straight and taut. The platform sank beneath him. Somewhere a crossbow snapped, and Jorian heard the swishing hum of the quarrel as it sped past.

Below, the crowd was in a frenzied uproar. Soldiers scrambled up the stair. As they reached the top, Karadur, who had been performing another incantation, dropped spryly off the edge of the platform. Jorian had only a brief glimpse of the wizard; he saw, however, that as Karadur reached the ground his appearance changed. Instead of a deep-brown, white-haired Mulvanian holy man, he was now, to all appearances, a member of the lower Xylarian priesthood, clad in a neat black robe of good stuff. The crowd swallowed him up.

Again came the twang of a bowstring. The missile grazed Jorian's shoulder, raising a welt. The soldiers had reached the platform and were looking doubtfully at the lower end of the rope. The thought flashed across Jorian's racing mind that they would try either to pull it down or to climb up after him.

Sweat poured down his face and his massive, hairy torso as he mounted the last few feet of the rope. He reached the place where the rope turned hazy and disappeared. As his head came level with this terminus, he found that the rope remained as solid and clear as ever, while below him the scene became dim and hazy, as if seen through a gathering fog.

A final, heart-wrenching heave, and the scene below vanished. Around him, instead of empty air, stretched an utterly strange landscape. He lowered his feet and felt earth and grass beneath them.

For the moment, he had not time to examine his new surroundings. Karadur had repeatedly warned him of the importance of recovering the magical rope, the upper end of which still stuck up stiffly from the grass to nearly Jorian's own height. He seized the rope with both hands and pulled. Up it came, as if out of an invisible hole in the ground. As he pulled, the visible part of the rope lost its stiffness, drooped, and hung limply, like any other rope.

Then Jorian felt a check, as if someone below were holding the rope. One of the soldiers must have nerved himself to seize it as he saw it rising into the air. Since the man was heavy, it was all that Jorian, still panting from his climb, could do to haul him up.

Then a better idea struck him. Rather than pull an armed foe up into this new world about him, he let the rope run loosely through his hands, dropping the man at the other end back on the scaffold. Very faintly, he heard a crash and a yell. Then he pulled quickly, hand over hand. This time the rope came up without resistance until it all lay in a heap on the grass before him.

Jorian drew his forearm across his forehead and sat down heavily. His heart still pounded from his exertions and from the excitement of this narrow escape. Now that he looked back, he could scarcely believe that he had survived.

Although Jorian was a young man of unusual size, strength, and agility, he entertained few illusions about the chances of a bound, unarmed man's escaping from the midst of his foes, even with the help of magical spells. Having practiced with arms for years and having fought in two real battles and several skirmishes, he knew the limitations of one man's powers. Moreover, spells were notoriously erratic and untrustworthy, and Jorian's break for life required perfect surprise, coördination and timing. Perhaps, he thought, Karadur's Mulvanian gods had helped after all.

He glanced swiftly about, thinking: So this is the afterworld, whither souls released from our own plane are sent for their next incarnations! He stood on a strip of artificially smooth grass, perhaps forty feet wide. The strip was bounded on either side by a broad strip of pavement, in turn about twenty feet in breadth.

More grass lay beyond these roadways. Beyond these lawns rose tree-covered hills, on some of which Jorian thought he discerned houses. The question struck him: Why should anybody in his right mind build two splendid roads side by side?

Then a swiftly rising, whirring, purring, swishing sound drew his attention. It reminded him unpleasantly of the sound of a crossbow bolt, but much louder. In a flash, his roving glance fixed itself upon the source of the sound.

Along one of the paved strips, an object was hurtling towards him. At first he thought it a monster of legend:

a low, humpbacked thing with a pair of great, glaring, glassy eyes in front. Below the eyes and just above the ground, a row of silvery fangs was bared in a fiendish grin.

Jorian's courage sank; but, as he backed away from the road, drawing the little knife and preparing to sell his life dearly, the thing whizzed by at incredible speed—a speed like that of a hawk swooping at its prey. As the object passed, Jorian saw that it had wheels; that it was, in fact, no monster but a vehicle. He glimpsed the head and shoulders of a man within, and then the carriage was gone with a diminishing whirr and sigh.

As Jorian, disconcerted, stood staring, another whirr behind him made him spin around. There went another vehicle—and yet another, a huge one with a towering, boxlike body and many wheels. In his own world, he was deemed a man of signal courage; but even the bravest loses his assurance in totally strange surroundings, where he knows not whence or in what guise danger may come.

Trapped between the two roads, Jorian wondered how he could ever escape to join Karadur. The roads extended in either direction as far as the eye could reach, neither converging nor diverging. It seemed as though he could walk along the grassy median strip for leagues in either direction without finding a safe means of exit.

After several more vehicles had passed, Jorian realized that one road was for eastbound traffic only and the other for westbound; and that, furthermore, the cars did not leave the pavement. So he was safe for the nonce. It might even be possible, by choosing a moment when no chariots were in sight, to dash across one of the roads to safety.

Jorian nerved himself to approach one of the paved strips. The road appeared to be made of some cement or stucco, with periodic narrow, black, transverse lines of a stuff resembling pitch. He jumped back as a huge vehicle roared past, buffeting him with the wind of its passage.

Jorian was appalled. He hoped that his soul would never have to live out an incarnation on this plane. One of those vehicles could squash him like a bug. How ironic to escape from the headsman's ax in his own world only to be run over in this! He wondered that anyone here survived long enough to become a driver of these chariots—unless the natives lived their entire lives in them, never setting foot on the ground. Perhaps they had no feet to set on the ground . . .

An approaching vehicle drew up and stopped with a thin, mouselike squeak. A door opened and a man got out. He had, Jorian saw, normal legs, encased in gray pantaloons that hung down to his shoes. He wore a hat with a broad, flat brim; and from a stout belt depended a small leather case. From this case projected the curved handle of some instrument, which Jorian guessed to be a carpenter's tool.

The man approached Jorian and spoke, but Jorian could make nothing of his words. Although he knew several languages, that of the man in the pantaloons was strange to him.

"I am Jorian of Aradamai, son of Evor the clockmaker," he said. This had been his name until that day, five years before, when he had innocently caught a human head hurtling through the air and found himself king of Xylar.

Staring intently at Jorian's golden crown, the man shook his head and said something else. Jorian repeated his statement in Mulvanian and in Shvenic. Looking blank, the man uttered more sounds.

Then another voice sounded, Jorian jumped, for he had not seen anyone else nearby. The voice, speaking unintelligible words in a squawking, metallic tone, seemed to come from the man's vehicle. The man smiled a forced smile of reassurance, and said something more to Jorian, and went back to his carriage, which soon roared off.

Jorian turned back to his rope and began to coil it around his waist. He recalled his instructions: Walk southeast one league, lower himself back to his own world, and await Karadur, if the holy man had not already reached the rendezvous.

But which way was southeast? Luckily the sky was clear, as it had been in Xylar. The execution had been timed for noon, and little time had elapsed since Jorian had placed his neck upon the block. Soon, however, the sun's motion would make it useless as a directional guide. He would have to risk crossing one of these roads despite the danger.

Looking along the nearest paved strip to make sure that no more vehicles approached, Jorian darted across. He continued to the edge of the lawnlike sward, where plants grew more naturally. He broke off a stem of long field grass, found a patch of bare earth, and set the stem in it upright. Then, with the point of the little knife, he traced a line where the shadow of the grass stem fell. He drew a transverse line, then bisected the near left angle by still another line. That gave him his direction.

As he set out, Jorian paused now and then to cut a tree seedling and trim it to a wand two or three feet long. The first of these sticks he kept, cutting a notch in it every hundred steps. By thrusting the other sticks into the ground every fifty or hundred paces and back-sighting, he kept in a fairly straight line. Every thousand steps, he checked his direction with the sun.

When he had cut fifty notches in his first wand, he halted in a gully between two wooded hillsides. Although he had seen houses in the distance, he was thankful that his march had not taken him close to any.

He counted the notches to make sure, unwound the rope from his waist, and took a turn with it around a tree. Then he uttered the Mulvanian incantation that Karadur had taught him:

*Mansalmu darm rau antarau,*
*Nodō zaro terakh hiä zor rau ...*

He felt his feet sinking, as if the solid ground beneath him were turning to quicksand. Then it gave way, and Jorian fell. He fetched up with a jerk, hanging suspended by the rope between earth—his own earth— and the clear blue heavens.

Above him, the two strands of rope arose, diverging slightly, until they faded out a yard above his head. Below, he was disconcerted to see the dark, stagnant waters of the Marsh of Moru. Karadur had told him that their rendezvous would be near the swamp, but he had not expected to come out right over it. To the north rolled the fields and woodlots of Xylar. To the south rose the foothills of the mighty Lograms, and beyond them the snow-topped peaks of that range, which sundered the Novarian city-states from the tropical empire of Mulvan.

He thought of climbing back up and trying again from another tree but decided against it. He was not sure how long the "soft spot" that his spell had created between the two planes would remain soft. It could not do to have the earth solidify just as he was climbing through it. On the other hand, he was a good swimmer and did not fear the three-foot dwarf crocodiles found in Moru Marsh.

He lowered himself to where the ends of the rope dangled. If he had tied one end around the tree with an ordinary loop, the rope would have been long enough to reach the surface of his world. In that case, however, he would not have been able to recover the precious rope after his descent. Therefore he had applied the middle of the rope to the tree and let both ends hang down an equal distance.

The dark, odorous water lay about twenty feet beneath him. A look around showed no sign of the wizard. Here we go, Jorian thought, and released one end of the rope.

He struck with a tremendous splash. The rope poured down after him, striking the water in loops and coils. Taking one end of it in his teeth, Jorian struck out for the nearest shore.

This proved to be a floating bank of reeds. Jorian hauled himself out, brown water running off his shoulders. When he stood up, the surface beneath him quivered, gave, and sank in alarming fashion. The safest mode of progress, he decided, was on all fours. Trailing the rope, he crept towards higher ground, where willows and dark cypresses grew thickly. At last he felt firm soil beneath him and rose to his feet. A water weed trailed from one of the spikes of his crown.

"Karadur!" he called, pulling loose the weed and scraping the swamp water off his skin with his fingers.

He was not surprised when there was no reply. A league-long hike would be hard on the old fellow, and he might not arrive until nightfall. Since Jorian saw nothing else of a useful nature to do, he found a spot masked by ferns, took off his crown, stretched out, and was soon fast asleep.

The sun was farther down in the sky, although still far from the horizon, when a voice awakened Jorian. He sprang up to face Karadur, who stood before him in his normal guise, leaning on a staff and breathing heavily.

"Hail!" said Jorian. "How did you find me, old man?"

"You—ah—snored, O King—I mean, Master Jorian."

"Are we followed hither?"

"Nay, not so far as my arts reveal. Ah me, I am spent! Suffer me to rest." The wizard sank with a sigh into the ferns. "Not in years have I been so fordone. Working two spells at once wellnigh slew me, and this march through forest has finished me off." He rested his head in his hands.

"Where have you hidden the gear?"

"Alack, I am too spent to think. How found you the afterworld?"

"*Oi!* Ghastly, from what little I saw," said Jorian. He described the double road of cement and the monstrous vehicles that whizzed along it. "By Thio's horns, life must be riskier there by far than in our own world, with all its wars, plagues, robbers, sorceries, and wild beasts! I'd rather take a chance on one of your Mulvanian hells, where one has to cope merely with a few nice, bloodthirsty demons."

"Saw you—met you any of the inhabitants?"

"Aye; a fellow whom I took to a carpenter stopped his carriage and bespoke me, albeit neither could understand the other's lingo. He stared at me as the Xylarians would stare if a man-ape from Komilakh were to stroll amongst 'em." Jorian described the man.

Karadur gave a faint chuckle. "That was no carpenter but a peace officer—a man trained in the use of arms but employed solely against evildoers of his own nation instead of against a foreign foe. I believe some of your Novarian city-states possess corps of such stalwarts. It is a plane of great wealth and many curious devices, but I hope never to spend an incarnation there."

"Wherefore not?"

"Because it is a dimension of base materialism, wherein magic is so feeble as to be wellnigh useless; so what scope were there for an accomplished thaumaturge like myself? Those who pass for magicians on that plane, I am informed, are mostly fakers. Why, even the gods of that world are but debile wraiths, able to work but little weal or woe, beyond causing petty strokes of luck, upon those they love and hate."

"Have these folk no religion, then?"

"Aye, or say they do. They also patronize magicians—astrologers and necromancers and such. The reason is not that the gods and wizards of that plane can do them much good or ill, but that they come into incarnation there with buried memories of their previous lives in this world, where such things in sooth are mighty and fell. But, on the whole, the folk of that dimension are blind in spiritual matters."

Jorian slapped a gnat. "Then I, having no more psychic powers than a head of cabbage, should do right well there."

"Not so, but far otherwise."

"Why?"

"Your strength and nimbleness—your strongest resources here—would avail you nought, because all tasks calling for such virtues in this world are there performed by soulless machines. What boots it if you can ride forty leagues between sunrise and sunset, when one of those mechanical cars you saw can cover thrice the distance in that time? Your strength were as useless as my moral purity and knowledge of spiritual forces."

"I'm not quite a halfwit, even though my thews be a trifle larger than most men's," said Jorian. "Natheless, belike you speak truth. In any case, old man, daylight will not last forever. So let us forth to find our cache, if you now be fit for walking."

"Aye, I am fit; albeit the prospect gives me no joy." With a groan, the wizard heaved himself to his feet and started poking in the nearest bushes with his staff, muttering:

"Now, let me see, where did I hide that accursed thing? Tsk, tsk. It was under the overhang of a boulder, I am sure, with a layer of leaves to conceal it ..."

"No boulders here," said Jorian with a touch of impatience.

"True, true; methinks the place lay a furlong or so to the north, on higher ground. Let us look."

They moved off in the direction indicated and for the next two hours scoured the woods, looking for a boulder. Karadur mumbled:

"Let me see; let me see ... It was a boulder of

granite, with patches of moss, about as high as your shoulder, O Jorian . . . I am sure . . . I think . . ."

"Did you not blaze a nearby tree, or otherwise leave a marking to guide our search."

"Let me think. Ah, yes, I marked three trees, on three sides of the cache. But there are so cursed many trees . . ."

"Why not find it by divination?"

"Because my spiritual powers are spent for the nonce. We must use our material senses or none."

They went back to the swamp and started off in a slightly different direction. Insects danced in level spears of light, shining through the forest, when Jorian said:

"Is this one of your blazes?"

"Why, yes, it is!" said Karadur. "Now, let me see, where are the others . . ."

"There are no more boulders here than there are fishes in the desert of Fedirun."

"Boulder? Boulder? Why—ah—I remember now! I left it not beneath a boulder at all, but under a tree trunk. There!"

Karadur pointed to a big trunk lying athwart the forest floor. In an instant they had scraped aside the concealing leaves and dragged out a canvas bag. Jorian let a hiss of annoyance escape through his teeth, for the wizard's vague ways often exasperated him. Still, he told himself, one should not be too critical of a man who has saved one's life.

As the sun set, Jorian arose. He was now clad like any forester, in coarse brown tunic and breeks, high laced boots in place of his tattered silken slippers, and sweat-stained green hat with a battered pheasant's feather stuck in the band. In his left hand he balanced a crossbow. A short, heavy, hunting falchion, better suited to gutting game and hacking brush than to swordplay, hung at his girdle.

"What shall we do with this?" he said, holding up the crown of Xylar. "It would fetch a pretty stack of lions."

"Never, my boy!" said Karadur. "If aught would betray you, that surely would. Show it to any goldsmith or jeweler or money changer within a hundred leagues, and with the speed of a pigeon's flight the news would fly to Xylar."

"Why not melt it down ourselves?"

"We have no furnace or crucible, and to seek to buy such things would direct suspicion upon us almost as surely as the crown itself. Besides, so ancient a golden artifact ought to have subsumed spiritual qualities from its surroundings, which could prove useful in making magic. It were a shame to destroy these qualities by melting."

"What, then?"

"Best we hide it here with your discarded garments. If circumstance favor, you can recover these articles some day. Or, belike, you could compact with the Xylarians, your head for directions to find their crown. I thought you had money hidden on your person?"

"I have; one hundred golden lions, fresh from the royal mint, in this belt inside my breeches. Any more would have sunk me to the bottom of the Marsh of Moru. But one can always use a little more."

"But that is a sizeable fortune, my son! The gods grant that no robbers hear that you bear such wealth upon your person."

"Well, as things stand, there is no good place where I could bank the stuff for safekeeping."

"True. In any event, to seek additional gain from this crown were not worth the risk. And now I must trim your hair ere darkness fall. Sit here."

Jorian sat on the tree trunk while Karadur went over his head with scissors and comb. He repeatedly warned Jorian to stop talking, but the former king could not be stilled for long.

"It grieves me," said Jorian, "to have robbed my

people—my people that was, I mean—of all their fun:
the beheading, and the coronation, and the scattering
of largesse, and the contests at running and shooting and
wrestling and football and hockey, and the singing and
dancing, and the feast."

"Followed, I doubt not, by a most wicked and sinful
orgy of drunkenness and fornication," said Karadur, "so
you may have accomplished some good despite yourself. You can always change your mind and go back."
He worked around Jorian's right ear.

"Na, na. I'm satisfied with things as they are. And
the gods must approve my course, or they'd not have
let me travel so far along it, now would they?"

"Your argument were cogent if you assumed that the
gods concerned themselves with single mortal beings—
a point the philosophers have hotly disputed for thousands of years. Methinks the main factors in your
escape were my thaumaturgy, reinforced by my moral
purity; the favorable aspect of the planets; and your
own strength and mettle. But he who seeks a single
cause for an event would more easily trim a flea's
whiskers. And, speaking of which, I must needs abate
that monstrous mustache."

"You would jealously rob me of every vestige of my
youthful beauty, you old villain!" grinned Jorian. "But
the drowning man who seizes a log cannot be fussy
about the quality of the wood. Proceed!"

The ex-king's flowing mane had now become a bris-
tling brush, nowhere longer than a finger's breadth. Karadur trimmed the mustache closely, as he had the hair.

"Now," he said, "let beard and mustache grow out
together, and none shall know you."

"Unless they noted my height, my weight, my voice,
or the scar on my nose," said Jorian. "Can't you cast a
spell to lend me the semblance of some slender, flaxen-
haired stripling?"

"I could, had I not already cast two spells today. But
it would accomplish nought, for such illusions last only

an hour or two at most. You will meet none between here and the house of Rhithos the smith but an occasional hunter, charcoal-burner, or lonesome cotter. And what good would your disguise do then?"

"It might hinder them from putting the judiciary of Xylar on my track."

"Aye; but suppose you appeared as a stripling and then resumed your true shape before their very eyes? That, if aught, would arouse suspicion."

Jorian pulled a large, leathern wallet out of the canvas bag, and out of the wallet produced a loaf of bread and a piece of smoked venison. He ate heartily of both, while Karadur contented himself with a modest morsel of bread.

The wizard said: "You must bridle that voracious appetite, my boy."

"Me, voracious?" said Jorian with his mouth full. "By Franda's golden locks, this is but a snack for one of my poundage! Would you think to keep an elephant on one honey-bun a day?"

"Base material appetites were meant to be subdued; and, anyway, those victuals must needs last you until you reach the smith's abode, where they await your coming. Dig deeper and you shall find a sketch map, showing the trails thereunto."

"Good, albeit I already know the country hereabouts, from chasing brigands through it. Dol lies not a league hence."

Karadur continued: "They say Rhithos has a niece or daughter, on whom rakish young oafs like you cast lustful eyes. Avert yours from her, for every sensual sin makes my magical tasks more difficult."

"Me, sensual?" said Jorian, raising an eyebrow. "With five ravishing young wives, what need have I for venery? Dip me in dung, but I shall enjoy a respite—although I shall miss the toddlers climbing all over me. But let us speak of this Rhithos the smith. What gives you such confidence that he'll not betray me to the

Xylarians? A man could turn a pretty penny by putting them on my trail."

"Sirrah! No initiated member of the Forces of Progress would be so base as to betray the trust of another member!"

"Natheless, you once implied that this Rhithos belongs to the faction opposed to yours. And my five years as king, if it has taught me nought else, has taught me not to trust any man overmuch."

"True that he is of the Black Faction, or Benefactors, and so would keep the mighty powers of magic mewed up within our guild, whilst I, of the White Faction, or Altruists, would fain spread it abroad to aid the toiling masses. But, howsoever we quarrel amongst ourselves, we close ranks in dealing with the world outside our learned order, and I am as sure of Rhithos' honor as of my own."

"Judging from the names of your factions, you're all as pure as spring water. Still and all, from what I saw of men during my reign—"

Karadur laid a bony brown hand on Jorian's knee. "You trusted me perforce in the matter of saving your head, my boy. Trust me likewise in this."

"Oh, well, you know what you do," grumbled Jorian. "Holy Father, let me thank you now for saving my worthless head."

"You are welcome; but, as well you know, you shall yet earn that head."

Jorian grinned slyly. "What if I find a wizard to work a counter-spell, nullifying that which you and your fellow-sorcerers have so unscrupulously put upon me?"

"There is no such counter-spell. I warn you that the combination of our spell with that of some bungling outsider bids fair to be fatal. The geas was laid upon you by the leader of our faction, Vorko of Hendau, and can only be lifted by him.

"Now, forget not: One month from today, we meet at the—ah—the Silver Dragon of Othomae, then on to

Trimandilam to fetch the Kist of Avlen, and lastly to the Conclave of my fellow-adepts in the Goblin Tower of Metouro. We must not tarry, for the Conclave meets in the Month of the Pike."

"That should give us ample time."

"Nay, but unforeseen events oft spoil the most promising plans. First, howsomever, we must get to Othomae."

"Why shouldn't I wend thither with you, instead of wandering through the wildwood?"

"Because the Xylarians will be watching the rods for you, and you need time to let your whiskers grow. Rhithos knows of your coming, so you can tarry there for a few days to rest and replenish your provisions."

"I shall be there, if no calamity befall. If I be late, leave a message for me with the taverner, under a fictitious name."

Karadur: "A false name? Tsk Tsk! Not ethical, my son."

"So? You forget that, ere I was king of Xylar, I served a year in the Grand Bastard's foot guards. Many in Othomae will remember me if encouraged to do so."

"You need not fear. The Grand Duke and the Grand Bastard are both alike opposed to Xylar, because the land they rule is wedged betwixt your former kingdom and the Republic of Vindium, which has an alliance with Xylar against Othomae. The lords of Othomae would not turn you over to the Xylarians."

"Perhaps not, but they might not be able to stop kidnappers from Xylar. The judiciary will stick at nought to complete their bloody ceremony Besides, what's more unethical about a false name than about coercing me into stealing that damned trunk full of mouldering magical parchments from the king of Mulvan, as your Forces of Progress has done?"

"Why—ah—there are many differences . . ."

"Name one," said Jorian.

"That were easy—it is to say—oh, you are not spiritually advanced enough to understand. It is a matter of purity of motives—"

"I understand well enough that, if I'm caught between here and Trimandilam because of some silly scruple of yours, you shall get no chest of wizardly screeds. A headless man makes a feckless burglar."

"Ah, well, your contention has a certain plausibility, although were I not so fatigued I could doubtless think of a counter-argument."

"What name will you adopt, if you can bring yourself to do anything so unethical?"

"I shall call myself—ah—Mabahandula."

"By Imbal's iron pizzle! That's a mouthful. But I suppose 'twere useless to feign yourself other than a Mulvani." Jorian repeated the name several times to memorize it.

Karadur winced. "Tsk, tsk. I would you did not blaspheme so freely, even in the names of your pretty local godlets. What shall your name be, if you arrive first?"

"Hmm—Nikko of Kortoli. I had an Uncle Nikko."

"Why not pass yourself off as a Zolonian? The isle of Zolon is farther away and hence safer."

"I have never been to Zolon and cannot feign their foul dialect. But I was reared in Kortoli, and a use the Kortolian country speech when a speak withouten thinking. How now, old kimmer, canst tha riddle me?"

"It is well. If I fail to appear at the Silver Dragon, inquire about the town for the wizardess Goania. She has custody of the instruments we shall need to liberate the Kist of Avlen from the wicked wight who now wrongfully holds it—the so-called King of Kings."

"Goania, said you? That I will. And you, my friend, do not in your absent way forget the name of the city and wander off to Govannian or Vindium and then wonder why I fail to join you."

"Never mind my absent way!" snapped the wizard. "Simply follow my injunctions and leave the rest to me. And guard that flapping tongue. On the scaffold, I thought your cheerful chatter had surely undone us. You had better drink nought but water, since wine and beer loosen your tongue at both ends."

"And if I wander about drinking strange waters, I shall come down with some fearful flux or fever and be wellnigh as useless to you as without my head."

"Well, at least measure your drinks; liquor and loquacity are your besetting weakness. And now, let us bow our heads in prayer to the true gods: the gods of Mulvan."

The wise man droned a prayer to Vurnu the Creator, Kradha the Preserver, and Ashaka the Destroyer. Then Jorian uttered a short prayer of his own to Thio, the Novarian forest god. He shook hands with Karadur, who said:

"Be wary and discreet; subdue the lusts of the flesh; seek moral perfection and spiritual enlightenment. All the true gods go with you, my son."

"I thank you, Father," said Jorian. "I'll be as discreet as a clam and as pure as a snowflake."

He strode off into the deepening gloom of the forest. Karadur, looking after him, began winding the magical rope around his waist. The song of nocturnal insects soared through the gathering darkness.

# II

# The Grand Bastard's Sword

The Month of the Bear had begun when Jorian reached the house of Rhithos the smith. In the foothills of the Lograms, all the leaves of the hardwoods had now turned to brown and scarlet and gold, while on the higher slopes the evergreens retained their somber, dark-green hue. Beyond these green-clad ridges looking black beneath the overcast, clouds half hid the white peaks of the central chain. A rain of red and yellow leaves, slanting down through the gray autumnal air and rocking and spinning in their fall like little boats on a stormy sea, drifted athwart the clearing where stood the house of Rhithos the smith.

The smith's house was larger and more substantial than one would expect for the dwelling of a solitary man. It had a first story of mortared stone and above it a half-story of logs, with a high-peaked roof. Besides the main house, a one-story extension or shed, at right angles to the main axis of the building, contained the smithy. Thence came the clang of hammer on anvil.

At the other end, against the house wall, stood a large wooden cage. Huddled in the cage was an ape-man from the jungles of Komilakh, far to the southeast. Near the edge of the clearing rose the stone curbing of a well, whence a young woman was drawing water. As Jorian arrived with his crossbow on his shoulder, she had just raised a bucketful by the windlass and was resting the bucket on the curb preparatory to emptying it into the jar. Across the clearing from the well, a tethered ass was munching hay.

As Jorian started across the clearing, the girl gave a startled movement, water slopped out of the bucket. Jorian called:

"God den! Let me give you a hand with that, lass!"

"Who are you?" she said, still poised on the edge of flight.

"Jorian son of Evor. Is this the house of Rhithos the smith?"

"Aye. We've heard you were coming, but we expected you many days ago."

"I got lost in the damned woods," said Jorian. "With this blanket of cloud I could not find myself again. Hold the jar whilst I tip the bucket!"

As he poured the water, Jorian looked the girl over. She was tall—within a hand's breadth of his own height—and had a mane of black hair. Her features were a little too coarse and irregular to be called pretty, but she was still a striking, forceful-looking woman with fine gray eyes. She said, in a rather deep, harsh voice:

"No wonder you got lost! Rhithos maintains a confusion spell over all the land you can see from here, to keep hunters and woodsmen out."

"Why?"

"For the silvans. In return, they fetch us food."

"I thought I glimpsed a little fellow with long, hairy ears," said Jorian, carrying the jar towards the house in the girl's wake. The ape-man awoke and growled at Jorian, but a word from the girl quieted the creature.

"The spell was supposed to have been lifted to let you in," continued the girl. "But one cannot turn off a spell as neatly as snuffing a candle. You have nice manners at least, Master Jorian."

"Na, na, we former kings must keep up our good repute." Jorian broke into his rustic Kortolian accent. "And sin a be no king the now, a needs must swink for ma supper."

The girl opened the door to a large room. Scrolls, crucibles, and magical instruments were scattered about on tables, chairs, and benches. The house furnished solid rustic comfort, like the hunting lodge that Jorian had inherited from his predecessors as king of Xylar. The floor was of wooden planks. Weapons hung on the walls, skins of bears and other beasts carpeted the floor, and decorated cushions bestrewed the benches.

The girl led the way along a passage to the kitchen. Jorian staggered as he hoisted the jar to the counter beside the sink.

"What ails you?" asked Vanora sharply. "Tell me not that the weight of that jar has unmanned a strapping fellow like you!"

"No, my dear young lady. It's just that I haven't eaten in three days."

"Great Zevatas! We must remedy that." She rummaged in the bread box, the apple bin, and elsewhere.

"What shall I call you?" asked Jorian, setting down his crossbow and his pack. "It seems not meet to refer to one who has saved one's life as 'Ho, you!'"

"I haven't saved your life."

"You will have, when you get me something to eat. Well?"

"My name is Vanora." As Jorian looked a question, she added: "Vanora of Govannian, if you like."

"I thought I knew the accent. Is Rhithos your father or uncle?"

"He, a kinsman?" She gave a short, derisive laugh. "He is my master. Know that he bought me as a bonded maid-of-all-work in Govannian."

"How so?"

"I had stabbed my lover, the worthless vagabond. I know not why, but I always fall in love with drunken louts who mistreat me. Anyway, this oaf died, and they were going to chop off my head to teach me not to do it again. But in Govannian they let outsiders buy condemned criminals as slaves, provided they take

them out of the country. If I returned to thither, they'd
have my head yet."

"How does Rhithos entreat you?"

She set down on the counter a plate bearing a small
loaf of bread, a slab of smoked meat, a wedge of
cheese, and an apple. Standing close to him, she said:
"He doesn't—at least, not what you'd call 'entreat.' So
long as I obey, he pays me no more heed than a stick
of furniture—not even at bedtime, for he says his magical works require celibacy. Now he's in his smithy, fid-
dling with Daunas' new sword; won't put his head out
of the shed until supper time."

She looked up at him from close by with half-opened
lips and swayed so that her full breast rubbed gently
against his arm. He could hear the faint whistle of her
breathing. Then his eyes strayed to the laden platter.

"If you'll excuse me, Mistress Vanora," he said,
reaching around her, "what I need right now is food,
ere I drop dead of starvation. Where would you like
me to eat it?"

"Food!" she snapped. "Sit at yon little table. Here's
some cider. Don't gulp it down; it has more power
than you would think."

"I thank you, Mistress." Jorian bolted several large
mouthfuls, then cleared his mouth long enough to say:
"Do I understand that Rhithos is making a magical
sword for the Grand Bastard?"

"I can't linger for light talk, Master Jorian. I have
work to do." She strode out of the kitchen, the heels
of her boots banging.

Jorian looked after her with a smile curling his stub-
bly new beard. Now what, he thought, is she angry
about? Is it what I suspect? He ate heartily, drank
deeply, and wandered back into the cluttered living
room. Here Rhithos the smith found him hours later,
rolled up in a bearskin on the floor and snoring.

\*      \*      \*

The faint sound of the opening door roused Jorian. As the smith entered his house, Jorian scrambled to his feet and bowed.

"Hail, Master Rhithos!" he said. "Your servant is humbly grateful for your hospitality."

The smith was shorter than Vanora, who entered after him; but he had the widest shoulders Jorian had ever seen. The huge hand on the end of his long arm had a grip that made even Jorian wince. The face under his tousled gray hair was seamed and wrinkled and brown, and out of it a pair of heavy-lidded, cold gray eyes looked without expression.

"Welcome to my house," rumbled Rhithos, "I regret that your arrival was delayed by a trifling misfunction in one of my protective spells. Vanora tells me you arrived half-starved."

"True. I exhausted the provender I had with me and sought to kill some game to replace it. I'm not altogether incompetent with the crossbow; but not so much as a hare did I see."

"The silvans must have driven the beasts out of your way. They guard them from hunters—not for sentimental love of the creatures, but to hunt themselves. Sit down there, Master Jorian. For the evening you may take your ease, although tomorrow I shall find ways for you to earn your keep whilst you tarry here."

As Vanora poured wine, Rhithos continued: "Now tell me how you got into this strange predicament."

"It began five years ago," said Jorian, glad of a chance to talk after the long silence of the forest. "But I must go back further yet. My father was Evor the clockmaker, who passed his last years in Ardamai."

"Where is that?"

"A village of Kortoli, near the capital. He tried to apprentice me in the making of clepsydras. But my hands, while steady enough on bridle, sword, plow, or tiller, proved too big and clumsy for such fine work. I mastered the theory, but the practice eluded me. He gave up at last, albeit not before I had traveled with him to several of the Twelve Cities where he had contracts to install water clocks.

"Next, he apprenticed me to Fimbri the carpenter, in Ardamai. But after a month Fimbri sent me home with a bill for all the tools that I, not having yet learned to control my strength, had broken.

"Then my father apprenticed me to Rubio, a merchant of Kortoli. This lasted a year, until one day I made a bad error in adding Rubio's accounts. Now Rubio was a bitter and hasty man, and things had lately gone badly for him. So he took his rage out on me, forgetting that in the year I had been with him I had grown from a stripling to a youth taller than he was. He laid into me with his walking stick, and I took it away and broke it over his head. It only stunned him; but I, thinking I had slain the man, fled back to Ardamai.

"My father hid me until it transpired that Rubio was not seriously hurt. Then he got me into the house of a childless peasant, one Onnus. He told me that, if I moved my draughtsmen aright, I might inherit the farm, since widower Onnus had no known kin. But Onnus was a skinflint who would try to sell the squeal of a pig when he butchered it. He worked me sixteen hours a day and nearly starved me. At last, when he caught me sneaking off from work to spark a neighbor's girl, he laid into me with his horsewhip. Of course I had to take it away from him—"

"And flog him with it?" said Rhithos.

"No, sir, I did not. All I did was to throw him head-first into his own dungheap, so hard he came out the other side, and went along home."

Warmed by the wine, Jorian became gay, speaking rapidly with animated gestures. "My poor father was in despair of finding a livelihood for me. My older brothers had grown up to be good, competent clockmakers, and my sisters were married off, but what to do with me? 'If you had two heads,' quoth he, 'we could charge admission to see you; but you're only a great, clumsy young lout, good only for clodhopping.' So we bethought us of Syballa, the local wise woman.

"The witch put herbs in her pot and powders in her fire, and there was a lot of smoke and flickering shadows with nothing visible to cast them. She went into a trance, muttering and mumbling. Then at last she said:

" 'Jorian, my lad, meseems you're fit only to be either a king or a wandering adventurer.'

" 'How so?' quoth I. 'All I want is to be a respectable craftsman, like my dear father, and make a decent living.'

" 'Your trouble,' she went on, 'is that you are too good at too many things to push a plow handle or to sweep the streets of Kortoli City. Yet you are not so surpassingly good at any one thing that it is plainly the work wherefor the gods intended you. For such a one, if he be not born to wealth and rank, the only careers are those of adventurer and ruler. Betimes the one leads to the other.'

" 'How about soldiering?' said I.

" 'That is classed with adventuring.'

" 'Then soldiering it shall be,' I said.

"My father sought to dissuade me, saying that I had too much brains for so routine a career, which would prove nine parts insufferable boredom to one part stark terror. But I said my brain had so far availed me little and set out natheless. Kortoli rejected my application; I think Rubio must have put in a bad word for me.

"So I hiked to Othomae and joined the Grand Bastard's pikemen. For a year I marched back and forth on the drill ground while officers bawled: 'Slant *pikes!* Forward, *'arch!'* We had one battle, with a Free Company that thought to sack Othomae. But the Grand Bastard routed them with a charge of his newfangled lobster-plated knights on their great, puffing plowhorses, so that no foe came within bowshot of us foot.

At the end of my enlistment I agreed with my father that the mercenary's life was not for me.

"When my time was up, I wandered into Xylar. I arrived on the day they were executing the king and choosing his successor. I suppose I had heard of this curious custom from my schoolmaster, years before; but I had never been to Xylar and hence had forgotten it. So, when a round, dark thing the size of a football came hurtling through the air at my face, I caught it. Then I found to my horror that I held a human head, freshly severed so that the blood ran up my arms. Ugh! And I learnt that I was the new king of Xylar.

"At first, I was in a daze as they clad me in shining raiment, plied me with delicious food and drink, and chose beautiful wives for me. But it did not take me long to learn what the catch was—that after five years I, too, should lose my head.

"Well, there are always more garments and food and drink and women to be had, but if a man loses his head he cannot grow another. After a year of going through the motions of kingship, as old Grallon and Turonus instructed me, I resolved to escape from this gin by fair means or foul.

"The first method I tried was simply to sneak out and run for it. But the Xylarians were used to this and easily caught me; a whole company of the army—the so-called Royal Guard—is made up of men expert with the net and the lariat, whose task it is to see that the king escape not. I tried to enlist confederates; they betrayed me. I tried to bribe my guards; they pocketed my money and betrayed me.

"The third year, I essayed to be so good a king that the Xylarians would relent and change their custom. I made many reforms. I studied the law and strove to see justice done. I studied finance and learnt to lower taxes without weakening the kingdom. I studied the military art and put down the brigands who had gathered around Dol and the pirates that had been raiding our coast. I don't mind admitting that battles fill me with trepidation—

"Who joys in the galloping destrier's gait?
        Not I!
Who's happy to ride with a pot on his pate?
        Not I!
Who loves to bear on his body the weight
Of iron apparel of mail or of plate,
And seek in a bloody encounter his fate?
        Not I!

"Who yearns to thrust with the sword
        and the spear?
        Not I!
Or draw the goose-feathered shaft to the ear?
        Not I!
Who's filled by the clatter of battle with fear,
Preferring a peaceable flagon of beer,
But lacks the astuteness to bolt for the rear?
        'Tis I!

"But the thought of the ax dismayed me even more, so that I ended by making these evildoers fear me even more than I feared them."

"Whose verse did you quote?" asked Rhithos.

"A certain obscure poetaster, hight Jorian of Ardamai. But to continue: At the end of the year, all agreed that King Jorian, despite his youth, was the best ruler they had had in many a reign.

"But would the Xylarians change their stupid law? Not for anything. In fact, they posted extra guards to make sure that I did not escape. I couldn't go for a ride, to hunt or to chase bandits or just for pleasure, without a squad of lariat-men from the steppes of Shven surrounding me lest I make a break for freedom.

"For a time I was in despair. I abandoned myself to the pleasures of the flesh—to food, drink, women, and all-night revels. Hence, by the end of my fourth year, I was a fat, flabby wreck.

"I caught cold that winter, and the cold grew into a fever that wellnigh slew me. Whilst I was raving in a delirium, a man appeared unto me in a vision. Sometimes he looked like my father, who had died that year. I had been sending my parents ample money for their comfort but durst not invite them to Xylar, lest I have a chance to escape but be unable to take 'it lest my parents be held as hostages for my return.

"Sometimes the man in the vision seemed to be one of the great gods: Heryx, or Psaan, or even old Zevatas himself. Whoever he was, he said: 'Jorian, lad, I am ashamed of thee, with all thy gifts of mind and body, giving up in the face of a little threat like the loss of thy head. Up and at them, boy! Thou mayst or mayst not escape if thou try, but thou wilt certainly not if thou try not. So what hast thou to lose?'

"When I got well, I took the vision's words to heart. I sent away all the women save my four legal wives, to whom I added a fifth of my own choice. I trained in the gymnasium and the tilt yard until I was more fit than ever. And I read everything in the royal library that might possibly help me to escape. I spent a year in training and study. And 'tis easier for an eel to play the bagpipes than for a man to train and study at the same time. When you train, you're too spent to study of evens; and when you study, you find you lack the requisite time for training. I could only do my best.

"Reasoning that, if the gods had in sooth condemned me to the life of a wandering adventurer, I had best be a good one, I studied whatever might be useful for that career. I learnt to speak Mulvani and Feridi and Shvenic. I practised not only with the conventional arms but also with the implements of men beyond the law: the sandbag, the knuckle duster, the strangler's cord, the poison ring, and so on. I hired Merlois the actor to teach me the arts of disguise, impersonation, and dialectical speech.

"During the last year of my reign, also, I gathered a squad of the most unsavory rogues in the Twelve Cities: a cutpurse, a swindler, a forger, a bandit, a founder of cults and secret societies, a smuggler, a blackmailer, and two burglars. I kept them in luxury whilst they taught me all their tricks. Now I can scale the front of a building, force a window, pick a lock, open a strong-box, and—if caught in the act—convince the house-holder that I am a good spirit sent by the gods to report on his conduct.

"As a result of these studies, I have become, one might say, a good second-rater in a variety of fields. Thus I am not so deadly a fencer as Tartonio, my for-mer master-at-arms; nor so skilled a rider as Korkuin, my master of the horse; nor so adept a burglar as the master thief Enas; nor so learned in the law as Justice Grallon; nor so efficient an administrator as Chancellor Turonus; nor so fluent a linguist as Stimber, my librar-ian. But I can beat all of them *save* Tartonio with sword and buckler, and out-ride all *save* Korkuin, and speak more tongues than any *save* Stimber, and so on.

"Through my readings, I learnt of the Forces of Progress. One of my predecessors had closed the Col-lege of Magical Arts and banished all magicians from Xylar, and his successors had maintained this prohibi-tion—"

"I know that," growled Rhithos. "Why think you I dwell up here in the wilds? To escape the net of laws and regulations that the Cities fling about the student of the higher wisdom. True, in none of the other Twelve Cities is the law so stringent as in Xylar; but in all of 'em are rules and licenses and inspectors to cope with. To the forty-nine Mulvanian hells with 'em! Go on."

Jorian: "Hence the only such practitioners in Xylar

are mere witches and hedge-wizards—furtive lawbreakers, eking out a shadowy existence by amulets and potions and predictions, half of 'em fake. After I had tried several local witches of both sexes, with unpleasing results, I got in touch with Doctor Karadur, who came to Xylar as a holy man and as such beyond reach of our law. My escape from the scaffold was his doing."

"Karadur has his good points," said Rhithos. "Were it not for his foolish ideas and impractical ideals—"

A scratching at the door interrupted the smith. Vanora opened it, and in bounced an animal. With a start of surprise, Jorian saw that it was a squirrel the size of a dog, weighing over twenty pounds. Long, black, glossy fur covered the beast. It chirped at Rhithos, rubbed its head against his leg, and let him scratch it behind the ears, and trotted out to the kitchen.

"My familiar, Ixus," said Rhithos. "The body is that of the giant squirrel of Yelizova; the spirit, that of a minor demon from the Fourth Plane."

"Where is Yelizova?" asked Jorian.

"A land far to the south, beyond the equatorial jungles south of Mulvan. 'Tis only in recent years that daring mariners from Zolon have sailed thither and returned the tale to tell. Ixus cost me a pretty penny, I assure you. Some of my colleagues prefer that their familiars possess the bodies of beasts of the ape kind, because of their dexterity. I, however, demur. In the first place, these animals are delicate, easily destroyed by cold; in the second, being near kin to mankind, they have minds of their own and so often escape the control of the spirit." The smith spoke in a coldly controlled voice, without expression of face or of tone. Now he addressed himself to his dinner.

"You were saying about Karadur?" said Jorian.

"Only that he is full of ideals that, however appealing

to the emotions, are impractical in the real world. The same applies to his faction."

"I heard there was a difference of opinion. Could you explain your point of view?"

"His faction, which call themselves the Altruists—"

"Or White Faction, do I understand?"

"*They* term themselves and us the White and Black Factions respectively; but we admit not the distinction. 'Tis but their own pejorious usage, to bias the case in their favor. To resume: these self-styled Altruists would fain release the secrets of the arcane arts to the vulgus, broadcast. Thus, they say, all mankind shall benefit from this knowledge. Every man shall have a warm back and a full belly; he shall enjoy a passionate youth, a teeming family, and a hale old age.

"Now, were all men as conscientious as we of the Forces of Progress, who must study many years and give up some of life's choicest pleasures to master our arts, who are straitly examined by the senior members ere being admitted to our fraternity, and who are bound by dreadful oaths to use our knowledge for the good of mankind—were all other men so sternly trained and strictly admitted to this arcanum, then might something be said for the Altruists' ideal.

"But as you have seen, Master Jorian, not all men are so minded. Some are stupid, some lazy, and some downright wicked. Most of 'em choose their own self-interest over that of the general; most of 'em elect the pleasure of the moment over what is good for them, and theirs in the long run. Loose this deadly knowledge on such a feckless rabble of fools, knaves, and lubbards? As well put a razor into the chubby fingers of a toddling wean! There are men who, possessing the fellest spells, would not scruple to use them to blast an entire city, if by so doing they could burke a single personal foe. Hence to this proposal are we Benefactors adamantinely opposed."

However emphatic his words, Rhithos never raised

his voice, speaking in the same expressionless monotone. There seemed to be something mechanical about
him, which reminded Jorian of the legend of the
mechanical servant that Vaisus, the divine smith, had
made for the other gods, and of the troubles that
ensued when the clockwork man wanted to be ranked
as a god, too.

"What of your current project?" he said as they finished their repast.

"'Twill do no harm to tell you, since it will be finished in three days at most. It is the sword Randir,
which I am forging for the Grand Bastard. When the
spells that go into its tempering are complete, it will
cut through ordinary armor like cheese.

"The trick, I may say, is to apply the spells during
the tempering stage. Some apply them earlier, during
the initial heating and forging. Most such spells, however, are wasted because the heating and pounding nul-
lify them.

"But tell us of your escape. What price did Karadur
exact? Despite his hypocritical piety, I know the old
didderer would not work so taxing and risky a magical
opus without a price."

"Oh, he said that your Forces of Progress demanded
that I go to the capital of Mulvan and there seek out
an ancient coffer called the Kist of Avlen, said to be
filled with portentous spells from olden times. Karadur
then wants me to lug this box back to the Goblin Tower
of Metouro, where, I understand, your society is to
hold a great Conclave."

"Aha! Now it comes out. If he told you that the
order as a whole demanded this thing, he lied, or I
should have heard of it ere now. It is his own faction,
the so-called Altruists, who lust after this chest in order
to force us Benefactors to accede to their mad proposals. How do they enforce this command?"

"By a geas that gives me a frightful headache and

nightmares if I keep not on the road to Trimandilam. I have tested this spell and know that it works."

"I might have guessed. But continue, good sir, with the tale of your escape."

While telling of his abortive execution, Jorian silently cursed himself for a rattlepate. He had wrongly assumed that Rhithos was in on his project for the theft of the Kist of Avlen, or at least that there would be no harm in telling him about it. Now it transpired that Jorian had involved himself in strife between the two factions of the magicians' fraternity. Rhithos might well try to put sand in the works. Jorian's wine-loosened tongue had betrayed him, and not for the first time.

Jorian got what little comfort he could from the thought that his indiscretion was also partly Karadur's fault. The old wizard had managed to give Jorian the impression, without actually saying so, that his whole society was behind this raid and not merely his own faction. Jorian sighed at the thought that even Karadur, despite his lofty talk of purity of morals and ethics, was himself not absolutely beyond all forms of perfidy and deception.

Rhithos listened without expression to the rest of Jorian's narrative. At last he said: "Bravely done, good my sir. Now let us to bed, for there will be plenty to do on the morrow."

Jorian spent most of the next day eating, resting, and taking a much-needed bath in Rhithos' wooden tub. He watched Rhithos holding the blade Randir by its tang wrapped in rags, for the hilt had not yet been attached. The smith repeatedly heated the blade to cherry-red. Then he laid it on the anvil and struck it, now here, now there, to take the least curvature or unevenness out of it.

A day later, Jorian had fully recovered. He helped Rhithos with the sword, holding with pincers the ends of the wires wound around the grip, polishing the blade and the silvered brass knuckle-guard, and otherwise helping to give Randir its final touches. He turned the crank of the grindstone as the smith administered the blade's preliminary sharpening.

The imp Ixus hopped about the smithy, fetching and carrying to Rhithos' orders. It chattered angrily at Jorian and bared its squirrel's chisel-teeth at his leg until a sharp word from the smith subdued it.

"He's jealous," said Rhithos. "You had better go out and help Vanora. I am about to put a minor spell on the hilt and prefer to do so alone."

Jorian spent some time in chopping wood, hauling water, kneading dough, and weeding the garden without winning more than a few curt words from the girl. He tried flattery and stories:

"Did you ever hear," he said, "about the great wrastle betwixt King Fusas of Kortoli and his twin brother Fusor? This king, you see, was a great athlete—almost as great as Kadvan the Strong in Xylar, with the additional advantage that they didn't amputate his head after five years. I have never heard of a headless athlete who was worth a piece of mouldy straw in a contest.

"Well, Fusas wanted to put on a grand celebration to mark the five-hundredth anniversary of the polis. Of course he cheated a little, for that there was a gap in this fine history, when for several years Ardyman the Terrible of Govannian united all the Twelve Cities under his rule, but the Kortolians thought it more seemly to ignore this break, and who shall blame them?

"Being himself a mighty man, King Fusas thought to please his folk by staging, at the climax of the celebration, an athletic contest between himself and another man. Now, the king's favorite sport was wrastling. But that presented a problem. For, you see, the king thought it bad for his royal dignity to be worsted in such a public contest. On the other hand, if his opponent were warned in advance to lose, the word might leak out, or the other man might too patently let himself be thrown. At best this would give a dull show, and at worst it might cause the king to be jeered, even worse for the royal dignity.

"Belike the king could match himself against a man so much smaller than himself that he were sure to win in any case. But again, the people would see their king flinging a mere shrimp of an opponent about and would jeer him.

"So King Fusas took counsel with his wise man, the wizard Thorynx. And Thorynx reminded Fusas that he had a twin brother, Fusor, living a quiet life in a small country house in the hills of southern Kortoli—or as quiet a life as one can lead when surrounded by spies and informers watching for a chance to denounce one for plotting to seize the throne from one's brother. Luckily for him, Fusor—the younger of the twain by a quarter-hour—was of a retiring disposition. He cared for little but fishing and so never gave the informers any suspicious acts to report upon.

"Now, said Thorynx, Fusor and Fusas were identical twins and therefore a perfect match as wrastlers, albeit Fusor might be in better physical trim as a result of the simple outdoor life he led, not having papers to sign and lawsuits to judge and banquets to eat and balls to keep him up late. So let him be brought to Kortoli City and there wrastle with Fusas at the climax of the festival. Both would be clad identically, so that the viewers could not distinguish them. Whichever won, it would be announced that King Fusas was the winner, and who should gainsay it? Then Fusor could be sent back to his country house with a handsome gift to keep him quiet.

"And so it was done. Prince Fusor was fetched to Kortoli City and lodged in the palace for a month preceding the festival. And at the high point of the celebration, a grand wrastle it was, with the king and his brother rolling over and over on the mat in a tangle of limbs and grunting like a pair of boars at the same trough. And at last one of the twain pinned the other and was declared the winner. He was also declared to be the king.

"But no sooner had they returned to the palace and passed out of the view of the throngs than they burst into a furious quarrel, with shaken fists and menaces. Each, both winner and loser, claimed to be King Fusas and, since they looked just alike and were clad in the same purple loincloths, there was no easy way to tell which spake sooth.

"First, the chancellor tried by questioning them separately about the affairs of the kingdom, But each claimant readily answered the questions. It transpired that Fusor—whichever of the twain he was—had made the most of his month's residence in the palace to familiarize himself with such matters, whilst his royal brother had been occupied with training in the gymnasium for the bout.

"Then the chancellor asked Thorynx if he had any ideas. 'Aye,' said Thorynx. 'I can settle the question. Give each claimant a sheet of reed paper and let him write an account of the last time he went in unto Queen Zeldé, with full particulars. Then show these two screeds to the Queen and let her say which is that of the true king.' For, unlike the southern tier of the Twelve Cities, the Kortolians do not allow even kings to take more than one lawful wife. It must be the Mulvanian influence that leads you southrons to permit such liberty.

"Anyway, so it was done. The Queen glanced over the two writings and forthwith declared that one was true and the other false. So the one she had declared the true king was restored to his crown and throne and dignities, whilst the other, still indignantly protesting his royalty, was beheaded for high treason.

"That had been the end of it, save that many years later, when the king had died and the aged Queen Zeldé was on her deathbed, she confessed that she had wantonly chosen the wrong screed—that penned by Prince Fusor and not that by King Fusas.

" 'But grandmother!' cried the young princess to whom she made this avowal. 'Why did you ever do such a wicked thing?"

" 'Because,' said Queen Mother Zeldé, 'I never liked that pig Fusas. His breath smelt bad, and when he made love he was always finished before I had even begun to warm up. I thought that by trading him for his brother I might get somebody more to my taste. But alas! Fusor proved identical with his brother in these as in other respects.' And so she died."

Vanora, however, remained scornful. "You're a fearful braggart, Master Jorian," she said at last. "I'll wager you cannot do one half the feats whereof you boast."

Jorian smiled ingratiatingly. "Well, any man would wish to put his best foot forward with an attractive girl, now wouldn't he?"

She snorted. "To what end? You are not even man enough to enjoy the fruits of gallantry, unless you are first stoked with enough victuals to sate a lion."

"I could show you—"

"Never mind, sirrah, you don't appeal to me."

"I am wounded unto death, as by one of the silvans' poisoned shafts!" cried Jorian, clasping his heart and pretending to faint. "What else would you like me to demonstrate?"

"That lock-picking skill, for example. See you the door of yonder cage?"

Jorian approached the cage. The ape-man, an exceptionally ugly one covered with short, grizzled hair, growled at him. Then, as Vanora came up to the bars, she extended a hand through them. The ape-man took the hand in his own and kissed it.

"A real gallant, this Komilakhian!" said Jorian, examining the lock. "What does Rhithos keep him for? He does not work the creature, as he does the squirrel, and the beast-man must be fed. What's the purpose?"

Vanora had been speaking to the ape-man in the latter's own clucking, hissing tongue. She said: "Rhithos means to use Zor here in the final stage of the making of the sword Randir. The concluding spell calls for thrusting the red-hot blade through the poor creature and leaving it there until it has cooled; then its edge is tested by striking off Zor's head. The spell should properly be performed with a human captive, but Rhithos assures me 'twill work as well with Zor, who is at least halfway to humanhood and is less likely to embroil us with vengeful kinfolk than would a man."

"The poor halfling! Zor seems to like you."

"More than that; he's in love with me."

"How do you know?"

"Look at him, stupid!"

"Oh, I see what you mean." Jorian fumbled in a small pouch, pinned to the inner side of his breeches, and brought out a short length of stout, bent wire. "I think this will take care of Zor's lock. Hold the cage door."

He inserted the wire into the lock, felt about, and twisted. The bolt clicked back.

"Beware!" said Jorian. "Zor might—"

Instead of helping Jorian to hold the cage door shut, Vanora stepped back and uttered a word in Zor's language. With a roar, the ape-man hurled himself against the door. He was even heavier and stronger than Jorian, and the force of his impact was irresistible. Sent staggering back, Jorian caught his heel and sat down in the dirt, while the door flew open and Zor rushed out.

"Stop him!" cried Jorian, scrambling to his feet. But Vanora only stood with fists on hips, watching complacently as Zor raced off into the woods and vanished.

"You did that on purpose!" cried Jorian, scrambling up. "By Zevatas's brazen beard, why—"

"What's this?" barked the voice of the smith as

Rhithos emerged from the smithy. "Great Zevatas, you've enlarged Zor! Are you mad, man? Why should you do this to me?"

"He was showing off his skill at picking locks," said Vanora.

"Why, you teat-sucking idiot—" raved the smith, shaking his fists. It was the first time that Jorian had seen the man express emotion of any kind.

"I like not to blame a woman, sir," said Jorian, "but your young lady here did suggest—"

"I did nought of the sort!" screamed Vanora, " 'Twas your own self-conceit that drove you to the deed, despite my remonstrance—"

"Why, you little liar!" said Jorian. "Dip me in dung if I don't spank your—"

"You shall do nought of the sort, sirrah!" roared Rhithos. "Look at me!"

Jorian did, then belatedly tried to snatch his gaze away and found that he could not. The smith held up something in the palm of his hand—whether a gem, a mirror, or a magical light, Jorian could not tell. It glowed and sparkled with a myriad of rays. The very soul seemed to be drawn out of his body as he watched in stupefied fascination. A corner of his mind kept telling him to tear his gaze away, to resist, to strike down the smith and flee; but he could not.

Closer and closer came the smith; brighter and more confusing came the sparkle of lights. The world around Jorian seemed to fade and vanish, so that he stood in empty space, bathed in flickering, coruscating lights of all the known colors and some unknown ones.

"Hold still!" said the smith, his voice toneless again. Jorian found himself unable to move at all. He felt the smith's free hand searching his clothing. His dagger was taken, and his purse, and then the smith extracted the money belt and the little bag of pick-locks.

"Now back!" said the Smith. "Back! Another step!

And another!" He continued until he had Jorian backed through the door of the cage.

Dimly, Jorian heard the door clang and the lock click. The dazzle faded and he was in Zor's cage.

"Now," said Rhithos, "since you have robbed me of Zor, you shall take his place."

"Are you serious, Master Rhithos?" said Jorian.

"You shall see how serious I am. I shall be ready to cast the final spell tomorrow, and in that spell you shall play a vital role."

"You mean you intend to temper the blade by skewering me with it and testing it on my neck?"

"Certes. The poets will sing of this blade for centuries; so, if it's any comfort, know that you die in a noble cause."

"By Imbal's brazen balls, that's unreasonable! Whilst I own to some small blame in Zor's escape, no civilized man would deem my blunder capital offense."

"What are you or any other man to me? No more than insects to be trodden down when they cross my path. What is important is the perfection of my art."

"My friend," said Jorian in his most winning tone, "were you not better advised to send me to Komilakh to fetch you back another man-ape? You can assure my return by one of your spells, like that which Karadur's colleagues have laid upon me. Besides, how shall I seek the Kist of Avlen—"

"Your faction seeks to put this Kist to some foolish use, so better you did not live to carry out your quest. Besides, the next twenty-four hours are astrologically auspicious, and such a favorable conjunction will not recur for years." The smith turned to Vanora. "Meseems, girl, you've been talking too freely with our guest, or he'd not have known so much about the making of Randir. I shall have somewhat to say to you later. Meanwhile, back to your chores. Leave this lout to contemplate the fruits of his folly, for even this meager pleasure will not long remain him."

"Master Rhithos!" cried Jorian in desperation. "Faction or no faction, to slay the servant of a fellow member of your fraternity will bring troubles upon you. Karadur will avenge—"

The smith snorted, turned his broad back, and marched off to the smithy. Vanora disappeared. Overhead, the blanket of thick, gray cloud seemed to press closer than ever, and the clearing seemed darker than could even be explained by the heavy overcast. Bare branches stood up like withered black hands against the darkling sky.

Jorian felt a brooding tension, as he sometimes did before a heavy thunderstorm. He paced nervously about the cage, trying his muscles on the bars and hoisting himself up by the bars that formed the roof. He poked in vain at the lock with his thick, hairy fingers.

Later, when the light dimmed, Vanora passed the cage with a jar of water.

"Mistress Vanora!" called Jorian. "Don't I get anything more to eat?"

"To what end? Tomorrow you'll never need food again—at least, not on this plane of existence. Better to spend your time making peace with your gods and forget that bottomless pit of a belly."

She passed out of sight. Presently she was back, thrusting a loaf of bread and a crock of water through the bars.

"Quiet!" she whispered. "Rhithos would take it ill if he knew I wasted his victuals, as he'd say. As 'tis, he's like to stripe my back for telling you about the sword spell. He never remembers a favor or forgets an injury."

"An unlikeable wight. Can you get me out of here?"

"At eventide, when he's absorbed in his spells."

"I thought the final spell came tomorrow?"

"It does; this is but the penultimate cantrip."

\*　　　\*　　　\*

The smith ate early and returned to his smithy, whence presently issued the sound of a drum and of Rhithos' voice raised in a chant. The shadows seemed to deepen about the shed even more swiftly than elsewhere. As full darkness fell, curious sounds came forth—croaks unlike any made by a human voice, and other noises unlike anything Jorian had ever heard. Now and then the voice of the smith rose in a shouted command. Strange lights of a ghastly bluish radiance flickered through the cracks between the boards of the shed. Jorian's skin tingled until he felt as if he could jump right out of it. He wanted to explode with tension.

Vanora, a blur in the darkness, reappeared at the bars of the cage: "T-take this!" she whispered, extending a trembling hand. "And drop it not, test it be lost for aye in the mud."

It was the pick-lock with which Jorian had opened the cage door earlier. "You dropped it when Zor escaped," she said, "and Rhithos marked it not when he took the rest of your gear."

Jorian felt for the keyhole on the outer side of the lock plate and inserted the wire. His hand shook so that he could hardly find the hole. Manipulating the wire from inside the cage proved awkward, but after some fumbling the bolt clicked back. He put away the wire and opened the door. Another blue flash lit up the smithy.

"Here!" said Vanora, thrusting something cold into his hand. It was the hilt of his falchion. "You must slay Rhithos whilst he is sunken in his spell."

"Couldn't we just flee to Othomae? Your smith is no mean wizard, and I crave not to be turned into a spider."

"Faintheart! You're no gallant cavalier, ardent for a fight at whatever odds, but a common, calculating kern, weighing pros and contras as a moneychanger weighs out grains of gold dust."

"I've never claimed to be a gallant cavalier. These gambols affright me silly."

"Well, play the man for once! Rhithos will be weakened by his spell-casting."

"I still like it not; I do not enjoy killing people without necessity. Why can't we just flee through the woods?"

"Because the instant Rhithos learns of our escape, he'll cast a spell to fetch us back, or send his demons to herd us hither like sheep. And back we shall be forced if we're within five leagues of his house. Even if that fail, he's allied with the silvans, who at his command will fill us with their envenomed arrows. Since flight were fatal, there's nothing for it but to kill him, and that right speedily."

Jorian hefted the short, curved blade. "This is not an ideal utensil for the purpose, especially as he'll have that great brand Randir ready to hand. With this butcher's tool, I shall need some defense for the left hand. Give me your cloak."

"You mean to get my one good garment all hacked and slashed in the fray? I will not! Oh, you villain!" she cried as Jorian shot out a long arm and wrenched the cloak from her shoulders. He whipped the garment around his left arm.

"Now *you* be quiet!" he whispered, as he glided towards the shed.

Rhithos had closed the shutters over the windows of the smithy. The louvers of these shutters were also closed, lying flat against one another like the feathers in a bird's wing. One louver, however, had been broken at one end and sagged from its socket at the other. Jorian put his eye to the narrow triangle of light.

Within, the anvil had been moved to one side. Where it had stood, near the forge, three pentacles had been drawn with charcoal: one large flanked by two small. Rhithos stood in one small pentacle, Ixus in the other. Six black candles, at the apices of the triangles of the main pentacle, shed a fitful light, to which a dull-red glow from the banked fire in the forge added but little. The sword Randir lay in the center of the large central pentacle.

In that circle, also, stood something else, although Jorian could not quite make it out. It was dark and wavering, like a misshapen cloud, man-high and man-wide but without any definite limbs or organs. A pallid glow, like a witch fire or a will-o'-the-wisp, flickered through the thing from time to time.

Rhithos was waving a sword and chanting. Ixus, facing him across the large circle, beat time with a wand.

"His back is to the door," breathed Vanora. "You can thrust it open and sink your blade in his back with one bound."

"What of that spirit in the pentacle?"

" 'Tis not yet wholly materialized; interrupt the cantrip and 'twill vanish. Come, one swift stab—"

"Not quite what a gallant cavalier would do, but—come on?" Jorian stepped to the door. "Does it squeak?"

"Nay. Hating rust, Rhithos keeps the hinges oiled."

"Then grasp the knob and open, gently."

She did as he bade. As the door swung silently open, Jorian took a short running step. One long bound would sink the falchion in Rhithos' back, to the left of the spine and below the shoulder blade . . .

But Jorian had forgotten Ixus, who stood facing the door. As Jorian started his spring, the familiar screeched and pointed. Without turning his head, the smith bounded to one side. As he did so, he kicked one of the six candles. The candlestick went clattering one way; the candle flew another and went out. The cloudy thing in the large pentacle vanished.

Jorian's rush carried him through the space where Rhithos had stood and across the main pentacle. He tripped over the sword Randir, staggered, and almost trod on Ixus, who dodged and went for Jorian with bared chisel-teeth.

Jorian struck at the hurtling, black, furry body just before the teeth reached his leg. The blow hurled the giant squirrel against the forge, where it lay, twitching and bleeding. The blow had cut it nearly in half.

Rhithos recovered from his leap. He stepped back to the main pentacle and snatched up the sword Randir. By the time Jorian had turned from his blow at the familiar, the smith was upon him, whirling the sword in great full-armed, figure-eight cuts.

Rhithos' wrinkled face was pale in the candle light and sparkled with drops of sweat. He moved heavily and breathed hard, for his sorcerous operation had taken its toll of his strength. Nevertheless, so vast had been that strength to begin with that Jorian found the man, even in his fatigued condition, all he could handle and a little more.

Since the smith's blade was nearly twice the length of the falchion, Jorian was tempted to fall back before the onslaught. But he knew that, if he did, the smith would soon corner him. Therefore he stood his ground, catching the blows alternately on the falchion and the rolled-up cloak.

At first the blows came so fast and furiously that Jorian had no time for a return cut or thrust. The smith seemed determined to squander his remaining strength in a whole-hog effort to beat down Jorian's defense by sheer weight of blade and fury of attack.

Soon, however, age and exhaustion slowed the smith's windmill assault. As he parried one slash with the cloak, Jorian sent a forehand cut at Rhithos' chest. The tip of the falchion slit Rhithos' tunic and pinked the skin beneath.

Gasping, Rhithos fell back a pace. Now he fought more craftily, in proper fencing style, with his right foot forward and his left arm up and back. Since Jorian had to use his left hand, he employed the two-hand stance, facing directly forward with feet apart and knees slightly bent. The two were well matched. As they advanced, retreated, feinted, thrust, cut, and parried, they circled the main pentacle.

Jorian found that now he could fight an adequate defensive fight against Rhithos, but the other's length of blade kept him out of reach. When he tried to close, Rhithos' long blade licked out in a thrust at his exposed right arm. The point caught the fabric of Jorian's sleeve and tore a small rip in it. For an instant, Jorian felt the cold flat of the blade against his skin.

Around they went again. Both breathed in quick pants, watching each other's eyes. Jorian accidentally kicked over another candle, which also went out.

Now the smith seemed to have gotten his second wind, and it was Jorian who was beginning to tire. Again and again the smith sent thrusts and slashes at Jorian's right arm. Jorian avoided these attacks, but by narrower and narrower margins.

In the course of their circling, the smith once more had his back to the door. Vanora, who had been hovering in the background, stepped forward with the sword that Rhithos had been holding when first attacked, and which he had dropped. It was not a fighting weapon but a magical accessory—a straight, thirty-inch blade with little point and less edge, of well-polished soft iron, with a smooth ivory grip and a cross-guard in the form of a copper crescent. Practically speaking, it was useless for anything but spells and evocations.

Nonetheless, Vanora took the weapon in both hands and thrust the blunt point into Rhithos' back. The smith started, grunted, and half turned. Instantly Jorian closed with him. He whipped the tattered end of Vanora's cloak around the sword Randir, immobilizing it for an instant, and drove his falchion into Rhithos' chest. He jerked out the blade, thrust it into the smith's belly, withdrew it again, and slashed deeply into Rhithos' neck.

Like an aged oak, Rhithos swayed and crashed to the floor. Jorian stood over him, gasping for breath. When he could breathe normally, he took a rag from the pile that lay near the forge, wiped his blade, and sheathed it. He tossed the bloody rag on the banked forge fire, where it smoked, burst into flame, and was quickly consumed.

"By Imbal's bronzen arse, that was close," said Jorian. "Lucky for me he was already spent from his sorcery; I misdoubt I could have handled him fresh."

"Are you all right?" said Vanora.

"Aye. I'm relieved to see he has real blood inside him. From his cold, mechanical manner, I wondered if he'd prove to be full of cogwheels and pulleys, like one of my father's water clocks." He picked up Randir, squinted along the blade, and cut the air with it. It was a handsome, single-edged, cut-and-thrust sword with a basket hilt. "It won't have magical properties, since we broke into the spell. Still, a pretty blade. Do you suppose he has a scabbard for it?"

"He doesn't make his own scabbards but orders them from an armorer in Othomae. But one of those in the main hall might fit."

"I'll try them. Fit is important; nothing so embarrasses a hero as to confront a dragon or an ogre and find his sword firmly stuck in its scabbard. I do not suppose we need fear the law here?"

"Nay; there's none, save as each can make his own. Both Xylar and Othomae lay a claim to these hills, but they never send officers hither to sustain their claims or enforce their statutes."

With the toe of his boot, Jorian stirred the body of the giant squirrel. "I'm sorry to have slain his pet. It did but defend its master."

" 'Tis well you did, Master Jorian. Otherwise Ixus

would have told the silvans, and they would have slaughtered us in reprisal for their ally's death. As it is, they will learn of Rhithos' demise soon enough."

"How?"

"By the nullification of the confusion spell, whereby he's kept woodsmen out of their territory. As soon as some hunter wanders into this demesne—and now is the hunting season—they'll come running to this house to learn what ails their sorcerer."

"Then we had best start for Othmae forthwith," he said.

"First we must gather our gear. I shall need a cloak; your set-to has reduced mine to tatters. One of the smith's will serve."

Taking three of the remaining candles, they returned to the house. Jorian said:

"I do not think it were well to start such a journey on empty stomachs. Can you whip up a meal whilst I collect my belongings?"

"All you think of is food!" said Vanora. "I could not down a crumb after all this excitement. But you shall have what you ask. Linger not over it, for despite the darkness we should put as much distance as we can betwixt ourselves and the house by dawn, when the silvans begin to stir." She busied herself with the fire and the pots.

"Do you know the trails hereabouts?" asked Jorian, watching her. "I have a map, but on such a starless night 'tis of little avail."

"I know the way to Othomae. We go thither every month to sell Rhithos' swords and other ironmongery, to take orders for more, and to purchase supplies."

"How do you carry the load?"

"The ass bears it. Here's your repast, Master Eat-all."

"Aren't you having anything?"

"Nay; I told you I couldn't. But now the damned tyrant is dead and good riddance, we need not drink cider." She poured a flagon of wine for Jorian and another for herself and drank hers greedily.

"If you so bitterly hated Rhithos," said Jorian, "how is it that you never fled from him?"

"I told you, he had spells for fetching back runaways."

"But if you set out directly the old spooker fell asleep some night, by dawn you'd be beyond the range of his spells. And you say you know the trails."

"I couldn't traverse these woods alone, at night."

"Why not? The leopard will not attack if you put up a bold front."

"I might meet a serpent."

"Oh, come! The serpents in these hills are neither venomous, like those of the lowlands, nor huge, like those of the jungles of Mulvan, but small and harmless."

"Natheless, I have a deathly fear of all snakes." She gulped more wine. "Speak you no more of the matter; the mere thought of a serpent turns my veins to ice."

"Well then, shall we bury the smith?" asked Jorian.

"Indeed we must, and hide his grave, lest the silvans see his body lying in the smithy."

"Then we must needs do it tonight, albeit the scoundrel deserves it not."

"He was not a wholly wicked man, in the sense of doing that which he knew to be wrong." She hiccupped. "Though I hated his bowels, I would do him justice."

"He'd have murdered me for convenience in his swordmaking, and if that be not a villain, I shudder to think of the crimes that would arouse your disapproval."

"Oh, people were nothing to him. All he cared for was his swordsmith's art. He had no lust for wealth, or power, or glory, or women; his consuming ambition was to be the greatest swordmaker of all time. This ambition drove him so hard that all other human feelings were squeezed out, save perhaps some small affection for Ixus the imp." She drank heavily again.

"Mistress!" said Jorian. "If you swill thus on an empty stomach, you'll be in no shape to march through the woods."

"'Tis my affair, what I drink!" shouted Vanora. "Tend your business and I'll tend mine."

Jorian shrugged and addressed himself to his food. He did well by a rewarmed roast, another loaf of bread, half a cabbage, a fistful of onions, and an apple pie. He asked, "Why did you turn Zor loose?"

"For one, the creature loved me—and cursed few there have been who did. I include not all the lustful young men like yourself, who prate of love but only seek to sheathe their fleshy poniards. So it grieved me to see Rhithos sacrifice him to his mad ambition.

"For another, I—I took pleasure in thwarting Rhithos, to gratify my hatred. Lastly, because I wished to escape. Had Rhithos not died, I had spent my life here. He was as lively company as a granite boulder. The years of a wizard are not as those of a common man, and he might have survived me, old and shriveled. I durst not attack him myself, even in slumber, because the imp would have warned him; I durst not flee, for the reason I've given. So, thought I, I'll stir up strife betwixt these twain, and whichever win, I may escape in the confusion."

"You'd not have cared if I—a harmless stranger—had perished in this strife?"

"Oh, I hoped you'd conquer, if—if only because I should have gained no pleasure from your death. But if you'd lost," she shrugged, "that had been nought to me. What has the world of men done for me that I should bear them that all-embracing, indiscriminate love the priests of Astis counsel?" She gulped more wine.

"By Astis' ivory teats, you're frank, at least," he said,

wiping his mouth. "I do not think we need wash these dishes, since we purpose to abandon the house. If you'll tell me where Rhithos keeps his shovel, I will bury him and his pet."

"On—on a peg to the right of the door of the smithy, ash—as you enter." Her voice had become blurred. "He wash a mos'—most particular man, with a peg for each tool, and woe betide the wretch who returned one to the wrong peg!"

"Good! Collect your dunnage whilst I perform this task." Carrying a candle, Jorian went out.

Half an hour later he returned, to find Vanora sprawled ungracefully on the floor, with her skirt up to her middle and an overturned flagon beside her. He spoke to her, nudged her, shook her, slapped her, and poured cold water on her face. Her only responses were a drunken mumble and a rasping snore.

"Damned fool woman," growled Jorian. "We're in such haste to flee the silvans, so you must needs get potulated!"

He stood scowling and thinking. He could not set forth without her, since he did not know the way. He could not carry her . . .

He gave up, stretched out on a bench, and pulled a bearskin over himself. The next thing he knew, dawn was graying the windows. He was being aroused by Vanora, who was showering moist, slobbery kisses upon him, breathing hard, and fumbling with his garments.

As the sun rose, they stepped out, closing the doors of Rhithos' house and smithy. Jorian wore the sword Randir in a scabbard from Rhithos' living room. He also bore a dagger of Rhithos' make: a deadly affair, with a broad, cubit-long blade and a catch that prevented its coming out of its sheath unless one pressed a stud. The pommel was no gaudy gem but a simple ball of lead. When held by the sheathed blade, the weapon made a handy bludgeon in case one wished merely to stun a foe.

Jorian also carried his crossbow, and under his tunic he wore a vest of fine mesh mail, also looted from Rhithos' house. Feeling as if he could knock an elephant down with his fist, he expanded his huge chest and said:

"We shall have to take our chances with the silvans. Perhaps they won't soon discover Rhithos' disappearance. But I don't care." While loading provisions on Rhithos' ass, he burst into a threshing song in the Kortolian dialect.

"What are you singing about?" snapped Vanora. "You'll rouse every silvan within leagues, with that big bass voice."

"Just happy, that's all. Happy because a've found ma true love."

"Love!" she snorted.

"Couldn't you feel a little love for me? I'm head over heals in love with you, wench. And you did give me your all, as they say."

"Rubbish! The fact that I needed to be well futtered after long deprivation has nought to do with love."

"But, darling—"

"Darling me no darlings! I'm not the woman for you. I am just a drunken slut with a hot cleft, and forget it not."

"Oh," he said, his exalted mood punctured.

"Get me to a city and buy me some decent clothes, and then if you want to talk of love, I don't suppose I can stop you."

Jorian sighed, and his broad shoulders dropped. "You're nobody's sweet little innocent honey-bun, I will grant. I'm a bigger fool for loving you than Doctor Karadur was in trusting Rhithos. But there it is, damn it. Let's say a prayer to Thio and go."

# III

# The Silver Dragon

Rhuys's tavern, the silver dragon, stood just off the main square of Othomae City, behind the Guildhall. The main taproom accommodated six tables, each flanked by a pair of benches, while to one side a pair of curtained alcoves served as private rooms for patrons of quality. Facing the entrance was Rhuys's bar: a counter with four large holes in the marble top, each closed by a circular wooden lid with a handle. Below each hole hung a cask of one of the cheaper beverages: beer, ale, white wine, and red wine, each with its own dipper. Choicer drinkables stood in a row in bottles on a shelf behind the taverner.

To the left of the bar, as one entered, was the door to the kitchen; Rhuys would have his wife cook dinner for patrons who ordered in advance. To the right were the stairs leading up to the dormitory and the three private bedrooms that the tavern rented. Rhuys himself occupied the fourth. Several oil lamps shed a soft yellow light about the room.

Although he bore the same name as a former king of Xylar, known as Rhuys the Ugly, Rhuys the taverner was not really ugly. He was a small, wiry, seedy-looking man, with thinning, graying hair and pouched eyes. He leant his elbows on the bar and watched his few customers. There were only five, for the morrow was a working day and few Othomaeans were out late that night. In addition, a huge, gross, porcine man sprawled in a corner.

The door opened, and Jorian and Vanora came in.

Jorian, looking worn from his fiftnight's hike from Rhithos's house, approached the counter.

"Good even," he said. "I am Nikko of Kortoli. Has a Doctor Ma—Mabahandula left word for me?"

"Why, yes, so he has," said Rhuys. "He was in today, saying he'd be here right after the supper hour; but he has not come."

"Then we'll wait. We have given our ass in charge of your boy in the back."

"What will you have?"

"Ale for me." Jorian looked a question at Vanora, who said:

"Red wine for me."

"Have you aught to eat?" said Jorian. "We've come a long way."

"Plenty of bread, cheese, and apples. The fire is out, so we cannot cook a hot repast for you."

"Bread, cheese and apples will do fine." Jorian turned away to lead Vanora to one of the tables.

"Master Nikko!" called Rhuys. "Have you a permit to carry that hanger?" He indicated Jorian's sword, the hilt of which was now attached to the scabbard by a wire. The ends of the wire were crimped together by a small leaden seal bearing the two-headed eagle of Othomae.

"They gave me one at the city gate," said Jorian, waving a piece of reed paper. "I'm a traveler on his way to Vindium."

Of the other customers, two men were drinking and arguing in low tones. Jorian and Vanora leisurely ate and drank. Other customers came and went, but the pair in the corner continued their dispute.

Long after Jorian and Vanora had finished their supper, the other pair were still at it. One of these men raised his voice in anger. Presently he stood up, leaned over the bench, shook his fist, and shouted:

"You son of a eunuch, you will cheat me of my commission, will you? Any man who so entreats me has cause to rue his deed! I have warned you for the last time! Now will you pay me my share, or—"

"Futter you," said the seated man.

With a shrill squawk, the standing man hurled the contents of his mug in the other's face. Sputtering, the other man tried to rise and reach for his dagger, but his robe had become entangled with the bench. While he struggled and the standing man screamed threats and denunciations, the huge, stout man in the corner caught Rhuys's eye. Rhuys nodded. The stout man lumbered to his feet, took three steps, picked the standing man up bodily by the slack of his garments, strode to the door; and tossed the man into the street. Brushing his hands together, he returned to his seat without a word.

Vanora gave the stout man a long look as she said to Jorian: "I wonder they did not notice the Grand Bastard's name on your sw—"

"*Hush!* Don't mention that. When I get a chance, I'll have it filed off."

She waved to Rhuys to refill her glass, asking Jorian: "What is this title of Grand Bastard? It does not sound like a real title. I've heard of the Grand Duke and the Grand Bastard, but none has ever explained it to me. Which rules Othomae?"

"They are corulers. According to Othomaean custom, the eldest legitimate son of the late Grand Duke becomes the new Grand Duke and hereditary ruler of the kingdom in civil affairs, whilst the eldest illegitimate son of that same late Grand Duke becomes the Grand Bastard and hereditary commander-in-chief of the army. Since the Othomaeans set great store by legitimacy, the Grand Bastard knows that 'twould avail him nought to try to seize the civil power, for none would then obey him."

"What a curious way to run a country!"

"The Othomaeans set it up long ago, so that no one

ruler should become too powerful and oppress his subjects. Now, Vanora, you are not going to get drunk again, I hope?"

"I'll drink what I please. How are you going to steal this Kist in Trimandilam?"

"That's for Karadur and me to decide when we get there. The plan for the nonce is for me to make up to the serpent princess."

"Serpent princess? What's that?"

"An immortal—or at least monstrously long-lived—being who is a luscious princess by day and a gigantic serpent by night, Karadur tells me she has the disconcerting habit of changing shape and devouring the poor wight who has just been making love to her, as I shall have to do."

She banged her mug on the table. "You mean, after giving me sweet talk of love all the way from Rhithos' house, you knew all the time you were going to try to seduce this—this snake-woman?"

"Please! I have no choice in the matter—"

"You're just another lying prick-hound! I should have known better than to listen to you. Farewell!" She started to rise.

"My dear, girl, what in the name of Zevatas's horse is there to get so excited about? Surely you do not make an idol of chastity—"

Furiously, she replied: "I should not much have minded your futtering a proper human dame; but a *snake*! Ugh! Goodbye! That looks like the kind of man I understand!"

She staggered over to where the stout man sprawled and sat down beside him. The man's little, piggy eyes opened, and his thick lips wreathed themselves in a smile through his stubble. Jorian followed her, saying:

"Pray, Vanora, be reasonable!"

"Oh, hold your tongue! You bore me." She turned to the ejector. "What's your name, big man?"

"Huh? My name?"

"Aye, handsome! Your name."

"Boso son of Triis. Is this fellow bothering you?"

"He won't if he knows what is good for him."

"Who are you, fellow?" growled Boso at Jorian.

"Nikko of Kortoli, if it is any concern of yours. This young lady was with me, but she is her own woman. If she prefers you, I might question her taste but would not thwart her choice."

"Oh," grunted Boso, settling back in his corner once more. But Vanora burst out:

"He is not Nikko of Kortoli! He is Jorian son of Evor—"

"Wait!" said Boso, opening his eyes and jerking upright once more. "That makes me think of something. Let me see . . ." He peered up through narrowed lids. "Not Evor the clockmaker?"

"Aye; he's told me many a tale of his sire—"

With a roar, Boso heaved up out of his seat, stooping to fumble for the two-foot bludgeon that lay at his feet. "So you're the son of the man who cost me my livelihood!"

"What in the forty-nine Mulvanian hells do you mean?" said Jorian, stepping back and laying a hand on his hilt. When he tried to draw, he realized that he could not because of the peace wire threaded through the guard.

Boso bellowed: "I was chief gongringer of Othomae, and a damned good one! My helpers and I sounded the hours in the city hall tower and never missed a stroke. Twenty years ago—or was it ten? No matter—your perverted father sold a water clock to the town council, and there it stands in the tower; going *bong, bong* with its wheels and levers. Since then I've had to live by odd jobs, and life has been hell. I cannot beat your fornicating father to a pulp, but you'll do!"

"Boso!" said Rhuys sharply. "Behave yourself, you stupid lout, if you want your job!"

"Bugger you, boss," said Boso and went for Jorian with his club.

Unable to draw the sword Randir, Jorian had hoisted the baldric over his head and now gripped the hilt of the scabbarded blade in both hands. As Boso lumbered forward like an enraged behemoth on the banks of the Bharma, Jorian feinted at his head. As Boso raised the bludgeon to parry, Jorian poked him in the midriff with the chape on the end of the scabbard.

"*Oof!*" said Boso, doubling up and giving back a step.

Since Jorian and Boso were by far the two largest men in the room, the remaining customers crowded back to the walls to get out of the way. Cautiously, the two combatants advanced and retreated in the space between the two rows of tables, which was too narrow to permit them to circle. Every time Boso tried to close to bring his bludgeon into range, the threat of the scabbarded blade drove him back.

Boso made a determined lunge; Jorian whacked him above the ear. The blow knocked him sideways, but he recovered. His little eyes blazing with rage, he stepped forward and aimed a terrific forehand swing.

The bludgeon whispered through the air as Jorian jerked back; the end of the club missed his face by the thickness of a sheet of parchment. The force of the missed blow swung Boso halfway around. Before he could recover, Jorian stepped forward and to the left and brought his knee hard up against Boso's back, over his right kidney. As Boso staggered, clutching for support at a table top, Jorian, now behind him, slipped the loop of the baldric over Boso's head. He tightened the strap around the ejector's neck, twisting it with all the strength of his powerful hands.

Boso opened his mouth, but only a faint wheeze came forth. Eyes popping, he stamped and kicked and waved his arms, trying to reach the foe behind him. But his arms were too short and thick. He plunged and staggered about the confined space, dragging Jorian with him, but Jorian's grip never loosened.

Boso's struggles weakened as his face turned blue. He clutched the edge of a table, then slid to the floor.

The door flew open, and several people crowded in. One was Karadur, with his long, white beard and bulbous turban. With him was a tall, gray-haired woman in a shabby black gown. After them came a squad of the night watch: four men armed with halberds and an officer. The latter said, "Master Rhuys! We heard there was a disturbance. Who is that? What has befallen?"

"That is Boso, my ejector—my former ejector, that is. He picked a fight with this customer and got thrashed."

"Was he alone to blame?"

"As far as I could see, he was."

The officer turned to Jorian. "Are you fain to submit a complaint against this man?"

Vanora had pulled Boso's head up so that it lay in her lap, and she was tricking a little wine down his throat to its normal hue. As Jorian hesitated, Karadur said:

"Do not—ah—send the fellow to prison, Jorian—"

"Nikko."

"Of course; how stupid of me! Do not send this poor fellow to prison. You have chastised him enough by strangling him nigh unto death."

"How do I know he'll not set upon me with that club as soon as he gets his breath back?"

"You must disarm him by your kindness. Remember, the best way to destroy an enemy is to make him your friend."

"All very pretty I suppose next you'll want me to find him another job."

"A splendid idea!" Karadur clapped his old hands together. To the officer he said: "I think, sir, you may leave us without a formal complaint." Then to Rhuys, "What is this man good for, save as an ejector?"

"For nought! He is too stupid," said the taverner. "If some big building construction were under way, he could carry a hod; but there is none just now."

The gray-haired woman spoke: "I can use one of thick thews but weak wits. Besides gardening and household tasks, he can protect me against those ignorant oafs who betimes raise the cry of 'witch!' against me, not withstanding that I am a fully licensed wizardess."

"I have not had the pleasure of meeting you, madam," said Jorian. "I am Nikko of Kortoli."

"And I, Goania daughter of Aristor." She leaned over and shook Boso's shoulder. "Get up, man!"

Boso and Vanora climbed unsteadily to their feet. Goania said sharply:

"Do you understand, Boso? You have lost your post here."

"Huh? You mean lost my job?" wheezed Boso.

"Certes. Will you work for me for what Master Rhuys paid you: sixpence a day and found?"

"Me work for you?"

"Aye. Must I repeat the terms?"

Boso ran a hand over his chin with a rasp of stubble. "Oh, I guess it's all right. But first, I'll just knock the pumpkin off this fornicating clockmaker, who goes around putting honest workmen out of their jobs."

"You shall do nothing of the sort! Sit down and calm yourself."

"Now, lady! I don't let no woman tell me—"

"I am not a lady; I am a wizardess who can turn you into a toad if you misbehave. And I say there shall be no more quarreling. We are all friends, henceforth."

"Him? Friend?"

"Verily. He could have sent you to prison but chose not to, thinking you more useful out than in."

Boso glowered at Jorian, spat on the floor, and mumbled under his breath. But he let Vanora lead him over to the far side of the room, where the girl soothed and comforted him while he drank beer and fingered his sore neck.

Jorian, Karadur, and Goania sat in the opposite corner. Jorian asked Karadur, "Where in the forty-nine Mulvanian hells have you been, man? We have been here for hours."

"I obtained access to the Grand Ducal library," said Karadur, "and became so—ah—absorbed in reading that I forgot about time. But you look as if you had had a hard time of it, lad. You have lost weight—not that you could not afford to lose a little."

"I have had a hard time; had to kill Rhithos—"

With sharp exclamations, the other two bent closer. "Keep your voice down, Master Nikko," said Goania. "I know your true name but think it unwise to utter it here, unless you wish the taverner to set the Xylarians on your trail. Tell us how this calamity came to pass."

Jorian told his tale. "So we hiked to Othomae on the trails Vanora knows, and here we are. The ass is stabled in the rear."

"What sort of traveling companion did the lass make?" asked Goania.

"*Oi!*" Jorian rolled his eyes. "She once called herself a drunken slut with a hot cleft—begging your pardon, madam—and I fear she did but speak the truth. Since she makes no bones about her love of fornication, I besmirch no lady's name in telling you. Daily we quarreled and made up. Nightly she demanded that I dip my wick, and then she'd taunt me by boasting of some former lover who, she said, could stroke three to my one. When I was king, I flatter myself that I kept five wives happy; but now I could not satisfy one. She's careless with her contraceptive spells, too. Altogether—well, I own I am the world's greatest fool for falling in love with the drab, but there it is."

"She hardly sounds beguiling, from what you say," said Goania. "Why should you, who have known the pick of a kingdom, love so cross-grained a hussy?"

Jorian scratched his new beard. "A kind of painful pleasure. There's something about her—a blunt honesty, a forceful vigor, and an intelligence that, were it but cultivated, could hold its own with learned doctors ... When in a good humor she can be more fun than a cage of monkeys. And when is love controlled by rational calculations? But the last few days have wellnigh cured me. I made a little verse about it, which she did not like at all:

"O lady fair,
    Why must you be
So sharp with me,
    When all can see
For you I care?

I'm not aware
    That nagging me
And ragging me
    Is how to be
My lady fair.

If handsome is
    As handsome does
(The saying was),
    Then cease to buzz
And sting and whiz.

Or else, beware!
    If like a flea
You pester me,
    You shall not be
My lady fair!"

"Only wellnigh cured, said you?"
"Just that. If she came hither now and pleaded and flattered, promising to be sweet and kind and to stay sober, and begging me to keep her with me throughout

my journey, I should be her pliant slave again, though I knew her promises to be so much straw. Thank Zevatas, she seems to have found someone more to her taste."

Goania glanced towards the corner, where Boso and Vanora had fallen into drunken slumber, the girl's head on the man's shoulder. "O Karadur, you had better get the lad out of Othomae forthwith, ere the wench change her mind. Know you any member of our order in Vindium?"

"I stayed with Porrex on my way to Xylar, last year. A delightful colleague—so kind and considerate."

"He is also tricky; beware of him."

"Oh, I am sure so good a man is to be trusted, as far as one can trust anyone in this wicked world. I had a chance of witnessing his kindness and generosity at first hand."

Jorian asked, "Why can't you perform a divination to find the results of our intercourse with Master Porrex?"

Goania shook her head. "The practice of magic introduces into the lifeline of the practitioner too many factors from other planes and dimensions. I can divine somewhat of the luck of a layman like yourself, Master Nikko, but not those of Doctors Karadur or Porrex."

"Well then," said Jorian eagerly, "tell me what lies before *me!*"

"Give me your hand. When and where were you born?"

"In Ardamai, Kortoli, on the fifteenth of the Month of the Lion, in the twelfth year of King Fealin the Second, about sunrise."

Goania examined Jorian's palm and thought silently for a moment. Then she held her goblet so that she could see the reflection of one of the lamps in the surface of the wine. With her other hand she made passes over the vessel, moving her fingers in complex patterns and softly whispering. At last she said:

"Beware of a bedroom window, a tinkling man, and a tiger-headed god."

"Is that all?"

"It is all I see at this time."

Familiar with the vagueness and ambiguity of oracles, Jorian did not press the wizardess for more detail. Karadur spoke, "And now, madam, or ever I forget, have you that which you promised me?"

Goania felt in her purse and brought out a small packet. "The Powder of Discord—pollen of the spotted fireweed, gathered when the Red Planet was in conjunction with the White in the Wolf. Blown into any group of men, it will cause them to bicker and fight."

"Gramercy, Mistress Goania. This may prove a mighty help in Trimandilam."

Jorian: "With the Xylarians hunting us, I would not try to walk to Vindium. We can afford horses, and we can lead the ass with our little baggage."

"No horse for me!" said Karadur. "A fall from so tall a beast would break my old bones like flowerpots. Get me another ass, instead."

"An ass would slow us."

"No more than the one you already have."

"So be it, then. When does the horse market open tomorrow?"

The folk of Vindium City observed their harvest festival, the Feast of Spooks, by dressing up as supernatural beings and dancing in their streets. Since the day was a holiday, masked Vindines began to appear in their costumes well before the early autumnal sunset. Before the dinner hour, they paraded the streets, admiring one another's costumes and trying to guess which notables were concealed by especially ornate and costly garb. The livelier events—the parade, the dancing and singing, and the costume contest—would come later.

Arriving at the West Gate while the sun was still a red ball over the tilled fields of Vindium behind them,

Jorian and Karadur halted at the gate for questioning. Then they rode on into the city, Jorian on the elderly black he had bought in Othomae, Karadur riding an ass and leading another. The main street, Republic Avenue, sloped gently down from the West Gate to the waterfront. They passed the Senate House, the Magistracy, and other public buildings, wherein the austere plainness of the classical Novarian style was adulterated by a touch of florid, fanciful Mulvanian ornateness.

Porrex's dwelling, said Karadur, was near the waterfront, so thither they threaded their way through swarms of gods, demons, ghosts, ghouls, skeltons, witches, elves, trolls, werewolves, and vampires, and some clad as supernatural beings from Mulvanian legendry. Mulvanian influence showed in Vindium not only in the architecture and the costumes but also in the swarthiness of the people. When one reveler, dressed as the war god Heryx, hit Jorian's horse with a bladder on the end of a stick, Jorian had much ado to keep the beast under control.

They took a room near the waterfront, stabled their animals, and sought out the dwelling of Porrex the magician. Porrex lived in a rented room above a draper's shop.

"Come in, good my sirs, come in!" cried Porrex at the head of the stair. He was a short, round, bald man with blue eyes almost buried in fat. "Dear old Karadur! How good to see you again! And your companion—tell me not, let me guess—is Jorian son of Evor, former king of Xylar! Come in, come in. Sit down. Let me fetch you a drop of beer; that is all I have in the place."

The room was small and sparsely furnished, with an unmade bed, a rickety chair, a table, and a small bookcase with a few tattered scrolls in the pigeonholes and a few dogeared codices on top. A couple of chests along the wall and a water-stained drawing of the god Psaan driving his chariot on the waves of the sea completed the meager appointments. A single candle inside a

small lanthorn with glass windows shed a wan illumination. When silence fell, the patter of mice in their runs
could be heard.

"My name, sir," said Jorian, "is Nikko of Kortoli.
Who told you otherwise?"

"My dear sir, what good should I be as a diviner if
I could not ascertain such simple facts? But, if you
prefer to be known as Nikko, then Nikko you shall be."
Porrex winked. "I grieve that I cannot receive you in
a palace, with feasts and dancing girls; but my business
affairs have not prospered of late as is their usual wont.
Hence, I must retrench. This condition, I assure you,
is only temporary; within a month I shall get some
new clients, who will put me back among the rich.
Meanwhile, I live as I can, not as I would. But tell me
of your affairs. I take it that Master Nikko is fain to
put a goodly distance between himself and Xylar?"

"Not exactly," said Karadur, sitting cross-legged on
the bed. "Know you that project that we Altruists have
mulled for several years?"

"You mean to lift the Kist of Avlen? Ah, now light
dawns! You are on your way to Trimandilam, hoping
with the help of this mighty youth to effect this righteous expropriation. Well, strength to arms and stealth
to your feet! You two have no engagements for dinner,
have you?"

"Nay," said Karadur. "We hoped you would give us
the pleasure—"

"Indeed, indeed I will! Would that I could entertain
you in style, but at the moment my purse contains
exactly one farthing. When my new contracts are signed
next month, I shall repay you a hundredfold. Let us go
to Cheuro's; there one need not order the meal in
advance. What do you purpose to do for Mulvanian
money?"

"How mean you?" asked Karadur.

"Oh, have you not heard? Since you left Mulvan, the
Great King has promulgated new laws about money.

Only Mulvanian coins may be accepted by his subjects. All foreigners entering the land are made to give up their foreign money and precious metal in exchange for coin of the realm. The rate of exchange, however, is murderous; the traveler loses half the value of his coins. If he fail to turn in all his foreign gold and silver and is later caught, he is put to death in various ingenious ways, whereof being trampled by the king's elephants is one of the simpler."

"That is a nuisance," said Karadur. "We had thought ourselves well provided, but if the King of Kings is going to rob us of half our funds—"

Porrex cocked his head and winked. "I might be able to help you in this matter. There are, naturally, those to whom an ounce of gold is an ounce of gold, and what matter if it bear the head of Shaju of Mulvan or Jorian of Xylar? Such persons smuggle foreign money into the empire and Mulvanian coins out—at the risk of their heads—to sell abroad at a premium. Or they coin Mulvanian coins—not base-metal counterfeits, but gold pieces—themselves. One can, with the right connections, buy enough of such coins, at a more favorable rate of exchange, to tide one through one's visit to mighty Mulvan."

"Do King Shaju's folk let one bring Mulvanian coins into the empire at face value?" asked Jorian.

"Indeed they do; for the endeavor of their government is to get all their coins into the empire and keep them there. In sooth, if their policy did not make such smuggling profitable, it would not occur in the first place. But Shaju's treasurer is obsessed with monetary theories, which he must put into effect willy-nilly, no matter if they cut athwart the grain of human nature. Wait here and help yourselves to the beer whilst I sally forth to see if the man I know can be found."

When Porrex had vanished, Karadur said, "Have you still your hundred Xylarian lions, my son? Methinks we should change them as Porrex proposes."

"All but two or three, spent on the road hither. But I prefer to confirm Doctor Porrex's statement before entrusting any money to him. I mean, his assertion about this new Mulvanian law."

"Oh, surely so kind a little man, and a member of my virtuous faction, were trustworthy—"

"Mayhap, but I still prefer to ask. Wait here."

Jorian in his turn went out. He soon returned, saying, "Your little butterball of a wizard is right. I spoke to several knowledgeable folk—taverners and the like—and they all confirmed what he said."

"I told you we could trust him. Here he comes now."

Porrex rëentered the room. "It is all arranged, gentles. My man awaits without. How much have you to exchange in gold or silver? Copper and bronze count not."

Jorian had ninety-seven lions and some silver; Karadur, much less gold but more silver. Porrex did some calculations on an abacus.

"I can get you forty-two-and-a-half Mulvanian crowns for that," he said. "That is deducting a mere sixth part for the broker's commission, compared to half at the border. If you will let me take this money downstairs; my man does not care to be seen . . ."

Karadur handed over his purse without demur, but Jorian held his. "You may change his money that way," said Jorian, "but I want to see your Mulvanian gold first."

"Oh, certes; it shall be as you say, dear lad. Wait." Out went Porrex again. This time he was gone somewhat longer. Karadur said:

"His gold speculator must be as suspicious of letting his money out of his hands as you are, Jorian."

"Better safe than sorry."

There was a clatter of feet on the stair, and Porrex came back in with another man. With a beaming smile, Porrex cried:

"Fortune is with us tonight! Let me present my dear

old friend Laziendo. These are Doctor Karadur and Master Nikko, of whom I told you."

Laziendo was a rather small man, a little older than Jorian, bronzed and swarthy, with a sweeping mustache. He bowed formally to the travelers and gave them a charming smile.

"Master Laziendo is supercargo on one of Benniver Sons' ships," continued Porrex. "He sails tomorrow and was searching for somebody with whom to celebrate his last evening ashore. Now you need not buy my dinner; friend Laziendo insists upon treating us all."

"The pleasure will be all mine, fair sirs," murmured Laziendo.

"Now," said Porrex, "here is your gold, Doctor; and here is yours, Master Nikko. Count it. If you will now give me yours, O Nikko . . . Laziendo, old boy, would you be so good as to step out and hand this sack to him who waits in the shadow below? It were not well for me to climb these stairs so often. Good! Whilst he is out, gentles, I must find masks for us, lest we be pestered by drunken revelers for not being in costume."

Porrex rummaged in a chest and produced four devil masks with staring eyes and scowls and fangs. Jorian examined several square Mulvanian gold pieces, with the crowned head of Shaju or of his father on one side and an elephant trampling a tiger on the other. Then he took the mask that Porrex gave him and adjusted the string to fit his head. Laziendo returned, saying:

"It is done, fair sirs. Allow your servant to lead you to Cheuro's. We shan't need lights, the town being illuminated for the festival."

Located on Republic Avenue, Cheuro's was a much larger establishment then the Silver Dragon in Othomae. At the door, a one-legged beggar accosted the four. Porrex fumbled in his purse and handed the man one small copper coin. Karadur said:

"If that was your last farthing, O Porrex, what will you eat on after we have departed?"

Porrex shrugged. "I suppose I shall raise a loan on one of my remaining books, which my forthcoming new contracts will soon enable me to redeem. This way, gentles."

The main dining room had a clear space in the middle for entertainers. The dinner was excellent, the wine sound, and the naked dancing girls supple. As the table was cleared, Laziendo said:

"If we kill time here for another hour, our foreign guests will see the parade by merely stepping out the front door. It passes in front of Cheuro's. Stay, fair sirs, and try some more of Cheuro's liquors. Since Vindium is the busiest port on the Inner Sea, we get the best vintages from all over."

Porrex yawned. "You will excuse me, I pray, dear friends; the years have leached away my capacity for late hours. I am sure that Master Laziendo can show you the delights of our city. Good night."

When Porrex had gone, Jorian asked Laziendo, "We seek the road to Trimandilam, and you should be able to advise us of the best way thither."

Laziendo stroked his mustache and smiled. "Why, this is a stroke of good fortune! I sail tomorrow on the *Talaris*, a gaggle of slave girls for Rennum Kezymar and marble, copper, wool, and miscellaneous cargo for Janareth. The deck will be a thought crowded until we discharge the lassies at Rennum Kezymar, but I'm sure we can find room for you. From Janareth you can ascend the Bharma by river boat to the capital."

Jorian asked about fares and said: "What is this Rennum Kezymar, and why are you taking slave girls thither?"

"The name means 'Ax Castle' in the dialect of Janareth. It is a small island off the mouth of the Jhukna, ruled by Mulvan. A couple of centuries ago, the then

King of Kings chose it as a home for retired executioners."

"What!"

"Aye, and with good reason. Be an executioner never so gentle and pleasant and virtuous in his private capacity, people still care not to befriend him, Hence the Great King found he had many headsmen, too old to swing the ax or knot the rope or turn the windlass of the rack, living in misery despite their pensions, because no man would treat with them. Betimes the locals would not even sell them food, so that they starved to death.

"Rennum Kezymar was then but a barren islet, good only for a winter pasture for the flocks of a few shepherds. It bore the ruins of an ancient castle, built many centuries back, in the time of the Three Kingdoms. The king had the castle rebuilt and gathered his executioners there, and there they have dwelt ever since."

"If they are old and retired, what need have they for young slave girls?" said Jorian. "As well go tilting with a lance of asparagus."

Laziendo shrugged. "To fetch and carry, peradventure. Some have wives, but of their own age. In any case, my duty is but to play sheep dog to these girls and deliver them to the destination averred in the manifest."

"What of the land route from Vindium to Trimandilam?"

Laziendo held up his hands. "Fair sirs! Although the map shows a road from here to Janareth along the coast, as a practical matter it's plain impossible."

"How so?"

"Because an easterly spur of the Lograms follows the coast for nigh a hundred leagues. The road is a mere track, winding up and down precipices, crossing swift mountain torrents like the Jhukna by swaying bridges of rope, and here and there ceasing entirely where a landslide has destroyed it. Besides which, the coastal country swarms with brigands and tigers. Nay, rather try to steal the emerald gold of Tarxia than essay this route!"

"Is not that coast under the rule of the mighty King of Kings, who maintains such fine roads and swift postal service?"

"Aye, but all these amenities you'll find in the interior, within a few score leagues of Trimandilam. The emperor neglects the borderlands—I think designedly, lest some invader take advantage of such improvements. In any case, better that you should go on my ship. This voyage is late in the season, but its very lateness, while it augments the danger of storms, lessens that of piracy."

"I thank you for your warning," said Jorian. "We may visit your ship early on the morrow to book passage. Tell us how to find her."

Laziendo gave directions and added: "Excuse me, fair sirs; all this wine necessitates a visit to the jakes. I shall return."

Jorian and Karadur sat over their flagons so long that sounds outside and the actions of Cheuro's other guests implied that the parade would soon begin. At last Jorian said:

"Is that fellow playing a jape on us? Wait here."

He went through the kitchen door, to be confronted by a fat cook.

"Aye," said the cook, "I saw such a man as you describe, a half-hour past. He went straight through and out the back, without stopping at the jakes. Why, is aught amiss?"

"No, nothing's wrong," said Jorian. He returned to their table, muttering: "The vermin has bilked us; slithered out and left us to pay the scot. Well, thank Zevatas we have the means."

"Speaking of which," said Karadur, "our host has in his eye the look of a man about to tender his bill."

Jorian pulled out his purse, which held a few of the

Mulvanian crowns, the rest being stowed in his money belt. He shook out one and almost dropped it.

"By all the gods!" he whispered, eyes wide. "Look at this, O Karadur! Keep your voice down."

Jorian held out the object, which was no Mulvanian golden crown but a square of lead of the same approximate size. Hoping against hope, he dug into the purse and brought out several more coins—all of which turned out to be leaden slugs.

Karadur stared in horror, then frantically clawed at his own purse. His gold had likewise turned to leaden squares. His mouth sagged open.

"That's the bastard you wanted us to trust!" hissed Jorian furiously. "Goania warned us he was tricky; and now, by Imbal's brazen balls, you know what she meant! I could have lived comfortably on that pelf for years!"

Tears rolled down Karadur's wrinkled brown cheeks. "True. It is all my fault, my son. I knew of that deception spell, too. I am a useless old dodderer. Never will I trust a strange man again, however fair and upright he seem."

"Well, how in the forty-nine Mulvanian hells shall we get out of here? If we try to walk out, there will be a fracas, and the watch will pitch us into the Vindine jail, where the Xylarians will presently discover me and request extradition. And 'twere easier to make pies out of stones than to wheedle credit from this Cheuro."

"Go along, my son, and leave me to take the blame."

"Don't talk nonsense. I cannot assail the Mulvanian Empire singlehanded, so we must fight our way out together. Oh-oh, here comes Cheuro now." Jorian hastily swept up the slugs.

Cheuro leant his fists upon the table. "Have you gentlemen enjoyed your repast and entertainment?"

"We surely have, sir taverner," replied Jorian with a jovial grin. "I'm only sorry that our companions had to leave early. How much do we owe you?"

"Two marks and six. May I serve you a round on the house?"

"Delighted! Let me see, we should finish the evening with something special. Have you any of that liqueur they brew in Paalua, called *olikau*? Betimes we get it on the western coast."

Cheuro frowned. "I know the drink to which you refer, but I know not whether I have a bottle."

"Well, do us the kindness to make sure, whilst we reckon who owes what to whom."

When Cheuro had gone back to his bar, Jorian whispered; "What magic have you for us now? I've gained us a little time. How about an invisibility spell?"

"That calls for lengthy preparations, with far more apparatus than we have to hand. Furthermore, it does but make one's flesh and bone transparent, not one's raiment. Hence one must either go about nude—which the coolth of the present weather renders impractical—or present the arresting sight of a suit of garments walking about with no one inside it. Moreover, to see in this condition, one must exempt one's eyeballs from the spell. But let me think. Ah, I have it!"

Moving quickly, the old magician produced a wallet divided inside into many compartments. From several of these pockets he withdrew pinches of powder, which he sprinkled into his empty flagon. He stirred the powders with his finger and placed the mug on the floor between his feet.

"Be ready to cry 'Fire!' " he said.

"Hasten!" said Jorian. "Cheuro is coming back, and without his Paaluan liqueur."

Karadur mumbled as he raced through a spell, while the fingers of his two hands fluttered through figures on the tabletop, like the legs of a pair of agitated brown spiders. When Cheuro was halfway from the bar to their table, there was a hiss from the flagon. A tremendous cloud of thick, black smoke billowed up out of it, surging up against the underside of the table, spreading out in all directions, and hiding the table and the two travelers in its ever-widening billows.

"Fire!" cried Jorian.

There was a clatter of overturned benches and running feet, as the other customers stampeded towards the entrance. Jorian and Karadur snatched their masks and cloaks and joined the throng. Since smoke now filled the room, they waited until the jam at the door had cleared and so got through without being squeezed or trampled.

Outside, they lost themselves in the crowd, which had lined up along Republic Avenue to watch the parade. As they walked away from Cheuro's, they passed a fire company running the other way. In the lead came the fire engine, a wooden tub with handles at the corners and a large pump rising in the middle. Eight stalwarts carried the engine by its handles, and after them pelted the rest of the company, bearing buckets with which to fill the tub from the nearest fountain.

"Let's make for Porrex's room," said Jorian. "If I catch that knave, do you counter his spells whilst I turn him inside out."

Porrex's door stood open, and his room was dark and quiet. Jorian got out his flint and steel, struck sparks into tinder, and lighted a piece of taper. The light showed the room to be not only empty but also stripped. The bed, the bookcase, the chair, the table, and the chests had vanished. A mouse whisked out of sight.

"That's the spryest removal I have ever seen," said Jorian. "He's cleaned the place out."

"Not quite," said Karadur, grunting as he stooped to pick up the little glass-sided lanthorn. "They forgot this. Aha me! The candle seems to have burnt all the way down. With a proper candle, I might do something yet."

"Let me look in the cupboard," said Jorian, stamping

on a roach as it raced across the floor. "Here we are, two usable candle stubs. What have you in mind, esteemed Doctor?"

"There is a spell, and I can remember it, which causes the light of a candle or similar source to pierce all disguises. Now leave me to my thoughts, my son."

Karadur took an eternity, it seemed to Jorian, to remember his spell and then to cast it, with a pentacle and chants and passes and powders burning in a broken saucer from the same cupboard. The candle flame in the lanthorn writhed and flickered as if blown upon by unseen lips, though no air stirred in the room. Faces seemed to form and dissolve in the smoke. Karadur, exhausted, had to rest for a time after the spell had been wound up.

"Now," said Karadur, picking up the lanthorn, "we shall see what we shall see."

Along Republic Avenue, the Vindines still stood deeply ranked, awaiting the parade; for this procession, like so many others, was late in starting. Wearing their demon masks, Jorian and Karadur walked slowly along the edge of the crowd. As Karadur held up the lanthorn, both peered at the faces of the crowd. Where the light of the candle fell, it seemed to Jorian as if the costumes and masks and false beards became almost transparent—mere smoky shadows of themselves, through which the Vindines' features stood out clearly.

They walked and walked, up one side of Republic Avenue westward and then down the other towards the harbor. Jorian looked at thousands of faces, but nowhere did he see that of Porrex or that of Laziendo. As they ambled towards the waterfront, Jorian heard band music, coming from the west and growing louder.

"Here they come," he said.

A group of men in the uniform of the Republican Guard, wearing shiny silvered breastplates and bearing halberds, walked down Republic Avenue, shouting to clear the street. Now and then they poked some laggard spectator with the butts of their weapons to hasten him.

As Karadur held up the lanthorn for another look at the crowd, Jorian's eye was caught by a little knot of men without masks or costumes—men in dark, plain garb, with a burly, self-confident bearing. One glanced at Jorian, stared, touched one of his companions, and spoke out of the side of his mouth. Recognizing the man, Jorian said in a low, tense voice:

"Karadur! See you those fellows in black? My Royal Guard. Their leader is a captain who twice caught me when I tried to flee Xylar. Across the street, quickly!"

Jorian plunged through the crowd, dragging Karadur after him. They came out on Republic Avenue in the midst of the guardsmen clearing the street. The band music grew louder, and over the heads of the guardsmen Jorian saw the leading units of the parade, with flags and silvered weapons.

Some guardsmen shouted angrily as Jorian and Karadur zigzagged through them and plunged into the packed mass of spectators on the other side. Jorian, being tall enough to see over the heads of most Vindines, looked back. The knot of men in black were pushing through the spectators on the far side. When they debouched on the avenue, however, they were blocked by a group of guardsmen. There was argument, lost in the growing noise. Arms waved; fists shook. The guardsmen roughly pushed the men in black back into the crowd and threatened them with their halberds. Then the parade arrived.

Gilt and tinsel flashed in the warm light of thousands of lamps, lanthorns, tapers, and torches. Bands brayed; soldiers tramped; pretty girls, riding on ornate floats, threw kisses to the crowd.

Jorian and Karadur did not wait to enjoy the spectacle. With a brief backward glance, they set off briskly down a side street. Karadur muttered:

"The parade will hold them up for a little while, at least. What I cannot understand is this: How did these men recognize us in our masks?"

"If you don't understand it, I do," said Jorian. "We forgot that the rays of this little magic lanthorn would have the same effect upon our own disguises as on others'."

"Ah me, I grow senile, not to have thought of that! But whither away, now? We are moneyless in a strange city, with your keepers searching for us."

"Let's find Laziendo's ship and hide in a nearby warehouse. If Laziendo appear, I shall know what to do. If he come not, we'll board the vessel, which is going our way."

Hours later, the parade had ended. The costume contest had been held, with prizes for the most beautiful, the most elaborate, the most humorous, and so forth. The soberer citizens had returned to their homes; the less sober raced and reeled the streets of Vindium City, yelling and singing. There was much hasty, hole-and-corner adultery, as husbands whose wives had grown fat and shrewish, and wives whose husbands neglected them for their trade or craft, sought excitement or comfort with strangers. As the lights of the city went out one by one, the late-rising crescent moon shed a wan illumination in their place. A fog crept softly up the streets from the harbor.

Jorian and Karadur huddled in a warehouse near the *Talaris*'s dock. The warehouse was supposed to be guarded, but the watchman had left his post to join the revelry. Piles of bales and boxes bulked dimly in the darkness. Jorian whispered:

"That's what we get for trusting one of your fellow spookers. I'll swear by Zevatas's brazen beard: It's the old fellows like you who are supposed to be cautious and crafty, whereas the young springalds like me are trusting and credulous and easily put upon. But here we seem to have the opposite."

"Could we not appeal the Vindine Senate to protect us from your Royal Guard?" replied Karadur. "Surely they do not wish harmless visitors kidnapped out of their proud city!"

"Not a chance! Othomae might have protected us, but Vindium is allied with Xylar against Othomae, glad to turn us over. The Twelve Cities are forever forming and breaking these alliances, so that yesterday's implacable foe is today's staunch ally and contrariwise. Like one of those courtly dances, Where you trade partners with every measure."

"You Novarians need an emperor to rule the turbulent lot of you, to stop you from wasting your energies in cutting one another's throats. We have a saying: Get three men from the Twelve Cities together and they will form four factions and fight it out to the death."

"Rabbits will chase wolves or ever the Novarians submit to such an overlord. Ardyman the Terrible once tried it, but he did not long abide. Besides, there are virtues in a group of squabbling little city-states, over against a big, monolithic empire like yours."

"To what advantage are your eternal, cruel and destructive internecine wars?"

"Well, each of the Twelve Cities is small enough so that a man feels that what he does matters. So our people take a lively interest in creative effort and in their respective governments. In Mulvan, the state is so huge and so rigidly organized that the individual feels lost and powerless. So you let Shaju and his like do as they please, be they never such idlers or debauchees or idiots or monsters. Now, in the Twelve Cities we have all kinds of governments—kingdoms, duchies, republics, theocracies, and so on— and if somebody invents a new and better one, all the others are eager to see how it works and whether they should consider imitating it."

"But if only there were a supreme ruler to stop your

fighting and direct your energies into constructive channels—"

"Then we should soon be just like Mulvan, with the supreme ruler directing all these energies towards the enhancement of his own power and glory."

"But at least we have internal peace, which is no small boon."

"And what has Mulvan done with its internal peace? From all I hear, your customs and usages and beliefs are exactly the same as a thousand years ago. Why think you the Twelve Cities so easily routed the vast army that Shaju's sire, King Sirvasha, sent to conquer them? Because the Mulvanians still rely upon the weapons and tactics of the days of Ghish the Great. So our cavalry made mincemeat of your scythed chariots, whilst our archers swept your slingers and darters from the field. Compare unchanging Mulvan with the Twelve Cities; consider what in the last century we have accomplished in the arts and sciences, in literature and drama, in law and government, and you will see what I mean."

"All very well, if one deem such material things important," grumbled Karadur. "I suppose it is partly a matter of age. When I was young, such turbulence and change appealed to me, also; but now I find safety and stability fairer to contemplate. Mark my words, my son, some day one of the Twelve Cities will call in the hordes of Shven to help it against its neighbor, and soon you will find a Gending cham ruling all of Novaria. Such things have happened before."

"But at least—" Jorian broke off, listening. There were footsteps and a murmur of talk outside. Jorian pulled Karadur behind a pile of bales.

Two persons entered the warehouse. From their sizes, Jorian took them to be a man and a woman, although the predawn light was too dim to tell any more. The man was speaking:

". . . here we are, fair mistress. Your servant will find

you a comfortable bed amongst all these piles of cargo, I swear; for there is scant romance in doing it standing up ... Ah, here we are, my sweetling: a pile of new sacking, just the thing for—*unh!*"

The final grunt followed the thud of the leaden pommel of Jorian's dagger on the man's skull. The man fell heavily to the stone floor. The woman was drawing her dress off over her head and so could not see what had happened. She completed her disrobing and stood for three heartbeats naked, holding the dress in her hands. The light was now strong enough for Jorian to perceive that she was a comely wench. A mask, which she had just dropped, lay at her feet.

Seeing her lover lying prone on the pave and Jorian's huge, shadowy form behind him, she uttered a thin little scream, fled out the door with her dress in her hands, and vanished into the fog. Jorian turned over the body and pulled off the mask.

"I was right," he said, squatting beside the body. "It was Master Laziendo, may dogs devour his vitals. I knew his voice. Let's hope the wench does not set the watch upon us."

"Is—is he dead?" quavered Karadur.

"No; his pate's only dented, not cracked, and his heart beats strongly." He looked up. "I have an idea that may save our hides. Can you sell a horse and a brace of asses?"

"I have never done horse trading, but I suppose I could."

"Then hie you to our room to fetch our gear and to the stable where our creatures dwell. Tell the stableman you wish to sell. It's early, but with luck he will know a couple of buyers ready for a quick bargain. The horse is worth at least two Mulvanian crowns or the equivalent, and the asses a quarter or a third as much apiece. Since it is a forced sale, you will have to take less, but at least do not accept the first offer."

"And you, my son?"

"I must bind and gag this rascal to keep him out of circulation until we have departed. When life stirs aboard the *Talaris*, I shall board the ship and see what my flapping tongue can do."

Two hours later, the risen sun was burning off the last wisps of fog, and Water Street was awakening. Carrying Jorian's pack and crossbow, Karadur shuffled across Water Street to the dock where the *Talaris* lay. The ship—a one-sticker of moderate size—was lively with longshoremen loading last-minute cargo, sailors handling ropes, and a dozen comely young slave girls chattering like a flock of starlings. Jorian stood at the rail, leaning on his elbows as if he had no cares. When Karadur climbed the companionway, Jorian helped him down, murmuring:

"How much did you get?"

"One crown, two and six for the lot."

"I could have done better, but we cannot be choosy. Let me present you. Captain Strasso, this is my friend, Doctor Karadur of Trimandilam, of whom I told you. Doctor, pay the captain ten marks for your passage and board to Janareth."

"Glad to have you aboard, sir," growled the captain. "Remember: no spitting, puking, or pissing from the weather rail! And no garbage on deck, either. I keep a clean ship. Get your girls out of the way, Master Maltho; we are about to shove off."

Later, when Vindium was small in the distance and the ship was heeling to the pressure of the wind on the striped triangular sail, Karadur and Jorian ate breakfast in the tiny cabin they occupied in the deckhouse aft. The cabin hummed with the splash, splash of the stem-cutting waves, the gurgle of water against the hull, the creak of the ship's timbers, and the thrum of wind-quivered cordage. Karadur asked:

"What in the name of Vurnu's heaven have you done, my son?"

Jorian grinned. "I found paper and ink in the warehouseman's desk and persuaded Master Laziendo to pen a note to Captain Strasso, saying he'd broken an ankle during the Feast of Spooks, and would the captain please ship his friend Maltho of Kortoli—an experienced commercial man from the Western Ocean—in his place?"

"How could you compel him to do that?"

"There are ways." Jorian chuckled. "I also found nine of our missing Xylarian lions in his purse and repossessed them. Porrex must have given him ten for his part in the swindle, and he'd spent one on his lady love. Of course, he denied all, if not convincingly. What most infuriated him was my cutting his fine velvet mantle into strips to bind him. He didn't lack courage, for he called me all sorts of foul names with my dagger at his throat. But he wrote the note, which was the main thing.

"Captain Strasso didn't much like it, but he did not wish to lose a day's sail by going ashore to rout Benniver's Sons out of bed to demand another supercargo. And when Belius, the slave dealer, arrived with his twelve little love-lies, I signed for them without a qualm.

"Now, forget not my new name: Maltho of Kortoli. I thought Nikko and Jorian had worn out their usefulness. Which philosopher said: The best equipment for life is effrontery?"

"Were it not wiser to give your origin as some western land, like Ir? You claim you've sailed those waters."

"Not with my accent! I can ape some of the others with fair skill if I try; but that, methinks, were a little too much effrontery for our own good!"

# IV

# The Castle of the Ax

A cold north wind from the steppes of shven stirred the Inner Sea and swiftly bore the *Talaris* southeast. The coast was a thin black line on the southwestern horizon. The dragon-spine of the Lograms should have been visible above this dark streak, but a blanket of winter cloud concealed it.

On the ship, Jorian stood on the roof of the deckhouse with the captain and the two steersmen, one to each of the quarter rudders. Karadur was confined to his cabin and the slave girls to their tent by seasickness.

"You seem to have a good stomach for a blow," said Captain Strasso.

"I've seen worse on the Western Ocean," replied Jorian. "Why, one time when I was chasing pirates—ah—I mean, when pirates were chasing my ship—well, anyway, the sea made this one look like a millpond. This sea saved us, for it swamped the pirate galley, whilst we came through with nothing worse than some wreckage on deck."

"And I suppose, mighty Master Maltho, that you were not seasick?" said Strasso.

Jorian laughed. "Spare your sarcasms, friend. On the contrary. I was as sick as a dying dog. But I think great Psaan decided that I had had enough of this affliction for one life, because I've never been seasick since. How much farther south must we sail ere the weather warms?"

"Janareth is warmer—it never snows there—but you'll find no truly tropical clime until you cross the

99

Lograms. On the hither side of those peaks, the summers are dry and the winters wet. On the farther side, they tell me, it is the opposite ... There's one of your chickabiddies now, dragging herself to the rail as to the scaffold."

"I must below, to see how the wenches do."

Strasso leered. "And perchance to improve an idle hour in their embraces?"

"A good supercargo does not handle the merchandise more than he must to insure its safe delivery." Jorian lowered himself to the deck and accosted the girl. It was Mnevis, who by force of personality had become spokeswoman for the twelve. She looked bedraggled and woebegone, having lost weight from not being able to keep food down.

"Good Master Maltho," she said, "I fear some dreadful doom awaits us."

"Oh, come! Anyone feels thus after a bout of seasickness."

"Nay, 'tis not the sea I fear, but these fearsome men to whom we've been sold. Headsmen—*ugh!*" She shuddered. "I shall see their hands dripping blood whenever I look upon them."

"Executioners are just like other men, save that their bloody but necessary trade arouses prejudice in unthinking minds. And these men have quit their profession for peaceful retirement."

"Natheless, the thought of them gives me the horrors. Could we not prevail upon you to engineer our escape? Or at least, our sale to men of more normal bent. We have nought to bribe you with, save our poor bodies; but these have been thought not uncomely ..."

"I'm sorry, Mnevis; impossible. I have promised to deliver you to Chairman Khuravela, of the retired headsmen of Rennum Kezymar, and delivered you shall be."

Later, Jorian said to Karadur: "You know, Doctor,

never before have I thought of the problem that executioners face in everyday living; yet such people are necessary, just as are collectors of taxes and of offal—two other much maligned classes:

"Oh, I am a headsman; they blanch at my name;
I chop and I hang and I stretch and I maim;
But that I be shunned, it is really a shame—
    I'm a virtuous fellow at heart!

My tools are the ax and the rope and the rack;
I execute rogues with my head in a sack;
I swink at my trade and I've never been slack;
    It's a fearfully difficult art.

At home, I am good to my children and wife;
I pay all my taxes and keep out of strife—
The kindliest man that you've seen in your life!
    Oh, why must they set us apart?"

The morning after the *Talaris* left Vindium, gray clouds covered the sky and the shore. Captain Strasso, turning his sun stone this way and that to catch the gleam that betrayed the sun's direction, grumbled to Jorian, "If the weather worsen, we may have to lay up at Janareth for the winter, 'stead of returning to our home port. And then will Benniver's Sons give me a wigging! That's the way of it with shipowners. Take a chance, and they berate you for risking their priceless property; take not a chance, and they betongue you for wasting their precious time and costing them profits."

"Island ahead!" called the lookout.

Captain Strasso looked pleased. "After sailing all night by the feel of wind and wave, that's not a bad landfall, now is it?" To the helmsman: "A hair to starboard ... Steady as you go." To Jorian again: "No proper harbor, but two anchorages, on the north and south sides of the island. At this season, ships use the south anchorage."

It was after noon when the *Talaris* dropped anchors in the small bay on the south side of Rennum Kezymar. The dinghy was lowered to transfer the slave girls ashore. With two sailors to row, Jorian, Karadur, and two of the girls went first. As they climbed out on the rickety little small-boat pier and the dinghy returned to the ship, a group of men approached from the shoreward end of the pier. They were brown-skinned, turbaned, and wrapped in many layers of wool and cotton, draped and tucked in various ways with loose ends fluttering in the wind.

The man in the lead was as tall as Jorian and much more massive—a mountain of muscle, now somewhat shrunken and sagging with age, with a big potbelly straining at his wrappings. Long, white hair hung down from under his turban, and a vast white beard covered his chest when the breeze did not blow it aside.

"Are you Chairman Khuravela, sir?" said Jorian in Mulvani.

"Aye." It was more a grunt than a word.

"Maltho of Kortoli, supercargo for Benniver's Sons. I have come to deliver the twelve slave girls you ordered from the dealer Belius in Vindium."

Another grunt.

"That is the second load, coming ashore now. One more trip will complete the task."

Grunt.

"My friend, the eminent Doctor Karadur."

Grunt.

This, thought Jorian, was becoming difficult. He continued to stand in the wind, trying to make conversation. But, what with his limited fluency in the language and the wooden unresponsiveness of the giant, he had little success. The other executioners—like their chief, big, burly men of advanced years—stood about silently, fidgeting and shifting their feet.

Jorian's gaze wandered from the sands of the shore, where clumps of sedge nodded in the wind, to the higher ground of the interior. The island bore no trees, only long grass, now dead and dried, and dark clumps of ilex and spreading holly. Around the castle on the highest point of the isle, cabbage patches added a touch of color to an otherwise sad, gray, washed-out landscape. The castle was gray against the darker gray of the overcast sky.

At last the dinghy arrived on its third shoreward journey. The rest of the slave girls climbed out on the pier.

"That is all," said Jorian.

Chairman Khuravela jerked his head. "Come."

They straggled up the slope to the castle. A few former headsmen were working in the cabbage patches. A dry ditch, half filled with rubbish and spanned by a lowered draw bridge, surrounded the castle.

The procession crossed the drawbridge, passed under the portcullis set in a vaulted archway with murder holes, traversed a short vestibule into which a gatehouse was built, and entered the main hall. Here, no artificial light relieved the dimness. Although the towers and walls had windows instead of arrow slits—the edifice not being now meant for serious defense—these windows were closed by sashes paned with oiled paper, and the gloomy day did not shed much light within. A pair of executioners sat over a game of draughts, ignoring the newcomers. On the other side of the hall, a huge bronze gong hung from a frame. Long tables stood against the walls.

When all were inside, Khuravela led the way to a big table with a massive oaken armchair at one end. He sat down heavily and said:

"Line them up."

Jorian did so. Khuravela counted them, wagging his thick forefinger and silently moving his lips. At last he said:

"They will do. Here is your money. At two hundred and forty silver marks apiece, the lot is worth ninety-six Mulvanian crowns at the current rate."

Khuravela spilled a heap of crowns, double-crowns, and five-crown and ten-crown pieces out on the table and counted out the amount. Jorian checked his addition and swept the heap of square golden coins into his own purse. Then he handed the chairman a receipt, saying:

"Sign here, pray."

"Oh, dung!" groaned the giant. "Fetch a pen. You two must witness my mark."

Khuravela made his mark, and Jorian and Karadur witnessed it. Khuravela said:

"Big feast this even. You and the doctor invited; so is your captain. Brother Chambra, send word to Strasso. Brother Tilakia, take the slaves away." He turned back to Jorian. "Time for our nap. Mehru can show you the castle. See you in three hours."

Khuravela heaved himself out of his chair and marched off into the shadowy corridors. The other Brothers wandered off until Jorian and Karadur were left with a single Brother. Karadur muttered in Novarian:

"O Jorian, I would fain not stay for this feast. Suffer me to return to the ship."

"What's the matter? Don't you want a real repast for a change?"

"It is not that. I feel an evil aura about this place."

"Nonsense! Forsooth, it's a gloomy old pile, but the dwellers therein seem normal enough."

"Nay, I have an astral sense about such things."

"Stay for a while, anyway. You can't leave me to face these fellows alone!"

The remaining executioner, Mehru, was a man of medium size and build. Unlike most of the rest, he was bare-headed and clean-shaven. Although gray showed in his topknot, he seemed younger than most of his retired colleagues. With a toothy grin, he said:

"If you gentlemen will come with me, I will show you the Castle of the Ax. You shall see sights you will long remember—mementoes of historic events which our mighty king—may he reign forever!—has graciously suffered us to bring hither upon our retirement."

"I do not think I wish to, thank you," said Karadur. "I am weary. Is there a place where I might lie down?"

"Surely: this chamber here. Make yourself at ease, Doctor, whilst I show Master Maltho around."

In contrast to Khuravela, Mehru proved a garrulous host. "If you look closely," he said, "you can see the difference in color between the lowest courses of this wall and those higher up. The lower courses are those of the original castle; the higher, those of the rebuilding under Cholanki the Third . . . This is our kitchen; those are the wives of the wedded Brothers, readying tonight's gorge . . . ."

"Is one of them yours?" asked Jorian, looking at a dozen stout, middle-aged women.

"Me? Ha! Women mean nought to me. I was wedded to my art."

"Why did you leave it so young?"

"A soreness developed in my right shoulder joint, so that my hand was no longer so true as erstwhile. It still bothers me betimes in damp weather. I am good enough with rope and bowstring and chopper, but not with the two-handed sword. That polluted crowbar is the nemesis of every aging headsman."

"How so?"

"Know that amongst the Chosen of the Gods, each class has its appropriate form of execution, and the sword is deemed the only honorable instrument for royalty and nobility. For nobles the sword, for warriors the ax, for officials the bowstring, for merchants the noose, the artisans the stake, and so on—albeit special crimes sometimes incur special chastisements, such as trampling by an elephant.

"Well, one of the wives of King Shaju—may he reign forever!—had committed adultery with a nobleman, and it was decreed that both should die by my hand. This Lord Valshaka's head flew off as pretty as you please. But when I swung at the woman, a twinge in that cursed right shoulder caused the heavy sword to strike low, against her shoulder blades. As you can well perceive, all this did was to open a great gash across her back and hurl her prone upon the platform. My helpers dragged her, shrieking and bleeding, to her knees again and held her long enough for a second swing.

"This time, all went well. The head I presented to His Majesty—may he reign forever!—was the most perfect I ever saw—no biased cut, no ragged edges of skin. *Perfect.* But Shaju decreed that, in view of that one blunder, I had served out my time."

They had come out on the roof of one of the corner turrets. Mehru pointed: "That way lies the estuary of the Jhukna, a nest of pirates. In summer, we see their galleys swarming out as thick as water bugs when a trading fleet between Vindium and Janareth goes by. That is why Vindium now convoys these fleets with its war galleys."

"Why does not King Shaju build a fleet and help to put down the sea thieves? Why should the Novarian cities bear all the burden?"

Mehru stared. "My good man! A pious Mulvanian go to sea? Know you not that it entails a religious pollution, to be expiated by elaborate and costly ceremonies of purification?"

"You had to cross the sea to get here."

"Ah, but that was only once, and the burden was light. If I took to the sea for my livelihood, I should have to spend all my time ashore in purification. It is different with you barbarians."

"Doctor Karadur does not seem to mind."

"That is his affair. Mayhap he is religiously heterodox, or else his spells neutralize the polluting effects

of sea travel. But let us go below, or ever I freeze
to death."

"You Mulvanians are as sensitive to cold as tropic
blooms," said Jorian, following Mehru down the winding stair. "The slightest draft, and you shiver and wilt.
To me, that wind was only pleasantly cool."

"I will match you, then, against one of the Chosen
of the Gods in the dank jungles of southern Mulvan,
where the heat is such that no life but that of insects
stirs abroad during the day. Now, where is that polluted
key? Ah, here! This room holds the machine that works
our drawbridge."

They looked into a room containing the mechanism
of a large water clock. Water trickled from a spout into
one of a circle of buckets affixed to the rim of a wheel.
Jorian saw at once how the mechanism worked. When
the bucket filled, the weight caused the wheel to rotate
a few degrees until checked by an escapement. Then
the next bucket filled, and so on.

"The used water runs into a barrel hung from the
drawbridge mechanism," said Mehru. "At sunrise, the
weight of the barrel, released, lowers the drawbridge—
which, being counterweighted, takes little effort. When
this barrel has descended, it empties, and the water
flows into another, which raises the drawbridge. A
clockmaster named Evor of Ardamai came by here
some years ago, they tell me—"

"Why," burst out Jorian, he was my ff—" he checked
himself. "I mean, he was a friend of my father. But
go on."

Mehru gave Jorian a sharp look. "That is all. This
man set up the mechanism, and ever since then it has
raised and lowered the drawbridge. We need not turn
a hand, save to pump water up into the tank in the
room above. This we do by a treadwheel in the cellar."

"Can the bridge be sundered from the water clock,
in case of emergencies?"

"Aye. The windless in the gatehouse can be used to

override the clock. But that happens seldom, for we have few visitors to Rennum Kezymar."

They descended another stair. Mehru unlocked another door, saying: "This chamber, Master Maltho, is our armory—but it is not an armory in the usual sense. It holds our choicest mementoes. Behold!"

"Good gods!" said Jorian, staring.

The mementoes were a collection of the instruments with which the headsmen carried out their duties. There were axes and blocks, swords, hangman's ropes, strangler's cords, and throat-cutter's hook-bladed knives. There were two complete racks and a cauldron for boiling oil. There were fetters and thongs and staves and scourges and branding irons. There were special instruments whose purpose was not at once apparent.

To one side, an elderly, whiskery Brother sat on a stool, lovingly whetting one of the axes with a faraway look in his eyes.

"How now, Brother Dhaong?" said Mehru. "Think you your edge will have the trueness tonight's contest demands?"

The ancient gave a dreamy smile and continued to bursh the whetstone back and forth, *wheep-wheep*.

"What contest?" asked Jorian uncomfortably.

"You shall see," grinned Mehru. "Behold here, the very block whereon Genera Vijjayan's head was smitted off, after his revolt against King Sirvasha failed. Let me show you some of our more specialized instruments. This is a set of matched eye-gougers belonging to Brother Parhbai. This iron boot is very persuasive when placed in the fire with the suspect's leg inside it. This is an ingenious device for crushing a suspect's leg to a jelly. King Laditya employed it on a brother whom he suspected of plotting against him. Since then our kings have become more practical; they have all their brothers slain upon their accession."

"That sounds hard on the brothers."

"True, but it makes work for us. Now here is Brother

Ghos's wheel, with the hammer for breaking prisoners on it. Here is a fine thumbscrew; see the gold and silver inlay on the steel ... Brother Dhaong was one of the lucky ones in the draw; so was I. Hence we shall have a chance—but I must not spoil your pleasure by telling you now."

"I have seen enough, thank you," said Jorian. "Like Doctor Karadur, I crave rest."

"Oh, certes," said Mehru. "In that case, let us return to the main hall, where a chamber has been set aside for you."

Jorian was silent on his way back to the main hall. Mehru, still chattering pleasantly, showed him to the chamber whither Karadur had retired. Inside were two beds, on one of which the old wizard lay on his back, snoring.

Jorian closed the door and lay down on the other bed. He found, however, that he could not sleep. After a while he got up, went out, and did some exploring on his own. The castle was silent save for the sounds of cookery from the kitchen and the snores that issued from behind various doors.

Beside the stairs that led up from the main hall, a stair led down from it. Pursuing it, at the bottom Jorian found a long passage, lit by a single candle on a wall bracket, with rooms opening off from it. Some of these, to judge by the massive padlocks on their doors, seemed to be storerooms for valuables. A couple were barred cells, and from one of these burst a chorus of familiar squeals. The cell contained the twelve slave girls.

"O Maltho! Master Maltho! Dear, kind Maltho!" they cried. "Why have they locked us up here? What do they with us? Can't you get us out?"

"Tell me what's happened," he said. All spoke at once, but the gist was that they had been taken directly to the cell from the main hall, given food and drink, and left in silence and solitude.

"I know not what these men intend," he said, "but I'll try to find out and, if it be evil, to thwart their plans. Be good girls!"

Jorian went back upstairs to the tower room that housed the clockwork. The locked door quickly yielded to one of his pick-locks. Thanking his gods that he was familiar with his father's mechanisms, he pulled out one of the keys that governed the raising of the drawbridge and inserted it into another hole. Then he returned to the chamber where Karadur slept and shook the wizard.

"Wake up!" he said. "I think you were right about your evil aura."

"Well?" said Karadur, yawning and rubbing his eyes.

"Unless I much mistake, these headsmen plan to stage a contest with their banquet this even, to exhibit their specialties in the practice of their calling."

"How mean you? To swing their axes and such-like to show they have not lost their form?"

"More than that. I think they plan to demonstrate their skills on those twelve slave girls we brought."

"You mean to chop and choke—Kradha preserve us! I will not stay here an instant longer to witness such wickedness!" Karadur began winding his turban, but so agitated was he that the thing repeatedly fell down in loops about his neck. "And you are he who has been talking about headsmen's being but human like all other men!"

"Now whither are you going so suddenly?" said Jorian. "If I am to rescue the lassies, I shall need your help."

"Rescue them? Are you mad, my son? How can one man rescue them from a castle full of these hulking brutes?"

"I know not, yet, but something may turn up. At

least, I mean to see it through. I brought the girls hither."

"But—but—do not throw your life away!" Karadur clutched Jorian's huge hand, and tears ran down his wrinkled, brown cheeks into his silky white beard. "It will avail your lassies nought and ruin our chances of obtaining the Kist of Avlen!"

"If I perish, it matters not a whit to me what befalls the Kist of Avlen. If I succeed, I shall still be available for your bit of high-class burglary."

"But you have no true moral obligation! What are these wenches to you? Why risk your life for them?"

"Shame on you for talking like one of those selfish materialists you are always denouncing!"

"Never mind me. Give me a good reason for what you plan to attempt."

"Say it infuriates me to see the poor little harmless dears put to pain and death for frivolous reasons. I never allowed that sort of thing when I was king, and I won't begin now."

"But the women are the Brothers' lawful property, to rob them of which were theft and in itself a sin."

"Then I'm a sinner. Besides, they are Novarians and so, according to the philosopher Achaemo, should never have been held in servitude by other Novarians in the first place. Now calm yourself and help me to plan."

"I will not! I cannot!" chattered Karadur, making a sudden rush for the door. Jorian, being the quicker, got there first and set his broad back against the door.

"Coward!" he snarled. "With all your lofty talk of altruism and self-sacrifice and moral purity, you turn tail at the first chance to practice your preachments!"

"Nay, nay, my beloved son!" wailed Karadur. "I am no warrior, inured to bloodshed and deadly hazards! I am but a peaceful philosopher and student of the occult arts, long past the age of combat."

"Rubbish! I'm no warrior, either, but a common artisan masquerading as one. These adventures affright me half out of my wits. If I can face it, surely you can. You showed mettle enough at my execution in Xylar."

But Karadur only babbled: "Nay! Nay! Let me go, I say! If it be wrong of you to risk yourself uselessly, it were doubly wrong to involve me in your suicide!"

Karadur, thought Jorian, would be useless in his present panic. He said: "I'll make a compact with you. Let me see what magical properties you have with you, and tell me what each one does."

"Well," said Karadur, sinking down upon his bed and fumbling in his robe, "this phial contains the essence of covetousness; a drop in the soup of him to whom you would sell a thing, and your suit is two-thirds won. It requires no incantation and is very popular with horse traders. Next, I have here a ring with a beryl wherein is imprisoned the demon Gorax. When threatened by malevolent spirits, such as the swamp devils of Moru, you have but to utter the right incantation, and Gorax will come forth and put those beings to rout. Afterwards another spell will compel him to return to the ring. The cantrips, however, are long and difficult, and the commands to Gorax must be phrased with the nicest accuracy, since he is stupid even for a demon and can wreak grave havoc through misunderstanding. Now here . . ."

Eventually, Karadur came to a packet of powder. "This is the Powder of Discord, which I obtained from Goania in Othomae. But—ah—you may not have it, because we shall need it in Trimandilam."

"It's just what I need," said Jorian. "For the others, I can see no use in my present plight. But your Powder of Discord would, methinks, serve very neatly here."

"No, no! I have told you why I cannot—"

"No powder, no escape. I'll hold you here until dinnertime. Then the drawbridge will be up, and you'll not be able to leave."

"But—but if you plan to abide beyond that time, how shall *you* escape?"

"Leave that to me. You may go when you give me the powder, not before—what's that?"

A hollow, metallic boom resounded through the edifice. Karadur squeaked: "That is the gong that summons the Brothers to meat! Let me go at once!"

Jorian held out his hand. Muttering something that—had he not known Karadur's stern views on blasphemy—Jorian would have suspected of being a Mulvani curse, the wizard put the packet into Jorian's hand. Saying: "Tell Strasso to send his dinghy in close to shore to await me." Jorian opened the door.

The lamps in the main hall had been lit, and a fire crackled in the fireplace. Some of the Brothers, yawning and stretching, were drifting into the hall, where tables had been pulled out from the walls. Prominent among them was the gigantic chairman. As Jorian and Karadur emerged from their chamber, Khuravela caught Jorian's eye and beckoned.

"Doctor Karadur is unwell," said Jorian smoothly. "He begs to return to the ship, where his medicines are."

Khuravela grunted. "If he will, he will. Your captain, also, sent word he could not attend. Hmph. Too many think themselves better than their origins."

While Karadur scuttled out, Jorian accepted a flagon of spiced wine and answered questions about the news from the Twelve Cities of Novaria. He was tempted to give a thrilling account of the escape of the king of Xylar but suppressed the urge.

When the chairman took his seat, the other Brothers sat down also. They seemed a taciturn lot, communicating in grunts. Jorian, however, found himself next to a tall, lean, skull-faced man with a fondness for gossip. The latter whispered:

"See how Mehru strives to bait the chairman, and how Khuravela ignores him. Mehru is ambitious to become chairman in the other's room. He is eternally buzzing about our ears, saying that Khuravela is but an old, dead oak—impressive to look at, but without sap in its bark. And, in truth, none knows if any thoughts do stir behind our chairman's noble brow, for he goes for days on end without uttering a word. On the other hand, see you Brother Ghos, he of the purple turban? He heads a third faction . . ."

The tale of the endless bickering and intrigues of this ingrown little world became boring at last. Jorian finished a plain but plentiful repast in a silence unusual for him.

When the women had taken away the plates, wiped the tables, and poured fresh mugs of beer, a buzz of talk arose. Chairman Khuravela, in his armchair, made a sign. Several Brothers rose and left the hall. Presently two came back, one balancing a red-painted heads-man's block on his brawny shoulder while the other bore an ax. Another man returned with a coil of rope, with a noose on its end, over his arm. He climbed on a table and tossed the noose end of the rope over a beam. Jorian said to his neighbor:

"Tell me, sir: Are the Brothers about to demonstrate their skills?"

"Why, of course!" said the skull-faced man. "Me-thought you knew."

"Using those slave girls as subjects?"

"Certes! We cannot practice on free men like your-self; that were a crime. Do you think us murderers?"

"Is this a contest?"

"Aye; the other Brothers will judge the skill and dex-terity displayed in each execution. Thank the true gods of Mulvan, it is the first break in the maddening bore-dom of life here in many a moon."

"Why does not everybody take a turn?"

"The Brothers refused to vote money for a larger number of slaves; a matter of internal politics. Khura-vela ordered the largest number for which funds were to hand, and we cast lots to see which amongst us should be chosen to take part in the contest."

Two men staggered into the hall, bearing a rack from the armory. Jorian stood up and watched Khurevela. When the latter glanced in his direction, Jorian caught his eye and called:

"Master Chairman, may I speak?"

"Speak!" growled Khuravela. "Silence, pigs."

"Gentlemen!" said Jorian. "Permit me to thank you from the bottom of my heart for the sumptuous repast and the delicious potations you have served me. In fact, I am so full I can scarcely stand. Though I live to be as old as the eldest amongst you, I shall always remember this even as one of the high spots of my life—"

"If he have aught to say, I wish he would say it," growled a Brother to his neighbor. Jorian heard it but continued:

"And so, to make a very meager and inadequate repayment for this delightful entertainment, I should like to tell you a story."

The Brothers straightened up. The boredom vanished from their faces, and their eyes shone with new interest. Jorian stepped out into the clear space, in the midst of the tables.

"This story," he said, "is called the Tale of the Teeth of Gimnor. Many centuries ago, it is said that there reigned in Kortoli a small but lively and quick-witted king named Fusinian, sometimes called Fusinian the Fox. The son of Filoman the Well-Meaning, he came to the throne quite young and wedded the daughter of the High Admiral of Zolon. If you know not, Zolon is an isle in the Western Ocean, off the far coast of Novaria, and Zolon counts as one of the Twelve Cities. Being an island, it is a maritime power; and being a maritime power, it is ruled by a High Admiral. Therefore, it was a suitable match for the king of Kortoli.

"This maid, who hight Thanuda, was divinely tall and

famous for her beauty. King Fusinian fell in love with her picture and dispatched his chamberlain to sue for her hand. She made no objections, despite the fact that she was the taller of the two. They were wed with all the usual pomp and settled down to such happiness as is granted to royalty, who marry for reasons of statecraft.

"Soon thereafter, war broke out betwixt Kortoli and its northern neighbor Aussar. It was some footling squabble over a bit of territory, and as usual, between them the two combatants had soon spent blood and treasure worth a hundredfold as much as the land. And in these struggles, Aussar, which began the hostilities, had the better of it. First the Aussarians drove the Kortolians out of the disputed area. Then, when Fusinian counterattacked, they routed him in two great battles. Fusinian's sire, Filoman the Well-Meaning, had been full of humane ideas about reducing the army and spending the money thus saved to uplift the masses, so that Kortoli had fallen behind the other Twelve Cities in the arts of war.

"Had Fusinian been older and craftier, he might have yielded to Aussar at the outset and used the time thus gained to strengthen his army, eventually to take the land back. But, being young and ardent and full of romantical notions of honor, he plunged into a war to which his forces were not equal. So he was beaten three times running. And then word came that the Aussarians meant to invade Kortoli proper, to get rid of Fusinian and put some puppet on his throne.

"In desperation, Fusinian went with a small escort to a witch named Gloé, who dwelt in the rugged hills that sunder Kortoli from its southern neighbor Vindium. The witch harkened to his plea for succor and said:

" 'As a patriotic Kortolian, I will of course help Your Majesty to my utmost. Howsomever, there is the matter of my license.'

" 'Eh? What is this?' said the king. 'My kingdom totters on the brink of ruin, and you babble of licenses?'

" 'It is no mean matter, sire,' replied Gloé. 'Know that I am no illicit practitioner of magic through choice. Thrice I have applied to your Bureau of Commerce and Licenses, and thrice they have turned me down. They demand a diploma from the Lyceum of Metouro or other institution of higher learning, or that I pass an examination, or take a refresher course, or some other nonsense of this sort, when I have been successfully healing the sick, summoning spirits, finding lost articles, and foreseeing the future for sixty years!'

" 'But what has all that to do with the peril of Kortoli?' asked the king.

" 'Because the efficacy of magic depends upon the state of mind of the magician. Did I but know that you would summarily command your finicking clerks to issue me a proper license as wizardess forthwith, the relief to me would enhance my chance of success.'

"The king frowned. 'I like not to interfere in the orderly processes of administration, nor yet to urge partiality upon my officials,' he said. 'But in this extreme, I suppose I must swallow my scruples. Very well, if your spell work, you shall have your license, though you know not a zoömorph from a zodiac. Pray, madam, proceed.'

"So the witch went into a trance and writhed and mumbled and spoke in strange voices, and shadows flickered about her cave without material objects to cast them, and strange, dissolving faces appeared in mid-air, and the king was seized by freezing cold, whether from some being from outer space or from simple fright is not known. When the king had stopped shivering and the shadows had gone away, the witch said:

" 'Know, O King, that you must slay the dragon Grimnor, who sleeps under a mountain nine leagues hence. Then you must take out every one of this dragon's teeth. On a night of a full moon, you must show these teeth on a plowed field, and there shall spring up from these teeth that which will enable you to vanquish Aussar.'

"So King Fusinian journeyed westward, following Gloé's directions, until he came to the mountain. The dragon lay snoring in a cave, which opened into a ravine at the root of the mountain. Fusinian feared that neither his arrows nor his lance nor his sword would pierce the dragon's scales—which are, as everyone knows, so hard that they make excellent mail, provided that one can obtain a dragon's hide to begin with—especially since Fusinian stood only three finger-breadths above five feet. At last Fusinian and his men found a boulder of the right size and drove an iron spike into it, and to this spike they belayed a long rope. Then they balanced this boulder precariously over the mouth of Grimnor's cave.

"Then Fusinian went to the mouth of the cave and shouted a challenge to Grimnor. And the dragon awoke and came looping and hissing out of the cave. Fusinian ran back before him, and when he saw that the head and a few feet of the neck were out of the cave, he jerked the rope. Down came the boulder, with a snapping of draconic skull bones. The thrashing and writhing of that beast were fearful; they shook the mountain and brought down a small landslide. But at length Grimnor lay still and dead.

"Fusinian discovered that the dragon had forty-seven teeth in each side of each jaw, making a total of one hundred and eighty-eight. He had thoughtfully brought along the royal dentist, who extracted these teeth. Fusinian put the teeth in a bag and, on the night of the next full moon, he sowed these teeth on a plowed field. He sowed and sowed, thus."

Jorian strode about the hall, making sowing gestures. Actually, he was tossing into the air above the heads of the diners pinches of the Powder of Discord, the packet of which he concealed in his left hand. He continued:

"Just as Gloé had predicted, the points of spears could presently be discerned, sticking up through the soil and shining in the moonlight. And then came the crests of helms, and soon there stood up, in the moonlight, one hundred and eighty-eight giants, eight feet tall and armed to the teeth.

" 'We are the Teeth of Grimnor,' said the tallest of the giants in a voice of thunder. 'What would you of us, little man?'

"Clenching his jaw to keep his teeth from chattering, Fusinian said: 'Your task, O Teeth, is to vanquish the armies of Aussar, which are overrunning my fair kingdom.'

" 'Harkening and obedience,' thundered the giant who had spoken. And off they marched towards the Aussarian border, so fast that they soon left King Fusinian and his escort behind. So Fusinian returned to Kortoli City to see how things fared there. And when he arrived, he found that the Teeth were there ahead of him. They had routed the Aussarians so utterly that those who escaped the carnage ran all the way back to Aussar City before stopping to draw breath. For it transpired the Teeth had hides of such toughness that the blows of swords and the thrusts of spears were no more to them than the scratches of a kitten are to one of us.

"Well, a pair of the giants at the West Gate admitted King Fusinian and his escort. But when Fusinian got to the palace, he was taken aback to find the biggest of the Teeth sitting on his throne—or rather, on a table top laid across the arms of his throne, for the throne itself was too small to accommodate that monstrous arse.

" 'What,' quoth he, 'in all the heavens and hells are you doing in my chair?'

" 'I am not in it, I am on it,' said the Tooth. 'And

as for what I am doing, we have decided to run your kingdom for ourselves. This is but natural, since we are so much stronger than you that it were ridiculous for us to take orders from you. Besides, only thus can we assure ourselves enough to eat, for our appetites are to yours like those of tigers to those of titmice. I have taken your queen for my concubine, and now I shall make you my body slave—'

"But Fusinian, with that quickness of wit that long served him so well, raced out of the throne room, dodged a giant or two who tried to snatch him up, vaulted on his horse, and spurred like a madman for the gate. He was out and on his way ere the Teeth could prepare themselves to stop him. They set out a pursuit; but, although they could run as fast afoot as Fusinian's horse could gallop, he knew the country better than they. By weaving back and forth like a fox dodging the hounds, he got over the border to Govannian.

"Fusinian had been on good terms with the Hereditary Usurper of Govannian until the latter refused to aid him against Aussar, as he had once promised to do. Fusinian's news, however, was ominous enought to patch up the quarrel. No fool, the Hereditary Usurper raised an army to scotch the Teeth before they decided to annex his realm as well as Kortoli.

"Fusinian meanwhile went from one to another of the Twelve Cities with his story. In most of them he got contingents for the army of liberation, although the Syndics of Ir demurred on the ground that it would cost too much, and the Senate of Vindium debated endlessly without deciding aught, and the Tyrant of Boaktis declared it was all a hoax by Fusinian to subvert his own enlightened and progressive rule and restore the reactionary exploiters.

"At length an army, with contingents from all the remaining Twelve Cities—even from Aussar—gathered on the border of Govannian and marched into Kortoli.

But alas! The army halted in dismay when the forces of the Teeth approached them. Some of the Teeth were riding on mammoths, which they had bought from the cham of the Gendings, in Shven. The beasts had been towed down the coast on rafts. Other Teeth fought on foot as officers of platoons of Kortalians, whom by terror they had trained to obey their slightest command.

"Fusinian was not altogether unprepared for such a reception. Knowing the might of the giants, he had constructed a battery of the largest wheeled catapults that anybody had built up to that time. The catapults went off with great bangs, hurling sixty-pound balls of stone. Some missed and some plowed into the hapless Kortolians, but one came straight at one of the Teeth. The Tooth leisurely caught it, as one catches a handball, and threw it back as accurately as it had been shot at him and with somewhat greater force. For it struck the Hereditary Usurper of Govannian, where he sat his horse in the midst of his host, and took off his helmet with the head inside it.

"After that, there was not much of a battle. The mammoths on the wings closed in, and Fusinian's mighty array dissolved into a mass of shrieking fugitives, among whom the Teeth amused themselves by striding and riding and smashing people like so many bugs with their ten-foot clubs.

"For some months, little was heard of Fusinian save rumors of his appearing and vanishing like a ghost along the borders of Kortoli. At length he sought the cave of Gloé the witch.

" 'Well, King,' she said, stirring her cauldron, 'How about my license?'

" 'Bugger your license madam!' quoth he. 'That cure you gave me was worse than the disease.'

" 'That was your fault, laddie,' she said. 'When you gave the Teeth their orders, you forgot to tell them to vanish or to turn back into dragon's teeth after they had routed the Aussarians. As it was, they were free of all obligation as soon as they had carried out your complete command.'

" 'How in the forty-nine Mulvanian hells was I to know that?' he yelled. 'You never told me!'

" 'Why should I?' said she. 'Knowing you for a king and a smart one at that, I assumed you would have the common sense to do so without my telling you.' And they fell to shouting and shaking fists at each other in most unkingly wise until they ran out of breath.

" 'Well, let us forget what has been said and be practical,' said Gloé. 'You want more help, yea?'

"Fusinian muttered something about damned women who can never give precise directions, but aloud he said: 'Yea, but Zevatas help us if it avail us no better than the last time! These creatures are eating my kingdom bare, not to mention niggling the wives of all the leading men, including mine.'

" 'Their voracity is explained by their draconic origin,' quoth Gloé. 'Now, I know a spell to call an army of aërial demons from the Sixth Plane. It is a spell of the utmost difficulty and danger. It also requires human sacrifice. Whom are you prepared to dispense with?'

"The king looked at his escort, and each member of the escort looked as if his keenest wish were to become invisible. But one man spoke up at last, saying 'Take me, O King. The physician assures me that, with my leaky heart, I have not long to live anyway.'

" 'Nobly spoken!' cried Fusinian. 'You shall have a monument when I have reconquered my kingdom.' And in a good sooth, this monument was duly erected and stands in Kortoli City even yet. 'So, madam.'

" 'Just a moment, sire,' said Gloé. 'I need something for myself as well, to put me in the right mood to cast an effective spell.'

" 'Here we go again,' said the king. 'What is it this time?'

" 'I want not only a proper license as wizardess, but also to be made your court magician.'

"They argued, but in the end Fusinian gave in, not having much choice in the matter. So the spell was cast. The moon turned to blood, and the earth shook, the forests were filled with weird wailings, and down from the sky swooped a horde of demons in the form of bat-winged lizard-men, to assail the Teeth.

"But, when a demon or other spirit takes material form, it is bound by the laws of matter. The Teeth merely laughed and seized the demons out of the air and tore them to bits like a bad boy dismembering a butterfly. And the survivors of the demons fled back to the Sixth Plane and have refused to be invoked from that day to this.

"Disgusted with Gloé and her spells, Fusinian disappeared again. From time to time he would be seen, in worn, patched garments, in one or another of the Twelve Cities, for he had friends and partisans everywhere. At last, whilst idling in the marketplace at Metouro, he saw a gang of boys raid the stall of a greengrocer, snatching fruit and dashing away ere the wretched merchant could summon aid. The thing that struck him about this incident was the fact that the greengrocer was so enormously fat that he could not even squeeze out of his stall in time to call for assistance.

"That made Fusinian think, and he recalled the tales he had heard of the monstrous appetites of the Teeth. Soon thereafter, the Faceless Five, who rule Metouro summoned Fusinian to ask his advice about a demand for tribute, which they had received from the Teeth in Kortoli. Fusinian looked at the five black masks and said:

" 'Send them not only what they ask, but also twice as much.'

" 'You are mad!' cried one of the Five. 'It would beggar us!'

" 'Have you had a good harvest?' asked Fusinian.

"Aye; but so what?"

" 'Then pay what I advise in farm produce. Let me explain . . .'

"Then for a while Fusinian went from city to city, expounding his plan. So food poured into Kortoli in groaning oxcart loads. This continued for six whole months. When one of the Twelve Cities ran short of agricultural produce, it borrowed money to import more from another of the Twelve or even from Shven and Mulvan.

"And at length came the day when King Fusinian rode into Kortoli at the head of his army while the Teeth, now grown so fat they could scarcely move, looked on helplessly and mouthed futile threats. And, whereas the skins of the Teeth were still too tough for ordinary weapons to do more than scratch, the Kortolians bound the giants by massive chains to huge blocks of Othomaean granite, towed them out to the deep sea on rafts, and overturned the rafts. And that was the end of that.

"Or nearly so. Fusinian had an affecting reunion with his queen, the lovely Thanuda. But sometimes, when he had finished making love to her, he would catch her looking at him with a curious expression—a trace of disappointment, or as if she were comparing him unfavorably with someone else. And once during a quarrel she called him 'shrimp.' So his later life was perturbed by the thought that, whatever the faults of the Tooth who had borrowed his wife, the giant must have had certain superhuman capacities that he, Fusinian, lacked. But, being a philosophical man, he made the best of things. And the moral is: Choking a cat with butter may not be the most obvious way of killing it, but sometimes it is the only one that works."

A moment later, Jorian picked the lock of the door of the cell that held the slave girls. They threw themselves upon him; Mnevis caught him round the neck and smothered him with kisses.

"Na, na, easy all, lassies," he said. "I'll get you out of this, but you must be absolutely quiet. No talking, whispering, laughing, giggling, squealing or other sounds! Now come along. Keep behind me and watch my signals. Softly now."

He led the twelve on tiptoe down the corridor. At the first of the locked doors he halted, picked the padlock, and went in. A quick look showed that the room was full of agricultural implements. The second storeroom proved to be full of heavy winter clothing: felt boots, woolen cloaks, and sheepskin greatcoats.

The third storeroom had shelves on which stood rows of objects that glimmered in the gloom, while on the floor a line of coffers ran around the wall.

"This," said Jorian, "is what I sought. One of you girls fetch that candle in from outside. Careful lest you blow it out. Ah!"

The girls echoed Jorian's ejaculation, for this was the treasury of the Brotherhood. The objects on the shelves were jeweled goblets of gold and silver, pictures in jeweled frames, golden candlesticks and lamps, and similar precious artifacts. The coffers, as Jorian soon discovered by picking the lock on one, contained money and jewels. Some of the Brothers must have saved up tidy fortunes—probably, Jorian suspected, by taking bribes from prisoners not to cause them much pain.

Jorian took out and crammed his money belt full of Mulvanian golden coins; without taking the time to count, he thought he had well over a hundred crowns' worth. He gave handfuls to each of the slave girls, with instructions to stow them as securely as possible. From the shelves and the jewel boxes he selected several handsome gauds, including a jeweled golden cup, a jeweled pendant, and several rings and bracelets. These he likewise gave to the girls to carry.

"Now come," he said. "We're going up yonder stair, but not all the way. Blow out that candle."

At the head of his little procession, Jorian stole up the stair to the main hall, until over the top he could see into the hall. Keeping back out of the lamplight, he silently watched events unfold.

The sound of talk in the hall had risen to a roar. Everywhere the Brothers were engaged in hot disputes, pounding their tables, smiting their fists into their palms, and wagging forefingers under one another's noses. Several more instruments of execution had been brought into the hall. As Jorian watched, two men came in carrying a little portable forge and a set of iron implements. They put the forge down, and one of them set about building a fire in it with stone coals and kindling. The other joined one of the raging arguments.

A louder shout drew Jorian's attention. One Brother had just thrown his beer into another's face. With a scream of rage, the victim hurled his mug at the first man's head and drew his dagger. The other man retreated to the space in the midst of the tables, now occupied by the instruments. He wrenched a beheading ax from its block and, as the other man rushed upon him with uplifted dagger, brought the blade down upon the attacker's head, cleaving his skull to the teeth.

The hall exploded into violent action. Everywhere men madly went for one another with whatever weapon came to hand. All the instruments fit for such use— axes, swords, knives, and the sledge hammer used in breaking prisoners on the wheel—were snatched up. Blood and brains spattered the tables and the floor; bodies fell right and left. Men grappled, rolling over and over on the floor, stabbing with knives and tearing with nails and teeth. The noise rose to a deafening pitch.

Jorian beckoned the girls. Sword out, he led the way to the top of the stair. By skirting the walls of the hall, he kept as much in the shadow as he could. He made the half-circuit to the vestibule that led to the outside. There he paused, waving the girls ahead of him.

As he did so, a figure detached itself from the bloody chaos in the hall and rushed towards him. It was Mehru, his erstwhile guide, waving his two-handed sword. Blood ran down his face from a cut, and his eyes gleamed wildly.

"Get along down to the pier and signal the dinghy," Jorian told the slave girls. "I shall be with you shortly." Then he faced the garrulous Brother.

"You did this, by some sorcery!" screamed Mehru, aiming a slash at Jorian's head.

Jorian parried with a clang, and again and again. The blows came so fast that he had no time for a counterattack. Although Mehru was the smaller man, he wielded his heavy weapon as if it were a lath, and his length of blade kept Jorian beyond the latter's reach. Jorian tried to catch the blows slantwise, so that the headsman's blade glanced off his own, but the force of them numbed his arm.

Step by step, Jorian backed into the vestibule and then into the archway that supported the portcullis. He kept glancing right and left, measuring the distances from side to side of the archway. Now he had backed out on the planks of the drawbridge, which, contrary to the custom of the Brothers, was down despite the darkness.

There he halted his retreat. Mehru, still attacking, was slowing down and panting heavily. Jorian permitted himself a smile, calling out:

"Why do you not fight, sister-impregnator?"

It was the ultimate insult in Mulvani. With a piercing scream, Mehru wound up for a terrific cut intended to shear Jorian in two at the waist.

The archway, however, was a little too narrow for such tactics. As a result, the tip of the long blade hit the masonry, striking sparks. The stonework stopped the blow; Jorian leaping in, sent Randir in a full-arm slash at the executioner's neck. Mehru's head leaped from his shoulders in a shower of blood. The body fell; the head bounced and rolled.

Jorian wiped and sheathed his sword. He sprang to the windlass for manual operation of the drawbridge and heaved. After a couple of turns, something went *clank*, and the wheel began to spin of its own accord from the weight of the unseen barrel of water. Jorian ran up the ever-steepening slope of the rising drawbridge, leaped to the path beyond, and trotted for the pier.

"Ten thousand devils!" growled Captain Strasso. "What means this, Master Maltho?"

"I've told you, sir captain: They refused the shipment. Something about trouble with their wives. We argued for hours. I insisted that a bargain was a bargain, whilst they said they would be damned if they'd pay for merchandise for which they had no use. At last they gave in and paid the amount agreed upon. Here are Belius' ninety-six crowns; pray give them to him when you return to Vindium, as Doctor Karadur and I plan to leave you at Janareth. Since the Brothers averred that they had no use for the lassies, they commissioned me to take them to Janareth to sell, retaining one-fourth of the money thus earned as my commission and returning the rest by your hand."

"Mmp. Be you through with the Castle of the Ax?"

"Aye. Sail when you list."

"Then I'll up-anchor and away. My lads fear the ghosts they say haunt this isle. Besides, there's less chance of meeting pirates in these waters at night. With this moon, we can hold a true course."

Later, in the cabin, Karadur said: "Ah me, I must practice austerities to atone for my craven conduct ashore today."

"You may forgive yourself, Doctor," said Jorian. "As

things fell out, you'd only have been in the way when the butchery started."

"What took place, my son?"

Jorian, sitting on his bunk and patiently whetting the edge of Randir where the blows of Mehru's sword had nicked or dulled it, told his tale.

Karadur: "Why, after so deceiving Captain Strasso as to the course of events, did you return Belius' money to him? Why not send the girls back to Vindium and keep the gold, which in the circumstance were scarcely theft?"

"I have other plans for them. Besides, we're rich again. I got more than the price of the wenches out of the Brothers' coffers; here's your share. And I need the girls more than I need the gold."

"How did you ever escape from the castle, with the drawbridge up?"

"It wasn't up. I moved one of the keys of the mechanism that controls it, to make it rise after midnight instead of at sunset. And now to bed; this has been a fatiguing day."

Karadur looked fondly at his young friend. "Do you remember, Jorian, when you told me of the witch's advice to you, to be either a king or a wandering adventurer?"

"Aye. What of it? I have tried the role of king, and once was enough."

"I fear you are not cut out for the adventurer's part, either."

"How so?"

"You are just not ruthlessly selfish enough to succeed at it. A true adventurer—and I have known several of the breed—would have embezzled Belius' gold and would never had tried to rescue those wenches, at least not at any risk to himself. And that brings us to the great moral question that for thousands of years had baffled the keenest minds amongst the philosophers of Mulvan: What is virtue? Some aver . . ."

But Jorian was already snoring.

# V

# The Butterfly Throne

Deep in its whitecapped, emerald bay, at the mouth of the mighty Bharma, Janareth lay in the sunshine, with white, red-roofed houses rising in tiers up the hillside amid the jade-green palms and dark cypresses, under the blue-and-white sky-bowl. A pilot boat, with the blue mermaid flag of Janareth fluttering from its masthead, came bouncing through the chop to guide the *Talaris* through the gap in the *mole* to the inner harbor.

Ships of many nations were anchored in this harbor or tied up at the quays. There were trim roundships from Vindium and Kortoli and Aussar and Tarxia. There were undecked craft from the Shvenic coast to the north, with their single square sails and high-pointed ends, like over-sized canoes. There were several black-hulled war galleys of Janareth, long, low, and lethal. There was a huge, high-sided, square-ended three-master, with slatted yellow lug-sails, from the Salimor Islands, far off in the Eastern Ocean.

Leaning on the rail and staring moodily at the craft, on the first day of the Month of the Wolf, Jorian gave a gusty sigh.

"At last we are getting back to a civilized clime!" said Karadur beside him. "Why sigh you?"

"I miss my wives. Nay, I'll take that back. I miss one of them: Estrildis, the little yellow-hair. The others are fine girls and fun in bed, but she is the one I chose for myself."

"How came that to pass?"

"She was the wench I was wooing in Kortoli when

130

Farmer Onnus made the mistake of trying to horsewhip me all day. After I had been king for three years, I learnt that she was yet unwed and got a message to her. I could not ride to Kortoli to claim her, as a proper hero of legend ought, because the Royal Guard would not let me over the boundaries of Xylar. But we managed. Some day I'll go back to Xylar and abduct her."

"If the Xylarians have not annulled your marriage and she have not wed some other man."

"I might snatch her anyway, were she willing. She was always my favorite. To preserve domestic harmony, I tried to hide the fact from the others, but I fear without complete success.

"Know, Doctor, that many a man has wished for a seraglio like mine, but I'll tell you how it works in practice. When the dames quarrel—which they do from time to time—the husband must act as judge and conciliator to settle their disputes. When they act in harmony—which occurs betimes—they get whatever they want from the poor wight by working upon him *seriatim*. And he must watch his every act, lest he give any one of them cause to think she has not been entreated so well as some other. If she do, then woe unto him! Scoldings, tears, complaints, and old scores raked up . . . Nay, if I ever achieve my modest ambitions to be a respectable craftsman earning a decent living, one wife will be plenty for me. But I could use at least one right now."

"Have you not been—ah—amusing yourself with Belius' maidens?"

"No, although how long I shall remain in this unwonted state of virtue is problematical. I haven't known a woman since I parted from that wild wench Vanora in Othomae."

"Your continence does you great spiritual credit, my son."

"Oh, bugger my spiritual credit! I've kept my hands off the poor little dears because it seemed unworthy to take advantage of their servile condition. Since I have, in a manner of speaking, inherited them from the Brotherhood of Rennum Kezymar, they could hardly have refused me."

"What is this mysterious plan you have for them?"

Jorian winked. "For four whole days I've held my flapping tongue, although bursting with my wonderful scheme. I feared that, did I get to talking, Strasso or one of his men might overhear. Once our good captain is on his way back to Vindium, I shall be overjoyed to share the plan with you, Holy Father."

Sailors were furling the sail, whose yard had been lowered into its crutches. Captain Strasso and the skipper of a tugboat exchanged shouts as the tug, propelled by ten brawny oarsmen, pushed against the side of the *Talaris* by means of a cushion of rope draped over the stem, nudging the ship into dock at one of the quays.

As the *Talaris* inched up against the bumpers of rope along the quay and was made fast, a pair of officials climbed aboard. One questioned Captain Strasso, checking the entries of his manifest, while the other scurried about, asking Jorian and Karadur their names, vanishing into the hold and reappearing, and consulting in an undertone with his colleague. By the time the inquisition was over and the officials had departed, a swarm of touts, pimps, peddlers, beggars, porters, donkey boys, and would-be guides had gathered around the shoreward end of the plank, crying:

"Come, my masters, to the tavern with the strongest liquors, the loudest music, and the nakedest dancing girls in Janareth ..." "... my nice, clean sister ..." "... to view the newly discovered grave of the demigod Pteroun, the ruined Temple of the Serpent Gods, and other fascinating wonders of antiquity ..." "Succor the child of misfortune!" "Buy my amulets: sure protection against the pox, the ague, and evil witchcraft ..." "Simha's Inn is so clean that not one bug has been seen there since the time of Ghish the Great ..."

Wearing his haughtiest royal expression—which he had used as King of Xylar to get rid of bores—Jorian strode down the plank and addressed the tout for Simha's Inn: "My good man, I have with me twelve ladies of quality, traveling *incognito* to Trimandilam. They will remain in Janareth about a fiftnight. Can your inn accommodate them in a style befitting their station?"

"Oh, my lord! But of course, my lord!" The tout bowed over his clasped hands again and again, as if worked by strings. "Do but deign to visit our worthy establishment . . ."

"Your performance had better match your promises," said Jorian, coldly eyeing the man. "Pick me a few porters of strong back and simple mind—four should do. What is the current porterage fee? . . ."

The waterfront of Janareth swarmed with the motley, many-tongued crowds of Janareth. Here were Novarians in short tunics and tight breeches; turbaned Mulvanians in skirts or baggy pantaloons of bright-hued silks; cameleers from the desert of Fedirun in brown robes and white head cloths; tall seamen from Shven, with lank, tow-colored hair and garments of sheepskin and coarse brown wool; slant-eyed, flat-faced men from far Salimor. There were semi-human slaves from the jungles of Komilakh, led on leashes. There were men of even more exotic racial types, whom Jorian could not identify.

Although Janareth paid tribute to the king of Mulvan, it retained self-government and still called itself a free city. The ferocious factional conflicts that flared up from time to time gave the Great King ample excuses for meddling, yet King Shaju had so far refrained. For one thing, the factions would instantly unite and fiercely oppose any such attempt. For another, conservative Mulvanians looked upon the great trading port as a necessary evil—a commercial convenience, but a repulsive one because of its mixed population of disgusting foreigners. They were glad it existed but also glad that it did not form part of their vast, orderly, minutely organized empire.

The tout cried back over his shoulder: "Beware! To the wall!"

Jorian and his companions crowded to one side as a cavalcade cantered through. The leader was a Mulvanian in scarlet silken garments, with a jeweled spray of plumes at the front of his turban. A squad of horsemen in spired, silvered steel caps, armed with light lances and little round shields, jingled after him.

"One of our local squires," said the tout after the horsemen had passed. "These landowners are always trying to worm and bluster their way into our governing council and so in time to rule the city—albeit they live out in the hills and come to town only for shopping and whoring." The man spat.

The following day, Jorian was eating his midday meal in the refectory of Simha's Inn when Captain Strasso came in.

"Good Master Maltho!" said the Captain. "The oracle promises fair weather for the next fiftnight, and I've been lucky in finding a good cargo for Vindium, ready to load. So *Talaris* will put out on her last voyage of the season the morn."

"Fine," said Jorian.

"But, there's the matter of the payment to the Brothers. Have you sold the wenches yet, so that I can take the money with me?"

"No, I haven't; nor am I in a hurry to."

Strasso frowned. "How so?"

"Naturally, I crave the highest price; for the higher the price, the larger my commission. Therefore, I've hired a man skilled in such matters to make highly trained ladies' maids out of the girls. This may take a month."

"Then how shall I convey the money?"

"Know you an honest banker in Janareth?"

"Oh, certes. I bank here with Ujjai and Sons. Ujjai seems trustworthy even if a Mulvanian."

"Then present me to him. When I sell, I shall deposit the money with him, and you can pick it up on your first voyage next spring."

Strasso clapped Jorian on the back. "Admirably thought of! But won't the Brothers chafe at the delay?"

"Judging by their actions when last I saw them, I think not. When I finish this narange, I'll forth to Ujjai's stall."

Jorian met the banker Ujjai, bade farewell to Captain Strasso, and returned to Simha's Inn. This time he went upstairs to the suite that had been turned over to the twelve.

Here, a man was coaching the girls in the rôles that Jorian had invented for them. Although slightly stooped with age, the man was even taller than Jorian. He had large, handsome features and flowing white hair. His piercing gray eyes and lordly, carefully mannered gestures instantly caught the vision of anyone in the same room with him. He spoke in a rich, rolling voice to Mnevis, who was walking back and forth in the middle of the room while the other eleven sat about, comparing their fine new clothes.

"Remember!" he said, "you are a queen. You are conscious every instant of status and worth far above those with whom you hold intercourse. At the same time, you wish them well and would not for worlds hurt their feelings—unless they presumed to undue familiarity. To express just that right combination of hauteur and graciousness calls for a veritable triumph of the actor's skill.

"I recall that when I played King Magonius, opposite that great actress Janoria, in Physo's *The Tinsel Crown* she struck just the right note." He sighed and shook his head. "There will never be another Janoria, even if she *would* throw things at her colleagues off-stage. Greetings, Master Jorian. As you see, I strive to obey your commands. Now come, Mistress Mnevis—Queen Mnevis, I should say—and try that walk once more."

Jorian was watching the work when Karadur knocked and slipped in, saying, "I was searching for you, my son. I was in the library at the Temple of Narzes and—ah—forgot about lunch in my absorption. Then I chanced upon Strasso, who told me you had returned hither. What takes place here?"

Jorian: "Doctor Karadur, allow me to present Master Pselles of Aussar, a leading ornament of the Novarian stage, now fallen upon certain—ah—temporary embarrassments. I've retained him to coach my girls."

"It does not look to me as if they were being trained as ladies' maids, as Strasso said."

Jorian winked. "Na, na, this is the scheme I promised to reveal to you. Know that these are no ladies' maids, but Queen Mnevis of Algarth and her eleven noble ladies-in-waiting."

"But—but you told me in Xylar that Algarth was only a nest of pirates! How can it have a queen?"

"Mnevis, tell the doctor who you are and what you purpose to do."

"My good sage," said Mnevis in a queenly voice, "know that we, Mnevis widow of Serli, are the rightful queen of Algarth, which is an archipelago off the western coast of Shven, far to the north of the Twelve Cities. A few years ago, these pirates whereof you speak seized our isles for their own fell purposes, slew our husband the king, and kept us captive as a puppet queen, to dance to their strings.

"Lately, with the help of loyal subjects—who have been reduced to serfdom by these bloody corsairs—we escaped from Algarth with these our ladies. Hearing that the mightiest and justest monarch in the entire world was the Great King of Mulvan, we have come hither to pray His Majesty, that he will render us aid in regaining our rightful throne."

Jorian applauded. "Splendid! You should have been

an actress in the first place." He turned to Karadur.
"Can you think of a better way to ingratiate ourselves
into the haughty court at Trimandilam, to whom ordinary foreigners are less than dirt?"

Karadur shook his head sorrowfully. "I know not ...
I know not. When you get these wild ideas, my son ...
Will not this imposture be speedily punctured?"

"I think not. They have never even heard of Algarth
in Mulvan."

"But what of you?"

"I am now Jorian of Kortoli, their factotum. Since
the lassies speak no Mulvani, they will need my constant attendance."

"What if King Shaju says: 'Very good, you shall have
the help you require.' What then?"

"We'll make the queen's demands so steep that there
shall be no danger of that. How can Shaju send a fleet
and an army to Algarth, when Mulvan has no ports on
the Western Ocean? They must need cross the desert
of Fedirun or the Twelve Cities or the steppes of Shven
to come to that sea, and then what should they do for
ships to get to Algarth? 'Tis preposterous on the face
of it. And a little skillful exaggeration of the rigors of
the boreal Algarthian clime will scare off any Mulvanian
tempted to join the ladies from motives of knight-
errantry."

Karadur shook his head again. "Meseems I spoke in
haste when I denigrated your talent for adventurehood,
my son. But it is safe to resume your name again so
soon?"

"I think so. We shall be far enough from Xylar so
that no report of the doings there will circulate. And
I weary of being addressed by other names and not
recognizing them, so that people get the notion I'm
deaf. Besides, since my name is not uncommon, 'Jorian
of Kortoli' might be any one of many persons. 'Jorian
of Ardamai' would give me away, Ardamai being a
mere village."

"Well, may the gods of Novaria and of Mulvan aid you."

The Bharma wound through the Pushkana Gap in the eastern Lograms, which here had dwindled to a mere range of forested hills. Laboring upstream under sail, the river boat *Jhimu* was towed by big, black buffaloes around the great serpentine bends of the river where it traversed the gap, the current here being too swift for the sail alone to make headway against. The steep, dark-green slopes soared into the sky on either hand, with no sign of animal life save a thread of blue smoke from a woodcutter's clearing, or a vulture hanging like a black mote in the blue. At night, however, the *Jhimu*'s passengers could sometimes hear the grunt of a tiger or the toot of a wild elephant.

Beyond the bends, the river ran more slowly and comparatively straight between stairlike rises on the east and west to wooded plateaus. Sometimes it widened into marshes where behemoths lay awash, with only their ears, eyes, and nostrils exposed. At night, snorting and grunting, these animals trooped ashore to graze or to raid the Mulvanian peasants' plantings.

From time to time, roads followed the river. On these roads, Mulvanians were always moving, from single wayfarers to parties of fifty to a hundred. There were holy men, religious pilgrims, merchants with laden pack animals, farmers with loads of produce, detachments of jingling soldiery, and miscellaneous travelers of high and low degree. There were people afoot, on asses, in carriages, in oxcarts, on horseback, on camels, and on elephants.

Every league or so, the *Jhimu* passed a temple to one of Mulvan's multifarious gods. The main structure might be shaped like a dome, a cylinder, a cone, a cube, a pyramid, or a tapering spire; each god had his preferred architectural style. All were encrusted with minutely detailed carvings. The erotic statuary that covered a temple of Laxara, the goddess of love and hate, so embarrassed Karadur when they went near it during a stop that the old man kept his face averted. Looking up at the carvings, Jorian stood with fists on hips, grinning through his beard.

"By Imbal's brazen balls!" he cried. "I didn't know one *could* do it in so many positions!"

Some temples were in crumbling ruin; others were active. At night, points of yellow lamplight flickered about these fanes and the sound of music and song came to the travelers, sometimes slow and solemn, sometimes fast and frenzied.

Aboard the *Jhimu,* Karadur studied a magical scroll he had obtained in Janareth, while Jorian rehearsed his girls in their roles. On the sixth day after leaving Janareth, the *Jhimu* neared the confluence of the Bharma and the Pennerath. In the fork rose the vast city of Trimandilam on its nine hills. The massive wall was of black basalt. Over it the travelers could see the hills, topped by gleaming palaces and temples of marble and alabaster, with gilded roof tiles ablaze in the sun. Below these structures spread thousands of the dun-colored, mud-brick houses of the common folk.

As they tied up, the girls, full of giggling excitement, wanted to scramble ashore. But Jorian sternly ordered them back.

"Queens and their ladies do not plunge into a strange city unescorted," he told them. "You shall wait here until I procure an escort suitable to your station."

Away he strode, leaving the captain of the *Jhimu* to dispute with an official from the city and the girls to watch the brown-skinned waterfront crowd. Unlike Janareth, the population of Trimandilam was fairly homogenous. The people were smaller than the Novarians and darker, with straight or wavy black hair. Most went barefoot. The main garment for both sexes was a long skirt, which most of the men tucked up between the legs to make a floppy loincloth. Both sexes left the upper body bare in the balmy air. Outside of the poorest classes, all wore masses of jewelry: necklaces of beads and pearls, bracelets, anklets, fillets, earrings, finger rings, nose rings, and toe rings.

An hour later, Jorian was back on a tall, big-boned chestnut-roan stallion, at the head of a score of lancers in spired helmets and jingling mail. After these followed three immense elephants with gaudily painted heads, howdahs on their backs, and their riders clad in drapes bordered with cloth-of-gold.

Jorian vaulted to the ground and bowed low before Mnevis. When the officer of the troop dismounted more slowly, Jorian said:

"May it please Your Majesty, I would fain present to you the gallant Captain Yaushka, veteran of many fierce battles!" He repeated the sentence in Mulvani.

For an instant, the captain and the queen confronted each other, haughty suspicion on one side and regal self-assurance on the other. Regal self-assurance won. The captain dropped to both knees on the granite blocks of the quay and bent down until his forehead touched the pave. Mnevis allowed herself a tiny nod and a small smile.

"Tell the gallant captain," she said to Jorian, "that if his bravery equals his courtesy, the empire has nought to fear."

Grinning, Captain Yaushka rose and signaled the mahouts. These in turn whacked their elephants over the head with their goads. The blows made hollow sounds, like beating a log drum. The three elephants knelt and then lowered their bellies and elbows to the ground. One mahout produced a small ladder, which he placed against the side of the foremost elephant. Captain Yaushka helped the queen up the ladder into the howdah. The eleven ladies-in-waiting gave a few squeals and giggles at the prospect of riding these beasts, but Jorian scowled at them so fiercely that they quickly fell silent.

When each elephant bore four women, the drivers signaled the beasts to rise. The sudden tilting of the howdahs elicited more squeals. Jorian vaulted back on his horse, while a trooper gave Karadur a leg-up for the latter to climb aboard a big white ass. Captain Yaushka blew a trumpet, and the cavalcade started off.

They jingled through endless, narrow, winding streets, where strange smells hung in the air, the elephants' drapes scraped against the house walls as they rounded corners, and people squeezed into doorways and arcades to let them pass. They passed mansions and hovels, temples and shops, inns and emporia, shacks and tenements, taverns and brothels, all jumbled together.

At last they reached the foot of the hill on which stood the royal palace. A wall ran around the base of the hill, and a massive, fortified gate in this wall gave access to the interior. To one side of the gate stood an inclosure in which an elephant mill operated a huge pump. A pair of elephants, one on each end of a long boom pivoted in the center, walked the boom round and round, while bearings squealed and the pump grumbled in its housing.

At the gate, Jorian and his party were scrutinized, questioned, and passed through the gate while the sentries touched their foreheads to the ground in salute to Queen Mnevis. The horses, the ass, and the elephants plodded up a long, sloping avenue, fifty feet wide, which had been hewn out of a cliff that formed that side of the hill. The cliff had been cut down to form an evenly sloping stone ramp and then roughened by transverse grooves, a fingerbreadth apart, to provide traction for the feet of men and animals.

As the avenue rose, the solid stone gave way to a built-up structure of well-fitted stone blocks. The road came up to the level of the main inner fortification

wall, of rose-red stone, rising from the top of the cliff
and on the right as one ascended the slope. Along the
outer side of the avenue, where the cliff fell away, a
bronzen pipe, green with verdegris and as thick as a
man's leg, passing through holes in stone blocks, carried the water pumped by the elephant mill to the
palace and also served as a railing.

The procession reached the gate in the fortification
wall and was again passed through. Inside, they faced
another gate. Whereas the outer gate was a massive,
military structure with arrow-slitted towers, portcullis,
murder holes, and other accessories for defense, the
inner gate was an ornamental edifice of many-colored
stone, with a huge central arch flanked by smaller portals. Under the arch, on the left, a raised platform
allowed horsemen easy mounting and dismounting. On
the right, a higher platform enabled elephant riders to
step on and off their mounts without using a ladder.

As the party gathered afoot under the main arch, a
small, wizened brown man came up, bowing repeatedly
over clasped hands. "Will Your Highness deign to follow your humble slave?" he said. "I am Harichumbra,
your unworthy adviser."

They followed Harichumbra through a series of halls
and courts, until Jorian was hopelessly lost. Centuries
ago, a king of Mulvan had ordered the entire top of
the hill planed off to build this palace, as large in itself
as a small city. Hall after hall had been added until the
entire hilltop inside the upper wall was now cut up
into square and rectangular courts, ranging in size from
ball courts to parade grounds.

The halls that divided these courts were long, narrow
buildings, mostly of three-story height. They were mar-
vels of Mulvanian architecture. In most of the courts,
there had been an effort to give the stonework on all
four sides an artistic unity. Thus some courts were
walled by white and red stone, some by white and
black, some by white and blue, some by white and

green, and some by other combinations. Everywhere
were arches: plain semicircular arches, pointed arches,
segmental arches, basket-handle arches, ogee arches,
horseshoe arches, and cusped arches in every possible
combination. They topped monumental gates and ordinary doors and windows. Little balconies projected here
and there from the upper stories of the halls. Broad eaves
extended out from the flat roofs to provide the courts
with shadowed spaces against the fierce tropical sun.
Domes, spires, and gazebos rose from the roofs.

Everywhere the stonework was enriched by carving
and by inlays of mother-of-pearl and stones of con-
trasting colors, making designs of flowers, beasts,
heroes, and gods. Sayings attributed to former kings
and holy men were carved in bands of stone or inlaid
in polished metal and semiprecious stones in the characters of the Mulvani language.

"These are your apartments," said Harichumbra,
indicating a hall whose third story was walled by deli-
cately carved marble screens, so that it was open to
the breeze but shielded from the vision of those outside. "Her Majesty will occupy the main chamber at
the end of this hall; her ladies, these rooms; my lords,
this chamber . . ."

He showed them the amenities of the place. "This
hall is called the Tiger Cub, in case you get lost and have
difficulty finding your way back to it. When you have
rested and refreshed yourselves, I shall return. Shall
we say in one hour? Or two? It shall be as you desire. I
shall now summon servants to minister to your wants."

He clapped his hands, and a score of women and
several men appeared through the door at the end of
the hall. Harichumbra bowed himself out.

Soon, Jorian and Karadur sat facing each other from
the ends of a huge tub, while pretty little brown Mulvanian girls soaped their backs. Speaking Novarian,
Karadur said:

"All right so far, my son. You managed the escort very featly."

Jorian grunted. "Save that the damned horse had no stirrups, only a pair of handgrips on the front of the saddle. Not having ridden bareback since I was a stripling on Onnus' farm, I nearly fell off twice. They kindly said I might use the beast during my stay, but I must have stirrups added to the saddle. 'Tis a big, strong beast, though. I think I'll call him 'Oser' after my schoolmaster in Ardamai. Those knobby joints and feet like platters remind me of the old boy. He gives a rough ride, but at least he's willing. Tell me: why don't Mulvanians use stirrups? They've been known in the Twelve Cities for centuries."

"Mulvanians pride themselves on preserving the ancient ways and ignoring the devices dreamt up by barbarians. Did you note that elephant mill outside the palace?"

"I surely did, and an admirable device I thought it."

"Well, that was installed by King Shaju's grandfather, King Sivroka, and it has been a source of contention ever since. Whenever discontent arises against the reigning monarch, those who seek to take advantage of this condition set up the cry: Destroy this unholy foreign contraption, which robs honest water-carriers of their livelihood! When the mill wears out, I do not think it will be repaired or rebuilt."

"And then the Mulvanians wonder why their history is a catalogue of invasions and conquests by loot-hungry barbarians," growled Jorian. "When I was king of Xylar, I tried to keep up with new things."

"And what good did that do you, my son?" asked Karadur gently. Jorian snorted. Karadur continued: "I advise you to get rid of that beard."

"By Zevatas, I've come to like the thing!"

"But in Mulvan it is the badge of either a holy ascetic, an ancient in retirement, or a low-class worker, and you do not wish to pass for any of those."

\*     \*     \*

Two hours later, the adviser returned. Bathed, shaved, and smelling sweetly of ointments and perfumes, Jorian listened as Harichumbra said:

"Now, my lord, my first task is to instruct you in the rules governing intercourse at the court of the King of Kings. To what class did you belong in your native land?"

"The lesser nobility. So?"

"The manner in which you greet and converse with others depends upon your own rank and that of your interlocutor. In other words, you must use one form of greeting to an equal, another to an inferior, and so on. The same applies to speech. Court Mulvani has eight grades of politeness, depending upon the relative status of the persons speaking. One must master them lest one give unwitting offense—or at least expose onself as an ignorant boor, unworthy of one's own class.

"This applies particularly to your noble self, because their ladyships appear to speak none of our tongue. You must, therefore, interpret for them, using the forms of speech that they would use in addressing Mulvanians of various classes, from the King of Kings down to the lowly classless ones who clean out latrines.

"As one of the lesser nobility of your own country, you will rank below our own nobility but above the official class. You are, of course, aware of the importance of class distinctions in this well-ordered land. Bodily contact between persons of widely separated classes is permitted only in line of duty, as when a barber cuts a nobleman's hair. Otherwise, he of the higher class is religiously polluted and must seek ritual purification. Fraternization is likewise limited, and intermarriage is to us utterly abhorrent.

"Now, let me begin your instructions. First of all, when you approach the Great King—may he reign forever!—the disparity in your ranks requires that you advance no nearer than nine paces from him, and that you touch your forehead to the ground thrice. By the way, that hat you wore upon your arrival would be unsuitable, because of the brim."

"Then I will go bareheaded. This clime is too warm for hats, anyway."

"Oh, sir!" Harichumbra looked shocked. "That were indeed an unseemly act! Respect for the king requires that men remain covered in his presence. Suppose I get you a turban."

"I know not how to wind those cursed things, and I should find them too hot. Is there no small, brimless cap I might wear?"

Harichumbra pondered. "Ah, I have it! I will get you a cap such as members of the Dancing Saints, an ecstatic religious sect, wear. It should meet your requirements.

"And now the grammar. In addressing His Majesty, you will naturally use the politest form. Sentences whereof His Majesty is the subject or the object are put in the third person singular subjunctive . . .

"In approaching a member of the king's immediate family, or a member of the priesthood in his official capacity, you must halt six paces from the person and touch your forehead to the ground once. In addressing such persons, the third person singular indicative is used with the suffix *ye*.

"In approaching a member of the Mulvanian nobility, you must halt three paces from the person and bow so that your body is parallel to the ground. In addressing such persons, the third person singular indicative is used without the honorific suffix. The nobleman should return your bow, but only by inclining his body at half a right angle to the ground . . ."

Before taking his leave, Harichumbra informed Jorian that Queen Mnevis would be presented to the king in a public audience the second day after their arrival, that a private audience with the king and his advisers was being set up for the day after that, and that on the tenth day they were all bidden to a court ball.

"Barbarians," said Harichumbra, "sometimes expect to be bidden to feasts, not knowing that amongst us Chosen of the Gods, eating is deemed an unseemly act, to be performed in private or, at most, with one's immediate family. We do, however, have balls—albeit our dancing is much more decorous and decent than in some lands. This ball celebrates the seven hundred and fiftieth anniversary of the Serpent Princess."

"Will the princess attend?"

"I believe she will; it is the only occasion during the year that she leaves her apartment. By the bye, are you an addict of fermented liquors?"

Jorian stared. "I like wine and my ale, but I should hardly term myself an addict. I can do without them if need be. Why?"

"Barbarians oft have a passion for these fluids, which are forbidden to Mulvanians—save the classless, to whom they are allowed to brighten the otherwise cheerless lives they lead as punishment for some sin in an earlier incarnation. If you require these poisons—" (Harichumbra gave a delicate shudder) "—and will write a petition to the effect that you are addicted to them and if deprived of them are liable to go mad and become a danger to the community, I can arrange a regular ration for you."

"I will think about it," said Jorian. After Harichumbra had gone, he asked Karadur: "What sort of man is this King Shaju, as a man and not as a king?"

"Your question, my son, means little, for in Mulvan the role of king is so exacting that the man, as a distinct entity, has little chance of emerging. From morn to night he is busied, if not with state business and the hearing of petitions, then with religious ceremonies. For he is supposed to please both the millions of Mulvanians beneath his sway and, at the same time, the hundreds of gods in the heavens above—a task to daunt the hardiest."

"How is he with his intimates, then?"

"He has no intimates—no friends, as you would use the term. The formality of courtly usage rules every aspect of his life and excludes him from true intimacy. When he summons one of his wives to his bed, she must perform the same prostrations on approaching him that the rest of us do in his throne room. Perhaps, after he has sown the royal seed and ere he goes to sleep, he engages in some small informal talk with the woman—but who would know about that?"

"We managed things better in Xylar; the king was allowed to be halfway human. What sort of man, then, would Shaju be if he weren't king?"

Karadur shrugged. "Who can tell? For the office molds the man as much as the man molds the office— and more so, if the office be so overwhelming as that of Great King. But from what I have seen of King Shaju, I suspect he would be a well-meaning and not unable mediocrity—the kind who, were he your neighbor, you might describe as 'a good fellow but dull.' Of course, he can be cruel and violent as circumstances require, and he showed no qualms about killing off a score of brothers upon his accession. Had he not, one of them would probably have slain him, so he would not be here for us to criticize. But that is kingship for you."

The public audience proved an interesting example of Mulvanian courtly techniques. Every word and gesture had been prescribed by Harichumbra and rehearsed by Jorian and his women. The replies and gestures of the Great King were just as artificial.

Shaju sat on a golden throne at the end of a long hall, whose air was blue with the smoke of incense burners. Behind a screen, musicians twanged and tootled.

Suppressing an urge to cough on the fragrant smoke, Jorian and his girls followed the usher down the hall. At the prescribed distance, Jorian and the eleven ladies-in-waiting prostrated themselves, while queen Mnevis, as a fellow sovran, merely bowed low. While they were in this position, a grinding noise made itself heard. When Jorian looked up from his crouch, the throne bearing King Shaju had risen on a pillar to a fathom above its normal height. With a grinding of gearwheels, the throne sank back to its former level.

This throne was an amazing structure. The back had the form of a gigantic butterfly, as high as a man. The wings of the insect, made of a kind of gold mesh, blazed with jewels, which formed a pattern like that of a real butterfly.

King Shaju was taller than most Mulvanians, albeit shorter by nearly a head than Jorian. He was middle-aged and a little overweight, with a shaven chin and a long, black, drooping mustache. Cosmetics failed to hide a sad, weary expression. In a high-pitched, expressionless voice he said:

"The Great King graciously condescends to receive the homage of the charming queen of Algarth. It pleases the King of Kings to see that other monarchs of the world acknowledge his primacy. My Majesty accepts the gift of Your Majesty with thanks and would have Your Majesty know that you shall not suffer for your generosity." The king turned over the gift—the best of the golden cups from the treasure room of Rennum Kezymar—and said: "This looks like Mulvanian work." He glanced inquiringly at Jorian, who responded:

"May it please Your Majesty, it probably is. Trade has carried the peerless products of Mulvanian handicrafts far and wide, even to distant Algarth."

"I see. Well, for the discussion of matters of state, the Great King will entertain the charming queen in the room of private audience at a time to be fixed by our servants. May the gods of Mulvan and those of Algarth smile upon the gracious queen!"

"Now we back out!" hissed Harichumbra.

The private audience proved more interesting. Besides the ubiquitous guards, there were only five persons: King Shaju, his minister Ishvarnam, Queen Mnevis, Jorian, and Harichumbra. Ishvarnam opened by asking:

"Lord Jorian, one has heard rumors of a king of your name, in one of the more distant Novarian cities. It is called Zy—nay, Xylar. Is your lordship perchance connected with this monarch, who one hears has died, or been slain, or fled the kingdom, or some such thing? The tales contradict one another, and we have no secure source of news from there."

Heart pounding, Jorian answered evenly: "One suspects we are distant cousins, Excellency. One was born in Kortoli City, whereas one believes this other Jorian came from the village of Ardamai, several leagues distant from the capital. One's own forebears moved from Ardamai to Kortoli two generations ago; but there might be a connection, could one take time to trace it down."

"One thanks your lordship for your information," said Ishvarnam. "Now let us to business . . ."

Translating Mnevis' speech, Jorian made his plea for a vast armed force to recapture the Algarth Archipelago from the freebooters. In actual fact, the pirates had been there since they first appeared in Novarian history. The Twelve Cities knew nothing of any line of legitimate sovrans in those isles. As Jorian expected, however, the Mulvanians had never even heard of Algarth and so were in no position to contradict him.

When he had finished, Ishvarnam and the king exchanged whispers. Then the minister spoke:

"My dear Lord Jorian, much as His Majesty would be delighted to restore Her charming Majesty to her rightful throne, what she proposes is beyond the powers of even such a world-bestriding realm as Mulvan. What with the pirates of the Inner Sea, and raids by the desert riders of Fedirun, and incursions by the savages of the equatorial jungles of Beraoti, we have all we can do to maintain order in our own realm. One fears Her Majesty asks the impossible."

Jorian and Mnevis put on suitably downcast expressions. Ishvarnam said: "The Great King will, however, see to it that Her Majesty go not hence empty-handed. He will, moreover, provide her with an escort back to Janareth suitable to her rank. Thence she can proceed to places where conditions are more favorable for finding succor. For example, we hear that in the Twelve Cities are many turbulent rogues, always eager for such adventure."

"How shall they reach Vindium, now that shipping on the Inner Sea has closed down for the winter?" asked Jorian.

"The escort will convey Her Majesty and her attendants to Vindium by the land route."

"One has heard—no doubt from some misinformed source—that this route is perilous."

"The escort will be large enough to master such contingencies as arise."

"One sees. It would, in one's humble opinion, be wise for them to set out forthwith, to get through the Lograms before full winter sets in."

"We can speed them on their way tomorrow, if that be Her charming Majesty's wish," said Ishvarnam.

"That will be excellent. One would like, however, to beg His Majesty's indulgence to the extent of allowing one to linger in Trimandilam for a few days after Her Majesty's departure. One would like to see more of His Majesty's world-famous city and to attend the ball to which he was so gracious as to invite one. Since ladies of noble birth and tender upbringing cannot be expected to travel swiftly, one should easily overtake them."

More whispers; then Ishvarnam said: "His Majesty graciously grants the plea of the noble Lord Jorian, in the hope that, by observing the customs and usages of a truly civilized realm, he will be moved to adopt these habits as his own and to spread Mulvanian enlightenment among the backward peoples who dwell beyond our marches. You have His Majesty's gracious leave to withdraw."

The girls left two days later in horse litters, guarded by gleaming cavalry commanded by Captain Yaushka, who had escorted them to the palace upon their arrival. Jorian had lectured Mnevis on the dangers she faced:

"I don't mistrust King Shaju or Captain Yaushka—at least not in this matter. The danger will come when you cross into Vindium. You won't be able to carry on this imposture of being a queen, but you mustn't drop it so suddenly that Yaushka hears about it and carries the word back to Trimandilam. You will have to hire men to tend your gear, guide your animals, and guard your precious persons whilst on your way to your homes. Unless you are both shrewd and lucky, your servants may turn on you, rape you, cut your throats, and make off with your money. Ere you hire anybody, get references to previous employers and follow them through.

"In case a former owner tries to seize you, I've made out documents of manumission for all twelve of you. Some might question whether I was ever your rightful owner, but short of going to Rennum Kezymar to query the people there, there is no way to disprove these documents. If you are serious about a career on the stage, look up my friend Merlois son of Gaus, in Govannian. He taught me such of the actor's tricks as I know.

"Here is the gift from King Shaju to Her charming Majesty, and something over from my own purse. Divide it into twelve equal parts, one for each girl, and give each girl her document. Don't let any of them show their new wealth around, lest its glitter draw evildoers."

"We should be much safer with you," said Mnevis.

"No doubt, and I should be much easier in my mind about you too. But that's impossible, so you must do the best you can and trust to the gods. Now, curse it, Mnevis, don't cry! I have told you why I cannot take wife, concubine, or bondmaid with me."

"B-but l-last night—"

"Na, na, never mind last night. Fun be fun, but a have deadly business before me. Get tha going, lass!"

When the weeping girl had left, Karadur said, "Last night, my son? Methought you had set your feet firmly on the path of virtue."

Jorian sighed and shrugged. "I held out as long as I could; but what is a healthy man of my age to do when a pretty creature like that crawls unasked into bed with him? I may not be the worst man in the world, but I am no saint—dancing or otherwise."


As the time of the ball approached, Jorian and Karadur plotted ways to gain access to the apartment of the Serpent Princess. They had made discreet inquiries here and there, some from Harichumbra, some from other members of the court.

They learnt that the Serpent Princess, Yargali, dwelt in an apartment directly over the ballroom, in a hall called the Green Serpent. Having been an adjunct of the court for many centuries, she stayed in this apartment year in and year out, save on a few special occasions like the forthcoming birthday party. Her function was to guard the Kist of Avlen, which had been brought to Trimandilam from Vindium by the wizard-king Avlen the Fourth, at the time of the Shvenic invasion. The invaders from the northern steppes had overthrown the Three Kingdoms of Old Novaria and brought about the dark age that preceded the rise of the Twelve Cities.

Fleeing these invaders, King Avlen had brought with him a chest of his most precious magical manuscripts, with which he sought to bargain with Ghish the Great of Mulvan for help in recovering his kingdom. Ghish, a nomad from the deserts of Fedirun, had just united by conquest the successor states that had grown up on the ruins of the former kingdom of Tirao. With barbarian practicality, Ghish had strangled Avlen with his own hands and put the Kist under guard, to preserve it for his own use in time of need. None was allowed to read the contents save the chief wizard of Mulvan. A few centuries later, when Yargali arrived at the court of Trimandilam, King Venu had entrusted to her the task of guarding the Kist.

It was said that various noble Mulvanians, from the king on down, visited Yargali late at night, allegedly to seek supernatural wisdom from her lips, although rumor credited her with giving them more tangible favors. There were no recent accounts of her turning into a serpent and devouring her visitors, as tales current in the Twelve Cities credited her with doing.

So Jorian and Karadur plotted and planned but without result. Jorian hurled his embroidered Dancing Saint's cap to the floor with a yell of frustration, saying:

"The curse of Zevatas and Franda and Heryx and all the other deities of the Twelve Cities upon you and your fellow he-witches! I'm minded to walk out and strike for Vindium despite all the aches and pains and nightmares you can send upon me. If your damned princess doesn't turn into a snake and swallow me, Shaju's guardsmen will fill me with arrows until I look like a hedgehog. I should be more usefully employed shepherding those poor girls back to their homes. Why can't you silly Progressives compose your own spells instead of copying those of some ancient wizard—whose magic was evidently not strong enough to keep the barbarians out of his kingdom?"

"Peace, my son, peace. Well you know that you cannot abandon your quest, save at the cost of your life. I would have helped you to escape from Xylar without exacting a price, but my fellow Altruists insisted. Know that at the time of the conquest of Old Novaria, much ancient magical knowledge was lost, and we hope to recover some of it. Perchance some of Avlen's spells have been rediscovered in the centuries since the fall of Old Vindium; but we shall never know until we compare the original documents with those of later times." He sighed, "But things are as they are. Perhaps something will turn up during this ball."

"Will you attend the ball?"

"I had not thought so. I am reading old manuscripts in the royal library and had hoped to spend the evening so occupied."

"But *could* you attend the ball?"

"Surely; as a member of the priestly class I can go anywhere. I outrank every layman in Mulvan, save the king himself."

"Then come to this party. I may want you to distract the king's attention whilst I make friends with the princess."

## VI

# The Serpent Princess

Wearing a fine new red satin coat with jeweled buttons,
Jorian followed Harichumbra through the maze of
courts and halls to the Hall of the Green Serpent. Karadur tottered along behind. As a nobleman and a traveler, Jorian was allowed to wear his sword in
Trimandilam, but he had to check it at the entrance to
the ballroom. The Mulvanians did not use peace wires.
Jorian caught a glimpse of Randir standing in the corner of the cloakroom, the only straight blade in a host
of scimitars. The brand was further conspicuous by its
plain guard of silvered brass amid the jeweled hilts of
the Mulvanians.

The ballroom occupied most of the ground floor of
the Hall of the Green Serpent. It had a polished floor
of brown marble and long windows, filled with little
leaded panes of many shapes, which opened on a terrace. Most of the windows were open to the mild evening air, admitting hosts of insects, which whirled in
suicidal circles around the flames of the many lamps
and candles. A couple of low-class Mulvanians were
kept busy with broom and dustpan, sweeping up little
charred corpses from the marble.

The terrace overlooked a large court in the form of
a sunken garden, where hedges and bushes loomed
dark in the fading twilight and fountains tinkled. On
the side of the hall away from the balcony, a huge
carpet had been rolled up.

Several score of the nobility of Mulvan and their
women were already standing about the ballroom, talking, drinking fruit juice, and nibbling sweetmeats from

a long table to one side. The men were gorgeous in silks and satins, plumes and jewels. Lords from the east and south favored skirts, while those from the west and north encased their legs in baggy pantaloons, gathered in at the ankle. Their ladies stood among them, their bangles clashing musically when they moved. The younger ones had flowers, stars, eyes, and other figures painted on their bare breasts.

Harichumbra introduced Jorian to various lords, to whom he bowed deeply until he was dizzy. He sipped fruit juice, wished for something more sustaining, and exchanged words with a young Mulvanian as large as himself. This man, Lord Chavero of Kolkai, wore pantaloons of a brilliant saffron yellow and a spray of peacock plumes in his turban. Jorian said:

"The weather is delightful this time of year in Trimandilam, I find, my lord."

Chavero yawned. "It will do, though you foreigners always complain of the heat in summer. Are you from Novaria or some barbarous place?"

"That is right, although we do not deem it so barbarous as all that."

"Perhaps not, but how would you know, without having visited Mulvan to form a standard of comparison?"

"A good question, but I might ask you the same."

The man pulled a long mustachio. "It stands to reason that, since Mulvan is the center and fount of civilization, all other places must be inferior to it in culture. But you, as a barbarian, cannot be expected to understand logic."

Jorian fought down a temptation to answer back in kind, but temptation won. "It is interesting to hear you speak thus, my lord. For we have a saying in Kortoli, that the most ignorant man is he who thinks he knows it all."

Chavero puzzled over this statement for an instant. Then his look of perplexity changed to anger as he replied, "And we have a saying, my good man, that the yapping dog must not mind if it get itself kicked. Let us hope it will not be necessary to—"

A trumpet sang, cutting short this speech. A eunuch smote the pave with his staff and cried: "The Great King!"

Shaju, blazing with jewels, stood in the doorway. All the Mulvanians, and Jorian, too, dropped to their knees and touched their foreheads to the ground three times. The king called out:

"Rise, my friends! For the remainder of this even, consider your obeisances to My Majesty as made."

Behind him, Karadur whispered: "That means we can speak to him without prostrating ourselves first." The wizard pulled at Jorian's sleeve. "Come away from that Kolkaian, quickly, ere he embroil you in a quarrel! He is a dangerous man. He would fain be Yargali's next lover, and if he knew of our intentions . . ."

"Some have thought me a dangerous man, too," muttered Jorian, but he let Karadur lead him off through the crowd. He asked Karadur: "Do His Majesty's wives attend such functions?"

"They used to, but since the distressing affair of the Lady Radmini and Lord Valshaka, he has shut them up, the way they did before the time of King Sivroka. The queens are watching the show now from behind that screened balcony." Karadur nodded his turban towards a marble screen high up at one end of the hall. "And doubtless wishing they could descend to mingle with the rest of us. When—"

Another trumpet interrupted. From the end of the hall opposite to that by which the king had entered, a eunuch struck the marble and called out, "Her Supernatural Highness, the Serpent Princess Yargali!"

Everybody bowed low. In the door stood a woman as tall as Jorian himself—well over six feet—and weighing, as far as he could judge, a good deal more. Her skin, exposed by Mulvanian fashions to just above her delta, was almost black, like that of a Mulvanian peasant. Huge jewels gleamed in her tiara and earrings; a triple rope of pearls ranging up to the size of crab-apples hung down between her enormous breasts.

Jorian had never seen so voluptuous a figure; he could hardly believe his eyes. Those breasts were the most astonishing of his experience. Larger than melons—in fact, as big and round as the udder of a milch cow—they stood out from her massive body without any sag at all. Below them, the body curved in to a waist which, while normal for a small woman, looked impossibly slender on this creature. Then the body widened out to broad, heavy hips and a slightly bulging belly. A cloth-of-gold embroidered skirt hung from her hips, just above groin level, to her ankles, and more gems blazed on the buckles of her slippers. The face beneath the tiara was round and plump, like that of Jorian's Estrildis, but not fat; in fact, if one could ignore her size and tear one's eyes away from her extraordinary bodily development, she was a remarkably beautiful woman.

"By Imbal's iron yard!" breathed Jorian. "With a basin-bone like that, she could bear giants and heroes—"

"Hush!" said Karadur. "The dancing is about to begin. Will you take part?"

"The ladies all seem to be paired off already, so I don't know how to obtain a partner. Anyway, I am not sure I know the steps well enough, for all of Harichumbra's coaching."

The orchestra struck up, and the couples lined up for the grand march. The king and the Serpent Princess led the march, the king holding one arm out so that the tips of his fingers just touched those of the princess. Mulvanian dancing frowned upon any bodily contact other than fingertips. Jorian remained by the fruit-juice table with a few other non-dancers. Karadur said:

"I will present you to Lord Hirayaxa. He has brought

both his wives, and I am sure he will let you dance with one—"

"No, no, never mind," said Jorian with a sudden rush of shyness. "I had rather just watch."

The grand march ended, and a eunuch cried: "Take position for the *nriga!*"

The male dancers lined up on one side of the ballroom, the female on the other. The musicians played; the eunuch called the figures. Everybody advanced three steps. The men and the women bowed to each other. They stepped back two steps and bowed. They advanced three steps and bowed. They formed squares and everybody bowed to everybody . . .

It went on for half an hour at the same slow, stately pace, stepping this way and that and bowing to the eunuch's commands. Compared to the hearty Novarian dances, Jorian found it a tedious performance.

As the music ended and the dance broke up in a frenzy of bows, a startling figure stepped in through one of the long windows opening on the balcony. This was a thin, dark-skinned man, completely naked, with his scrawny body covered with ash. His matted hair streamed down his back, his dirty beard cascaded down his breast, and his white eyeballs rolled wildly. He burst into a tirade in a dialect that Jorian could only half follow.

To Jorian's surprise, nobody moved to suppress or remove the man. Everyone, from the king down, seemed to listen respectfully to the outburst. The naked man raved, foamed at the mouth, and shook his fists. He castigated them all as vile sinners for departing from the ways of their ancestors. He denounced the heathen custom of dancing. He anathematized the elephant mill and demanded that it be broken up. He commanded that all women, and not just those of the king, be shut up in their houses as they were in the days before the wicked innovations of King Sivroka of cursed memory. He called down the wrath of the true gods upon this congregation of sensual sinners. Then he disappeared into the night.

Jorian turned to Harichumbra, who had just bustled up, and asked, "Explain to me, pray, Master Harichumbra, how the king can allow such an affront to his royal dignity?"

"Oh, that is a holy man. He may do as he likes. But come, my lord. The Princess Yargali has expressed the wish to meet you."

Jorian caught Karadur's eye and made a slight but significant jerk of his head. He found the super-voluptuous supernatural being standing beside the fruit-juice table, with the king beside her.

"Your Majesty!" said Jorian, bowing low "Your radiant Highness! This is indeed a pleasure."

"It iss my pleasure, also," said Yargali, speaking Mulvani with an accent that centuries of dwelling in Trimandilam had not affected. "You are a Novarian, no?"

Karadur materialized like one of his spirits and engaged the king in a low-voiced discussion of the state of organized magic in the empire, while Jorian answered the princess: "Aye, Highness. A subject of the king of Kortoli, to be exact."

"Know you any of those lively Novarian dances? I find the Mulvanian kind all too stately for an active person like myself."

"Permit one to think. One used to be pretty good at our local peasant dance, the *volka*."

"Oh, I know that one! That iss the one that goes *one—two—three—four—five—six—turn, one—two—three—four—five—six—turn*, no?"

"Like this?" said Jorian, walking the fingers of his right hand across the palm of his left.

"But yess! In the reign of King Sirvasha, there was an ambassador from Kortoli here, who showed me. Will you ask me to dance the volka with you, my lord Jorian?"

"One wonders if our musicians know any suitable tune?"

"Oh, we can dance it to any tune that iss loud and fast, with a strong one-two beat, no? Come, let us speak to them about it."

Yargali started off across the marble floor towards the orchestra. Jorian followed, feebly protesting: "But, Your Highness! One is sure the king's other guests will not know—"

"Oh, to the next incarnation with them! Thiss will be for just you and me. We will show them barbarians are better dancers than they! We will make them look like the bumps of the logs, no?"

Soon Jorian found himself alone on the dance floor with the princess, the other guests having drawn to the sides. Each placed his hands on the other's shoulders, and off they went in the vigorous, stamping, and whirling steps of the volka. On and on they went, round and round. Having noted that Mulvanian musical compositions were apt to run on for half-hours or even for hours, Jorian feared that he would be compelled to dance until morning.

After a mere quarter-hour, however, the orchestra stopped. Both Jorian and his partner were breathing hard and sweating freely. The noble lords and ladies snapped their fingers by way of applause, while the pair bowed in all directions and Lord Chavero scowled and pulled his long mustache.

"One suggests," said Jorian, "that we could use a bit of that fruit punch."

"An excellent idea, my lord. And you need not use those stilted, ultra-polite forms of speech with me. It iss all very well for these Mulvanians; but my people, who were wise when your forebears were sitting on a bough and scratching, do not bother with such useless refinements. Life iss complicated enough without going out of one's way to make it more so, no?"

A team of sixteen professional dancing girls, wearing

a multitude of beads and bangles and nothing else, had come out on the floor and were performing a dance with little, shuffling steps and rhythmic jerkings of their arms and heads. Jorian said:

"How would Your Highness like to step out on the terrace to cool off?"

"By all means."

When they were outside under the stars, Jorian said: "The holy man's outburst does not seem to have discouraged the festivities."

"Oh, these Mulvanians! Always they are talking about their moral purity. No wine, no meat, no fornication, and so on. But when one comes to know them, they are just as sinful in their own little ways as everybody else. Now they will go home feeling very virtuous because they let the holy man harangue them without taking offense, and they will go right on doing the things they always do."

"We had a Mulvanian saint like that in Kortoli once," said Jorian. "He all but ruined the kingdom before they got rid of him."

"Tell me about thiss holy man!"

"Gladly. This took place back in the reign of King Filoman the Well-Meaning—the father of the more famous King Fusinian.

"King Filoman had without doubt the noblest emotions and the best intentions of any king who ever reigned in Novaria. Nor was he stupid; but alas! he had no common sense whatever. One version of the legend says that this was the result of a peculiar planetary conjunction at the time of his birth. Another says that, when the fairies gathered for his naming ceremony, the fairy who was supposed to confer common sense upon him became enraged when she saw that another fairy wore a gown just like her own and left in a huff without bestowing her gift. So Filoman grew up with all the virtues—courage, honesty, diligence, kindliness, and so forth—except common sense.

"It was after the bankruptcy of the kingdom, as a result of the pension scheme of the ghost that Filoman had retained as his minister, that this holy man, Ajimbalin, came to Kortoli. Filoman's new minister, Oinax, had just been promoted from a mere clerk in the Treasury and was too much in awe of the king to tell him aught that Filoman did not wish to hear. So Ajimbalin was soon ensconced in the palace, pouring advice into Filoman's ears.

"Filoman lent these ears willingly enough, for he felt guilty about the collapse of the pension scheme and the hardships that ensued, and even more guilty about his failure to make all the Kortolians as pure and upright and virtuous as himself. 'It is no wonder,' said Ajimbalin, 'when you and your entire people engage in so many vile, sinful habits.'

"'I thought I lived a reasonably virtuous life,' said Filoman. 'But, holy Father, perhaps you can persuade me to the contrary.'

"'To achieve salvation for yourself and your folk,' said the ascetic, 'you must follow the path to moral perfection on which I shall guide you. By setting an example, we may hope to persuade all your subjects to do likewise; and if example and precept avail not, then stronger measures may be needed. First you must give up fermented beverages, your—ugh!—wine and—ugh!—beer.'

"'If you mean drinking to excess,' said Filoman, 'I do not believe I am guilty of that. I have never been drunk in my life.'

"'Nay,' quoth Ajimbalin, 'I mean you must give them up entirely.' So he presently had the court on a regimen of fruit juice, like the punch we have been drinking. Can I get you another?"

"No; please go on with your story."

"Ajimbalin then wished to extend this prohibition to

all Kortolians, but Oinax stood up to him and averted that the kingdom needed the tax revenue after its recent disasters. So the general prohibition of wine and beer was put off for the time being.

"Then Ajimbalin told the king: 'You must give up this revolting custom of eating the flesh of slain animals. It shows a lack of proper respect for life. How know you if the cow or pig your servants butcher for your table be not an incarnation of one of your own ancestors?' So the king and the court went on a diet of breadstuffs and greens, like that to which I have been subjected during my stay here.

"Then the holy man said: 'Next, my son, you must give up the vile, sensual pleasure of going in unto your wife. Since desire is the source of all sorrow, you can attain happiness and escape sorrow only by extinguishing desire and relinquishing all bonds to earthly things and persons.'

" 'But I am chiefly concerned, not with my own happiness, but with my subjects' welfare!' protested Filoman.

" 'All the better,' said Ajimbalin. 'By following my rules of life, you will not only achieve a state of indescribable bliss yourself, but also attain such strength and wisdom that you will easily solve your kingdom's problems. You will be able to push over a city wall or pick up an elephant. You will know the secrets of the forty-nine Mulvanian heavens of the gods and of the forty-nine hells of the demons. You will no longer need an army, for you will be able to rout any foe singlehanded. But you cannot have these things and the mingling of your vile flesh with that of a woman, too.'

" 'But,' said Filoman, 'if all my subjects gave up conjugal relations, there would soon be no people in Kortoli at all.'

" 'All the better,' said the sage. 'If people ceased to be born on this plane, then all the souls would perforce be promoted to the next one, instead of being sent back again and again to this vale of suffering and sorrow. So you and the queen, to set an example, must henceforth live like brother and sister.'

"Filoman gave in. The queen, however, did not take kindly to this scheme. Within the year she had eloped with a sea captain from Salimor, who became a notorious pirate. She left behind her young son, who grew up to be the famous King Fusinian.

"Next, Ajimbalin made Filoman relinquish his fine raiment and wear a piece of sacking pinned about his body, as Ajimbalin himself was wont to do. He made him sleep on the ground in the palace courtyard and spend all his waking hours memorizing Ajimbalin's moral precepts. Filoman's idea of wild revelry had been to sit up till midnight over a flagon of ale and a game of draughts with some crony; but even these simple pleasures were denied him.

"Strangely enough, this regiment did not produce in King Filoman the state of perfect bliss that Ajimbalin had promised. It only made him unhappier than ever. He missed his wife—for all that she had nagged him—and he missed his son, who had been sent off to the court of the Grand Duke of Othomae to serve as a page. He missed his cronies and he missed the hunting and fishing and dancing and the good food and drink he used to enjoy. Instead of the promised strength and wisdom, he found himself enfeebled in body and bewildered in mind. Weeping, he told Ajimbalin that he must be a hopeless sinner, because the life of perfect virtue had not made him happy but the reverse.

" 'Then, my son,' said the holy man, 'I see that you are now ready for the final and most drastic step. First you shall make out a document of abdication, naming me king in your room.'

"This startled Filoman, and he argued. But Ajimbalin soon talked him round, for the holy man had so gotten Filoman under his thumb that the king no longer had will of his own. So Filoman wrote out the document.

" 'Now,' said Ajimbalin, 'you shall utter a prayer to the true god of Mulvan and slay yourself. Only thus can you promote the welfare of your people and end your own sorrow, for you lack the mettle to impose upon Kortoli the reforms required for its salvation, The gods have therefore chosen me as their humble instrument to effect these improvements. Here is a dagger from your armory; one quick thrust and it is done.'

"Filoman took the dagger, looked dubiously at it, and tried its point on his thumb. Then he pricked his breast a little, said 'Ouch!' and cast the blade from him, for he could not quite summon the courage to thrust it home. Nor could he nerve himself to drink the poison that Ajimbalin thoughtfully proffered him. He broke down into sobs and tears; and indeed he was a pitiful sight, gaunt from starvation, in rags, and covered with sores and dirt from the ascetic life he had led under Ajimbalin's spiritual guidance.

" 'I will get Oinax to do the deed,' he said. So the minister was summoned, and a sword that King Filoman had worn in former days was fetched from the armory.

"Filoman explained the plan to Oinax, who fell on his knees and begged the king to reconsider. But Filoman, to whom death now seemed a welcome relief from his misery, was firm.

" 'I shall kneel here,' he said, 'and when I say, "Strike!" you shall cut off my head. It will be your last act as my loyal subject, and I do but ask that you make the stroke swift and sure. Thenceforth, your loyalty shall be transferred to the future king, the holy father Ajimbalin.'

"So King Filoman knelt and bowed his head, and Oinax, trembling with fear and horror, took up the sword. Being a small man, he had to wield it in both hands. He took his stance, made a practice swing, and glanced at Ajimbalin. The holy man was crouched nearby, glaring at the king with a strange gleam in his eyes and spittle running from his mouth. Now whether this was some form of holy ecstasy, or whether it was a simple, worldly lust for the power he now saw nearly within his grasp, was never known. For Oinax pivoted suddenly on his heel and struck with all his might at the neck of Ajimbalin, whose head went bouncing and rolling across the floor like a football.

"Horrified, Filoman tried to wrest the sword from Oinax, but so weak was he from his austerities that the minister easily frustrated him. Then the king burst into a fit of mad weeping. And when he had finished that, he seemed to come to himself.

" 'How fares the kingdom, Master Oinax?' he said. 'It has been months since I heard aught about it.'

" 'In some ways well, in others not so well,' quoth the minister. 'The leopards, from not being hunted, have become so bold that they snatch children from the streets of the villages. We need to raise the tax on luxurious imports from Mulvan, and we need a new dam on the river Phodon. I have done what I could, but there is much that has necessarily awaited Your Majesty's return from his—ah—quest for spiritual perfection. And I urge that Your Majesty recall his son from Othomae, where I hear he has fallen in with a wild young crowd and bids fair to acquire dissolute habits.'

"So they buried Ajimbalin and tried to pretend he had never existed. And Filoman returned to his former way of life, and Kortoli, to its normal state."

"Did your King Filoman ever get his wife back?"

"No. She preferred to be the mistress of a pirate king. She said that Filoman, though nice in his way, bored her, and she wanted excitement for a change."

"Did he learn common sense from his tribulations?"

"Oh, no, nothing could give him that. Luckily for Kortoli, a few years later he fell from his horse during a hunt and broke his neck. Fusinian—who proved a very different sort—succeeded him."

* * *

Yargali: "You tell fascinating tales, Lord Jorian. Do you know many more?"

"Many more indeed. But—" Jorian glanced through the long windows to the interior of the ballroom. "—I fear I should be discourteous to our royal host if I kept you out here for the rest of the ball. Perhaps I might call upon you later . . . ?"

Yargali pointed up to the windows of the upper story of the Hall of the Green Serpent, where lamplights showed through the diamond panes. "Yonder iss my abode, and it would pleasure me to receive you there. But I fear it were impossible."

"Why so?"

"How would you gain access? All the doors and windows leading into this hall are locked after the ball, with armed guards posted at the doors."

"Suppose I could fly and appeared before your window after the ball. Should I be admitted?"

"If you came bearing such tales, aye. But I do not see how you can. You have no wings, and the wall iss without carvings to climb by. You would have to walk up the smooth stone like a fly, no?"

"Leave it to me, Highness. Now, perhaps we had bet—"

"One moment, Master Jorian," said a voice, and a hand was laid, none too gently, on Jorian's arm. It was Lord Chavero, the disagreeable Mulvanian. "I have somewhat to discuss with you."

Jorian twisted his arm free. "I believe I am called Lord Jorian by those would entreat me with courtesy."

"That is one of the things I wish to discuss. But this were a poor place. You will excuse us, Princess? Will you be so good as to descend this stair to the garden, Master Jorian?"

They went down the marble steps at the end of the terrace into the sunken garden, which was six cubits below the level of the terrace. Then Lord Chavero faced Jorian. Although there was no moon—this being the end of the Month of the Wolf—enough light escaped from the ballroom to show each plainly to the other.

"Well?" said Jorian.

"*Master* Jorian," began Chavero, "this ball was to have been for members of the true nobility—that is to say, the nobility of Mulvan, not the self-styled 'nobles' of upstart barbarian realms, who to us of the genuine birth are no more than dirt. We were willing to put up with you as long as it was necessary for you to interpret for Queen Mnevis. Now, however, that condition no longer obtains. Since your presence here is offensive to us of superior blood, you are requested to leave the premises forthwith."

"Quite a speech," said Jorian. "But since I was invited by His Majesty himself, and since His Majesty—may he reign forever!—did not withdraw his invitation upon the queen's departure, I have no intention of complying with your wish. What do you propose to do about it?"

"For the last time, dog, get out!"

"Put me out!"

"I will!" Chavero stooped and fumbled behind a shrub. He straightened up with a naked scimitar in his hand. He stalked towards Jorian on the balls of his feet, blade poised for a quick slash.

Having neither sword, nor cloak, nor dagger to defend himself with, Jorian backed away. As Chavero started a quick rush, Jorian dodged around a fountain. For a few minutes they darted back and forth on opposite sides of the fountain, circumambulating it now clockwise and now contra-clockwise. Although a big, powerful man, the Mulvanian was shorter in the legs and bigger in the belly than Jorian, so the latter managed to keep the fountain between him and his foe.

Then he heard a low call from the balcony: "Lord Jorian! Here!"

A glance showed him Yargali leaning over the marble rail, extending his own sword to him. He left the fountain, bounded over to the foot of the terrace, and caught Randir by the hilt as she tossed it to him.

He spun to face the onrushing Chavero. Their blades met in a whirl of steel; they clashed and sang and struck sparks. Jorian easily parried the whirlwind, slashing attack of the Mulvanian until shortness of breath forced the other to slow down. Then he feinted a backhand cut, reversed it, and slashed diagonally down and to the left, so that the tip of his blade sliced through the sash that upheld the saffron pantaloons.

Jorian then leaped back. Chavero began a quick advance; but what Jorian hoped for happened. Deprived of their support, Chavero's trousers fell down, and Chavero fell prone on the greensward, right at Jorian's feet.

Jorian planted his foot on Chavero's sword. "Now, my lord," he said smoothly, "I think I will carve my name on your pretty little bare, brown arse—"

"Swine!" yelled Chavero, letting go his sword and rolling to his feet. He grabbed for the trousers wound about his ankles and, at the same time, tried to leap back out of reach of Jorian's blade. But he missed the garment and fell into the fountain. He emerged from the water, blowing and coughing, and hauled himself out on the side opposite to Jorian.

The latter darted around the fountain and caught up with Chavero as the latter, now trouserless, gained his feet. Jorian brought the flat of his sword with a loud whack against the Mulvanian's buttocks. Screaming curses and yelling for help, Chavero ran around the paths of the garden with Jorian after him, now and then getting in another blow.

Jorian was almost having too much fun to realize that the noise had aroused the attention of others. Light and motion from the terrace caught his eye. Then he heard the voice of the king, raised in anger:

"Stop this at once!"

Jorian and Chavero stood side by side, looking up at the terrace. Thence the king, surrounded by the plumed and bejeweled nobility of the realm, glared down. Chavero kept pulling down the lower front edge of his shirt to preserve his decency. Shaju pointed to Chavero and barked:

"Explain!"

"This—this b-beastly—(*cough*)—barbarian grossly insulted my honor, sire, and then t-tried to m-m-m- . . ." Chavero's voice trailed away into spasms of coughing and incoherent stammers and squawks. Between his rage and the water he had taken into his lungs, he could not speak intelligibly. A mutter of anger at the barbarous foreigner ran through the nobles.

While Chavero still sputtered, the king pointed to Jorian. "You, then!"

Jorian gave his best bow. "Your Majesty, since anything one said might be interpreted as self-serving, one prays that you ask the Princess Yargali for an account of this unfortunate event. Having witnessed the whole incident, she can give Your Majesty an objective account."

"Well?" said the king, turning to Yargali, who told a truthful tale of what happened. She explained that, when she saw Chavero chasing Jorian with a scimitar, which he had evidently hidden ahead of time in the shrubbery, she realized that she could not explain to the king or his officials what was happening in time to save Jorian's neck. So she had gone straight to the cloakroom and thence fetched Jorian his sword.

The king's lips twitched, and then he burst into a hearty guffaw, throwing his head back and rocking on his heels. For once he seemed almost human. All the nobles laughed even louder, for it went without saying that a joke by royalty was always ten times as funny as the same joke told by someone else. King Shaju said something to Minister Ishvarnam, turned his back and reentered the ballroom. Ishvarnam leant over the marble balustrade and called out:

"My lord Chavero! His Majesty instructs me to tell you that you have incurred his august displeasure by your unmannerly conduct. You shall return at once to your estates at Kolkai and remain there until further notice. Lord Jorian, you have His Majesty's forgiveness for any breach of courtly etiquette that you may have committed in defending yourself, against Lord Chavero, and His Majesty commands you to remain at the ball as long as you wish and to forget tonight's incident."

Chavero cast one last sneer in Jorian's direction. He muttered, "You shall yet rue your insolence, dog!" before stalking away through the darkened garden.

Jorian joined Karadur on the terrace. The latter said in Novarian: "Lucky for you, my son, that you slew not the miscreant. Had you done so, not even Yargali's tale could have saved you from punishment."

"I figured that out whilst he was chasing me round the fountain. So, when a chance offered to make him ridiculous without killing him, I seized what the gods offered. But by Zevatas's brazen beard, was I frightened!"

"My son!" said Karadur in tones of gentle reproof. "If you would play the role of nobleman, you must not go about telling everybody how terrified you were under this or that circumstance. I know you have more courage in one finger than most of these popinjays have in their whole bodies, but you spoil the impression you make by this harping on your own timidity. Desist!"

" 'Tis the simple truth, though, and don't you urge men to utter the simple truth?"

"Mayhap, but in this case we must make an exception. I have known men of many kinds, and I believe that noblemen suffer from fright just as much as the rest. The difference is that their sense of honor forbids them to admit their fear."

"But I am no nobleman, only a—"

"Hush! Whilst you play the part, you must follow the customs, however silly they seem. But now we must beware of Lord Chavero's vengeance. The remaining nobles may befriend you, for that Chavero was much disliked for his quarrelsome and overbearing nature. But he may still hire a poisoner to slip into your soup that which is no elixir of life."

"I hope we can be on our way before the morning's light. Have you that magical rope?"

"Aye, in our quarters."

"Well, fetch it here at midnight. Can you gain access to yon garden without passing the sentries who guard the Hall of the Green Serpent?"

"That were easy; the door in the hall opposite is not guarded."

"So be here with that rope. When I have entered Yargali's lair, go quickly to the stables and take out our mounts. Will the city gates still be open?"

"With luck, since this is a holy day."

"Well then, take the beasts outside the city wall and tether them in some safe place."

"Which gate?"

"Let me think—the East."

"Why not the North or the West? We are going back to Vindium, I trust."

"Fool!" exploded Jorian. "That's the first direction they'll look. We're going up the Pennerath to the first ford or bridge, then east towards Komilakh. Then north across the Fangs of Halgir to Shven and west again to the Twelve Cities."

"You mean to travel right around the Inner Sea? A frightful journey! We shall never get to Metouro in time for the meeting."

"With luck, we shall; I've studied the maps. If we are trampled by King Shaju's elephants, we shall never get there at all."

"But Shaju has elephants trained as trackers, as

hounds are employed in other lands. Of all beasts, the elephant has the keenest sense of smell."

"Well, we shall have to chance it. When the beasts are secure, gather our gear and meet me at the Inner Gate of the palace."

"Why not outside the city? Prolonged questioning at the gates is to be avoided."

"I know not my way about this damned monster of a city and should get lost without you as a guide."

"Then let us meet outside the outer palace gate, thus avoiding at least two scrutinies. Use the rope to get over the walls."

"Very well. If they stop you, tell 'em we're on a secret mission for Ishvarnam, or whatever you think they'll believe. Now I'm going in to fraternize with the beauty and chivalry of Mulvan."

Inside, Jorian found that Karadur's prediction had been right. Nobles crowded about him, pressed goblets of fruit juice upon him, and told him that for a barbarian he was indeed a man of parts. One said that Jorian had merely done to Chavero what many others at court had long yearned to do themselves.

As he sipped fruit punch, Jorian reflected that at a Novarian ball he would probably have drunk himself dizzy in his triumph and so be useless for the desperate adventure ahead. Even Mulvanian asceticism, he concluded, had its uses.

At midnight, the princess Yargali heard a tap on the window panes of her bedroom. She opened the window to see Jorian, hanging by one hand from a vertical rope, about which his legs were locked, while he tapped with the other hand. As she helped him over the sill and led him into the adjoining living room, she asked:

"Good my lord, to what iss the upper end of yonder rope affixed, that it upheld you so firmly?"

"It is affixed to the afterworld, Highness. I do not fully understand the matter myself, although a magician could doubtless tell you. What have we here?" He picked up a pitcher and sniffed. "Tell me not that this is real wine, in this desert of austerity!"

"It iss indeed." She whisked the cover off a pair of golden plates, disclosing steaks. "Real flesh, also."

"By all the gods and demons of Mulvan! How do you manage it?"

She shrugged her huge shoulders, making her great globes quiver. "It iss part of the agreement betwixt myself and the Great Kings. I guard their cursed Kist, whilst they provide me with the meat and drink I wish. I should soon waste away on this Mulvanian diet, which may be good for rabbits but not for me. Now sit and devour, ere your provender cool."

Jorian did so. Between ravenous bites he asked: "How came you by this agreement, Princess?"

"Know that my people are an ancient race, who dwell in the far-off jungles of Beraoti. But, albeit longer-lived than your folk they beget few offspring. And so they have dwindled during the last myriad of years, until there be but a handful left. As a result of a quarrel—into whose nature I will not go—I wass cast out from amongst them. And I arrived, weary and footsore, in Trimandilam in the reign of King Venu, or Venu the Apprehensive as he was called.

"King Venu greeted me hospitably, but after a while he began to worry over the fact that I ate thrice as much as did he and his better-fed subjects and insisted, moreover, upon forbidden flesh. As his sobriquet implies, he wass one of those who are not happy unless they are unhappy over some impending peril, if you understand me, no? He wass a worrier.

"He also worried about the Kist of Avlen, since there had been two attempts to steal it—one by stealth, the other by bribing those who guarded it. The latter attempt would have succeeded had not one of the bribe-takers suffered a rush of conscience and betrayed the plot. For this, he wass promoted to captain whilst the others were trampled by the king's elephants—an eventuality which hiss so-sensitive conscience had doubtless foreseen.

"So King Venu conceived the idea of skewering two worries with one lance, by making me official guardian of the Kist, in return for which he furnished me with this apartment and with food, drink, and servants to enable me to live in comfort. And that agreement has now been in effect more than five hundred years."

"I should think," said Jorian, "that Your Supernatural Highness would find it oppressive to be cooped up in this one suite, day after day."

"I do not mind, for I do not have the traveler's itching foot, as you men so often have. I have seen Trimandilam and need not refresh my view of it. And I like not the way the Mulvanians of the lower classes stare at me as if I were some sort of monster. My servants bring me news of the outer world, and I am content with this place, which I have redecorated every century to my taste. Now sit beside me on this divan and tell me some of the tales you promised." She refilled the goblets. "For ensample, the tale of the disaster that your King Filoman brought upon Kortoli, when he had a ghost for his minister. I have never heard of putting a ghost to such a use."

Jorian quaffed deeply. "This was early in his reign, when he had occasion to appoint a new minister to replace one who had died. He had reigned for several years in a fair state of justice, order, and prosperity, but it grieved him that some Kortolians still lived lives of vice and crime, for all he had done by precept and example to better things. To remedy this state of affairs, he determined to enlist the services of the wisest man in the Twelve Cities.

"By diligent inquiry, he learnt that the man with the repute of such wisdom was a philosopher from Govannian, named Tsaidar, who was said to be the most learned man in all Novaria.

"But, when Filoman sent a messenger to Govannian, to tender an offer of honorable employment to this Tsaidar, the messenger learnt that the learned doctor had but lately died. When word of this reached King Filoman, he wept with frustration. But his chamberlain said that all hope had not yet fled. There dwelt in the hills of southern Kortoli a witch hight Gloé, who was an able sorceress and a person of good repute, notwithstanding that she had never been able to obtain a licence as lawful wizardess from Filoman's government. Since Tsaidar had but recently died, his spirit might not yet have passed on to its next incarnation, either on this plane or on the next, and therefore could possibly be raised by Gloé to advise the king.

"So Filoman sent to fetch Gloé to Kortoli City, promising immunity for her illicit practice of magic. And Gloé burnt her powders and stirred her cauldron, and shadows gathered without material objects to cast them, and the flames of the candles flickered although there was no breeze to flutter them, and hideous faces, dissolving into one another, appeared in the smoke, and the palace trembled, and the king was seized with freezing cold. And there in the pentacle stood the ghost of Tsaidar the philosopher.

" 'Why disturb you me?' said the ghost in the thin, squeaky voice that ghosts have. 'I was studying a treatise on logic amongst the neglected old manuscripts in the library of the Grand Bastard of Othomae and had just come upon a new statement of the law of the excluded middle, when you snatched me hither.'

"Well, Gloé explained King Filoman's purpose. The ghost said: 'Minister, eh? Well, now, that is different. All my life I sought to find a ruler who would accept my advice and run his realm by logic, but I never found one. I gladly accept your offer, sire. What is the first problem I can solve for you?'

" 'I would fain put an end to crime and vice amongst the Kortolians,' said the king, and went on to describe conditions in the kingdom and the failure of his previous efforts.

" 'Well now, ahem ahem, I have a theory about crime,' quoth the ghost. 'It is obvious to me that criminals are compelled to commit their felonies by want. Men steal to avert starvation. Men rape because they are too poor to afford lawful wives, or even the modest fees of harlots. Remove the cause—namely, the want—and you instantly end the crimes. I wonder that nobody else has thought for so simple a solution.'

" 'But how shall I alleviate their want?' asked the King.

" 'Simple again; give every convicted criminal a modest but adequate pension and turn him loose. That is logical, now is it not?'

"The king could see no flaw in Tsaidar's reasoning and so permitted Gloé to dismiss him. And he ordered that criminals, instead of being punished, should be given pensions. And so it was done.

"This pension scheme, however, had unexpected results. True, a few of the pensioners reformed, and some even became a credit to the state—like Glous, our leading poet, or Soser the shipping magnate.

"A larger number did nothing either very good or very bad. They settled down to loafing and amusing themselves in more or less harmless ways. What really astonished good King Filoman, however, was that many kept right on committing crimes when, being pensioned, they no longer had to do so.

"Furthermore, the amount of crime actually waxed as Filoman's subjects discovered that to be convicted was the best way to get a regular stipend from the treasury. People robbed and raped and assaulted all over the place and made no attempt to evade capture. Thus, two merchants accused each other of theft; the hatter said the antique dealer had stolen a dozen of his hats, whilst the antique dealer accused the hatter of making off with a costly vase. Even odder, each had his loot in plain sight in his own shop. It was plain to every one save Filoman the Well-Meaning and his ghostly minister that the twain had cooked up this scheme between them, to get on the pension rolls.

"When, during a seance with Gloé, Filoman complained of these unwonted events, Tsaidar's ghost would not admit any flaw in his logic. 'It must,' he said, 'be that the emoluments you pay your felons are not enough to relieve their want. Double all pensions at once, and you shall see.'

"Then so great became the demands on the treasury that Filoman was forced to borrow abroad and then to debase the currency to pay his promised stipends. Soon, Kortolian money contained so much lead and tin mingled with the silver, and copper with the gold, that no knowing person would accept it. The sound money from earlier times went into hiding, whilst all Kortolians sought to rid themselves of Filoman's counterfeits, as they were called. And soon all trade ground to a halt, for none would take the new money and none would part with the old. There were bread riots in Kortoli City and other distressing events.

"At length, King Filoman determined to seek advice from the living to find out what was wrong. He asked many of those arrested for crime why they had so conducted themselves. Some answered with glib lies. Some admitted that they wanted pensions, too. But one scarred old rogue with a missing ear, who had slain and robbed a merchant on the road, at last revealed to the king what was truly in the minds of many of his kind.

" 'You see, Your Majesty,' said the robber, 'it is not just the money. To sit at home and live on my pension were too dull to be borne. I should go mad with boredom.'

" 'But,' quoth the king, 'there are many worthy occupations, such as soldier or hunter or messenger, which would provide you with healthful activity and enable you to do good at the same time.'

" 'You do not understand, sire. I do not want to do good; I want to do bad. I want to rob and hurt and slay people.'

" 'Good gods, why should you wish that?' said the king.

" 'Well, sire, one of man's deepest desires is to put himself above his fellow men—to compel them to admit his superiority, is it not?'

" 'One might say so,' replied the king cautiously. 'But I seek to attain superiority by virtue.'

" 'You do, but I do not. Now, a living man is, in general, superior to a dead one, is he not?'

" 'Aye, it would seem reasonable to say so.'

" 'Then, if I slay a man, and I live whilst he dies, I am obviously his superior by the mere fact of being alive, am I not?'

" 'I never thought of that,' said the king, greatly troubled.

" 'The same,' said the scoundrel, 'applies to assault, robbery, and other deeds that I delight in. If I give something to a man, or accept a free gift from him, or barter things of equal value with him, that proves nought about who is the better man. But if I take from him that which is his, against his wish, I have proved that my power is greater than his. Every time I make another unhappy, without his being able to retaliate, I have proved my superiority.'

" 'You must be mad!' cried the king. 'Never have I heard so monstrous a philosophy!'

" 'Nay, sire, I do assure you that I am but a normal human being like yourself.'

" 'If you are normal, then I cannot be, and contrariwise,' said the king, 'for our views are as different as day and night.'

" 'Ah, but Your Majesty, I said not that we were alike! People are so various that there is no one normal kind, all others being lunatics and antic characters. And most folk have in them different urges, which pull them now one way and now the other. In you, the urge to do good is so much stronger than the urge to do evil that the latter can be neglected, whereas with me and many like me it is the opposite. But amongst the general, you will find, these motives are more evenly balanced, so that they do now good, now ill. And, when one of your subjects has grown to manhood with these urges in a certain proportion, I do not think you will change this proportion thereafter, no matter what you do to or for him.'

"The king sank back on his throne, aghast. At last he said: 'And where, my good murderer, did you learn to reason so philosophically?'

" 'When I was a boy, I went to school in Metouro under your esteemed minister, Tsaidar of Govannian, who was then not a disembodied spirit but a young schoolmaster. And now, sire, if you will summon your treasurer to put me on his pension roll—'

" 'I cannot,' said the king, 'because you have convinced me of the error of my whole scheme. I cannot call in the headsman to shorten you by the appropriate amount, as you deserve, because you have done me a favor by giving me a deeper insight into my fellow men. On the other hand, I cannot permit you to continue your villainies in Kortoli. So you will be given a horse, a small purse, and twenty-four hours to quit the land, on pain of death if ever you return.'

"And so it was done, not without some soul-searching on the part of Filoman, who felt guilty about turning this rascal loose on one of the neighboring states. He dismissed Tsaidar's ghost and paid off the witch Gloé, whereupon she cried out:

" 'Sire! I am bilked! These are those worthless adulterated coins you have been striking lately!'

" 'Well, the advice of your ghost proved equally

worthless, so we are quits,' said Filoman. 'Now get along back to your cave and bother me no more.'

"And Gloé departed, muttering maledictions, although whether these had aught to do with the king's death in a riding accident some years afterwards is not known. And Filoman appointed Oinax his new minister, and for a while Kortoli returned to its former condition. But then King Filoman fell under the sway of the so-called holy man Ajimbalin, with results whereof I have already told you."

Jorian had inched closer to the princess, and now had an arm about her vast, bare torso. She put up her face to be kissed, then seized him in a grip of pythonic power.

"Gramercy for your story, man," she murmured. "And now we shall see whether you are a better man than those pygmies of Mulvanians, with their tools like toothpicks, no? Come!"

Three hours later, Princess Yargali lay on her side, facing the window by which Jorian had entered and breathing slow, deep breaths. Jorian slid quietly out of the huge bed. He quickly donned his garments, except for his boots, which he thrust into his sash.

Then he searched the bedroom for the Kist of Avlen. The candle in this room had burnt down and gone out, but enough light came through the doorway from the living room, where a pair of butter lamps still burnt, for his purpose. He found that none of the chests ranged around the walls was that which he sought. Nor did there seem to be any closets or secret compartments in the walls. A search of the princess's bathroom proved equally fruitless.

At last Jorian discovered the Kist in the most obvious place: under Yargali's bed. It was a battered little chest, about a cubit and a half long and a cubit in height and depth, with an old leather strap buckled around it to reinforce its brass clasps. It lay under the side of the bed away from the window. Jorian had lain on that side after making love to Yargali. Evidently he would have to pull the chest out from under the bed from that side, tiptoe around the bed to the window, and let himself out.

Moving as if treading on razors, Jorian knelt beside the bed Slowly he pulled the Kist towards himself by one of the brass handles. It did not prove very heavy. Fingerbreadth by fingerbreadth, almost holding his breath, he teased the chest out from under the bed. At last it lay before him. Grasping the two handles, he stood up and stepped back.

Then, to his utter horror, the princess Yargali muttered in her sleep and rolled over. Her eyes opened. She cast off the coverlet, exposing her huge, brown body with its exaggerated curves.

"Sssso!" she said.

For an instant, Jorian—still a little drunk from Yargali's wine—was rooted to the spot. In that instant, Yargali changed. Her body elongated; her limbs shrank. The dark-brown skin changed to an epidermis of olive-green scales, with a reticulated pattern of russet and yellow stripes. Her face bulged out and became a long, scaly muzzle. A musky odor filled the bedroom.

She was a serpent—but such a serpent as Jorian had never heard of outside myths and legends. The head, as large as that of a horse, reared up from the pile of coils. A forked tongue flicked out from the jaws. In the middle, the serpent's body was as big around as Jorian's waist.

Sobered abruptly and shaking himself out of his momentary paralysis, Jorian thought with lightning speed. If he tried to run around the bed to get to the window, he would come within easy lunging distance of the head. If he had only caused Karadur to send the rope up to one of the living-room windows, he could have fled that way; but now his retreat was cut off. Too late, he remembered Goania's warning against bedroom windows. If he tried to get out the living-room windows, he would probably give himself a fifteen-cubit fall on the marble of the terrace and break a leg or a neck. The stonework outside was smooth, and there was no ivy to climb by or tree into whose branches to leap.

As the serpent poured off the creaking bed and came for Jorian, he fled into the living room. There were two exits from this parlor. One door, he supposed, opened into the third story of the adjacent hall; there was probably a guard on the far side of it. The other, whose door stood ajar, revealed a descending flight of stairs, down which Yargali had earlier come on her way from her apartment to the ballroom.

Jorian raced across the living room and through the door at the head of the stairs. Down he went; and after him, hissing like a giant's kettle, poured Yargali—all forty cubits of her. The thought crossed Jorian's mind that, in assuming her serpent form, the princess had at least deprived herself of her ability to shout for help.

The ballroom was dark but for one small oil lamp, which burnt on a bracket. The king's servants had unrolled the huge rug that covered the marble when the floor was not being used for balls.

Jorian dashed to the nearest of the long windows opening on the terrace. The window had, however, been not only closed but also locked. The feeble light showed him the keyhole. Yargali's serpent head appeared from the doorway at the foot of the stairs.

Given a few minutes, Jorian was sure he could pick the lock of any of the long windows. Given time and no interference, he could probably batter the glass panes out of the window and burst his way through. But the panes were small and the leads between them were stout and closely set, so that this operation would take many blows with some heavy object, such as a chair, and the noise would fetch the guards who stood outside the big doors at the end of the ballroom.

If he tried to get out one of his pick-locks and pick a window lock, Yargali would seize him from behind, throw a coil around him, smother him in her serpentine embrace, and swallow him little by little, head first like a frog. Now Jorian saw why no one had succeeded for five hundred years in stealing the Kist from her somewhat casual guardianship.

As Yargali's head came towards him, her forked tongue flickering, Jorian set the Kist of Avlen down upon the carpet. Seizing the corner of the rug, he heaved and tugged his way down the side of the ballroom, past the long windows, pulling the carpet with him. It buckled into folds and became frightfully heavy to move, since the whole thing weighed several times as much as Jorian. A smaller or weaker man could not have moved it at all. But, straining and sweating and with muscles cracking with the effort, Jorian hauled the whole carpet down to the far end of the ballroom, where he left it in a crumpled heap.

Then he picked up the Kist—which had come along with the carpet—and went back to one of the long windows. Yargali had now slithered all the way down the stairs and out on the bare, brown marble floor. But here, lacking any roughness or solid objects to exert a horizontal force against, she found herself unable to advance further. Her vast serpentine body rippled; wave after wave flowed from her wedge-shaped head to her tapering tail, but to no avail. Like a flag fluttering in the breeze, she moved but did not progress. Hissing in a fury of frustration, she doubled the speed and violence of her writhings, but her scales slithered futilely back and forth on the polished marble floor.

Meanwhile, Jorian picked the lock of the window at the far end, slipped out with the Kist, and closed the window behind him. He ran to where the magical rope still stood upright on the pave and uttered the

simple cantrip that nullified its spell and brought it
tumbling down in coils.

A quarter-hour later, Jorian rejoined Karadur outside
the main gate, around the elephant mill out of sight of
the sentries. He whispered:

"Have you all our gear? My sword? Thanks . . . Curse
it, you forgot my hat! They'll give it to their hound-
elephants to smell. Oh, well, no matter; I have this silly
cap. Can we make a sling of your magical rope, so I
can carry this damned chest on my back?"

Karadur fingered the rope. "Aye, might as well. The
rope's magical powers are exhausted, and until it be
ensorcelled again it is no more than a common rope."

Another hour saw them riding southward on the road
up the left bank of the Pennerath. Jorian told Karadur
the essentials of his adventure. The wizard asked:

"How did you ever think of that extraordinary expedient for immobilizing Yargali, my son?"

"I remembered when I was a boy, I caught a harmless little snake and kept it for a few days. Then I went
with my father to the house of a squire of Ardamai,
where my father was installing a water clock. And whilst
I was there, helping my father, the serpent escaped from
my purse and fell to the squire's polished hardwood floor.
The squire's wife carried on like a crazy woman until
I removed the poor little snake, and I was sent to bed
that night without my supper. But I remembered that,
on this floor, the snake had been unable to move from
here to there for want of traction, and so was easily
caught. And I thought it might work the same way with
the black wench."

"How found you your—ah—sensuous escapade?"

"Bumpy, a little like serving a cow elephant mad-
dened by passion. I could have used stirrups there, too;
I was almost thrown out on my head on the floor."

Karadur shuddered. "Was she pleased?"

"She seemed to be, albeit meseems she would have

been receptive to more bouts than I was prepared to give. I was but a mere mortal man and a badly frightened one at that."

"Jorian! I have told you not to talk—"

"Oh, very well. But hereafter I'll confine my venery to human women. If I could only get back my little Estrildis ..." He wiped away a tear, then turned a startled face to the wizard. "Gods! I just thought: what if the seed take root?"

"Fear not, my son. A hybrid betwixt a man and one of the serpent people were impossible, which is perhaps as well. I tremble to think what a being combining her shape-changing powers and your craft and daring might do to the world!"

# VII

# The Ruin in the Jungle

In the jungles of Komilakh, which stretched for more than a hundred leagues from the marches of Mulvan to the Eastern Ocean, enormous trees of many species towered over a hundred cubits into the sky. In the upper branches, squirrels and monkeys scrambled and chattered; gaudy birds whirled and flapped and screeched. Lower down, beneath the permanent waves of this green sea of leaves, vines as thick as a man's leg hung in loops and braids and tangles. Along these lianas, hairy spiders as big as crabs, with eyes like octets of little diamonds, crept in search of prey. Parasitic plants with flowers of ghostly colors sprouted from the trunks and branches of the trees.

Still lower, in the permanent gloom of the ground level, an undulating surface of brown leaf mold stretched away among the tree trunks. Here and there this surface was broken by saplings—most of them dead—or clumps of ferns. From the ground, only an occasional fleck of blue sky could be seen through the all-covering ceiling of green; but now and then a golden gleam ahead through the trees gave the direction of the morning sun. Men seldom saw the larger denizens of this level—elephant, buffalo, tiger, rhinoceros, deer, antelope, tapir, and wild pig—because the beasts heard man afar off and made themselves scarce.

Through this somber, silent world, Jorian and Karadur rode, winding among the tree trunks and around the fern clumps, swaying and ducking to avoid the branches of saplings and the dangling loops of lianas.

Jorian rode the tall roan, Oser; Karadur, the white ass. Their mounts' heads hung with fatigue, and their riders had to kick and beat them to prevent them from stopping every other step to snatch a mouthful of greenery.

They had been riding since well before dawn. When the brush was thin enough to permit, they forced the animals to a trot. They also kept turning their heads to look back and listen.

For several days they had fled from their pursuers, who consisted of two tracking elephants and ten well-armed mounted soldiers. At the beginning, the fugitives had had a start of several hours, because the first pursuit had been sent in the obvious direction, down the Bharma. But King Shaju had quickly corrected this mistake and dispatched another force up the Pennerath.

Although the pursuers' speed was limited by the elephants, who could not go long distances faster than a horse's trot, nevertheless the pursuers' familiarity with the country and the fact that they led spare horses enabled them to close the gap. When the farmlands of eastern Mulvan turned to isolated clearings and then gave way to roadless jungle, they were only an hour behind.

Since then, the fugitives had fled almost continuously, sleeping in snatches, sometimes on the backs of their animals. Both looked worn and weary. The fine clothes in which Jorian had begun his flight were now dirty, dusty, and stained by rain and sweat. This was the so-called dry season in Komilakh, when rain occurred only every two or three days in place of the continual downpour of summer.

Jorian was stripped to breeches and boots against the damp heat. His left arm was in a crude sling, and he handled the reins with his right hand. Two days earlier, in making camp, he had stepped into a hole, reached out to steady himself, and seized a branch of a small tree covered with long, needle-sharp spines. A few hours later, his left hand had been swollen to twice its

normal size and had turned a fiery red. At the moment
it was still too painful to use. Any sudden jerk sent
sharp pains lancing up Jorian's arm, so that trotting his
horse was one long agony. But the thought of being
trampled by King Shaju's elephants urged him on.

From time to time he reined in his mount, to breathe
the animals and to listen for pursuers. The night before,
the rumbling purr of elephants had warned him of their
approach. Luckily, this had occurred in a patch of jungle so dense that neither party had sighted the other.
Galloping recklessly and riding the animals along a
stream bed for several furlongs, Jorian thought they had
thrown off the pursuit; but he was taking no chances.

Now, as he halted and let his horse munch ferns, he
raised a hand. Karadur froze. To their ears came, far
but unmistakable, the squeal of an elephant and the
jingle of harness.

"Doctor," said Jorian, "another run, ere our beasts
have rested and fed, will kill them. Now's the time for
your confusion spell."

"It will be the last time," mumbled Karadur, "for I
have materials for but one such spell. Help me down
from this ass, and I will do what I can."

Soon the old wizard had a tiny fire going. "Dry twigs,
dry twigs!" he muttered. "Nothing wet, for that we
want as little smoke as possible. Now, let me see, where
did I put the powders for Confusion Number Three?"

He fumbled in his garments and at length produced
one of his compartmented purses. When he opened
this, however, he exclaimed in horror, "Ah, woe! I have
none of the powder of the yellow mushroom of Hroth!"
He searched frantically. "I must have forgotten it when
I made up this battery of powders. We are lost!"

"Can't you use any old mushroom? Like this one?"

"I know not how it would work. But let us try; it
can scarcely put us into a worse predicament."

Karadur crumbled the mushroom into the tiny cal-
dron, added other substances, and stirred. Leaves rus-
tled without any detectable breeze, and the green

canopy overhead seemed to press down upon them, closer and darker . . .

At last Karadur leant back against a tree trunk. "Water!" he croaked in a ghost of a voice. "I am spent."

Jorian passed him the leathern water bottle. As Karadur drank, Jorian sniffed the air.

"What in the name of Zevatas is that stench?" said Jorian. He sniffed again. "It's you—nay, it's both of us! Your spell must have gone awry. We stink like a gymnasium, a slaughterhouse, and a dunghill, all rolled into one. The gods grant that a wind carry not this odor to our pursuers . . . Oh, plague! There it goes!"

A wind had swung up, rustling the leaves of the vast green awning overhead and swaying the smaller branches. Only a light breeze could be felt at ground level, but such as it was, it came from the east and blew towards King Shaju's men.

"Mount! And be yare about it!" snapped Jorian.

"I cannot; I am fordone—"

"You damned old fool, get on that ass or I'll haul you on by your beard! Here they come!"

Through the forest came the loud, brassy cry of an elephant. This was echoed by a trumpet's blast and the sound of voices and movement. Jorian picked up Karadur bodily and set him down on the ass. Then he mounted himself.

"Hold tight!" he said. "They're galloping. They'll probably spread out, thinking to catch us with one quick rush. Off!"

The brief rest had given the animals back some of their strength. Jorian led the way at an easy canter, curving around obstacles, swaying and ducking, while the ass rocked along behind. Groaning, Karadur bounced along on the ass, clutching the saddle. He had little control over the animal; but the ass, being used to following the horse, did so with little guidance.

The sounds of galloping diminished as the pursuers spread out. There were more trumpetings, but farther away, as the elephants were left behind in the pursuit. After Jorian had cantered for some time in silence, he held up an arm and slowed. He led the way to the far side of an enormous tree, whose trunk at the base measured over twenty cubits through.

"There's but one man close behind us," he said. "The others have spread too far and lost touch with each other. They'll have to rally back at the elephants to pick up our trail again. Here, take your cursed Kist!"

"What mean you to do?"

"To await our pursuer behind this tree, whilst you go on. I can't shoot, with this polluted hand, but I can still handle a sword. Not, however, with that thing on my back. Get along!" he snarled as Karadur started to protest.

The ass trotted off, with Karadur bouncing in the saddle and the Kist, slung over one shoulder by its rope sling, bumping against the wizard's back. Unable to grasp the reins firmly enough with his swollen hand, Jorian wound them around his left forearm and drew the sword Randir. Then he waited.

Nearer and nearer came the galloping horse. When it seemed as if Jorian could bear the suspense no longer, the rider appeared: a Mulvanian trooper in scarlet silken pantaloons, hauberk of silvered chain mail, and spired helmet. A quiver of light twirl-spears hung across his back, and he balanced one of these darts in his right hand.

Jorian kicked his horse's flanks. The roan started forward, but not so quickly as Jorian intended, because its rider was not wearing spurs. The delay gave the soldier time to twist about in his saddle and fling his javelin.

Jorian, bouncing in the saddle as Oser broke into his rough gallop, ducked down behind his horse's head. The missile hissed past, missing him by a fingerbreadth.

The soldier made a tentative snatch at his quiver, then changed his mind and reached instead for the scimitar at his hip. But his horse, seeing Oser bearing down upon him, shied a little. Lacking stirrups, the soldier was shaken in his seat. His hand missed the hilt, and he was forced to grab at one of the hand-holds on the saddle to steady himself. He was still fumbling for his sword when Jorian's point took him in the throat. He fell into the leaf mold, while his horse, snorting, galloped off.

When Jorian caught up with Karadur, the wizard looked up at him from under his sweat-stained turban. "Well?"

"Dead," said Jorian, "thanks to the fact that I had stirrups and he did not. The way this nag bounces one, 'tis a wonder I hit the fellow at all. I'll relieve you of that chest now, if you like. Curse it, my hand is hurting again."

"Have you thought of the moral aspects of your slaying that trooper?" said Karadur. "Doubtless he was as good and pious a man as yourself—"

"*Oi!*" cried Jorian. "I save your wretched neck and your box of worthless spells, and you read me a damned sermon! Dip me in dung, but if you do not agree it was he or us, you can turn back and give yourself up."

"Nay, nay, my son, be not wroth with me for indulging my bent for speculation. The question of what to do when one is confronted by a man no worse than oneself, and whom one must slay to achieve a goal as worthy as his, has long beguiled me. Portentous questions, like that of war and peace, hinge upon it."

"Well," said Jorian, "I don't go out of my way to kill King Shaju's soldiers; but when 'tis a question of him or me, I strike first and argue ethics later. Did I not, I should not be here to discuss the matter. Meseems that, when one takes the king's coin as a soldier, one accepts the risk that, sooner or later, one may suddenly depart this life. None compelled that ill-starred horse-darter to chase and shoot at me. Having done so, he has no legitimate complaint—assuming his spirit will be vouchsafed a chance to protest in one of your multifarious Mulvanian afterworlds."

"The trooper's officer compelled him to pursue and attack you, so he was not a free agent."

"But he put himself under the officer's orders voluntarily, when he joined the army."

"Not so simple, my son. In Mulvan, all must follow their sires' occupations. So this man, born the son of a soldier, had no option but to become a trooper in his turn."

"Then the blame lies, not on me, but on your polluted custom of hereditary occupations."

"But that, in turn, has many advantages. It provides a stable social order, lessens the bitterness of competition for advancement, and furnishes each man with a secure position on the social stair."

"All very well, Doctor, when the sons' natural bent lies in the same channel as their sires'. But when 'tis otherwise? I know from my own life. Esteeming my father as a good and kindly man, I had been well content to follow his trade of clockmaking; but whilst my mind could grasp the principles, my hands proved too clumsy for the practice. In Mulvan, I had been bound to this profession for aye, and starved in consequence."

Karadur: "But even when there's a free choice of livelihood, as in the Twelve Cities, the same dilemma presents itself, when the general levy is called up for war. Then you will find yourself opposed to another, each of you convinced his cause is just, and no way to settle the question but spear and sword."

"Well, when one fighter is slain, he ceases to have any cause at all, just or otherwise. So justice resides *ipso facto* in the winner."

"A frivolous answer, O Jorian, unworthy of one who has ruled a state! Well you know that, for all your prayers to your various gods, the winner is determined by strength, or skill at arms, or luck—none having aught to do with justice."

"Holy Father," said Jorian, "when you persuade all my quarrelsome fellow-Novarians to submit their disputes to a tribunal of the wisest and most learned minds and to accept without cavil this court's decisions, I will gladly bow to such judgments. But behemoths will fly or ever that happens, and meanwhile I must fend for myself as best I can. But hold! Here's a dingle athwart our path, with a brook running through it. I'll wade the stream for a few furlongs, to see if I can throw them off the scent again. You may follow if you like."

He turned his horse's head downstream and set off at a rapid amble, water splashing in fountains about the roan's fetlocks. Karadur followed.

The stream gathered volume as it flowed, and around noon it joined another. Below this confluence, the united stream formed a small river, a fathom or two in width—small enough for easy fording but too voluminous to use as a path. Because of the density of the vegetation along the banks, Jorian and Karadur followed the stream at some distance, glimpsing the water through the trees.

"Methinks this is an affluent of the Shrindola," said Karadur. "The Shrindola flows into the Inner Sea, they say, albeit no man to my knowledge has ever followed it to its mouth to make sure."

"Then it must curve northward somewhere, in which case we're on the right side to get to Halgir," said Jorian. "Stop and hush for a moment whilst I listen."

There was no sound save the hum of insects and the chatter of birds and monkeys. They rode on. Then Jorian noticed something about his surroundings. Stones or small boulders appeared, scattered about the forest floor. Presently, as these objects became more frequent, he realized that they were too regular in shape and arrangement to be products of nature. Although often half buried and covered with patches of moss, algae, and lichen, they still showed flat faces at right angles, evidently the work of a mason's chisel. Moreover, they lay in lines—wavering, broken lines, but lines nonetheless.

Now the ancient masonry became denser and better preserved. Peering into shadowy, silvan distances, Jorian saw pieces of megalithic wall and the stumps of tumbled towers. Here a structure had been invaded by the roots of a tree growing out of its top, groping downwards between the individual stones and prying them apart, like the tentacles of some vegetable octopus, until the tree supported the remains of the structure rather than the building the tree. There rose a megalithic wall, bedight with sculptured reliefs in riotous profusion. Intricately carven towers of sandstone blocks loomed up through the forest, their tops lost in the masses of greenery overhead. Trees grew out of a monumental staircase, whose massive blocks their roots had heaved and tumbled.

Sinister, scowling stone faces peered out from behind the fronds of palms and ferns. An immense statue, fallen and broken into three pieces, lay among ruined walls and towering tree trunks, its finer details largely hidden by splotches of moss. For a while, the animals walked along a raised causeway paved with large, square slabs of slate and supported on either hand by cyclopean walls made of blocks weighing hundreds of tons.

On either hand stretched endless galleries bounding vast, overgrown courtyards. The entrances to these galleries were stone portals lacking the true arch. Instead, the openings were headed by corbelled arches, each course of masonry overhanging the one beneath until they met at the top, forming tall isosceles triangles. Among the sculptures that decorated the walls of these galleries, Jorian glimpsed scenes of armies on the march, demons and gods in supernatural combat, dancing girls entertaining kings, and workers at their daily tasks.

A flock of small green parrots rose from the ruins and whirred away, screaming. Monkeys scampered over the tottering roofs. Little lizards, some green with purple throats, some yellow, and some of other hues, scuttled over the stones. Huge butterflies came to rest on the tumbled masonry, fanning the air with their gold-and-purple wings before flitting away once more.

"What ruin is this?" Jorian asked.

"Culbagarh," groaned the wizard. "Can we stop here? I shall soon be dead else."

"Methinks we've gained a few hours upon them," said Jorian, dismounting at the base of a headless statue. The head that belonged to the statue lay nearby, but so covered with moss and mold that its precise nature was not evident. As he helped Karadur, groaning, down from the ass, Jorian said: "Tell me about this Culbagarh."

While Jorian staked out the animals where long grass grew in a ruined courtyard and prepared a frugal meal, Karadur told the story:

"This city goes back to the kingdom of Tirao, which preceded the empire of Mulvan. When the last king of Tirao, Vrujja the Fiend, came to the throne, his first concern was to have all his siblings slain, lest any should aspire to usurp his seat. This massacre later became the usual procedure in Mulvan and is now a custom hallowed by time. But in the days of Vrujja—more than a thousand years ago—it caused much comment.

"Hearing of the fate in store for him, one of these brothers, Naharju, gathered his followers and fled eastward into the wilds of Komilakh. They marched eastward for many leagues, until they came to a few scattered ruins, on this very spot. Those ruins were, however, much less extensive than these about us and more dilapidated, because this earlier city had stood abandoned much longer than the mere thousand-odd years since of the fall of Culbagarh.

"None in Prince Naharju's party knew what city

those scattered stones were the remains of, although
some opined that this had been a city of the serpent
people ere they migrated thence into the denser jungles of Beraoti. Amid these scanty ruins stood a worn,
moss-grown altar, and beyond the altar the remains of
a statue, so weathered that none could be certain what
sort of creature it had depicted. Some thought it a
figure of an ape-man, like unto the ape-men who are
the native inhabitants of Komilakh, and of whom the
party had caught glimpses. Others thought the statue
not that of one of the higher animals at all, but something nearer to a spider or a cuttlefish.

"Naharju had with him a priest of Kradha the Preserver, to minister to the spiritual needs of his people.
It seemed to Naharju that preservation of their lives
was the most urgent task confronting the refugees and
that, therefore, Kradha were the most suitable god to
worship. A modern theologian might argue that Vurnu,
Kradha, and Ashaka are all merely aspects or avatars
of the same godhead; but in those days thinkers had
not yet reached such heights of metaphysical subtlety.

"On the first night they spent in the ruins, the
priest, whose name was Ayonar, had a dream. In this
dream, he reported, the god whereof the ruined
statue had been the image appeared unto him. The
folk pressed Ayonar for a description of this god—
whether it had the form of a man, an ape, a tiger, a
crab, or what; but when Ayonar tried to answer their
questions, he turned pale and stuttered so that nothing intelligible came forth. And when they saw that
merely to think about the appearance of this god so
troubled their holy priest, they left off questioning him
and asked instead, what this god demanded of them.

"So Ayonar told the people that the god was named
Murugong, and he had indeed been the god of the folk
who had dwelt in the city ere it became a ruin, and
that he was the chief god of Komilakh and never mind
what the priests of Tirao said about their holy trinity's

ruling the world. Komilakh was his; other gods, despite their ecumenical pretensions, knew better than to quarrel with him. Therefore Naharju's colonists had better worship him and forget all other gods.

"Then it transpired that Murugong was worshiped with exceedingly barbarous and bloody sacrifices, wherein a chosen victim was flayed alive on his altars. Murugong had explained to Ayonar that, not having tasted the pain of such a sacrifice for thousands of years, he was nigh unto starvation, and they should find a victim to flay right speedily.

"Naharju and his men were troubled, for such usages had long been abandoned in Tirao, and they were not eager to take them up again, let alone to slay one of their own in this uncouth manner. So they took counsel, and whilst they disputed, the priest Ayonar said: 'May it please Your Highness, I have thought how to gratify the mighty Murugong and preserve our own skins intact. Let us go into the forest, seize one of the ape-men, and sacrifice it in the manner prescribed. For, if not so intelligent as a true man, the ape-man stands high enough in the scale of life so that it will suffer quite as acutely as any human being. And, since Murugong thrives on the pain of his victims, he should be just as well satisfied as if one of us had perished in this manner.'

"The men of Naharju's faction agreed that the priest had spoken sound sense, and a hunting party was made up at once. After the ape-man had been devoted to the god, Murugong appeared unto Ayonar in a dream and said he was well pleased with the sacrifice and would adopt the Tiraonian refugees as his chosen people as long as they continued the sacrifices. And so it went for many years. Under Naharju and his son of the same name, the people waxed in numbers and built the city of Culbagarh on the ruins of the older, nameless city.

"Meanwhile the leading men of Tirao, desperate

over the enormities of Vrujja the Fiend, sought for a prince to head a rebellion against their sovran. They had trouble in this, for that Vrujja had made a clean sweep of his kinsmen, executing them unto third and fourth cousins and sending men to murder those who had fled to Novaria and other barbarian lands.

"At length, however, the rebels discovered a chief of the desert-dwellers of Fedirun, hight Waqith, who boasted one-thirty-second part of royal Tiraonian blood in his veins. And they invited him to invade Tirao and become king in Vrujja's room. The invasion went briskly, for most of Vrujja's men deserted. Soon Vrujja was slain in an interesting manner that perturbs me too much to describe, and Waqith was crowned king.

"But Waqith did not prove so great an improvement over Vrujja as his supporters had hoped. His first public act was to arrest all the chief nobles of Tirao and have their heads piled in a pyramid in the public square. Having, as he thought, terrified the rest into being docile subjects, he next commanded that the contents of the treasury be dumped on the floor of the throne room. And the sight of so much wealth drove Waqith—who had all his life been a bare-arsed desert thief, to whom one silver mark was a fortune—clean out of his mind. They found him sitting on a heap of coins, tossing jewels in the air and laughing and babbling like an unweaned babe.

"So they slew Waqith and sought for someone to replace him. But now the word of Tirao's troubles had blown hither and yon about the deserts of Fedirun, and other bands of nomads irrupted into the fertile plains of Tirao, where the surviving nobles fought amongst themselves to see who should rule the land. And soon the kingdom went down in blood and fire, and owls and bats and serpents nested in the ruins of the palaces and fortresses of former times. And so things remained until the coming of Ghish the Great.

"Meanwhile, Culbagarh grew and grew, as fugitives

from the fall of Tirao sought sanctuary there. But under Naharju's grandson, Darganj, it became even more difficult to catch enough ape-men to keep up the sacrifices to Murugong. For the ape-men had become wary of Culbagarh and gave it a wide berth, so that the Culbagarhis were forced to keep hundreds of men constantly employed on hunts for these beings. And there was talk of choosing victims by lot from amongst the new arrivals in Culbagarh, in case the supply of ape-men failed altogether.

"Amongst the refugees from Tirao was a man named Jainini, who preached a new god, called Yish. This new god, said Jainini, had appeared to him in dreams to expound a religion of love instead of blood and terror. If only everybody, said Jainini, would love everybody else, all their troubles would be over. Furthermore Yish, being a mightier god than Murugong, would protect them more effectively than Murugong ever had.

"The priesthood of Murugong, now grown rich, corrupt, and powerful, sought to sacrifice Jainini on the altar of Murugong as a dangerous heretic. But Jainini had many followers, especially amongst the new immigrants, who had not been pleased to hear of the priests' intention of devoting them to Murugong. And it looked as if the two factions would have to fight it out.

"But then King Darganj went over to the side of Yish and his prophet Jainini. Some said Darganj was interested, not in any religion of love, but in getting his hands on the treasures of the temple of Murugong.

"Be that as it may, Yish became the chief god of Culbagarh, and Murugong was forsaken. And for a while the city enjoyed the benefits of the religion of love. The army was put to such civilian tasks as cleaning the streets of the city. Evildoers, instead of having a hand or a head sliced off by the executioner, were lectured on the virtues of love and turned loose with the admonition to sin no more—although it is said that few of them heeded this advice; the rest continued their careers of robbery, rape, and murder with greater gusto than ever.

"Then, without warning, a horde of ape-men overran and sacked the city and slaughtered its dwellers. For the continued raids of the Culbagarhis for three generations had filled these creatures with hatred, and at last this persecution had driven the many little clans of ape-men to unite against their persecutors. The fact that the hunts for sacrificial victims had been halted made no difference; centuries would have had to pass before the ape-men lost their lust for vengeance.

"The invaders were armed only with crude wooden spears and clubs and sharpened stones, but they were very many, and the Culbagarhis under the influence of Jainini had put away their arms, melting them up and reforging them into the tools of husbandry. A few, including King Darganj and Jainini, escaped the massacre and fled westward. And the next day, the prophet told the king that the abandoned god Murugong had appeared to him in his sleep. No more than Ayonar, could Jainini describe this god; but natheless he had somewhat to tell of him.

" 'He said,' quoth Jainini, 'that it serves us right for deserting him.'

" 'Would he take us back under his wing if we resumed his worship?' asked King Darganj.

" 'I asked him that,' said Jainini, and he said nay; we had proven such faithless and fickle rascals that he would have no more truck with us. The ape-men, on the other hand, would suit him as worshipers very well, being too simple-minded to question his authority by theological theorizing.'

" 'What of your mighty god Yish, who was supposed to ward us?'

" 'Murugong has trounced Yish and driven him out of Komilakh. I complained that Yish had told me he was the mightier of the two, whereas this did not appear to be the fact. But how could a god lie? Easily, said Murugong, as easily as any mortal. But, I said, I always understood that gods never lied. Who had told me that? said Murugong. The gods themselves, I said. But, said Murugong, if a god be a liar, what hinders him from lying about this as about other matters? Then I was stricken with horror at the thought of living in a universe where not only the men lie, but the gods as well. It was unfair, I protested. Quite true, said Murugong, but then, existence is unfair.

" 'Thereupon I fell to cursing the gods and dared Murugong to slay me, but he only laughed and vanished from my dreams. So there we are, sire. And I pray you to flay me forthwith as a sacrifice to Murugong, that some at least of his wrath be turned from this sorry remnant of your people, which my folly had brought to this pass; and that, moreover, that I shall be quit of this dreadful world, where not even the gods are to be trusted.'

"But Darganj told Jainini not to talk rubbish but to flee with the rest of them to the West, in hopes of finding some corner of the former kingdom of Tirao where they could settle without attracting the notice of the barbarians who now fought one another on the ruins of that land. And they had just taken up their march again when a horde of ape-men appeared behind them. Whilst the rest of the Tiraonians fled in terror, Jainini walked boldly into the midst of the pursuers.

"This act so astonished the savages that the other fugitives had time to escape ere the creatures recovered their wits. The last that was seen of Jainini, the ape-men had seized him. It is not known what they did with him, but it is deemed unlikely that he converted them to the worship of Yish. And the city of Culbagarh has lain derelict ever since."

"The moral would seem to be," said Jorian, "to trust nobody—not even a god."

"Nay, that is not quite right, my son. The moral is,

rather, to exercise a nice discrimination in all one's dealings, both with gods and with men, and to trust only the trustworthy."

"That's fine, could one only discover which they be. Holla! What's this?"

Jorian's boot struck a half-buried stone. Something about this stone led him to bend over and examine it. He kicked and pulled at it until it came loose in his hand. It was a statuette of a small, rotund, bald, grinning god, seated cross-legged on a plinth. The whole thing was less than half a foot high and weighed about a pound. Being made of an exceedingly hard, translucent green stone, it was in good condition, its outlines only slightly softened by weathering.

Jorian peered at the worn inscription on the plinth. "What's this?" he said, turning the statuette towards Karadur. "I do not recognize the writing; the characters are not those of modern Mulvani."

Karadur, peering through his reading glass, puzzled in his turn. "This," he said at last, "is Tiraonian, from the latter times of that kingdom. Modern Mulvani is derived from Tiraonian, with an admixture of Fediruni words. Evidently, one of the folk of Culbagarh dropped this statue here ere the city fell to the ape-men."

"What says it?"

Karadur traced the characters with his fingers. "It says 'Tvasha,' which I believe to be the name of a very minor god of the Tiraonian pantheon. There were so many that it is hard to remember which was which."

"Well, belike we should worship this Tvasha and ask him for help and guidance. After lying here in the mold for a thousand years, he ought to be glad of a worshiper or two, and I misdoubt the gods of my own Novaria have jurisdiction so far from their own demesne."

"If he have not died from neglect."

"How should we go about it? Catch one of these little green lizards and cut its throat?"

"Not until we know his wishes. Some gods are highly

offended by blood sacrifices. Pray that he will appear unto you and advise you."

"He'd better find us something to eat. This is the last of our journey cake. Tomorrow we shall be reduced to catching lizards and serpents for our supper."

Jorian thought he was standing on a black marble pavement in a hall of some kind, although he could not see the walls or the ceiling. Before him in the dimness glimmered the pale-green form of Tvasha, sitting on his plinth in the same attitude as he took in the little statue. The god's head seemed to be on a level with Jorian's own. But, although he tried to focus his eyes, Jorian could never be sure whether the god was the same size as himself at a distance of ten or fifteen paces, or much smaller at arm's length, or much larger and furlongs away. The god's lips moved, and a voice spoke in Jorian's mind:

"Greetings, Jorian son of Evor! If thou but knew how good it is to have a worshiper once again! Before the fall of Culbagarh, I had a worshiper like unto thee; let me think, what was his name? I cannot recall, but he was a big, handsome wight, always in some fantastic scrape, wherefrom he ever expected me to rescue him. I remember one time—"

"Thy pardon, lord!" Jorian, not without trepidation, interrupted the garrulous deity. "We are hotly pursued by men who wish us ill. Canst save us?"

"Let me see . . ." The god vanished from his plinth, leaving Jorian alone in his dark, misty space. A few heartbeats later, Tvasha was back again. "Fear nought, my son. Though thy ill-wishers are but a bowshot away, they shall do thee no scathe—"

"A bowshot away!" cried Jorian. "I must needs awaken at once, to flee! Let me go, O god!"

"Be not so hasty, dear Jorian," said Tvasha, smiling broadly. "It is so long since I have had a mortal to converse with that I am fain to continue our talk. I will take care of the Mulvanians and their trained elephants. Tell me, how fareth the empire of Mulvan these days?"

"First, lord, tell me how thou wouldst be worshiped."

"An occasional offer of a flower and a nightly prayer suffice me. Tell me how mighty I am. In sooth— betwixt thee and me—I am but a feeble little godlet; but, being like all deities exceedingly vain, I drink flattery as thou drinkest fine wine. Now that—"

The dark, misty hall vanished, and Jorian found himself awake, with Karadur shaking his shoulder. Through the massed leaves overhead, the silver shield of the full moon sent a few ghostly gleams.

"Awaken, my son!" whispered the wizard. "I hear elephants; and if my weak old ears can detect them, they must be close—"

Jorian scrambled up. "Could they be wild elephants? We have seen the signs of many such in this forest . . . Nay, I hear the jingle of horse trappings. It's the Mulvanians."

He started for the courtyard where the animals were tethered, then paused. The squeals of the elephants, the creak and jingle of harness, the muffled sound of horses' hooves on the forest floor, and the low-pitched snatches of talk receded. Soon they were so faint that he could barely hear them. Then they died away altogether. Jorian returned to the wizard.

"He's done it," he said.

"Who?"

"Tvasha. He said he would take care of the Mulvanians. I had my doubts, since he seemed a gabby old party and none too sharp. But whatever he did, it seems to have worked. We might as well go back to sleep, for if we go blundering about in the jungle in the dark we may run head-on into our pursuers by sheer mischance."

The air had cooled, so Jorian donned his upper garments, wrapped himself in his cloak, and lay down again. For a long time, however, sleep failed to come.

His injured hand throbbed, and he thought about the problem of getting along with one's private god. He was still making up imaginary conversations with the deity when he found himself back in the dark, misty hall, before Tvasha on his pedestal.

"How didst thou do it, lord?" asked Jorian.

"Simply, my son. I cast an illusion upon the tracking elephants, so that they saw and smelt a beautiful cow elephant in heat, beckoning to them with her trunk. They rushed off to take advantage of her offer; and the Mulvanians, thinking their beasts were on a hot trail leading to you and your companion, harkened them on. Now they are leagues hence."

The god smiled smugly. "And now, my dear Jorian, let us resume the discussion we were having when the holy Karadur snatched thee away to thy own plane of existence. How fareth the empire of Mulvan? For the statuette thou foundest in the ruins is the only one of me still in fair enough condition to permit me to use it as a point of intersection between my world and thine. Hence, in my visits to thy plane, I am limited to a short distance from the ruins of Culbagarh. Say on."

Jorian gave the god a brief account of the state and recent history of Mulvan, as far as he knew it. When he told of the death of Shaju's father, King Sirvasha, Tvasha chuckled.

"That reminds me," said the god, "of one of the last kings of Tirao—Vrujja's great-grandfather, but I cannot recall his name. Dear me, what was it? No matter. Anyhow, I will tell thee a very funny story about this king, whose name—bless me, what was that name? It is on the tip of my tongue—anyway, this king . . ."

Tvasha went off into a rambling tale that seemed to have neither point nor end. Nor could Jorian see anything funny about it. A quarter-hour later, it seemed, he was fidgeting with boredom and impatience while Tvasha rambled on.

Then the god seemed to cast a glance over his shoulder and cry: "Oh, dear me! I have been so absorbed in telling thee this story that I have not noticed the dire peril that creepeth upon thee! And, alas, this time I cannot save thee, for they who menace thee are under the protection of the mighty Murugong, whereas I am but a small, weak god . . ."

Jorian frantically tried to wake himself up. It was like straining at physical bonds. And then a physical shock awoke him all at once. Hairy hands gripped his arms and legs: he yelped as one seized his still tender left hand. A few paces distant, a swarm of the ape-men of Komilakh had likewise pinioned Karadur. To the east, a ruby gleam through the jungle told of the rising sun.

The ape-men were about five feet tall, but very stocky and muscular. Their necks jutted forwards, and their chins and foreheads receded, and their wide, thick lips parted to show rows of large, yellow teeth. They went naked, were almost as hairy as the beasts of the wild, and stank.

Gathering his muscles, Jorian made a furious effort to tear himself loose. But, great as was his strength compared to most men, that of each of his captors was equal to his own. Hairy hands with blackened, broken nails gripped him all the more tightly, and a couple of the ape-men pounded him with their fists until he became quiet. As he lay in the ape-men's grip, he found himself looking at the half-buried head of the nearby headless statue. He suddenly realized that the stone face was that, not of a man, but of a tiger. Goania's warning . . .

"Resist not!" said Karadur. "It does but madden them the more."

"What are they going to do with us?" said Jorian.

"How should I know? Do you understand aught of their speech?"

"No. Do you?"

"Nay, though I speak five or six tongues besides my own Mulvani."

"Can you cast a spell upon them?"

"Not whilst they hold me, for no spell worthy of the name is effected by a simple babbling of magical words."

Jorian: "Tvasha told me they're under Murugong's protection."

"Ah, woe! Then what Jainini told King Darganj a thousand years ago is still true. I do fear the worst."

"You mean they'll skin—"

Jorian was interrupted by a movement among the ape-men. In response to a barked command from one of their number, they heaved Jorian to his feet and half-led, half-dragged him through the overgrown ways of Culbagarh. Others bore Karadur. They zigzagged through ruins until Jorian was lost.

They stopped before some large stones. The nearer and smaller of these was a simple block, two cubits high and twice as wide, weathered until its ancient edges and corners had all been rounded off, so that it might almost be mistaken for a natural boulder.

Beyond the low block rose a large, squat pedestal or plinth, atop which something had once been sculptured; but so worn was this statue that one could no longer tell for sure what it had depicted. Its general shape was that of a seated man, but no definitely human limbs or members could be discerned. It was low and squat and rounded, with here and there a mere suggestion of carving. A large, red-and-black banded snake, lying at the base of the statue, slithered away and vanished into a hole.

"This must be the statue of Murugong, whereof you told me," said Jorian.

"Ah me, I fear you are right. I do blame myself for bringing this doom upon you. Farewell, my son!"

An ape-man appeared, holding a rusty iron knife. This was the only metal tool or weapon in sight, all others being of wood, stone, or bone. The aboriginal whetted the edge on the altar block, *wheep-wheep*.

"Blame not yourself, Doctor," said Jorian. "We must all take our chances. If they'd only just tie us up and go off and leave us a bit, perchance I could do something . . ."

*Wheep-wheep* went the knife. The ape-men had no intention of tying up their captives. Instead, they stood or squatted about them, firmly gripping their arms and legs with ominous patience.

At last the ape-man with the knife completed his whetting, tested the edge with his thumb, and stood up. At a grunted word, the ape-men holding Jorian dragged him to the altar and laid him supine upon it, still holding him firmly. He of the knife, standing before the statue, raised his arms and intoned a speech wherein Jorian caught the word "Murugong."

Then the ape-man turned back to Jorian and bent over the victim. He raised the knife, then drew the blade in a long, deliberate slash along Jorian's breastbone from throat to waist, bearing down hard. Jorian tensed himself to bear the pain manfully.

The knife cut neatly through Jorian's tunic but was stopped by the shirt of fine mesh mail beneath. With a guttural exclamation, the sacrificer bent over, flipping the severed sides of Jorian's tunic aside to examine this garment. Words broke out among the ape-men holding Jorian, and a couple began tugging at the mail shirt to pull it off over his head. While they struggled and argued and got in one another's way, an altercation sprang up out of range of Jorian's vision. Soon all the ape-men were shouting unintelligibly.

Gradually the noise died down. The ape-men holding Jorian pulled him up, so that he was sitting on the altar. He confronted a peculiarly ugly, middle-aged ape-man, who thrust a thick, hairy forefinger at him.

"You Jorian?" said this one in barely comprehensible Novarian.

"Aye. Who are you?"

"Me Zor. You remember? You save my life."

"By Imbal's brazen balls!" cried Jorian. "Of course I remember, O Zor. Tell me not that after you got out of that cage, you marched afoot all the way from the western Lograms to Komilakh!"

"Me strong. Me walk."

"Good for you! How have you fared?"

"Me do well. Me chief."

"And now, what of us?"

"You help me, I help you. Where you go?"

"We should like to get to Halgir, to cross the strait."

"You go."

Zor pushed aside the ape-men holding Jorian and threw a thick, hairy arm around Jorian's shoulders. Jorian winced from the bruises he had received from his captors' fists. Gesticulating with the other arm, Zor made a short but emphatic speech to the other ape-men. Although he could not understand a word, Jorian thought the speech meant that he was Zor's friend, and nobody should harm him on pain of Zor's displeasure.

"How about my friend?" said Jorian.

"You go, he stay. He not help us. We kill him."

"Either let us both go, or neither."

Zor scowled into Jorian's face. "What for you say that?"

"He is my friend. You would do the same for your friend, would you not?"

Zor scratched his head. "You speak good. All right, he go, too."

The next day, having left the banks of the Shrindola, they jogged across country northeast through a thunderstorm, with a squad of ape-men trotting along to show them the way and fetch food for them. Karadur said:

"An I have ever criticized you, my son, I humbly ask forgiveness now."

"What?" shouted Jorian over a roar or thunder. Karadur repeated.

"Why, Doctor?" said Jorian.

"You came within a hairbreadth of letting yourself be sacrificed—in a singularly painful manner—rather than abandon me, when you had an excellent opportunity to escape alone. I humble myself before you."

"Oh, nonsense! It just came out. Had I stopped to think, I should probably not have had the courage. As it was, I was so terrified of that skinning knife—oh, very well, very well, I'll say nought of my own fears aloud."

"Have you our new god with you?"

" 'Tis in the pack, though how much good Tvasha will do us is open to question. I think we ought to invent a new religion: the worship of the god of the absurd. If any force rule the universe, it is surely absurdity. Consider: you cast a confusion spell that goes awry and brings the foe right down upon us."

"That was not the fault of the spell. We lacked the proper ingredients."

"Then I stumble upon the statue of Tvasha. The god saves us from the Mulvanians—only to let us fall into the clutches of the ape-men because he's too busy telling me some long, boring tale about a king of olden times to notice them. When he does observe them, he's too fearful of the greater god Murugong to interfere.

"Then we are saved from painful deaths by Zor's happening along, and happening, moreover, to recognize me, when I should never have known him; these aboriginals look all alike to me. Zor believes I purposely released him from the cage of Rhithos' house. Truth to tell, that was a pure accident, resulting from my own stupidity, and for which Rhithos would have slain me had not the wench released me.

"Nor is that all. Were this a tale of some minstrel's fancy, Vanora and I should have been predestined mates and lovers—whereas, after trying me at stud, she finds she can't bear the sight of me and goes off with that halfwit Boso, who would be right at home amongst these escorts of ours. Now try to tell me that the universe makes sense!"

"I am sure it makes most excellent sense, were our puny mortal minds strong enough to grasp its entirety."

"Ha! Howsomever, one more dinner of roots and fungi, served in a sauce made of mashed bugs, and I may tell our friends to take me back to Culbagarh and sacrifice me. From such a diet, death were a welcome relief!"

# VIII

# The Sea of Grass

In the month of the ram, a cold wind roared across the steppe of Shven. The gently rolling plain stretched away northward to a flat horizon unbroken by tree, house, or hill. The long grass was a faded yellow-gray, for the new spring crop had not yet come up. When the grass was scanty, it showed the wet, black soil beneath. An occasional water course traced a shallow, winding dale across the plain; here grew small willows and alders along the swollen stream. Snow lingered in patches in the shade of these trees.

Riding the same animals on which they had set out from Trimandilam over three months before, Jorian and Karadur trotted briskly across the steppe. They were coated with mud to their middles, for every *plop* of their animals' hooves sent up a little black fountain of liquid mud.

Arriving at Halgir, at the strait that divided the Inner Sea from the smaller Sea of Sikhon, they had been compelled to waste a month until the weather moderated enough for them to cross the water. The enforced rest, however, had been welcome, for Karadur had been near to death from exhaustion. Even Jorian, whose strength was beyond that of most men, had been badly fatigued, as much from the ape-men's diet as from physical effort.

During this pause, Jorian's injured hand had healed, and they had outfitted themselves for the journey around the northern shores of the Inner Sea. Jorian's boots, which had been falling apart from the dampness of Komilakh, had been repaired. Karadur had obtained a pair of felt boots in place of his sandals. Both had procured knee-length sheep-skin coats and fur caps.

Leaving Gilgir, across the strait from Halgir, they had followed the coast, except where they could save distance by cutting across the base of a cape or peninsula. They counted themselves lucky to have seen scarcely another human being for nearly a month.

Once they had passed the burnt-out rains of a village in a dell. One of the peasants who had dwelt there lived long enough to tell his tale. The village had supposedly been under the protection of Hnidmar, the cham of the Eylings. But they had prospered too obviously, so Hnidmar ordered them destroyed, lest their success draw more settlers to the steppe, which would thus be fenced and plowed and ruined as a grazing ground.

They slept near streams, where they could cut enough brushwood to make beds that at least kept them up out of the mud. Twice, Jorian had supplemented the food they had brought with them by shooting a steppe antelope with his crossbow. Once they sighted a small herd of mammoths, beginning their northward spring migration to the distant forests of Hroth, but they prudently let these animals alone. They also gave a wide berth to the unicorn, a huge, hairy, short-legged, barrel-bodied beast not unlike the nosehorn of the tropics, save that its single horn arose from the middle of its skull, over the eyes.

Few towns arose along the north shore of the Inner Sea. There was Gilgir, at the end of a long, tapering peninsula—one of the "Fangs of Halgir"—facing Halgir across the Strait of Halgir. Gilgir and Halgir were muddy shipping and fishing villages, whose people were mainly of the flat-faced, slant-eyed type found in Ijo and Salimor. Through these settlements passed a small trickle of trade, and ships plying between Salimor and the ports of the Inner Sea often stopped there. But

Halgir's trade with the hinterland was scanty; since the ape-men of Komilakh were hardly profitable customers.

The largest port of the north shore of the Inner Sea was Istheun, at the head of the Bay of Norli. It was the only Shvenic city to boast a wall and a fair degree of self-government. This was possible because of the protection of the cham of the Gendings, the strongest of the Shvenic hordes. Jorian and Karadur trotted along the coast towards Istheun in hope of finding a ship for Tarxia there.

They were riding through a depression in the steppe, when Jorian remarked, "This damned jade's canter is fairly smooth on the nigh foot but rough on the off. On the latter, every time the saddle goes up I feel as if I were on my way to heaven. I'm trying to train the idiot to run only on the nigh ..."

The wind moaned and fluttered the dry grass. Jorian said: "There is nothing like travel to teach one of the beauties of home.

"Oh, some like the steaming jungle hot,
Where serpents swarm and the sun shines not,
And sweat runs off and your garments rot;
But I prefer a more temperate spot—
    Novaria, sweet Novaria.

Some yearn for the boundless, grassy plain,
Where rolls the nomad's creaking wain,
And horsemen gallop through wind and rain:
But I love the land of fruit and grain—
    Novaria, sweet Novaria.

And some to the sea with its howling gales,
And mountainous waves and wallowing whales
Where tall ships heel till they dip their rails;
But I'll take the friendly hills and dales
    Of Novaria, my Novaria."

"You have omitted the mountains and deserts," said Karadur.

"If I ever climb the High Lograms or travel to Fedirun, I'll add some stanzas ..." Jorian paused, reined in, and held up a hand. "Man ahead," he said in a low voice. "Hold Óser for a moment."

Slipping off the roan, Jorian handed the reins to Karadur. Then he took off his cap and ran up the next rise, bending double lest his head show against the skyline. Soon he was back.

"Just a couple of herders, watching horses. We must be getting close to one of the hordes. We'd best double back to the last stream and camp, whilst I ask Tvasha whether to ride in boldly or to slink around their flanks. Dip me in dung, but by all my reckoning we ought to have reached Istheun long since!"

"As Cidam the philosopher said: 'A journey and a sickness always last longer than expected, a purse and a jug of wine shorter,'" said Karadur. "At this pace, we may yet get to Metouro in time for the Conclave. We shall need to stop in Tarxia to draw breath. One of my faction dwells there."

"Who's he?"

"An old magician, hight Valdonius."

"Can he be trusted?"

"Certes; Valdonius is known as a man of strictest integrity."

"Well, let's hope he prove of more probity than Rhithos and Porrex, of whom you were equally confident!"

Karadur was silent for a while, then said: "Oh Jorian!"

"Yes?"

"Would the magical profession beguile you? I need an apprentice, for that my last one died years ago."

"What did he die of?"

"The poor ninny left a gap in his pentacle when

invoking a hostile demon. I am sure you would have better sense. How say you?"

"By Thio's horns, me, a magician? I know not. I've harbored ambitions to be a clockmaster, merchant, farmer, soldier, and poet, but never a spooker."

"Well, you will have a chance to judge my colleagues at the Conclave."

Looking less cheerful than was his wont, the green god Tvasha asked Jorian: "Where are my flowers?"

"Oh lord," said Jorian, "How canst thou expect me to find flowers at this season on this cold prairie? If thou wilt but wait a fiftnight, I will give thee enough flowers to make up for all arrears."

"I still want my posies," said the god pettishly. "In Tirao there was never any difficulty about offerings of flowers the year round."

"This is not Tirao," said Jorian, trying to stifle his impatience with this childish deity. "Here flowers bloom at certain seasons only."

"Then I hate this place! Take me back to my dear, familiar jungle!"

"Look here, O god," said Jorian, "I dug thee out of the dirt of Culbagarh, and faithfully have I worshiped thee daily ever since. If thou wilt not act thy divine age, I'll tell thee what I shall do. The next time we pass an arm of the Inner Sea, I will fling thee as far out into the waters as I can. Belike thou wilt find the sturgeon and the herring more congenial worshipers."

"Oh, very well, very well," grumbled Tvasha. "I will let thee owe me the flowers. What wouldst thou of me this time?"

"I fain would know about the horde that lieth across our path: who they be and who be their cham."

Tvasha vanished from his plinth, leaving Jorian alone in the dark, misty hall. Then the god reappeared.

"It is the horde of the Gendings, camped about the city of Istheun, and their cham is Vilimir."

"Oh! Is this the same man who was a refugee at the court of Xylar last year?"

"That I know not, albeit I could doubtless find out. Was thy Vilimir a lean man of middling height, clean-shaven, with long, hay-colored hair streaked with gray, and scars on his face and his right hand?"

"That was he. The old cham must have died or been overthrown. Canst thou advise me whether, having once befriended the fellow in his need, to trust myself within his grasp now?"

"Oh, I think thou wilt be safe enough, my dear Jorian. At least, I detected no thoughts of villainy passing through his mind when I looked in upon him just now. I did get the impression of a shrewd, hard-headed wight."

"That was my impression of him, when he visited Xylar. Farewell!"

When Jorian awoke, he told Karadur of his latest interview with Tvasha. "I am still not altogether sure of a friendly welcome," he said. "Vilimir seemed to me too much of a cold-blooded realist to be swayed by gratitude. What would you advise?"

"Oh, Jorian, let us by all means trust ourselves to him! Only thus can we find a ship to Tarxia, and my poor old bones will not endure much more jouncing and shaking across this endless plain. Besides, if we tried to circle about his array, that would delay us for days as well as compelling us to make the journey by land. This in turn might make us late for the Conclave."

"Very well," said Jorian, and saddled up. By noon they had reached the main camp of the Gendings, on a slight rise in the land north of the seaport of Istheun. Beyond Istheun could be seen the steely glitter of the sun on the waters of the Bay of Norli, where several of the undecked, canoelike little ships of this region were setting out on their first voyage of the season under their single brown, square sails. Istheun itself was a crescent-shaped town embracing the end of the bay. A wall of rough fieldstone, atop which a score of windmills whirled merrily in the brisk breeze from the steppe, surrounded the town.

The black tents of the Gendings covered a vast area. Outside this space, troops of nomad soldiery were exercising. They practiced charges, feigned retreats, and shooting from the saddle at full gallop. The bulk of the Gending army was composed of light-armed horse-archers, but the richer among Cham Vilimir's subjects made up squadrons of heavy-armed lancers, covered from head to foot in chain or scale mail and riding big horses, also partly armored. High officers watched the exercises from the backs of tame mammoths.

Nobody paid any special heed to the two nondescript riders, covered with dust and dried mud, who ambled up to the huge red-and-black pavilion in the midst of the array. Jorian and Karadur hitched their beasts to a post, and Jorian told one of the sentries, in Shvenic:

"King Jorian of Xylar is fain to pay his respects to the Grand Cham of the Gendings. He knows us."

"Said you *king*?" replied the sentry, looking Jorian up and down. "I have seen kings ere this, but never one clad as a beggar, with no escort but a diddering ancient on a spavined ass." He was a big young man, almost Jorian's size, with long golden hair in braids and a mustache that hung down to his collar bones on either side. He wore baggy woolens, a mail shirt, a fur cape, and a bronzen helmet with a wheel-shaped crest.

"The fact is as we have stated," said Jorian evenly. "Will you have the goodness to announce us?"

"His Terribility is exercising his troops. Will Your High and Mighty Majesty have a seat in the vestibule until his return?" The sentry gave a low, mocking bow.

"We thank you, soldier. We shall have things to say to you anon."

The sentry turned away with a sneering laugh. After a wait of an hour, a party of Gendings approached the pavilion on mammoths. The drivers made the huge beasts lie down in front of the pavilion, while the riders leaped to the ground. The mammoths rose and moved off while the riders entered the vestibule.

In the lead came Prince Vilimir, wearing a gold-trimmed helmet and closely followed by officers and bodyguards. Knowing at once that narrow, clean-shaven face, Jorian rose. Vilimir paused, then said; "By Greipnek's bowels! Are you not Jorian—" (he pronounced it "Zhorian") "—who was king of Xylar?"

"Quite so, Your Terribility."

Vilimir gave a wolfish smile. "Well, this is a surprise! We beheld your escape from Xylar—an artful feat, that—but never expected to see you here. Come on in."

Presently they were seated on carpets in the main tent, where Jorian received a flagon of ale. His golden ornaments tinkling when he moved, Vilimir said:

"And now, king-that-was, what brings you to Shven?"

"A small errand for the holy father Karadur, here. This is a fine case of turnabout, is it not? How long have you been cham?"

"Three months, since one of our uncle's wives poisoned the old scoundrel. We could never ascertain which one, so we had to kill them all to make sure that justice was done."

"How prospers the horde?"

"Just now, we are preparing for war against the Eylings. Hnidmar needs to be taught a lesson. We sent an envoy to protest a raid into our territory, and he sent the man back without his hands. But tell us of yourself."

"Well, for one thing, your sentry—the young one with the foot-long mustachios—used me in a most insolent manner when I approached your tent."

Vilimir shrugged. "You cannot expect a simple nomad to treat any sessor as a fellow human being." Jorian looked sharply at Vilimir, wondering if the cham, too, meant to insult him. But Vilimir went smoothly on, "You must have seen some strange sights in your journey through the unknown southern lands."

"That I have!" Jorian began to narrate some of the high spots of his journey, when he became aware of a curious languor creeping over him. He scarcely had the strength to hold up the flagon. Great Zevatas, he thought, surely I haven't drunk *that* much?

He tried to go on, but his tongue seemed reluctant to obey his brain. The hand holding the flagon relaxed, spilling ale. Jorian glanced at Vilimir with sudden suspicion.

The cham snapped his fingers, and a noose dropped over Jorian's shoulders and tightened, pinning his arms. A second snaked out and added its grip to the first. With a muffled roar, Jorian staggered to his feet. But the Gendings who held the other ends of the lariats were big, powerful men, who easily checked Jorian's befuddled lunges.

"What is this?" he ground out at Vilimir, who sat smiling.

"Why, only that we need money for this war with Hnidmar, and the reward offered by Xylar for your return will serve this purpose."

Jorian's tongue seemed to have swollen to twice its normal size, but he forced it to obey. "You damned trencher! By Imbal's iron yard, I could have sent you back to your uncle likewise, when you came to Xylar."

"No doubt; but, being a silly, sentimental sessor, you missed the chance. It only goes to prove that the greatest sessor is no more than a bug beneath the heel of the lowliest nomad. Put our new fetters on him."

A pair of heavy manacles of shiny new steel, joined by a foot of chain, were snapped on Jorian's wrists and locked with a key.

"The best Tarxian workmanship," said Vilimir. "You should feel complimented, my good Jorian." The cham turned to Karadur, who sat trembling. "And now, O wizard, what of you? The Xylarians would doubtless like to get their hands on the he-witch who compassed their ruler's escape; but, being vile money-grubbers like all sessors, they would probably add nought to the reward. On the other hand, we need a competent wizard. The last one we had, we slew when he could not answer the question of who poisoned our uncle. As a third alternative, we can simply order your head smitten off right now; perhaps that were the simplest solution. Which is your choice?"

"I—I will remain your humble servant."

Jorian cast a bitter look at Karadur, who avoided his eye. The cham said:

"Brakki! Place Master Jorian in the pen and put a trustworthy guard over him. He is, I warn you, skilled at escape from such gyves. Sequester all property of value with him, save his raiment. Make up an escort— ten men should do—to carry him hence to Xylar. Let me think—Xylar is allied with Vindium against Othomae; Othamae is allied with Metouro against Govannian; Metouro is allied with Tarxia against Boaktis; Govannian is allied with Aussar against Metouro. Therefore, Xylar is allied with Vindium, Govannian, and Boaktis against Othomae, Metouro, Assar, and Tarxia, whilst Solymbria, Kortoli, Zolon, and Ir are neutral. The best route were, therefore, through the Ellornas into Boaktis, avoiding Tarxian land, and thence through Solymbria and Ir into Xylar. Is that clear?"

"Aye, Your Terribility," said the man addressed as Brakki.

Then Jorian's legs folded beneath him, and he sank to the carpet unconscious. In his swoon, he found himself again facing the green god Tvasha. Instead of approaching the deity reverently, he roared:

"Why didst thou not warn me this knave lay in wait for me?"

Weeping, the god blubbered, "A thousand pardons, good Jorian! I am but a small, weak god, of limited powers. Do not, I pray thee, think hard of me! I could not bear it. And now farewell, for they are robbing thee of the little green idol, and I must perforce serve this villainous cham henceforth, May stronger gods than I go with thee!"

With Jorian in the middle, the escort wound along trails that snaked up and down the valleys of the eastern Ellornas. Moisture dripped from trees which, just bursting into leaf, loomed up out of the mist. Early wildflowers spangled the wet earth with little stars of yellow and blue and white. When the mist lifted, the higher peaks on either hand were seen to be still covered with snow.

The Ellorna Mountains and the Lograms further south formed twin barriers, walling off the land of Novaria between them. This land formed a broad peninsula, which joined Shven to the north with Fedirun and Mulvan to the south, and which also sundered the Inner Sea from the Western Ocean. Between these two mighty ranges lay the roughly rectangular stretch of hill and plain called Novaria, the Land of the Twelve Cities.

The existence of these ranges had allowed the twelve city-states of Novaria to flourish, constantly squabbling and warring with one another, despite the menace of the nomadic hordes of Shven to the north, the predatory desert-dwellers of Fedirun to the south, and the might of Mulvan to the southeast. The few passes through these mountains were easy to defend.

Since both the fierce steppe-dwellers of Shven and the teeming, docile multitudes of Mulvan looked upon the sea with horror, shipping in the Inner Sea was largely in the hands of Novarians and the mixed folk of Janareth and Istheun. Hence there was little danger of a seaborne invasion of Novaria from the greater powers to north and south—unless one of the Twelve Cities, blinded by hatred of some neighbor, brought in shiploads of these dangerous outsiders to help it in a local quarrel. This possibility kept Novarian chancellors and ministers awake nights, for they knew their own folk. They knew that, when their passions were sufficiently aroused, there was no perfidy they would not commit and no risk they would not run to gain an advantage over the immediate object of their wrath.

Jorian still rode his big chestnut roan, Oser, although his hands were manacled. Another rider led Oser, and the loop of a lariat, in the hands of still another, encircled Jorian's neck. Brakki had wanted to send Jorian on a sorry nag and keep Oser for the cham's herds, since horses big enough to carry a large, armored man were highly valued on the steppe. But the commander of the escort, a Captain Glaum, pointed out that Jorian was the heaviest man in the party. If they mounted him on some worn out little rabbit, the beast would collapse, and they would have to buy or steal another mount along the way. Therefore, Brakki had sent Jorian on Oser, warning Glaum that he was to defend the life of the horse with his own.

So they wound among the hills. As day succeeded day, the peaks on the right grew taller and more snow-covered. This was the main spine of the Ellornas. The party kept to the southern foothills, skirting the lands of the Twelve Cities. Jorian, glancing to his left at the forested ridges, was sure that if he could only get over a few of them, he would be in Tarxian territory.

And what then? Being allied against Xylar, Tarxia would probably not extradite him. But he had no money and no weapons. The gold he had taken from Rennum Kezymar, his sword, dagger, crossbow, and mailshirt—even his little green god—had all been taken from him. He knew nobody in Tarxia, which stood at the farthest remove from Xylar of any of the Twelve.

Jorian repeated the one Tarxian name he had heard from Karadur—the wizard Valdonius. If the project of fetching the Kist of Avlen to Metouro was now dead, Jorian would presumably be free to go about his business. But he had better make sure that his geas was lifted and that he knew what his business was. In any case, Valdonius of Tarxia seemed as good a person to start with as any.

For the first few days after leaving Istheun, there had been little talk between the Gendings of the escort and their prisoner. They had not treated him badly, but their attitude was that of an unfeeling but practical man towards his domestic animals. They did not wish to injure him, because such hurts might diminish his value; but they did not mean to take any nonsense from him, either.

As the party left the plains of Shven and climbed into the lower Ellornas, relations thawed as Jorian's ebullient spirit asserted itself. The fact that he spoke fairly good Shvenic and could make small jokes helped. And Jorian resorted to crafty tricks to arouse their interest. For instance, while his escort made camp, he remarked:

"These ridges look much like those of the Lograms, a hundred leagues south of here. They remind me of the time that wizard-smith was going to temper his blade by running it red-hot up my—but that would not interest you."

"What mean you?" said Glaum. "Go ahead, tell us."

"Oh, you nomads know all and believe nothing a sessor says. Why should I bore you with my tales?"

"We will not let you arouse our curiosity and then tease us, for one thing," said Glaum. "Now talk, or by Greipnek's prick, I will twist this rope until you do!"

"Oh, very well," and Jorian was off on the tale of his adventure with Rhithos the smith.

By the time they were well into the Ellornas, it had become an evening routine for the Gendings to demand: "Jorian! Tell us a story!"

Glaum made sure that, at any time, at least two men were watching Jorian with weapons ready. He divided the night into watches, during which two watched Jorian while two others stood regular sentry duty.

"We might run across a bear newly emerged from its den," he explained, "and in the higher mountains, the cave men attack small parties. Please Greipnek, neither shall befall us; but we mean to be ready if it come."

One day, Jorian caught snatches of talk that made him suspect that the party would soon turn south, threading its way through the passes into Boaktis. Therefore, he had better escape forthwith if he wished to reach friendly Tarxian territory. That evening he outdid himself as a storyteller.

"If I did but have the wit of King Fusinian of Kortoli," he said, "I should have given you thickheads the slip long since; but alas! I fear I am as stupid as you. You remember my telling you about Fusinian, the son of Filoman the Well-Meaning, a few nights ago? He was a small man, but lively and quick-witted, so that they called him Fusinian the Fox. And I have told you of the time he sowed the Teeth of Grimnor and was driven out of Kortoli.

"After he recovered his kingdom and his lovely queen, Thanuda, all went well for a time. And then one day, the queen vanished, leaving her boudoir in confusion, as if she had been carried off by violence. Naturally, Fusinian was much distressed. Their two children aggravated his grief by tugging at his garments and asking, when was mummy coming home?

"As soon as this disappearance transpired, Fusinian sent out searchers, and issued proclamations, and offered rewards, and consulted knowledgeable persons to try to find out what had become of his beloved. One of the first of whom he inquired was his court wizard, Doctor Aichos, who cast horoscopes and studied the flight of birds and evoked spirits, all to no avail. Then Fusinian consulted with all the other licensed wizards and wizardesses in the kingdom, with no more success.

"At last he resorted to the one person he had sworn

he would never hire again: the witch Gloé, who dwelt in a cave in the mountains of southern Kortoli. Gloé had been giving the Kortolian monarchy bad advice for two generations. Moreover, she was determined to make herself the court wizard in place of old Aichos, and this was the price she had exacted from the kings of Kortoli on the previous occasions of her employment by them. As things fell out, her spells had always failed in one respect or another, so the kings had never felt obliged to give her this post.

"Now, rendered desperate, King Fusinian rode south and sought out Gloé's cave. When he asked her what had befallen his consort, she answered readily:

" 'Oh, that. A troll, who has lately moved hither from the Ellorna Mountains, has taken up his abode in the Marvelous Caverns. A fiftnight ago, I received word from one of my familiar demons that this troll had brought a woman thither.'

"Now, the Marvelous Caverns were well known to Fusinian, for his father, Filoman the Well-Meaning, had caused them to he explored and mapped, and Fusinian himself had visited them as a youth. They were a series of limestone caves, opening into a ravine a few leagues from Gloé's cave. Few, however, had visited them, because they were very difficult to get into and had the repute of being haunted by evil spirits. Fusinian asked Gloé:

" 'Can you cast a spell upon this troll, to draw him forth from his cave and destroy him?'

" 'Alas, nay, sire!' replied the witch. 'Know that, whereas trolls have no inherent supernatural powers, they are singularly proof against spells cast upon them by others. The only spells of mine that might work require lengthy preparations, and also require that the object of the spell hold still during the operation.'

" 'Then I suppose I shall have to pursue this monster into its cave myself and seek to slay it,' quoth the king.

" 'I advise that not,' said Gloé. 'This is an egregiously

tough old troll, yclept Vuum. Your weapons will glance from his scaly hide as from a granite statue, and such is his strength that he could pick you up and tear you in pieces, limb from limb, and scatter the pieces about his ravine.'

" 'Then I will come with a company of my doughtiest soldiers, and overwhelm him by numbers.'

" 'That will not do either, Your Majesty. For the Marvelous Caverns open out midway up a cliff, and they can be entered only by lowering oneself down by ropes from the top of the cliff. Furthermore, the single entrance to the caverns is narrow, so that your men could come at Vuum only one at a time and thus be destroyed in detail.'

" 'If this is so, then how does Vuum come in and out?'

" 'Because he is a troll, his fingernails and toenails are so thick and talonlike that he can force them into cracks in the rocks that your eye would never notice. Thus he can scale the cliff as easily as a squirrel runs up a tree trunk.'

" 'How about mounting a ballista across the gorge from the cave and skewering him with a dart when he shows his head?'

" 'So keen are his senses and so great his agility that he would see your missile coming and dodge back into the cave.'

" 'Well,' said Fusinian, 'if my time has come, it has come. Whatever the odds, my honor will not permit me to leave this vermin in possession of my dear wife.'

" 'What do you purpose to do?' asked Gloé.

" 'Why, to fare to the Marvelous Caverns, have myself lowered down the cliff, enter the cave, and essay to slay this Vuum.'

" 'Oh, sire! Whatever will Kortoli do without you? We nearly perished under your dear but foolish father. If you die now, we shall face a long regency ere your eldest wean reaches manhood, and you know what perils that entails. Had you any chance at all, I would bless your undertaking. But consider: this troll is half again as tall as you, and twice as wide, and weighs thrice as much. His hide is as hard as that of the crocodiles of Mulvan, and he can crumble rocks with his fingers—'

" 'Wait,' said the king. 'Twice as wide as I, said you?'

" 'Aye, and all made of thews of iron—'

" 'Let me think,' said Fusinian. 'I am trying to remember the map of the Marvelous Caverns prepared in my father's reign. Look at you, O Gloé: If I immobilize this Vuum, can you blast him with some spell or other?

" 'Well, sire, there is a lightning spell I long ago learnt from a holy man of Mulvan. It is nearly as dangerous to the user as to the victim; but in this case I should be willing to try it. However, I want your word that, if I succeed, I shall be granted my license and made your court magician—'

" 'Yes, yes, I knew that was coming,' quoth Fusinian. 'You shall have what you ask if, and only if, your levin bolt perform as you have promised. Now I go to prepare my assault.'

"So the king rode back to his capital, and there he selected his swiftest steed, and his keenest weapons, and a hundred of his most stalwart warriors. And another thing he took with him was a set of bagpipes, such as are used by the shepherds of the hills of Govannian, which the king had been trying to learn to play. The general opinion in Kortoli was that the sound of this instrument was hideous enough when played by a competent piper, but when the king made noises upon it the result was ghastly beyond all description.

"Since Fusinian was king, nobody but Thanuda dared to tell him to his face what they thought of his piping; but from the way they hemmed and hawed when he asked their views, he very soon wist their true opinion. So he took to practicing in a cell of his dungeon, where nobody would be bothered save a prisoner or two. Being a humane man, Fusinian allowed them time off their sentences in return for their having to listen to his playing.

"The king also took the map of the Marvelous Caverns prepared under Filoman and studied it as he traveled. And in due time he came to the ravine whereunto opened the entrance to the Caverns. He took a position on the bluff over against the ravine from the cave entrance and played his bagpipes.

"After he had played for a while, and his hundred stalwart warriors had covered their ears, the troll appeared at the mouth of his cave, roaring: 'What is that hellish racket?'

" 'It is no hellish racket, but the sweet strains of my bagpipes,' said Fusinian.

" 'Well, why are you subjecting me to them?' said Vuum.

" 'Because I am King Fusinian, whose queen you have abducted, I want her back, and I want you out of my kingdom.'

" 'Oho!' said the troll. 'So it is our little mouse of a king, is it? Know, worm, that I mean to keep your woman for myself, and if you do not stop pestering me, it will be the worse for you.'

"After they had bandied words thus for a time, Vuum came out of the cave, climbing down the sheer cliff by his nails like a bat, and came roaring up the other side of the gorge to destroy Fusinian and his men. The men loosed a volley of quarrels from their crossbows, but these merely bounced off the scaly hide of the troll. Then Fusinian and his party vaulted into their saddles and galloped off, and the troll could not catch them. But as soon as Vuum returned to his cave, Fusinian was back at his post, serenading him again.

"And so it continued for many days, with the king making both days and nights hideous with his pipes and then fleeing away whenever Vuum sought to retaliate. At length even the iron strength of the troll began to fail, and he contented himself with lurking in the mouth of his cave, hurling stones and insults at his tormentor. Fusinian took cover when the stones came whizzing over, and the insults bothered him not a whit.

"At last the troll called across the ravine: 'O King, if you would fain have your wife again, then agree to fight me man to troll! I will wrastle, or box, or fence, or fight with spears, axes, clubs, or knives, or duel at a distance with the longbow or the crossbow or the sling or the twirl-spear. Can you think of any more ways for us to settle our difference?'

"'Since I am the challenged party,' quoth Fusinian, 'it is mine to choose the weapons. And I will not wrastle, or box, or fight with swords, spears, et cetera, because I know your strength and hardihood all too well. But I will undertake a fair contest with you.'

"'And what might that be?'"

"'We shall have a foot race, in your own caverns. We shall start at the entrance, and run back along the main corridor, and around the big loop, and out to the entrance again.'

"After some argument over details, the troll agreed that this was a fair contest. Then Fusinian said: 'Now, as to terms. If you win, I will go away and leave you in undisturbed possession of the Marvelous Caverns and of Thanuda. If I win, you shall yield me Thanuda and depart forthwith from my kingdom.'

"Again they argued, but when Fusinian began to blow up the bag of pipes, Vuum quickly assented. Then Fusinian said: 'Not that I mistrust you, my good troll, but to make sure that there occur no untoward event when I am in your cave, you shall bring Thanuda to the bottom of the ravine and leave her there whilst we stage our contest. My men have orders, in case of treachery on your part, to take the woman and flee, not even trying to rescue me.'

" 'But what about treachery on your part, my lord King?'

" 'The mere fact of my being within your reach takes care of that,' said Fusinian. 'You could squash me like a bug if I played you false.'

"So Fusinian descended to the bottom of the ravine, and Vuum did likewise, carrying Thanuda on his shoulder. And then the troll took Fusinian on his shoulder, and bore him up the cliff again to the mouth of the cave, and Fusinian said afterwards that the journey on this stinking monster's scaly shoulder was the hardest of all his trials to bear. But at last they reached the cave, and the troll gave Fusinian one of the little lanthorns lit by captive glowworms that he used to illumine the darkness, whilst he took another one. Then Fusinian put his head out of the cave and called down to his wife:

" 'All right, dear, you may give the signal.'

"So she called up: 'Ready! Set! Go!' and Vuum and Fusinian were off like the wind, or as nearly like the wind as they could in the darkness of the cave, with its uneven floor and the stalactites and stalagmites to dodge.

"Being a small man and fast on his feet, Fusinian knew he could get off at the very start faster than his lumbering antagonist, who was a fine runner once he got going but slower to reach his best speed. And sure enough, Fusinian found himself bounding along two paces ahead of Vuum. Vuum had the advantage of knowing the Caverns better than Fusinian, who had not been there in a decade, and he began to gain upon Fusinian. But then he ran his head into a stalactite, so that it broke off and huge chunks of limestone rained down upon him. Being a troll, he was not gravely hurt, but the accident threw him off his stride and enabled Fusinian to gain another pace upon him.

"Now, Fusinian knew from his study of the map of the cave that in the main loop, whereof he had spoken, there was a narrow place. And when he got to this strait, he turned his body sideways and nimbly slipped through. But Vuum, following him, got stuck. He must have known about this narrow place, but it would seem that he had never tried to see if he could pass through it. Fusinian paused to call back a few choice insults, whereupon the troll, roaring savagely, tried even harder to push through the strait but only jammed himself in more tightly than ever. As you can see, trolls are not a highly intelligent race, ranking somewhere near the ape-men of Komilakh in this regard.

"And so Fusinian reached the entrance once more and called up to his men—some of whom had come around to the top of the cliff above the cave—to drop a rope down into the ravine. And when Fusinian got his breath back, he let himself down by the rope and seized Thanuda in a loving embrace. Then they climbed to the other side of the gorge, and the king called upon the witch Gloé to perform.

"Gloé had been bringing her cauldron to a boil and putting into it the eye of a newt, and the toe of a frog, and other unwholesome substances. And she uttered a mighty spell and incantation, so that the sky darkened, and a cold wind blew, and rain fell, and the air was filled with the rustle of unseen wings, and a foetor as of the Pit filled the air. And she pointed her wand at the entrance to the cave, and a bolt of lightning flashed from the cloud overhead and struck the side of the mountain—but not the cave entrance. She tried again, and the lightning struck the other side. For an hour she aimed her wand and spoke the words of power, and each time the lightning flashed and the thunder boomed, but never could she seem to hit the mouth of the Marvelous Caverns. When the thunder was not crashing, they could hear the bellows of the trapped troll inside the Caverns.

"Then the thunder cloud wafted away, and Gloé collapsed in exhaustion, without having once struck the target. And whilst Fusinian and Thanuda and the warriors stood about in a daze, half deafened by the thunder and wholly soaked by the shower, a deep rumble was heard. The earth trembled and moved, and the cliff crumbled with a mighty roar, and the entrance to the Marvelous Caverns vanished in a roaring slide of rock and gravel, and the air was filled with choking dust. Some of the other side of the ravine gave way, too, and had not Fusinian snatched his queen away from the brink, they would have fallen with it. As it was, the ravine was now half filled with rubble, and no trace of the Caverns or of the troll could be seen, save a peculiarly sticky green fluid, which oozed out from between the rocks.

"So that was the end of the Caverns and of Vuum, and they returned to Kortoli City rejoicing. Then Gloé demanded the post of court magician, and Fusinian refused on the ground that she had not in fact slain the troll by her levin bolts, which had all gone awry. The coming of the earthquake at that opportune moment, he said, had been a happenstance. Gloé, on the other hand, maintained that, even if her lightnings had not gone into the cave and struck Vuum, they had so disturbed the balance of natural forces as to bring about the earthquake. Hence, she had really performed her part of the bargain, even if not quite the way she had intended.

"The dispute waxed bitter, for Fusinian was too just a king to order Gloé summarily suppressed for dunning him. At last Thanuda suggested that they bring in an impartial outsider to arbitrate. So they put the question to the theocrat of Tarxia, who decided in favor of Gloé. Since Doctor Aichos was ripe for retirement anyway, it looked as if the change could be effected with the least possible disturbance. But Gloé had not enjoyed her new post a fiftnight when she caught a phthisic from some other courtier and died in three days. So Aichos' retirement proved only temporary after all.

"Thanuda assured her consort that Vuum had done nothing worse to her than to make her play draughts with him by the hour. But presently it transpired that she was with child. And when the child was born, it was bigger and more robust than any child ever seen in Kortoli. Moreover, as it grew, its skin developed a rough, scaly appearance, not unlike the hide of a crocodile.

"Happily, the boy was not the heir apparent, having two older brothers; and, if not especially intelligent, he was good-natured and docile. Named Fusarius, he grew up to be a famous warrior, being twice as strong as the average man, with a hide of such remarkable toughness that he hardly needed armor, although he wore it in battle, disliking the scratches and bruises that would have been mortal wounds had they befallen other men.

"About the paternity of Fusarius, Fusinian doubtless had his own private thoughts. But, being a philosophical man, he made the best of things."

Jorian glanced around. One of his escorts had gone quietly to sleep, curled up against the base of a tree. Of the rest, several should have been sleeping so as to be wide awake when their watches began. Instead, they were all hanging eagerly on his words.

"They tell a tale," he went on, "about this Fusarius and the lonesome lion . . ."

So he continued for hours, reeling off story after story: some dredged out of his memory, some made up on the spot. Speaking in a low, undramatic voice, he shamelessly padded the tales and strung them out, deliberately keeping them from becoming too exciting. In consequence, by midnight every man of the escort was asleep. Watches had not been posted, because Glaum had dozed off before he thought to do so. The clearing buzzed gently with the snores of the Gendings.

Jorian rose to his feet. He searched inside his waistband for the one possession, besides his clothes, of which he had not been robbed: the little bag of picklocks. The Gendings had been so elated over his weapons and money belt that they had neglected to search his garments more minutely. Once Jorian had one of the bent wires in his hands, it was only a matter of a few breaths before the manacles opened.

He laid the fetters down carefully to keep the chain from clanking, and picked up the scabbarded sword that one of the escort had laid on the ground beside him. It was a straight, two-edged horseman's blade, even longer than Randir, with a plain cross-hilt. Jorian did not like it so well as the one he had taken from Rhithos the smith, but it would do.

He would like to have stolen one or more purses from the Gendings. They had, he knew, brought a considerable sum of money wherewith to bribe the officials of Solymbria and Ir if it should prove necessary in order to hustle Jorian through those countries without interference. But, since each man had his purse firmly tied to his girdle, Jorian did not see how he could do this without the risk of awakening somebody.

Oser swiveled his ears and made a small equine sound as Jorian, moving like a shadow, stepped to him, stroked his nose, and untied him. For such nocturnal work, he would have preferred a horse of a darker color than the chestnut roan, but this factor was much outweighed by the fact that this animal knew him, whereas the others did not and might make a row if he tried to lead one of them away.

Holding the reins in one hand and the stolen sword in the other, he quietly led Oser out from among the other animals and up the nearest ridge to the south. Atop the ridge, out of sight of the camp, he paused to study the stars. The crescent moon had set two hours before, but the stars, visible through the branches of trees not yet in leaf, gave him his direction. With a quiet smile to himself, he set off down the further slope towards Tarxia.

# IX

# The Smaragdine God

The river Spherdar meandered through the central plain of Tarxia, where teams of buffalos pulled wooden plows through the wet, black earth. The meadows and the borders of roads and fields, where the plow had not trenched, were gay with millions of wildflowers.

Beside the Spherdar, a few leagues from the Inner Sea and at the head of navigation for seagoing ships, stood Tarxia City. Its wall looked imposing from a distance but a closer view showed that it was out of date and in poor repair. It was made of brick instead of stone and hence would not stand up under the battering of modern seige engines. Many merlons had crumbled away, and here and there a big crack, caused by uneven settling, ran zigzag through the brickwork. For defense, the Tarxians relied more on their god and the supernatural powers of his priesthood than on arms and fortifications. Since the establishment of the theocracy, Tarxia's neighbors had held these powers too much in awe to test them seriously.

The city itself was smaller and shabbier than one would have expected of a major port of the Inner Sea. The streets were narrow, winding, and filthy. Most of the houses were either tall, jam-packed tenements or hovels patched together with odd pieces of brick and board. Even the houses of the richer Tarxians were modest in size and subdued in décor. The streets swarmed with drably clad laymen and black-robed priests of the god Gorgolor.

The city was dominated by one huge, towering structure: the temple of Gorgolor, the patron god of Tarxia and—according to the theocracy—the supreme god of the universe. It was the largest, costliest, and gaudiest temple in all Novaria, not even excepting the splendid fane of Zevatas in Solymbria. The salient feature of this temple was the enormous dome at the center of the cruciform structure.

Supported on a drum and pendentives and braced by half-domes and buttresses, this dome soared over 350 feet into the air. The spring sun blazed blindingly on its gilded tiles. Four slender towers, whence the priests of Gorgolor called the Tarxians to prayer thrice a day, stood in a square at the corners of the structure. Around the temple spread a temenos of park and subsidiary buildings, including the theocrat's palace.

From the temple of Gorgolor, the ground sloped downwards to the waterfront, with its docks and ships and sailors' haunts. Swollen by several tributaries, which joined it above and below Tarxia City, the Spherdar meandered eastward through the great Swamp of Spraa to the sea. Sea cows were strictly protected in Tarxian waters because, by feeding on the swamp plants, the creatures helped to keep them from blocking the river.

On the sloping ground between the temple and the waterfront rose a multitude of dwellings of Tarxia's more prosperous laymen, including that of Valdonius the magician. Around noon on the nineteenth of the Month of the Crow, Jorian knocked on the door of Valdonius' house. When the porter opened the peephole, Jorian said:

"Is Doctor Valdonius at home?"

"What if he is?" said the porter, eyeing Jorian's ragged garments and shaggy hair and beard with distaste. On Jorian's left arm a yellow band was tied, bearing the words, in the archaic characters used in Tarxia:

"Pray tell him a messenger from Doctor Karadur is without."

The peephole closed, and presently the door opened. As Jorian stepped inside, the porter recoiled with a wrinkled nose. Jorian grumbled:

"If you hadn't a bath in two months, old boy, you'd stink, too!"

When the porter led Jorian down a hall and into a handsome living room, Jorian stopped and stared in amazement. Of the two men seated at lunch, one—a huge, bald, fat man—he took to be Valdonius. The other was Karadur. Valdonius said:

"Greetings, Master Jorian. One need not see a mouse through a millstone to perceive that you somehow gave the barbarians the slip." Then, to Karadur: "You see, old man, my divination worked. Said I not he would be here around midday?"

"Greetings, Doctor Valdonius," said Jorian; then, to Karadur: "What in the forty-nine Mulvanian hells are you doing here? The last I saw of you, you had abandoned me and your mission to become Cham Vilimir's hired spooker!"

A tear rolled down Karadur's wrinkled brown face. "Ah, my son, blame me not over-harshly! It would have availed you nought for me to have been sent back to Xylar with you, or to have been slain on the spot. What else could I—with the most morally upright intentions—have done?"

"You could at least have pleaded with Vilimir, or threatened him with some nameless supernatural doom. All you did was to squeak: 'Aye, aye, sir!' and let me be dragged off to my fate without a word of protest."

"But you escaped your doom!"

"No thanks to you. And now I suppose that, having learnt that Vilimir wanted you to go galloping over the steppe with him in his war with that other horde, you found it better for your health and comfort to slip away and continue your journey, eh?"

"Ah, no indeed, my dear son! I had to say what I

did to befool the barbarian, so that I could escape and essay to reach you—"

Valdonius interrupted with a roar of laughter. "Your young man has grown an old head on his shoulders, Karadur!" he cried jovially. "Master Jorian, I think that shaft went close to the clout. Natheless, if an older if not wiser man may offer a word of advice, assume not that the motive you ascribe to a man, even if your guess be true, is the only one. For men's motives are commonly mixed, with self-interest jostling righteousness and fears mingled with hopes. What if the good Father Karadur allowed self-interest for the moment to overcome all other considerations? Has the same never befallen you? Besides, he is old and infirm, no puissant young hero like yourself. Therefore, the adamantine valor of a Ghish the Great or a Fusinian the Fox should not be expected of him."

"I'm no hero," growled Jorian. "I am only a simple craftsman who would like to settle down and earn a decent living. Natheless, I didn't run off and leave Karadur in the jungles and steppes we have lately traversed, although I could easily have done so. But what's done is done. What is the present state of affairs?"

Valdonius grinned. "Events have taken a most interesting turn. But, my good Jorian, I need hardly summon fell spirits from forbidden planes and unholy dimensions across nighted gulfs of space and time, to discern that you would fain have three things: a solid repast, a bath, and the ministrations of a barber. Is my speculation correct?"

"Eminently, sir. If my hair be allowed to grow any longer, I shall trip on it as I walk. As for the bath, your poor porter wellnigh swooned when he got a close whiff of me. But of all these desiderata, the meal stands foremost, or, I, too, shall swoon."

"How have you subsisted since your escape?"

"When a farmer had firewood to be chopped, I chopped for fodder, for myself and my horse. When he did not, having not the price of a patch for my breeches upon me, I stole one of his fowls. That's an art to which I devoted much study in training for my escape from Xylar. I thank you, fair one," he said as a pretty girl tendered him a goblet of wine and another brought in a hearty meal for him.

"Peradventure you will be known as Jorian the Fox for that accomplishment," said Valdonius with a chuckle.

"Or at least as Jorian the chicken thief."

"What befell you at the Tarxian frontier?"

Between ravenous bites, Jorian said: "I told them I was Maltho of Kortoli, seeking honest employment as a mercenary. They plainly didn't like my looks—or perhaps my smell, or my empty purse—but after some muttering and whispering they let me in on a thirty-day permit. The priest in command of the post tied this damned brassard upon me, as if I carried some fatal and contagious pox."

"From their point of view, you do," said Valdonius. "You bear in your head all sorts of unauthorized thoughts, which if not checked might spread amongst the general populace and imperil that delicate state of mindless acceptance of the True Faith, which the theocracy has so long and so earnestly striven to impose upon the Tarxian populace."

"I know; they made me promise not to discuss religious or philosophical matters with any Tarxian during my sojourn. I trust I have not already violated this injunction?"

"It matters not. For thrice a hundred years, the theocracy succeeded in sealing the borders to such subversive influences. Now, however, the country seethes with restlessness and discontent, for many of the priests have become mere cassocked lechers and grafters, and the benefits they have promised have not come to pass. Ideas have a way of leaking across frontiers despite walls and sentinels. Be reasonably discreet in your subversive utterances and you will have little to fear."

"I wonder they let me in at all?"

"Belike they were impressed despite themselves by that aristocratic manner you learnt as king. They took you for a gentleman fallen upon hard times, who if kindly entreated might be useful to them."

"Which, in a sense, I suppose I am." Jorian finished his plate and sat back with a sigh of repletion. "Zevatas! that was good. There's no sauce like a ravenous appetite. And now, my learned colleagues, pray tell me: How fares the Kist of Avlen and the project concerning it?"

Valdonius chuckled. He seemed to be always laughing or chuckling or smiling, but Jorian found his mirth not especially kindly.

"Well, now," he said, "the Kist of Avlen—" (he pronounced it, "Aulen" in the northern manner) "—is safe and well guarded in my cellar and shall remain there until you gentlemen have assisted me in a certain enterprise."

Jorian glanced at Karadur, who was shedding another tear. "Fool that I was!" said the Mulvanian. "If ever I survive past the Conclave, I will withdraw from all association with my colleagues and become a hermit, so rare is good faith among them."

"Now, now, old man," said Valdonius, "do not carry on so. After all, what I am doing for the magical profession here in Tarxia is quite as important as what my fellow Altruists propose to do in Metouro."

"And what is it that you would do here?" asked Jorian.

"Ere I go further, let me warn you that this discussion shall not go beyond the three of us, and I have ways of dealing with any who play me false. Karadur tells me you are a bit of a blabbermouth."

"Not when I have a real secret to keep. I will keep yours."

"Very well, then. Have you visited the temple of Gorgolor?"

"Nay; I've only glanced at it in passing on my way hither."

"Well, in this temple stands an altar, and beyond this altar rises a pedestal, and on this pedestal stands one of the wonders of the world."

"The smaragdine statue of Gorgolor? I've heard of it."

"Aye. This statue is in the form of a frog, carved from a single emerald—but this frog is the size of a lion or a bear. It is the largest emerald ever known to have existed, and its value may be greater than that of all the other jewels in the world together. The priests make much of the brilliant radiance of this statue, which they say will blind unbelievers who look upon it. But I have seen it often, and my eyesight is as sound as ever. When Gorgolor manifests himself on this plane, they say, he takes possession of the statue, and to the statue are the prayers of the theocrat and the rest of the hierachy directed. Now, what think you would ensue if this statue vanished?"

Jorian peered out at Valdonius from under his heavy brows. "It would cause much scurry and flurry amongst the priesthood, I should think."

"That, my dear young man, is a magnificent understatement."

"Why make the statue disappear?"

"As you have gathered, many intelligent Tarxians are less than enchanted by the rule of the theocracy. Look at me, for example. The priests allow only a very limited practice of magic: nought but divination and sympathetic magic. No sorcery or necromancy, no matter how laudable their purposes or beneficial their results. And why? Because their theologians assert, on no scientific basis but solely from their convoluted casuistical reasoning, that any spirits so invoked are by definition evil entities opposed to the good god Gorgolor. Therefore, traffic with such beings is a damnable heresy, to be punished by stake and faggot. So I, who could mightily advance the supernatural sciences if permitted freedom of research, must confine my activities to such trivial pastimes as casting horoscopes and sending my spirit forth in trances to search for my clients' lost bangles.

"Others have other complaints, but they all come to the same thing. We are fettered hand and foot by these obsolete theological gyves. Our polis stagnates, whilst the other Twelve Cities advance in the arts and sciences. I could give you endless instances of the stupid oppressions of literature and the arts, the ban on free discussion, and so on. Why, only last month—"

"Pardon," said Jorian, not wishing to hear all the woes of the Tarxians. "I think I understand your complaints. Let us return to the statue. A carving of that size can't be carried out of the temple in one's pocket; so what will you do?"

"The Kist, which your good colleague has fetched hither so opportunely, contains a useful shrinking spell, which should be applicable in this case. It is better than the modern shrinking spells, which leave the weight of the shrunken object unchanged. If this statue weighs, say, ten talents, to shrink it to pocket size whilst its weight remained constant would leave it as hard to move as it now is. It might even cause it to crack its plinth, because of the concentration of weight in a small space. I must warn you, if you should be called upon to handle the statue, that the lessened weight leaves the mass unchanged."

"What's the difference?"

"Weight is the force wherewith the planet draws objects like yourself and Gorgolor to its bosom. Mass is the quality that makes an object resist a sudden change in motion, as in starting or stopping. The two maintain a constant proportion—save when interfered with by a puissant spell. If you run with the shrunken statue, think not that you can stop it in its flight as readily as you could a simple brick or stone. If you do, its momentum will toss you arse-over-apex."

"What's my part in this escapade?"

"That we must discuss this even, to make sure that every detail has been planned and every contingency anticipated."

"But I," said Jorian, "am weary of this whole business. What makes you think I'll have any part of your scheme?"

"Because, my dear Jorian, you are still subject to the geas that my fellow adepts put upon you. Hence you have really no choice in the matter. Whereas the geas compels you to help, in every way you can, in getting the Kist to Metouro, and whereas the only way you can do this is to fall in with my wishes, you defy me on pain of those torments of which you have already experienced small samples."

"Not if you no longer live," gritted Jorian, seizing the hilt of his sword and tugging.

As he did so, however, Valdonius shouted words of power, threw a handful of powder towards him, and made some quick passes. The Shvenic sword came out of the scabbard only a few fingerbreadths and then stuck fast. Jorian's powerful arm muscles swelled and knotted, and sweat furrowed the dirt on his forehead, but the blade would not budge. He finally let go with a gasp. The sword snapped back to the bottom of the scabbard with a click.

"You see?" said Valdonius, chuckling. "But come! I am not your foe, so let us make your sojourn here as pleasant as we can. That long-desired bath awaits you. You shall be not only scrubbed but also oiled, massaged, and perfumed like one of the good spirits of the Mulvanian heavens. And I have sent for a washerwoman to cleanse and mend your garments and a barber to give you the look of a civilized mortal and not a club-waving caveman from the Ellornas.

"As for the remaining form of recreation, which I know is in your mind from the glances you gave my maid servants, I fear you must needs wait until you have left Tarxia. Relations between the sexes are governed by strict regulations here, and casual fornication is not permitted even to sailors from the ships that call here. This fact makes Tarxia an unpopular seaport, notwithstanding the profits to be made here."

"Has this government actually succeeded in stopping all lechery and harlotry?"

"Practically speaking, yes. The only ones who get away with such illicit amusements are certain members of the priesthood. Our dear old theocrat is always promising to end this abuse, but somehow he never seems to get around to it."

The following evening, they approached the temple of Gorgolor with Valdonius bearing a lanthorn. In a low voice, the magician explained:

"We are in luck. The theocrat and his hierachy have been disputing whether to send missionaries to Mulvan or Shven. So, when I told them you had just come from those lands, they arranged an audience at once. You had better review what you know of the religions of those countries."

"I know not much," said Jorian. "Had I been warned that such questions would be asked of me, I could have inquired; but now 'tis too late."

"Well, make up what you do not know, but make it plausible. This audience cost me a pretty penny, and I would have my money's worth."

"They charged for it, even though it's to their advantage?"

"Certes! The first principle of the cult is that every operation shall pay for itself and more. Why else maintain so strict a monopoly in supernatural matters?"

"What's the status of the other gods?"

"At first, after the fall of the Ignadian dynasty, the

rule was one of toleration for all faiths. In fact, the promise of such liberty was one tactic whereby the priesthood of Gorgolor—theretofore an obscure minor god—attained power. You have tried kings, they said, and the kings became tyrants; you have tried democracy, and the republic became a cauldron of anarchy and mob rule. There remains but theocracy: rule by the holy gods through their virtuous and moral vicars.

"The Gorgolorians had not long been in power, however, than they began to arrogate unto themselves a monopoly of the supernatural. First they enacted stringent laws against witchcraft. Then a few small, eccentric cults were suppressed. Then the priesthoods of Zevatas and Franda and the other major gods were placed under the orders of the high priest of Gorgolor, who thus became the theocrat.

"Then the theocrat announced a series of revelations from the gods. Each revelation enlarged the power and glory of Gorgolor and shrank those of the other gods. At last the other gods were reduced to mere lackeys of Gorgolor. One by one their temples have been converted to other uses or torn down, and their statues have been destroyed or hidden away on one pretext or another, until they no longer have any separate cults apart from that of Gorgolor."

"I wonder what the gods themselves think of this," said Jorian.

"So do I. Nowadays the other gods are not even named separately in the rites to Gorgolor, but are merely spoken of collectively as Gorgolor's attendant spirits."

"What if a Tarxian tried to revive the worship of Zevatas?"

"They would burn him as a heretic. You as a foreigner are allowed to exist here, but for a limited time only. If you wished to settle permanently, you would have have to accept the True Faith. Now let us see:

How shall I introduce you? I told the priests little about you."

"I am calling myself Maltho of Kortoli," said Jorian.

"Not distinguished enough; Maltho is a common name. How about Lord Maltho of Kortoli?"

"Kortoli has no nobility. Save for the king, it is a one-class polis. I persuaded the Mulvanians that I was a Kortolian noble, but that might not work with these priests."

"Well, then, Doctor Maltho?"

"If you like. I did once take a course at the Academy in Othomae, when I soldiered for the Grand Bastard."

"What did you study?"

"Versification. I once harbored an ambition to be a poet."

"Then you shall be Maltho of Kortoli, Doctor of Literature from the Academy of Othomae. Now, we shall arrive just after vespers. As soon as that is over, most of the priests will go about their own business; hence they will not much infest the temple.

"Your audience will be in the theocrat's palace. The theocrat is Kylo of Anneia, who aside from his office is not a bad fellow. I take him for a perfectly sincere and rather simple-minded old man, who believes all the moonshine his priests dole out to the faithful.

"When you have satisfied their curiosity regarding the ripeness of the foreigners for conversion, you might utter some leading remarks about the temple. Hint that you might be ready for conversion yourself, if you could but see its wonders. If I know Kylo, he will insist on showing the edifice to you in person. He redecorated it a few years ago and is monstrously proud of his handiwork.

"Armed guards are posted around the outside of the temple, and inside a couple of priests are supposed to keep a constant vigil, praying to Gorgolor and incidentally watching to see that nobody steals the furnishings. But in these degenerate days, one who suddenly intrudes upon these priests is likely to find them engrossed in dicing or draughts.

"As your party passes near the emerald statue, I wish you to display your storytelling talent. You must so fascinate all within earshot that the priests on watch will leave their posts and follow your party. Dear old Kylo will not, I am sure, rebuke them.

"Meanwhile, Karadur and I will slip behind the pedestal of the statue of Gorgolor. Whilst your party drifts out the main entrance, with you talking your head off, we shall try the shrinking spell. When we rejoin you, it will, the gods permitting, be with a much diminished Gorgolor in our pockets. Even if the theft transpire ere we leave the temenos, it is unlikely that we shall be searched, for the priests will be looking for a crew of twenty to thirty men and a team of oxen, which would be needed to rape away the statue in its present form."

As the party, consisting of Jorian, Karadur, Valdonius, the theocrat, four of his episcopals, and one ordinary priest who was his secretary, approached the main entrance to the temple of Gorgolor, its spear-bearing guards dropped with a clang to one knee. At a word from the high priest, they sprang to the great bronzen doors and pushed them groaningly open.

Kylo of Anneia was a short, stout man with a large, hooked nose, wearing a white silken robe and a tall headdress of white felt, trimmed with gold and gleaming with jewels. The episcopals were in crimson; the ordinary priest, in black.

Jorian, now barbered, sweet smelling, and clad in clean garments, was saying ". . . and so, I cannot extend much hope to Your Holiness in this matter. The nomads of Shven hold all sessors, as they call them, in such contempt that, if you send missionaries thither, they will either laugh at them or slay them out of hand.

"The Mulvanians present no more hope, although their response would be more amiable. They would say:

Welcome, O priests; we already have hundreds of gods but are always glad to add another. And they would enroll Gorgolor in their own teeming pantheon, where he would be lost in the throng. When you complained that they had perverted your meticulous theology, they would simply smile and promise to do better—and then go on doing as they have always done."

Jorian paused inside the temple to look around. "Marvelous!" he cried. "Incredible! Such taste! Such artistry! Surely, Your Holiness, your god must be a great and wise god indeed, to inspire men to such an achievement!"

"It is good of you to say so, my son," said Kylo, beaming and speaking with a broad Tarxian peasant accent. "You would be surprised at the trouble I had with some conservative members of my own hierachy, who thought mosaics of mortals and spiritual beings in a state of nudity indecent."

The central portion of the temple was square, with a colossal stone pier at each corner of the square. Huge arches and pendentives sprang from the tops of these piers. From the pendentives a low drum arose, and above the drum, the central dome soared up into dimness. The interior of the dome and its flanking half-domes were covered with gilded, brightly colored mosaics illustrating scenes from Gorgolorian mythology. At the floor level, numerous lamps shed adequate lighting. Further up, the light became fainter, until it picked out only an occasional bit of gilding.

On the floor, an altar stood to one side of the square. From the square, three short arms projected, allowing space for the worshipers to stand; for in Gorgolorism the laymen were allowed inside the temple. On the fourth side of the square, where the altar rested, was the holy of holies to which only the priests had access. This side could be closed off from profane eyes by a sliding screen. This screen was now drawn back, showing the cubical plinth, about six feet on an edge, and on the plinth the image of Gorgolor, carved from a single boulder of emerald.

As the party approached, two black-clad priests hastily rose. One tucked something that might have been a gaming device into his robe. Then they genuflected.

"Incredible!" repeated Jorian, looking up at the lion-sized smaragdine frog, in whose depths green lights seemed to glow and waver. "My only reservation, if Your Holiness will pardon my saying so, is that so much beauty might distract a man from the contemplation of the higher truths."

"True, Doctor Maltho," said Kylo. "With some worshipers, it may have that effect. But with others, it predisposes them all the more to harken unto our edifying homilies. We cannot, alas, divide the faithful into categories and furnish each group with a temple of the most suitable kind. So we seek a moderate approach, which will save the greatest number of faithful souls."

"Ah yes, Holy Father," said Jorian. "In my city, we long ago decided that the best safeguard against such perils was moderation. Even beauty, we found, can be overdone. Know you the tale of King Forimar of Kortoli—Forimar the Esthete?"

"Nay, my son, albeit I recall the name from histories of Novaria. Speak, an you would."

Jorian drew a long breath. Moving a leisurely half-pace at a time towards the main entrance, so as to draw the clerical crowd—including the two priests on vigil—with him, he began:

"This Forimar was a predecessor of Fusinian the Fox, of whom so many tales are told. It seems a rule of royalty that, out of every six kings, a land gets one hero, one scoundrel, one fool, and three mediocrities. Forimar was one of the fools, as his great-grandnephew Filoman the Well-Meaning was after him.

"But Forimar's folly took a special form. State business bored him to distraction. He cared little for law and justice, less for commerce and finance, and nothing at all for war and preparations therefor."

"Would that all sovrans and governments shared your king's distaste for war!" said the theocrat. "Then would men live in peace and devote themselves to leading good lives and worshipping the true god."

"True, Your Holiness; but the problem is, how do you get them all to give up war at once? Especially with so quarrelsome and factious a folk as the Novarians? And if one lay aside his arms before the rest, the rest reward his good example by leaping at his throat.

"Forimar, howsomever, was not a profound thinker about such matters. His passion for art and beauty overpowered all else. When he should have been reading state papers, he was playing the flageolet in the palace sextet. When he ought to have been receiving envoys, he was overseeing the building of a new temple or otherwise beautifying Kortoli City. When he should have been inspecting the troops, he was composing a sonnet to the beauties of the sunset.

"What made such matters more difficult was that he was really competent at all these arts. He was a fair architect, an accomplished musician, a worthy composer, a fine singer, and an excellent painter. Some of his poems are the glories of Kortolian literature to this day. But he could not do all these things and king it, too.

"Hence he left the governance of the polis to a succession of chancellors, chosen neither for probity nor for competence but for their admiration of their sovran's artistic achievements. After the kingdom had long suffered under a series of thieves and bunglers, Forimar's younger brother Fusonio took him to task.

" 'My dear brother and sire,' quoth Fusonio, 'this cannot go on.' After he had lectured Forimar on the iniquities of the recent ministers, he added: 'Furthermore, you are nearly thirty but have not yet chosen a queen, to provide legitimate heirs to the throne.'

" 'That is my affair!' said Forimar hotly. 'I have long cast an eye upon eligible members of the other sex but have never seen one who qualified. For my sensibilities are so acute that the slightest blemish of mind or of body, which a lesser man could put up with, were to me intolerable. So I am, and shall probably remain, wedded to my art. But fear not the failure of our line, Fusonio. If I die, you will succeed me, and you have already begotten five healthy children upon your spouse.'

"Fusonio argued some more, but Forimar put him off, saying: 'Nay; my only true live is Astis, the goddess of love and beauty, herself. Her I have loved with a consuming passion for many years, and no mere mortal wench can compare with her.'

" 'Then,' said Fusonio, 'your duty is to abdicate in my favor, ere your obsession with beauty bring disaster upon us. You would be permitted to pursue your artistic career undisturbed.'

" 'I will think upon that,' said Forimar. But the more he thought about it, the less he liked it. Although he and his brother had always gotten along well enough, they had little in common. Fusonio was a bluff, hearty, sensual type, blind to what Forimar deemed the higher things of life. Fusonio's idea of a large evening was to go incognito to some low tavern frequented by the rougher element and spend the even swilling ale and roaring ribald songs with unwashed peasants and ruffianly muleteers.

"Morever, the idea occurred to Forimar that his brother was seeking to oust him from base motives of ambition. Once he resigned, he feared, nought would stop Fusonio from getting rid of him by *force majeure*. On the other hand, as long as he kept the crown, the state's revenues provided him with means of pursuing his arts that he could hardly expect to enjoy as a private person.

"Not wishing to quarrel openly with Fusonio, he

devised a scheme to get rid of his brother. He made him admiral of a fleet, to explore the Eastern Ocean as far as the fabled isles of Salimor. Fusonio sailed off without demur, for this kind of adventure appealed to him. And Forimar returned to his arts.

"But the remark he had made to Fusonio, of being in love with the goddess Astis, came little by little to signify a real condition. He could think of little save the goddess. Many an all-night vigil he spent in her temple, praying that she would appear unto him. But the goddess failed to manifest herself.

"In a frantic effort to lure the goddess into his arms Forimar inaugurated a contest: to sculpture a statue of Astis that should, by its ineffable beauty, overcome the goddess's scruples about mating with a mortal. The treasurer was aghast at the rewards that Forimar offered; but, with Fusonio's influence gone, there was nothing to stop Forimar. He offered not only a huge prize for first place, but also rewards for all the other sculptors, win or lose.

"Consequently, a number of persons entered the contest who had never sculptured anything in their lives, and some very strange works of art were submitted. One was an untrimmed log with the bark on, whose submitter averred that the spirits had told him that this symbolized the true inward nature of the goddess. Another brought a simple boulder, and another a tangle of iron straps riveted together.

"These were too much even for Forimar, who decided that he was being made sport of. He had these self-styled sculptors whipped out of town and their productions thrown into the sea. He did the same with a sculpture showing, with utmost realism, the goddess being impregnated by the war god Heryx, albeit I have seen the like taken for granted in Mulvan. One had, he said, to draw the line somewhere.

"Natheless, many excellent sculptures were made, in bronze and in marble and in pottery. Nearly all showed the goddess in the likeness of a beautiful naked woman, for such had long been the convention of Novarian art. In due course, Forimar awarded the first prize to a certain Lukisto of Zolon, and lesser prizes to the other contestants. And all the hundreds of statues were placed in the temple of Astis, whose priests could scarcely perform their sacred functions, being compelled to worm their way amid masses of statuary.

"Now it happened that, contemporary with the reign of Forimar in Kortoli, Aussar was under the rule of a priest of Selindé, one Doubri. The priest had turned politician to overthrow the hereditary despots who had for a century cruelly oppressed the folk of Aussar. The new ruler called himself Doubri the Faultless, meaning that he had utterly conquered sin and lust in himself.

Doubri did, in fact, make many improvements in affairs in Aussar. But he took what many thought an overly rigid and censorious attitude towards those common human weaknesses that are deemed sins by theologians of the stricter sort. Please understand, Your Holiness, that I imply no criticism of your own regime in Tarxia; I do but strive to relate events as they happened.

"Moreover, this Doubri was not satisfied with 'cleaning up' Aussar, as he called his forceful suppression of drinking, dicing, wenching, and other manifestations of sin. The gods, he averred, had laid upon him the duty of liberating other nations from their slough of sin and error. And, when he looked about him, it seemed that Kortoli was most in need of his virtuous intervention. Its king was wholly absorbed in his pursuit of beauty; its people were sinning on a huge and raffish scale; its army had fallen into decay from neglect.

"So the Aussarians marched into Kortoli to right the wrongs they said were rampant in that kingdom. The Kortolian army fled without striking a blow and sought refuge in the capital, which was presently invested by the forces of Doubri. The Aussarians readied battering rams and wheeled belfries and other engines of war to break down or overswarm the walls. Although these events took place before the invention of the catapult, the besiegers managed natheless to deploy a terrifying array of equipment.

"When it looked as if all were lost, the fleet commanded by Forimar's brother Fusonio sailed into the harbor. Fusonio had gone to fabled Salimor and negotiated, a treaty of friendship with the Sophi of that land. When he entered the city, King Forimar ran to him without formality and embraced him, calling upon him to save them all.

"When Fusonio took stock of the situation, he was not encouraged, for the army had become a cowardly rabble, the arsenals contained few usable weapons, the walls were weak and tottery and needed but a few good pokes from a ram to bring them down, and the treasury was all but empty.

" 'Wherefore have we no money?' demanded Fusonio. 'There was an adequate balance when I left.'

"So Forimar told of the great sculpture contest. Fusonio refrained from saying what an idiot he thought his brother, although his glance conveyed the message. And he said: 'Before we surrender, let me see that proclamation Doubri issued when he attacked us.' And he read the document, noting the vile acts whereof Doubri the Faultless accused the Kortolians:

" '... men, and sometimes women, also, resort to mug-houses, where they consume fermented liquors, instead of drinking healthful boiled water. They waste their substance in games of chance. They indulge in croquet and other frivolous pastimes on the days sacred to gods, instead of spending all their free time in contemplation of their sins and prayers for forgiveness. Men and women openly bathe together in the public bath, which the degenerate King Forimar has erected, exposing their persons not only to those of their own sex, which is bad enough, but even to those of the other, which is an unspeakable abomination. They commit fornication and adultery unpunished. Even when lawfully wedded, they copulate in a state of nudity, for sensual pleasure instead of for the righteous purpose of creating offspring to praise the gods. They wear gaudy raiment and wasteful jewelry instead of the chaste and sober garments that please the gods. They lend money at interest, which is sinful as against nature. They exploit the working class by wringing a profit from the labor of these unfortunates. They sell goods by lying about the virtues of their commodities, excusing this mendacity by calling it "salesmanship" . . .'

" 'Well!' said Fusonio, 'if this priest overcome us, I see we can look forward to a jolly time under his rule. What is this about the bath house? We Kortolians have always bathed together.'

" 'Oh,' said Forimar, 'Doubri is an utter fanatic on nudity. To him it is actually worse than fornication. Why, in Aussar, everybody is supposed to bathe in his shirt, even in privacy. Married couples are commanded to wear long gowns to bed, these being furnished with slits in the appropriate places for those who wish to beget children for the glory of the gods.'

"Fusonio thought a while, then said: 'Let me see those statues of Astis, for which you so rashly squandered our treasury.' And the king took his brother to the temple of Astis, where Fusonio spent some time, now and then passing an appreciative hand over a particularly well-rounded curve of one of the statues.

" 'All right,' said Fusonio at last. 'I think I know what to do. But lest I merely rescue you from one such predicament, dear brother, only to have you plunge us all into another, I must ask that you abdicate in my favor. Otherwise, I will return to my ships and sail away, for an excellent post as minister for western affairs awaits me in Salimor if I choose to return thither.'

"Forimar pleaded and wept to no avail. He cursed

and threatened and stamped and pulled his own hair in rage and frustration. But Fusonio would not bulge a finger-breadth. When Forimar commanded his body-guards to seize his brother, they suddenly became deaf, saying: 'What is that, sire? I cannot understand you.' So at last Forimar signed the document of abdication, threw the royal seal at his brother, and stamped off to compose a piece of music that is still known as the Angry Sonata.

"King Fusonio then commanded that all the statues of Astis be covered with wrappings and set up on the wall. And when the assault began, the wrappings were pulled off, and there stood those hundreds of statues of the naked Astis.

"Doubri was watching from beyond bowshot. Being near-sighted, he asked his men what was toward. And when he learnt, he was filled with horror. For, plainly, his soldiers could not scale the walls without coming face to face with all these lewd statues. Arrows could indeed be shot at them, but these would merely chip and mar them slightly, and meanwhile the minds of the archers would be filled with unholy sensual thoughts. Since the catapult did not yet exist, he could not smash the statues with stone balls from a distance, as he could today.

"Doubri remained encamped for a few more days. He made a half-hearted attack on the wall, wheeling up a ram tortoise to batter it. But, not needing to take cover from arrow-shot, the defenders easily caught the head of the ram in the bight of a chain and upset the whole engine. Doubri also tried tunnelling, but the defenders flooded the tunnels.

"Doubri knew he could not starve out the defenders, because the Kortolian navy, reinforced by Fusonio's squadron, still commanded the local waters. When a sickness broke out among the Aussarians, Doubri raised the siege and marched away, only to find on his return to Aussar City that his government had fallen, and that one of the more promising younger members of the despot's family had been made ruler in his place.

"And that is the tale of Forimar the Esthete and Doubri the Faultless. The moral, as we see it in Kortoli, is that both Forimar's artistry and Doubri's morality would have been good things in their way, had they been applied in moderation. But any virtue can be turned into a vice by indulging it with excessive rigor and consistency."

Jorian and his audience now stood in the portico of the temple, outside the great bronze doors. Bit by bit, as he unfolded his tale, he had edged away from the central square, along the nave, and out the main doors. As he did so, he kept an ear cocked towards the holy of holies. At any moment, he expected Karadur and Valdonius to sidle quietly up and rejoin the group. The theocrat was saying:

"A most edifying and amusing tale, Doctor Maltho. Even in our holy cultus, we must sometimes curb the excessive zeal of some of our colleagues. We know that we alone possess the ultimate truth, and that it is incumbent upon us to propagate this verity and to extirpate error; but in this extirpation, excessive violence sometimes defeats its own—"

GLOOP! An extraordinary sound issued from the temple: a sound like a frog's croak, but augmented to the loudness of a lion's roar or a buffalo's bellow.

"Good Gorgolor, what is that?" cried one of the episcopals, turning to look back through the doors. Then the crimson-clad priest staggered back with a shriek, clapping a hand to his forehead. "The Holy Frog save us! The statue has come to life!"

GLOOP! came the bellow, closer, and a squashy, thumping sound accompanied it. Then out through the bronzen doors leaped the emerald god, the same size as he had been on his pedestal but now informed with life. Gorgolor landed among the group outside the doorway. Jorian leaped aside, but several others, including the theocrat, were bowled over. With a final GLOOP, the gigantic frog took off on another soaring leap into the darkness.

Jorian hastily gave Kylo a hand up and picked up the theocrat's battered white felt crown. But Kylo paid no heed, either to Jorian or to his sacerdotal headpiece.

"Send men in pursuit!" he screamed, dancing on the marble. "The god headed for the Swamp of Spraa, and if he gets there we shall never catch him. Turn out the army! Fetch nets! Hurry! Hurry! Are you all turned to stone? You, Eades, send out the pursuit! The rest of you follow me!"

The little fat man set off at a run down the path through the temenos that led eastward, his white robe fluttering. As they ran, others rushed out of the dark to ask the cause of the commotion. When they heard, they joined the pursuit with cries of horror and lamentation. Within a few breaths, a motley throng, many in nightdress, was streaming away eastward along one of Tarxia's winding streets.

Jorian, Karadur, and Valdonius remained alone in the portico. Karadur was weeping again. Beyond the temenos they could glimpse the movement of torches and lanthorns, as the word of the transformation of their god spread swiftly through Tarxia City and hundreds dropped whatever they were doing to run towards the East Gate.

"Well," said Jorian, eyeing his companions, "I suppose your damned spells went agley again?"

"One might say so; one might say so," replied Valdonius, ostentatiously preserving his poise. "Peradventure we mistranslated a word in that old scroll, which is writ in a very archaic form of the language. Natheless, the results will be nearly as satisfactory."

"In any case," said Jorian, "methinks Karadur and I had best flee whilst the Tarxians are preoccupied with catching their god. Where's your ass, Karadur?"

"I abandoned it in the camp of the Gendings, to give myself more time before the barbarians suspected I had left them. I came to Tarxia by a ship from Istheun."

"Do you own a beast of burden, Doctor Valdonius?"

"Why," said Valdonius, "I have a matched pair of whites to draw my chariot. But I cannot break the pair—"

"Oh, yes you can! Either you turn one of those animals over to Karadur to ride, or the theocrat shall hear of your part in this even's events."

"You would not inform on your confederates, would you?"

"Try me and see. I'll talk Kylo into thinking the blame is all yours. Now that I think of it, I'll also tell them you've been practicing sorcery, which is true; I know enough of magic to know that swords do not stick in their scabbards on a word of command, without the aid of a spirit."

"My masters," said Karadur, wiping his eyes on his sleeve, "why does not Doctor Valdonius drive his chariot to Metouro, to attend the Conclave with us? Then he could carry me in his car. The Altruists will need every vote."

"I cannot," said Valdonius. "I must forgather with those of my opinion, to see if we cannot overthrow this priestly tyranny with one sharp blow. Such a chance may not recur during my lifetime. I will lend you the horse; but I expect you to stable it in Metouro until I can send a servant to fetch it back— if I do not end up standing on a pile of faggots."

"Or you may have to flee to Metouro yourself," said Jorian. "When the hierarchy recovers its wits, it will soon infer that you must have had something to do with the theophany of their god. Meanwhile, let's be on our way whilst the gates are still open."

# X

# The Faceless Five

Jorian and Karadur rode down the vale of the Kyamos on the fifth of the Month of the Pike. Spring was in full tide. Flowers of a hundred hues bloomed everywhere, every pond resounded to the croaking of frogs, and all the trees were in leaf. Although the drowsy heat of summer had not yet arrived, the warmth of the air hinted at its coming.

The two riders—Jorian on his faithful if bumpy Oser, Karadur on the white pony borrowed from Valdonius in Tarxia—no longer wore the heavy sheepskin coats that had seen them across the steppes of Shven. These garments were rolled up and lashed to their saddles behind them. The journey had taken them twice as long as it would have taken Jorian alone, because Karadur did not dare to move at more than a fast walk. Between fear of falling and fear of being late for the Conclave, the old magician was in a constant swivet.

The Kyamos was a small river, which presently widened out into the broad Lake Volkina. On the north shore of the lake stood Metouro City—or New Metouro as it was more exactly called. A bowshot from the shore, directly in front of the city, rose an islet, on which stood the Goblin Tower.

Lake Volkina was of relatively recent origin. A landslide in the western part of the valley had blocked the course of the Kyamos a few centuries before, flooding the original Metouro City and creating the lake. In time, the lake had overflowed the natural dam formed by the landslide, and the Kyamos had resumed its course across Ir to the Western Ocean.

At the East Gate, as they dismounted and gave their names to the sentries, a small man in gray appeared. "Doctor Karadur?"

"Aye."

"Drakomas of Phthai, at your service. Our colleague, Doctor Vorko, has asked me to conduct you to your quarters in the Goblin Tower."

"I feared," said Karadur, "that, because of our lateness, all space in the Tower would be taken."

"A thousand nays, fair sir! Knowing the worth of yourself and your companion and the burden you bear, we reserved a suite for you early. Pray come!" To the sentries, Drakomas said: "We vouch for these men."

The sentries waved Jorian and Karadur through. Metouro proved a larger and handsomer city than Tarxia, with straight streets crossing at right angles instead of Tarxia's tangle of winding alleys. While more prosperous-looking than those of Tarxia, the people seemed dour, reserved, and tight-lipped, giving the strangers brief, sidelong glances without any change of expression.

Drakomas led the two travelers, not directly to the boat landing for the Tower, but to an inn. He saw to the stabling of their mounts. In an upstairs room, they found a man and two nonhuman beings. Karadur said:

"Master Vorko, permit me to present my apprentice, Jorian of Ardamai. Jorian, know that this is Vorko of Hendau, the head of our White Faction."

"Your apprentice?" said Vorko, in a voice even deeper than Jorian's. "Is this not the former king of Xylar, who accompanied you as bodyguard and factotum?"

"Aye."

"Has he then determined to enter the profession?" Vorko of Hendau was an extremely tall, lean, knobby man, with a big, hooked nose and a jutting chin. His two attendants were of about human size and shape, but they had scales, tails, muzzles, fangs, talons, pointed ears, and mustaches consisting of a pair of fleshy tendrils, which constantly curled and uncurled and waved about like the tentacles of a small squid. Their big, yellow eyes had slit pupils.

Jorian was staring at the nonhumans as Karadur replied: "Nay, he has not taken the vows. But I hope that, by exposing him to the exoteric side of magic at the Conclave, I shall arouse his curiosity to the point where he will wish to do so. Meanwhile, by your leave, I will continue to call him 'apprentice' to make his admission easy. I trust that none will take technical umbrage at my so doing."

"I think not," said Vorko. "The rules are pretty loose these days. But what of your mission?"

"Esteemed colleague, we are happy to report success. The Kist, Jorian!"

Jorian unslung the little chest from his back and handed it to Vorko by its rope sling. "Here you are, sir," he said. "And now, since I have performed the task for which you laid me under a geas, may I ask that you lift this geas forthwith?"

"Oh, murrain!" said the enchanter. "You're entitled to it, youngling, and you shall have it—but not just now, for want of time. We must needs forth at once to the Tower, without even pausing to wash up. We shall be late as it is. Of course, Master Jorian, you need not attend the Conclave if you do not wish."

"Oh, I will indeed attend, forsooth! 'Tis a small enough reward for the risks and hardships I've undergone for you and your colleagues in the past half-year."

"Very good; off we go. The Kist will be safe here, with my servants to guard it."

"What *are* they?" asked Jorian.

"Demons from the Twelfth Plane, hight Zoth and Frig, fixed in material form on this plane and bound to my service for nine years. They are good, faithful guardians, albeit not very intelligent. Their main complaint is that I should invoke a demoness or two for them to consort with. But let us hasten; the ferry service is incredible." Vorko spoke a few syllables in an unknown tongue to Zoth and Frig, who bobbed their fanged heads in acknowledgment. Zoth picked up the duffel of the two travelers and silently followed them through the streets to the lake shore.

The lake shore of Metouro had several boathouses for small boats, a stretch of bathing beach, and a few small piers for pleasure craft. Lake Volkina was not large enough to carry commerce. On one pier, scores of men in dark robes and cloaks were lined up. Jorian, Karadur, and Vorko took their places in the line. The pier pointed towards the Goblin Tower, a bowshot away. A pair of rowboats, each pulled by a single rower, plied the water between the pier and the tower, taking passengers across three at a time.

"We've complained of this pediculous ferry service to the Faceless Five," said Vorko in a fretful tone, "but they as much as invited us to move our Conclave elsewhither. They've run the polis so long as they pleased that they are not accustomed to advice or complaints from anybody."

"The Metourians seem a grim lot," said Jorian.

"You would be grim, too, an you had to watch every word lest some nark bear tales to your rulers," said Vorko. "That's what it is to live in a land ruled by a secret society. Suspicion is the way of life here. They would not suffer us to meet in Metouro at all, save that we promised to confine our activities to the Tower. They recall the events that led up to the building of the Tower in the first place."

"I know not that tale," said Jorian.

A magician, robe fluttering, glided in on a broomstick to a landing on the beach. As he approached the shoreward end of the pier, with a carpetbag in one hand and his broomstick in the other, Vorko called out:

"Hail, Sir Fendix! You were asking me, Master Jorian?"

"About the Gob—"

"Certes! I will tell you the whole story—God den, good Doctor Bhulla! How fares the art of Thaumaturgy in Janareth? To resume, Master Jorian: Once upon a time, Metouro was a republic, with a constitution like that of Vindium today. There was an elected archon, and a senate of heads of propertied families, and an assembly of the people. This scheme worked very well for many years, so long as Metouro was poor and backward, having just risen from the dark age that followed the fall of the Three Kingdoms. Ah, greeting, good Master Nors!"

This salutation was addressed to another magician, who first appeared in the form of a whirlwind of dust. This dust column danced along the beach until it neared the pier, when it collapsed into a brown-robed man.

"The trouble with all these flying spells," said Vorko, "is that they leave the thaumaturge so spent that he can do little for days thereafter. Watch Doctor Nors and Sir Fendix—the latter is an authentic Othomaean knight, turned to magic—and you'll see them dozing through all the sessions—some of which, I confess, are hard enough to wake in anyway.

"As I was saying, the republic flourished until wealth accumulated. Then the leading families gathered more and more land and coin into their hands, until a small clique of the rich ruled the polis, squeezing the much more numerous poor until the latter could barely survive. Behold, here comes Antonerius of Ir on his dragon! He is always fain to make a show of his arrival, but I'll wager he will have trouble stabling his monster."

The magician Antonerius glided into a landing on the back of a wyvern, a flying reptile with a forty-foot wingspread. The wind of the creature's wings fluttered the robes and cloaks of the magicians on the pier. A couple of attendants ran up to take the reptile's reins but shrank back when the beast arched its neck and snapped at them, disclosing fearsome fangs. Its rider whacked it over the head with a goad until it quieted.

"Why do they all land here instead of at the Tower?" asked Jorian.

"Because our good president, Aello of Gortii, has laid a preventive spell upon the Tower, lest in the heat of debate some colleague be tempted to launch a thunderbolt at his opponent or otherwise to wreak magical woe upon him. Hence no spell works in the Tower. If Doctor Sir Fendix, for ensample, were to seek to alight on the battlements, his broom might lose its power just before he touched down and dash him to his death on the rocks below.

"To resume: There arose in Metouro a man named Charens, one of the rich who had lost his wealth. He said the other oligarchs had swindled him out of his property. They said he had lost it by profligacy and dissipation, and we cannot now tell which had the right of it.

"This Charens became a leader of the poor, demanding reforms: such as compelling the rich to pay taxes, which irksome duty they had thitherto managed most featly to shirk. And he demanded that public moneys be spent on amenities for the poor, such as a public lazaretto and an orphanage, instead of things that benefited the rich only, hike hunting lodges and banquet halls. At the next vote, Charens was elected archon despite the efforts of the rich to intimidate the voters and miscount the ballots."

The wyvern had at last been brought under control. While several attendants held its head by ropes, the rider dismounted and tied the animal's wings in the furled position, so that it could no longer flap. Then the attendants dragged away the reptile, hissing and bucking. A huge black vulture now glided in, flopped down on the sand, and changed into another wizard.

"As soon as Charens got power," continued Vorko, "he began to effect his reforms. This so enraged the rich that they hired a gang of bravos to slay Charens as he walked home from the marketplace. Since, under the then constitution, the man having the second largest number of votes became vice-archon, the candidate of the rich became archon and rescinded all of Charens' reforms.

"The oligarchs, howsomever, had not reckoned on Charens' younger brother, Charenzo. This Charenzo had greatly loved and admired his brother, and now he swore to devote his life to vengeance. And soon he had gathered a secret following. One year after the murder of his brother, he led a revolt, which slaughtered many of the rich and forced the rest to flee. This was the first of the great massacres, which for the next few years convulsed the history of Metouro, with heads piled in heaps in the marketplace, and howling mobs cheering on the torture of captives and tearing their opponents' women and children to pieces.

"Charenzo proved a less able and enlightened and much more violent man than his brother. Reforms and public amenities interested him less than vengeance upon his brother's slayers—a class which he little by little expanded to include everybody who opposed him. Hardly a day passed in Metouro but that some unfortunate was led out to death at his command as a suspected oligarch, or at least as a factor of oligarchy.

"With each execution, Charenzo made more enemies, and even his friends began to be bored and alarmed by the endless charges of treason and oligarchical leanings. When a party of exiled oligarchs appeared with an army of Shvenic mercenaries, they routed Charenzo's armed rabble and seized control of Metouro once more. Then they had their turn at massacre and execution.

"Charenzo escaped from Metouro. Since his people had failed him, he determined to seek supernatural aid. So he sought out the sorcerer Synelius in Govannian. This Synelius was a Metourian, exiled because he was under sentence as a witch. One of Charenzo's own judges had sentenced him in his absence, Synelius having learnt from his spirits what was toward and having prudently fled.

"Now, however, Charenzo made common cause with his former foe. And Synelius said that, yes, he could summon an army of goblins—the vulgar name for demons of the Ninth Plane—to oust the present regime in Metouro. The new oligarchical government, like their predecessors, had learnt nought from experience and were oppressing and exploiting the poor as ruthlessly as ever.

"So Charenzo and Synelius and a host of goblins suddenly appeared amongst the Metourians. Terrified of supernatural beings, the terrible Shvenic mercenaries fled. So did many Metourians, until Charenzo closed the gates and posted goblins as sentinels.

"So began another period of rule by the fierce and implacable Charenzo. Being nocturnal, the goblins were seldom seen in the daytime. But at night everybody cowered behind locked and barred doors, lest one of these bouncing, huge-headed creatures enter to drag him off to some nameless doom.

"Charenzo resumed his reign of terror, until at length Synelius warned him that he was killing off the Metourians faster that they were being born, and that if he continued this process long enough he would have no subjects left to rule. This advice aroused Charenzo's suspicions of his ally, or perhaps he had planned all along to rid himself of Synelius as too dangerous to let live.

"Professing great interest in Synelius' magic, he flattered the old man until the latter revealed the spells and words of power whereby he controlled the goblins.

Then Charenzo had Synelius arrested and thrown into a dungeon in the bowels of the citadel, which stood on a hill in the midst of the city. Synelius called upon his goblins to rescue him, but Charenzo countermanded the order. So the goblins did nothing. Not having his magical paraphernalia in his cell, Synelius could not work a spell to free himself by other magical means.

"Meanwhile, a conspiracy had arisen among a group of Metourians, which included representatives of men of all degrees: rich, poor, and intermediate. These people formed a secret society, called simply the Brotherhood, with passwords and oaths and other mummery. They chose a committee of five to command the society, including representatives from Metourians of as many different kinds as possible: rich and poor, young and old, male and female. Thus, if one was a rich old woman, another would be a poor young man to balance her.

"Through one of its members who was also a member of the prison guard, this Brotherhood heard about the imprisonment of Synelius. With the help of this member, they gained access to the dungeon and presented forged documents apparently signed by Charenzo, commanding the warder to deliver Synelius to them. Thus they got the sorcerer out of jail. And when they had taken him to a place of refuge, they urged him to throw in his lot with them. When he agreed to this, they demanded to know if he could get rid of the goblins. Alas no, he said, for that Charenzo now controlled them and could countermand his orders that they return to their own plane.

"Things were not, however, hopeless, for he knew a mighty spell that would turn the goblins to stone. When he said it required human sacrifice, the conspirators drew lots. And when a promising youth drew the fatal lot, the oldest conspirator, who had been an oligarch, insisted on taking his place, saying he was not for many

years and was too full of obsolete ideas and prejudices
to be useful in the new regime.

"So the spell was cast. There was a mighty flash of
lightning, and a deafening roar of thunder, and a shaking of the earth. The citadel collapsed with a frightful
crash, burying Charenzo in the ruins, and a landslide
blocked the Kyamos below Metouro City. On that
instant, every goblin in Metouro was turned into stone.
When the conspirators ran to see how Synelius fared,
they found the old sorcerer dead with a peaceful look
on his face.

"The Brotherhood then reorganized the city
according to their own ideas. They insisted on
remaining secret, and this is why Metouro is ruled
today by a committee of the Brotherhood called the
Faceless Five. These appear in their official capacity
wearing black masks, and nobody is supposed to know
who they are. When the blocking of the Kyamos created Lake Volkina and flooded the old Metouro City,
they built a new one, laid out by an architect with
straight, wide streets. Since the citadel was in ruins and
the hill whereon it stood was become a mere islet in
Lake Volkina, they cleared away the rubbish and built
a new stronghold, in which they used not only the
unbroken stones from the former citadel but also the
hundreds of stones into which the goblins had been
turned. Thus this edifice became known as the Goblin Tower.

"Originally, the Faceless Five dwelt in the Goblin
Tower. But a century ago they gave up this habit, partly
because it made their comings and goings too conspicuous, so that their anonymity was hard to preserve, and
partly because the Tower itself was uncomfortable, having been designed more as a fortress than as a
human abode."

"How have the Metourians made out under their
Faceless Five?" asked Jorian.

"Well in some ways, not so well in others. Like all such self-perpetuating cliques, the main concern of the Five had been to keep all power firmly in their own hands. On the whole, they have given the polis an efficient government, with a fair degree of prosperity. They still have rich and poor, but no industrious man need starve. Not having a glittering court like Mulvan's or an extravagant temple like Tarxia's to keep up, they have not felt the need to squeeze every last farthing out of their subjects. And the custom of choosing members of the Five to represent persons of as many different kinds as possible has made their rule fairly even-handed.

"On the other hand, there is precious little personal freedom in Metouro. The ordinary citizen says little, lest his interlocutor be an informer, and he looks over his shoulder before answering a question about the time of day. Personally I prefer Vindium, with all its disorder and corruption, to quite so oppressively virtuous a regime. Unless—" (the enchanter smiled wryly) "—I myself could be the ruler!"

During this story, Jorian and his companions had inched forward along the pier. As Vorko finished, one of the rowboats drew up, and the three stepped aboard. Zoth dropped Jorian's and Karadur's bundles of gear into the boat, nodded silently to Vorko, and started back for shore.

# XI

# The Goblin Tower

As the surly, silent boatman rowed them towards the island, the Goblin Tower loomed up over their bow. It was a simple structure in the form of a narrow ellipse with forty-foot curtain walls. At each end, a single large round tower rose another twenty-odd feet higher. A slender arched stone bridge joined these towers near the summits. The shape of the islet dictated the extreme narrowness of the structure.

The Tower had a drawbridge, which, however, did not join anything at its outer end. It merely hung out over the water and served as a landing pier. Jorian climbed out with his companions and followed them through the gate, under the portcullis, and into a hall. There was no open court inside this tower; the edifice was completely roofed over and built up inside.

In the hall, magicians stood in line before a desk, at which sat a man in a black robe, with a red, conical cap of stiff paper on his head. On the front of this cap was written, in large letters with a broad-pointed pen, the words:

FORCES OF
PROGRESS
SIXTY-FIRST
ANNUAL
CONCLAVE
GNOUX,
RECEPTION

275

A bulletin board, listing the events of the convention, stood near Receptionist Gnoux.

As Vorko and Karadur reached the desk, the receptionist asked their names, wrote them on a piece of paper, and pasted the slips to the fronts of conical caps like his own but black. He handed them their caps and room keys. When Jorian's turn came, Karadur told Gnoux:

"This is Jorian of Kortoli, my apprentice. I have paid your registration fee, Jorian."

"Welcome, Master Jorian," said Gnoux. "How spell you that? ... Here you are." Gnoux handed Jorian a dunce cap like the others, but white to denote Jorian's rank as apprentice, with his name written on the front. "You shall room in twenty-three, with Doctor Karadur."

"Have you an extra key?" asked Jorian. "The good doctor and I may come and go at different times."

"Here you are. Welcome again to this learned assemblage!"

Jorian asked: "Has one Porrex of Vindium registered?"

Gnoux consulted a list. "Nay, though you're the third conventioner to ask me that."

"Peradventure he's swindled the others, too, and they hope to take it out of his hide."

"Well—ah—" said Gnoux, trying to hide a smile, "'tis not my affair, but I did overhear some remarks about red-hot pincers applied to sensitive areas."

Jorian followed Vorko to the ballroom at the end of the hall, which had been turned into an auditorium. It was full of seated male and female magicians, wearing conical caps. When they had found seats, Vorko whispered to Jorian:

"That's President Aello, up there."

The president, wearing a golden dunce cap, was a tall, stooped old man with a long white beard cascading down the front of his black gown. He was introducing celebrities, each of whom received a patter of applause:

". . . and I am informed that we have with us the distinguished necromancer, Omphes of Thamoe, whose stable of spirits includes some of the most eminent shades not yet reincarnated. Will you stand, Doctor Omphes? Thank you . . . And we also have the preëminent wizardess, Goania of Othomae; will you take a bow, Mistress Goania? . . ."

Jorian remembered the gray-haired woman and tried to catch her eyes, but she was too distant. He squirmed on his bench, looking about him. A figure standing against the back wall, near the door, caught his attention. This was a burly, porcine man wearing a red cap. With a shock, Jorian recognized Boso, son of Triis, the ex-gongringer with whom he had fought in Othomae, and whom Goania had taken into her service. Boso not only carried a cudgel but also wore a sword. Jorian wondered if Vanora, too, would be there. Aello of Gortii droned on:

". . . the worthy astrologer, Ktessis of Psara; will you stand, Master Ktessis? . . ."

Increasingly bored and hungry, Jorian wondered if he had been so clever to insist on attending the Conclave after all. He soon lost track of the names. His eyelids became heavy, and twice he caught himself falling forward from his sitting position. He was pinching himself to keep awake when Aello mercifully ended the introductions and announced:

"The first item on the program will be a paper by the learned Bhulla of Janareth on 'Familial Organization and Kinship Nomenclature amongst Demons of the Eighth Plane.' Doctor Bhulla."

Amid scattered applause, a small, potbellied, brown man took Aello's place on the dais and began to read a paper, in a squeaky monotone with a strong Mulvanian accent. Although Jorian, if largely self-educated, was fairly well-read, the discourse was completely unintelligible to him. When he found himself nodding again, he whispered to Karadur:

"I'm going out for a while. Where's our room?"

"One flight up at the west end. I shall accompany you, for the next item is an auction of magical properties, old manuscripts, and historic mementoes of our profession. I think I will absent myself therefrom, also."

"Is there any place to eat in this pile?"

"There will be a dinner here, in this ballroom, one hour ere sunset. A costume ball will follow."

Jorian suppressed a groan. "That's three hours yet! I shall starve meanwhile. Lend me a few pence, will you?"

He followed Karadur out into the main hall but paused to look the company over while the old magician tottered off towards his quarters. In the main hall, Jorian discovered that many others at the Conclave, too, were playing truant from the lecture. Little groups of magicians stood in knots, discussing professional matters with expressive gestures and grimaces. The shrill laughs of women cut the air; there were several such groups, from young to old, some wearing the conical caps of registered magicians and some not. The latter, Jorian supposed, were attached to the magicians in one capacity or another. He wondered about Karadur's insistence that celibacy was an absolute requirement for rising high in the profession.

A small, dimly lit room was filled with magicians sitting at tables, munching dried chick-peas and drinking wine or beer. Jorian squeezed in and took an empty seat. The three men at the table were in the midst of a hot technical discussion. They smiled and nodded to Jorian with absent-minded politeness and went on with their talk:

". . . that astral movement being circular, every azotic or magnetic emission which does not encounter its medium returns with force to its point of departure, does it not?"

"Aye," said another, "but you must admit that the duodenary, being a complete and cyclic number in the

universal analogies of nature, invariably attracts and
absorbs the thirteenth, which is regarded as a sinister
and superfluous number. Hence your cycles will fail to
recapitulate their elements in synchronous order—"

"You are both wrong," said the third, "having forgotten that in nature there are two forces producing equi-
librium, and these three constitute a single law. Here,
then, is the triad resumed in unity, and by adding the
conception of unity to that of the triad we are brought
to the tetrad, the first square and perfect number, the
source of all numerical combinations and the principle
of all forms. Hence the astral currents will cycle homo-
geneously . . ."

Jorian became so uncomfortable at being compelled
to listen to this incomprehensible talk, while being
completely ignored, that he left as soon as he had finished his ale. Outside, he paused before the bulletin
board. The board listed the lecture now in progress
and the auction to follow it. After that would come a
panel discussion on "Invisibility," followed in turn by
an informal dinner and a costume ball.

The next morning would be taken up with a debate
over the Altruists' proposal to end all secrecy surrounding magic, offering its benefits freely to the general public. There would be a testimonial luncheon to
Aello as outgoing president. In the afternoon there
would be several learned papers, including a demon-
stration of evoking a fiend from the thirty-third Mulvanian hell. A small red star after the name of this
experiment indicated that it was dangerous.

The evening would see the formal dinner, with
awards to deserving magicians and a speech by Doctor
Yseldia of Metouro, the guest of honor. Madame Yseldia would talk of recent advances in the enchantment
of flying broomsticks. After the banquet would come a
series of small closed meetings, to which master magicians only were admitted.

The third and final day would have a couple of

papers in the morning and then the business meeting, at which a new president would be elected, the site of the next year's Conclave chosen, and amendments to the constitution of the Forces of Progress considered.

Having absorbed this information, Jorian began to walk away from the board. Then he started and stared as he sighted Vanora, talking with a group of women. The tall, angular girl wore a long gown of emerald-green silk, with a little round cap on her long, black, glossy hair. She was much changed from the bedraggled wench he had left in Othomae. Despite the irregularity of her features, she looked almost pretty and certainly attractive.

"Good morrow, Mistress Vanora!" he said.

"Well, Jorian!" she cried. "Your pardon, girls; here's an old gossip of mine." She took Jorian's arm and walked down the hall. "Did you really rescue that box of moldy screeds from the King of Kings?"

"Aye, that we did and got away with whole skins. How wags thy world?"

She made a face. "That stinkard Boso ... But Goania's a dear. I stay with him more for her sake than for his." She pinched a piece of the emerald gown and pulled it out from her body. "She got me this."

"Very pretty. Didn't I see Boso in the ballroom just now?"

"Aye; he's been made sergeant-at-arms, which is to say the same post as ejector that he held at the Silver Dragon in Othomae. But never mind me, who have led a tame enough existence for the past sixmonth. Tell me of your adventures! Rumor has gone out of your hairbreadth escapes."

Jorian grimaced. "Most of these escapades I should have been most heartily glad to be quit of whilst they were happening, I can tell you, however jolly they sound in the later retelling."

"I suppose you'll say you were frightened half to death?"

"'Tis the simple truth. After all, I'm no swaggering gallant, but a simple craftsman who would like to settle—but ere I bore you with a four-hour account of my doings, can you find me something to eat? I have scarcely bared a fang since dawn. We rode from Thamoe to Metouro this morn and then came directly hither without stopping to eat or wash. So I'll not utter another word until I'm fed."

Vanora showed Jorian to the kitchen and wheedled a bun and a flagon of beer from the chief cook. Between bites, Jorian told of some of his experiences in Mulvan and Shven.

Two hours later, he paused to say: "Time is passing, and here I waste our time in self-conceited narration of my own petty affairs! I can resist almost any temptation, save an invitation to talk. Methinks the session nears its end, and I had best rejoin my master."

"Have you become Karadur's apprentice in fact as well as in name?"

"Nay, though a reason for attending this Conclave is to see how I like the profession of magic. But I doubt if the rewards of high magic will persuade me to give up women."

"By giving up all the pleasures of the flesh, Goania tells me, the most skillful adepts can prolong their lives to twice or thrice that of common mortals."

"Or perhaps it only seems twice or thrice as long, without wine or women."

Vanora looked at Jorian in a marked manner. "Ah— it is about such matters that I would speak to you in conf—"

"Your pardon, Mistress Vanora, but I really must go, instanter!" Jorian handed his empty flagon to a cook. "I'm stinking filthy from travel and must remedy this condition before dinner."

He gave the girl his arm and started briskly for the main hall. There he excused himself and found room twenty-three. He let himself in with his key and found a small sitting room and a small bedroom with two narrow beds. Karadur had been to the suite but had gone out again. Jorian cleaned himself up, trimmed his beard to a dashing point, put on his one clean shirt, tried to shine his battered boots, and returned to the ballroom.

There he found that the auction had ended and the panel discussion on invisibility was in progress. The panelists, who sat in a row on the platform, had finished their prepared statements and were answering questions from the audience. President Aello sat at one end of the row and pointed his wand at auditors he wished to recognize. As Jorian entered, a man stood up, beginning:

"I should like to ask—"

"State your name and specialty, pray," said Aello.

"Merkon of Boaktis, theurgic sorcerer. I should like to ask the honorable members what the advantage would be to making all of themselves but their eyeballs invisible? I should find a pair of disembodied eyeballs following me around quite as obvious as a visible man, and much more disconcerting."

"As I thought I had explained," said one panelist, "total invisibility, while achievable, has the disadvantage of blinding the person employing it, because there is no interaction betwixt the rays of visible light and the substance of human eyes to produce the sensory phenomenon we know as 'sight.' I thought this was known to every apprentice. Hence total invisibility is practical only as a measure for extreme emergencies, when one is hotly pursued. Since the invisible one cannot see until he lifts the spell, he must needs rely upon other senses to warn him of the close approach of his foes— especially his astral sight. But this faculty is poorly developed in most mortals. With visible eyeballs, on the other hand, one can at leisure examine forbidden things, provided one stays far enough from the nearest observer that one's eyes are not noticeable. . ."

Jorian kept looking for Karadur but could not see him. Hundreds of dunce-capped magicians looked much alike from the back, and Karadur had shifted his place. Jorian began tiptoeing around the aisle at the edge of the hall, in order to see the faces of the audience from the side. In so doing, he came face to face with Boso.

"You!" whispered the sergeant-at-arms, reaching for his sword, "I ought to—"

"Behave yourself, Boso!" said Jorian.

"Futter you! You behave *yourself,* or I'll—"

"Shh!" said several magicians, facing towards the pair and scowling.

Boso quieted, and Jorian continued his search, sweeping his glance back and forth against row after row of faces—pink faces, gray faces, tan faces, brown faces; clean-shaven faces, mustached faces, bearded faces; young faces, middle-aged faces, old faces; male faces and female faces. At last, when he thought he would have to give up, he sighted Karadur across the auditorium, sitting with his conical cap on his head and his turban in his lap. The wizardess Goania sat next to him. Jorian quietly joined them.

The panel discussion was nearly over. When Aello declared the session adjourned, hundreds of magicians rose and stretched.

"Whither now?" said Jorian.

"There will be an aperitif in the library," said Karadur, "but I take no fermented beverages. I think I will rest until dinner. Why do you not escort Goania thither?"

"Colossal idea!" said Jorian. "Mistress Goania, may I have the honor?"

"One thing in parting," said Karadur. "Here, of all places, guard that flapping tongue!"

"I'll try," said Jorian.

\* \* \*

In the library, Jorian drank spiced wine and nibbled snacks of salt fish and cookies with Goania, who introduced him to countless wizards, sorcerers, necromancers, diviners, and other practitioners of the magical arts. He soon lost track of names and faces. During a pause, he asked the wizardess:

"How is Vanora making out With Boso?"

"Oh, they had a terrible quarrel yesterday and are not speaking today. But that is how things go with them. Tomorrow they will have forgotten what they were fighting over."

"She gave me the impression she wasn't happy with him. After all, she is a person of some intelligence, if badly organized, whereas he lacks the brains of a polliwog."

"That she is unhappy most of the time I grant. The question is would she be happier with anyone else? I doubt it, for it is her nature to be unhappy and to make those about her unhappy. All of us have some of this in our natures and she, poor girl, has more than most." Goania looked sharply at Jorian. "You and she were close at one time, weren't you?"

"Aye, though it was a painful pleasure."

"Are you nurturing sentimental ideas of 'taking her away from all this,' or otherwise sacrificing yourself to make her happy?"

"No-o," said Jorian hesitantly, because such ideas had in fact been flitting through his mind.

"Well, if any have, dismiss them at once. You cannot change the basic nature of a grown man or woman, even by magical spells. If you took up with her again, you would find you had acquired, not a lover, but a sparring partner—a rôle for which Boso's grossness and stupidity fit him far better than your qualities fit you."

Jorian drew himself up. "You forget, Mistress Goania, that I left five lovely wives behind in Xylar. One of them at least—my little Estrildis—I hope to fetch away some day, to settle down and lead a simple crafts-man's uneventful life."

Goania shook her head. "I have cast your nativity and studied your palm, and I fear that a quiet crafts-man's life is the one boon the gods do not have in store for you. As for the wenches, I suggest that you adhere to your resolve to regain your Estrildis when you are lured into other bypaths." She glanced across to where Vanora stood, surrounded by young men. "From the way she is guzzling, I suspect we have one of Vanora's lively evenings ahead of us."

"What mean you by that?"

The wizardess sighed. "You shall see."

The library became more and more crowded, as more conventioners drifted in. The noise rose, as each speaker found he needed to raise his voice to make himself heard. Soon the room was packed with magi-cians and their helpers, all shouting at the tops of their lungs.

Jorian tried to introduce himself and engage those about him in talk but, despite his natural gregariousness and garrulity, with little success. He had to bellow to make himself heard, and the replies, when they came, were mostly unintelligible. He could catch only an occasional word, and that word was often so distorted that he could not tell whether it was a common word misunderstood or some esoteric magical term.

After a while, Jorian became bored by this noncom-munication. He tried an experiment. To a long-bearded, dignified wizard, he solemnly shouted:

"Sir, did you know that the ultifang had metisold the otch whangle."

The wizard's bushy, white eyebrows rose, and he uttered what sounded like: "You do not say so! We mist certimate glasso in the thourimar!"

"Aye, sir, I had it from the bolimbrig gazoo. No

doubt abung it. When is the flolling gebisht in vemony?"

"On the fenty-nifth, I shink."

"Perzactly, perzactly. It's been a mosure, sir!"

But even this amusement palled in time. Jorian's feet were tired from standing and his head rang with the uproar when dinner was at long last announced. He took Goania in, but as an apprentice he ate with the others of his rank, while Goania joined Karadur to sup with the other master magicians. Remembering Karadur's last injunction, Jorian refrained from an account of his adventures. Instead, he confined himself to polite replies, leading questions to encourage the others to talk, and occasional quips and humorous verses to turn aside their curiosity about him.

"Are you donning a costume tonight?" asked one of his table mates.

"Alas! My master and I arrived late, without time to gather materials. Now I could only go as one shabby travel-worn apprentice. But tell me how this contest works, since this is my first Conclave."

"We must clear this hall to allow the servitors to remove the tables and push the benches back along the walls," said another apprentice. "A long platform is erected against yonder wall. Then those in costume assemble on the floor, whilst those not so clad sit on the benches. There is always a fuss over folk who stand up, blocking others' view, or inch forward into the press of the costume wearers.

"The master of ceremonies takes the names of all those in costume and calls upon them, one by one, to parade up one end of the platform and down the other, whilst the judges sit, looking judicious and marking their tablets. After all have paraded, the few best are called back to parade again, and from these the judges choose the prize winners."

"We have some comical rules," said another apprentice. "To give an example: human beings may parade

in the guise of spirits, but demons, spirits, or other
denizens of other planes and dimensions may not enter
the contest at all. You'll see old Aello standing at one
end of the platform and waving his wand at each con-
testant as he goes by. His great protective spell is supposed to make disguise by spirits impossible, but he
wants to make doubly sure."

"And then," resumed the first apprentice, "there is
a rule against complete nudity."

"Why?" said Jorian. "I have always thought that well-
formed women looked their best that way."

"So did some of our lady conventioners. It got to be
that twenty or thirty of these dames would parade as
nude as frogs, so that the event bade fair to degenerate
into a body-beauty contest and not a costume contest
at all. There was a terrific row, with factions shaking
fists and threatening maleficent spells. So a panel of the
oldest and wisest magicians was appointed to arbitrate.
These decided that a naked person is not, by definition,
wearing a costume."

"In other words," said Jorian, "no costume is no costume. A fine philosophical and grammatical point."

"Precisely," beamed the apprentice. "Hence, naked
human beings might not enter, not being in costume.
But that didn't end the matter. There was a squabble
only last year, when Madame Tarlustia, the Kortolian
sorceress, paraded with no adornment other than a
large jewel pasted into her navel. Did she qualify or
didn't she? They ruled that she qualified but won no
prizes, her garb displaying neither sufficient ingenuity,
nor effort, not esthetic appeal. But 'twas a near thing.
Had she been twenty years younger and twenty pounds
lighter, the decision might have gone the other way,
for she was still a fine figure of a woman."

Two hours after dinner, the company filed back into
the ballroom. Jorian noted that most of those in costume—as far as he could see their faces at all—tended

to be the younger element at the Conclave: the apprentices and assistants. The older wizards and wizardesses, by and large, preferred to sit sedately on the benches around the walls.

After an hour of milling about and getting the parade organized, the master of ceremonies mounted the platform. On the farther side of this platform, with their backs against the wall, sat the nine judges. President Aello stood at one end of the platform with his wand. The master of ceremonies looked at a list and called:

"Master Teleinos of Tarxia!"

An apprentice, dressed like a demon from the Fourth Plane, climbed the steps at one end of the platform, walked slowly past the judges, and descended the steps at the other end. While he paraded around the hall past the spectators, the master of ceremonies called:

"Masters Annyx and Forion of Solymbria!"

A dragon of cloth and lacquer, borne by two apprentices who represented the monster's legs, mounted the platform.

"Mistress Vanora of Govannian!"

Vanora, flushed but not staggering, marched up the platform in the guise of an undine. This consisited of a knee-length shift of transparent green gauze. Lengths of artificial seaweed were braided into her long black hair. She wore green gloves with webbing between the fingers, and her eyelids, lips, and toenails were painted green.

"Doctor Vingalfi of Istheun ..."

And so it went for three hours. In the end, Vanora won a third prize. Then an orchestra played. Jorian came up to congratulate Vanora, who was again surrounded by apprentices. Boso hovered, glowering unhappily, in the background. She was saying:

"They're playing a Kortolian volka. Which of you knows how to dance it."

"I was once deemed an expert," said Jorian,

extending his elbow for her to take. He nodded politely to Boso, saying: "With your kind permission, sir . . ."

"Oh, to the next incarnation with him!" said Vanora, seizing Jorian's arm and tugging him out upon the floor. "The witling can't dance a step."

Off they went, stamping and whirling. Although Vanora's breath was heavy with wine, the liquor she had drunk did not seem to have affected her excellent dancing. But the volka is vigorous, and the air was warm and balmy. By the end of the piece, both Jorian and Vanora were bathed in sweat. They found a refreshment table, where Vanora gulped down enough iced wine at one draft to have laid an ordinary drinker flat.

"Jorian dear," she said, "I was a damned fool to carry on about your serpent princess, as I did in Othomae. As if a drunken slut with a hot cleft, like me, should take umbrage at whom you frike on a mattress with! But it's my curse, to rail at every decent man and to bed with swine like Boso."

As she spoke, Jorian's eyes traveled over her body. Vanora wore nothing under the gauzy shift, whose sheerness bent the nudity rule as far as it would bend without snapping. Jorian tried to focus his mind on his lost Estrildis, but the blood poured into his loins.

"Say no more," he said, realizing his voice had thickened. "I'm sure I should have enjoyed it more with you than with her. At least, you wouldn't have tossed a man clear out of bed on the floor!"

"Did she, actually?"

"No, but it was a near thing. And the postures those Mulvanians use! But come, isn't it stuffy in here with all these people?"

"Aye. Have you been up to the battlements?"

"No, I haven't. Let's go."

On the battlements the moon, in its first quarter, was just setting. Stars glowed overhead, while in the south a mass of cloud was fitfully lit by the flicker of distant lightning.

"Isn't it warm for this time of year?" he said, sliding an arm around her waist.

"It is rather. Methinks we shall be in for a rainy spell." She turned slowly towards him and tipped back her head. "What of those Mulvanian postures?"

Soon afterwards, they walked lightly down the corridor leading to room twenty-three. Jorian's pulse pounded in his temples. He whispered:

"I haven't seen old Karadur all evening. If he's in our room, we shall have to try yours. If he's not, I'll lock him out."

"I know where some pallets for late-arriving guests are kept," she whispered. "We could drag one up to the roof."

"We shall see." Jorian tried the door of his suite and found it locked. He inserted the key he had received upon registration and quietly unlocked the door. He pushed it open a crack, then froze, listening. Vanora began:

"What is—"

Jorian made a quick chopping motion with his hand. The look of feral lust on his face had vanished, replaced by a hunter's stealthy alertness.

He pushed the door open a little wider, and a little wider yet, until it was open enough for him to slip through. The sitting room was dark, but a candle was lit in the bedroom. The door between the two was ajar, so that a narrow wedge of light slashed across the sitting room. Voices came from the bedroom, and between the snatches of speech the crackle of old parchment could be heard.

"Here's our scroll," said a voice. "By all the gods and demons! 'Tis a version of the sorcerer Rendivar's great counter-spell, thought to have been lost for aye."

"There's our answer," boomed the deep voice of the

magician Vorko. "As I see it; we shall have to proceed by three stages. The first, to be performed tomorrow at the start of the debate, will be to work this counter-spell, thereby opening the way for subsequent actions—"

An old voice with a Mulvanian accent—Karadur's—spoke. In a tone of shocked surprise, this voice said: "You intend to assail our opponents by magic, in despite of all the laws and customs of the Forces of Progress?"

"Certes; what thought you? We've counted noses and know that our proposal has no chance of passage. We do but lack the votes."

"But—but—you were always such a stickler for ethics—"

"Be no bigger a fool than the gods made you! When it's a question of doing something for the masses of mankind, one quibbles not about rules and ethics."

"But are you not being a little—ah—precipitate?" said Karadur.

Vorko snorted. "If you're concerned about every Maltho, Baltho, and Zaltho getting his hands on all the deadliest spells in the grimoire, you can stop worrying. I am not an utter idiot. I know as well as you that some of the reactionaries' claims—that ignorant men are not to be trusted with such powers—have a mort of truth in them. But offering magic free to all is the way to get power.

"Once we control the Forces of Progress, we can have Altruist governments in every one of the Twelve Cities within a year. I have my plans all laid and agents in those places—"

"But the Forces have always eschewed the politics of laymen!" said Karadur, in a voice that was almost a wail.

"The more fools they. Once we're in power, of course, we must needs proceed with caution, letting the masses in on only the most elemental secrets of magic—which they could learn for themselves in any good library—until they prove themselves worthy of more trust: But getting absolute power is the main thing. Once we have crushed all opposition, we can do whatever seems expedient. And, since I know that my own motives are pure and my plans are logically sound, it is my duty to seek the power to carry them out!

"Now, back to business: The second step will be to collect the names of the leaders of the Benefactors and all those who speak on their side of the question on the morrow. Rheits, you shall perform this task whilst the rest of us work the counter-spell. The session is supposed to last two hours—ample time."

Another voice said: "Are you sure, leader, that the old Rendivar spell will be strong enough? Aello's spell is no petty cantrip."

"As cast by one, belike not," said Vorko; "but by three or four of us simultaneously, I'm sure it will do. Now, as to the third step, if we could collect possessions or parts of the body from all these persons, we could attack them by sympathetic magic: impossible in the time at our disposal. Therefore, Magnas, you shall summon a flight of demons from—"

Jorian, standing in darkness near the connecting door, was horrified to hear a loud hiccup from Vanora behind him. Her consumption of wine had caught up with her. She hiccupped again.

"What's that?" said a voice from the bedroom.

To Jorian's helpless horror, Vanora staggered past him, banged open the connecting door, and cried in a hoarse voice:

" 'Tis I, that's who it is! And why don't you impotent old shlobs get to the afterworld out of here, so Jorian and I—*hic*—can use a bed for what a bed's meant for?"

As the door flew open, Jorian had a fleeting impression of several men, besides Karadur, Drakomas, and Vorko, sitting on beds and chairs. Then Vorko's voice spoke a harsh, unintelligible word. Something warned

Jorian of danger on his right. As he started to turn, out of the corner of his eye, in the suddenly augmented light, he saw one of Vorko's demons. The demon was stepping towards him and raising a bludgeon. Fast though Jorian's reactions were, the attack came so swiftly that he did not even have time to dodge before the universe exploded.

When Jorian came to, the room was lit by gray daylight through the arrow slit, furnished with a shutter and a casement sash, which served as a window. It took him some time to realize that the flashes and the rumbling were not inside his head but were caused by a violent storm outside. Rain drove against the little diamond panes of the sash and crawled down the glass like tiny, transparent snakes.

Jorian rolled over, wincing at the pain in cramped muscles and at the sharp stab of headache that accompanied each movement. He found that his wrists and ankles were bound and his mouth was full of gag. As his bleary vision adjusted itself, he saw that Vanora and Karadur were likewise trussed.

Vanora, still wearing her shift of green gauze, looked at him from bloodshot eyes over her gag. About Karadur he could not tell; the Mulvanian looked like a heap of old clothes in the corner.

Although Jorian's assailants had done a sound job of tying him up, they had not reckoned on the practice he had had in Xylar at escaping from such gyves. His first step was simply to chew. A few minutes of vigorous chewing parted the rag that held the gag in place and enabled him to spit out the gag.

"Vanora!" he said thickly. "Are you all right?"

"Gmpff, glmpff," she said through her gag.

"Karadur, how fare you?"

A groan answered. Jorian looked across the room, as best he could from his position on the floor. His sword still hung by its baldric from a hatrack by the door.

It is hard for a man whose ankles are tied together and whose writs have been lashed behind him to rise from the floor, but it can be done. Several times, Jorian almost got to his feet and then crashed down again with bruising force. Little puffs of dust arose from the cracks between the floor boards. At last he made it. He hopped over to the hatrack and butted it over. Then he squatted down and got his hands on the hilt of his sword. A couple of grotesque hops took him to where Vanora lay.

"Seize the sheath with your feet," he growled. When she had done so, he hopped away from her, drawing the sword from its scabbard. Then he thrust the hilt between her feet.

"Now hold that blade steady. If you let go, 'twill skewer me."

He began squatting and rising again, holding the cords that bound his wrists behind him against the blade. When after twenty-odd squats a cord parted, the lashings came quickly off. For a few moments, Jorian stood rubbing his wrists and feeling the lump on his skull. Then he took the sword and quickly severed his and his companions' remaining bonds.

"That's how I once saved my head," he said. "The moral is to keep your sword well honed. These knaves were tyros after all, or they'd never have left aught sharp where we could come upon it."

"Remember, my son," said Karadur, "that they are accustomed to coping with foes, not by such crude devices as swords and cords, but by spirits, spells, and the transcendental wisdom of magic."

"So much the worse for them. What time is it?"

"Good gods!" said Karadur. "It must be after the fourth hour. That means the debate on the Altruist proposal will be under way in the ballroom. Vorko will be working that counter-spell he got from the Kist. Where is the wretched thing? Alas, they have taken it with them. Ah, me, shall I ever cease being a trusting, credulous ninny? But we must hasten to the ballroom to warn the Forces!"

"Gods, what a hangover!" moaned Vanora, holding her head. She did not look at all attractive this morning.

"Are you changing sides, Doctor?" asked Jorian.

"Nay; I have always been on the side of virtue and order. Say rather than Vorko and his minions have deserted me." The old man groaned as he tried to rise. Jorian helped him up. He failed to find his key but got out his pick-locks and went to work on the door, which soon swung open.

"We must lose no time, feeble though I be this morn," said Karadur.

"We?" said Jorian. "Why should I concern myself with the squabbles amongst your spookers? My work for you is done, and I don't intend to join your profession."

"You heard what Vorko said. An you care not for me and other honest magicians, think of Vorko's tyranny, blacker than those of Mulvan, Tarxia, and Metouro combined, But I cannot stop to argue; follow me who will."

The old magician hobbled out the door. After a heartbeat's hesitation, the other two followed him.

The doors of the main ballroom opened to Jorian's vigorous push. Karadur tottered in and down the central aisle between the rows of benches. One of the debaters was on his feet, saying:

". . . and if you believe not that the common man be unworthy to be trusted with such fell secrets, let me cite instances of his stupid, swinish conduct from the history of our host country. When the kings of Metouro were overthrown and the Republic established—"

The speaker broke off as he became aware of Karadur, limping down the aisle bareheaded, his eyes glaring.

"Treason!" croaked the old Mulvanian. "A cabal of

our members plots to overthrow the governance of this brotherhood and seize all power! Master Rheits, yonder, is gathering the names of the Benefactors, to further this attack! Seize him, an you believe me not—"

As Karadur spoke, Jorian and Vanora started to push through the door after him. As they did so, Boso confronted them. Seeing Jorian first, Boso started to say:

"Apprentices in the balcony for this meeting. Only master magicians down here—"

Then the sergeant-at-arms sighted Vanora. "You!" he barked. His face turned red, and his eyes glared with an insane rage. "You two spend—you spend the night in high diddle, and then you have the nerve—the g-gall—I'll fuff-fix you, strumpet!"

With an inarticulate snarl, he tore out his sword, shouldered Jorian aside, and rushed at Vanora. With a scream, the girl fled back into the main hall.

Torn two ways, Jorian hesitated for a heartbeat. In the ballroom, Karadur seemed to have things well in hand. He poured out his denunciation, while turmoil erupted around him. Several members of the Forces had seized Master Rheits. Jorian turned and ran after Boso.

He came out into the main hall in time to see Vanora vanish up the stair at the end of the hall with Boso in pursuit. After them he went, drawing his own sword— the same long blade he had taken from the sleeping Gending in the Ellornas.

Up he went, flight after flight until he began to pant, at each turn catching a glimpse of those he pursued. Soon he came out on the roof. Low clouds scudded overhead; rain beat slantwise to the flagstones. Lightning flashed, and booms of thunder periodically drowned out the whistle of the wind and the rattle of the rain.

Looking anxiously around, with his left hand up to keep the rain from blinding him, Jorian saw Boso enter the door to one of the two big round towers—the twin keeps—of the castle and slam it behind him. Slipping on the wet flags, Jorian ran to the door and tried it; but Boso had shot the heavy bolt inside.

Boso, thought Jorian, would chase Vanora up to the top of this tower and, if he did not catch her there, out across the bridge that joined the two towers and down the spiral stair in the other tower. So he ran back to the base of the other tower, whose door had not been locked.

Entering the other door, he trotted up the stair. As he came out on the roof, he almost collided with Vanora, who, gasping for breath and with her transparent shift clinging wetly to her, arrived at the same moment on the tower top from the bridge. Behind her came Boso, sword and teeth bared.

"Get back down and get help!" Jorian barked at Vanora over his shoulder as he sprang out on the bridge. The wet, gray stones under Jorian's feet vibrated in the gale like a fiddle string.

The structure was not quite so spidery-slender as it looked from below. The footway was four feet wide, and there was a low, crenelated parapet, a little over waist high, on each side. One was not likely to fall off merely from the effects of wind and rain. On the other hand, it would not be hard to fall out of one of the embrasures during a hand-to-hand fight.

The swords met with a whirl and a multiple clang, which was lost in a roar of thunder. The two powerful men stood on the bridge, still panting from their climb and glaring into each other's eyes, cutting, thrusting, and parrying. For an instant they backed off, breathing heavily, then they were at it again, clang-tzing-zip-clang. There was little footwork, because of the limitations of space and the slipperiness of the wet stones.

Their right arms worked like pistons, until Jorian's began to ache. The wind howled and drove the rain scudding almost horizontally. It staggered both fighters so that they had to clutch at the merlons with their free hands for support, even while they hacked and lunged. Lightning glared and thunder boomed.

Jorian found his horseman's blade a little too long for this kind of work, especially since its hilt was too short for both hands. Boso's blade was of about the same length and weight as the sword Randir, now the loot of the cham of the Gendings. The burly ruffian handled it well, whereas Jorian's parries, doubles, and one-twos were a little slow. Boso easily parried them, no matter how complex an attack Jorian launched. On the other hand, Jorian's extra inches of arm and blade kept Boso a little too far away to take advantage of his greater speed of blade. His stout, short-legged build made him too slow on his feet to slip in by a quick advance-lunge to get inside Jorian's guard.

Moreover, Boso had the bad habit of parrying in the obsolete seconde. Jorian swore that, the next time his foe did it, he would double and skewer him properly . . .

A new sound and sensation made itself felt. This was neither the crash of thunder, nor the whistle of the wind, nor the humming vibration of the bridge. It was a deep rumble, combined with a heavy shaking as of an earthquake. From below came a rising uproar of thumps, rumbles, rattles, clatters, crashes, shrieks, howls, screams, and bellows. Behind Jorian, Vanora screamed:

*"The tower is falling!"*

Jorian cast a quick look at Boso, who had withdrawn a couple of paces and stood, clutching a merlon with one hand and his sword with the other. The sergeant-at-arms's face was pale, and his hair was wetly plastered to his low forehead.

Jorian risked a backward glance. Vanora stood a couple of strides from him, clutching the merlons of the parapet of the tower.

"Why didn't you go down—" began Jorian, but then the stones lurched under his feet. With a frightful, grinding roar, both towers and the bridge that joined them began to sway outward, over the rain-lashed water of Lake Volkina.

Jorian sprang to the parapet, where the bridge joined the tower top. "Jump as far out as you can!" he yelled.

As he gathered himself to spring, Jorian took one last look at Boso. The latter was not looking at Jorian at all, but at a being that had appeared behind him. One of the merlons of the bridge parapet had burst into pieces. One stone, falling to the footway of the bridge, had changed into the being. Five feet tall and spindle-legged, it had an enormous head, larger than a pumpkin, and a huge, froglike gash of a mouth. It wore no clothes, and its skin had a moist, froglike appearance. It had no visible organs of sex.

That was all that Jorian saw as the towers leant further and further out over the water. He hurled himself out with a mighty bound, felt the wind whistle in his hair and rain in his face—curious, he thought in a flash, that rain should seem to be falling up; but of course he was overtaking the raindrops on their way down. Then he saw the slate-gray water coming up at him. *Smack!*

He reached the surface, feeling as if a giant had swatted him with a paddle. On either side of him, someone was splashing. As he got the water out of his eyes and regained his breath, he saw that one of these was Vanora, who, unhampered by her negligible costume, was striking out for shore. The other was Boso, ineffectually wallowing and thrashing and trying to choke out the word: "*Help!*"

Jorian had dropped his sword during his dive. Two strokes took him to where Boso thrashed, bobbing under water and out again with each frantic effort. Jorian hooked an arm under the sergeant-at-arms's chin, secured a crushing hold, and began swimming on his back towards the shore.

A few strokes and he touched down. He dragged Boso to shore and dropped the man on his back in the mud. Boso lay with his eyes closed, coughing, spitting water, and breathing in racking gasps. Then Jorian looked around.

The Goblin Tower had collapsed into a vast heap of stone blocks. From under a few of the nearer blocks, human hands and feet protruded. All around the isle, hundreds of magicians and their helpers stood in the water, up to their ankles, knees, waists, or even chins. Some poked among the ruins of the castle. Injured persons moaned.

The rain had slackened to a steady drizzle. Nearby, Vanora stood naked at the edge of the lake, wringing the water out of her flimsy garment.

"Jorian!" He looked up to see Karadur and Goania wading towards him.

"What in the forty-nine Mulvanian hells happened?" Jorian cried.

Karadur was too winded and frightened to do more than gasp, but Goania explained: "You know how the Goblin Tower got its name? Well, when Vorko worked his counter-spell, this nullified not only Aello's protective spell, but also the original spell put upon the goblins by Synelius, back in the days of the tyrant Charenzo. Since the castle had been partly built of these stones, when they were changed back into goblins, the walls collapsed because there were so many gaps in them. Most of the goblin stones seem to have been on the south side, and that is why the towers fell this way."

"I saw one of the things whilst I was up on the bridge, fighting with Boso," said Jorian.

"There must have been many hundreds of them in the lower parts of the castle."

"Where are they now?"

"Karadur released the demon Gorax from his ring and set Gorax on the goblins, whereupon they all whisked back to the Ninth Plane. I think they were worse frightened by awakening from their sleep of enchantment in the midst of the collapsing Tower than we were frightened of them."

"How did you escape?"

"When Karadur told what he knew of Vorko's counter-spell, old Aello instantly knew what was up. He screamed to us to get out of the Tower instanter. Most of us got out, although some were caught, and some were struck by falling stones after they had left the edifice. Luckily, the water on the other side is shallow all the way to shore. Vorko and his minions seem to have been amongst those destroyed; at least, I have seen nought of them."

"And Aello?"

"Dead in the ruins, I fear. He went to the kitchen and the servants' quarters to get those folk out, too, and was last seen poking about there to make sure that none was left behind. But what is this?" She indicated Boso, who was beginning to revive.

"I dragged him out of the lake. He would have slain Vanora up on the roof, out of jealousy. I was fighting with him on the bridge when the castle crumbled."

"Fighting him to death, and then you saved his life?"

Jorian clapped a hand to his forehead. "By Imbal's brazen balls! Why do I *do* these stupid things? Oh, well, I didn't really crave to kill the poor halfwit." Glancing about, he glimpsed a dull, metallic gleam in the shallow water. It was Boso's sword, lying in the mud. Jorian picked it up and shoved it into his own scabbard.

"My own is out in the lake somewhere," he said. "Will you go to law with me about it, Boso, or shall we forget the whole sorry business?"

Boso, now sitting up, shook his head and mumbled: "I hurt my back."

"Well, back or no back, get up! We have work to do." Jorian led the groaning Boso around the isle to where the magicians, standing up to their knees and waists in the water, were loading injured persons into rowboats that had come out to pick them up.

"Vanora!" said Goania severely. "Get some clothes on, child, ere you catch your death of cold."

When evening had fallen on Metouro, Jorian sat in the tavern that Vorko had occupied, with Karadur and Goania. Karadur had lost his turban in the collapse of the Goblin Tower and, feeling uncomfortable without it, had wound a strip of rag around his head as a substitute. Boso and Vanora, the latter wearing a new dress purchased that day by Goania, sat by themselves two tables away. Jorian said:

"Now I've done what your Altruists demanded, Doctor, even if your cursed Kist is buried in the ruins of the Goblin Tower, where at least it won't cause trouble for a long time to come. Since I have performed my part of the bargain, how do I get this geas lifted?"

"It is already lifted, my son. Since Vorko imposed it, his death cancelled it. But we must consider your future. If you would become my apprentice in fact as well as in name, I could make a prime magician out of you in fifteen or twenty years—provided I pass not to my next incarnation in the interim."

"No, thank you. I have my own plans, the first of which is to get back my dear little Estrildis."

"How will you accomplish that, without the help of magic?"

"I know not, old boy, but I shall find a way. During our journey, I observed that when I relied upon my own mundane powers, I usually succeeded; whereas, when I leant on the supernatural, I usually ended up worse off than when I started.

"I used to think that magic was the key to life's charade,
And therefore of its learned devotees I sought the aid:

Of necromancers whom the ghosts of men of yore
   obeyed.

Of hoary seers who, they said, the future could
   foretell,
Of sorcerers who to their lairs could summon
   spirits fell,

And wizards who could utter many a dark and
   deadly spell.
But when it was all done, I found a better spell
   was made
By counting on my own resource of eye and arm
   and blade,
My native reason, and between my knees a sturdy
   jade.

So now I'm through with horoscopes and pentacles
   as well,
And words to summon spirits who in strange
   dimensions dwell.
To every kind of spookery, I bid a last farewell!

"Horses will play the fiddle before I count on your
arcane arts again."

Karadur began to argue: "The most ignorant man is
he who knows it all. Without my arcane arts, you would
have no head on your shoulders to harbor that wit
whereof you boast. An ethical man gives just credit
to—"

But Goania cut him off: "Let the lad be, old colleague. His mind is made up and from his point of
view, rightly. When he attains our age and the blood
runs less hotly in his veins, he may find our mysteries
more beguiling. What shall be your first step, O Jorian?
The Faceless Five demand that we all quit Metouro
on the morrow, ere we destroy the city by another ill-
directed enchantment."

Jorian grinned. "I have a horse and a sword—both

of middling quality—but no money. My first task is to get some of the last-named; and for that I shall need a hat. My fur cap and my wizard's headpiece are buried in the ruins of the Tower."

"A hat?" said Karadur vaguely. "I suppose you might find one in Vorko's room, upstairs. But how can a hat—"

"You shall see." Jorian rose and started for the stair.

"Jorian!" called Vanora. "Wait." She hurried across the room and spoke in a low voice. "Leaving us?"

"Soon."

"Well—ah—I am, as you know, a tough and useful traveling companion—"

Jorian shook his head. "I thank you, Mistress Vanora, but I have other plans. It has been very interesting to know you. Na, na, weep not, lass; 'twill but redden thy nose to none avail. A needs must forth the morn, and ma nag can bear but one."

He ran up the steps and presently reappeared with Vorko's hat on his head.

"How got you into his room?" asked Goania.

Jorian smiled. "Know you not that I do but make a mystical pass, and all locks open unto me?"

She glanced over to where Vanora sat beside Boso with tears running down her face. Vanora and her companion both stared morosely into space. "I take it she asked to become your leman again, and you denied her?"

"That's right. Thrice I've come close to being killed on that young woman's behalf, and that is twice more than enough. I'm no hero—merely a simple craftsman—oh, all right, Father Karadur, I won't say the rest."

The glare that Karadur had given Jorian softened, and the old magician said: "But the hat—how—"

"Come out into the marketplace in a little while, and you will see how I do it. Did not the philosopher

Achaemo say that the superior man uses his very faults and weaknesses to advantage? Fare you well!"

Half an hour later, Karadur, Goania, Boso, and Vanora strolled out to the marketplace. The rain had ceased, although puddles among the cobblestones still reflected the yellow light of link and lanthorn. A crowd was gathered around the Fountain of Drexis in the center of the open space. When the four approached, they saw that the crowd surrounded Jorian, sitting on the curb of the fountain. As they came up, he was saying:

". . . and so ends the tale of King Fusinian the Fox and the enchanted shovel. And the moral is, that more woe is wrought by stupidity than by villainy."

Jorian fanned himself with Vorko's hat, for the night was warm. "Would you like some more? Let's say, the tale of ex-king Forimar and the waxen wife? Yes? Then let us see if you cannot prime the pump a little, to spur my sluggish memory . . ."

He passed the hat around the circle, to the clink of coins. "A little more priming, good gentles; money is the grease that lubricates the storyteller's clockwork. Ah, better.

"Well, it seems that after King Forimar the Esthete had abdicated in favor of his brother Fusonio, a man set up an exhibition of waxworks in Kortoli City. This man, whose name was Zevager, asked the former king to allow such an effigy to be made of His Highness and displayed with the rest . . ."

# Part II

## The Clocks Of Iraz

*To John and Ann Ashmead*

# CONTENTS

# CONTENTS

# I

# The Scarlet Mammoth

It was the Hour of the Goat, on the thirteenth of the Month of the Unicorn, in the republic of Ir, one of the twelve city-states of Novaria.

In the tavern called the Scarlet Mammoth, in the city of Orynx, a slim, well-dressed young man toyed absently with a glass of wine and watched the door. Although this man wore Novarian garb, there was about him a suggestion of the exotic. His skin was darker than that of most Novarians, although the latter were a mainly brunet folk. Furthermore, his ornaments were gaudier than those of the Land of the Twelve Cities.

Across the common room sat an older man: a chunky fellow of medium height, with a plain, nondescript face, clad in garments of sober black. If the first man looked foppish; the second looked ostentatiously austere.

While the tall youth watched the door, the chunky man, now and then sipping from a leathern drinking jack of ale, watched the tall youth. Sweat beaded the foreheads of both men, for the weather was unseasonably hot.

The door flew open. In stamped six noisy, rough-looking men, covered with sweat and dust and cursing the heat. They seized the largest table in the common room and hammered on it. The tallest man, a burly, ruddy fellow with deep-set dark eyes under heavy black brows and a close-cut black beard, shouted:

"Ho, Theudus! Can't a gang of honest workmen get a drink, when their throats are caked with dust thick enough to raise a crop in?"

311

"Coming, coming, Master Nikko, if you'll stop that hellish racket," grumbled the taverner, appearing with his fists full of jacks of ale, a thick finger hooked around each handle. As he set the vessels down, he asked: "Be this your last day, working out of Orynx?"

"That's right," said the big man, across whose face a sword-cut had left a scar and put a kink in his nose. "We move to Evrodium on the morrow. Our orders are to make the aqueduct swing south, following the high ground, before reaching Ir City."

"I should think you'd cut directly across to Ir," said Theudus, "to shorten the total length."

"We would, but the Syndicate would have to pay for an arcade several leagues long, and you know how they are with money; they give it out as a glacier gives out heat. When the thing is built, they'll doubtless complain that the grade is too low and the channel clogs up. I warned 'em, but they wouldn't listen. No matter what route we pick, we poor surveyors get blamed."

"They've been talking about this project for years," said the taverner.

"Aye. They should have built it years agone, but I suppose they hoped that Zevatas would send enough rain to fill the old aqueducts. They did nought till water got so scarce that they had to ration baths. You ought to smell the air in that underground city! They could cut it up and sell it for fertilizer. Well, what's for dinner?"

As the men gave their orders, the slim young man approached the surveyors' table. Standing behind the big man, he rapped the latter on the shoulder with a peremptory forefinger. As the chief surveyor looked up, the younger man, speaking Novarian with an accent, said:

"You, there! Are you not Jorian of Ardamai?"

The big man's eyes narrowed, but his face remained blank and his voice level. "Never heard of him. I'm Nikko of Kortoli, as my mates here will attest."

"But that is—well, come over to my table, where we can talk."

"Certes, my unknown friend," said the surveyor in no friendly tone. Carrying his ale, he rose and followed the other back to his table. He sat down beside the younger one, while his hand strayed to the knife at his belt. "Now, sir, what can I do for you?"

The other gave a high-pitched giggle. "Come, good my sir. Everyone has heard of Jorian of Ardamai, once king of Xylar, who fled his official decapitation and has been hiding—*ow!*"

"Be quiet," murmured the big man, who had slid an arm around the younger man's waist and then, with his other hand, had thrust his knife so that its point gently pricked the skin of the other's belly.

"How—how dare you!" cried the slim young man. "You cannot order me around! You durst not harm one of my rank!"

"Want to find out? An you'd not mess up Theudus' nice clean floor with your guts, you shall do exactly as told."

"B-but, my dear Jorian, I know you! Doctor Karadur said that Nikko of Kortoli was one of your false names, and that is how I tracked you hither—*eh*, stop that!"

"Then shut up, idiot! What has Karadur to do with this? Keep your voice down!"

"He gave me a letter to you—"

"Who are you, anyway?"

"M-my name is Zerlik son of Doerumik son of—"

"An uncouth name, if ever I heard one. Whence come you? Penembei?"

"Precisely, sir. The great city of Iraz, in fact. Now—"

"And Karadur is in Iraz?"

"Aye, Master Jor—*ow!*"

"The next time you speak that name aloud, I'll let you have it up to the hilt. Let's see this letter."

Zerlik looked down his long, hooked, high-bridged

nose. "Really, sir, a gentleman like myself is not accustomed to such unmannerly—"

"The letter, your lordship, unless you want steel in your guts. Did Karadur hire you as messenger?"

"Really, good my sir! Persons of my quality do not work for pay. It is our duty to serve the court, and my task is that of royal messenger. When His Majesty, knowing me fluent in Novarian, commanded me to bear Karadur's missive . . ."

During this speech, the big man had pried the seal off the letter and unfolded the sheet of reed paper. He frowned at the spidery writing on the crackly, golden-brown surface, then called:

"O Theudus! A candle, if you please."

When the candle had been brought, the big man read the following epistle:

Karadur the Mulvanian to his stout comrade in the adventure of the Kist of Avlen, greetings.

If you would recover your little Estrildis, and if you remember enough of your early training in clockmaking to put in order the clocks on the Tower of Kumashar, then come to Iraz with Master Zerlik. The task should not be difficult, for I understand that these clocks were installed by your sire in the first place. Farewell.

Jorian of Ardamai murmured: "The old fellow has better sense than you, Zerlik my boy. You'll notice he mentioned no names—"

He broke off as a movement on the other side of the room caught his eye. The man in plain, dark clothing laid a coin on his table, rose, and walked quietly out. Jorian caught a glimpse of his profile against the darkening sky, and then the door closed on the man.

"Theudus!" Jorian called.

"Aye, Master Nikko?"

"Who was that who just left?"

The taverner shrugged. "I know not. He's been here all afternoon, sipping a little ale and watching about him."

"Could you place him by his speech?"

"He said little; but what he said was, meseemed, with a southern accent."

Jorian grunted. "With those clothes and a southern accent, he has 'Xylar' written all over him, as surely as if he bore the crimson hourglass on his tunic."

"Are you not jumping to conclusions on scant evidence?" said Zerlik.

"Mayhap, but in my position one becomes sensitive to such things. If it make you happy, Master Zerlik, know that you're not the only stupid man in the room. I should have noticed this wight as soon as I came in, but I was thinking of other things."

"Mean you the Xylarians are still fain to cut your head off and throw it up for grabs, by way of choosing the next king? A beastly custom, I always thought."

"You'd find it even beastlier if it were your head. Well, I shall have to accept Karadur's invitation instanter. But travel costs money, and I have but little of the precious stuff."

"That is all right. Doctor Karadur entrusted me with a sum adequate for the purpose."

"Good. How came you hither?"

"In my chariot," said Zerlik.

"You drove all the way from Iraz? I knew not that the coastal road was good for wheeled traffic."

"It is not. My man and I had to dismount a hundred times, to manhandle the thing over rocks and out of holes. But we made it."

"Where is this man of yours?"

"Ayuir is in the kitchen. You would not expect him to dine with his master, would you?"

Jorian shrugged. After a pause, Zerlik said: "Well, sir, and what next?"

"I'm thinking. We have perhaps half an hour wherein

to flee the Scarlet Mammoth ere a squad of Royal Guardsmen from Xylar arrives with nets and lariats. Are you staying here?"

"Aye. I have a private room. But surely you do not propose to leave tonight?"

"Yes I do, and forthwith."

"But my dinner!" cried Zerlik.

"Bugger your dinner; corpses have no appetite. If you hadn't blabbed my name ... Anyway, command your man to hitch up your chariot whilst we gather our gear. What's your idea of whither we should go?"

"Why, back the way I came—through Xylar and along the coastal road, at the foot of the Lograms, and down the coast to Penembei to Iraz."

Jorian shook his head grimly. "You'll never see me in Xylar—not whilst they seek to chop off my head."

"What, then? Shall we send eastward to Vindium and around the other end of the Lograms?"

"Not practical. 'Twould take months, and the valley of the Jhukna is wild, roadless land. Methinks we needs must go by sea."

"By sea!" Zerlik's voice rose to a squeak. "I hate the sea. Besides, what would become of my beautiful chariot?"

"You and your man can take it back the way you came. I'll join you in Iraz as soon as I can find passage."

"From what I hear, there is not much coastal shipping just now, with the pirates of Algarth active off the coast. Besides, I was commanded to accompany you, to render aid and assistance."

Jorian thought that if any help were called for, it would be he who rendered aid to this spoilt young fop rather than the other way round. But he merely said:

"Then come with me, whilst your man takes the chariot. If we cannot find passage on a coaster, we may have to sail our own ship, and that takes at least two."

"Ayuir might steal my car and run off with it!"

"That, young sir, is your problem."

"Nor can I be expected to flit about the world without a single attendant, like some wretched vagrant—"

"You'll learn, laddie. You'd be surprised what one can do when one puts one's mind to it." Jorian rose. "In any event, we cannot sit here havering all night. I go to pack and shall meet you back here in a quarter-hour. Tell your man to be ready to drive us down the river road to Chemnis." He stepped back to the large table and touched one of the surveyors on the arm. "Come up to the dormitory a moment, Ikadion."

With a puzzled frown, the other followed Jorian up the creaking stairs. In the dormitory, Jorian pulled his spare clothing, sword, and other possessions out from under the bed. He donned the scabbard and jammed the other gear into a stout canvas bag. As he worked he said:

"I fear I must run out on you, as the pard said to the lioness when the lion returned home."

"You mean—you mean to leave the gang?"

"Aye. That makes you head surveyor. The Syndicate owes me for the work I've done so far. Pray collect my pay and keep it against my return."

"When will that be, Nikko?"

"I know not. Perchance in a fortnight, perchance in a year."

"Whither away? Why the haste and mystery?"

"Say that I fear the blast of the wintry winds and the drip, drip, drip of the rain. When and if I return, I'll seek you out and tell you about it—and also collect my pay."

"The boys will be sorry to see you go. You drive them hard, but they think you're a good boss."

" 'Tis good of you to say so. By rights you should have had my job."

"True, but I never could get the work out of them as you do. Did I hear that foreign fellow call you 'Jorian'?"

"Aye, but he had confused me with another man entirely."

\*　　\*　　\*

With his duffel bag slung over his back and Ikadion following, Jorian strode to the head of the stair. Glancing over the scene below, he muttered: "Where's that Zerlik?" Then he stepped back and knocked on the door of the private room occupied by the Irazi.

"Coming, coming," said Zerlik's voice.

"Well, hurry up! Have you sent your man to get out the car?"

"Nay, Ayuir is in here helping me. You do not expect me to pack my own gear, do you?"

Jorian sucked his breath through his teeth. "I've just packed mine without dying of the effects. What do you want, an egg in your beer? Send the fellow out; we have no time to squander."

The door jerked open. Zerlik said: "My good man, if you think I will do my own chores like a common lout, just to meet your convenience—"

Jorian flushed a dangerous red. At that moment, Zerlik's servant, a small, swarthy man, spoke timidly in his own tongue. Zerlik briefly replied. Ayuir picked up the massive wooden chest and issued from the room.

"One moment," said Zerlik. "I needs must give the room a last inspection, lest I forget aught."

Jorian waited while the servant staggered down the stairs with the chest. Ayuir set the box down near the door and scuttled out.

Zerlik came out of his room; he, Jorian, and Ikadion started down the stairs. As they did so, five men in plain black clothing entered the Scarlet Mammoth. In the lead came the chunky man, who pointed to Jorian and shouted:

"There he is, boys! Take him! King Jorian, I command you in the name of the kingdom of Xylar to surrender!"

The five rushed across the floor, circling around the table at which the gaping surveyors sat. As one of the former started up the stairs, Jorian swung his duffel bag off his shoulder and hurled it at the man. The missile bowled the fellow over, and the man behind him tripped over his body.

Before they could recover, Jorian's sword came out with a *wheep*. Jorian hurdled the two sprawling figures and brought the blade down in a whistling cut on the shoulder of the next intruder. The man screamed and staggered back, cloven halfway to the breastbone. He sank to the floor in a swiftly widening pool of blood.

Another black-clad man threw a net over Jorian's head. Jorian slashed at the net but only entangled his sword in its meshes. He struggled to tear off the net, but the men in black expertly drew it tighter about him, while one stepped up behind him with a bludgeon.

"Surveyors, to me," roared Jorian. "Help! Zerlik, bear a hand! Theudus!"

Coming out of their daze, the surveyors rose to attack the men in black. Three of the latter pulled out short swords. The surveyor had only daggers, but one picked up a stool and smote the nearest Xylarian over the head.

Theudus appeared with a mallet. After hesitating to see who was fighting whom, he waded in with the surveyors. Zerlik, after dancing excitedly about on the fringe of the fray, ran to his chest, fumbled with a key, opened the chest, and took out a light scimitar.

Assailed from all sides, the Xylarians left off cocooning Jorian to defend themselves. Jorian tore and cut his way out of the net and fell upon the foe. Since not only was he the largest man in the room but also his sword had much the longest reach, his reëntry into the fray tipped the odds against the kidnappers.

The combatants swayed back and forth, stabbing, punching, grappling, falling down and scrambling up again, hurling crockery, thrusting, slashing, swinging, and kicking. The room resounded with the shouts of the fighters, the boom of overturned furniture, and the crash of breaking tableware. Red blood spattered the floor and stained the fighters' garments. The Red Mammoth trembled to the stamping of feet. The din of roars, yells, curses, and threats wafted into the street, so that several Oryncians gathered about the door.

Outnumbered, the newcomers were soon overborne. Jorian sped a fierce thrust through the body of one, while the Xylarian was engaged with Zerlik. As the man fell, the remaining four set up a cry:

"Out! Flee! Save himself who can!"

The four burst through their opponents and out the door. Two dragged another, half-stunned by a blow from Theudus' mallet. The three still on their feet displayed slashed clothing and oozing wounds. The faces of two were masks of blood from head wounds. A flourish of weapons sent the spectators fleeing, and the quartet vanished into the gathering dark.

Inside, two surveyors bound up cuts, while Ikadion sat with head in hands, nursing a growing lump on his pate from a Xylarian bludgeon. The first man whom Jorian had struck down was dead; the other coughed bloody froth.

"My nice tavern!" wailed Theudus, surveying the wreckage.

"We didn't do it wantonly, Master Theudus," said Jorian, leaning on his sword and breathing hard. "Bear a hand with cleaning up, Floro. You, too, Vilerias. Tot up the cost of breakage, mine host, and Master Zerlik will pay."

"What?" shrilled Zerlik.

"Charge it against the sum Karadur entrusted to you on my behalf."

"Are you in sooth the fugitive King Jorian of Xylar?" said a surveyor in an awed tone.

Jorian ignored the question and turned to Theudus, who stood over the wounded Xylarian. The taverner said:

"This fellow may linger for hours, but I misdoubt he'll survive. Someone should fetch the constable; there must be an inquest on these manslayings."

"Inquest all you like, but without me," said Jorian. "I'm off with Master Zerlik."

Theudus shook his head. " 'Tis not lawful, to leave town ere the magistrate has dismissed you. There might be charges."

"I'm sorry. Whereas I am a reasonably law-abiding wight, I can't wait around for another gang to lay me by the heels, whilst your men of the law mumble gravely in their beards. Pay Master Theudus, O Zerlik." While Zerlik fumbled with his purse, Jorian donned his hat and shouldered his duffel bag. "Now let's forth!"

"But, Master Jorian!" said Zerlik. "It is all but dark."

"So much the better."

"But we shall get lost or overset the chariot—"

"Fear not; I'll drive. There's a moon, and I know the roads hereabouts."

Heavily laden with three men and their gear, Zerlik's chariot, drawn by a pair of handsome Fediruni whites, reached the village of Evrodium around midnight. Zerlik climbed down shakily, saying:

"Methought my last moment had come a hundred times, Master Jorian. Where got you that skill with driving a car?"

Jorian laughed. "I can do many things, some passing well and some not so well. I'm probably the only wandering adventurer especially trained for the rôle."

When they had secured quarters, Zerlik asked Jorian to elucidate his last remark. Over dinner, Jorian—who had a weakness for talk—explained.

"I got into the king business by happenstance. I was about your age and had been apprenticed to various crafts, such as clockmaking and carpentry, and had served a hitch in the army of Othomae. When that was over, I wandered into Xylar to see what might turn up.

I happened upon the drill field outside Xylar City on the day of the casting of the Lot of Imbal, when they behead the old king and toss his head to the crowd.

"When, not knowing this curious custom, I saw this dark, round thing whirling towards me, I caught it without thinking. To my horror I found that I was the new king of Xylar, having caught my predecessor's gory head.

"As soon as I learnt that the same fate awaited me five years thence, I sought means to escape. I tried to flee, to bribe my way out, to persuade the Xylarians to change their damned system, and even to drink myself to death, all without avail.

"Then I learnt that, with the help of Doctor Karadur's spells, I might just possibly escape, in return for a favor I was able to do him. Did I succeed, howsomever, the Xylarians would pursue me to the ends of the earth, since their laws suffer not a new king to be chosen by any but the prescribed method, and therefore they must essay to drag me back and resume their interrupted rite to permit public business to go on."

"How if the king die in office?" asked Zerlik. "Or if you die ere they can recapture you?"

"They have other procedures in such cases; but they are irrelevant to me, since I'm not yet dead and have no yearning to become so. To resume: Knowing that I was virtually condemned—should my escape succeed—to the life of a wandering adventurer, I prepared myself therefore by the practice of such arts as acting, rough-and-tumble fighting, sleight-of-hand, cozenage, and burglary. For these, I had the tutoring of some of the most unsavory rogues in the Twelve Cities. But some of their lessons have proven most serviceable."

Zerlik: "Do you like this irregulous life?"

"Nay. My real ambition is to be a respectable craftsman or tradesman—a surveyor, for ensample—earning a decent if modest living, rearing a family, meeting my obligations, and plaguing no man. A peaceful bourgeois life would suit me well, but it seems to flee before me like the end of a rainbow."

"If you knew the Xylarians were after you, why took you this post in Ir, next door to Xylar? Why not work in some more distant place, like Zolon or Tarxia?"

"Because the Xylarians hold something I wish: to wit, my wife. Therefore I skulk about their borders, seeking means to get her out."

"Oh. Is this the Estrildis whereof the letter from Karadur speaks?"

Jorian gave Zerlik a hard look. "By Imbal's iron pizzle, young sir, you seem to have made rather free with my private correspondence!"

"Oh, but Jorian, Doctor Karadur requested that I memorize the message, in case the letter were lost or destroyed!"

"Ah, that's different. Ay, 'tis she."

"Oh. I have heard that you Novarians entertain romantical notions about women. When one has several wives, as I have, one takes a particular woman less seriously."

"I had several wives, too, when I was king. Five, in fact; the Xylarians allow a plurality of wives to the king but not to his subjects. Mulvanian or Penembic influence in the southern tier, I suppose. But this was the last, and the one I chose myself."

"Really?" Zerlik patted a yawn. "It is hard for me to imagine going to such trouble and risk over any woman. After all, they are all basically alike."

"I have not found them so."

Zerlik shrugged. "But why? It cannot be that you were otherwise condemned to a celibate life, for you Novarians seem to have no such rigid interdicts against fornication and adultery as, I am told, obtain among the Mulvanians. Is it that this woman is rich, and you wish to possess yourself of her property?"

"Not at all; she's a Kortolian farmer's daughter."

"Is she then of extraordinary beauty?"

"Not even that. She's a pretty little thing, with golden hair like a Shvenite; but of stocky build and too thick in the ankles to please the connoisseur of female beauty. No, Zerlik, it's what we call love."

"Oh, we have this 'love' amongst us, too. In our land, however, to fall in love is accounted a misfortune—a kind of madness. It leads men to entangle themselves with unsuitable women, causing their kin distress and embarrassment. Ordinarily, our parents choose our wives for us, very sensibly, by go-betweens, with the advice of astrologers and haruspices."

"This is not quite the same as your falling in love, laddie. Let me merely say that I enjoy Estrildis' company more than that of any other person I have known, and I am fain to have more of it, until death do us part."

"Well, I wish you joy of it. But does not one become bored with a single woman?"

"That depends. Having tried your system, I have no faith in it, either."

"How so?"

"There's a jingle that explains:

"Oh, pity the man with a score of wives!
For when they're at outs, however he strives
To gentle them down, the quarrel revives,
With curses and blows, and even with knives,
Till among them 'tis wonder that he survives.

"Oh, weep for the fellow with multiple mates!
For when they're in concord, with garrulous spates
Of chatter, they seek their desiderates
And wear him away by alternates,
Until the poor devil capitulates.

"Condole with the poor polygamist!
For every night he must keep a tryst
With one of the wives on the harem's list,

And he dare not repose or leave one unkissed,
Lest the peace of his family cease to exist."

"Whose verse is that?"

"An obscure poetaster, hight Jorian son of Evor. Anyway, one woman at a time's enough for me. When I get mine back, one wife, one house, and one honest trade will suffice me." Jorian yawned. "We must to bed, to be up ere dawn."

"But that will give us scarce four hours' sleep!"

"Aye, but Chemnis is a long day's drive hence."

"You mean to make Chemnis in one day?"

"Certes. Since four of those rogues escaped, the Xylarians will soon be on my trail again."

"You'll slay my poor horses!"

"I think not; and if I did, a self-proclaimed gentleman like you could afford another pair."

Beyond Evrodium, the road swung north to join the main road from Ir City to Chemnis, the main port of the republic at the mouth of the Kyamos. As Zerlik's chariot thundered down the river road to where Chemnis arose on the margin of the estuary, a forest of masts and yards loomed over the houses along the waterfront. Many ships had been laid up for the winter earlier than usual, since the depredations of the Algarthian pirates had depressed seaborne traffic.

The day after the arrival of Jorian and his companions in Chemnis, they walked to the waterfront in the early morning. Zerlik still staggered from the jolting of the previous day's headlong drive. Jorian growled:

"When I was king, we kept the sea thieves down. I built up our little fleet and commanded it myself. Betwixt us in the South and the navy of Zolon in the North, no pirate dared to show his sail off the western coast of Novaria. But they've let the fleet go to the shipworms since I fled, whilst Zolon has a new High Admiral who dotes on fancy uniforms but never goes to sea."

Zerlik looked more and more unhappy. At last he said: "Master Jorian, I fear that when His Majesty sent me forth on this errand, he did not mean me to get my throat cut by pirates."

"Afraid?"

"Sirrah, a man of my rank does not brook insults!"

"Keep your doublet on, young fellow. I did but ask."

"I bloodied my scimitar on your side against the kidnappers. But meseems it were pure madness for us twain to set forth in some cockleshell craft alone. If these bloody freebooters caught up with us, what earthly chance should we have?"

Jorian frowned. "Well, no regular ships sail now to Iraz; so 'tis either buy or rent a ship of our own or not go at all. Rental were impractical, they say, for the owner would demand so large a deposit that one might as well buy the craft. Still, what you say makes sense of a sort.

"I have it! We'll be a pair of poor fishermen with but a meager catch to show for our pains." They reached the waterfront, and Jorian consulted a list of ships for sale. "Let's see; the *Divrunia* should lie yonder, with the *Flying Fish* beyond and the *Psaanius* in the other direction . . ."

Jorian hunted up a ship broker whose name he had. The broker took them on a tour of the waterfront. After a morning of inspecting ships, Jorian bid the broker farewell for the nonce. While he and Zerlik ate at a waterfront tavern, Jorian said:

"Meseems the *Flying Fish* is our craft, an we can beat Master Gatorix down to a reasonable price."

"That dirty little tub!" cried Zerlik. "Why—"

"You forget, laddie, that we shall be a pair of indigent fishers. So a craft like the *Divrunia,* as spick as a royal yacht, were the last thing we want. We must look the part."

"Well, the *Flying Fish* certainly stinks of fish. Why cannot we get a proper warship—say, one of those Irian biremes anchored out yonder? Then, with a well-armed crew, we should have nought to fear from corsairs."

"Imprimis, those galleys are the property of the Republic of Ir, and I have no reason to think the Syndicate would wish to sell one. Secundus, such a deal would at best require months of negotiation, during which time the Xylarians would be upon me. And tertius, have you a hundred thousand marks wherewith to buy the ship, with an equal amount for the hire of the crew?"

"Unh. But my good clothes—"

"We shall, naturally, wear garb suitable to our assumed rank. So fear not for your finery. We shall be ragged and stinking."

"Ugh!"

"Moreover, the *Flying Fish* is sound of hull and rigging. With her beam she may be slow, but she'll get us whither we fain would go. Finish your repast, so that we can sally forth to seek Master Gatorix."

When they found the ship broker again, Jorian said: "We should like another look at your *Flying Fish;* albeit a thousand marks is beyond the vault to heaven. Why, I could buy a surplus Zolonian trireme for that . . ."

After two hours of haggling, Jorian brought the price down to 650 marks. He said: "Methinks we can do business, Master Gatorix. Of course, you'll throw in a sun stone, a chart, and an astrolabe . . ."

After further chaffering, Jorian asked the broker about distances, winds, and currents between Chemnis and Iraz. Gatorix advised him that even with favorable weather, the voyage would take at least a sennight. Jorian calculated and dispatched Zerlik and Ayuir to buy supplies. When they returned, followed by longshoremen laden with sacks of biscuits, salt pork, apples, salted fish, salt, a fish net, two poles with lines and extra hooks, and suits of rough, worn seamen's garb,

Jorian was again engrossed in an argument with Gatorix.

"I'm trying to get him to include this spyglass in the deal," he explained. "He wants a hundred marks extra for the thing."

"Great Ughroluk!" cried Zerlik. "In Iraz, one can buy a good glass for a fraction of that."

"Naturally," said Gatorix, "since you Irazians invented the contraption and make it, 'tis cheaper there than here."

Jorian had raised the brass tube to his eye and trained it eastward. He stood silently for a moment, then closed the telescope with a snap and said in a changed voice:

"Pay Gatorix his hundred marks, Zerlik."

"But—"

"No buts! We're taking the glass without further argument."

"But—"

"And help me to get this stuff aboard, yarely."

"Surely, sirs," said Gatorix, "you're not putting to sea so late in the day?"

"No help for it," said Jorian. "Hop to it, Ayuir; you, too, Zerlik."

Between a quarter and a half of an hour later, the *Flying Fish* cast off and wallowed out into the estuary. The ship was a two-masted lateener, with a blue hull and yellow sails. She flew a large mainsail forward and a smaller mizzen aft. Seated abreast on the thwarts abaft the cabin, Jorian and Zerlik each heaved on an oar. Jorian had to exert only a fraction of his normal strength to keep the craft going in a straight line. He was so much stronger than Zerlik that, if he had put his back into it, he would have made the *Flying Fish* spin in circles.

As they drew away with exasperating slowness, Ayuir waved from the quay before disappearing towards their inn. The *Flying Fish* heaved and bounced on a brisk chop, driven up the estuary by a steady west wind. The afternoon sun blazed in a clear blue sky.

"I hope he makes it back to Penembei safely," said Zerlik in a worried tone. The young Irazi was already looking green. "He speaks but few words of Novarian."

"Poor fellow! I would have given him lessons."

"Oh, it is not with him that I am concerned, but with my beautiful car and team. I can always get another manservant."

Jorian grunted. Zerlik said: "Excuse me. I have heard of these curious ideals that are rife in Novaria, of consideration for the lower classes, and I suppose I should guard my tongue with more care. Why put we not up the sails now?"

"We ought to get farther from that lee shore first, lest this sea breeze blow us back thither and pile us up."

They rowed for a while in silence, until Zerlik said: "Let me rest for a moment; I am fordone."

"Very well. What sort of speech do you use in Penembei?"

"Why, Penembic, of course."

"Is it related to Fediruni? I speak fair Fediruni, as well as Mulvani and Shvenic."

"Nay; Penembic is related to no other tongue—at least, in this part of the world—albeit it contains not a few words of Fediruni and Novarian origin. Our dynasty is of remotely Fediruni origin, you know; King Juktar was a nomadic chieftain in Fedirun. And before that, a Novarian adventurer founded the city and begat a dynasty. But Penembic is a much more precise and logical tongue than your congeries of Novarian dialects. Most of us speak a little Fediruni, since that is the tongue of the cult of the supreme god Ughroluk."

"You must teach me Penembic."

"I shall be pleased to. At least it will take my mind off this damnable stench of fish. Tell me: Why took you Gatorix's exhorbitant price for his glass? And why the sudden haste?"

Jorian chuckled. "I looked through the telescope up the Kyamos and saw a squad of horsemen riding hard down the river road. They were mere specks in the glass, but natheless they gave the impression of Xylarian guardsmen ... Hola!" Jorian reached behind him into the cabin and took the spyglass from its rack. He peered through it shoreward. "By Astis' ivory teats, those losels are on the quay now!"

"Let me see," said Zerlik.

On shore, the telescope showed a group of black-clad men, one of whom held the horses while the others expostulated with several Chemnites. Their vigorous gestures could be seen.

"Let's hope they don't find a barge and put to sea after us," muttered Jorian. "Eight oars could easily overhaul two. Row harder!"

After a while, Zerlik asked: "Could we not put up the sails now?"

"We shall, but count not too heavily upon them. With this onshore wind, we shall have to tack out to sea, and I know not how high our little tub will point. Here, give me the glass. Ten thousand demons, but they've already found a barge and are putting out! Now we're for it!"

## II

# The Flying Fish

"We must hoist the sails instanter," said Jorian.

Zerlik asked: "How do we that? I have never sailed."

"First, we heave to in the eye of the wind." With powerful strokes of his oar, Jorian turned the bow of the *Flying Fish* westward. The little ship pitched wildly as she took the waves bow-on. Jorian shipped his oar.

"Now," he said, "keep her in this position whilst I raise the sails. Oh, dip me in dung!"

"What is the matter?"

"I forgot that these sails had their covers on."

"I thought you were a nautical expert?"

"Do be quiet and let me think!" Jorian quickly unhooked the lashing of the mizzen cover.

"It is my skin, too," said Zerlik plaintively.

"Fear not for your precious skin. 'Tis I whom they're after."

"But if a fight develop, they will not draw subtle distinctions . . ."

Jorian, heaving on the mizzen halyard, forbore to answer. The mizzen yard went up by jerks. The yellow sail flapped and boomed as it luffed. Jorian shouted:

"Keep her head into the wind!"

"Why not sail on this sail alone?"

"Too far aft; she'd give us too much weather helm."

"I know not your nautical terms. Here come our pursuers!"

The black-hulled barge, rowed by eight men, had covered half the distance from the quay to the *Flying Fish*. Zerlik asked:

"Then why did you not put up that big front sail first?"

"One must hoist sail from stern forward. If one hoists the foremost sail first, the wind takes charge and sweeps one downwind—which in this case is upriver, whither we are fain not to go. There!"

Jorian belayed the halyard and worked his way forward to the mainmast. An instant later, Zerlik heard a wild yell. He called:

"What is the matter now?"

"May fiends torment, for a million eternities, the bastard who lashed this sail cover! He tied it in a hard knot, around to the front where I can't see it."

"Hasten, or the Xylarians will be upon us." The pursuers were now close enough for their faces to be discerned.

"I do my utmost. Shut up and hold her bow steady!"

The mainsail yard, swathed in the canvas sail cover, extended out for several feet beyond the bow. The knot that secured the lashing was at the forward end of this yard. To reach it, Jorian had to sprawl out lizardlike on the yard, gripping for dear life with his left arm, with his feet on the anchor, while he felt around the butt end of the yard with his free hand. To untie a hard knot with one hand takes doing even when one can see the knot, let alone when one has to work solely by touch.

The freshening wind drove larger and larger waves up the estuary. The *Flying Fish* leaped to each impact like a horse at a fence. Smash! smash! went the little ship's bow as she came down from each pitch.

Tossed up and down, eight or ten feet to each toss, Jorian had much ado to keep his grip on the yard. The sun, near to setting, turned the seaward waves to gold, which glared in Jorian's eyes like the glow from a furnace.

The barge drew closer. The Xylarians were within easy bowshot, but Jorian was sure they would not try archery. For one thing, the wind would carry their shafts awry; for another, they wanted him alive.

"Zevatas damn it!" he screamed as his hat blew off, alighted gently on a wave, and went sailing up the estuary on its own.

"Jorian!" called Zerlik. "A man is readying a lariat."

When it seemed hopeless, Jorian felt the knot yield to his straining fingers. The black pursuing barge was almost within spitting distance. The knot came loose at last. Feverishly, Jorian unhooked the sail cover, bundled it up, and tossed it aft. It came down on Zerlik and wrapped itself pythonlike about him. In trying to free himself from the canvas, he let go his oar.

"Keep her head into the wind!" bellowed Jorian, heaving on the main halyard.

Zerlik bundled up the sail cover and returned his attention to his oar. "Here comes the noose!" he called.

One Xylarian cast his lariat, but the cast fell short, into the heaving blue water. The yellow mainsail went up. Its luffing in the strong wind shook the ship. Jorian shouted:

"Point her to starboard!"

"Which is that?"

"Oh, my gods! Back water, stupid!"

Zerlik caught a crab with his oar but at last did as commanded. As the bow fell off to starboard, the wind, with sharp cracks, filled the sails on the port tack. The *Flying Fish* heeled to starboard and began to pick up speed.

As Jorian scrambled aft, he saw that the Kylarian with the lariat was again whirling his noose. The man's black hood had fallen back, exposing a head of long, wheat-colored hair. The man, Jorian thought, was probably a nomad from the steppes of Shven. Xylar often hired these Northerners for the Royal Guard because of their skill with the lariat, since the principal duty of the Guard was, not to protect the king, but to keep him from escaping and to catch him alive if he tried.

This time, Jorian was within easy casting distance. He scuttled into the cockpit.

"Ship your oar," he said, "and catch hold of my belt in back."

"Why?"

"Just do it."

The oar clattered inboard. Jorian stood up in the cockpit, with one hand on the mizzen backstay, and thumbed his nose at the Xylarians. Zerlik caught his belt from behind. The Xylarian put one foot on his gunwale to make his cast.

Helped by the wind, the noose whirled through the air and settled around Jorian's shoulders. Jorian seized the rope in both hands and gave a mighty heave. Zerlik pulled at the same time. The Xylarian was jerked clear out of the barge, splash!

With cries of rage and alarm, the pursuers stopped rowing. Those on the near side of the barge rose and stretched out their oars to the man in the water. One, in his zeal, hit the swimmer over the head. The head vanished but soon bobbed up again.

The *Flying Fish* gained speed. Jorian crouched in the cockpit, holding the tiller with one hand and with the other, reeling in the rope. He grinned at Zerlik.

"One can never have too much good rope on shipboard," he said.

The barge fell astern, while the Xylarians hauled their dripping comrade aboard. Zerlik asked:

"Are we safe, now?"

"I know not. She seems to point pretty well on this tack; but we have yet to learn how featly she comes about and how well she pointed with the sails taken aback."

"What means that?"

Jorian explained the features of lateen sails and the good and bad points of shifting the yards to the leeward of the masts with each tack. He cast a worried glance ahead, where the far side of the estuary was opening out as they neared it: a long, low green line of marshes and woods, interspersed with croplands and villages.

"Get forward, Zerlik," he said, "and watch for shoal water. All we need now is to run aground."

"How shall I do that?"

"Look straight down and yell when you think you see bottom."

After a while, Jorian called a warning, put the helm sharply down, and brought the *Flying Fish* about on the starboard tack. The little ship responded well and pointed almost as high on this tack as on the other. Zerlik called:

"The Xylarians have not yet given up, O Jorian. They seek to cut us off."

Jorian shaded his eyes. Laboring into the teeth of the wind, the pursuers were forging seaward. Although the *Flying Fish* moved much faster than the barge, the angle at which the lateener was forced to sail by the direction of the wind brought the two vessels on converging courses.

"Should we not tack again, ere we come close?" asked Zerlik.

"Mayhap; but they'd still be south of us. They'd run farther out to sea and intercept us on the next tack. I have a better idea."

With a dangerous glint in his eye, Jorian held his course. Closer came the barge.

"Now," said Jorian, "take the trumpet, go forward, and shout a warning, that we mean to exercise our right of way. Let them stand off if they would not be run down."

"Jorian! The collision would smash both ships!"

"Do as I say!"

Shaking his head, Zerlik went forward and shouted his warning. The Xylarians turned faces towards the *Flying Fish*, swiftly bearing down upon them. There was motion aboard the craft as some of the pursuers readied their nets and lariats. The *Flying Fish* kept on.

"Can you swim, Zerlik?" asked Jorian.

"A little, but not from here to shore! My gods, Jorian, would you really ram them?"

"You shall see. Repeat your warning."

At the last minute, the barge burst into action. The rowers backed water, the sea foaming over their oars. The *Flying Fish* raced past so close to windward that the barge rocked in her wake. One Xylarian stood up to shake a fist until his comrades pulled him down again.

"Whew!" breathed Zerlik. "Would you have truly run them down?"

Jorian grinned. "You'll never know. But, with that much way on, 'twould not have been hard to dodge them. Anyway, we can now devote ourselves to the sea road to Iraz—if storms, calms, sea monsters, and pirates interfere not. Now excuse me whilst I pray to Psaan to avert these perils."

Night fell, but the brisk wind held. Having lost his lunch and being unable to eat any dinner, Zerlik sat moaning with his head in his hands.

"How do you stand it?" he asked, watching with revulsion as Jorian, one hand on the tiller, put away a hearty supper. "You eat enough for two."

Jorian bit a piece out of an apple, swallowed, and replied: "Oh, I used to get seasick, too. On my first cruise against pirates, as king of Xylar, I was sick as a dying dog. I was like that fellow in the operetta, *The Good Ship Petticoat,* by Galliben and Silfero—you know, the one who sings about being a pirate captain bold."

"I know it not. Could you give it to me?"

"I can try, albeit vocal training is one skill wherefore I've not had time." in a heavy bass voice, slightly off key, Jorian sang:

"Oh, I am a pirate captain bold;
I fill my vessel with jewels and gold

And slaughter my captives, young and old,
To rule the raging sea, oh!

"And whether the blast be hot or cold,
And the tossing main be deep or shoaled,
I'm master of all that I behold
As I cruise the ocean free, oh!

"But although with treasure I fill my hold,
And my loot at a bountiful price is sold,
I harbor a secret that's never been told:
I'm sick as a dog at sea, oh!"

"That is good!" said Zerlik. "I would learn it; for I know no Novarian songs." He started off in a high but well-controlled tenor.

"You sing better than I ever shall," said Jorian after he had helped his comrade through the lyrics.

"Ah, but amongst us, to carry a tune well is deemed one of the accomplishments of a gentleman! How got you over your seasickness?"

"Well, thanks to Psaan—"

"Thanks to whom?"

"Psaan, the Novarian sea god. Anyway, my system adjusted, and I've never been seasick since. Perhaps you will adapt likewise. That reminds me: Is my—ah—colorful past known in Iraz?"

"Nay, at least so far as I know."

"Then how did you learn of it?"

"Doctor Karadur told me about your having been king of Xylar and accompanying him to Mulvan and Shven, to make it easier for me to find you. He swore me to secrecy, howsomever."

"Good for him! Karadur is a wise old man, if sometimes absent-minded. Now, when we reach your homeland, I want no word of my former kingship or aught else breathed abroad. To the Irazis I shall be merely a respectable technician. Do you understand?"

"Aye, sir."

"Then come hither and take the tiller. It must be the hour of the owl already, and I needs must get some sleep."

"May I run her closer to shore? I can barely see the coast, and so much water around me makes me nervous."

Zerlik gestured to eastward, where the Xylarian coast formed a black strip between sky and sea, both illuminated by the rising moon. The moon cast a million silvery spangles on the waves between the *Flying Fish* and the shore.

"Gods, no!" said Jorian. "Off a lee shore like this, the more water around us the better. Keep her as far from shore as we are now, and wake me if aught happens."

Next day, the west wind continued, blowing little cotton-wool clouds across the deep-blue sky. Zerlik still complained of headache but summoned enough strength to eat. Jorian, with a scarf tied around his head in piratical fashion in place of his lost hat, took the tiller. As he guided the *Flying Fish*, he quizzed Zerlik about the language of Penembei. After an hour of explanation, he clapped a hand to his forehead.

"Gods and goddesses!" he cried. "How do little Penembians ever master so complicated a tongue? I can understand having indicative, interrogative, imperative, conditional, and subjunctive moods; but when you add to those the optative, causative, dubitative, reportative, accelerative, narrative, continuative, and—"

"But of course, my good Jorian! That is why we deem our speech superior to all others, for one can say exactly what one means. Now, to go over the aorist perfect reportative of the verb 'to sleep' again. In Novarian you would say: 'They say that I used to sleep' but in Penembic we do all that with a single word—"

"A single word with fifty-three suffixes," growled Jorian. Later he said: "Perhaps you'd better merely teach me common expressions, like 'Good morning' and 'How much?' I used to think myself a fair linguist; but your grammar baffles me."

"Ah, but once you learn the rules, you have but to follow them to speak correctly. There is none of those irregularities and exceptions that make your Novarian tongue so maddening."

By mid-afternoon, the wind and the sea had moderated. Feeling better, Zerlik moved about, learning the spars, the lines, and the other parts of the ship.

"I shall be a true mariner yet!" he exclaimed in a rush of enthusiasm. Standing on the gunwale abeam of the mizzenmast, he burst into the song from *The Good Ship Petticoat.* As he reached the final "oh!" he let go the mizzen stay to make a dramatic gesture. At that instant, the *Flying Fish* lurched to a large wave. With a yell of dismay, Zerlik fell into the sea.

"By Vaisus' brazen arse!" cried Jorian as he put the helm down. The *Flying Fish* turned into the wind, lost way, and luffed. Jorian gathered up the rope he had taken from the Xylarians, belayed one end to a cleat, and hurled the rest of it to Zerlik, whose head bobbed into sight and out again with the rise and fall of the waves.

With the third cast, Zerlik got his hands on the rope. Jorian hauled him by the slack of his fisherman's blouse up over the counter. While Zerlik, bent into a knot of misery, retched, coughed, spat, and sneezed, Jorian said: "That'll teach you to keep a grip on something all the time you're out of the cockpit! Remember the rule: one hand for yourself, one for the ship."

"*Ghrlp,*" said Zerlik.

The wind fell. The sun set behind a bank of fog, which rolled in from the sea. Jorian said:

"We shall be becalmed in that fog. We'd better head into shore and anchor."

An hour later, as the first tendrils of fog drifted past the *Flying Fish,* Jorian dropped anchor and furled sail. The wind died. The waves became smooth little oily swells, just big enough to rock the *Flying Fish* gently. Jorian and Zerlik bailed out the bilge water with sponge and bucket.

When daylight vanished, utter darkness settled down, since the moon did not rise until hours after sunset. Jorian lit a small lanthorn. When he and his companion tired of language lessons, they played skillet by the feeble light. Jorian won several marks.

"Never bluff more than once at a sitting," he said. "Would you like me to take first watch?"

"Nay; I could not sleep, with all the salt water I have swallowed."

Later, Jorian was awakened. Zerlik whispered: "I hear something!"

Yawning and rubbing his eyes, Jorian ducked out of the cabin. A pearly opalescence in the fog showed that the moon had risen. The ocean was still as a pond, so that Jorian could not tell direction.

The sound was a rhythmic thump. Jorian, listening, said: "Galley oars."

"Whose galley?"

Jorian shrugged. "Belike Ir; belike Xylar; belike Algarthian pirates."

"What were the galleys of Ir or Xylar doing out in this murk?"

"I know not. The sea power of both states is at ebb— Ir because their pinchpenny Syndicate won't keep up their fleet; Xylar because they don't have me to keep 'em on their toes. Hence I surmise that all the ships of both are snug in harbor, and that the oars we hear are piratical."

"I should think the Algarthians would fear running aground as much as we do."

"They have wizards whose second sight enables them

to warn their ships away from rocks and shoals. They can also see storms and fogs approaching from afar. Now let's be quiet, lest they hear us."

"A Penembic gentleman," muttered Zerlik, "would scorn to let such scum frighten him into silence."

"Be as knightly as you please, when you're on your own. Just now, 'tis my skin, too—as you remarked the other day. Since I am neither a Penembian nor a gentleman, I prefer saving my hide to parading my courage. Now shut up."

"You ought not to speak to me like that—" began Zerlik indignantly, but Jorian shot him so fierce a look that he subsided.

The sound of the oars grew louder. Mingled with them was the splash of the oar blades, the tap of the coxswain's drum, and an occasional snatch of speech. Jorian cocked an ear.

"I cannot quite make out their language," he breathed.

The sounds receded and died. Zerlik said: "May we speak, now?"

"I think so."

"Well, if these Algarthian wizards can foresee the weather, why cannot they control it?"

"Seeing is one thing; doing, quite another. There have been but few wizards who could control the winds and the waves, and their efforts have gone awry as often as not. Take the case of King Fusinian and the tides."

"What story is this?"

Jorian settled himself. "Fusinian was a former king of my native Kortoli. A son of Filoman the Well-Meaning, he was called Fusinian the Fox on account of his small stature, agility, and quickness of wit.

"Once, King Fusinian invited the leading members of his court to a picnic on the beach of Sigrum, a few leagues from Kortoli City, where the waves of the Inner

Sea break on the silvery sands. A fine beach for picnicking, swimming, and like amusements it is. The beach lies in a long curve at the foot of a low bluff. Thither went Fusinian, with his lovely queen Thanuda and the royal children, and his high officers of state with their wives and children, too.

"Now, one of the guests was Fusinian's distant cousin Forvil, then enjoying a sinecure as curator of the royal art gallery. Being fat and lazy, Forvil impressed those who knew him—including the king—as a harmless nonentity. But the fact was that Forvil cherished royal ambitions of his own and, at the time of the picnic, had already begun to put forth tendrils of intrigue.

"In Fusinian's presence, however, the Honorable Forvil was full of unctuous flattery. This time he outdid himself, for he said: 'Your Majesty, your servants have placed the picnic chairs and tables where the rising tide will inundate us all.'

"'Really?' said Fusinian, staring. 'By Zevatas, I do believe you're right! I shall order all this gear moved to higher ground forthwith.'

"'Oh, sire, that will not be needed,' quoth Forvil. 'So great are Your Serene Majesty's powers that you have but to command the tides, and they will obey you.' For the tides in the Inner Sea, while smaller than those along this coast, are still big enough to drench a crew of picnickers who carelessly site their feast below the high-water mark."

"'Don't talk nonsense,' said Fusinian, and turned to give the command to move the chairs and tables.

"'Oh, but sire! 'Tis a simple fact!' persisted Forvil. 'An you believe me not, command the sea, and you shall see!'

"'Damn it, I will!' said Fusinian, no little annoyed, for he suspected that Forvil essayed to make a fool of him. 'And you, dear cousin, shall see what nugacities you are uttering.' So Fusinian stood up and waved his hands in mystic passes and cried:

"Hocus pocus
Keep your locus
Do not soak us!"

"Then he sat down and resumed eating, saying: 'If we get wet, O Forvil, you shall pay for the damage to our raiment.'

"The guests likewise remained seated and ate, albeit nervously, since they did not wish on one hand to wet their finery, nor on the other to entreat their king discourteously by fleeing the tide whilst he faced it unflinching. And so things went for a time, whilst the picnic was consumed and the sweet wines were poured.

"But, strangely, the tide failed to rise at the appointed time. People looked surreptitiously at pocket sundials and at one another and—with deepening awe—at their lively little king, who ate and drank unconcerned. At last there was no doubt about it, that the tide had been halted in its wonted rise. Forvil stared at his king with his fat face the color of gypsum plaster.

"Fusinian was perturbed by this phenomenon, for he knew well enough that he had uttered no real magical spell, nor summoned a horde of demons to hold back the tide. And, whilst he pondered—keeping a straight face the whiles—one of his children approached him, saying: 'Daddy, a lady up on the hill asked us to give this to you.'

"Fusinian saw that the note was from the witch Gloé, who dwelt in the hills of southern Kortoli and had long coveted the post of chief magician of the kingdom. The fact was that she was not even a licensed wizardess, because of a long-standing feud betwixt her and Fusinian's Bureau of Commerce and Licenses. She had come uninvited to the picnic in hope of persuading King Fusinian to intervene with his bureaucrats. When, by her super-normal powers, she overheard the colloquy between Fusinian and Forvil, she seized the opportunity and, concealed in the woods above the bluff, cast her mightiest spell, to hold back the tide.

"Gloé's powers were, however, limited, as are those of all sentient beings. For most of an hour she held back the tide but then felt her authority weakening. She therefore scribbled this note and called to her the young prince, who was playing tag with the other children on the slope of the bluff. The note said: 'Gloé to His Majesty: Sire, my spell has slipped, and the waters are returning. Get you to higher ground.'

"Fusinian divined what had happened. But, if he confessed the truth, all the effect of retarding the tide would be lost, and Forvil would win this round. So he stood up and cried:

" 'My friends, we have sat here gorging and swilling longer than is good for us. To settle our stomachs, I ordain a race to the top of yonder bluff. There shall be three classes: first, the children below the age of thirteen; the winner shall have a pony from the royal stables. Second: the ladies, for whom the prize shall be a silver tiara from the royal coffers. Third: the men, the swiftest of whom shall receive a crossbow from the royal armory. I warn you that I shall take part in the third race. Since, howsomever, 'twere ridiculous to award a prize to myself, I will, if I win, bestow it upon him who comes in second. Line up, children! Ready, set, go!' And the children were off like the wind in a yelling mob. Then he said: 'Line up, girls! You'd better hike those gowns up to the knee, if you would make any speed. Ready, set, go! And now, gentlemen . . .' And he repeated the performance with the men."

Zerlik put in: "If the king were competing, would not all the courtiers make a point of losing?"

"With some kings, aye; but not with Fusinian, whom they knew to be a true sportsman. They knew that he would resent it if he caught anyone patronizing him by deliberately holding back. So they all ran their best.

Being very wiry and active, Fusinian did in sooth reach the top of the bluff the first of the men. But poor Forvil, being fat, was puffing and waddling along at the base of the bluff when the tide came in with a rush, knocked him down, rolled him over, and half drowned him before a pair of servants pulled him out of the water.

"Fusinian always disclaimed any hand in the phenomenon of the tides, saying that it must have been the libration of the moon or some such thing. But his folk believed not these disclaimers and looked upon him with more awe than ever."

"Did he reward the witch?"

"Nay; for he said that she'd acted without authorization and, moreover, had given him a very uncomfortable time whilst trying to think his way out of the predicament into which she had plunged him. When he came down with a persistent itch on the soles of his feet, he suspected that Gloé in revenge had sent it upon him by goëtic magic. But nought could be proven; and his chief wizard, Doctor Aichos, managed to cure it."

"And the Honorable Forvil?"

"In consequence of these events, Fusinian entertained a lively suspicion of his cousin. Being Fusinian, he thought of an original way to discourage Forvil from hanging about the court and intriguing for power. Pretending that Forvil was a connoisseur of all the arts, he invited him down to the dungeon beneath his palace to listen to Fusinian practicing on his bagpipes. Forvil's perceptive criticisms of his playing, he said, would soon make him the finest piper in Novaria. After three days of this, Forvil 'got religion,' as they say, and became a priest of Astis. Thereafter his sacerdotal duties furnished him with a legitimate excuse for not listening to the howls of the royal instrument. In any case, he gave up his intrigues lest worse befall him."

\* \* \*

An hour after sunrise, the fog thinned. A land breeze sprang up. The fog dissolved into patches and dwindled away; the sun blazed forth. Jorian hoisted the anchor and broke out the yellow sails. When they were well out to sea, Zerlik said:

"How convenient, that the wind should take us out to sea again when we wish to go thither! Did you pray to your Psaan?"

Jorian shook his head. "I like it not. A regular land breeze springs up at night and takes coasters and fishermen out to sea ere dawn. This feels like the kind of easter that heralds a storm . . . Murrain! Do I see ships off our starboard bow?"

Zerlik ducked around the mizzen. "Aye, that you do! One is a sailing ship; the other looks like some sort of galley but is also under sail."

"Take the tiller." Through the spyglass, Jorian examined the ships, which were bearing briskly down upon the *Flying Fish.* "Fry my balls, but I'm a dolt for not keeping a sharper watch! I ought to have seen them as soon as their mastheads showed. Now they've seen us."

"Pirates?"

"Indubitably. That blue thing they fly is the Algarthian flag."

"Can we flee?"

"No chance, curse it. If I knew the rocks and shoals hereabouts, I might seek refuge in water too shallow for them to follow; but I don't. If we had Karadur, belike he could cast a glamor on us to make us invisible, or at least to make us look like a rock in the sea. But we have him not."

"Why do the Twelve Cities not get together to extirpate this nuisance?"

"Because they're too busy quarreling amongst themselves, and one is ever hiring the pirates to plague another. Some years ago, in the reign of Tonio of Xylar, the Syndicate of Ir did hire the Zolonian navy to root the rascals out. But then the Novarians lapsed into their

old ways, and the pirates sprang up in the archipelago again."

"You need an all-powerful emperor, like our king.
What shall we do if they stop us?"

"We're humble fishermen, remember? Get a line
over the side and troll."

The approaching ships were now near enough for
details to be made out. One was a carack, converted
from merchant service. The other had been a bireme,
which now had her lower oar ports blocked to make
her more serviceable in rough weather. Her oars had
been shipped, but now several were thrust out through
the upper ports on each side to add to her speed.

"I will not!" said Zerlik.

Jorian turned a puzzled frown. "Will not what?"

"Pretend to be a humble fisherman! I have been
running and hiding ever since I met you, and I am sick
of it. I will defy these scoundrels to do their worst!"

"Calm down, you idiot! You can't fight a whole ship-
load of freebooters."

"I care not!" cried Zerlik, becoming ever more
excited. "At least, I shall take a few of these wretches
with me!"

He ducked into the cabin and reappeared with his
scimitar, which he unwrapped from its oilskin covering
and drew from its sheath. He waved it at the
approaching ships, forcing Jorian to duck to avoid getting slashed.

"Come on!" shrilled Zerlik. "I defy you! Come, and
you shall taste the steel of a gentleman of—"

A heavy thump cut off his words, and he slumped
to the floor of the cockpit, his sword clanging beside
him. Jorian had struck him on the head with the heavy
leaden ball forming the pommel of his dagger. He
lashed the tiller, sheathed and put away the scimitar,
got out the fishing tackle, and let a line trail astern.

"Heave to!" came a shout through a speaking trumpet from the forecastle of the galley.

A sharp tug on Jorian's fishing pole told of a strike. He jerked the pole and felt a solid, quivering pull.

"Heave to, I said!" came the cry from the galley. "Are you fain to be run down?"

"Can ye na see that I've got a fish?" yelled Jorian, struggling with line and pole.

There was a buzz of talk on the galley. Some sportsman among the Algarthians was arguing that Jorian should be given a chance to land his catch before being pirated. The galley swung to starboard, backing water with her starboard oars. She furled her sail and rowed parallel to the *Flying Fish,* twenty paces away. The carack trimmed sail to follow more distantly.

Jorian landed a mackerel. Leaving the fish to flop in the bottom of the cockpit beside the unconscious Zerlik, he brought the *Flying Fish* into the wind and luffed.

"God den, me buckos, and what would ye with me?" he said in down-west Xylarian dialect. "Would ye buy some of me fish? There be this bonny fresh one ye seen me catch, and a dozen or three more salted in the hold. What would ye?"

More muttering on the galley. The man with the trumpet called: "We'll take your fish, Master Fisherman." As the galley maneuvered close to the *Flying Fish,* the man said: "What ails the other fellow, lying in the bilge?"

"Ah, the poor spalpeen—me nephew, he be—had no better sense than to try to drink the port dry, afore we cast off. So now he be as ye see him. He'll be jimp in an hour."

Someone on the galley lowered a basket on a line over the side. While several pirates with boathooks held the two vessels apart, Jorian tossed his fresh mackerel into the basket and followed it with salted fish from the hold. When the basket had been hoisted back aboard the galley, Jorian said:

"Now about me price . . ."

The pirate with the trumpet grinned over his rail.

"Oh, we'll give you something vastly more precious than money."

"Eh? And what might that be?"

"Namely, your life. Farewell, Master Fisherman. Shove off!"

Jorian sat scowling up and moving his mouth in silent curses as the galley rowed away and broke out its sails. Then his scowl changed to a smile as he put his tiller to starboard, so that the little ship, as she backed before the shore wind, swung clockwise. The sails filled, and the *Flying Fish* resumed her southward course. Zerlik stirred, groaned, and pulled himself up on the thwart. He asked:

"What did you hit me with?"

Jorian unhooked his dagger from his belt. "See this? The blade won't come out unless you press this button. Hence I can use it as a bludgeon, holding the sheath and striking with this leaden pommel. I had one a couple of years ago, when I was adventuring with Karadur. I lost it later, but I liked the design so well that I had another made. It comes in handy when I wish, not to slay a man, but merely to stop him from doing something foolish—like getting my throat cut so that he can show what a fearless, gallant gentleman he is."

"I will get even with you for that blow, you insolent bully!"

"You'd better save your revenge until after we reach Iraz. I doubt if I could handle this craft alone; and if I could not, I'm sure you couldn't."

"Are you always so invincibly practical? Have you no human emotions? Are you a man or a machine of cogs and wires?"

Jorian chuckled. "Oh, I daresay I could make as big a fool of myself as the next, did I let myself go. When I was a young lad like you—"

"You are no doddering graybeard!"

"Forsooth, I'm not yet thirty; but the vicissitudes of an irregulous life have forced maturity upon me. If

you're lucky, you will grow up fast, too, ere some childish blunder puts you into your next incarnation—as has
almost happened thrice on this little voyage."

"Humph!" Zerlik ducked into the cabin, where he
sat, holding his head and sulking, for the rest of the
day.

Next day, however, he was cheerful again. He
obeyed orders and performed his duties on the ship as
if nothing had happened.

# III

# The Tower of Kumashar

For nearly a hundred leagues, the mighty lograms marched along the western coast. The dragon-spine of the range, clad in evergreen forests of somber hue, continued down into the sea. Hence, this part of the Western Ocean was spangled with islets and sea-washed reefs and rocks, forcing ships to detour to seaward. Then the Lograms dwindled into the hills of Penembei, green in spring but a drab dun color, with only a faint speckling of green, in autumn.

As the sun arose above these green-spotted brown hills on the twenty-fourth of the Month of the Unicorn, Jorian aimed his spyglass southward along the coast. He said:

"Take a look, Zerlik. Is that your clock tower—that little thing that sticks up where the shoreline meets the horizon?"

Zerlik looked. "It could be . . . I do believe that it is . . . Aye, I see a plume of smoke from the top. That is the veritable Tower of Kumashar."

"Named for some former king, I suppose?"

"Nay, not so. It is a curious story as to how this came to pass."

"Say on."

"Know that Kumashar was an eminent architect and engineer, over a century ago in the reign of Shashtai the Third, otherwise called Shashtai the Crotchety. Now, Kumashar persuaded King Shashtai to hire him to build this lighthouse tower—without the clocks, however; those were installed later."

"I know," said Jorian. "My own dear father installed them when I was a little fellow."

"Really? Now that I think, I believe Karadur said something of that in this letter. Did your father take you to Iraz with him?"

"Nay; we dwelt in Ardamai, in Kortoli, and he was gone for several months on this contract. He claimed your king cheated him out of most of his fee, too; some confiscatory tax on money taken out of the kingdom. But go on with the tale."

"Well, King Shashtai wished his own name—not that of the architect—inscribed on the masonry for all to see. When Kumashar said that his name, too, ought to appear, the king waxed wroth. He told Kumashar that he was getting above himself and had better mend his ways.

"But Kumashar was not so easily balked. He built the tower with a shallow recess on one side, and on the masonry of the recess he personally chiseled: 'Erected by Kumashar the Son of Yuinda in the Two Hundred and Thirtieth Year of the Juktarian Dynasty.' Then he covered this inscription with a coating of plaster, flush with the rest of that side of the tower, and on the plaster he inscribed the name of the king as commanded.

"For some years, the tower bore the name of King Shashtai. But then the plaster softened in the brumal rains and peeled away, exposing the name of the architect.

"King Shashtai was furious when he learnt how he had been flouted. It would have gone hard with Kumashar had he not—fortunately or unfortunately, depending upon how one looks at it—already died of natural causes.

"So the king commanded that the offending inscription be chiseled out and one more to his liking substituted. But his officials had esteemed Kumashar highly and did not much like Shashtai the Crotchety, who was by this time old and infirm himself. So they politely acceded to the king's commands but then found endless pretexts for delaying the work. There was never quite enough money in the treasury, or unforeseen technical problems had arisen, or something. And soon King Shashtai died in his turn, leaving the inscription still unmodified."

"Showing that the power even of these mighty monarchs is limited by human factors," said Jorian. "I went all through that as king of Xylar. 'Tis one thing to say to one's minion: 'Do this,' and have him reply: 'Yes, sire; I hear and obey'; and quite another to follow one's order down the chain of command and see that it be not mislaid along the way. What sort of king have you now?"

"King Ishabar?" Zerlik's features took on a stiff controlled expression. He gave a mechanical smile, such as Jorian had often seen on the faces of courtiers and officials during his own reign in Xylar. "Oh, sir, what a splendid monarch he is! Quite a paragon of wisdom, justice, courage, morality, prudence, dignity, generosity, and nobility."

"Sounds too good to be true. Has he *no* faults?"

"Ughroluk preserve us! Nay, not a fault. Of course, he *is* a bit of a gourmet. He sensibly devotes himself to the harmless pleasures of the table and leaves the details of running the state to experts, over whom he merely exercises a benevolent supervision. Moreoever, he is too prudent to risk his precious person by buzzing about the kingdom, forcing heavy expenses upon the locals to entertain him and upsetting the provincial officials and military commanders by importunate interference. Like a good king, he stays home in his palace and minds his business."

In other words, thought Jorian, the fellow is a lazy, self-indulgent hog who sits gorging in his gilded sty and lets the kingdom shift for itself.

\* \* \*

The hills leveled off into the broad valley of the river Lyap, at the mouth of which sprawled vast Iraz. The *Flying Fish* sailed serenely past the suburb of Zaktan, on the northern side of the river. Zerlik pointed to a large, many-spired building, on whose gilded domes and turrets the midday sun flashed.

"The temple of Nubalyaga," he said.

"Who or what is Nubalyaga?"

"Our goddess of the moon and of love and fertility. The racecourse lies behind it. There is supposed to be a secret tunnel under the river, joining that temple with the royal palace. It is reported to have been dug at vast expense in the reign of King Hoshcha, to serve the king on the occasions of the Divine Marriage; but I know of none who will admit having actually seen it."

"If it ever existed, it must have filled up with water," said Jorian. "Those things always leak, and it would take an army with mops and buckets to keep it dry. But what's this Divine Marriage?"

"On the night of the full moon, the temple of Nubalyaga celebrates the wedding of Nubalyaga to Ughroluk, the god of the sun, of storms, and of war. The king plays the rôle of Ughroluk and the high priestess, that of Nubalyaga. Chaluish, the high priest of Ughroluk, and High Priestess Sahmet are nominally husband and wife, as required by their offices; but they have long been at bitter enmity, each trying to rape away some of the other's power. They fell out over the Prophecies of Salvation, a decade agone."

"What prophecies were these?"

"Oh, Sahmet announced that Nubalyaga had revealed to her in a dream that the salvation of Iraz depended on a barbarian savior from the North." Zerlik looked sharply at Jorian. "Would you qualify as a barbarian savior from the North?"

"Me? By Astis' ivory teats, no! I'm no barbarian, and I have all I can do to save my own hide, let alone a city's. But the other prophecy?"

"Well, not to be outdone, Chaluish proclaimed that all this about barbarian saviors was nonsense. His god Ughroluk had appeared to him in a trance and avouched that the salvation of Iraz depended on keeping the clocks in Kumashar's Tower running. And there things rest—albeit 'rest' is not the word I want, since the twain have continued to plot and intrigue against each other from that day to this."

They sailed past the mouth of the Lyap, where scores of ships, large and small, lay at anchor. There were high-sided merchant galleons, smaller caracks and caravels, little coasters and fishermen, barges and wherries, and the long, low, lethal, black-hulled forms of war galleys. Preëminent among these were several huge catamarans, capable of carrying thousands of rowers, sailors, and marines in each twin-hulled ship. The sun gleamed on the gold-plated ornaments of the galleys. The Penembic flag, with a golden torch on a blue field, flew from their jackstaffs.

"I shouldn't think Algarthian pirates would venture near Iraz, in the face of that fleet," said Jorian.

Zerlik shrugged. "It is not, alas, so formidable as it looks."

"Wherefore so?"

"The costs of labor have been rising, so that His Majesty has been unable to afford full crews. And one of those monster double-hulled battleships, if its oars be not fully manned, is too slow and unwieldly to cope with pirates. There have in fact been several piracies within a few leagues of Iraz during the past year. Now there is talk of ships of black freebooters from Paalua, across the ocean, joining in the game. They once invaded Ir, did they not?"

"Aye, and not so long past."

The cries of sailormen came faintly across the water as some ships furled sails and were towed to their anchorages by tug-wherries. Others were towed out, broke out their sails, and put to sea.

The *Flying Fish* sailed past the river mouth and reached the waterfront of Iraz proper. Here, ships pushed off from the piers and quays, while others sought places at them, with much shouting and cursing.

Along the shore, wooden cranes slowly rotated and raised and lowered their loads, like long-necked water birds. They were powered by huge treadwheels, which in turn were manned by convicts. Behind them rose the sea wall guarding the city, and over the wall could be seen the domes and spires of Iraz. The hot sun flashed on roof plates of copper, or of copper plated with silver and gold. Beyond the city, on a ridge of higher ground, a row of windmills turned lazily in the gentle breeze.

"Where should we dock?" asked Jorian.

"I—I believe the fishing wharves are at the south end," said Zerlik.

The *Flying Fish* passed the Tower of Kumashar, soaring up over a furlong. Halfway up, on all four sides, the circle of a clock face interrupted the sweep of the buff-colored masonry. The single hand of all four clocks showed the Hour of the Otter. Jorian took out a ring with a short length of fine chain, held it suspended, and turned it slowly against the sun. A pinhole in the upper part of the ring let a tiny shaft of light through to illumine the hours marked on the inner side of the lower half of the ring.

"As I thought, 'tis past the Hour of the Turtle," said Jorian.

"If that be designed for measuring times in Ir," said Zerlik, "you must needs correct it for the distance you have come southward."

"I know that; but even with such a correction, 'tis plain that your clocks are out of order."

"They have not run for months. Old Yiyim, the clockmaster, kept saying that he would get them fixed any day. At length His Majesty lost patience. Doctor Karadur had been pressing him to let him take over the task, and now the king told him to go ahead. So the good doctor requested His Majesty to dispatch me to fetch you to Iraz. And behold, here we are! Excuse me whilst I don more seemly garb."

Zerlik vanished into the cabin, whence he presently emerged with a complete change of clothes. He wore a silken shirt with full sleeves and over it a short, embroidered, sleeveless vest. A knee-length pleated skirt clad his legs; slippers with turned-up toes, his feet. On his head sat the cylindrical, brimless, felt Irazi cap, like a small inverted bucket.

"You had better don your more respectable raiment, also," he said. "Even though you disclaim the status of gentleman, it were well as a practical matter to look like one."

"I daresay you're right," replied Jorian. In his turn, he got out his one decent suit of shirt, jacket, hose tights, and soft boots.

"You are obviously a foreigner," said Zerlik, surveying him, "but that is no matter. Iraz is a cosmopolitan city, and the folk are used to exotic garb."

The *Flying Fish* came abreast of the fishing wharves, where nets spread like gigantic bats from house to house to dry. Jorian guided the little ship to within a score of yards of the first empty quay, then hove to and lowered the sails.

"Why sail we not right up to the mooring?" asked Zerlik. "It would make a better impression than laboring into shore by our oars, like a pair of base lumpers."

"If I knew the ship and the waterfront better, I might. As it is, I might miscalculate. Then we should smash into the quay and damage our ship. That would make a far worse impression than rowing."

As the *Flying Fish* touched gently against the quay, Jorian and Zerlik scrambled ashore and made fast to the bollards. While they were tying up, an official-looking person with brass buttons on his dark-blue vest and a short, curved sword at his side bustled up and spoke in Penembic. Zerlik answered. Although he could now make up a few simple sentences in the complex Penembic tongue, Jorian could not understand the language when spoken rapidly.

"He is a deputy port inspector," said Zerlik as the man climbed aboard the *Flying Fish*. "He will collect the harbor tax and issue you a temporary pass. Then you must apply at the Bureau of Travel and Immigration for a permit as a resident alien."

"Can we leave the ship tied up here?"

"I do not believe we are supposed to leave it overnight, but for a small bribe I think I can arrange it. He will not make things difficult for one of my rank."

"How shall I find Karadur?"

"Oh, I will take care of that. Instead of lugging our gear to our quarters like navvies, let you remain with the ship, guarding it, whilst I go to inform Doctor Karadur of our arrival. He will send transportation suitable for persons of our quality."

Jorian was not much taken with this plan, fearing being stranded in a strange city where he neither knew his way nor spoke the language. While he pondered his reply, the inspector sprang ashore again and chattered with Zerlik. Next, the inspector produced writing materials, including several small sheets of reed paper.

"He wants your name and nationality," said Zerlik.

With Zerlik translating, Jorian furnished the needed information, while the inspector filled in blanks on his form in duplicate. At last Jorian was asked to sign both copies.

"Will you kindly read this to me?" he said. "I like not to sign my name to aught I can't read; and your Penembic script looks like a tangle of fishhooks."

Zerlik translated the text: a statement of Jorian's identity, the purpose of his visit, and other elementary matters. At length he signed. The official handed him one copy and departed. Zerlik shouted across the water-front street, and a donkey boy came running with his animal behind him.

"Farewell for the nonce!" cried Zerlik, swinging aboard the ass. "Guard well our impedimenta!"

He jogged off along the waterfront street, with the boy running beside him. Then he turned and vanished through one of the huge fortified gates in the sea wall, which rose behind the row of slatternly houses on the landward side of the street.

Jorian shaded his eyes against the low westering sun and gazed out to sea, which had become an undulating carpet of golden flakes. Then he examined his surroundings.

Men came and went along the waterfront. Most were Penembians in felt caps. Some wore a pleated knee-length skirt like Zerlik's, while others encased their legs in baggy trousers, gathered at the ankle. There was a sprinkling of Fedirunis in head cloths and robes, and an occasional Mulvanian in a bulbous turban. Now and then came a black man—a Paaluan with wavy hair and beard, wearing a feather cloak, or perhaps a kinky-haired, scar-faced man from the tropical jungles of Beraoti, swathed in animal skins or in a loosely-pinned rectangle of cloth. A train of laden camels swayed past, their bells chiming.

Jorian waited.

And he waited.

He took a turn along the waterfront, peering in the doors of the taverns and lodging houses that backed against the sea wall and looking in shop windows. He tried to ask a few Irazis the way to Doctor Karadur's dwelling. He had put together the words comprising a simple question; but each time, the native came back with a long, rattling sentence, too fast for Jorian to understand. He stopped a man in a head cloth and queried him in Fediruni, but all the reply he got was:

"I am sorry, good sir, but I am a stranger here, too."

Jorian returned to the *Flying Fish* and waited some more. The sun set. He prepared a dinner from the supplies on the ship, ate, waited some more, and went to sleep in the cabin.

Next morning, there was still no sign of Zerlik. Jorian wondered whether the young man had fallen victim to an accident, or to foul play, or whether he had deliberately abandoned his companion.

Jorian would have liked to stroll about the neighborhood, to learn the layout of the nearby streets. On the other hand, he durst not leave his gear unguarded aboard the *Flying Fish*. Although the cabin door had a lock, it was of the sort that any enterprising thief could pick with a bent pin. To prove that this was the case, Jorian took out of a leathern inside pocket in his hose one of several pieces of bent wire and opened the locked door with ease. He had learnt to pick locks in preparing for his flight from Xylar.

To find a man in a strange city, without guide or map, where one did not speak the language, was a formidable task. (If he had known about street signs and house numbers, he would have added their lack to the hazards facing him. Never having heard of them, he did not miss them.) The task was perhaps not quite so hazardous as slaying a dragon or competing in spells with a first-class wizard, but it was still one to daunt all but the boldest.

When a merchantman pulled into a neighboring berth and several travelers stepped ashore, a tout hurried up to offer his services. Jorian, however, had a profound distrust of such gentry. The more eager one of them seemed to take the stranger in tow, the more likely he was to be planning robbery or murder.

The Hour of the Hare came, and Jorian still turned over plans. For instance, if he could accost a port official with whom he had some speech in common, he could then ask advice about trustworthy guides. Of course the fellow might hand him over to some cut-throat with whom he had an arrangement for sharing the loot . . .

As Jorian, seated in the cockpit of the *Flying Fish*, thought about these matters, a familiar figure appeared in the distance, ambling towards the *Flying Fish* on the back of an ass. It was a thin, dark-skinned old man with long white hair and beard, clad in a coarse brown robe and a bulbous white turban. He was followed by a youth mounted on another ass and leading a third.

Jorian bounded out of his ship. "Karadur!" he shouted.

The oldster drew rein and stiffly dismounted. Jorian folded him in a bearlike hug. Then they held each other out by the arms.

"By Imbal's brazen balls!" cried Jorian. "It's been over a year!"

"You look well, my son," said Karadur, on the middle finger of whose left hand shone a golden ring with a large, round, blue stone. "The sun has burnt you as dark as a black from the jungles of Beraoti."

"I've been conning this little tub for ten days, without a hat. And by the way, Holy Father, she's yours."

"What mean you, O Jorian?"

"The *Flying Fish* belongs to you. You furnished the wherewithal to buy her in Chemnis."

"Now, really, my son, what should I ever do with a ship like that? I am too old to take up fishing as a means of livelihood. So keep the ship; I relinquish her to you."

Jorian chuckled. "The same impractical old Karadur! Well, I'm no fisherman, either, so perhaps your feelings won't be hurt if I sell her . . . On second thought, perhaps I had better keep her. When one becomes involved in one of your enterprises, one never knows when a speedy scape will be needed. But tell me:

Where in the forty-nine Mulvanian hells is that ninny Zerlik? He was supposed to fetch me away yesterday."

Karadur shook his head. "A light-minded wight, I fear. I encountered him by happenstance this morn at the palace, whither he had come to deliver his report to the king. When he saw me, he clapped a hand to his forehead and cried: 'Oh, my gods, I forgot all about your friend Jorian! I left him awaiting me on the waterfront!' And then the tale came out."

"What had he been doing?"

"When he left you, he hastened home to greet his household and to see whether his charioteer had yet returned with his car and team. As it fell out, they had come in the day before; and so excited was Zerlik by the reunion with his beloved horses that he forgot about you."

"And also, I daresay, by the pleasant prospect of futtering his wives all night," said Jorian. "If I never see that young ass again, 'twill be too soon."

"Oh, but he greatly admires you! He talked me deaf about what a splendid comrade you were in a tight place: so masterful and omnicompetent. When you have completed your work here, if you embark upon another journey, he would fain accompany you, to play squire to your knight."

" 'Tis good to know that someone esteems me, but he'd only be in the way. I suppose he is not a bad lad; just a damned fool. But then, I doubtless committed equal follies at his age. Now whither away? I need a bath."

"To my quarters, where you shall lodge. Put your bags on the spare ass, and we will deliver Zerlik's at his house on the way."

Over lunch at Karadur's apartment, in a rooming house near the palace, Jorian said: "As I understand it, you wish me to fix the clocks in the Tower of

Kumashar, and this will somehow free Estrildis from Xylar. What's the connection?"

"My son, I have no instant method of recovering your spouse—"

"Then why haul me a hundred leagues down the coast? Of course, if the job pay well—"

"But I confidently expect to obtain such a method as a result of your success with the clocks. The little lady has not become some other's wife, has she?"

"I'm sure not. I got word to her by one of my brothers, who traveled through Xylar, selling and repairing clocks, and smuggled a note in to her. The note urged her, if she still loved me, to hold out; that I should find a way to bring her forth. But how will my repairing Irazi clocks do that?"

"It is thus. The high priest of Ughroluk once uttered a prophecy, that these clocks should save the city from destruction, provided that they were kept running on time. Last year the clocks stopped; nor could Clockmaster Yiyim prevail upon them to function again. This is not surprising, since Yiyim was an impoverished cousin of the king, who had been appointed to this post because he was in penury and not because he knew aught about clocks."

"What's the state of the horological art in Iraz?"

"None exists, beyond a few water clocks imported from Novaria and the grand one that your father installed in the tower. In the House of Learning, several savants strive to master the art. They have attained to the point where one of their clocks loses or gains no more than a quarter-hour a day. In a few years, methinks, Iraz will make clocks as good as any. Till then, the Irazis must make do with sundials, hourglasses, and time candles."

"What's this House of Learning?" asked Jorian.

"It is a great institution, set up over a century ago under—ah—who was that king?" Karadur snapped his fingers. "Drat it! My memory worsens every day. Ah!

I remember: King Hoshcha. It has two divisions: the School of Spirit and the School of Matter. The former deals with the magical arts; the latter, with the mechanical arts. Each school includes libraries, laboratories, and classrooms wherein the savants impart their principles to students."

"Like the Academy at Othomae, but on a grander scale," said Jorian.

"Exactly, my son, exactly; save that the Academy—ah—devotes itself mainly to literary and theological studies, whereas the House of Learning deals with more utilitarian matters. I have a post in the School of Spirit."

"Come to think, I heard of this House when I was studying poetry at the Academy. Wasn't it they who developed the modern windmill?"

"Aye, it was. But the House of Learning is not what it was erstwhiles."

"How so?" asked Jorian.

"Hoshcha and his immediate successors were enthusiasts for the sciences, both material and spiritual. Under them, the House received lavish subsidies and achieved great advances. But later kings discovered that, for all the achievements of their laboratories, they were still bound by mortal limitations. A more efficient draft harness did not keep the king's officials from grafting and peculating and oppressing the people. A spell against smallpox did not cure the king of lusts, follies, and errors of judgment. An improved water wheel did not stop his kinsmen from trying to poison him to usurp the throne."

"If you fellows are given your heads, you'll have this world as mechanized as that afterworld, whither our souls go after death and where all tasks are done by machinery. You'll remember that I glimpsed it in my flight from Xylar."

Karadur shrugged and continued: "Discovering that life, even though materially better in some ways, was not really happier, the kings began to lose interest in the House of Learning. During the last half-century, appropriations have been steadily lessened. There have been no great advances since the invention of the telescope, thirty-odd years ago.

"The present head of the House of Learning is one Borai—another sinecurist, unqualified for his task. Because of the prophecy concerning the clocks, the king and his advisers have been greatly exercised over their malfunction. The king has brought pressure to bear upon Borai, who in turn has brought it upon the dean of the School of Matter, who in his turn has applied it to Yiyim the Clockmaster—all to no avail.

"None of these gentlemen can admit the principle that appointments to the House of Learning ought to be on a basis of merit and knowledge, for then their own posts would be endangered. The expert, they assert, is too full of prejudices and convictions that this or that is impossible. Only the gentlemanly amateur can view these arcane arts in a judgmatical spirit. And so things have buzzed along for months, with much loquacity but no action.

"Last month, His Majesty gave a banquet to the professors of the School of Spirit. The king entertained us with such gustatory rarities as the tongues of the fatuliva bird of distant Burang—gods of Mulvan, how that man eats! Being myself a man of very simple tastes, I paid little heed to these exotic delicacies but seized the opportunity to broach some of my own ideas to His Majesty. I implied that, had I Borai's authority, I could eftsoons have his tower clocks put in order.

"We beat around the bush somewhat, since prudent commoners utter not blunt truths to kings, nor do wise kings reveal their full minds to commoners. King Ishbahar, howsomever, is not an unreasonable individual when one can get his mind off his stomach. He conceded that something must be done about his nontimekeeping timepieces. On the other hand, he could not simply dismiss Borai, who has powerful friends among the nobility, on the mere say-so of a junior professor and a foreigner at that.

"At last we reached a compromise. Ishbahar would grant me a special commission as Friend of the King, which in practice means king's errand boy. I might then make my own arrangements for fixing the clocks. If they worked, the king would pension off Borai and appoint me in his room. On the strength of my commission, I sent Zerlik to find you, having approximately located you by divination."

"But how does this get my little darling out of that gilded gaol in Xylar?"

"See you not, my son? As director of the House of Learning, I can direct the efforts of the scientists and magicians under my command in such directions as would prove most efficacious in abducting your wife. With all that intellectual power—"

"I wonder that you haven't figured out some magical method of your own."

"That is not possible in my present situation. The dean of the School of Spirit, Fahramak, is of the same kidney as Borai and Yiyim. To make sure that I did not—ah—'show him up,' as the vulgar put it, he assigned me to one of the most useless tasks he could find: compiling a dictionary of the language of the demons of the Fifth Plane. He visits me betimes to make certain that I waste not my time on other researches."

"What had you in mind as a method of rescue?"

"A magical flying vehicle seems the most promising. You have certainly heard of flying brooms and carpets. We have investigated these and found that, while it is possible to imprison a demon in one of these objects and compel him to bear it aloft, they leave much to be desired as aërial vehicles."

"What do they do?"

"They wobble, overturn, go into a spin like that of a

falling leaf, and otherwise misbehave, with usually fatal results for the would-be flier. Some of Fahramak's savants are working on the problem now. If you will repair the clocks, I shall be in a position to assign more of my colleagues to the problem, and I doubt not that we shall soon achieve our goal."

"Who will pay me," asked Jorian, "and how much?"

"I shall pay you from the fund set aside for my use as King's Friend. Would half a Penembic royal a day suit you?"

"How much is that in Novarian?"

"A Penembic royal is worth about two and a half Irian marks, or a sixth of a Xylarian lion."

"Half a royal a day will do nicely, then."

"It is not so much as it seems at first blink, for these great cities are costly to dwell in. If you find yourself running short, confer with me."

"Meseems I shall do well to invest my first pay in some local garb, to be less conspicuous."

Karadur looked sharply. "That brings up a question. Dress has political significance here."

"*Oi!* How's that?"

"There are two racing factions, the Pants and the Kilts—"

"I beg your pardon. Said you racing factions?"

"Aye. Belike I had best begin at the beginning. Know that of all mankind, the folk of Iraz are the greatest sport fanatics, and their favorite sport is racing. They race beasts of divers kinds—even tortoises."

"What? Were a snail race not more thrilling?"

"Spare me your jests, my son. These are giant tortoises, from distant isles. Men ride them around the Hippodrome. Now there are two factions, distinguished by their garb. One faction wears kilts, like that which you saw on Master Zerlik; the other, trousers. It is a rare race that is not followed by a riot betwixt the factions, with knifings and other outrages; and there are affrays between factionists apart from the races."

"What's the political angle?"

"With so much rabid partisanship afloat, the factions have acquired political colorings. One might call the Pants the liberals and the Kilts the conservatives, since the kilt is the more traditional garment. Trews have come into fashion only in the last century, being copied from those worn in northern Mulvan."

"Then I shall perforce have to be enrolled as a liberal," said Jorian, "for I prefer trousers. Where stands the king in this?"

"He is supposed to be neutral, since the factions have public status and furnish companies of the Civic Guard. In fact, he leans to the Kilts, who are vociferous supporters of absolute monarchy, whereas the Pants would fain limit the king's power by an elective council. The Pants are in bad odor just now, for a dissident faction of them has fled Iraz, it is feared to foment revolt in the countryside. It were wiser for you, therefore, to dress as a Kilt."

Jorian stubbornly shook his head. "I shall wear trousers, for I should never feel comfortable in a skirt. Too drafty. You will have to explain that, as a foreigner, the garment has no political significance for me."

Karadur sighed. "I will try. As I said, King Ishbahar is not an unreasonable wight, if one interfere not with his gustatory pleasures."

# IV

# The Master of the Clocks

Clad in his baggy new Irazi trousers, Jorian stood in the courtyard of the Tower of Kumashar and tipped his head back, squinting against the brightness of the sky.

"By Vaisus' brazen arse!" he said. "Those clocks must be thirty stories above us. Am I doomed to run up and down thirty flights of steps every day?"

"Nay, my son," said Karadur. "As the tower was originally built in the days of Shashtai the Third, men had to toil up all seventy-odd stories to bear fuel for the beacon. But so many workmen perished of heart failure that, when Joshcha established the House of Learning, he commanded the savants to devise a method of hoisting men and materials up and down the tower. Come with me, and you shall see."

The twain approached the vast entrance on the north side, where the huge teakwood doors were flanked and surmounted by sculptured lions, dragons, and gryphons. The soldier leaning against the stone of the door frame straightened up, stepped in front of the door, and clicked his greaves together as he came to attention. He barked a challenge in Penembic.

Karadur peered nearsightedly. "Oh," he said, and replied in the same tongue. "Here!"

The old Mulvanian produced a scroll of parchment, which he handed to the soldier. The latter, needing both hands to unroll the stiff sheet, had to balance his halberd awkwardly in the crook of his arm as he read. He let the parchment roll up again with a snap and handed it back.

"Pass, sirs!" he said, bringing his fist up to his bronzen breastplate in salute. He turned the big brass door handle with a clank and pushed open one of the teakwood valves. The hinges squealed.

The interior was cavernous and dusty. After the brilliance of the sun outside, it seemed dark, although windows at every story let in light. The light was dimmed, however, by the dirt on the windowpanes.

To the right, the main staircase rose from the floor. It circled round and round the tower as it rose, with landings at every story to give access to the many small chambers built into the structure. The hollow shaft of the interior rose into dimness far above.

On the ground floor were pieces of apparatus: chains and ropes hanging down from above and, to one side, a horse mill. This comprised a vertical shaft with a horizontal crosspiece on top. From each end of the crosspiece dangled a set of straps and a horse collar. No animals now occupied the harness.

"What's that?" asked Jorian.

"When the clocks are running, the water that drives them must needs be daily pumped from the sump back up into the reservoir. A pair of mules, attached to yon mill, turns the shaft, which drives the pump by means of those chains and sprockets and things. You would understand them better than I. Since the clocks have stopped, howsomever, the mules have been put to other tasks. Hola, Saghol!"

A bundle of rags in a corner stirred and resolved itself into a sleeping workman. As the man rose, a grin split the brown face and showed an irregular row of yellow teeth.

"Ah, Doctor Karadur!" said the man and went on in Penembic. Jorian thought he said: "Do you wish to go up?"

"Aye," said Karadur and turned to Jorian. "How much do you weigh, my son?"

"A hundred and ninety the last time I weighed. When I get over two hundred, I begin to worry. Why?"

"Your weight must be counterbalanced." Karadur turned to the lift attendant. "Allow us three hundred and a quarter."

Saghol pulled one of the cords that hung from above, whence a bell tinkled faintly.

"Stand in this thing with me," said Karadur. The wizard stepped into a large, open-topped wooden box or tray, six feet on a side, with a handrail around it and a gantrylike structure arching over their heads. Attached to this structure was a chain, which extended upward out of sight.

Saghol grasped another cord and jerked it thirteen times, with a pause between jerks. Then he pulled the first cord again, twice. The bell tinkled.

"Whatever is he doing?" asked Jorian.

"He is signaling his colleagues above to set counterweights weighing three hundred and twenty-five pounds in the other car, to balance our weight. Hold tight!"

Jorian gripped the stanchion on his side of the box, which trembled and rose. "By Zevatas' golden whiskers!" he exclaimed as he peered over the edge.

"Make no sharp movements," said Karadur, "lest you set this car to swinging like a pendulum."

The stairs and chambers of the tower sank past as the lift rose. The walls came slowly closer, since the tower tapered upward. At the sixteenth story, the other car, laden with cast-iron weights, sank past them. The sounds of gearwheels and ratchets from above waxed louder.

The car stopped, and Karadur stepped briskly out. Jorian followed. A pair of brawny, sweating Irazis rested from turning a pair of large flywheels by means of crank handles.

The shaft bearing these wheels was united by gearing with a huge sprocket wheel mounted over the center of the hollow shaft of the tower. The lift car that had carried Jorian up hung from one end of the chain that passed over the sprocket, while the weighted car that had passed them hung from the other. A dog locked the gearing in place.

"*Whew!*" said Jorian, peering uneasily down the shaft. "That scared me worse than when the princess Yargali turned into a monster serpent whilst I was in bed with her."

"Now, now, my son!" said Karadur. "Do you still practise your old vice of self-deprecation?"

Jorian grinned weakly. "Not very often, Holy Father. Anyway, I misdoubt these fellows understand Novarian." He stepped to one of the windows. Beneath him, vast Iraz lay spread out, with broad, straight processional avenues cutting at various angles through the tangle of lesser streets and alleys. Amid the sea of redtiled roofs, the metallic roof-plates of temples and other public buildings flashed blindingly in the sunlight, like gems scattered about a red-patterned counterpane.

"*Oi!*" said Jorian. "Karadur, tell me: is that the palace? And that the temple of Ughroluk? And that the House of Learning? Where lies our tenement?"

Karadur pointed out landmarks. Jorian said: "I wonder the king add not a few coppers to his treasury by letting the vulgus up the tower for a small fee, to enjoy the view."

"One of Ishbahar's predecessors did that; but so many young people, disappointed in love, ascended the tower to jump from the top that the privilege was rescinded. If you have seen enough, follow me."

The old man led Jorian up a narrow stair to the next level, cluttered by a mass of machinery. To one side rose another lift, like the one that had brought them halfway up the tower but smaller.

"That takes fuel up to the beacon," said Karadur. "There is Yiyim now."

A metallic tapping came from the clockwork. Then

a small, gnomish man with a graying beard popped out of the gearing. In one hand he gripped a hammer, with which he had been tapping one of the huge brass gear-wheels.

"O Yiyim," said Karadur, "this is Jorian the Kortolian, whom the king has commanded to repair the clocks. Jorian, I present Clockmaster Yiyim."

Yiyim stood glaring with fists on hips, silent but for the hiss of breath in his nostrils. Then he hurled his hammer to the floor with a clang.

"You cursed old pickthank!" he screeched. "Offspring of a demon and a sow! Incondite meddler!" He added several more epithets; for which Jorian's limited Penembic was inadequate. "So your plot finally came to a boil, eh? And you think I'll show this young mountebank how these clocks work, so that he can steal the credit for starting them and cozen me out of my post, eh? Well, not one word of help shall you have from me! If the twain of you get caught in the gears and ground to sausage, so much the better. May the gods piss on you!"

Yiyim vanished down the stairs. The sounds of the lift told of his departure.

"Something tells me I had better not stand at the base of the tower whilst that fellow's at the top," said Jorian, "where he could drop something on me."

"Oh, he is harmless. If you succeed, Ishbahar will pension him off; and he surely would not risk loss of his pension by fomenting trouble."

"Yes? Umm. I've seen what happened before when you trusted somebody to be upright and reasonable." Jorian picked up the hammer. "Here's one tool, anyway. There's a tool rack on yonder wall, but with nary a tool in it."

"They have all been mislaid or purloined over the years," said Karadur. "You needs must furnish your own."

"I shall, when I've looked over the works . . ."

For an hour, Karadur sat cross-legged on the floor, absorbed in meditation, while Jorian tapped and pried and fingered the clockwork. At last he said:

"I haven't worked on clocks for years, but it is plain as your whiskers why this machine won't run."

"What is the cause, my son?"

"Causes, you mean. For one thing, one of the pallets of the escapement is bent. For another, somebody must have struck this gear in the train a heavy blow and marred one of the teeth. For three, the oil in the bearings has been allowed to dry and get sticky, so the wheels wouldn't turn even if all the other faults were righted."

"Can you rectify these deficiencies?"

"I think so. But first I must order tools. Who would be the best man in Iraz for that?"

On the twenty-third of the Month of the Stag, a procession arrived at the courtyard of the Tower of Kumashar. First marched a musical band. Then came a company of the royal guard, consisting of one platoon each of pikemen, swordsmen, and arbalesters. Then came the royal litter, borne on the shoulders, not of slaves, but of the leading gentlemen of the court, half of them in kilts and half in trousers. A squadron of cavalry brought up the rear.

The courtiers set down the litter in front of the main entrance. As the curtains of the litter-parted, the soldiers clanged to salute, while the civilians dropped to one knee.

An enormously fat man in a gold-embroidered white robe, with a curly wig on his head and a serpent crown on top of that, emerged slowly from the litter. The effort made him puff and wheeze.

When King Ishbahar had caught his breath, he made an upward gesture, so that the sun flashed on the huge ruby seal stone on the middle finger of his left hand. In a high, wheezy voice he said:

"Rise, good people! Ah, Doctor Karadur!"

The king waddled forward. In his path lay a puddle from yesterday's rain, but one of the gentlemen quickly threw his mantle over it.

Karadur bowed. The king said: "And is this your young—ah—Master—ah—"

"Jorian, Your Majesty," said Karadur.

"Master Jorian? A pleasure to know you, young sir, heh heh. Are the clocks running?"

"Aye, O King," said Jorian. "Would you fain see the works?"

"Indeed we would. Is the lift working?"

"Aye, sire."

"We trust all its parts are sound and solid, for we are not exactly a sylph, heh heh! Let us go; let us go."

The king puffed his way through the portal. Inside, the ground floor of the tower had received a hasty sweeping and cleaning. A pair of mules walked the boom of the mill around, while a muleteer from time to time cut at one or the other with his whip. The gears and shafting grumbled. The king stepped aboard the lift.

"Doctor Karadur!" he said. "It were inconsiderate to ask one of your years to climb thirty flights, so you shall ride with us. You, too, Master Jorian, to answer technical questions."

"Your Majesty!" said one of the gentlemen—a tall, thin man with a pointed gray beard. "No offense to Messires Karadur and Jorian, but it were risky to entrust yourself to the car without a bodyguard."

"Well, heh heh, one stalwart soldier ought to suffice."

"If lift will bear weight, sire," said Jorian.

"What is its limit?"

"I know not for sure, but methinks we press it."

"Ah, well, we cannot diet down in time for this ride. Colonel Chuivir!"

"Aye, sire?" replied the most glittering soldier of all, a strikingly handsome man as tall as Jorian.

"Detail a squad of the guard to ascend the tower by the stairs, keeping on a level with us as the lift bears us aloft. Pick strong men with sound hearts! We would not have them collapse halfway up, heh heh."

Like the tower, Saghol, the ground-floor lift attendant, had been cleaned up for the occasion, He jerked his cords, and the lift rose, groaning. The squad of guardsmen clattered up the stairs, keeping pace with the lift.

At the top, the king got off the lift, which wobbled as his weight left it, and wheezed his way up to the clockwork floor. Jorian followed. The soldiers, red-faced, sweating and gasping, filed into the clockwork chamber after him.

On the clockwork floor, the machinery was in full noisy operation. The shaft driven by the horse mill on the ground floor rotated, driving the pump that raised water from the sump to the reservoir above. Water ran from this reservoir through a pipe to a large wheel bearing a circle of buckets. As each bucket filled, the escapement released the wheel, allowing it to rotate just far enough to bring an empty bucket under the spout. At the bottom of their travel, the buckets tipped, spilling their water into the trough, whence it ran to the sump. The bucket wheel drove a gear train connected to the shafts of the four clocks on the four sides of the tower. Another mechanism struck a gong on the hour.

"We have not been up here in years, heh, heh," said King Ishbahar, raising his voice to be heard above the clatter and splashing. "Pray explain this to me, good Master Jorian."

Jorian's Penembic was now fairly fluent if ungrammatical. With Karadur helping to translate when he got stuck, Jorian told the king about clockwork. While

Jorian spoke, several gentlemen, having come up on the second trip of the lift, filed into the chamber.

"You should know Doctor Borai, O Jorian," said the king. "He is director of our House of Learning—at least for now."

Borai, potbellied, gray-bearded, and kilted, bowed to Jorian, mumbled something that Jorian could not hear, and shot a slit-eyed glare at Karadur.

"Pardon us a moment," said the king. "We would speak to him of plans for the city, and where better to discuss such things than this lofty eyrie, whence it is spread out below us like a map?"

The king waddled over to a window, where to Borai he pointed out various things below, talking animatedly. A plump, trousered man a little older than Jorian addressed him.

"Permit me, Master Jorian. I am Lord Vegh, stasiarch of the Pants. I see by your garb that you are a person of progressive ideas, like those of my honorable association. When you take out Penembic citizenship, perhaps you would care—"

"Soliciting a new member already, eh, Vegh?" said the tall, thin grandee with the pointed gray beard. "Not sporting, you know."

"First come, first served," said Vegh.

"Excuse me, my lords," said Jorian. "I be not up on Irazi politics. Explain, pray."

Vegh smiled. "This is Lord Amazluek, stasiarch of the Kilts. Naturally, he would prefer to enlist you in his—"

"Bah!" said Amazluek. "The poor fellow has but lately arrived in Iraz. How should he know the glories of our ancient traditions, which my association cherishes and upholds? Be advised, young sir, that if you would fain make your way amongst people of the better sort here, you ought to abandon those barbarous nether garments—"

"I believe I was conversing with Master Jorian, when

you cut in, Amazluek," said Vegh. "Will you kindly mind your business, whilst I—"

"It is my business!" cried Amazluek. "When I see three cozening an innocent young foreigner—"

"Cozening?" shouted Vegh. "Why, thou—"

"Gentlemen! Gentlemen!" said several courtiers, thrusting themselves between the angry stasiarchs.

"Anyway," said Amazluek, "none of *my* association has turned traitor and fled to the provinces to raise a rebellion!" He turned his back and stalked off.

"What he talk about?" said Jorian, looking innocent.

Vegh: "Oh, he alludes to that rascal Mazsan, leader of a dissident faction. He was a member of my honorable association ere we expelled him. There are always bloodthirsty extremists, and Mazsan is ours."

"Yes?"

"You see, Master Jorian, we—the Pants, that is—are the moderates of Iraz. We follow the middle way, in urging that the Royal Council be elected and given legislative powers. On one hand we have mossbacked conservatives, like Amazluek, who would hold back all progress. On the other, we have fanatics like Mazsan, who would abolish the monarchy altogether. We are the only sensible folk."

"What this about Mazsan disappearing?"

"He and some followers have dropped out of sight, and rumor says they fled the city when their attempt to unseat me failed. But none has seen them since. I suspect that some of Amazluek's rich young thugs caught the lot at a conspiratorial meeting, murdered them, and concocted the tale of their flight to discredit all the Pants. When—"

"Gentlemen!" wheezed the king. "We do believe we have seen enough for the nonce. Let us all return to the courtyard, where we shall have somewhat to say."

When they were drawn up in the courtyard in the middle of a hollow square of the Royal Guard, King Ishbahar said:

"It is our pleasure to announce that, in recognition of their services to our crown and state in repairing the clocks of the Tower of Kumashar, we hereby appoint Doctor Karadur of Mulvan director of the House of Learning, and Master Jorian of Kortoli our new clockmaster. In recognition of their many years of faithful service, Doctor Borai and Clockmaster Yiyim are retired on pension. Doctor Borai is hereby made honorary commissioner of city planning."

"*Oi!* Who said I wanted to be clockmaster?" Jorian whispered to Karadur.

"Do be quiet, my son. You needs must do something whilst I grapple with the problem of your wife, and the pay is fair."

"Oh, well. Borai doesn't seem to like being pensioned."

"That is not surprising, seeing that his income will be halved. The city-planning thing carries no salary."

"Then we have another enemy to watch out for."

"You are too suspicious—"

"And now, gentlemen," said the king, "we shall return to our humble home. Doctor Karadur and Master Jorian, it is our pleasure that you take lunch with us this noon."

On the way from the tower to the palace, Jorian and Karadur passed through a huge gate in the wall surrounding the palace grounds. From the top of the gate rose a row of iron spikes, one of which bore a human head.

"The Gate of Happiness," said Karadur.

"That wight up yonder doesn't look very happy," said Jorian, indicating the head.

"Oh, this is the traditional place where heads of malefactors are exhibited."

"A curious conceit, to attach such a name to such a place."

"You utter verities, my son. The present monarch,

howsomever, is mild and merciful, so that there is seldom more than one head on exhibition at a time. The conservatives grumble that such lenity encourages evildoers."

In the palace, the gentleman litter-bearers were dismissed by the king. Jorian and Karadur were conducted to a private dining room, where they ate with the king, alone but for a pair of guardsmen standing in the corners, a secretary who scribbled notes, and the king's food taster.

After amenities, Jorian brought up his brush with the pirates of Algarth on his voyage south. "From what I hear," he said, "they wax ever more aggressive along these coasts. I daresay Your Majesty knows what actions to take against them."

Looking unhappy, King Ishbahar spoke to the secretary: "Remind me to pass the word to Admiral Kyar, O Herekit." Then to Jorian: "Ah, that we could persuade these rogues to earn honest livings, like other men! Do you know that the ungrateful knaves have had the insolence to demand an increase in our annual largesse?"

"Means Your Majesty that you pay them trib—*unh!*" Jorian broke off as Karadur kicked his shin beneath the table. "I mean—ah—that your government subsidizes these gentry?"

"One might put it thus. One might. I know there is an argument for a hard policy; we have gone over it many a time and oft in council meetings. But our great philosopher Rebbim held that such men should not be blamed for their acts. The Algarthian Archipelago is a congeries of barren, sea-beaten rocks, where little food can be raised. The folk of that grim land must, therefore, resort to piracy or face starvation. So a subsidy, in return for immunity to our ships, seemed but a humane and benevolent act.

"Besides which, the subsidy was at first but a fraction of the cost of putting our navy on a war footing. Know

you that the stroke man of a bench of rowers now gets
three coppers a day? Some people are never satisfied."
The king shook his head, his jowls wobbling. "But let
us to a pleasanter subject. Do try this rhinoceros liver
with sauce of lamprey's brains. You will swear that you
have tasted nought like it, heh heh."

Jorian tried it. "Your Majesty is right," he said, swal-
lowing manfully. "Your servant has never tasted aught
like it. But, whilst Your Majesty's wish is my command,
I have come to point where I can still chew but not
swallow. I am full."

"Oh, come! A big, lusty swain like you? What you
have eaten would not keep a bird alive. Not a bird."

"That depends upon the kind of bird, sire. I have
already eaten thrice my usual lunch. Is like story of
King Fusinian and the Teeth of Grimnor, which I
told you."

The king's jowls quivered with laughter. "Ah, Master
Jorian! Would that, had the gods permitted us children,
we had a son like you!"

Startled, Jorian looked up. "Your Majesty's flattery
overwhelms me. But ..." he raised an inquiring
eyebrow.

Karadur said: "Master Jorian is new to Iraz, sire, and
he has been working night and day on the clocks. He
is therefore unfamiliar with your dynastic situation."

"Our dynastic situation, as the learned doctor deli-
cately puts it, is simple. We have had several wives, of
whom two survive; but with all of these available
females, we have begotten but one child, who died in
infancy. So now we face the prospect of passing our
crown on to one of a pair of worthless nephews.

"But let us speak of more cheerful things. In three
days comes the feast of Ughrotuk, with the major races
of the year. You two learned gentlemen shall occupy
reserved seats in the Hippodrome, directly below the
royal box. You will be safer there in case the factionists
make a disturbance."

The king sighed as he looked at the still heaped plates before him. "Would we could spend the afternoon enjoying the harmless delights of the palate and interfering with none. But, alas, we must depart for our nap, after which we have a tedious matter of a lawsuit to decide. Ah, the rues of royalty!

"Know, Master Jorian, that in our youth we were deemed a bit of a scholar. In the libraries, you will still find our treatise on the pronunciation of Penembic in the days of Juktar the Great. But all that, alas, is far behind us. For the past year, we have endeavored to write our memoirs, but so implacably does public business nibble at our time that we have not yet reached the third chapter."

"I can sympathize," said Jorian. "I, too, have sometimes wished that I could have been a scholar, as Doctor Karadur is, in sooth. I did once study briefly at the Academy of Othomas; but the exigencies and contingencies of life have never let me abide in any one place long enough to get my teeth into a program of serious study."

"Now that you are living amongst us," said the king, "we are sure that this difficulty can be overcome. And now we must away once more. Fare you well, our friends."

Later, Jorian said: "He seems like an amiable old duck."

"Amiable, yes," said Karadur. "But he neglects public business to pamper his stomach, and he has no more spine than a bowlful of jelly. From a strictly moral point of view, I applaud his pacific outlook; but I fear it is impractical in this wicked world."

Jorian grinned. "You're the one who was always twitting me on my juvenile cynicism, as you called it, and now 'tis you who voice acerb views."

"I have probably caught some of your acrimonious outlook, like a contagious tisic. So long as the kingdom ride on an even keel, King Ishbahar may do well enough. But if a crisis arise—well, we shall see."

"Is this fellow Mazsan likely to overthrow him? So feeble a rule impresses me not as perdurable."

"Mazsan has dwelt in Novaria and returned full of lofty ideas for setting up a republic on the lines of Vindium. His following is formidable, since oppression and corruption are rife amongst Ishbahar's officials. Let us hope Mazsan never succeeds,"

"Why so? The Vindines seem to do as well as the folk of any of the Twelve Cities, and things do not look good to me here."

"It is not Mazsan's ideas, which are not bad as such things go; it is the man himself. I know him. He is brilliant, energetic, and idealistic—but a hater, boiling with rancor and ferity. He has boasted that, when he attains power, there shall be displayed at the Gate of Happiness not one head but a thousand. There is a tale that he would even summon the wild nomads of Fedirun to help him to his goal,"

"'Tis too bad that we cannot somehow sunder the man from his ideas," said Jorian.

"Aye; but that is the rock whereon many noble political schemes have gone to wrack. Mazsan could proclaim the world's most enlightened constitution, but that would do the Irazis no good when he began decapitating them by the hundred, as he would the instant he had power."

"So then," said Jorian, "the choice between that kindly mass of wobbling royal jelly and the gifted but bloodthirsty Master Mazsan is like the choice between being hanged and beheaded."

"True, but that is the way of the world."

# The Tunnel of Hoshcha

The morning of the twenty-sixth was overcast, presaging another autumnal rain. The mouth of the Lyap was covered with small craft, plying back and forth like a swarm of water insects as they conveyed thousands of Irazis across the river to Zaktan.

Jorian and Karadur strolled up the street that led from the Zaktanian waterfront. The street ended at the edge of the temenos of the temple of Nubalyaga. Following the flow of the crowd, Jorian and Karadur proceeded around the temple grounds to the right. This brought them to the temple entrance at the eastern end of the temenos.

The temple was a huge structure of domes and spires. The silver plating of its tiles glowed softly under the gray sky. Flanking the entrance were two thirty-foot statues of Nubalyaga in the form of a beautiful naked woman. One statue showed her as bending a huge bow; the other, pouring water from a jar.

"The one on the left is chasing away the eclipse," said Karadur, "whilst the other controls the tides."

Jorian stopped to look. "That's funny," he said. "Last night I dreamt that a woman just like that sculptor's model appeared unto me."

"Oh? What did she?"

"She said something like: 'Beware the second crown, my son.' Since the dame was clad as you see those statues, and since I have been unwontedly virtuous since you and I parted in Metouro, I sought to make love to her; but she turned to smoke and vanished.

384

Since I thought the dream but a manifestation of my bridled lusts, and since the words did not seem to make sense, I paid no special heed and have now forgotten the rest of the vision."

"Hm. One needs must be alert to such things, because the gods—ah—really do appear to mortals thus, as you well know."

"If the advice of this goddess be no better than that of that little green god, Tvasha, who advised us in Shven, I can do without it."

Since the temple stood on an elevation, the street leading eastwards from it sloped downwards. Down this street flowed a river of folk: Irazis, the men in kilts or trousers and their women in enveloping robes; foreigners from Fedirun and Novaria and even—sweating in their furs and heavy woolens—blond barbarians from distant Shven. Among the Irazi men, kilt-wearing partisans sported the red and white colors of their faction, while adherents of the Pants wore blue and gold.

"It gratifies me to hear that you are subduing the lusts of the flesh," said Karadur. "It is the requisite preliminary step towards moral perfection and spiritual enlightenment. Have you, then, adhered to some ascetic philosophy or cultus?"

"Nay; I merely felt that Estrildis would mislike it if she knew I'd been dipping my wick. That's love for you. If I ever get her back, I'll make up for lost time."

They came to the outer wall of the Hippodrome, where rows of stone arches, one atop another, supported the tiers of seats. The crowd divided and flowed around the structure to the entrances. Jorian said:

"Our passes admit us through Entrance Four. Which is that?"

"To the right," replied Karadur.

Hawkers of flags, toy chariots, handwritten programs, and food and drink mingled with the crowd, crying their wares. Jorian and Karadur found Entrance Four and were swept in with the tide. An usher saluted as he saw the royal passes and directed their holders to seats below the royal box, at the halfway mark on one side of the long, elliptical course.

Jorian and Karadur settled in their seats and opened their lunch. On their left, where seats were reserved for active members of the Pants, the stands were a mass of blue and gold. On their right, red and white likewise filled the stands in the bloc composed of Kilts. Members of the two blocs scowled at each other across the intervening strip reserved for noblemen and officials, where sat Jorian and Karadur. Now and then, an epithet was shouted above the general din.

Jorian was finishing his beer when a fanfare announced the king. All in the stands arose as Ishbahar waddled into his box and lowered himself into the gilded throne. When the audience had sat again, the king motioned to his crier, who produced a speaking trumpet. The king held up a sheet of reed paper and a reading glass. He began to read in his wheezy squeak, pausing between sentences so that the crier could bellow his words.

It was a dull little speech, what Jorian could understand of it: "... auspicious occasion ... glorious nation ... gallant contestants ... good sportsmanship ... may the best team win ..."

As the king finished, a man arose from among the Pants and shouted: "When will Your Majesty bring the slayers of Sefer to book?"

The king replied through his crier: "Pray, good sir, do not bring up this question now. The time is inappropriate. We are pursuing the matter ..." But the voice even of the leather-lunged crier was lost in the chant of "Justice! Justice!" that rose from the massed Pants. In their turn, the Kilts began shouting in rhythm: "Down! Quiet! Down! Quiet!"

"Who's Sefer?" asked Jorian.

"An official of the Pants, who was found slain. The

Pants swear he was killed by a gang of Kilts; the Kilts deny all knowledge of it."

The shouts of the crier, together with a threatening move on the part of the squads of gleaming guardsmen in bronzen cuirasses and crested steel helmets, at length abated the shouts of the rival factionists.

"They are putting the tortoise race first," said Kara-dur, "to amuse the mob and take the factionists' minds—if that be the word I wish—off their feud."

At the starting post at one end of the course, Jorian sighted through his spyglass four huge tortoises. When they stood up on their thick, bowed legs, the tops of their shells were the height of a tall man from the ground. On the back of each tortoise was strapped a saddle, similar to a camel saddle. On each saddle sat a man in motley clown's costume.

At the blast of a trumpet, the four tortoises ambled forward. It took them a long time to reach the part of the track directly before Jorian. In the meantime, bets flew thick and fast.

As the tortoises plodded past at a slow walk, the crowd roared at the antics of the riders, of whom two wore the colors of the Kilts and two, those of the Pants. They reached out to thwack one another with slap-sticks, turned somersaults off their mounts and bounded back on, and indulged in a hundred zany gambols.

Jorian: "I feel a certain kinship for the Kilts, even though I wear trews."

"How so, my son? Are you becoming aristocratical-minded?"

"Not at all. Their colors, red and white, are those of the flag of Xylar. The Xylarian war cry, in fact, was 'red and white!'" Jorian sighed. "Betimes I regret that those lackwits wouldn't let me show what a good king I could be."

The tortoises passed on around to the other side of the course. A single circuit constituted their race. The good humor of the crowd seemed to have been restored.

Next came a race between two teams of zebras. Then a detachment of the Royal Guard, their metal polished to mirrorlike surfaces, marched around the course to the tune of a military band, stopping from time to time to perform a brief precision drill with their spears.

Six camels, ridden by brown-robed Fediruni desert men, raced four laps around the course. Then a float bearing a gilded image of the god Ughroluk, drawn by white oxen and preceded by a hundred priests singing a mighty hymn, passed slowly around the course. Many in the crowd joined the priests in singing. The god, crowned with ostrich plumes dyed scarlet and gold and emerald, bore a silver thunderbolt in one hand and a golden sunbeam in the other.

A pair of King Ishbahar's elephants, draped in purple and gold, lumbered around the track, not seeming to hurry much despite the yells of their mahouts and the whacks of their goads. Then two teams of unicorns raced.

"Now come the horses," said Karadur. "Being the fleetest draft animals, their race will decide the day as between the Pants and the Kilts."

Tension grew. A trumpet peal sent the four teams off. As the four chariots—two blue and gold, two crimson and silver—thundered past the roar from the blocks of factionists drowned out all other sounds.

There were seven laps to the race. With each lap, the excitement waxed. As the chariots whirled past, men stood up, shaking fists, sobbing, frothing, and screaming.

When the cluster of vehicles rounded the first turn on the fourth lap, there was a crash and a glimpse of pieces of chariot flying. Two cars had collided. A detached wheel continued along the course on its own for half a bowshot before toppling over. When the dust had blown away enough for Jorian to see, he glimpsed a pair of stretcher-bearers trotting across the sand to pick up a victim. There was also a glimpse of an injured horse struggling to rise.

By the time the two surviving cars approached on their next lap, the service crew had largely cleared away the wreckage. The two survivors passed and repassed on the straightaway, neither able to gain a definitive advantage. On the last lap, they whirled to the finish line abreast. As they sped past the royal box, Jorian could not see that either had the advantage.

Officials huddled in consultation at the edge of the track. Then a pair of them hastened up the steps to the royal box. More consultation, and the crier shouted:

"Driver Paltoi, of the Pants, wins!"

The Pants applauded. Jorian noted that the Penembians applauded like Novarians, by clapping their hands, not by snapping their fingers like Mulvanians.

A growl arose from the Kilts. It grew, mingled with cries of "Foul! Foul!" The Pants shouted back.

"Was there a foul?" asked Jorian.

Karadur shrugged. "Alas, I am no expert on sports; nor are my old eyes up to detecting such irregularities. Natheless, methinks we had better make ourselves scarce."

"Why?"

"The races are over, all but the awards to the winners; but my spiritual senses tell me a riot is brewing. Besides, it looks like rain."

"All right," said Jorian, rising.

As he did so, a large beer mug, turning over and over in the air, flew from the bloc of Kilts towards the Pants. It struck Jorian's head with a crash and shattered. Jorian slumped back into his seat.

"My boy!" cried Karadur. "Are you injured?"

Jorian shook his head. "That does not seem to have split what few brains I have left. Let's go."

He rose again, staggering a little, and started for the exit. A trickle of blood ran down one side of his face.

More missiles flew over the central strip between the two blocs of factionists. As the gentry in this strip left their seats to run for cover, the two blocs rose and rushed at each other, drawing hitherto hidden daggers and short swords. Trumpets blew. The crier screamed. Whistles sounded.

Squads of glittering guardsmen clattered hither and yon, striving to beat the combatants apart with spear shafts. Others fought their way to the royal box to protect the king, who sat quivering and helplessly waving his fat hands. Fighting spread all over the Hippodrome, while the more peaceable members of the audience ran for the exits. The noise grew deafening.

Pulling Karadur by one bony wrist Jorian forced his way through the crush at Entrance Four. In the concourse outside, knots of factionists were already hurling missiles, brandishing improvised clubs, kicking, punching, and stabbing.

Jorian tried to thread his way among the combatants to the main entrance without becoming embroiled. As he reached the gate, a fierce yell from behind made him turn.

"Kill the dirty foreigners!" shrieked a man. A flash of lightning revealed the man as Borai, the former director of the House of Learning. He was haranguing a group of armed Kilts. Beside him stood Yiyim, the former clockmaster. Thunder growled.

"The old witch cast a spell on our team!" screamed Borai. "That cost us our victory!"

"And the young one is his apprentice!" added Yiyim. "Slay them both! Tear them to pieces!"

The well-gnawed carcass of a chicken whirled through the air and missed Jorian; so did a horse turd. A paving stone, however, grazed Jorian's already bloody scalp and staggered him.

"Run, my son!" gasped Karadur.

"Whither?" shouted Jorian.

"The temple! To the temple of Nubalyaga! Demand sanctuary!"

The pair trotted across the street, just as rain began to fall. The gang of Kilts broke into a run behind them. As they reached the slope leading up to the temple, Karadur said:

"Go on, my son. I cannot run up yon hill."

"I won't leave you—"

"Go on, I say! I am old; you have many years—"

Without further words, Jorian gathered up the ancient bag of bones hill his arms and ran up the hill carrying Karadur, despite the Mulvanian's pleas. Jorian slipped on the rain-wet cobblestones and fell; Karadur's bulbous turban came off and rolled away. Jorian scrambled up again with his burden and ran on. The mob behind them gained.

At the entrance to the temple, a pair of eunuch guards, standing inside the gate, crossed their spears to bar the way. Jorian, his red face streaked with mingled rain, sweat, mud, and blood, was too winded to speak. Karadur cried:

"Admit us in the name of the lady Sahmet, sirs! I am Doctor Karadur of the House of Learning!"

The eunuchs lowered their spears. As soon as Jorian and Karadur were inside, the eunuchs clanged the bronzen gate valves shut. Other guards hastened from other parts of the temenos. In a trice, a dozen eunuchs, with cocked crossbows, stood in a line behind the gate.

"Begone, or we will shoot through the bars!" they shouted.

The mob milled and screamed but made no effort to assault the gate. Jorian and Karadur hastened towards the main temple building.

"I owe you my life," said Karadur.

"Oh, nonsense! Had I thought the matter out, I should probably have left you. You almost deserve it for assuring me that Borai and Yiyim were harmless. Where's this Lady Sahmet?"

"I will send in our names. If she be not engaged in ritual, methinks she will see us."

Despite the drizzle, the mob of Kilts, under the leadership of Borai and Yiyim, had spread out into a cordon, which seemed to be extending itself clear around the temenos.

"They're laying siege to the place," said Jorian.

"I am sure the king's men will clear them away. If not, belike Sahmet can solve our difficulty."

"If we had one of those flying things you have spoken of, we could flit over their heads. But then, if we had a carriage, we should have a horse and carriage, if we had a horse. Isn't that a fire?" Jorian pointed to a column of smoke and sparks, which rose above the nearby roofs.

"Aye; the fools will burn down the city if given a free hand."

High Priestess Sahmet received Jorian and Karadur in her chamber of audience. She was a tall, large-boned woman in her forties, handsome but too massive of jaw and beaklike of nose to be called beautiful. Clad in a gauzy robe of pale gray embroidered with symbols in silver thread, she sat in a chair of pretence and stared with large, dark eyes at the disheveled fugitives. A couple of lesser priestesses glided about.

"It is a pleasure to see you again, good Doctor Karadur," she said in a deep, resonant voice, "albeit one could wish the circumstances less frantic. And who is the young man?"

"I am Jorian the Kortolian," said Jorian, "presently clockmaster to His Majesty. I am honored to meet Your Sanctity."

The woman gave Jorian a penetrating stare. She snapped her fingers. "Inkyara! More light, if you please." When a branched candlestick had been set on a taboret and lit, Sahmet said:

"Master Jorian, methought I knew you."

"Madam! I misdoubt I have had the pleasure—"

"I mean not in the sense of knowing you on this material plane. But I have seen you in visions."

"Yes, madam?"

"You are the barbarian savior!"

"Eh? Oh, come now, Madam Sahmet. I am no barbarian! I learnt my letters when I was but five, in school in Ardamai; and I have studied at the Academy at Othomae. My table manners may not be up to courtly standards, but I do not make a pig of myself. I am only an honest craftsman, and in any case I am unqualified to save Iraz from any doom. But what mean you to do with us?"

"Not cast you to that slavering mob, certes." She spoke in an undertone to one of the lesser priestesses, who glided out and presently returned. After a whispered colloquy, Sahmet said:

"Fires have sprung up in several parts of Iraz as well as Zaktan, and the soldiers are too busy fighting them to control the mobs of factionists. The crowd of Kilts surrounding this temple has been reinforced, so you cannot leave by the streets."

"Neither have we magical power to fly over their heads," said Jorian.

"Let me think," said Sahmet. "I am loath to harbor you overnight, since for entire males to pass the night here, other than on the occasion of the Divine Marriage, would offend the goddess. Happily, there is another course. Ere I reveal it to you, howsomever, I must have your promise to do me a small favor in return."

Jorian's eyes narrowed. "Madam, I have been in and out of not a few tight places in my short life, and buying pigs in pokes is one thing I have learnt to avoid. If I can, I shall be glad to help you—but I must needs know about this favor."

"It amounts to little. I do but ask that you play a small part in one of our forthcoming observances."

"If you mean to make a eunuch of me, madam—"

"Bountiful heavens, nothing like that! I solemnly promise that it shall cost you not the least scrap of your splendid physique. More I cannot say now."

"Nor senses, faculties, and abilities?"

"Nor those, either. Well, sir?"

Jorian argued a little more, but no further details could he elicit from Sahmet. He exchanged glances with Karadur, but the old wizard was not helpful. Jorian did not like to promise anything under such vague conditions, but he saw no alternative.

"Very well, Madam Sahmet," he said, "I agree."

"Good! You shall not rue your choice. Now come with me."

An assistant priestess hurried up with a small lanthorn, which she handed to Sahmet. The high priestess led them out. They passed through halls and rooms and down steps until Jorian was lost. In an underground passage, dimly lit by a single sconce, Sahmet halted at a massive, bolted, wooden door.

"Master Jorian," she said, "I would not do this for any wight, even to save life. But, since this peril involves the barbarian savior, I have no choice." She slipped a massive ring off one finger. "Take this. When you come to the door at the far end of the tunnel, knock four times, thus." She tapped twice with a knuckle, paused, and tapped twice more. "When the peephole opens, show this ring—which, may I add, I wish returned when this peril has passed."

She drew back the bolt and opened the door. Then she held out a hand. "Fare you well, gentlemen." She gripped Jorian's hand longer and more forcibly than he expected. "I may see you again, Master Jorian—and sooner than you think."

She handed Jorian the lanthorn, whose single candle stub sent feeble rays through its windows of glass. The heavy door boomed shut behind Jorian and Karadur.

\* \* \*

The passageway sloped down and down and down. The stones lining the tunnel became wet and slimy. Jorian said:

"This must be that tunnel under the Lyap I've heard of. I am sure we're below the water table."

"The what, my son?"

"The water table. Know you not how, a certain distance below the surface, water fills up all the pores betwixt the grains of soil? Hence, if one digs below that level, one gets a well."

"Nay, I did not know, having devoted my life to the spiritual as opposed to the material sciences. How learnt you such things?"

"I picked them up when I was surveying for the Syndicate of Ir."

"You are assuredly a versatile fellow."

Jorian grinned in the gloom. "I suppose I am." He recited:

"Oh, Jorian was a man of many parts;
    He'd gallop on a fiery steed of war,
    Cross swords with desperados, or
Purloin from maidens fair their gentle hearts;
Whip up a sonnet, rondeau, or sestine,
    Discharge a deadly shaft, repair a clock,
    Administer a kingdom, pick a lock,
Survey a road, or sail a barquentine.

"For all his many skills, this artful man
    Could never reach the goal for which he played,
    Which was to settle with a loving wife,
Become a quiet, bourgeois artisan,
And prosecute some worthy, peaceful trade
    Throughout a long and uneventful life."

Jorian hastened to add: "I'm really not so self-conceited as all that. 'Tis just that the rhyme amused me."

Karadur chuckled. "My boy, you are all that you say; albeit I doubt that you are really so determined upon a quiet life as you proclaim. Otherwise you would not—"

"Oh, yes? And who dragged me from my quiet, peaceful surveying job to this hotbed of intrigue and insurrection?"

"Ah, but in your last letter you said you would do aught to recover your Estrildis."

"Oh, well, so I did. But now I'm sure we are below the Lyap. What keeps the water out? I see no pumps."

"The water is kept from Hoshcha's Tunnel by a trio of wizards, spell-casting night and day. They are Goelnush, Luekuz, and Firaven, in my Department of Applied Thaumaturgy. Just now the House of Learning is embroiled in a furious feud, which I am supposed to resolve and compose. So high has partisan feeling run that the deans of my two schools will not speak to each other."

"What's this?"

"Goelnush, Luekuz, and Firaven form part of the School of Spirit. Now, engineers in the School of Matter claim that with pumps of the latest design, they can keep the tunnel as dry as my three wonder-workers, at less cost and with less chance of failure. The dean of the School of Spirit retorts that pumps are quite as likely to break down as a group of well-trained thaumaturges; that besides labor to furnish power for the pumps, we should require plumbers to keep the pumps and pipes in order; and that the pumping apparatus with its pipes would occupy so much of the tunnel that it would impede the king's monthly journeys through it."

"Is this the Divine Marriage whereof Zerlik told me?"

"Aye. You know of that, then?"

"I know what Zerlik told me. Is this ritual marriage consummated?"

"Well—ah—yes, it is. In sooth, when the king can no longer play his manful part, he is disposed of."

"Good gods, this is as bad as Xylar! How is it done?"

"When the king can no longer—ah—carnally penetrate the high priestess, she reports the fact to her nominal husband, the high priest of Ughroluk. Then the high priest, with a delegation of lesser priests, waits upon the king and presents him with the sacred rope, wherewith to hang himself."

"And the silly ass does it?"

"Aye; although this suicide has taken place but once in the last century. All the other kings have perished in war, or by assassination, or from some common ill, ere the rope came into play."

Holding his lanthorn up, Jorian walked a few steps along the dark tunnel in silence. Then he said:

"By Thio's horns, you don't suppose that promise Sahmet exacted from me was to take the king's place in this ceremony?"

"I know not, my son, but I fear she had some such scheme in mind."

"There you are! I listen to your moral preachments on the virtues of continence and try to practise them; but the very gods conspire against my new-found virtue."

"True, O Jorian. Little though I esteem fornication, I fear I must condone it this once."

"Well, that's something. At least, I don't suppose Sahmet will turn into a gigantic serpent, as did the princess Yargali. Now, I can see why Sahmet might not find Ishbahar to her taste as a bedfellow. But why pick on me?"

"You were to hand; she has seen you—or claims she has seen you—in her visions; and perhaps she finds you attractive."

"If I'm attractive to her looking like this, she'll find me utterly ravishing when cleaned up. Well, I daresay I can hold up my end, in all senses of the phrase. We won't tell Estrildis about it and hope that, if she find out, she'll forgive me natheless."

"Your secret is safe with me, my son."

"Good. But why need the king anything so costly as this tunnel for his connubial visits? Why cannot he cross the Lyap in a boat, like everyone else?"

Karadur shrugged. "Some say that King Hoshcha—who was not of the line of Juktar the Great and whose right to the throne was therefore questioned—was full of fancies about being assassinated as he rode through the streets. Others aver that he wished the tunnel as a means of escape from his palace in the event of revolution. In any case, he began the use of the tunnel for the Divine Marriage, and his successors have imitated him."

"What finally happened to Hoshcha?"

"After all his precautions—which included wearing a steel breastplate under his robes—he slipped in getting out of his bath and fractured his skull."

At the head of the long, narrow flight of steps that ended Hoshcha's Tunnel, Jorian rapped four times on the heavy door. When the peephole opened, he held up Sahmet's ring.

A bolt clanked and the door groaned open. There stood King Ishbahar in a dressing gown, without his wig. The lamplight shone on his egg-bald pate. A pair of guardsmen stood behind him; beyond these, servants hovered.

"By Nubalyaga's cleft!" cried the king. "Jorian! Whatever befell you, my boy? Come in, come in! You, too, Doctor."

They stepped into the king's dressing room, and Jorian told briefly what had happened to him and his companion since the start of the riot. A guardsman closed the door, which became merely one more panel in the wall. The handle of the bolt that secured it looked like a piece of gilded ornamentation.

"You did the proper thing," said the king. "We shall order the arrest of those villains Borai and Yiyim. You two shall sup with us this even. But first, my dear Jorian, you must clean up. You look as if you had been fighting a dragon and getting the worst of it, heh heh. You shall have the use of our royal bathtub, no less!"

"Your Majesty's consideration overwhelms me," said Jorian.

"Stuff and nonsense, my boy! We are friends, not merely sovran and subject. Evvelik! Conduct these gentlemen to the bathroom and furnish them with the needfuls."

The royal bathtub was a huge affair of burnished copper. As Jorian soaked and soaped, he murmured to Karadur, who was washing his face and hands:

"O Karadur, is this king deemed a little queer?"

"Nay; barring his fondness for the table—"

"I mean, with a lust for boys or men in lieu of women."

"Oh, ah I see. Nay again. Whereas that aberration is rife in Irazi, I think not that the charge has ever been laid against Ishbahar. When young, he had several wives, of whom all but two have died or been cast off; but I know of no other outlet for his lusts. Forsooth, me-thinks his only present passion is for rare victuals. Why?"

"Why else should he seek to make a bosom friend and confidant of a nobody—a mere foreign artisan— like me? It makes no sense."

"Perchance he simply likes you, my son. Or again, perchance it is concerned with Sahmet's plans for you."

"Oh. We must look further into this matter. And by the bye, meseems this tub were an admirable flying vehicle for our foray into Xylar. If we kept the weight well down in it, 'twere stabler than the common flying carpet or broomstick."

Karadur shook his head dubiously. "It would take a mighty demon to loft such a weight, and demons resist being imprisoned in copper or silver, since they know it is difficult for them to escape therefrom.

"Why not try Gorax, whom you keep mewed up in that ring? He's the strongest demon I know of."

"Alas, Gorax owes me but one more labor. Then he will be free to return to his own plane. Hence I dare not release him save for the direst need."

"I should have thought that being chased by that mob this afternoon were a case of direst need."

"True; but so scattered were my old wits that I never thought of Gorax at all."

Over one of King Ishbahar's colossal repasts, Jorian asked: "How went the riots, Your Majesty?"

"Luckily for Iraz, the rain waxed so heavy that it dispersed the factionists. Hence only a few score were slain and a few houses looted and burnt. This factiousness is a dreadful thing, but we know not how to end it. Have some of these oysters, which have come all the way from the coast of Shven, packed in ice."

"Why not simply stop the races, sire?"

"Ah, one of our predecessors—Huirpalam the Second, as we recall—tried that. Then the two factions united to revolt, drag poor Huirpalam to the Hippodrome, and tear him to pieces—a small piece at a time. We would not invite a similar fate, heh heh."

"If you will pardon your servant's saying so, methinks Your Majesty will have to face these factions down, soon or late. But that is Your Majesty's concern. Tell me, sire, what is this about Madam Sahmet's wishing me to take part in a service to the moon goddess?"

The king looked startled. "She has told you already? One moment." He sighed to everybody present save Jorian and Karadur—even the bodyguards and the food taster—to leave the chamber. Then he said, barely above a whisper: "Know you the fate of a futterless king in Penembei?"

"I have been told of it, sire."

"It is true." The king pointed to a massive bracket overhead, whence hung a lamp. "All too true. They take away that lamp, and we are supposed to toss the rope over yon gallows. We stand on a table, make fast the knot, and overset the table—ugh! Thus they get rid of an unwanted monarch without laying impious hands on his sacred person."

"Is Your Majesty finding his sacerdotal duties—ah—"

"Arduous? Have we your solemn oath of secrecy?"

Jorian and Karadur both swore. Ishbahar went on: "Our life is in your hands. We would not entrust it to you gentlemen, save that desperate conditions demand desperate remedies. For several months, now, our lady Sahmet has been dissatisfied with our performance; and forsooth, we had as lief abandon such games, since our girth imposes mechanical difficulties upon the coital process, and the fires of youth have long since burnt low.

"So, you see, our life is already in the hands of Madam Sahmet. She has but to tell her nominal husband, High Priest Chaluish, and he will pay us a visit with the sacred rope. She refrains for two reasons: Imprimus, that she hates High Priest Chaluish and would do nought to favor him; secundus, that I have promised her a lusty springald with an iron yard as my surrogate, an she will keep tacit about my limitations. And you shall be he."

Jorian: "I trust I shall prove worthy of the honor. But we once had a king in Kortoli who faced a similar predicament."

"Tell us, dear boy."

"This was King Finjanius, who reigned just after the Dark Age following the fall of Old Novaria to nomadic invaders from Shven. The Kortolian rule was that, when the king was no longer for any reason deemed worthy to rule, the chief priests of the kingdom called upon him to present him with a goblet of poison to drink. If he drank not, they said, the magical nexus betwixt him and his land would be broken, and the crops would wither and the people starve.

"Now, Finjanius was sent to the Academy at Othomae for his higher education. The Academy was then a new institution with but a handful of professors—none of the ivy-clad buildings it now boasts. In the Academy, Finjanius absorbed what were then deemed heretical 'modern' ideas. Shortly after his return from Othomae, he succeeded to the throne when his uncle, the old king, died.

"For a year or so, Finjanius ran the affairs of Kortoli according to his best lights. Being young, he had little reverence for tradition and introduced many novelties, such as no longer requiring subjects to knock their heads on the ground nine times in approaching him, or no longer forbidding them to speak to him unless he spoke first. This last rule had nearly lost him a military campaign against Aussar, when none of his officers durst warn him of an ambush.

"Finjanius it was who introduced the public bath to Kortoli and encouraged all the people, regardless of age, sex, or rank, to mingle freely in these establishments. Moreover, he patronized them himself and did not scruple to indulge in vulgar horseplay with his subjects, splashing and ducking them and being splashed and ducked in turn.

"Such conduct made him popular with the commons but gravely offended the more conservative elements. These at length determined that Finjanius needs must go. Since the chief priests also belonged to the leading and most tradition-bound families, a concensus was soon obtained. Presently, a delegation of priests waited upon the king with the fatal draft.

" 'Oho!' quotha. 'what is this?'

" 'The gods,' said the high priest of Zevatas, 'have decided that Your Majesty is no longer worthy to rule.'

" 'How know you that, sirrah?' said Finjanius.

" 'They have informed us in visions and dreams, sire,'

replied the priest. 'They demand the life of the chiefest man of the kingdom, lest they loose their wrath upon the land.'

" 'So they crave the chiefest life, eh?' said the king. He counted the priests and found that there were eight in the party. 'Now, whereas I am doubtless the chief man in Kortoli, you holy fathers are also not without standing. Would you not agree, messires?'

" 'Aye, sire; else we were not qualified to pass the gods' commands on to you.'

" 'In sooth, let us suppose that the life of one of you is worth—ah—let us say, one eighth of mine. That were plausible, were it not?'

" 'Aye, milord king,' said the priest.

" 'Then,' said Finjanius, 'an the gods desire the chiefest life, they should be just as well satisfied with eight lives, each worth one eighth of mine. Ho, guards! Seize me these eight gentlemen and hang them forthwith!'

"And so it was done. Thereafter none durst broach such a proposal to the king again, and hence the custom fell into abeyance."

King Ishbahar said: "Do you propose, dear Jorian, that we adopt a course like unto your king's?"

"That is up to Your Majesty. It has been done; and what men have done, men can do again." Jorian turned to Karadur. "Is that not one of the proverbs of your Mulvanian sage, what is his name?"

"Cidam," said Karadur.

The king shuddered, his chins quivering. "Alas! Would—would that we had the hardihood to essay such an enterprise." A pair of tears trickled down his fat cheeks. "But we *could* not defy tradition. We fear we are not of the stuff of your Finjanius." The king burst into sobs and covered his face with his hands.

"Your Majesty!" said Karadur. "An your servitors and guardsmen return and find you weeping, they will think we have entreated you ill and slay us."

The king wiped his face with his napkin and smiled through his tears. "Let us forget our griefs, then. Have some more of this Vindine wine! Master Jorian, we trust you are an entire man, with the usual lusts and faculties?"

"Aye, sire."

"Then you should not find the task confronting you arduous or disagreeable. Whilst a trifle older than you, Sahmet is neither unattractive nor cold. Neither. Remember, it is not just your prick that you pleasure, but our royal neck, as well, that you save. We will have Herekit make you out a commission as Friend of the King forthwith, for such you will be in a most literal way."

"I thank Your Majesty," said Jorian. "When does this sacred orgy take place?"

"At the next full moon, eleven nights hence. Let us drink to your success. May you give Her Sanctity a night she shall remember to her grave!"

# VI

# The Golem General

Next morning, Jorian went to the tower of Kumashar to inspect his clocks. He was pleased to find that yesterday's disturbances had not reached the tower. Then he made his way through the bustling crowds to the House of Learning.

Knowing him by now, the sentries admitted him without question. As he walked through the halls, he lingered at the doors of several laboratories where experiments were in progress. In one, engineers of the School of Matter tinkered with a machine designed to run on the power from boiling water. The project was old, but none had yet succeeded in making the contraption do any useful work. In another, technicians worked on a telescope, like the ordinary spyglass but much larger, wherewith they hoped to investigate the heavenly bodies.

Other chambers were in use by wizards of the School of Spirit. In one, three such sages sought to train a demon from the tenth plane, a creature of low intelligence, to obey simple commands. In another, a wizard-physician experimented with a spell to cure plague; his subjects were condemned criminals who had volunteered for the task on the promise of freedom if they survived.

Besides these activities, many rooms stood empty. As a result of the decline of the kings' financial support of the House of Learning, the size of its personnel and the scale of its projects had greatly shrunk in recent decades.

"At least," said Jorian, seated in the director's office, "yesterday's misadventures finally led you to get a new turban. That old one was getting so decrepit that I expected to find mice nesting in it." He had had his own hair cut short to bandage the wounds on his scalp.

"Contemn not such old things, my son," said Kara-dur. "That turban had acquired some small magical potential, merely by being in the vicinity when so many fell incantations were uttered and spells were cast. Do your clocks run harmoniously?"

"As regularly as the heavenly bodies. I've just come from the Tower. There was never any real problem, had your predecessor hired a competent mechanic instead of a fumbler. My father did a good, workman-like job, as anyone who knew him could have told you. "What I've come for, howsomever, is not the state of the clocks but the state of Jorian of Ardamai. Have you a means for our raid into Xylar?"

"Gods of Mulvan, Jorian, be not so hasty! Here we have barely escaped with our lives from riot and insur-rection; we have traversed the most secret passageway in the kingdom; we have become embroiled in the con-flict amongst the king, Madam Sahmet, and High Priest Chaluish—"

"All the more reason for pressing on. What's Chalu-ish like?"

"A little gray-haired man—nobody whom one would look at twice. He was in that parade of priests yester-day, and I have encountered him at courtly functions. But—"

"I have the *Flying Fish* tied up in a private dock for a small monthly rental, but I fear she'd prove too slow if we really had to run for it. So we had better prepare some swifter magical vehicle—"

"My son, I have never said that I would accompany you on your mission of abduction. Much though I esteem the lady Estrildis, I cannot desert a responsible post for petty personal—"

"Petty!" barked Jorian. "I'll have you know—"

"Now, now, my son, I meant no offense. But you have seen how this kingdom totters along, and I—unworthy though I be—am in a position to lend it a little stability and rationality. It were irresponsible—"

"I quote," growled Jorian: " 'So convenient a thing it is to be a reasoning being, for it enables one to think up a plausible reason for whatever one wishes to do.' "

"The wise Cidam?"

"Nay; our home-grown Novarian philosopher Achaemo. But, my reverend old spooker, my task needs at least two persons."

"Take Zerlik," said Karadur. "The lad will be delighted."

"What, and have to wipe that idiot's nose at every step? No, thank you! He'd do something silly at the critical moment, such as challenging the captain of the guard to a duel just when I was trying to hoist Estrildis out undetected."

"At least, he is reasonably strong and agile. I am neither, nor am I any longer up to such desperate adventures. Another journey like ours around the Inner Sea would terminate this incarnation for me."

"You can still cast a dire spell, which Zerlik cannot. But let's leave the question of personnel for the nonce to discuss the vehicle. How about that royal copper bathtub?"

Karadur wagged his head. "Alas, I see no prospect of obtaining it for your purpose. Even supposing that I could persuade the king to lend it—"

"Build another like it, then."

"That were too costly. It would come to hundreds of royals, and I have no funds in this year's appropriation to cover it.

"Furthermore, you appear not to realize the practical difficulties. It would require months of the most puissant sorcery to entrap our demon and compel him to our will. For such an enterprise, my best men were

Goelnush, Luekuz, and Firaven, but they are fully occupied with keeping Hoshcha's Tunnel dry. The other sorcerers at my command are all less competent. Old Oinash, for ensample, is but a doddery old time-server awaiting his pension. Barch, a younger man, is gifted but careless. Twice he has barely escaped sudden death at the claws of a hostile demon he had evoked, through some silly error in his pentacle; but he never seems to learn. As for Yanmik—"

"Why not put these dimmer flames on the tunnel—which must now be mere routine—to release your best men for my spell?"

"The king has forbidden it. He is fain not to have the wizard on duty sneeze and let in the floods just as he is traversing the tunnel on his tryst with Sahmet. Therefore he insists that my best men be kept at this task. And speaking of the king, there is—ah—umm—another complication."

"What's this? Out with it!"

"The—ah—His Majesty but this morn forbade me to assist you in any way in leaving Iraz. He must be apprehensive as to what might befall him if you were not present at the next full moon to pleasure the priestess."

Jorian glowered. "Curse it, you hauled me away from a good, respectable job, where I was at least geographically near to my darling, to this distant and turbulent city, on the promise of getting me means to rescue her. All you needed, you said, was to become director of the House of Learning, and the fish was in the creel. Well, thanks to my clockery, you're now director—and what happens? You can't do this for this reason, and you can't do that for that, and so on. I can make things hot for people who betray me—"

"My son, my son! Pray, take not that harsh and hostile tone. At the moment, I admit I envisage no easy thoroughfare to your noble goal. Only have patience, and the gods will open the way for us. They have never met—yes, Nedef?" Karadur changed from Novarian to Penembic. "O Jorian, this is our official scryer; Master Nedef, I present Jorian the Kortolian, our new clockmaster. You were saying?"

"Doctor Karadur," said the scryer, "I fear I have portentous news."

"You may speak before Master Jorian."

"Iraz is threatened by a host of assailants."

"Eh? Vurnu, Kradha, and Ashaka! What assailants? We are at war with none."

"May I sit, sir? I am weak with what I have seen."

"By all means, sit. Now tell us forthwith."

The scryer drew a long breath. "North, east, south, and west—they converge upon us from all sides. From the west comes a fleet of Algarthian pirates; from the south, a rabble of armed peasants under Mazsan and his faction; from the east, a swarm of Fediruni nomads on camels; and from the north, a Free Company of mercenaries from Novaria."

"How nigh are they?"

"Some are nigher than others; they may reach us on the morrow."

"How got the Fedirunis past the army along our eastern borders? Have they defeated the frontier force?"

"I know not, Doctor. They were already well inside the border when I discovered them."

"We must notify the king instanter," said Karadur.

They found King Ishbahar at his afternoon repast, which he called "tea." "Sit down, sit down, our dear fellows!" he cried. "Have a cup of genuine tea, brought at vast expense from Kuramon in the Far East. Have some of these honey biscuits to go with it. Try some of these sardines. Have you tea in Novaria nowadays?"

"It can be obtained, Your Majesty," said Jorian, "but it has never really taken hold. Perhaps the fact that the upheavals in Salimor cut off the supply from time to time have discouraged its use. Howsomever—"

"The Novarians ought to take it up," said Ishbahar. "They are too much given to drunkenness, we hear. A pleasant but nonintoxicating drink were better for their health." The king bit off the end of a huge plantain from Beraoti. "Moderation in all things is our guiding principle. Temperance." The plantain rapidly diminished.

"No doubt, sire. But we have something important to—"

"In fact, dear boy, how would you like a royal concession, to freight tea up the coast to Xylar? You could build up a profitable trade—"

"Sire," said Jorian, "Iraz is about to be attacked. Had we not better break the impending siege ere discussing trade routes?"

"Iraz? Besieged?" said the king, holding an olive in front of his open mouth. "Nubalyaga save us, but what is this?"

Karadur explained the visions that the scryer had seen in his crystal ball.

"Oh, dear!" said the king, looking sadly at the piles of uneaten food. "To have to break off such a splendid tea in the middle! The sufferings we kings endure for the welfare of our people! Ho, Ebeji! Summon Colonel Chuivir!"

When the glittering commander of the Royal Guard had clanked in and saluted, Ishbahar asked Karadur to repeat his tale. Then he asked Chuivir:

"However did those barbarians get past the frontier undetected?"

"You forget, sire, that General Tereyai has assembled the frontier army for maneuvers in the foothills of the Lograms, leaving the border covered by only a skeleton force. The Fedirunis must have surprised one of the frontier fortresses and poured through ere the alarm could be spread."

"Where is Admiral Kyar?"

"I believe he has put to sea in his flagship, to exercise his rowers."

"Then, Colonel, you would seem to be the ranking officer in Iraz. Kindly get word to General Tereyai and Admiral Kyar as soon as you can. Meanwhile, you shall mobilize the Royal Guard and call up the companies of the factions."

"But, Your Majesty, how shall I—how do you wish me to carry out your commands? Shall I send a barge out to seek the admiral—"

Ishbahar slapped the table, making the cups and dishes dance. "Colonel Chuivir! Bother us not with those details; just carry out our orders! Now go and get to work!" When the crestfallen colonel had clanked out, the king shook his head. "Woe is us! We do believe we committed an error in appointing Chuivir to that command. He looked so magnificent on parade, but he has never fought a battle in his life."

"Then how did it happen, sire?" asked Jorian.

"He was a cousin of our third wife and well-liked in society. Since we relied upon the frontier force to keep the foe a decent distance from Iraz, we never expected that the actual defense of the city would devolve upon this amiable popinjay. Herekit!"

"Aye, sire?" said the secretary.

"Draft me a letter to Daunas, Grand Bastard of Othomae, inquiring whether he would hire out to us a few squadrons of his lobster-plated heavy cavalry, and on what terms. And command two of our swiftest couriers to stand by, booted and saddled. Draft another to Shaju, king of kings of Mulvan, urging him to invade the deserts of Fedirun from the east, since this land will be partly stripped of warriors. Suggest that he loot their sacred city of Ubar." The king turned back to his guests with a sigh. "Ah, well, we have done what we can. Now the fate of the city rests upon our gallant subjects."

"Does Your Majesty plan to take an active part in the defense?" asked Jorian.

"Bountiful heavens, dear boy, nay! Can you imagine us, with our girth, trading spear-thrusts on the battlements? Besides, we have always been a man of peace, with little use for fire-eating sword-rattlers. And now, meseems, our city and our life must needs depend upon these same swashbucklers. Doctor Karadur, you should muster your scientists and wizards to the work of defense. Have you, perchance, a spell to summon some unhuman race—say, the silvans of the Lograms—to our aid?"

"I will see what the House of Learning can do," said Karadur. "But let Your Majesty not count upon any such assistance. The unhumans have little love for mankind, having been harshly entreated by them. To seek to compel aid from them is like holding a sword by the wrong end, so that it wounds the hand of the wielder. But I go—"

"Stay, stay. Now that we have given the essential commands, there is no reason why we should not finish our tea."

"But, sire, I—"

"Nay, relax. A quarter-hour more or less will not decide the fate of the city. Do have some of these mushrooms, gathered in the jungles of Baraoti."

"If Your Majesty thinks them safe ..." said Jorian, staring uneasily at a yellow-spotted purple fungoid growth of singularly repulsive appearance.

"Nonsense! We have been eating these for years, and we have not lost a royal taster yet, heh heh."

Jorian manfully swallowed a mouthful of fungus. To give himself a pretext for not eating another, he said:

"Your Colonel Chuivir reminds your servant of the tale of King Filoman and the golem general."

"Go ahead, dear boy," said the king. "You will not mind if we steal a bit of your mushroom, will you?"

"Feel free, sire."

\*　　\*　　\*

"This king," began Jorian, "otherwise called Filoman the Well-Meaning, was the father of the celebrated Fusinian the Fox. King Filoman was also an outstanding ruler in his way. He had the noblest emotions and the best intentions of any Kortolian monarch. He was intelligent, courageous, honest, hard-working, moral, kind, and generous. His only fault was that he had no common sense, and in practice this fault often cancelled all his other virtues put together.

"One legend says that this fault was caused by an astrological conjunction at his birth. Another avers that, when the fairies gathered for his naming ceremony, the fairy who was supposed to confer common sense lost her temper when she beheld another fairy wearing a gauzy gown just like hers and flounced out in a rage without bestowing her gift.

"Early in his reign, King Filoman confronted the problem of the defense of his realm. Being a peace-loving man, he supposed that others felt likewise. In this opinion he was encouraged by his minister, an old-ster named Periax whom he had inherited from the previous reign.

"Periax urged Filoman to reduce the army to a mere royal guard. 'Wars,' quotha, 'are caused by mutual fears and suspicions, which in turn are caused by armaments. Get rid of the armaments and you will abolish war. When our neighbors see us disarming, they will know that we have no aggressive intentions towards them and lose their fear of us. Then they will follow our example, and peace and brotherhood shall reign forevermore.'

"Periax did not enlarge upon the real reason for his advice. This was that he was himself too old and creaky to sit a horse, brandish a sword, and perform other warlike acts. In these early times, the king and his min-isters were expected to lead charges in person. Periax reckoned that, as a result of his pacific policy, war would at least be deferred until after his natural death, and he cared not for what befell the kingdom thereafter.

"Periax's argument seemed to Filoman like sound sense, so he virtually disbanded his army. Now, at this time, Kortoli's southern neighbor, Vindium, was under the rule of Nevors the Daft, whose character is implied by his sobriquet. I need not detail the enormities of his reign: wasting his treasury on solid gold statues of himself; slaying ministers, kinsmen, and associates on the slightest pretext; whimseys like making his army dress up as frogs and go hopping about the parade ground on all fours, shouting '*Diddit! Diddit!*' while King Nevors rolled on the ground screaming with laughter.

"In time, a cabal of noblemen and officials got the king apart from his bodyguard, hacked him to pieces, and threw the pieces into the Inner Sea. Then the problem arose, who should take the unlamented Nevors' place? For he had slain all his near kin.

"As it happened, an astute and ambitious lawyer, Doctor Truentius, had foreseen these events and gathered a powerful following among the commons. When King Nevors was slain, Truentius marched to the palace at the head of thousands of his partisans, chased out the relics of the old reign, and proclaimed a republic with himself as First Consul.

"Truentius was the most brilliant man in Vindium. He had read all the historians and philosophers and prophets and had thought deeply on questions of government. He it was who, more or less singlehanded, invented republican government in Novaria. He drew up a constitution for Vindium which, considering its early date, is still acclaimed as a marvel of profound and original thought.

"Knowing himself the ablest man around, Truentius inferred that his decisions as to what was best for the Vindines were necessarily right. Therefore, anyone who opposed them was by definition an enemy of the people and hence a scoundrel for whom the direst punishment were too lenient. Soon Vindium City saw in its main square a large wooden block, served by a man with a black hood over his head and a large ax in his hands, wherewith to smite off the head of anyone so malign and perverse as to dispute the infallible reasoning of Doctor Truentius.

"After a couple of years of this, Truentius, finding that such domestic problems as the production and distribution of wealth and the reconciliation of order with liberty stubbornly resisted the best efforts of himself and his headsman, bethought him of spreading the blessings of popular government to the rest of Twelve Cities. Besides the benefits that such a program would confer upon the other Novarians, it would rally the Vindines, who were beginning to fall into seditious factions, behind their First Consul and furnish him with a pretext for making his rule even more absolute. He therefore sent an ultimatum to King Filoman of Kortoli, demanding that Filoman abdicate in favor of a popularly elected consul.

"Naturally perturbed, King Filoman sought advice. The advice he got from his councillors, however, was so contradictory that Filoman could make nought of it. Some were for arming every man in the kingdom and resisting to the last; but others pointed out that no such stock of arms existed.

"Some said to reactivate the old army and recall the retired officers to the colors. But it transpired that most of these officers had gone abroad to seek service as mercenaries. The former general of the Kortolian army, for instance, was now serving as a captain in the forces of the Grand Bastard of Othomae. It would take too long to recall them, even if they were willing to come.

"Old Periax urged Filoman to yield to Truentius' overwhelming force. But others said that, judging by his master's conduct, the new First Consul's first act would be to set up a chopping block in Kortoli City to shorten everybody who might possibly be a threat to him, which included all those present.

"At last it was decided to make some arms, and buy some, and call up the lustier young men, and hire such former officers as could be found to train them to use them.

"The only thing that saved Kortoli from conquest during this parlous time was the fact that Truentius, too, had his military troubles. For most of the officers of the Vindine army, as members of the old regime, either had been executed or had fled. Truentius knew that the mob of mechanics and merchants, with whose help he had seized power, would not be up to a real campaign without much organization and training.

"To gain time, Filoman was urged to seek a parley with Consul Truentius. To strengthen Filoman's hand, it was decided to hold a plebiscite of all adult male Kortolians, as to whether they wished to continue under the rule of King Filoman or to change to a republican system like that of Vindium. When the plebiscite was held, the Kortolians gave Filoman ninety-seven out of every hundred votes. This may have been the voters' honest opinion, since Filoman was then greatly beloved for his modesty, kindliness, and other virtues. Besides, Truentius' republican doctrines had been somewhat discredited by tales of his unbridled use of the ax.

"The question also arose, who should command the new Kortolian army? Several councillors put themselves forward for the post. But, whenever one proposed himself, the others shouted him down, crying that he was an ambitious schemer who sought to use his power to usurp the throne. So vehement was the opposition to any name proposed that Filoman felt he needs must leave his choice in abeyance for the time being.

"The parley with Truentius was duly arranged. It took place on an islet in the river Posaurus, which divided Vindium from Kortoli. Each was to bring no more than three armed men with him. In due course, the two met, ate lunch, and got down to business. Truentius said:

" 'My good Filoman, love you your people?'

" 'Certes!' replied the king. 'Have I not proven it an hundred times over?'

" 'Then, an you truly love them, you must yield your throne as I have demanded. Otherwise you will bring down upon them a brutal, sanguinary war. The choice is yours, and so is the responsibility.'

" 'And wherefore should I do that?'

" 'First, because I demand it and have the force to compel your compliance; second, because it is the good and righteous thing to do. Monarchy is an ancient superstition, an outmoded charade, an obsolete form of injustice and oppression.' And Truentius lectured Filoman on the reasons for a popular republic.

" 'But,' said Filoman, 'we have just polled the Kortolians, and they voted overwhelmingly to keep the monarchy.'

"Truentius laughed. 'My dear Filoman, do you expect me to take your vote seriously, when you held the plebiscite and counted the votes?'

" 'Do you insinuate that I cheated?' cried Filoman in wrath. 'Never has anyone so impugned my honesty in the five years of my reign!'

"Truentius merely laughed some more. 'Well, let us suppose that you did report the votes truthfully. You are a naive enough young fool to have done just that. It still makes no difference, since the *people* natheless voted for a republic.'

" 'How do you make that?'

" 'Why, it is simple. Any population is divided into two factions: the people, and the enemies of the people. Since my program is the best one for the people, anybody who opposes it must logically be an enemy of the people.'

" 'Mean you,' said Filoman, 'that if ninety-seven out

of every hundred vote for me and three for you, the three are the people and the other ninety-seven the enemies thereof?'

" 'Certes, my lad. Right glad am I to see that you learn the facts of politics so quickly.'

" 'But that is absurd!' cried Filoman. 'It is merely a pretext for the infinite expansion of your own power!'

"Truentius sighed. 'I will try once more to explain, albeit I fear your grasp of logic is inadequate. My guiding principle is: all power to the people. The people, I assume, are always right. Do you follow me so far?'

" 'Aye.'

" 'Then, if certain malevolent or misguided persons make a decision that is obviously wrong, it follows that they cannot belong to the people. Therefore they must be enemies of the people.'

" 'But who decides which decision is right?'

" 'No mere mortal mind decides that, but the iron laws of logic. For ensample, I have explained to you why a republican government is preferable to a monarchy. This is an objective fact, which no personal whim, error, or bias can alter, any more than they can change the sum of two and two. Therefore—'

"But Filoman interrupted: 'Never! I will die fighting ere I suffer you to put this monstrous doctrine into effect!"

" 'Oh, come, my dear King! That is quite unnecessary. You can abdicate and flee abroad with as much of the royal treasury as you can bear with you. In fact, I have your successor, the First Consul of Kortoli, already chosen. He is a muleteer named Knops: a good man who will promote your former people's welfare.'

" 'The people would never vote your puppet Knops into office!'

" 'Oh, yes they would, because he would have no opposition. Since I have chosen him, and since my logic is irrefutable, it follows that Master Knops is the best

man for the magistracy. Anybody opposing him would
be an enemy of the people, to be slain out of hand.'

" 'But Knops is not even a Kortolian!'

" 'Not now; but as your last official act, you can confer citzenship upon him. I like to keep things orderly—'

"Just then, a powerful sneeze came from a clump of
alders on the Vindine side of the Posaurus. Filoman
looked up, startled, and his eyes caught the glint of
the sun on steel. For once he acted with admirable
promptitude. He shouted to his men-at-arms: 'Treason!
Let us fly!' And he and his men sprang to their feet
and ran through the shallows to the Kortolian side of
the river, where a groom held their horses.

"Truentius' guards and the men he had hidden
rushed after them and brought down one of Filoman's
men with an arrow; but the king and the others got
away. It had not occurred to Filoman to have more
armed men waiting over the nearest hill to come to his
aid, so there was nought to do but ride hell-for-leather.
They galloped off into the hills of southern Kortoli and
lost their pursuers.

"They lost themselves, also. They were wandering
around, suffering hunger and thirst, when a woman of
early middle years called to them from a hillside.

" 'Hail, Your Majesty!' she cried. 'Can a loyal subject
be of service to you?'

" 'Methinks you can, good lady,' quoth Filoman. 'But
how know you me?'

" 'I have powers not of this mundane sphere,' she
said. 'But come on into my cave and refresh yourselves.'

" 'Mean you that you are a witch?'

" 'Nay, sire; a proper wizardess, hight Gloé. At least,
I should be but for a trifle of difficulty about my
license, which I am sure Your Majesty can put straight
with a snap of his finger.'

"When Filoman, his two surviving men-at-arms, and
the groom had refreshed themselves, Filoman said: 'I
am sure the difficulty whereof you speak can be ironed

out. But if you have in sooth magical powers, mayhap you can tell me how to find a commander-in-chief for my new army, which is even now drilling against the expected onslaught from Vindium.'

"Then he told her how, amongst his councillors, all those with warlike experience—and some without—coveted the post, but none wished for anyone else to have it. In sooth, King Filoman himself worried over the prospect that a successful general might oust him from his throne.

" 'Why not lead your army yourself?' asked Gloé.

" 'I am not qualified. Being a lover of peace and of my fellow men, I have not sought experience with the bloody art of war.'

" 'Well, then,' said Gloé, 'I needs must make you a golem general.'

" 'A what?'

" 'A golem is a manlike image of clay, animated by a demon from the Fifth Plane. I shall set this demon the task of defeating the Vindines. I shall promise him that, once that is done, he may return to his own plane, leaving the image lifeless and no threat to Your Majesty. If you would fain preserve the image, you can bake it to brick and stand it on a pedestal.'

" 'But,' said Filoman, 'will this demon of yours possess the needful military skill?'

" 'He will be adequate, sire. After all, the Vindine army is itself but a rabble of shopkeepers and artisans, since most of the Vindine knightly class who have not lost their heads have fled abroad. Moreover, Truentius, for all his bloodthirsty talk, is an arrant coward who cannot bear the sight of blood. He never attends those executions he orders so lavishly.'

"This seemed like a sound proposal, so Filoman assented. A sennight later, Gloé arrived in Kortoli City driving an oxcart wherein, padded by straw against damage, lay the image of a man seven feet tall. When the cart drew up in front of the palace, Gloé uttered a spell. Then the image threw off its straw and climbed creakily to its feet.

"It was the image of a mighty warrior in armor, wearing the insignia of a Kortolian general. Gloé had not stinted her preparations, for the clay that composed the armor and costume of the image was painted to resemble the real thing. In fact, one had to look closely to perceive that it was not in sooth a normal man of commanding aspect.

"In a hoarse, growling voice, the image said: 'General Golemius reporting for duty, Your Majesty.'

"And indeed, General Golemius proved a competent commander, even if the yellow-gray complexion of his face and hands made the soldiers uneasy.

"Another sennight passed, and word came that the Vindines had crossed the Posaurus into southern Kortoli. Filoman and his new army marched out to meet them. Filoman kept in the background and left the active commanding to General Golemius, who seemed to manage well enough.

"At length the two armies sighted each other, on a dank day of lowering clouds. General Golemius drew up his army. Filoman, mounted and attended by a small personal guard, watched admiringly from a nearby hilltop.

"When the golem general had gotten all his men in place, he stepped to the fore, waved his sword, and growled: 'Forward!' So the army clattered after their general, who tramped stolidly in the lead.

"Filoman walked his horse down the hill and followed the army at a leisurely pace. The force marched across the plain, which was broken here and there by a few small clumps of trees. As the two armies approached, Filoman saw that which startled him. Leading the Vindine army was, not First Consul Doctor Truentius, but another golem general. For Truentius, being as Gloé had said a physical coward, had had recourse to his own sorcerer. This thaumaturge had summoned another demon from the Fifth Plane to animate a general of clay.

"The armies moved slowly, because both were composed largely of green troops, whose alignment was often disordered by the trees that dotted the plain. When this happened, the two clay generals had to halt their forces and straighten them out again. And then it began to rain.

"As the armies came closer, the rain came down harder. It rang on helmets with a metallic sound; it trickled down inside hauberk and greave. And, just as the armies came within bowshot, they slowed and stopped.

"King Filoman pushed his horse forward through the rear ranks to see what had halted his host. Soon he observed that General Golemius was standing still in front of his army. Moreover, the general seemed to have lost in stature and gained in girth. As Filoman watched, the general dissolved into a mound of mud, as did the other general.

"That left both armies without commanders. Over against the Kortolians stood the Vindines, whose army was much larger. Behind the Vindine army, First Consul Truentius sat in his carriage, watching, for he had never learnt to ride a horse. When his army halted, he clambered up on the roof of his carriage to see what betid. Discovering that his general, like the other, had reverted to clay, he began to shout: 'Forward, my brave men! At them! Charge!'

"At first, his army milled and shuffled uncertainly. But then some officers, by blows and exhortations, got their units moving again.

"Meanwhile the Kortolian army, seeing a force of nearly twice their own strength bearing down upon them, began to edge backwards. Here and there a man broke from the ranks and ran. Vindine arrows began to fall amongst the Kortolians.

"King Filoman had drawn up his horse beneath a

tree, to keep out of the rain. And in this tree was a hornets' nest. Because of the rain, the hornets were all huddled inside their nest and minding their own affairs, when an arrow aimed at the king flew high and skewered their nest. I know not if Penembei have insects like these, but our Novarian hornets most fiercely resent any tampering with their nests and take stern measures against the tamperer.

"As the hornets swarmed out, the first animate thing they beheld was King Filoman. He was sitting his horse right under their bough, waving his sword and trying by cries and appeals to stem the rout of his army, in much the same vein as Truentius on the other side was harkening on his host. Presently Filoman gave an even louder yell as a hornet stung him on the wrist and another on the cheek. Then his horse whinnied, as another stung it on the arse, and bounded forward.

"Filoman's guard put spurs to their steeds to keep up with the king. The soldiers saw their king galloping straight at the foe, brandishing his sword and followed by a handful of bodyguards. Someone set up a cry of: 'Save the king!' and started running after Filoman. When some did, all did, so that what had been a rout of the Kortotians was changed in a trice into a rout of the Vindines.

"Truentius commanded his coachman to turn the carriage around; but, finding this difficult in the press, the coachman lighted down from his seat and fled on foot. Truentius then climbed into the driver's seat and tried to take the reins himself. Having no knowledge of chariotry, however, he was unable to bring the frightened horses under control. Then he got down, too, but was overborne in the rout and trampled to death.

"The Vindines fled in disorder from Kortoli. When the survivors got home, they changed their constitution to allow for two elected consuls, in the hope that the twain would watch each other and keep each other from seizing unlawful power. And, despite interludes of turbulence and usurpation, they have kept to that scheme ever since.

"Filoman rode home in triumph, notwithstanding that his face was grotesquely swollen from the sting. He was hailed as the savior of Kortoli for his desperate charge into the heart of the foe. He disclaimed credit, saying that the victor was neither himself nor his golem general, but the hornet that had stung his horse's rump. But so great was the love for Filoman that people said, ah, that is just our hero-king being modest.

"In any case, Filoman decided to stick to flesh-and-blood generals thereafter. They might have their faults but at least would not dissolve into mud at the first wetting.

"Later, Filoman's reign became more and more eccentric. He retained a ghost as his minister; he tried to abolish crime by pensioning all criminals; and he fell under the influence of a Mulvanian ascetic, Ajimbalin. This man persuaded him to lead a life of utter self-denial and mortification of the flesh, to the neglect of his kingdom and of his queen, who eloped with a pirate captain.

"The Kortolians sometimes wondered if they had not been wiser to toss Filoman out and adopt a republican scheme like that urged upon them by Truentius. In fact, they might well have done so; but, ere matters could come to a head, Filoman lost his life in a riding accident and was succeeded by his much abler son Fusinian. King Fusinian restored the popularity of the monarchy, and it has persisted down to the present day."

The king laughed heartily until he got into a fit of coughing and wheezing and had to be slapped on the back by his taster and his secretary.

"At least," he said, "we have never appointed a general of clockwork or of clay, heh heh. Chuivir may not be any Juktar the Great, but at least he bleeds if one pricks him." The king's little black eyes stared sharply at Jorian out of his puffy, round face. "That brings up a problem. Yes, sir, a problem. Two days ago, our spies brought us a rumor that you, dear boy, were not quite what you seemed—that, in sooth, you were no mere mechanic but a former ruler of some Novarian city-state. Is that true?"

Jorian and Karadur exchanged glances. Jorian muttered: "Zerlik must have been flapping that long tongue of his." He turned to the king. "It is true, Your Majesty. Your servant was king of Xylar for five years. Know you their method of succession?"

"We once knew but have forgotten. Tell us."

"Every five years, they come together in a grand assembly, cut off the old king's head, and throw it up for grabs. I became king by catching my predecessor's head when I saw it flying towards me, not then realizing what the object was and what catching it implied. When my five years neared their end, Doctor Karadur devised a method for me to escape this drastic ritual."

"Bountiful heavens!" exclaimed the king. "Here, the ruler is at least granted more than five years of tenure; albeit the principle is not wholly different. How did the Xylarians take the escape of their human toss-ball?"

"They have been after me ever since, to drag me back and complete their interrupted ceremony. Therefore I beg Your Majesty not to reveal my former status, lest the Xylarians get wind of my whereabouts and kidnap me. I barely escaped one such attempt on my way hither."

The king clucked. "Too bad, too bad. An we could publicly proclaim that you were a former king, we could do fine things for you. What was the date of your birth?"

Jorian raised his bushy black eyebrows, but replied: "I was born in the twelfth year of King Fealin the Second of Kortoli, on the fifteenth of the Month of the Lion. Why, sire?"

"Have you taken that down, Herekit?" the king asked his secretary; then to Jorian: "We asked it so that our wise men can calculate what the fates have in store for you. Tell me: had you warlike experience during your kingship?"

"Aye, sire; quite a lot. I led Xylar's army in two pitched battles, at Dol and at Larunum, with brigands calling themselves free companies, as well as several skirmishes. I admiraled the Xylarian fleet in driving the Algarthian pirates away from our shores. Besides, I had already seen battle whilst serving a hitch in the Foot Guards of the Grand Bastard of Othomae."

"Then, my dear Jorian, you would seem to be the answer to a fat old man's prayer."

"How so, sire?"

"Look you. We know nought of warfare and make no pretense of doing so. Our senior officer, Colonel Chuivir, is, for practical purposes, as ignorant as we. He, howsomever, is not fain to admit it. For that matter, it would do the spirits of the defenders no good for their commander to avouch himself a military ninny.

"We lack time to find a replacement for Chuivir. Most of the officers in his command are, we suspect, as innocent of war as he. Our seasoned commanders are all with the frontier army. Nor can we appoint you in Chuivir's place. You are a foreigner and a commoner, whom the militia would not obey with any zeal. Moreover, Chuivir has influential friends among the nobility and officials, who would be affronted by our abruptly dismissing him ere he has had time to commit any gross blunder. Even a king with theoretically unlimited power, you know, must constantly make sure of his political support, heh heh."

"Well, sire?" said Jorian as Ishbahar hesitated.

"So we—ah—the thought has come to us: How would you like to be our military aide?"

"What would that entail?"

"Oh, you would wear a fancy uniform. In theory,

you would be merely our messenger boy, to carry our commands to the forces and bring us reports of the fighting. In practice, we shall ask you to look over the military situation every day, decide what needs to be done, and advise us accordingly. We shall put your recommendations in the form of royal commands, which you shall convey to Chuivir or whomever else we designate. You will not seem to have any power over the defense but in fact will be in full command thereof. How does that strike you?"

"All I can say, sire, is that I will try my best."

"Good." Ishbahar spoke to the secretary: "Herekit! Draw up a commission for Master Jorian—yes, Ebeji?"

"Sire," said the attendant, who had just come in, "a ship's officer would speak with you on urgent business."

"Oh, curse this churlish world, that will not let a man eat a simple snack in peace! Send him in."

The visitor was a young naval officer with a drawn, ghastly look, who dropped to one knee. "Sire!"

"Well, sir?"

"Admiral Kyar is lost, and the pirates of Algarth are upon us!"

"Eh? Eh? Oh, good gods! How did this happen?"

"The—the admiral took the flagship *Ressam* out this morn for exercises, accompanied by two small dispatch galleys, the *Onuech* and the *Byari*. At sea, we encountered a patch of fog, which some said had the look of sorcerous fog. Then, of a sudden, a swarm of Algarthian craft sped out of the fog and surrounded the *Ressam*. Being undermanned, she could not work up enough speed to fight clear. The freebooters also took the *Onuech;* but the *Byari*, by putting the marines on the oars, won free."

"Were you in command of the *Byari?*" asked the king.

"Aye, sire. If Your Majesty thinks I ought to have stayed and perished with the admiral—"

"Nay, nay, you did right. Someone had to bring us

word. In fact, you are hereby promoted to admiral in place of Kyar. Prepare the rest of our navy for battle." To the secretary, the king said: "Draw up a royal commission for this officer and bring it to us to sign. Now, Admiral, do sit down and try some of this—by Ughroluk's toenails, the young man has fainted! Pour water on him, somebody!"

That evening, Jorian and Karadur stood on the floor of the Tower of Kumashar that housed the clockwork. They looked towards the sea, where the Penembic navy was locked in battle with a fleet of Algarthian pirates. The largest Penembic ships, the huge catamarans, were not even sent into action for want of rowers to man them. The ships that did take part in the battle moved sluggishly for lack of oar power.

"There goes another one," said Jorian as ruddy flames enveloped a ship.

"One of ours or theirs?" said Karadur.

"One of ours, I fear; but 'tis hard to be sure in this failing light."

"How did that young fellow—what's his name—the officer whom the king of a sudden promoted to admiral, how effective has he proven?"

Jorian shrugged. "Considering the generally unprepared state of the fleet and the lack of time, there's no way to tell. Not even Diodis of Zolon, the greatest Novarian sea commander, could have done much in this man's room."

"How do you with Colonel Chuivir?"

"Methinks he suspects the true state of affairs. He seems to take the king's commands with ill grace, even if he had not yet flouted any of them. What worries me is that, if he learn that the Xylarians are after me, he may get word to them to come and take me."

"They could hardly do that, with the city surrounded and under siege."

"True, Doctor. So I'm in a pretty pass, am I not?

I'm safe whilst the siege lasts. My duty, howsomever, is to defeat and break it, which will place me again in jeopardy. If on the other hand the besiegers take the city, I shall probably lose my head in that case, too." He reached up and tugged at his head. "Just making sure 'tis firmly fixed in place."

"An we win here, I am sure the king could protect you."

"Perhaps, perhaps. But suppose he find himself straightened for money to pay the cost of the war and hear of the price the Xylarians have placed on my head?"

"Oh, he is a kindly man—"

"For the present; but the day may come when he loves his little Jorian less than the cash I could bring. My taste of kingship has taught me never to trust any ruler. They can always justify any perfidy by saying, 'It's for the people's good.'"

The battle continued for hours in ever-deepening darkness and confusion. Then the surviving Penembic ships broke off and fled up the Lyap. The pirates swept the decks of the anchored ships, both naval and merchant, and invested the shoreline outside the wall of the city.

Next day, a Free Company in flashing armor marched down the Novarian Road from the north; Mazsan's peasant army straggled up from the south; and a swarm of robed, camel-riding nomads from Fedirun approached from the east. The siege had begun.

# VII

# The Siege of Iraz

The besiegers spread around Iraz, out of catapult range, and set up their camps. That of the Free Company was an orderly fortified square of tents, surrounded by a ditch and an embankment. It stood in the fields northeast of the city, where a bend in the Lyap gave the mercenaries room to camp between the river and the wall.

The camp of the Fedirunis was a sprawling city of brown camel's hair tents set every which way, whence sounds of drums and wailing music arose at night. From eastward, a stream of Fedirunis rode camels, horses, mules, and asses down the East Road to join the besiegers. The news that Iraz might be sacked had spread over the eastern deserts and had drawn all the sand thieves of Fedirun like flies to honey. The city of camel's-hair tents grew and spread like a fungus.

Mazasan's peasants had not brought tents. Instead, they built rude huts of fieldstone and brushwood or else slept, bundled in sheepskins, in the open. The Algarthian pirates slept aboard their ships.

The suburb of Zaktan across the Lyap, whose people had all fled to Iraz proper, was plundered and some of the houses were burnt; but a rainy spell prevented a general conflagration. The beacon atop the Tower of Kumashar was dark, for the only incoming ships were additions to the pirate fleet.

The besiegers assembled mantlets, which they extended in lines towards the city. From behind these defenses, their archers sniped at Irazis on the walls.

Since this part of Penembei had few trees, the besiegers' engineers broke up some of King Ishbahar's biggest war galleys for timber to build their engines.

Beyond the lines of mantlets, siege engines—catapults, tortoises (wheeled sheds), and belfries (movable siege towers)—began to take shape. The sounds of sawing and hammering continued day and night.

Meanwhile, the wizards on both sides tried out their arts. The besiegers' magicians conjured up illusions of vast, winged monsters, which swooped with bared fangs and fiery breath at the battlements. At first, the defenders scattered with cries of alarm. But Karadur and his assistant wizards quickly identified these monsters as mere harmless phantasms and dispersed them with counter-spells.

The besiegers' sorcerers then cast a mighty spell, which evoked a horde of bat-winged, scaly demons from the Sixth Plane, to assail the defenders with fangs and talons. But the defending thaumaturgists cast a counter-spell. This spell caused all the bees, wasps, and hornets within ten leagues of Iraz to swarm to the city and attack the demons. With shrieks of pain and croaks of outrage, the demons fled and vanished back to their own plane.

The men of the Free Company, as the best-disciplined soldiers among the attackers, were the first to complete a catapult. The skeins, slings, and fittings they had brought along in their baggage wagons, and for timbers they used wood from the dismantled battleships.

This catapult was of the two-armed, dart-throwing type. They levered it forward on its ponderous wheels. A big wooden shield, hung with green hides, was fastened in front of it to protect it against counter-bombardment. Karadur's wizards, collected on the wall, sweated and mumbled and gesticulated in attempts to cast a spell upon the device.

*     *     *

Early one morning, under an overcast sky, Karadur stood watching from the wall. He said to Jorian: "I fear me, alas, that they have already placed a protective spell over yonder engine, so that all my wizards' efforts will go for nought. The advances in magic of recent centuries have given the defense great advantages in wizardly conflict."

Jorian, in silvered scale mail, peered through his spyglass. "Methinks they're ready to shoot," he said. "Take a look."

"Ah, me! You are right."

"Get ready to duck. One of those darts would skewer you like an olive on a toothpick ... Here it comes!"

The Free Company's catapult discharged with a crash. The missile—a three-foot bolt of wood and iron, with wooden vanes—whistled over their heads, to curve down and fall inside the city.

"If that be the best they can do," said Karadur, "I doubt that they will soon beat us down by hurling darts at random into this vast city."

"You don't understand," said Jorian. "That was a mere ranging shot. When they get the elevation right, they'll use that engine to scatter defenders on the wall and thus hinder the servicing of our engines. Now, do you see that other catapult a-building, back of the first one?"

"Aye."

"That one will be twice as big and will throw balls of stone or brick instead of darts. They'll wheel it forward and set it to battering a breach in our wall, whilst the dart-thrower protects it 'gainst our counter-measures by a covering bombardment. It may take a fortnight; but soon or late, the wall will crumble and fall at that point."

"What can we do?"

"I've already told Colonel Chuivir to start his masons building a lune behind the threatened point. Whether he'll do it is another thing. He suspects that, when I tell him 'tis the king's will that he do thus-and-so, it is really my idea, and he bubbles with resentment."

"How is our defending army coming?"

Jorian spat. "Lousy! The Royal Guard have had at least formal training, but they're a mere handful. The militia companies are drilling; but the two stasiarchs are more interested in blackguarding and plotting against each other than they are in winning the war. There have been many affrays betwixt Pants and Kilts, with several wounded and a couple slain.

"They're just urban rabble anyway: splendid at rioting, looting, and arson, but as soldiers worth no more than so many rabbits. They argue every command and take a perverse pride in slovenliness and indiscipline. Had I but a few thousand of my sturdy Kortolian peasants . . ." Jorian laughed shortly. "Perdy, kimmer," he said, falling into his rustic Kortolian dialect, "a grew up in little Ardamai and kenned the farm folk well. Then a thought them the crassest clods, dullards, and skinflints on earth. When a first saw Kortoli City, a said, aha! City life be the life for me! And indeed, a still find city folk better company. But, when it come to the push of the pike, gie me yeomen wi' dung on their boots and na thought but the next harvest in their heads!

"Now, take those houses built against the West Wall, along the waterfront street. That was strictly illegal, since such dwellings provide cover for attackers; but Ishbahar's inspectors doubtless pocketed bribes to overlook . . ."

Jorian fell silent for a moment while he swept the besiegers' lines with his telescope. Then he said: "Were I boss of yon besiegers, 'stead of wasting time in building catapults and belfries, I'd make hundreds of scaling ladders and send the whole force against our walls at once."

"Why, my son? Such ladders are easily overthrown, to the scathe of the men clinging to them. I have never understood how any number of men could take a defended wall. Why cannot the defenders simply push over the ladders as fast as they are erected?"

"Were numbers anywhere near even, they could. Stout-hearted defenders can beat off several times their number of attackers. But the foe now outnumber us fifteen or twenty to one—at least as far as real soldiers are concerned; I count not Vegh's and Amazluek's rabble. With the defenders so few, they could not man all parts of the wall at once. By throwing up ladders against parts of the wall that are bare for the nonce, the assailants can get a lodgment on the top. Once a few sections are taken, the attackers can stream down into the city and make their numbers felt.

"If the foe strike now, he'll have an excellent chance of overrunning the city; whereas, an he fool around with all these beautiful engines, he may find his advantage lost by Tereyai's arrival . . . Speaking of whom, has your scryer, what's his name, found out whether our messengers have yet reached General Tereyai?"

"Nedef has been at his crystal from dawn to sunset, but the scrying has been poor. I daresay the foe's wizards have cast spells to block it. Now and then Nedef gets a fix on some spot in northern Penembei, but all he sees are bare brown hills, with no sign either of our frontier army or of the messengers."

"Hmm." Jorian stared so long through his spyglass that Karadur said:

"What is it, O Jorian?"

"See you that thing between the camps of the Free Company and that of the Fedirunis?"

"It looks like another line of mantlets, does it not? My dim old eyes—"

"Aye, but what are mantlets doing so far back? Even a catapult couldn't reach 'em. They seem inordinately high, and methinks I detect activity behind them." Jorian turned on Karadur. "Could your scryer get a glimpse behind that fence?"

"He can try, whilst I essay to counter the interference of the foe's magicians."

An hour later, Jorian and Karadur sat in Nedef's chamber in the House of Learning. The scryer sat cross-legged on a bench, hunched over his crystal sphere, which rested upon a small stand of ebony carved into coiling dragons. Karadur sat, also cross-legged, on a cushion on the floor, leaning back with his eyes closed and moving his lips. Jorian sat in a chair, holding a stylus and a waxed wooden tablet. He leaned forward tensely, holding the stylus poised.

The scryer spoke just above a whisper: "The scene ripples and shifts, although it is not so confused as yesterday's ... Methinks their wizards who cast interference upon me have been recalled to other tasks ... Ah, now I see Iraz ... The scene pitches and tosses, as if I were an insect riding an autumnal leaf borne along on the wind ... Steady, steady ... Nay, that is the wrong side of the besiegers' ring ... Now I have the nomads' tents in view ... More to the left! The left! Ah, here we are. Here is your fence, whereon I look down ... Curse this interference; it is like trying to see the bottom of a river through the waters of a rapid. I see a great pile of long things; long things with crosspieces ... Ah ... Now I see men working on these objects. ... From my height, they look like ants; but ... They hammer and saw ..."

"Ladders?" said Jorian.

"Ah, that is it! Ladders! I could not be sure, because of bad scrying, but ladders they are."

"Can you estimate their number?" said Jorian.

"Nay; but there must be hundreds ..."

Jorian looked at Karadur. "They're doing just what I said I should do in their place. The siege engines are a diversion, to make us think we have plenty of time to ready our defenses. Instead, they'll rush us early some morn with all those ladders and scramble over our walls ere we've rubbed the sleep out of our eyes. Once inside, they could stand off Tereyai for ay. With command of the sea, they could not be starved out.

"Keep Nedef at his crystal and command him to try to learn the foe's precise plans. If he could eavesdrop on a conference amongst the leaders, that might be helpful. Meanwhile, I must forth to tell Chuivir to build crutches."

"Crutches?"

"That's what we call those poles with a curved or forked crosspiece at the end, for pushing over ladders."

"Beware of arousing Chuivir's jealousy!"

Jorian had thitherto been careful to report back to the palace before issuing royal commands to Colonel Chuivir. But, as he strode through the streets between the House of Learning and the palace, an uproar drew his attention. A group of armed Kilts was chasing three Pants along the avenue, waving swords and shouting vengeance.

"Heryx blast them!" snarled Jorian to himself, stepping out into the street. As the Pants ran past him, he threw out his arms in a commanding gesture and roared: "Halt, in the king's name!"

At least, he thought, his glittering parade armor did have its uses. At the sight of his regalia, the pursuing Kilts halted. The three Pants clustered behind him, panting:

"They ... would ... slay us ... good sir! And ... for nought!"

"What is all this?" barked Jorian.

"Thieves!" screamed the leading Kilt. "We found them sneaking and snooping around our armory, to steal our weapons!"

"They lie!" cried a new voice. Jorian turned, and there was the plump Lord Vegh, stasiarch of the Pants. "I sent my trusty lads thither to ask a few civil questions of the other faction, as to what armament they thought most suitable—"

"Now it is ye who lie!" cried the gaunt, goateed Amazluek, pushing through the gathering crowd. "Civil questions, forsooth! Mere questioners need not try to pick the lock on the armory door—"

"There was no one on guard," shouted a Pant. "None to answer our questions, so we sought to—"

Amazluek: "Liar again! There is always a man—"

"Thou callest me liar?" yelled Vegh, drawing his sword.

"Liar, thief, and coward!" screamed Amazluek, drawing likewise.

"Stop it! Stop it!" shouted Jorian over the rising din. "Put up your blades, in the king's name!"

The clash and ring of sword against sword answered him. Spectators began to shout and to cheer on the combatants according to which faction they supported. They also began to bark threats and insults at each other. Jorian saw one man kick another's shins, another tweak another's nose, and a third seize another's hair and pull it. A full street battle was in the making. In desperation, Jorian drew his sword and knocked up the crossed blades of the stasiarchs.

"Keep out of this, dirty foreigner!" snarled Amazluek, making a thrust at Jorian's chest. Not expecting the attack, Jorian was slow in parrying. But his corselet saved his life as the stasiarch's point skittered off its scales and tore the sleeve of Jorian's jacket.

Vegh lunged at Amazluek, who had to leap back and make a hasty parry to save his own gore. Jorian unhooked his lead-pommeled dagger. Holding it by the sheath, he stopped behind Amazluek and brought the pommel down on the stasiarch's head.

Amazluek wilted to the cobblestones. When Vegh made to run the prostrate man through, Jorian knocked his blade aside and thrust his own point into Vegh's face.

"Get back, or I will give you some of the same!" he said.

"Who are you to order us about—" sputtered Vegh.

"I am who I am. You five Kilts, carry Lord Amazluek back to your headquarters. If water in the face fail to revive him, fetch a chirurgeon to tend him. Lord Vegh, will you be so good as to send your men back to their barracks? Meseems they need every waking hour for drill, if they are to withstand the foe."

The Kilts, cowed by Jorian's size and air of command, silently picked up their fallen leader and disappeared. Vegh grumbled some threat or curse under his breath. Being a full head shorter than Jorian, he seemed indisposed to carry the argument further. He and his trio also departed, and the crowd broke up.

Jorian hurried on to the palace. The sun had passed the meridian, and Jorian felt oppressed by the need for haste. The attack with scaling ladders might come at any time, and the disparity in numbers of hardened fighters grew with every additional Fediruni who halted his camel in the growing tent city east of Iraz.

It was urgent that the crutches be prepared forthwith. It was also urgent that something drastic be done about the command of the militia, before the factions began a civil war.

At the palace, Jorian was told that King Ishbahar was taking his nap after lunch and could not be disturbed. Jorian chewed his mustache in frustration. He considered forcing an entrance to the king's private chambers on grounds of emergency, waiting until the king awoke, or going directly to Chuivir without clearing his intentions with the king first. The dangers of the last course seemed to him the least.

He found the handsome colonel in his chamber in the topmost level of the huge, cylindrical keep built against the wall on the eastern side of the city. Thence Chuivir could watch the entire length of the East Wall, including the East Gate. Chuivir, wearing gilded lizard mail even more gorgeous than Jorian's, was checking payrolls.

Jorian saluted by bringing his fist to his chest. "Colonel," he said, "it is the king's pleasure that his forces prepare for an imminent assault on the walls by scaling ladders. In particular, he desires that hundreds of crutches be prepared and placed on the walls to overthrow these ladders."

Chuivir frowned. "Where got he any such idea, Captain Jorian? Any fool can see that they are readying a prolonged attack on the walls themselves, by catapults and ram tortoises, in order to make a breach before mounting his assault."

Jorian told of the scryer's discovery of the ladder work going on behind the fence to the northeast. Colonel Chuivir picked up his own spyglass and leaned out the window on that side of the tower. After a while, he said:

"Nay, your seer must have been mistaken. Even if they be preparing ladders, it were incredible that they should essay to use them so early upon our walls."

"His Majesty," said Jorian, "thinks they are fain to make a sudden assault in hope of carrying the city ere General Tereyai arrive with his army."

Chuivir stubbornly stuck to his point. "My good Captain, it says right here in Zayuit's *Military Manual*"—he waved a copy—"that the chances of carrying a wall over forty feet high with ladders alone were negligible. And our walls measure forty-five feet."

"A city this size should have at least sixty-foot walls," said Jorian.

"Perhaps; but that is beside the point."

"Well, are you going to set men to making crutches?"

"No. I need all the manpower I can get for practise at conventional drill, for arms making, and for strengthening the masonry."

"But, sir, His Majesty was quite positive—"

The colonel gave Jorian a sharp look. "Meseems that, to listen to you, His Majesty has been taking an entirely unwonted interest in the details of the defense—something he has never done hitherto. Did he give you such a message just now, from his own mouth?"

"Certes. You do not think I would give you orders on my own responsibility, do you?"

"On the contrary, that is just what I think. Know, good my sir, that I command the defense and none other—let alone foreign interlopers. If you would convince me that His Majesty has in sooth issued this silly command, you must bring me a written order in his own hand, or else persuade him to issue his dicta to me in person."

"Would you rather let the enemy in than yield on a bit of protocol?" said Jorian angrily. "If I must needs run back and forth all day bearing bits of paper—"

"Get out of here!" shouted Chuivir. "Any royal commands hereafter shall be in writing, or I will ignore them. Now off with you and stop pestering me, or I will have you arrested!"

"We shall see," growled Jorian. He left the tower fuming.

That evening over supper, he told Karadur of the day's events.

"When I got back to the palace," he said, "I found the King just waking up. I told him about the quarreling between the factions and about my troubles with Chuivir. I said I feared my supervision would come to nought unless I had direct and acknowledged command of the whole defense, with none to gainsay me. Even then, 'twould be a chancy thing.

"I told Ishbahar I wanted nothing less than commanding the defense of Iraz, which was not my city; but I was caught therein and stood to fall therewith. Hence, to save my own hide, I needs must do what I could to save it."

"Did he believe your—ah—protestations of virtue?"

"I know not, albeit they expressed my true sentiments. He flat refused, howsomever, to oust Chuivir and the stasiarchs and appoint me in their room, saying 'twere politically impossible.

"At length he summoned the three and me to tea this afternoon. Another gorge, naturally. If His Majesty keep on stuffing me like a sausage skin, I shall have to go on a fast; I've already gained ten pounds in Iraz.

"Well, at table, Amazluek, with a bandage round his head, glared daggers at Vegh and me. But I will say old Fatty did his best. He homilized us on the need for coöperation whilst the siege lasted. An we failed to work together, he reminded us, we should be tied to posts, tarred, and kindled to illumine the Fedirunis' victory feast. The desert dwellers have quaint notions of entreating their captives. At the end, he was blubbering great tears of self-pity and had even my three recalcitrant commanders looking solemn and wiping their eyes."

"Did he confirm your tale of having obtained the order about the crutches from him?"

"Aye; luckily, I had thought to prime him on this little white lie. So we all parted with expressions, if not of good will, at least of promises to work for the common goal. But nought has really been changed, and the morrow will doubtless see us at one another's throats again."

"How about those crutches?"

"Seeing a chance to score off his rival, Amazluek said he'd be responsible for them. His faction, he said, had many competent woodworkers, and he would set them to sawing and nailing night and day. Then Vegh said his Pants could make two crutches for every one turned out by the Kilts. The king said to go to it."

Karadur: "My son, I promised Nedef to look in at his sanctum this even. He is attempting to spy on a meeting of the hostile commanders, to learn what he can of their plans. Wilt—ah—accompany me? With all in confusion and arms handed out broadcast, the streets are none too safe o' nights."

"Surely, old man. Have you a lanthorn?"

Nedef murmured: "Nay, I see no gathering around the tent of the Fediruni chieftain ... That leaves the Algarthians ..."

For some minutes, the scryer sat silently with an intense expression, as he strove to guide the vision in the crystal seaward.

"It is easier this even," he said. "Belike all the wizards are at meat. Ah, here is the pirates' flagship, with longboats clustering about her. The council of war must be aboard ..." Then more silence. Nedef gasped: "Aid me, Doctor Karadur! The wizards have cast a protective spell about the admiral's cabin, so I cannot enter it."

Karadur mumbled and made passes. At last Nedef exclaimed: "Ah, now I am in! But it takes all my strength to remain ..."

"What see you?" asked Jorian.

"In sooth, it is a veritable council of war. I see Mazsan the factionist, and the pirate admiral—I think his name is Hrundikar, a great huge wight with a long red beard. I also see the leaders of the Free Company and of the nomads, whose names I know not."

"What do they?"

"They talk, with much gesticulation and pauses for the interpreters ... Mazsan says something about making an attack from all four sides at once, to stretch the defense thin ..."

Silence, then: "They argue the question of timing their attack. The Fediruni points heavenward; he—I cannot read his lips, for he speaks his native tongue. Ah, the interpreter asks how they can time their attacks with the sun hidden by clouds ...

"Now Mazsan speaks. He says something about the Tower of Kumashar ... He holds a spyglass to his eye.

The Fediruni asks a question, but I cannot catch it ... Mazsan demands something of Admiral Hrundikar. Everybody takes a drink ... Now a sailor brings in a sheet of something—parchment or paper. They spike it to the bulkhead; each of the four chieftains drives his dagger through one corner of the sheet. With a piece of charcoal, Mazsan draws a two-foot circle on the sheet. He marks a spot in the enter. He makes a set of marks around the edge of the circle. He draws an arrow, starting at the center and pointing to one of the marks ..."

"Which mark? Which mark?" demanded Jorian.

"It is on the right-hand side of the circle ... My vision is blurred ..."

"If it were a clock, what time would it tell?"

"Ah, I see! The clock hand points to the third hour. Now the scene grows wavery, as if their wizards had returned to their task ..."

Nedef's voice trailed off. The scryer slumped in a faint and rolled off his bench to the floor.

"Dear me, I hope he have not damaged his brain," said Karadur. "That is a hazard of his profession."

"His pulse seems normal," said Jorian, bending over the fallen man. "So now we know: the foe will attack at the third hour of the morning—or the Hour of the Otter, as we say in Novaria. They will time their assault by watching the Tower of Kumashar through telescopes."

"We know not the day of the attack," said Karadur.

"True, but we had better assume it to be tomorrow. I must get word to the king and the commanders."

"I cannot leave poor Nedef in a swoon ..."

"Take care of him, then, whilst I go about my business, which brooks no delay."

"Go you first to the king?"

"Nay, I think I'll drop in first on Chuivir to pass the news."

"What chance have we, with a few hundred guardsmen against their tens of thousands?"

"The chance of a pollywog in a pond full of pike. But the militia can push over ladders if nought else. Still, 'tis a muchel of city wall to cover with a small force. All they need is one good foothold . . ."

"I suppose we could stop the clocks in the Tower of Kumashar. Then they would lack means of coördinating their attack."

Jorian stared. "You're right, old man. But, by Heryx's iron yard, you've given me an even better idea! Each of the four parties plans to attack a different side and use a different one of the four clocks, does it not?"

"I suppose so."

"All right, you succor Master Nedef; I'm off."

When he had reported to the king, who was eating a late evening snack, Ishbahar asked the same question that Karadur had already posed: "What chance have we, lad, with their twenty or thirty thousand against our four hundred-odd guardsmen and a few thousand militiamen?"

"Not much, Your Majesty," said Jorian. "I do, howsomever, have an idea that may well throw their attack into confusion."

"What is it?"

"Ere I tell Your Majesty, your servant would like to beg a boon, in case my scheme work."

"Anything, my boy, anything! If it work not, none of us will have further use for material possessions anyway. An we defeat this siege, we have plans for you."

"All I ask, sire, is your copper bathtub."

"The gods bless our soul, what an extraordinary request! No cartload of gold? No high office? No noble maiden for your harem?"

"Nay, sire; I meant just what I said."

"Of course you shall have it, win or lose. But what is your scheme?"

Jorian told him.

# VIII

# The Barbarian Savior

As the overcast sky paled to pearly gray, Jorian told Colonel Chuivir: "The Fedirunis will attack the East Wall first, in about half an hour."

"How in the name of Ughroluk do you know?"

"Because at that time, the east clock will show the third hour."

"But will not the other clocks show the same—oh!" Chuivir stared round-eyed at Jorian. "You mean you have set them all to show different times!"

Jorian nodded, and Chuivir gave a command. Messengers departed on a run. Soon, nearly all the Royal Guard was assembled along the East Wall, with their armor gleaming dully in the gray light. Mingled with them were several companies of militia. Most of the militiamen bore either crutches or spears to whose butt-ends short crosspieces had been affixed. When all were in place, there was a man for every six feet of wall. A skeleton guard of militia was left on the other walls.

From the swarming, dun-colored camp of the Fedirunis, ram's horns gave their soft bleat. A flood of figures, robed in brown, sand color, and dirty white, poured out from the tent city and streamed towards the East Wall. They covered the earth like a swarm of ants. Foremost among them came hundreds of pairs of men, each pair carrying a ladder. Others gathered in knots and unlimbered the powerful, double-curved compound horn bows of Fedirun.

"Keep your heads down!" shouted Chuivir. The command was passed down the line.

The Fediruni bows twanged, and sheets of arrows shrieked up from their line. Some shafts soared over the battlements; others struck the stones and rebounded. A few struck home. Cries arose along the line of the defenders, and the physicians of Iraz ran up and down with their gowns flapping, seeking the wounded.

The swarm of foes flowed up to the wall. All along the line, hundreds of ladders were planted in the ground. Their other ends rose like the booms of cranes as the attackers pushed on them from behind with hands and spear points.

"Loose!" cried Chuivir.

All along the wall, arbalesters of the Royal Guard stepped out from behind their merlons to discharge their crossbows into the crowd below. Then they ducked back again to reload. Elsewhere, squads of militiamen placed boxes of heavy stones and cauldrons of boiling oil, molten lead, and red-hot sand in the embrasures and tipped them until the contents poured down on the heads beneath. Screams resounded.

Still the ladders rose until their upper ends, even with the top of the wall, came to rest.

"Wait until they are loaded, Colonel," said Jorian.

"Curse it, stop telling me how to run my business!" snapped Chuivir. "I was going to do just that." He raised his voice: "Crutch men, wait for the signal! How far up are they, Captain Jorian?"

Jorian risked a peek out an embrasure. "Three man-heights. Give them a little more . . . Now!"

As the heads of the most active climbers approached the top of the wall, the Fediruni archers ceased shooting for fear of hitting their own. Chuivir shouted: "O-o-over!"

All along the wall, militiamen hooked their crutches into the tops of the ladders and pushed. Here and there a man fell to a Fediruni arrow, but another took his place. The ladders swayed outward and fell, dropping their shrieking burdens into the crowd.

The Fediruni leaders dashed up and down, screaming commands and exhortations. Up went the ladders again. Again, swarms of brown-robed figures scrambled up them.

Jorian found himself next to an embrasure in front of which an Irazi militiaman had fallen with an arrow through his throat. The top of a ladder showed in the gap between the merlons. Before Jorian could gather his wits, a black-bearded brown face, surmounted by a white head cloth held in place by a camel's-hair rope, popped into the embrasure. Golden hoops hung gleaming and swaying from the man's ear lobes.

Jorian snatched up the crutch that the fallen Irazi had dropped. His first attempt to place it against one of the uprights of the ladder miscarried; he missed and almost hurled himself through the embrasure. Before he could recover and replace the implement, the Fediruni leaped like a cat through the embrasure and had at him with a scimitar.

Jorian threw up the crutch to parry a whistling cut, which drove into the wood and nearly severed the crutch. He struck at the man, but the crutch broke at its weakened point. The man slashed again; his blade clashed against Jorian's mail as Jorian leaped back.

By the time the man drew back his arm for a third blow, Jorian had his sword out. A straight thrust took the unarmored man in the ribs. The Fediruni still had the strength to complete his cut, which clanged on Jorian's helmet, knocking it down over his eyes and filling his head with stars.

Jorian pushed his helmet back into place, to see the Fediruni leaning against the merlon. The scimitar dropped from his lax fingers as the man slowly sagged to the pavement.

Meanwhile, another Fediruni had hoisted himself

through the embrasure. This man carried both a scimitar and a leathern buckler in his right hand. Over his brown robe he wore a crude cuirass of boiled leather, painted red and blue, and on his head a light steel cap with a slender spike on top. As he came, he shifted the buckler to his left hand and engaged Jorian. There was a quick exchange of cuts and thrusts; the man was a skilled fighter.

Out of the corner of his eye, Jorian saw a third Fediruni, with his shaven skull bare, climbing through. If the third man gained the wall and assailed him from behind, Jorian knew he would have little chance. Despite the hero tales, it was rare indeed that a single swordsman could defeat two competent foes at once. If Jorian took his attention for a heartbeat off the man he was fighting, the fellow would instantly have him.

He tried to speed up his cuts and lunges to kill the man before the other came. But the man caught the blows on his buckler and sent back one whistling counter-cut after another . . .

The third man had reached the wall and slithered around behind Jorian, who knew what was happening but could do nothing to stop it. Then a shriek arose behind him, and the sound of a falling body. The eyes of the man he was fighting shifted past him, and in an instant Jorian ran him through the throat.

"Here is another!" cried Chuivir, drawing a bloody sword from the Fediruni behind Jorian. "Help me!"

The colonel referred to a fourth Fediruni, now poised on the topmost rung of the leadder with a scimitar in his teeth. Jorian and Chuivir each drove the point of his sword into one of the two uprights.

"Over!" said Chuivir.

They shoved. The ladder swayed out. It seemed to stand balanced for an incredible time, while the topmost Fediruni looked down with eyes that widened with terror in his swarthy face. The last sight that Jorian had of him, as the ladder toppled, was of the man's opening his mouth to scream and dropping the sword he had held in his teeth.

"That was close," said Chuivir. "They have gained another foothold yonder; come along!"

The two rushed along the wall to where several Fedirunis had formed a solid knot with their backs to an embrasure, while others, climbing up the ladder from behind, tried to push in.

"Watch!" said Jorian.

He put a foot on the adjacent embrasure and hurled himself up on top of the merlon. A small, slender Fediruni was just pushing through the embrasure behind the knot of battlers. At the moment, he was on hands and knees in the embrasure.

Jorian swung up his arm and brought his sword down in a long, full-armed cut. He had the satisfaction of seeing the man's head fly off, to roll among the trampling feet of the fighters. The blood-spouting body collapsed in the embrasure, and through Jorian's mind flitted a fleeting thought of wonder that so small a man should contain so much blood. A scarlet pool spread out on the flagstones, so that the fighters slipped and staggered in it.

The body hindered the next climber, who pushed and tugged at it to clear it out of the way. While he was so engaged, Jorian caught him in the face with a backhand cut. The man fell off the ladder, carrying away those below him in a whole concatenation of screams and crashes.

"Hand me a crutch!" Jorian shouted.

A spear was at length passed up to him. With this he pried one of the uprights of the ladder away from the stone and sent it toppling. The Fedirunis on the wall, cut off from support and slipping and falling in the puddles of blood, were soon beaten down and hacked to pieces.

\* \* \*

Panting, Jorian, in dented helm and rent hauberk, confronted Colonel Chuivir, around whose left arm a physician was tying a bandage. Below, the Fedirunis sullenly flowed back towards their tent city. They carried many of their wounded; but many more were left behind, along with hundreds of corpses.

"Bad?" said Jorian.

"Scratch. You?"

"Never touched me. Thank you for your help."

"No trouble. When and whence is the next attack?" asked Chuivir.

"Soon, north. The north clock is set an hour after the east."

"The Free Company, eh?"

"Aye. Not many, but fell fighters."

"With that armor, they will not be able to climb so monkeylike. Adjutant, everybody but the skeleton guard to the North Wall!"

An hour later, the Free Company withdrew from the North Wall, leaving scores of armored figures lying like smashed beetles at its base. Jorian, bleeding from a cut on the side of his jaw, told Chuivir: "The pirates next."

The houses that had been illegally built against the West Wall, facing the waterfront, furnished the pirates with an easy means of getting halfway up the wall. They made several lodgments on the top of the wall and clung to them despite the hardest fighting; Jorian took another light wound, on his right arm. But the houses, being inflammable, soon blazed up under a shower of incendiary missiles from the wall. Pirates struggling to emplace short ladders on the roofs of the houses were engulfed in flames and died screaming.

By the time the clock on the south side of the Tower of Kumashar showed the third hour, Mazsan's peasant army had heard about the defeats of the other three forces. There was talk of a mysterious mixup in timing, and of the unexpected strength of the defenders. The yells of Mazsan's officers and even blows with the flats of swords failed to get the peasants to rush the wall. They stood sullenly muttering; some began to trickle away.

Trumpets blared in the hills. Little black specks grew to squadrons of the regular Penembic cavalry, riding down the East Road and deploying.

"Tereyai!" shouted voices along the wall, as the frontier army rolled into view.

As the word went round, Mazsan's peasants dissolved in mad flight. The Fedirunis, fearful of being cut off from their homeland, abandoned their camp, swarmed on their camels and horses, and scattered. The Algarthian pirates scrambled aboard their ships, cast off, and hoisted sail.

The Free Company struck its camp in orderly fashion. It formed three hollow squares, with pikes leveled outwards in all directions and crossbowmen inside the squares. The mercenaries marched leisurely away on the North Road, as if daring anybody to try to stop them. No one did.

"My boy!" cried the king. "You have saved Iraz! Nothing were too good for you! Noticing!"

"Oh, come, sire," said the bandaged Jorian, affecting more modesty than he really felt. "All your servant did was to sit up half the night tinkering with the clocks, to make the four dials register different hours."

"But that proves the prophecy. Or rather, both prophecies. You are the barbarian savior, and the salvation of the city depended upon the clocks' functioning—albeit not quite in the sense that one would expect, heh heh. Name your reward!"

"All I want, Your Majesty, is that copper bathtub."

"Forsooth? Well, it is a queer sort of reward; but if that is your desire, you shall have it. Shall we have it delivered to Doctor Karadur's quarters?"

"Nay, sire. Leave it where it is for the time being.

But one of these days I shall want it. And one other thing!"

"Yes? Yes?"

"Pray stop calling me a barbarian! I am only an honest craftsman, as civilized as the next wight."

"Oh," said the king. "We see the difficulty. You think of a 'barbarian' as a rude, uncouth, illiterate oaf from some backward land where they know not letters and cities. But in the prophecy, methinks, the word was used in its older sense, to mean any non-Penembian. The change in meaning took place during the century preceding this one; we told you we used to be a bit of a scholar.

"So, you see, in that sense you *are* a barbarian, however refined your manners and vast your erudition. And the prophecies are proven after all. By the way, it is fortunate that our victory took place when it did, and that you sustained no grievous wounds. In three nights, we shall have a full moon again."

Jorian wrinkled his forehead. "So, Your Majesty?"

"Have you forgotten? That is the monthly Divine Marriage of Nubalyaga!"

"Oh," said Jorian.

Three nights later, at the full of the moon, Jorian gave the ritual knock on the massive door at the north end of Hoshcha's Tunnel. The door swung open, and in it stood two minor priestesses in gauzy gowns. They bowed low, saying:

"All hail, Your Majesty, soon to be divine!"

Jorian nodded affably. "Whither away, lassies?"

"Follow us."

Jorian followed them through winding corridors, up stairs, and through portals. Once he passed the main chamber of the temple. Through an open door, he glimpsed scaffolding and saw men moving about. He heard the sounds of sawing and hammering and the clink of masons' chisels.

The Free Company and the Algarthians had looted the temple of all the gold and precious stones they could pry off the decorations. They might have destroyed the whole structure had not Mazsan's influence restrained them. Now craftsmen were working overtime to refurbish the fane.

"Priestesses!" said Jorian, "Where—ah—I mean when do I—ah—"

"Oh, sire!" murmured one. "You needs must be suitably clad ere the god incarnate himself in you!"

They led him at last into a smaller chamber, where garments were laid out on a divan.

"Now, sire," they said, "if Your Majesty will graciously sit . . ."

Jorian sat on the end of the divan while they pulled off his shoes and buskins.

"Now arise, sire, and stand still whilst we prepare you."

Jorian stood up, and they began to undress him. They took off his Irazi cap, unbuttoned his vest and shirt, and untied the drawstring of his trousers. Jorian soon stood in his breechclout, which one of the girls began to unfasten.

"Eek!" said Jorian. "Ladies, please!"

"Oh, but this, too, must come off!" said a priestess with a giggle. "Surely a man of Your Majesty's age and experience . . ."

"Oh, very well," grumbled Jorian. "I am an old married man, and in my native land we all bathe together. It just seemed odd."

Off came the breechclout. The appraising stares of the priestesses made Jorian wince. One said:

"Think you he will do, Gezma?"

The other priestess cocked her head thoughtfully. "He may. The gods have endowed him with length, but as for strength—well, the proof of the pudding is in the eating, they say, whilst the proof of the—"

"Ahem!" said Jorian. "If you must discuss me as if I

were a prize bull, I had rather you did it out of my hearing. Besides, it is cool for standing in one's skin."

With squeals of suppressed laughter, the priestesses draped Jorian in flame-colored gauzy robes, which they bound with a scarlet sash. They completed his raiment with a golden wreath on his head and pearl-sewn sandals on his feet.

"Oh, my, does he not look the very god?" said one.

"He *is!*" cried the other, sinking to her knees and touching her forehead to the floor. "Great Ughroluk!" she prayed. "Deign to look with favor upon thine humble subjects!"

"Deliver us from sin and evil!" said the other, prostrating herself likewise.

"Stretch forth thy divine hand over the pious priesthood of thine eternal consort!"

Jorian fidgeted while the two young women poured out their pleas. He did feel godlike. He certainly did not feel as if he could pass miracles to save anybody from sin and evil.

"Yes, yes, I will do my divine best," he said at last. "Now where do we . . .?"

The priestesses scrambled up. "Will Your Divine Majesty follow us?"

More corridors, and then he came to a chapel. One of the priestesses whispered: "Usually the rite is held in the main sanctum, but that is full of craftsmen."

As Jorian entered, a small orchestra of lyres and pipes played a delicate, tingling melody. In the center of the room stood a huge bed. The air was heavy with incense and perfume.

Before the altar at one side stood High Priestess Sahmet. Like Jorian, she was enveloped in gauze. On her noble brow, a silver tiara flashed with white gems. In the dim light of the little oil lamps hung from the ceiling, she looked almost beautiful. As Jorian approached, she bowed low, murmuring:

"All hail, divine consort! All hail, king of the gods!"

"All hail, Your Sanctity," said Jorian. "Here is your ring, madam."

The following morning, Jorian met Karadur in King Ishbahar's palace, whither the wizard had gone to report to his royal employer. The two set out afoot for Karadur's quarters. As they passed through the Gate of Happiness, Jorian squinted up at Mazsan's head, which occupied one of the spikes atop the gate. He said:

"Some of his ideas seemed sound to me. Too bad they couldn't have been tried out. If someone could persuade the king to command them ..."

"That has been tried," said Karadur. "Mazsan himself once urged Ishbahar to redistribute the lands of the great magnates amongst the peasants. But these lords are powerful men, with their own armed followings, and they would not without demur accede to the loss of their power and pelf. A hero-king might undertake it, were he willing to risk an uprising led by the magnates; but poor old Ishbahar ..." The Mulvanian shrugged. "How went things last night?"

Jorian laughed. "Damndest experience of my life, and I've had some beauties." He told of his robing and his being conducted to the wedding chapel. He continued: "They made me stand for hours, clad in those gauzy things like one of the he-whores you see mincing up and down Shashtai II Street, whilst they went through an eternity of ritual. They sang hymns and intoned prayers, whereof I could understand nought, since they were in an old form of the language. They handed me a silver thunderbolt and a golden sunbeam and bade me wave them about in prescribed motions.

"Well, I am not exactly decrepit, but 'tis hard to keep up one's interest for hours—if 'interest' be the word I seek. At last the mummery was over, and Sahmet and I were hailed as the lawfully wedded god and goddess. These deities had supposedly taken up their temporary abodes within our mortal frames."

"Felt you any divine possession?" asked Karadur.

"Nary a bit. Belike the true Ughroluk and Nubalyaga were otherwise occupied. Or, belike, when they feel like a bit of amorous libration, they can do it perfectly well in their own persons without employing mortals as surrogates.

"Anyway, Sahmet led me to the bed. I was taken aback by the thought of futtering the dame with all the company looking on bug-eyed. I wondered if I could—ah—rise to the occasion under those circumstances. But the priestesses hauled out screens, which they set up around the bed, and snuffed all but one of the lamps. I heard them swishing out of the chamber, and then the only sound was that of that damned orchestra, tweetling and plunking away in the corner.

"Well, even when I had a harem in Xylar, I never invited in the Royal Band to play whilst I plumbed the depths. I may be old-fashioned, but for some things I like privacy. Howsomever, necessity is a stern schoolmaster and Sahmet, a handsome woman. So I set about my business, with the usual kissing and fondling and disrobing. Presently we were one flesh, as say the preachers."

"How fared you?"

"Wherefore would you know, old ascetic? The details would shock your pure soul."

"Indulge my curiosity, my son. All human affairs are of moment to me, even though my spiritual profession limits my participation in worldly activities. Of course, such things are of but abstract concern to me, who must needs conserve his chastity to attain the highest levels of magical practise. But my knowledge of amatory matters is all gained at second hand, from books, and you can furnish knowledge the books overlook."

"Very well. The first try was not very successful. As a result of my year of virtuous conduct, I was like a crossbow on a hair trigger. Sahmet was disappointed, but I told her not to worry; that with a respite I should be able to repeat my performance.

"So, for the next half-hour, we ate and drank and talked of this and that. I told her of some of the deeds of King Fusinian. Then I was ready again, and this time I did a proper fifty-stroke job. The lady flopped beneath me like a fish on a hook. She said it was the first time in years that she had really enjoyed a man; in fact, ever since she had quarreled with Chaluish.

"But think you she was then ready to drop off to sleep? By Vaisus' brazen arse, nay! She lusted for more. After another half-hour, I managed to work up another stand and gave her a proper frigging.

"But then she wanted *still* more. Becoming weary, I pretended to go to sleep, which in sooth soon became the real thing. But this morn, at the dawn's first light, I was aroused by my holy bedmate, diddling with me in hopes of raising my temple column."

"Did she succeed?"

"Oh, aye, it worked; if anything, too well." Jorian yawned. "I could sleep the clock around. Afterwards she crushed me to her ample bosom with hot words of love. She swore I should never leave Iraz but remain here for ay, to riddle her night and day."

"You could fare further and do worse," said Karadur.

"What? Become a male concubine? And give up my little Estrildis? You must think me a mere tomcat, fornicating about the world as opportunity offers."

"Nay, my son. This is, after all, the lawful consummation of a sacerdotal rite and hence no—ah—fornication."

"Not so lawful. The ram in this holy tupping is supposed to be the king, and I'm not the king. If High Priest Chaluish find out and have a mind to make trouble . . . . No, thank you! These high intrigues are too chancy for a simple fellow like me.

"Besides, who knows what'll happen when Ishbahar dies? With all that fat, he looks not like a good risk.

Then the new king and the priestess might decide to have me quietly murdered—they're skillful with poison here—to rid themselves of my awkward presence.

"In any case, whilst I may not be of the stuff of heroes, I care not to be any lady's fancy man. Futtering is good healthy fun, but I'd rather earn my bread with my hands and head than with my prick. Besides, I like it better with my own dear little wife, with whom 'tis an act of love and not of mere lust. Now I have the king's promise of the copper bathtub, all I need is a proper spell from you to make it fly. Then ho for Xylar!"

"The spell is still incomplete," said Karadur.

"Well, hurry it up! Put more men on the job!"

"When I can, I will. But just now we at the House of Learning are occupied with preparations for the grand festival that the king has commanded for five days hence, to celebrate the salvation of Iraz. If you be not too busy with your clocks, I could employ your engineering skills at the House, in the designs of some of our stage effects."

"Glad to help," said Jorian.

# IX

# The Waxen Wife

As guests of the king, Jorian and Karadur followed Ishbahar's litter up the ramp to the royal box. At the top of the ramp, the litter bearers set the litter down. This time, the bearers were slaves—hairy apemen from the jungles of Komilakh—not aristocrats. King Ishbahar did not trust his poundage to amateurs on such slopes.

The king wriggled out of the litter like a broaching whale. He waved to the crowd and puffed through the entrance to his box, around which guardsmen were drawn tip. Jorian and Karadur followed.

"Sit anywhere you like, our dear fellows, anywhere you like!" said the king. "We needs must occupy this cursed throne, albeit it is far from comfortable. Now, where is lunch? Ah, steward, here you are! Doctor Karadur, will you move your chair, pray, to let the table be set up? Master Jorian, we have a real treat for you: minced scarlet monkey from Beraoti, fried in the fat of the giant tortoise of Burang. And wine made from the chokeberry of Salimor. Try it!"

Jorian thought that chokeberry wine was an excellent name for the fluid, but he drowned his potion. The king leaned confidentially towards him. "Are you in fine fettle today, dear boy?"

"As far as I know, sire. Why?"

"We have a little surprise for you later. We are sure that so stalwart a youth as yourself would hardly shriek and swoon with shock; but we thought it well to warn you."

"May I ask the nature of this—"

"Nay, you may not!" The king gave Jorian a heavy wink. "To tell you now were to spoil the fun, heh heh. You shall see in good time—in good time. Do you dance ?"

"I dance some Novarian dances, like the volka and the whirligig. Why, sire?"

"We are planning a grand ball. You can doubtless learn the Penembic steps. It has been years since we gave one; as you can see, dancing is not exactly our forte."

While the king shoveled in the food, and Jorian and Karadur ate modest portions, the stands below them filled. As before, the Pants sat on their left in blue and gold, while the Kilts, in red and white, sat on their right. Nobles and officials occupied the intermediate strip.

"Let us hope that we have not another factional disturbance," said Karadur.

The king swallowed a huge mouthful. "We had the stasiarchs before us just this morning, Doctor. We laid down the law to them, we assure you! They promised to love each other like brothers. Like brothers, they said."

"Brotherly love, sire, cannot always be counted upon," said Jorian, "as in the case of the kings Forimar and Fusonio of my native Kortoli."

"What is this tale, Master Jorian?" asked the king.

"It is called the Tale of the Waxen Wife. King Forimar was a collateral ancestor of the better-known King Filoman the Well-Meaning, who was the father of King Fusinian the Fox. This king was known as Forimar the Esthete. He was noted for his indifference to public affairs and for his passion for the arts, at which he was himself no mean performer. He was a fair architect, an accomplished musician, a worthy composer, a fine singer, and an excellent painter. Some of his poems are the glories of Kortolian literature to this day. He could not, alas, do all these things and at the same time run the kingdom.

"As a result of Forimar's neglect, public affairs in Kortoli got into a frightful mess. The army was a cowardly rabble, crime and corruption prevailed in the city, and the people were on the verge of revolt. Then the army of neighboring Aussar marched into Kortoli. The city was saved by a ruse devised by Forimar's brother Fusonio, who returned in the nick of time from a mission abroad.

"In saving the city, however, Fusonio demanded as his price that Forimar abdicate in his favor. This Forimar did with ill grace; but I will tell Your Majesty that story some other time.

"Anyway, the king was now Fusonio, who was of a very different character. Fusonio had none of his brother's esthetic sensitivities. He was a bluff, hearty, sensual type, whose idea of a large evening was to spend it incognito in some low tavern frequented by the rougher element, swilling ale and roaring ribald songs with unwashed peasants and ruffianly muleteers.

"Whereas Forimar was unwedded, Fusonio had a plump, peasantly, and not at all beautiful wife, named Ivrea, who had borne him five children. The twain would oft argue familial matters at the tops of their voices until the windows rattled; but woe betide the man who thought they were really quarreling and sought to take advantage of the fact! Both would turn upon him like tigers, and the children like tiger cubs.

"After his abdication, Forimar at first found it a relief not to be pestered by his ministers for decisions about public works, and hiring and firing, and foreign affairs, and law and order, and all those other tedious matters that take up a ruler's time."

"We know whereof you speak," said King Ishbahar.

"After a while, however, Forimar began to regret his lost kingship. Whilst his brother granted him an ample stipend, it was no longer enough to enable him to gratify his artistic whims. For ensample, he had an idea for an all-Novarian poetry contest, which he hoped to make into an annual affair and thus to place Kortoli in the front rank as a cultural center. As usual, he entertained grandiose ideas for the prizes. He had already spent his allowance on paintings, sculptures, and the like and had borrowed against it until his credit was exhausted. When he besought of his brother ten thousand golden marks for poetry prizes, Fusonio told him he was out of his mind.

" 'I have enough trouble rounding up tax money to repair the damages of your reign, dear brother.' quoth he. 'Get you gone and contemplate the beauty of a daisy in the field, or something equally cheap and harmless. You shall get no money for your schemes here, unless you save up your emolument.'

"It happened that a man named Zevager had lately set up an exhibition of waxworks in Kortoli City, showing such historical tableaux as King Finjanius defying the priests, the crowning of Ardyman the Terrible as emperor of Novaria, and the beheading of the rebel Roskianus. Zevager, who prided himself on the meticulous realism and authenticity of his exhibits, besought the former king to allow such an effigy to be made of His Highness and displayed. Forimar, who had never shown any sense about money but was now straitened by its lack, demanded a fee, which Zevager paid.

"Forimar took an interest in making the image, as he did in all the arts. Thus he discovered that Zevager, besides the usual techniques of making waxen effigies, knew something of magic. He cast a glamor spell upon the image, so that it looked even more like its living model then it otherwise would have. Forimar went to the Bureau of Commerce and Licenses and learnt that Zevager had no license to practise magic in Kortoli. This gave him a handle to use in dealing with the man.

"When the exhibit of the waxen Forimar proved popular, Forimar subtly insinuated into Zevager's mind the thought of making images of King Fusonio and Queen Ivrea. For a larger bribe, Forimar undertook to gain the permission of the royal couple to having their images put on display. He said it would cost him vast sums in bribes and contributions to worthy causes favored by his brother; but in fact it cost him nought. He simply asked his brother and sister-in-law at breakfast whether they would mind if he told his old friend Zevager that he might reproduce them in wax.

" 'Not at all,' said Fusonio, 'so long as his images do not make monsters of us. It will be good public relations.'

"Thus Forimar kept all the money that Zevager paid him, but he was still far short of the ten thousand marks needed for his poetry contest. So he became more and more intimate with Zevager. Soon he enticed the showman into a conspiracy against the throne. He inveigled the magician into his plot by, on one hand, dangling before him the post of Minister of Fine Arts when Forimar should become king, and on the other hinting that, if Zevager resisted his lure, he would denounce the showman for witchcraft or unlawful magic.

"In his magical arsenal, Zevager had a spell of immobility. To effect this spell, he had to get samples of Fusonio's hair and fingernail parings. Forimar got these for him.

"One night, when Fusonio was out on one of his pub-crawls, Zevager cast the spell upon him as he was passing near the waxwork museum. Zevager and Forimar dragged the statuesque Fusonio within, exchanged his garments with those on the waxwork, and set him up in place of the image. The effigy they hid in a lumber room.

"Then Forimar hastened to the palace, awoke his

sister-in-law, and gave her a document in his brother's
writing. The document stated:

My darling Ivrea:

I have departed the kingdom for a secret meeting
of all the heads of Novarian city-states in Xylar
City, about threatening moves by the nomads of
Shven. My absence should be kept quiet as long
as possible. Meanwhile, my brother Forimar is
named regent. Convey my love to the children and
promise them that I shall be back in a fortnight
or two.

Fusonio Rex

"Actually, the document was a clever forgery. Being
an artist, Forimar could feign the calligraphy of anyone
he chose. Ivrea was startled; but the tale sounded plausible, since there had been rumors of an invasion
from Shven.

"So Forimar ascended the throne as regent. His first
act was to announce his poetry contest and appoint a
committee of judges. He entered no poems of his own,
knowing that he would have an unfair advantage in
such a contest. This would militate against making the
contest a respected annual event. He was sincere in his
desire to advance the art of poetry and to promote
Kortoli as a center of culture.

"Forimar's next act was to begin a purge of his brother's adherents. He retired some, sent others to far
places, and demoted still others. The posts thus vacated
he filled with his own supporters. He moved cautiously,
not wishing to arouse suspicion. He calculated that in
a month, when Fusonio was due to return, he would
have the machinery of state firmly in his grip and could
declare himself king.

"As for Fusonio, now standing regally in Zevager's
waxworks, Forimar would decide what to do with him

later. He hesitated to slay his brother, since the family had an old tradition of presenting a united front to the world despite their internal differences. On the other hand, he knew his brother for a much abler man than he, who if left alive would surely devise means to usurp the throne from the usurper.

"He reckoned, however, without Queen Ivrea. When a fortnight had passed with no word of Fusonio, she became suspicious. She besought the aid of a scryer, who sent his mystic vision to Xylar and reported that there was no sign of an international conference in that city.

"Ivrea mourned, sure that foul play had befallen her man but uncertain what to do next. One day, missing him, she stopped at Zevager's museum to look at his waxworks. Fusonio's effigy, she thought, were better than no husband at all. Zevager was delighted that the queen and several of her ladies should patronize his establishment. He showed them about with much bowing and scraping.

"When Ivrea sighted the ostensible effigy of Fusonio, she exclaimed at its verisimilitude. In fact, she said, she could scarce believe that it was not her man in the flesh. When Zevager was talking to some of the other women at the other end of the chamber, she touched the hand of the image and found that it did not feel like wax.

"Then she conceived a daring plan. She made careful note of the costume on her own effigy.

"Back in the palace, she supped that even with her brother-in-law. 'I met your friend Master Zevager today,' she said, and artlessly told of her visit. 'He said something about seeing you there tomorrow.'

" 'Oh?' said Forimar. 'Methought it was the day after tomorrow—but then, I always get dates mixed up.'

"That night, Ivrea sallied forth with a single guardsman whom she trusted and another fellow lately released from gaol for burglary. For a suitable reward, the burglar picked the lock on the door of Zevager's museum, admitted her, and locked the door behind her. Ivrea climbed the stair to the loft where the images stood. Clad almost exactly like the waxwork, she hid the effigy of herself behind a curtain and took its place.

"When sounds announced the approach of Zevager and his first customers, she stiffened to immobility. One of the viewers said that the image of the queen was so lifelike that she could swear she saw it breathe. Luckily, Zevager took this as a compliment to his glamor spell.

"Later, when there were no regular customers in the museum, Regent Forimar arrived. Standing before the royal trio of images, he nervously asked Zevager what was up. 'Are our plans discovered?' he panted.

" 'Nay, my lord, not to my knowledge,' said the showman. 'True, there have been rumors that King Fusonio set out on some mysterious quest but never reached his destination. He vanished off the earth, they say.' Zevager glanced at the effigy of the king and chuckled. 'Of course, my lord, you and I know that he is in plain sight still—if one know where to look.'

" 'Hush up, you fool!' said Forimar. 'Even walls have ears. I may have to strike sooner than I expected. Therefore we may have to scrap one of your waxen images.' He in his turn looked at Fusonio. 'A pity, but we cannot risk having him turn up alive and vigorous.'

"The twain walked slowly down the loft, talking in low voices, so that Queen Iyres could no longer hear them. But she knew enough. Zevager saw his royal guest out and came back up the stairs.

"As he stepped out on the floor of the loft, a movement made him turn. He had just time to glimpse the queen's effigy, as he thought, swinging the ax from the tableau of the execution of Roskianus the rebel. He gave one horrified shriek ere the blade split his skull. Luckily for Ivrea, who was a strapping wench, the ax in the tableau was real and not an imitation of painted wood. Zevager had prided himself on authenticity.

"The showman's apprentice was at the door below to collect admission fees. When he heard the disturbance, he hurried up the stairs. When he saw Ivrea with a bloody ax in her hand and Zevager lying dead, he gave an even louder shriek and took to his heels.

"With the death of Zevager, the spell he had cast upon Fusonio quickly wore off. The king blinked and rubbed his eyes and began to breathe normally.

" 'Where am I?' he said. 'What in the forty-nine Mulvanian hells is going on?'

"When things had been explained, he said 'Hand me the ax, my dear. My reach is longer than yours.' And the pair marched post-haste back to the palace. The guards gaped at the sight of their king and queen approaching the palace unescorted, the king with a bloody ax on his shoulder; but none barred their way.

"Presently Fusonio came upon his brother, practising a flute solo in his study. Seeing what was toward, Forimar fell to his knees and begged for his life.

" 'Well,' said Fusonio, swinging the bloody ax about his head, 'I ought to give you what our ancestor gave Roskianus. No headless man has ever yet caused his sovran trouble.

" 'But then, we have our tradition of keeping a united front to the world, which I am loath to breach. So you shall depart forthwith as my ambassador to Salimor in the Far East. And I shall send a message to my old friend the Sophi of Salimor, that if he is fain to keep our profitable trade, he must hold you there for the rest of your days.'

"And so it was done. Face was saved by the appointment of Forimar as ambassador, none but a very few knowing that he was going into exile and genteel captivity. It is said that he wrought revolutions in several of the native arts of Salimor, but that I cannot vouch for."

"What of Forimar's poetry contest?" asked the king.

"Since the judges had been chosen, the announcements had been made, and the submissions were already pouring in, Fusonio forbore to cancel the event, lest in so doing he dishonor the government of Kortoli and bring to light the discord betwixt him and his brother. A few sennights later, after Forimar's departure, the judges announced their awards. First prize, they said, should go to Vatreno of Govannian for his poem, *Demonic Downfall*. This verse began:

"Temper the bejeweled interpleading,
Monotheistic, fair, letter-perfect;
Counterchange an alien thither.
We prevaricate, junket despumate,
And traverse plumate lanes.
Intercommunication is pixilated.
Explanation: liquoricity incorrigible . . .

"The judges brought the manuscripts of all the prize-winning poems to King Fusonio for his approval. He was supposed to bestow the prizes the following day. Fusonio read Vatreno's poem and said:

" 'What is this? Some kind of joke?'

" 'Oh, no, Your Majesty,' quoth the chief judge. 'It is a serious poem, very soul-revealing.'

" 'But,' said Fusonio, 'the thing has neither rhyme nor rhythm. Moreover, meseems it makes no sense. It is not my idea of a poem at all.'

" 'Oh, that!' said the judge. 'One can see that Your Majesty, with all due respect, has not kept up with late developments in the art of poesy. Rhyme and rhythm have been abandoned as archaic, artificial fetters on the artist's creativity.'

" 'But still, one expects a poem to make sense!'

" 'Not today, sire; one does not. We live in chaotic times, so poetry should reflect the chaos of the times. If the world fail to make sense, one cannot expect a poem to do so.'

" 'Perhaps you feel chaotic, messires,' said the king,

'but I do not. In fact, to me the world makes very good sense indeed.'

" 'Would that your humble servants had Your Majesty's divine omniscience!' said the chief judge with sarcasm.

" 'I claim no omniscience,' said Fusonio with ominous calm. 'The world is far too complicated for any one mortal mind to encompass in its entirety. The few things I do claim to understand seem to follow orderly natural laws—including the follies of my fellow men.' He flicked the paper with a finger. 'If you ask me, Master Vatreno composed this thing by opening a dictionary at random and pointing to words with his eyes closed.' "

" 'Well, ah,' said the judge, 'as a matter of fact, sire, that is just what he did. Afterwards he added a few auxiliary words like "the" to give it grammatical form. We thought it a brilliant poetical innovation. It is the coming thing.'

"Fusonio glanced through the poems to which the judges had awarded the lesser prizes, but they pleased him no more than did *Demonic Downfall.* At last he said:

" 'And I am supposed to pay ten thousand good marks out of my straitened treasury for this garbage! Well, when I order beer in a tavern, I at least expect beer for my coin and not horsepiss.' With that, he tore the manuscripts across with one wrench and roared: 'Get out, you dolts! Asses! Noodleheads!'

"The judges ran from the chamber with their robes flying and King Fusonio after them, thwacking their rumps with his scepter. The poetry contest was called off on the ground that nought worthy of award had been submitted. This act caused much discontent among the artists and the advanced thinkers, who called Fusonio a low-browed tyrant and a crass vulgarian. But Fusonio paid no heed and had, in fact, a long and successful reign."

\* \* \*

King Ishbahar laughed heartily. "Luckily for us, perhaps, we have no brothers; nor has poetry in Penembei ever reached such a pitch of refinement that none but the poet can ever understand one of his own compositions. But now the program is due to begin." To his secretary he said: "Herekit, hand us our reading glass and the proclamation."

Ishbahar stood up and read, while the crier bellowed his words through the speaking trumpet. The speech was the usual amass of clichés, and then the parades and clownings and races began.

# X

# The Crown of Penembei

The western half of the Hippodrome was in shadow when the last race had been run. King Ishbahar stood up to announce the winners. As before, the crier relayed his words.

"Leave not early, good people," said the king. "When the formalities are over, we shall have somewhat to say that will interest you."

The king went down the list of winners. As the crier called each name, the winner marched up the steps to the royal box, bent the knee, and, to general applause, received his prize from the king. For once, the rivalry of the Pants and the Kilts seemed in abeyance.

Then King Ishbahar cleared his throat. "Loyal subjects of the Penembic crown!" he said. "Amidst the turmoils of the last month, we have been delayed in bringing up a matter of moment to all of you: to wit, the succession.

"You are all aware that we have no heirs of our body, legitimate or otherwise, living. Therefore, as our reign nears its destined end, it behooves us, to assure an orderly succession, either to search amongst our more distant kinsmen for a suitable candidate or to resort to the extreme measure of adoption.

"Be not astonished at the mention of adoption, our friends. True, the succession has not passed by adoption for over a century. But some may have forgotten that the great King Hoshcha was an adopted son of his predecessor, Shashtai the Third. Hoshcha had not a drop of the blood of Juktar the Great in his veins. To retain the crown within our divine family, he wedded both of his predecessor's daughters, and the first of their sons to reach maturity was his successor.

"Now we are confronted by a similar situation. True, we have living male relatives, but amongst them we have failed to find any who qualify for the duties of king.

"The gods, however, have sent us a true hero—a man young enough to give the throne many years of vigorous occupancy, yet old enough to be past his youthful follies; a man of mighty thews, active mind, and solid character. He has already saved holy Iraz from the horde of miscreants who lately assailed her. Moreover, the fatidical and astrological indications agree that he was born on a lucky day.

"We have, therefore, this day signed and sealed the documents adopting this hero as our son and designating him as our lawful successor. Anon, we shall arrange for his marriage to one or more of our kinswomen, amongst whom are several of nubile age and winsomeness.

"This done, we shall abdicate the throne in favor of our adopted son, ere the holy father Chaluish find it needful to wait upon us with the sacred rope."

Sounds of disturbance began to swell from the throng.

"Nay, nay, good people," said the king, "be not surprised at talk of abdication! Jukar II did it, as historical records attest. Quiet, please! Quiet! We have not yet told you the name of our chosen successor."

Jorian, having inferred what was coming next, gave Karadur a desperate glare. The old Mulvanian only spread his hands helplessly.

"The hero in question," continued Ishbahar, "my adopted son and your next king, is Jorian the son of Evor! Rise, my son!"

Leaning towards Karadur, Jorian hissed: *"Oi!* Get me out of this, curse it!"

"I cannot," murmured Karadur. "I was surprised, also. Stand up as the king commands!"

"But I don't wish to be king—"

"Later, later. Stand up now!"

Jorian stood up. A slight pattering of applause was quickly drowned in a storm of boos and catcalls. From the benches occupied by the Pants arose a chant, growing louder with each repetition: "Dirty foreigner! Dirty foreigner! *Dirty foreigner!* DIRTY FOREIGNER!"

On the other side, the Kilts took up the cry until the Hippodrome rocked with it. The stasiarchs, Vegh and Amazluek, could be seen standing amid their factions, beating time like orchestra conductors. The chant spread to the rest of the audience until it became deafening.

King Ishbahar stood beside Jorian with tears running down his fat cheeks. "P-pray, good subjects—" he stammered. The crier shouted his words but was unheard in the din of "Dirty foreigner."

Missiles began to fly. Royal guardsmen rushed towards the royal box to protect the king. Colonel Chuivir appeared at the rear of the box.

"Your Majesty!" he shouted. "Come quickly, or all is lost! The factions have united in sedition against your throne. You must get back to your palace!"

"Come, our friends," said Ishbahar to Jorian and Karadur. The king waddled out of the box to the top of the ramp. His gilded litter lay, smashed, on one side.

"How shall we return to the palace without a conveyance?" he quavered.

"Walk!" said Chuivir.

Another guardsman rushed up clanking and spoke into the colonel's ear. Beyond the crowd of gleaming guardsmen, Jorian glimpsed a scud of mob, missiles flying, and weapons whirling. Chuivir said:

"The insurgents have seized the waterfront of Zaktan. Your Majesty will have to use Hoshcha's Tunnel."

"Must we climb that dreadful hill afoot?"

"It is that, or else," said the colonel with visible impatience.

"Ah, us! Let us hasten, then."

Followed by Jorian and Karadur and protected by a mass of guardsmen, the king puffed his way down the ramp. In the concourse, screams of rage and defiance and a rain of cobblestones, bricks, potsherds, and other missiles assailed the guardsmen. A knot of citizens rushed at the guards with clubs and knives. The guards easily beat off the attack, leaving a wrack of tumbled bodies. A few guards who bore crossbows began methodically shooting into the swirling, screaming crowds.

"This way!" yelled Chuivir.

Stumbling over corpses, they pushed across the street surrounding the Hippodrome and started up the slope to the Temple of Nubalyaga. After a few steps, the king halted, panting.

"We can no more," he moaned.

"Help me with him, Master Jorian," said the colonel.

Each of them draped one of the king's fat arms around his neck. With help on either side, the king dragged his monstrous weight slowly up the hill.

At the top, the eunuch guard was already drawn up behind their gate with crossbows ready. They opened the gate to admit the king and his escort.

At the temple, High Priestess Sahmet came running out. After a quick explanation, she said: "Follow me, sire!" and led the way towards the Tunnel of Hoshcha.

"Hold!" cried Colonel Chuivir. "I shall come with you as soon as I appoint a commander of the local detachment."

"Why?" asked the king.

"If I can regain the palace and take command of the main body of the Guard, belike I can keep the sedition from spreading across the river. Captain Saloi!"

"Aye, sir?"

"Take command of the guardsmen in Zaktan. Try to

guard the main points, like this temple. If you have enough men, send a flying squad to patrol and break up gatherings of rebels." He turned to the king. "If it please Your Majesty, we are ready to go now."

Sahmet clutched Jorian's arm and whispered: "You shall see me again at the next full moon!"

Four men moved through the Tunnel of Hoshcha: Jorian in front, bearing a lanthorn; then King Ishbahar, puffing and panting; then Karadur; and lastly Colonel Chuivir, with another lanthorn. To Jorian it seemed an eternity, for the king toddled along with tiny steps at a snail's pace.

They had come, he supposed, halfway across and were under the deepest part of the Lyap, when he saw something that made his hair rise. From the side of the tunnel, a tiny jet of water sprayed out, shooting halfway across at waist height before breaking up into discrete drops.

"Gods and goddesses!" he exclaimed. "Look at that, Karadur!"

"Here is another," said the wizard, pointing to the overhead, whence another trickle of water descended.

Everywhere they looked, forward and back, water appeared in drips and leaks and spurts. The floor of the tunnel became wet and slippery.

"What befalls, Doctor Karadur?" wheezed the king. "Have your hydrophobic spells failed? Should we have ordered pumps installed after all?"

"It must be," said Karadur, "that a mob has invaded the House of Learning and snatched my wizards Goelnush, Luekuz, and Firaven from their task. I hope they have not done the poor fellows to death."

"Yes, yes," said Jorian. "But hadn't we better hurry, ere this burrow fill with water?"

"Aye, my son, that we must." Karadur turned back. "Your Majesty—"

"We—are going (*puff*)—as fast—as we can," said the king. "If you fear drowning—go on—without us."

"Oh, come on, sire!" said Chuivir heartily. "Lengthen those royal strides!"

With every step, the leakage of water increased. Soon the four were splashing along ankle-deep. Groaning and gasping, the king made a desperate effort to speed up his uncouth waddle. Then he slipped and fell with a great splash.

"Your Majesty!" cried the three others at once.

Jorian and Karadur handed Chuivir their lanthorns. Grunting with effort, they got Ishbahar into a sitting position. The king's eyes were half closed, and his breath came in rattling snores. He did not answer at first. They pushed him so that his back rested against the side wall of the tunnel. The water was calf-deep.

At last the king opened his eyes. "Master Jorian!" he whispered.

"Aye, sire?"

"Lean over. Close."

Jorian leaned. With a last effort, the king reached up, plucked the serpent crown from his bewigged pate, and clapped it on Jorian's head.

"Now—my boy—you are king. These witnesses . . ."

The king's voice trailed off to a mumble and ceased. Karadur tried to feel his pulse.

"I cannot locate the blood vessel through all that fat," he grumbled. He thrust a hand inside the king's robe and then laid his ear against the king's breast.

"He is dead," said Karadur. "Methinks his heart succumbed."

"Not surprising, with all that blubber," said Jorian.

"Let us be off, Captain—ah—sire," said Chuivir, "ere we drown like rats."

"What of the king?" said Jorian. "It would look odd for him to have entered the tunnel with us but not to emerge. An we cannot show his unmarked body, men will say we slew him."

"You are right, my son," said Karadur. "Help Jorian to bear the body, Colonel."

Chuivir took an arm. "Take the other, Master—ah—King Jorian."

The two struggled and heaved. Between them, they got the body up. Grunting, they staggered a few steps. Then Jorian slipped. The two men and the corpse fell with a mighty splash. Karadur said:

"If the water become any deeper, the body will float. You two can haul it by the feet."

"O wise old man!" said Jorian. "Take his other ankle, Chuivir."

The water was soon knee-deep. Karadur, with his robe hiked up to his bony brown knees, went ahead. He held the two lanthorns, which gave off feeble yellow glows. Behind him waded Jorian and Chuivir, hauling on the body's ankles. The corpse still scraped along the floor of the tunnel, but with each rise in the water level, the body lightened.

"Are you sure we have the right tunnel?" said Chuivir. "We must have walked halfway to the Fediruni border."

"This is the tunnel, certes," said Jorian. "It is now sloping up. If we can keep ahead of the rise in the water level, we shall escape."

"The water gains," said Chuivir. "It is up to my waist. Would I had doffed this damned armor in the temple."

The deepening water floated the king's body off the floor and made it easy to tow. On the other hand, it impeded the movements of the three living men. They could only plod, plod under a continuous shower of jets and leaks and trickles from the parts of the tunnel not yet submerged.

"That is the trouble with magic," growled Jorian. "When folks think they can count on it, they skimp on proper engineering and maintenance."

The water continued to rise; it was now breast-high. Jorian and Chuivir tried to speed their progress by

making swimming motions with their free arms. Karadur, being smaller, was forced to hold the lanthorns
over his head to keep them from being drowned. His
white beard trailed in the water.

A spurt of water from the overhead struck one of
the lanthorns, which went out with a faint hiss. On they
plodded through the gloom. Jorian mutered:

"Any higher, and the cursed corpse will scrape the
roof."

"If the remaining light go, at least we can feel our
way," panted Chuivir. "There are no forks or branches
in this tunnel, are there?"

"Nay," said Karadur. "It runs straight to—glub?" The
water had been up to his chin, and a ripple filled his
mouth. He coughed and sputtered, shaking the
remaining lanthorn.

"Ho, don't put out our last light!" said Jorian. "Drowning is bad enough, but drowning in the dark . . ."

"Save your breath, King" said Chuivir.

Karadur, who had gained a little on the other two,
turned back long enough to say: "When my boy Jorian
ceases conversing, you will know he has terminated his
present incarnation."

"Can you talk without getting a mouthful of water?"
said Jorian.

"Now that you mention it, the water has not deepened recently."

The water level remained constant for a time, while
the only sounds in the tunnel were the heavy breathing
of the three men and the splashing of their slow progress. At last the water began to recede. Soon the king's
body was again scraping the bottom.

"At least, we are now above the river level," said
Jorian. "Now all we need worry about is being slaughtered by rebels at the far end."

"I could not fight a mouse," groaned Chuivir.

\*　　\*　　\*

Karadur knocked on the secret door to the king's bedchamber. When he had explained, the door opened. After some delay, several guards and palace servants came down the stair with a stretcher.

They found Jorian and Chuivir a furlong down the tunnel, sitting in half a foot of water with their backs to the wall, breathing heavily in a state of utter exhaustion. The monstrous corpse lay in the water near them.

When the people from the palace had rolled the body on the stretcher, tied it fast with straps, and borne it back up the tunnel, Jorian got to his feet with a groan. Chuivir, weighed down by his armor, had to be helped up. After another struggle, the two crept on hands and knees up the stair and entered the royal bedchamber. They collapsed into chairs and lay back, dripping puddles on the floor. Karadur already occupied another chair, with his turban on the floor beside him. The wizard's eyes were closed.

"Wine!" croaked Jorian. Servants scurried.

Jorian looked up from his goblet to see an officer of the Guard. "Sir!" said this man. "What means this? King Ishbahar is dead, and you wear his crown!"

"Do I, forsooth?" said Jorian. He pulled off the serpent crown and stared at it absently, as if he had never seen it before.

"Is it true what they say, that His late Majesty named you his sucessor?"

"It is," said Chuivir behind the officer. "His Majesty died of natural causes in the tunnel whilst fleeing the insurrection in Zaktan. Have the rebels attacked the palace yet?"

"Nay, Colonel. But some have crossed the river, and there is fighting and looting and arson along the waterfront. What are my orders?"

"Secure the palace against attack, first of all. I shall be with you presently to take active command. Now leave us. You servants, also." When the chamber had been cleared of all save Karadur, Jorian, and Chuivir, the last set down his goblet.

"Excellent wine," he said. "Vindine, methinks. I begin to feel like a human being again. Now, sir, you and I have some matters to straighten out."

"At your service, Colonel," said Jorian, also putting down his goblet.

He looked speculatively at Chuivir, wondering what chance he would have against the colonel in a fight. Chuivir wore armor and a sword against Jorian's mere dagger; but Chuivir had been much more exhausted by the ordeal in the tunnel.

Chuivir: "Do you really intend to exercise your king-ship, in view of the general revolt against you?"

"No longer than I must," said Jorian. "I wanted no crown. Ishbahar was a fool to name me without first making sure of political support for the move."

"A well-intentioned wight, but no monarch," said Chuivir. "Well, that relieves my mind. You may be the lawful sovran; but as a foreigner you are unpopular. Even if I threw my full weight behind you, I know not if I could keep you on your throne. How long is no longer than you must?"

"As long as it takes Doctor Karadur and me to take off in our flying bathtub."

"Eh? What is this?"

"Ishbahar promised me that great copper tub of his as an aërial vehicle."

"How will you make it fly?"

Jorian nodded towards Karadur, who was rewinding his turban. "The good doctor has in his ring a demon, who will bear us aloft."

"But, Jorian!" protested Karadur. "I told you I did not wish to liberate Gorax save in direst emergency, since this will be his last labor—"

Jorian snorted. "If this be not a dire emergency, with the whole city buzzing about our ears, then I know not an emergency when I see it. Wouldst rather be torn to bits by a mob whipped up to hatred of foreigners?"

"Oh. But, my son, think of all the good you could effect if you retained the crown! You could introduce those reforms that Mazsan preached. You could provide the House of Learning with adequate financial support—"

"Not when half the people I saw would wish to shoot, stab, or poison me. They've made it plain that they want no foreigner for king. This must be that 'second crown' whereof Nubalyaga warned me in the dream. The first was the crown of Xylar, which you and I buried near the Marshes of Moru."

"The Irazis would soon forget their xenophobia," persisted Karadur, "once you were firmly ensconced in power and demonstrated what a good king you could be and how well you adapted to their ways. You already speak better Penembic than I do. After all, Juktar the Great was not only a foreigner but also a barbarian, and this is a cosmopolitan city."

Jorian shook his head. "I tried to show the Xylarians what a good king I could be, too, but that didn't stop them from trying to cut off my head. Besides, how should I ever get firmly ensconced in power, without some foreign mercenary army at my back?"

"Surely there are loyal elements in the Guard and in the Frontier Army on whom you could rely. Once you dompted the factions—"

"And suppose I did, then what? Spend my life humping Her Sanctity Sahmet until the priests arrived with the sacred rope? No, thank you!"

"You could abolish that custom, as did that Kortolian king."

"Doubtless. But 'tis useless to try to argue me round, old man. I've had my taste of kinging it. Whilst 'twas fun in a way, I have no wish to go back to it. Many lust for the wealth, power, and glory that kingship entails, but I harbor no such lordly ambitions. A simple life, with a respectable trade, a snug house, plenty to eat and drink, a loving family, and congenial cronies will suffice me.

"Nor do I covet an Irazi wife. I already have one spouse, and that's a plenty. Besides, the more I travel, better I appreciate my native land.

"Oh, some like the mountains, rugged and grim,
Where the sleet storms howl
        and the low clouds skim,
And you hang by your toes from a ledge's rim,
But I'll warble a rondeau and carol a hymn
        To Novaria, dear Novaria.

"And some seek the desert, barren and dry,
Where the hot sun hangs in a cloudless sky
And your camel sways and your eyeballs fry,
But I to the land of my birth will hie:
        To Novaria, my Novaria.

"While some love the spires of vast Iraz
And admire its domes with oh's and ah's
And go to the races to shout hurrahs,
But the bonniest land that ever there was
        Is Novaria, fair Novaria.

"So let the factions fight it out; 'tis no affair of mine. To the forty-nine Mulvanian hells with the Penembic crown! I'm for Xylar to rescue my little darling, and that's that."

Looking worried, Chuivir passed a hand across his forehead. "Well then, sire, I wonder—ah—perhaps you can advise me. With you gone, the leading contenders for the crown will be the stasiarchs. But I deem neither Vegh nor Amazluek a man of kingly quality; whiles, of the late king's sister's sons, one is a wastrel and the other a halfwit. General Tereyai, to whom I have sent messengers, is old and soon to retire. Admiral Kyar is dead. Have you any thought as to whom I should back?"

Jorian stared at Chuivir. "Why not be king yourself? Methinks you would make not a bad one."

Chuivir's mouth fell open. "Really? You offer *me* the crown?"

"Why not? I thought you a harmless, feckless fop, but since the rebel assault you have learnt fast."

Chuivir shrugged. "I do my poor best."

"To make it legitimate, fetch writing materials, and I will sign over the sovranty, to take effect when we leave in our flying tub. Whether you can make it good is your problem."

Chuivir rose. "I thank you, sire, and will try to deserve your trust. Now I must go to command my men; but I shall soon return to see you off."

As Chuivir clanked out, Jorian raised his voice: "Servants! Hither, pray. I want a change of clothing—warm woolens, suitable for roughing it; not these pretty silky things. And fetch a dry robe for Doctor Karadur."

"Oh, my son, I need no—"

" 'Tis cold aloft, and I can't have you catching a tisic. You there, find the chief armorer and tell him to fetch me some weapons and armor to make a choice from. And where did King Ishbahar keep his privy purse? You! Tell the cook to whip up a dinner for the doctor and me. Not fancy, but substantial, and tell him to waste no time about it."

While the servants scurried, a guardsman entered, saying: "A courier named Zerlik would fain see Your Majesty."

"Send him in," said Jorian.

The young man entered and dramatically dropped to one knee. "Your Majesty!" he cried. "I have just returned from bearing the king's letter to Othomae. Nominating you was the best thing King Ishbahar ever did. My sword is at your service; your every wish is my command!"

"That is fine, but I fear I shan't be here long enough to profit from your loyalty."

"You are leaving? Take me with you as your s-squire!"

"Alas, our vehicle cannot carry three. Colonel Chuivir is my deputy and chosen successor, so transfer your loyalty to him."

"But there must be something, sire—"

"I will tell you. You have a big house. Set aside one small room as a refuge for me, should I ever have to flee Novaria and go into hiding here."

"It shall be done! May the gods bless Your Majesty!"

"Better ask them to bless Chuivir; he will need it. Farewell!"

An hour later, the streets of Iraz resounded to the tramp of feet, the roar of mobs, the clash of arms, and the screams of the stricken. Chuivir and several of his guardsmen stood on the roof of the palace, watching the bathtub carrying Jorian and Karadur wobble off into the heavens. The rays of the setting sun gleamed redly on the copper of the tub. The vehicle shrank until it became a mere crimson spark in the deepening blue of the heavens.

Chuivir, wearing the serpent crown of Penembei instead of his helmet, sighed and murmured: "There goes the man who should really have been king, were he not debarred by popular prejudice. Ah, well." He turned to the officers around him and began to receive reports and issue commands.

# Part III

# The Unbeheaded King

# CONTENTS

# CONTENTS

# I

# The Palace of Xylar

A large copper bathtub, its polished surface redly reflecting the light of the setting sun, soared above the snow-clad peaks of the Lograms. It wove around the loftiest summits and scraped over the lower ones, betimes with but a few cubits to spare.

"Gorax!" yelled one of the two men in the tub. "I have commanded thee not to miss those peaks so straitly! Wouldst stop my old heart from sheer fright? Next time, go around!"

"What's his answer!" asked the other man.

The first cocked his head as if listening. At last he spoke: "He says he is fain to get this journey over with. He also begs that I suffer him to alight one of these mountains to rest; but I know better. Did I permit him, his last labor for me were completed. Away the fiend would flit to his native dimension, leaving us stranded on an icy mountain top."

The speaker was a small, lean, brown-skinned man in a coarse brown robe. The wind of the tub's motion rippled the silky white hair that hung down beneath his bulbous white turban and fluttered his vast white beard. He was Karadur, a seer and wizard from Mulvan.

The other tub-rider was a large man in late youth, with a ruddy complexion further reddened by the mountain winds, deep-set dark eyes and black hair and beard, and a scar across his face that put a slight kink in his nose. This was Jorian of Ardamai in Kortoli, once King of Xylar and, before and since, a poet, mercenary soldier, professional taleteller, bookkeeper, clockmaker, and surveyor.

Continuing an argument that had begun before they narrowly missed the mountain peak, Karadur said: "But, my son! To rush unprepared into such an adventure were a sure formula for disaster. We should instruct Gorax to set us down in some safe land, where we have friends, and plan our next move."

"By the time we've done planning," said Jorian, "the Xylarians will have gotten word of my flight from Penembei. I know, because when I was King, the secret service was on its toes. Then they will set traps for me, hoping I'll try to rescue Estrildis. And then. . . ."

Jorian brought the edge of his hand sharply against his neck. He alluded to the bloody Xylarian custom of cutting off the king's head every five years and throwing it up for grabs, the catcher to be the next king. Karadur's magic had enabled Jorian to escape his own beheading. Ever since, Xylar had sought to recapture its fugitive king, to drag him back and resume their interrupted ceremony so that his successor could be chosen in the time-honored way.

"Besides," Jorian continued, "so long as Gorax remains your slave, we have this aerial vehicle to approach the palace from aloft. You yourself said that, if you permit him to alight, that were the end of his services. Any earthbound attempt were rendered that much harder. Why think you I brought this along?" He pointed to the coil of rope lying at one end of King Ishbahar's tub. "Could you magic that rope as you did the one in Xylar?"

Karadur shook his head. "Alas, nay! It requires the capture of a spirit from the Second Plane, for which I have no present facilities." Then Karadur tried another tack. In his high, nasal voice, he droned on: "But Jorian dear! The world harbors many attractive women. Why must you remain fixated upon this one? She is a nice girl; but you have enjoyed many women, both during your kinship and since. So it is not as if she were the only possible mate—"

"I've told you before," growled Jorian, "she's the one I chose myself. Those other four wives were picked for me by the Regency Council. Nought wrong with them; but 'twas an arrangement political. What would an ascetic old sage like you know of love?"

"You forget that I, too, was once young, difficult though you may find that to believe."

"Well, if King Fusinian of Kortoli could risk his life to rescue his beloved Thanuda from the troll Vuum, I were a recreant knave not to make an effort."

"There are still those other women of whom you have had carnal knowledge since your escape."

"You can't blame me about the high priestess. I had little choice in that matter."

"Aye; but there were others—"

Jorian snorted. "I try to be faithful to Estrildis; but I'm not yet able, after long abstinence, calmly to dismiss unplumbed a fair lass who crawls into bed with me, begging that I pleasure her. When I reach your age, perhaps my self-control will be equal to the challenge."

Karadur said: "How know you the Xylarians have not bestowed your Estrildis upon another?"

"They hadn't when my brother Kerin was there, repairing their clocks. I suspect they save her as bait for me. Through Kerin, I got word to her to hold out."

"Suppose her affections prove less perdurable than yours? Suppose she, too, has found agreeable the company of another of the opposite sex?"

"Ridiculous!" snapped Jorian. "She always told me I was her true love, and I trust her as far as I trust my mortal."

"Ah, but ofttimes Astis—the goddess whom we in Mulvan call Laxari—afflicts the steadiest of mortals with a passion that overrides the weightiest resolves and the most cogent reasonings. Misprize not the havoc that fate and the vagaries of human nature can make with our soberest plans. As said the wise Cidam, 'Blessed be he who expecteth the worst, for verily he shall ne'er be disappointed.' "

Jorian scowled. "You mean, let's suppose she has willingly suffered some knave to mount her in my absence? I suppose it could happen. Since I was the best swordsman in Xylar, excepting Tartonio, the fencing master who taught me, I should easily skewer the villain. Some would say to slay the woman, too, but I'm too chicken-hearted."

"You say you love her, right?"

"Aye, desperately."

"Then you would fain not wantonly render her unhappy, would you?"

"Of course not!"

"But suppose she really love this wight? Then you had broken her heart to no purpose. If by force or fraud you compelled her to live with you thereafter, your domestic scene were something less than heavenly."

Jorian shook his head. "Curse it, old man, but you think of some of the direst predicaments! Whatever I propose, you are endlessly fertile in reasons why it were a folly, a blunder, and a wicked knavery. Betimes you have reason; but if I harkened to all your cavils, I'd stand immobile until I sprouted roots. Methinks I must await the event and guide my actions accordingly."

Karadur sighed. "It is difficult for one so young to take the long view of what is best for all concerned."

Jorian glanced up. Overhead the stars were coming out. "Pray tell your demon to go slowly. We would not run into Mount Aravia in the dark."

"Mount Aravia? I believe a colleague of mine, named Shenderu, dwells there as a wise hermit. Could we not pay him a visit?" At Jorian's expression, Karadur sighed again. "Nay, I suppose not."

\*     \*     \*

A scarlet-and-golden dawn found the flying bathtub still over the Lograms, although the ridges became lower as the travelers flew northward. Soon the mountains ended, and for hours they soared above the vast Marshes of Moru. This dubious place was nominally part of Xylar. In practice it was a no-man's land, inhabited by a few desperate men, by dwarf crocodiles, and, it was rumored, by descendants of the dragons that the cannibal Paaluans once brought to Novaria. Generations before, these sophisticated cannibals sent a foraging expedition to Ir on the west coast of the broad Novarian peninsula.

Curious about everything, Jorian peered over the side of the tub. He looked in vain for a Paaluan dragon among the black pools and gray-green tussocks of this everglade, whence the approach of winter had bleached most of the color. Karadur cautioned:

"Lean not so far, my son! Gorax complains that you rock the tub and might overset it, despite his endeavors to fly it on an even keel."

"The tub has no keel," grinned Jorian. "But I get his point."

> "Two gentlemen fleeing away
> From warfare in doomed Penembei,
>     Their carriage capsized,
>     The marsh fertilized;
> Their bones molder there to this day!"

"Not your best, my son," said Karadur. "We know not whether Penembei in fact be doomed. If that fellow Chuivir, whom you nominated king, make good his claim, he may prove a good-to-middling king, make good his claim, he may prove a good-to-middling monarch. Besides, methinks you require a conjunction at the beginning of that last line."

"That would spoil the meter," said Jorian. "The first

foot should always be an iamb, according to Doctor Gwiderius."

"Who?"

"The professor who taught me prosody at the Academy of Othomae. Well, how's this?"

> "Two knaves in the royal washbasin
> O'er Moru's dank marshes did hasten,
>     But leaning too far,
>     They fell with a jar,
> And mud their presumption did chasten."

Karadur shook his head. "That implies that I, too, am leaning over the side. As you can perceive, I am careful to keep to the centerline."

"What a literal-minded gaffer you are! All right, let's see you compose a better!"

"Alas, Jorian, I am no poet, nor is Novarian my native tongue. To compose a verse incorporating the thoughts of yours in Mulvani, and obeying all sixty-three rules of Mulvanian versification, were a task requiring more comfort and leisure than the gods see fit at the moment to accord us."

By afternoon they had left the Marshes of Moru and soared above the forests of southern Xylar. By sunset the forest was giving way to farmland.

"Tell Gorax," said Jorian, "that we do not wish to arrive at Xylar City before midnight."

"He says we shall be fortunate to arrive ere dawn," said Karadur. "He groans—mentally of course—with fatigue."

"Then have him speed up. The last thing we wish is to find the sun rising just as I am shinnying down that rope."

"Just what do you intend, Jorian?" Karadur's voice expressed a growing tremor of apprehension.

"Simple. Kerin told me they have Estrildis quartered

in the penthouse apartment on the roof. They think that putting her up there will make it harder for me to get her—assuming that I shall approach the palace on the ground." Jorian chuckled. "So, when we reach the roof, I'll belay the rope to the faucet, drop the other end over the side, slide down, and carry off Estrildis before any mouse knows I'm there. I wish we had one of your ensorcelled ropes."

"If we ever alight long enough for the sorcerous operation, I will prepare one."

"This faucet was King Ishbahar's pride and joy," said Jorian. "An engineer in the House of Learning invented it. The only trouble was that the king's servants had to mix hot and cold water in a tank on the palace roof, and they could never get the proportions right. Poor Ishbahar was ever being either chilled or boiled. I proposed that he install two faucets, one for hot water and one for cold, so that he could adjust the mixture to suit himself. But, what with the siege of Iraz and the revolt of the racing factions, he never got around to trying my idea."

Karadur shook his head. "With all these new inventions pouring out of the House of Learning, in a few centuries our plane will be like the afterworld, where all is done by buzzing, clattering machines and magic is of no account. I pray never to spend an incarnation in such a world."

Jorian shrugged. "I try to make the best of things, be they magical or mechanical. At least we can thank King Ishbahar's monstrous fatness that we have so huge a tub, wherein the twain of us can comfortably sleep. Didst ever hear how he came to have it made?"

"Nay, my son. Tell me, pray."

"When Ishbahar acceded to the throne, he was already vastly obese, eating having been his favorite pastime from boyhood on. Well, the night following his coronation, he was, naturally, weary after a day of standing about and making ceremonial motions and uttering prescribed responses to the high priests of the leading cults. So he commanded his lackeys to prepare a bath for him, and told his favorite wife to await him in the royal bed.

"The royal bathtub, however, had been made for his predecessor, Shashtai the Eighth, who was a small, spare man. Ishbahar tested the water with his finger and found it just right. With a sigh of happy anticipation, he mounted the step that the lackeys had placed beside the tub and lowered himself into the water. But alas! As he sank down, he found himself firmly wedged between the sides of the tub. He called out to a servant: 'Ho, this won't do! We are squeezed to a jelly! Help us out, pray!' So the servitor caught the king's arm and heaved, but without effect. Between the king's vast weight and the wedging effect of the sloping sides of the tub, Ishbahar was stuck fast.

"They called more servants, and all together heaved on the king's arms—to no avail. A guardsman was called, to thrust the butt of his halberd over the edge of the tub and under the royal arse, to pry him up. Ishbahar bore the pain bravely except for a few groans, but still he remained stuck. Then two flunkeys added their weight to that of the guardsman on the head end of the halberd, but they only succeeded in breaking the spear shaft.

"Then the king had the chief engineer of the School of Matter in the House of Learning dragged out of bed. The engineer looked over the problem and told the king: 'Your Majesty, I can get you out. All we need do is bore a hole in the ceiling and install a hoist with compound pulleys. By looping ropes under your armpits and thighs, we shall have you out in a jiffy.'

" 'How long will this take?' asked King Ishbahar.

"The engineer thought a moment and said: 'May it please Your Majesty, allowing time for drawing up a plan and assembling materials, I am sure we can have you out in a fortnight.'

" 'And meanwhile we shall sit here soaking?' said Ishbahar. 'Come, come, my good fellow! Fetch us the head of the School of Spirit.'

"So they brought in the head wizard of the School of Spirit, a bitter rival of the chief engineer in the House of Learning. The enchanter said: 'Your Majesty, I have just the thing! It is my newly developed levitation spell, which can easily handle up to three talents avoirdupois. Let me fetch my instruments, and all shall be well.'

"So, after midnight, the wizard ordered all the others out of the bath chamber and began his spell. He burned mysterious powders in a brazier, whence arose many-hued smokes that writhed and twined like ghostly serpents. He chanted mystical phrases, and shadows chased each other about the walls, albeit there was no solid body in the chamber to cast them. The hangings rippled, and the candle flames flickered, although there was no wind in the chamber.

"At length the wizard cried three words of power, and King Ishbahar rose—but the tub rose with him, still firmly attached to the royal haunches. At length the wizard was compelled by sheer fatigue to let the king and his tub settle back to the floor. This tub, you understand, had no faucet and no pipes to let water in and out, so it could be freely moved.

"At length the favorite wife, named Haziran, came in to see what was keeping her lord so long. She found the king still in the tub, and the chief engineer and the chief wizard and the servants all standing about, muttering disconsolately at their failure to get the king unstuck. They were proposing desperate expedients, such as starving the king until he shrank enough no longer to fit so snugly, like a cork in a bottle.

"Haziran looked the situation over and said, 'You are all a pack of fools! This is a ceramic tub, is it not? Well, you lackeys, take the water out. Doctor Akraba—'

That was the chief engineer. '—fetch me a heavy hammer, forthwith!'

" 'Do as she says,' quoth Ishbahar. 'This damned tub is cutting off our circulation.'

"By the time the sledgehammer was brought, the servants, with dippers and pails and sponges, had removed nearly all the water. So Haziran smote the tub on the side where it gripped Ishbahar's hips, and with a loud crash the tub broke into several pieces. The king gave a yelp of pain from the impact, but he recked that a bruised hip were a small price for his freedom. He dried himself, embraced Haziran, and led her off to the bedchamber. She was a level-headed woman, and had she not died of a pox a few years later, she might have saved the kingdom much grief by giving Ishbahar good advice.

"Anyway, the king ordered another bathtub. This time he made sure it was large enough so that, no matter how fat he got, he would be in no danger of being entrapped. And in later years, when officials of the House of Learning complained of the king's cutting their appropriations, Ishbahar would say: 'Ha! For all your pretended wisdom, you geniuses could not even get us out of a bathtub!' "

"An edifying tale," said Karadur. "But why did he have it fabricated of copper? It must have been much more costly that way."

"That was a decision political. His officials were embroiled in a quarrel with the potters' guild over taxes, and ordering the tub from the coppersmiths' guild was Ishbahar's way of reminding the potters who was boss."

"Now back to our own plans," said Karadur. "How shall you get your queen up the rope and into the tub again? Mighty though you be, I misdoubt you could scale the rope with one hand whilst grasping your sweetling with the other."

Jorian frowned. "You have a point. I suppose the best way were to have her grasp me round the neck from behind, thus leaving my hands free."

"Do you ween you can hoist the weight of the twain of you?"

"If not, I shall have to remain clinging to the rope until you find us a safe place to alight."

"You cannot dangle until we are out of Xylar! The journey would require hours. And if we alight ere departing this land, Gorax will desert us, and we shall be forced to flee afoot."

"Hmm." After a moment of silence, Jorian said: "I know! There's a ruined castle, said to be haunted, a dozen leagues southeast of Xylar City. A certain Baron Lorc built it back in feudal days. Much of the main wall still stands. Gorax can drop us on the wall and then bring the tub down to the level of the parapet, so we can climb in. Be sure to tell him not to let the tub touch the wall, lest he deem himself freed from his last labor."

Karadur muttered: "I like it not. Demons are tricky beings, especially those we cannot see. And what is this about the castle's being haunted?"

"Just a rumor, a legend. There's probably nought to it; and if a malevolent spirit does abide there, I trust you to protect us from it by magical means."

Karadur dubiously wagged his beard. "Why not bring the tub to the edge of the palace roof, as you speak of doing at Baron Lorc's castle?"

"Because, save for a narrow walk around the penthouse and a little terrace, the roof slopes down on both sides, and there is nought to hang on to ere one reaches the eaves. By myself, I might chance sliding down the roof tiles and leaping into the tub, but I cannot ask that of Estrildis."

"Curse it, boy, could you not take me across the border into Othomae and leave me there? I would instruct Gorax to obey you until his final dismissal."

"Oh, no indeed!" said Jorian. "I need you to control this aerial chariot whilst I am below fetching my darling. Cheer up, old man! We've gotten each other out of more parlous plights."

"All very well for you, young master," grumbled Karadur. "You are constructed of steel springs and whalebone, but I am old and fragile. I know not how many more of these exploits I can endure ere joining the majority."

"Well, you can't complain that life in my company has been dull, now can you?"

"Nay. Betimes I lust for some nice, quiet, boresome dullness."

The time was past midnight and a silvery half-moon was rising when Jorian sighted a sprinkling of faint lights, far off to their left. He said: "Methinks that's Xylar City yonder. Tell our demon, hard to port! His deduced reckoning was off by half a league."

The tub changed course in obedience to the Mulvanian's mental command. Soon the lights grew and multiplied. Some came from the windows of houses; some from the oil lamps that Jorian, when king, had erected on posts at major street crossings. This was the city's first regular street lighting; before, citizens, unless rich enough to hire bodyguards and link boys, stayed home behind bolted doors at night.

"We must keep our voices down," whispered Jorian.

By whispered commands to Karadur, who passed them on mentally to Gorax, Jorian guided the tub to the royal palace. He circled the structure before coming close to the penthouse.

"No guards on the roof; good!" he murmured.

He brought the tub to a halt six cubits above the small square terrace at one end of the penthouse. While Karadur placed the tub just where Jorian wanted it, Jorian knotted one end of the rope around the faucet and dropped the rest over the side. He prepared to climb down.

"No sword?" whispered Karadur.

"Nay. It would clank, or bang the furniture, and give me away. If an alarum sound and the guards rush in, one sword were of no avail against several."

"In the epics," mused Karadur, "heroes are ever slaying a hundred fierce foes single-handed."

"Such tales are lies, as anyone who has done real sword fighting knows. Take a legendary hero like Dauric—but here I am talking when I should be acting."

"Your besetting weakness, my son. That runaway tongue will yet be our doom."

"Perhaps; but there are worse vices than garrulity. The reason I talk so much—"

"Jorian!" said Karadur with unusual vehemence. *"Shut up!"*

Silenced at last, Jorian went over the side and down the rope. The soles of his boots made scarcely a whisper as they touched the tiles of the terrace.

He stole to the door of the penthouse, feeling in his purse for his pick-locks. He had learned to use these implements during the year preceding his escape from Xylar. A wise woman had prophesied that Jorian was best fitted to be either king or a wandering adventurer. He had no special desire to be either, since his real ambition was to be a prosperous, respectable craftsman like his father, Evor the Clockmaker. But circumstances conspired to thrust him into these rôles willy-nilly.

Jorian had become King of Xylar by unintentionally catching the head of his predecessor when it was thrown from the execution scaffold. Since it was plain that he could not indefinitely continue as king in the face of the Xylarian law of succession, he had determined to be the ablest adventurer he could. So he had trained himself for the rôle as rationally and thoroughly as would any expert in science, art, or law.

He studied languages, practiced martial arts, and hired a group of rascals: a cutpurse, a swindler, a forger, a bandit, a cult leader, a smuggler, a black-mailer, and two burglars, to teach him their specialties. If the gods would not let him play the part of an indus-trious, law-abiding bourgeois, at least he would act the rôle they had forced upon him competently.

As it turned out, he did not, on this occasion, need his pick-locks, since the door was not locked. Jorian turned the knob, and the door opened with the faintest of squeals.

He well remembered the plan of the penthouse from the days when he had dwelt there. Each night he had one of his five wives sent to him. To allay jealousy, he companied with them in rotation. But the system broke down when one or more became ill or pregnant, and disputes arose over who should take the absent one's place. Finally Jorian settled the argument by saying that he was glad of a night or two off.

Now he found himself in the living room of the apartment. Before him, doors opened to two bedrooms, a bathroom, and the head of a stair leading down to the third story of the palace. In the mild air of an autumnal warm spell, the doors of the bedrooms stood open. One, Jorian supposed, contained Estrildis; the other her lady-in-waiting, whoever she was.

No light burned in these rooms, and little moonlight mitigated the darkness. Jorian wondered how to deter-mine which bedroom harbored which woman. It would not do to awaken the lady-in-waiting by mistake. He must tiptoe to the door of each room, peer in, and, if still in doubt, approach the bed closely enough to settle the question. While he did not know the lady-in-wait-ing, he hoped at least that she was a brunet, making it easy to distinguish her from the blond Estrildis.

He started toward the left-hand door and at once tripped over an unseen obstacle. He had assumed, without thinking much about the matter, that all the chairs and tables would be in the same places as when he had fled from Xylar. He had forgotten the womanly passion for rearranging the furniture.

The invisible object fell over with an apocalyptic crash. Jorian staggered and recovered, silently cursing a barked shin.

Before Jorian could take a step nearer the left-hand door, a terrific din of barks, growls, and snarls erupted from that bedroom. Jorian had a glimpse of the moon-lit, gleaming eyes and bared fangs of some beast bounding toward him.

Swordless, Jorian snatched up the chair he had stumbled over. He brought it up, legs pointing toward the charging watchdog. The animal fetched up against the chair, snapping at the legs, with a force that almost bowled Jorian over. When it fell back to the floor, it tried to circle round Jorian, who turned to keep the chair between himself and the dog.

Women's voices came from the bedrooms: "Who's there?" "Help!" "Who are you?" Then came the buzz of a wheel-lock lighter and a spark of light from the left-hand chamber.

A ghostly figure appeared at the door of the other bedroom. A woman's voice, unfamiliar to Jorian, cried, "Help! Help! Murder!" The woman rushed to the head of the stairway and vanished.

Estrildis, small, stocky, and blond, appeared at the door of the other bedroom, carrying a candle. Still holding off the dog, Jorian shouted: "Darling! It's Jorian! Call this beast off!"

"Oh!" shrieked the little queen. "What—where—come, Thöy! Come back! Come here, Thöy! Good dog! Come, Thöy!"

The dog, which the candlelight revealed as a huge Shvenic mastiff, backed off, growling. Seizing the dog's collar, Estrildis cried: "What do you here, Jorian? I did not expect—"

The cries of the lady-in-waiting came up the stair: "Help! Robbers! Murder! Save the Queen!"

"Sweetheart!" cried Jorian. "I've come to take you away. Come quickly, ere the guards arrive!"

"But how——"

"Never mind! Put down that candle and tie up the dog!"

"But I must know——"

"Damn it, woman, if you don't come instanter——"

A clatter of arms on the stair interrupted Jorian's plea. Men flooded into the living room, the candlelight striking golden gleams from their steel. "Get him!" roared a soldierly voice.

Jorian perceived three naked swords coming toward him, with reinforcements following. He ran out the door to the terrace. There he took three running steps and a flying leap to catch the dangling end of the rope as high up as he could.

"Karadur!" he shouted. "Take us up, fast!"

He began hoisting himself up the rope. The bathtub rose. Before the rope's end had cleared the terrace, a guardsman, putting his sword between his teeth, also caught the rope and began to climb.

The ascent of the tub slowed. On the terrace, other armed figures clustered. One caught the tip of the rope, but the end slipped out of his grasp.

Jorian looked down into the upturned face of the guardsman below him. He thought he recognized the upcurled mustache.

"You're Duvian, are you not?" said Jorian. "I'm Jorian; don't you know me?"

The guardsman, with the sword in his teeth, could only grunt. From below came cries: "Who has a crossbow?" "Well, fetch one, idiot!"

"You'd better let go," said Jorian. "If you are still there when we leave, I'll kick you loose or cut the rope above you. Then you will fall to your death."

The guardsman, holding the rope with his left hand

and with his legs clamped around it, took the sword in his right hand and swung it at Jorian's legs, saying: "'Tis my painful duty, O King!"

Jorian kicked, and the sword spun out of the guardsman's grasp. It struck the roof tiles, slid bumpily down the slope of the roof, disappeared over the edge, and landed with a crash on the paving below.

Jorian lowered himself on the rope and aimed another kick, at the guardsman's face. The kick missed, but the soldier relaxed his grip, slid down the rope to the end, and fell a few cubits to the terrace. He landed on one of his comrades, so that the two rolled on the terrace with a clashing of mail. Shouts of furious argument arose from the terrace, now dwindling beneath Jorian as the tub rose.

The jarring snap of a crossbow came up, and a bolt thrummed past. Jorian hoisted himself as fast as he could up to the tub and levered himself over the side. Another crossbow snapped, and a bolt hit the tub, making it ring like a bell. Jorian felt the side of the tub at the place whence the sound had come. His fingers found a bump where the bolt had dented the copper.

"Next thing," he panted, "they'll haul out a catapult. Tell Gorax to get us away with all demonic dispatch!"

"Whither?"

"To Othomae. Tell him to head east. As you said, we do have friends there."

Another crossbow quarrel hummed past below, but the tub was out of range. With the half-moon on their starboard bow, they flew eastward through the night. Jorian was silent, breathing deeply. Then he said:

"A plague, a murrian, and a pox on the Xylarians! By Imbal's brazen balls, I itch to burn their damned city down on their heads. What said your Mulvanian wiseacre about expecting the worst? I had the damnedest run of bad luck; Elidora must have it in for me. 'Twas like one of Physo's comedies. First I tripped over a chair in the dark. Then, Estrildis has somewhere obtained a watchdog the size of a lion, who knew me not. Then—"

"My son," moaned Karadur, "I pray you to reserve the tale till the morrow. I must needs get some sleep betwixt now and dawn. I cannot forgo rest as I could when I was your age."

The wizard curled up in his blanket and was soon snoring. When he calmed down, Jorian found he could smile at himself. He mentally composed a jingle:

> "A hero who wanted his wife
> To carry away without strife,
>     Fell over a chair,
>     With noise filled the air,
> And soon had to flee for his life!"

With nobody to listen to his tale of the abortive rescue, Jorian soon joined his companion in slumber.

# II

# The Grand Duke's Park

"Gorax insists he cannot persevere much longer," said Karadur, peering into the murk. After leaving Xylar City, they had flown all day and crossed the Othomaean border. The overcast thickened, and rain began to fall. Jorian and Karadur huddled in their cloaks. But the rain fell more and more heavily, soaking them. Water sloshed about the bottom of the tub.

"Have we nought to bail out our ship with?" quavered Karadur. "Gorax complains of the additional weight of the water."

"Now that you mention it," said Jorian, "the tub has an outlet drain with a plug. It should be under that rope."

He inched his way to the faucet end of the tub and pushed aside the coil of rope. The plug was a large cork, driven in so firmly that Jorian's powerful fingers could not dislodge it. He pried the plug out with his dagger, and the bilge water drained out. Night came on.

"I stated that Gorax nears his limit," said Karadur. "He avers that, if not soon permitted to alight, he will collapse and drop us from whatever height we be."

"Tell him to slow down," said Jorian. "I know this country well, but I cannot see my hand before my face, let alone landmarks. 'Tis blacker than the inside of a cow. By my reckoning, we should reach Othomae City in two or three hours."

"At least," said Karadur, "we shall not frighten the yokels below to death. As we cannot see them, neither can they perceive us."

Jorian laughed, "Remember that wagoner in Xylar, who leaped from his wain, ran across a field, and burrowed into a haystack to hide?"

"Aye. But your efficient secret service will hear thereof and know we departed to eastward."

"True. But methinks we shall be safe in Othomae. The Othomaeans are ever on bad terms with Xylar. 'Tis one of those silly things where a river changes course, leaving behind a sandbar that belonged to one nation, and now is claimed by another. The dispute had just arisen during my last days as king, so I had no chance to compose it. At any rate, I misdoubt the Othomaeans would extradite us."

"I hope you be right. A lavish bribe oft overrides such parochial passions."

"Then we must needs trust the Xylarian treasurer's parsimony. In my time the post was held by Prithio son of Pellitus, as tight with his golden lions as a Mulvanian tiger with its prey." Jorian peered into the murk, trying to discern some solid object. "Tell Gorax to fly low but slowly, so as not to collide with some tree or steeple. When the moon rises, belike we can find a road or a river to guide us."

Hours later, the rain had slackened to a drizzle. The moon, in its last quarter, gave a faint pearly glow to the clouds overhead. Time ground on.

Peering over the side, Jorian saw plowed fields and now and then a village, a cluster of black rectangles in the darkness. He failed to identify any landmark. Karadur said:

"Gorax avers he be fordone. He warns us to brace ourselves, for he must descend whether we will or no."

There was a feeling of lightness as the tub dropped. The darkness deepened as trees arose about them. With a slight jar, the tub settled on soft ground.

"He bids us farewell," said Karadur. "Know you where we be?"

"Somewhere in Othomae," said Jorian, "unless Gorax have flown us clear across the duchy into Vindium."

Jorian stood up, grunting at the stiffness of his limbs. The rain had ceased, but all around he heard the drip of water from branches.

He hoisted himself out of the tub. The ground seemed a green sward in a small clearing or glade, surrounded by huge trees. Jorian walked around the edges of the glade. Returning, he said:

"I still know not where we are. At least, let us wring the water from our clothes."

Standing in the tub, Jorian removed his garments and wrung them, holding them over the grass. He sneezed. "I hope," he grumbled, "they dry ere we freeze to death. . . . What's that?"

Something moved about the glade. Its footfalls were practically noiseless; but Jorian could see a darker shadow in the darkness and hear a faint hiss of breathing. Then something sniffed, close to the tub. Two spots of feeble luminosity, barely visible, appeared above the edge of the tub. Jorian recognized an odor.

He was sitting on the coil of rope at the faucet end of the tub. Suddenly he leaped up, waving his arms and uttering an earsplitting scream: "*Ye-ee-ow!*"

There was a spitting snarl and sounds of a body moving swiftly away. "A leopard, I think," said Jorian. "Are you all right, Father Karadur?"

The old wizard was gasping for breath. "Your screech well-nigh arrested my old heart for all eternity."

"Sorry, but I had to surprise the cat to get rid of it. The sky is lightening." Jorian felt his clothes; Karadur's were draped along the opposite side of the tub. "They're not yet dry, but we'd best do them on. The warmth of our bodies will dry them. How about a fire?"

"An excellent idea if feasible. With this all-pervading wet, I have doubts."

Jorian took out his lighter. "Plague! My tinder's wet,

and I see not how to get dry tinder. Would your magical fire spell work, think you?"

"If you will fetch fuel, I will essay it."

Soon Jorian had collected fallen branches and twigs. Standing in the tub, Karadur waved his wand, made mystic passes, and uttered words of power. A little blue flame appeared among Jorian's pile of fuel. The flame danced among the branches, now and then evoking a faint hiss; but the fuel would not ignite.

"Alas!" said Karadur. "We can do nought until our wood dries."

Jorian grunted. "I always thought magic was something one resorted to when material means failed; but wizardries seem to fail quite as often."

Karadur sighed. "My son, I fear you have penetrated the secret of secrets, the inmost arcanum."

"Meaning that all you spookers' professions of infinite powers are but a bluff to cozen us laymen?"

"True, alas. We fail as often as do the engineers in the House of Learning in Iraz. But I beseech you, reveal not this dread secret to the vulgus. We wizards have a hard enough time making a living."

Jorian grinned in the darkness. "Since you saved my life, old man, I'll keep your secret." He looked around. The light had grown strong enough to pick out twigs and leaves on trees, although the deciduous trees had lost most of their summer foliage. "By Astis' ivory breasts, what are those?"

To three of the trees surrounding the glade, wooden ladders had been affixed, reaching up until lost in the foliage. Jorian said: "I never heard of trees that grew ladders naturally. They must be the work of men."

"One can imagine erecting such ladders on fruit trees, to facilitate harvesting," said Karadur. "But these are nought but oaks, beeches, and lindens."

"There are beechnuts," said Jorian. "But two of the ladders I see go up oaks. Who would gather unripe acorns?"

"A breeder of swine, belike. But I am not convinced, when it were so much easier to pick them from the ground. Perchance the ladders lead to sentry posts, whence sentinels look out over the land to espy invaders."

"I never heard of aught like that when I served in the Grand Bastard's army," said Jorian. "But what other—oh-oh, Karadur, look behind you!"

The wizard turned and started in alarm. "A unicorn!" he breathed.

The head and forequarters of the animal appeared from out the shrubbery on one side of the glade. The unicorn of Jorian's world was no graceful pseudo-horse. Instead, it was a large member of the rhinoceros tribe, covered with golden-brown hair, with its single horn sprouting from its forehead, above the eyes, instead of its nose.

"If we keep still," whispered Jorian, "maybe he'll go away."

"I fear not," Karadur whispered back. "I detect emanations of rising rage. Methinks we had best prepare to make a dash for one of those ladders."

The unicorn gave an explosive snort, pawed the ground with a triple-hooved foot, and stepped forward.

Jorian murmured: "Soonest begun, soonest done, as said the wise Achaemo. Ready, set, go!"

He vaulted out of the tub and ran for a ladder across the glade from the beast. Karadur followed but, because of his age, fell behind. Jorian waited for him at the foot of the tree, calling: "'Faster! Here it comes!"

When the wizard, panting and staggering, reached the tree, Jorian put his large hands around Karadur's waist and boosted the slight oldster several steps up the ladder.

The unicorn made a thunderous charge, snorting like a volcano. It rushed the tub, jerking its head as its horn struck. With a loud *bongg*, the tub flew into the air, scattering the belongings of the two travelers.

"Up! Hasten!" barked Jorian, for the winded Karadur was climbing the ladder with difficulty. Below, Jorian was still in range of the thick, curved horn.

The unicorn lumbered back and forth about the glade, trampling the objects scattered about. It got Jorian's blanket caught on its horn and wheeled about, shaking its head so that the blanket flapped like a flag. When the blanket flew away, the unicorn charged the tub again, tossing it end over end.

Then the animal turned its attention to the travelers on the ladder. It trotted to the oak and tried by rearing up against the trunk to reach Jorian, but he was now beyond range of the horn.

Safely out of reach, Jorian and Karadur continued their climb at a more leisurely pace. When they reached a thick horizontal branch with many smaller boughs for handholds, Jorian climbed out on the branch and sat. Karadur nervously followed. Below, the unicorn cocked its head to keep them in sight.

"Something tells me," said Jorian, "that fellow likes us not. Anyway, I think I know where we are."

"Where?"

"When I served in the Grand Bastard's Foot Guards, there was talk of a plan the Grand Duke cherished. This was to unite his several hunting preserves south of Othomae City into a national park to exhibit wild life. Grand Duke Gwitlac was getting too old and fat to enjoy hunting; and the Grand Bastard Daunas, his half-brother, preferred the pursuit of women to that of deer and boar.

"In either case, they needed money to equip and train their lobster-plated heavy cavalry. So they reckoned that, by stocking the park with beasts both familiar and exotic, they could make a neat income by charging the rabble admission. Visitors would come from other lands to spend their money and thereby be taxed. Our friend below is one of the exotic beasts, since it is native to the northern prairies beyond the

Ellomas. Those ladders must have been emplaced for the purpose wherefor we used them, to escape the charge of some beast that misliked gawking visitors."

"All very well," said Karadur. "But how shall we persuade this dratted unicorn to begone?"

Jorian shrugged. "Sooner or later 'twill tire of watching us."

"If we weaken not from starvation and fall out of the tree first," grumbled the seer.

"Well, there was the method whereby King Fusinian escaped the Boar of Chinioc."

Karadur settled himself. "I thought I had heard all your tales of Fusinian the Fox, but this one I know not."

"When Fusinian was King of Kortoli," began Jorian, "he inherited a hunting preserve, like those of this Grand Duke. The preserve was called the Forest of Chinioc. Now, when Fusinian succeeded his father, the incompetent Filoman the Well-meaning, he was kept too busy for several years, what with the war with Aussar and the trouble with the giants called the Teeth of Grimnor, to have time for the Forest of Chinioc.

"After these events, Fusinian settled back to enjoy life, as far as any conscientious ruler can enjoy it despite the harassments of his position. Some of his gentlemen urged him to take up hunting in Chinioc, which, they said, was overrun by wild beasts. In particular, the forest harbored a wild boar of preternatural size, strength, and ferocity. As they described it, it sounded like a buffalo with tusks instead of horns, and the hangers-on filled Fusinian's ears with tales of the glory he would earn by slaying the beast, giving a feast with its flesh, and having its head stuffed and mounted on the palace wall.

"Fusinian did not much care for hunting, but he did like fishing. Moreover, he liked to get off by himself from time to time to mull over the stream of proposals, and bills, and acts, and requests, and treaties, and agreements, and petitions, and memorials constantly urged upon him. For such purposes, the sport of fishing was useful.

"So, one summer day, Fusinian set out with a bodyguard of four troopers and rode to the edge of the Forest of Chinioc. Here he left the troopers, commanding them to remain there unless he should fail to return by an hour before sunset, in which case they should come searching.

"The guards protested, warning the king against the bears, wolves, and leopards in the forest, not to mention the Boar of Chinioc. But Fusinian brushed aside their objections and set out along a trail which, he knew, led to a good trout stream. He bore a pair of fishing rods and a creel containing his luncheon, and he whistled gayly as he plunged into the wold.

"Ere he reached the stream, he heard a grunting, like that engine in the House of Learning in Iraz, whereby one of the servants hopes to get useful work by the power of steam. And then the Boar of Chinioc ambled out from between the trees. At the sight of Fusinian, the animal grunted, pawed the earth, and lowered its head to charge.

"The beast was not quite the size of a buffalo, but it was certainly large enough. The bristles on its back came up to the height of Fusinian's chin; and Fusinian had no arms save a knife for cleaning fish.

"As the monster bounded forward, the king dropped his fishing rods and sprang for the nearest tree, a big beech like that one yonder. Although a small man, he was wiry and active, and he scrambled up into the branches. Below, the boar reared up against the trunk; but it could not reach Fusinian, now perched on a branch as we are.

"Fusinian thought that, if he sat long enough, the boar would lose interest and go away. But hours passed, and the boar stubbornly remained below. Every time

Fusinian moved, the boar circled about, looking up and grunting ferociously.

"Fusinian began to worry about his guards and his wife and his kingdom, and he decided that he must escape in one way or another. He tried shouting, hoping his guards would hear; but they were too far away.

"He thought of other expedients, such as whittling a branch into a pole and tying his knife to it to make a spear. He actually cut one branch of about the right size for the purpose, but found it too limber. It would simply bend and break ere it drove a blade through the boar's thick hide.

"Next, he thought to make a diversion. He did off his hat, jerkin, and hose and constructed a dummy, using his fishhooks to pin these garments together and leafy branches for stuffing. Then he crept out along a branch and hung the dummy by means of his spare fishing line at such a height that the boar could not quite reach it.

"Creeping back, he shook the branch so that the dummy bobbed up and down and swayed from side to side. The boar, seeing what looked like Fusinian dancing in the air above it, went into a paroxysm of rage, snorting like a thunderstorm and leaping about beneath the dummy, striving to reach and slash it.

"Meanwhile Fusinian climbed down the tree on the side away from the boar and ran for his life. When he could no longer hear the thrashing and grunting of the boar, he stopped with the realization that he was lost.

"Steering by the sun, he headed back toward the edge of the Forest of Chinioc. In mid-afternoon, he came to a fence that marked the boundary. Continuing on, he found himself in cultivated fields; but he realized that he must be a long way from where he had entered the forest. The first person he saw was a farmer hoeing weeds. Approaching, he said: 'God den, goodman. May I—'

"At that, the farmer turned to shout toward his

house: 'Inogen! Run to fetch the constable! 'Tis a madman we have, running about the land naked!' For, indeed, Fusinian was naked but for his boots, underwear not having been in use in his time. Meanwhile the farmer ported his hoe like a weapon, in case Fusinian should come closer.

" 'My good man,' quoth Fusinian, 'you are mistaken—a natural error, belike, but a mistake natheless. Know that I am King Fusinian, your sovran lord. If you will be so kind as to lend me some garments—' Whereupon the rustic shouted louder than before: 'Inogen! Hasten! The madman is proclaiming himself king!'

"The farmer's wife ran out of the house, mounted a mule, and set out at a gallop. Fusinian tried to explain how he had fallen into this curious plight; but the more he talked, the more alarmed the rustic became, threatening Fusinian with his hoe until the king had to leap back to avoid being struck.

"Then came a clatter of hooves, and the farmer's wife reappeared on her mule, accompanied by a constable on horseback. The latter swung down with a jingle of mail and approached the king, saying: 'Easy, now, easy, fellow! Come with me to the lazarette, where our learned physicians will cure you. Come along, poor fellow!'

"The constable approached Fusinian and made a snatch at him, but the king leaped back and ran. The constable ran after, clanking and jingling, and so did the farmer. The farmer's two sons, just returning from school, joined the chase. So did other yokels. Soon Fusinian found himself pursued by a score of men and boys, some armed and all shouting: 'Seize the madman, ere he slay someone in his frenzy!'

"A swift runner, Fusinian long kept ahead of the pursuit. But, as one pursuer became winded and dropped back, another joined the chase, so that in time the little king faltered. Then men on horseback galloped up on either side of him, one being the constable whom the farmer's wife had summoned. So Fusinian stopped, holding up his hands to show he was harmless. Between gasps, he tried once more to explain, but none heeded his words.

"Instead, someone knotted a rope around his neck and gave the other end to the constable, who said: 'Now, poor fellow, ye shall come along whether ye will or no.' The constable turned his horse away and tugged on the rope, so that Fusinian was forced to trot along. And thus, at sunset, they came to the nearest village, called Dimilis.

"They fetched the magistrate, who arrived at the jail-house much put out by having to leave his dinner half-eaten. When he had heard the stories of the first farmer and the constable, he asked Fusinian: 'And what have ye to say, my featherless fowl?'

"Fusinian said: 'Your Honor, it is true that I am King Fusinian.'

"'Hah!' said the magistrate. "A likely story! Where are your crown, your robes of state, your train of attendants? Forsooth, we have here not merely insanity but also high treason. Clap this knave in irons!'

"'Your Honor!' quoth Fusinian. 'To prove my veracity, I can recite the coronation oath. I can list the ancestors of the royal line for fifteen generations. Fetch someone who knows me! Send word to the court!' But no heed did anyone pay.

"None knows how much further this farce would have gone, but just then two of Fusinian's guardsmen appeared, demanding news of their King. When they saw Fusinian, laden with chains, being led off to a cell, they dropped to one knee, crying: 'Your Majesty! What scoundrels have entreated you thus? Command us to slay them!'

"A great silence fell amongst the folk gathered in the jailhouse. Each tried to look as if he had just happened by on other business and knew nought of the dispute over the naked man's identity. Each tried to hide behind his fellows, and some of those near the door tiptoed out and ran for it, until one of the guardsmen blocked the door.

"Fusinian smiled through the dirt wherewith he was covered, saying: 'Hail, Baldolf and Cumber! Am I glad to see you! How came you so opportunely?'

"A guardsman spoke: 'Your Majesty, when the sun stood a hand's breadth from the horizon, we followed your trail into the forest. Soon we saw what we thought was Your Majesty hanged from a branch of a tree, which gave us a frightful shock; but we found this was merely Your Majesty's garments stuffed with brush. Although we could not imagine the reason for this, we agreed that two of us should continue to search the forest, whilst the other two hastened to Dimilis and spread the alarum for our King's disappearance.'

" 'I will explain,' said Fusinian, but at that moment the magistrate and all the other local folk fell on their knees and groveled, crying: 'Mercy, Great King! We meant no harm! We thought but to do our duty! We have wives and children! Mercy, we beseech thee!'

" 'Get up!' said Fusinian sharply. 'To say I am pleased by today's events were stretching the truth; but I do not massacre my subjects, however idiotically they comport themselves. Magistrate Colgrin! For your haste in passing judgment ere the evidence be in, I will levy a small fine upon you. You shall remove your jacket and trews and give them to me, instanter!'

"So pleased was the magistrate to get away with his life that he stripped off the garments and handed them over forthwith, leaving himself naked but for his shoes and chain of office. Fusinian donned the garments, which fitted him ill since Colgrin was fat. With his two guards, the king strode out of the jailhouse, mounted his horse—which the guards had led with them—and galloped away. But thereafter Fusinian was more cautious about leaving his guards and going off by himself."

Karadur said: "An edifying tale, showing how our

perceptions of rank and authority are swayed by super-
ficial things. But our unicorn shows no disposition to
depart, and I misdoubt we could distract it as your king
did with the boar."

Jorian put a finger to his lips, whispering: "I hear
voices." The voices waxed, and a swishing of branches
told of the movement of a large body. The unicorn
looked across the glade and snorted.

Out from the trees lumbered an elephant, a huge
Mulvanian tusker with people on its back. As the animal came closer, Jorian saw that a broad plank was
secured lengthwise along its spine. Eight people sat on
this plank in two rows, back to back, with their feet
resting on footboards along the elephant's sides. A turbaned Mulvanian sat astride the elephant's neck and
guided the beast.

One rider was a man in an unfamiliar uniform, who
was lecturing the seven others on the plank. In a sten-
torian voice, this man said: "There you see a unicorn
from the steppes of Shven. Its scientific name is *Elas-
motherium*, and the philosophers tell us it is related to
the rhinoceros of Beraoti. Although a grass-eater, it is
short-tempered and dangerous if approached on
foot. . . ."

The unicorn turned and trotted away from the glade.
Jorian quickly lost sight of it. A young elephant-rider
called out: "Master Ranger, what's that red thing yonder?" The child pointed to the battered bathtub.

The ranger spoke to the mahout, who guided the
elephant toward the tub and the debris of Jorian's and
Karadur's belongings. The ranger said: "By Zevatas'
brazen beard, what's this? It looks as if some vagabonds
had camped here and departed leaving their litter.
There is punishment for littering. But what's this
object? It looks like a large bathtub, but how could
such a thing get here?"

The child spoke again: "Master Ranger, there are your vagabonds, sitting in that big tree!"

"Oho!" said the ranger. He spoke to the mahout, who brought the elephant to stand beneath the branches of Jorian's tree. "Fry my guts, but here we have a brace of poachers, caught red-handed! But the game they flushed proved larger than they expected."

"Excuse me, sir," said Jorian, "but you are misinformed. We are not poachers, merely a pair of travelers dropped into your park by happenstance."

"A likely story!" The ranger turned to his sightseers. "Now you shall behold how we of the Ranger Corps dispose of such knaves." He raised a bugle to his mouth and blew a call. The call was answered from afar.

"How got you in?" the ranger asked. "You did not come in the gate and sign the register, or you would not be wandering the park unescorted. Your presence alone proves your guilt."

Jorian pointed to the bathtub, lying across the glade. "We came in yonder tub, upheld by sorcery. When our demon became exhausted, he dropped us into this glade. Since it was at night, we knew not where we were."

"Ha!" said the ranger. "Try to convince the judge of that!"

"Good my sir," persisted Jorian, "we are quite respectable folk, despite appearances. I have served in the Grand Bastard's Foot Guards and studied at the Academy. If you will ask Doctor Gwiderius—"

"You waste your breath, poacher," said the ranger. "If you shut not your gob, 'twill be the worse for you."

After a further wait, three rangers on horses cantered out from between the trees. After talk between them and the one on the elephant, the latter spoke to his mahout, and the elephant started off into the forest. Jorian could hear the ranger's voice, fading with distance:

". . . the unicorn is an animal of solitary habits, keeping company with another of its kind only at the mating season. . . ."

Of the three newly arrived rangers, two bore crossbows. The third, who appeared to be in command, said: "Come down now, poachers. But think not to run off through the woods, unless you crave a bolt in the brisket."

"May we gather our belongings, pray?" said Jorian, reaching the ground.

"Aye, but be quick about it!"

Half an hour later, Jorian and Karadur arrived at the park entrance. Some of their belongings, such as Jorian's set of small cooking utensils, had been smashed beyond repair. The rest were rolled up in blankets, which they bore on their backs like refugees.

Another elephant was being prepared for a sightseeing trip. It lay on its belly, and the next batch of sightseers was climbing a ladder placed against its side to take their places on its back. Several more of the animals were tethered to stakes in a row, rhythmically swaying and stuffing greenery into their mouths.

The two travelers were surrounded by rangers, disarmed, and hustled into a small detention room. "Here you shall wait, poachers," a ranger said, "until Ranger Ferrex returns from his tour."

The door was slammed and bolted on the outside. A bench was the only furniture; the only light came from a little window high up, about a handspan square.

"Now I know how your King Fusinian felt when none would listen to his rational explanation," said Karadur. "Could you open the door with your pick-locks?"

"If it were closed by a proper lock, yea; but my little teasers were useless against bolts."

During the wait, Jorian relieved his boredom by composing a poem on their latest misadventure. The first stanza ran:

"Two gallant adventurers, hardy and bold,
     To Othomae endeavored to fly;
But their demon gave out o'er the Grand Ducal wold,
     So now in the lockup they cry!"

Jorian had reached the fifth stanza when the door opened. Ranger Ferrex beckoned. "Come, poachers!"

They were handcuffed together, taken to a wagon with seats, and loaded aboard with their gear. Ranger Ferrex got in and sat facing them. The driver whipped up the horses. The wagon rattled over the dirt road for an hour, passing fields and villages, until Othomae City appeared on the horizon.

On the way, Jorian and Karadur conversed in Mulvanian. This made Ferrex scowl, but he did not try to stop them. They agreed that Jorian might as well give his true name, since he wanted to get in touch with people he knew.

At the jailhouse, the ranger told his story to the magistrate, Judge Flollo, and Jorian repeated the tale he had told the ranger. The magistrate said:

"I cannot let you out on bail, since as foreigners you have no local ties to assure your appearance for trial. You profess to have used sorcery to come hither; but if you be sorcerers, you could summon another demon or work spell with your sorcerous implements and escape."

"But Your Honor!" protested Jorian. "If we be sorcerers, then our tale is proven true. Hence we cannot be poachers."

"Nought hinders a sorcerer from trying his hand at poaching, if that be his bent." The magistrate hefted Jorian's purse and poured out its load of coins. "A veritable fortune! Whence got you this money? Have you robbed a royal treasury?"

"Not robbed, Your Honor. It's a long story. As you

see, the coins are of the Kingdom of Penembei, where I was employed to repair the clocks in the tower—"

"Never mind. The money shall be sequestered and returned to you, minus the cost of your prison victuals, when and if you are acquitted of the charge of poaching."

"But, Your Honor, if I be so well provided, I had no need to sit out in the rain all night in hope of snaring a hare. Let me tell you how—"

"I cannot take time to hear your tale, prisoner; I have many more cases to decide. Your presence unescorted in the park is *prima facie* evidence of wrongdoing; so whether your story be true or false will be for the trial judge to decide. Take them away, bailiff."

"Come, you two," said a heavyset, scar-faced man in a shabby black uniform. Jorian and Karadur were led down a corridor to another cell. This, Jorian found, had a single, heavily barred window, high up. As the bailiff closed the door, he said: "Did I hear you give your name as Jorian of Ardamai?"

"Aye. What about it?"

"Do ve not recall a fellow soldier named Malgo?"

"Yea, now that you mention it." Jorian looked sharply at the bailiff. "By Imbal's iron yard, methinks I see my old comrade-in-arms!"

"Comrade, hell!" snorted Malgo. "Ye be the bastard who gave me a beating. And now I have you where I want you! Ye'll be sorry ye ever laid a finger on me!"

"But that was seven years ago—" began Jorian. Malgo walked heavily away, paying no attention.

"What was all that?" asked Karadur.

"When Malgo and I were recruits in the Grand Bastard's army, Malgo was the company bully. He made life especially hard for one lad who, whatever he was good for, was not cut out for a soldier. He was a spindly little whelp and awkward, forever stepping off on the wrong foot or dropping his pike. So Malgo took delight in tormenting him.

"One day I found the lad backed into a corner, while Malgo poked, pinched, and otherwise mistreated him, all the while telling him how worthless he was. I suspected that Malgo had made certain demands of the youth and had been denied. Thinking it time for Malgo to receive a dose of his own physic, I hauled him round and gave him a drubbing. I got a bloody nose and a black eye, but you should have seen him!"

"All very gallant," said Karadur, "but it redounds not to our advantage now. Would we had used one of your pseudonyms, such as—what did you call yourself when you first fled hither from Xylar?"

"Nikko of Kortoli. You may be right, but it's too late now."

During the following days, Bailiff Malgo, while careful to keep out of Jorian's reach, found ingenious ways to torment the prisoners. He made sure that their food ration was but half that of the other prisoners, and consisted of the least edible parts of the day's serving. The food was delivered by Malgo's assistant, a huge, half-witted youth with a vacant smile.

When Jorian demanded to see the magistrate to complain, Malgo said he would carry the message. Soon he came back, saying that the magistrate refused. Jorian suspected that the message had never been delivered.

When Jorian asked for water, Malgo fetched a cup, then poured it on the floor outside the cell, laughing.

Jorian asked for writing materials, to send a note to Doctor Gwiderius and another to the wizardess Goania. Malgo furnished paper and pen. When Jorian had written the notes and handed them through the bars, Malgo tore them up, laughing.

Malgo refused to let his helper take out and empty the commode, so that the cell came to stink. The stench attracted swarms of flies. Malgo sometimes stood in the hall outside, laughing at the prisoners' efforts to slap the pests. "Let's hope this lasts not till next summer's heat," grumbled Jorian.

At last Jorian said: "Holy Father, can't you work up a spell to get us out of here?"

"Nay, my son. The little spells I could perform without my paraphernalia would accomplish nought. Besides, I sense that a contraspell has already been laid about this edifice, so that none of my spells would succeed. How about your pick-locks? The locks on these cells, meseems, are of the sort for which they are suited."

"Aye, but my little ticklers are in my wallet, which is in the magistrate's custody."

"He also has my magical accessories in his charge."

"This is ridiculous!" growled Jorian. "Here we are, two harmless travelers with local friends of influence and repute, locked up through a series of mischances, and we cannot even communicate with anyone who could help us!"

"If we shouted our message through yonder window, belike we could persuade someone to carry a message."

Jorian clapped a hand to his forehead. "Why didn't I think of this sooner? I'm a stupid clod. We've wasted a quarter-moon in this stinking cell. If I stand on one of the stools. . . ."

The stool brought Jorian's face up to the window. He found himself looking down from the second story of the jailhouse on to the street below.

"Methinks we're on Amaethius Street," he told Karadur. "There are a few passersby. Ho there, young man! You with the red cap! Wouldst earn a golden royal of Penembei by bearing a message?"

The boy hurried on. Jorian tried again and again with other pedestrians. At last he gave up. "They must be so used to hearing cries from prisoners that they heed them not."

A raucous laugh came from beyond the bars. Malgo stood there, saying: "Waste your breath if ye will, noble

Jorian! Know that there's a law against carrying messages for prisoners, and we keep an officer posted to see that none flouts the rule."

Jorian got down. When Malgo went away, Jorian said: "Still, there must be something." He sat frowning in thought and said at last: "Some have said that I have not a bad singing voice, albeit untrained. If I gave the folk below a little concert, at a regular hour each day, perchance I could draw a crowd who would gather to hear. Sooner or later the word would get out, and one of our friends would hear of it."

"I cannot see how it would hurt to try," said Karadur.

Jorian hoisted himself back on the stool and, in his powerful bass, began singing one of his jingles, to a tune from an operetta by Galliben and Silfero. The first stanza ran:

"Oh, some like the steaming jungle hot,
Where serpents swarm and the sun shines not,
And sweat runs off and your garments rot;
But I prefer a more temperate spot—
        Novaria, my Novaria."

By the end of the third stanza, a cluster of pedestrians had coagulated in the street below, staring up. Malgo appeared outside the bars, roaring: "Stop that hellish noise!"

Jorian grinned over his shoulder at the bailiff and continued on through the six stanzas he had previously composed. He added a new one:

"Some take to the ice-clad arctic waste,
Where man by the snow bear fierce is faced,
Or else by ravenous wolves is chased;
But as for me, I'd return in haste
        To Novaria, good Novaria."

Malgo continued to bawl objections, but he did not enter the cell. Jorian added several other songs, then stepped down. "It's a start," he said.

He spent the rest of the day and much of the night remembering the verses he had casually tossed off over the years and trying to match them to tunes he remembered. The following afternoon, at about the same time, he delivered another recital. Malgo shouted: "For this, I'll see to it ye never go free! Ye shall rot here for ay!"

Jorian ignored the threat and continued his singing. On the sixth day after the first recital, the half-wit appeared at the bars with keys. To Jorian's astonishment, the youth unlocked the cell door, saying: "Ye come, now."

They found Magistrate Flollo talking with Doctor Gwiderius. The professor beamed through his bushy gray beard. "Jorian! My onetime pupil! When I heard those songs with the quadruple-alpha rhyme scheme, I suspected 'twas you, since that was your favorite form despite its difficulties. You are free, and there are your effects. Who is your companion?"

Jorian introduced Karadur, adding: "What—how—"

"I shall tell you later. Have you a place to stay? I cannot lodge you in my own house, because we have visiting kinfolk."

Jorian shrugged. "I suppose I'll stay at Rhuys' inn, the Silver Dragon, as I did before." He turned to the magistrate. "Sir, where is Master Malgo?"

"Oh, when Doctor Gwiderius brought the order for your release, the bailiff was seized by sudden pains internal. Avouching that he suffered an affliction of the bowels, he begged the rest of the day off. So I let him go. Why, Master Jorian?"

Jorian looked at the knuckles of his fist. "Oh, I just thought I should like to bid him a fond farewell." He turned to Gwiderius. "Where's the public bathhouse?"

# III

# The Inn of the Silver Dragon

Jorian said: "Good Master Rhuys, I, too, am glad to see you again. I trust the dinner will make a pleasant contrast to those I've enjoyed as a guest of the Grand Duchy."

"I heard of your trouble with the park rangers," said Rhuys. The proprietor of the Silver Dragon was a small, seedy-looking man with thinning, graying hair and pouched eyes.

Jorian, Karadur, and Doctor Gwiderius occupied a table in Rhuys's common room, drinking wine and telling tales while awaiting their repast. Jorian had sent one of Rhuys's pot boys with a message to the wizardess Goania, whom he had met on his previous visit to Othomae. He said to Gwiderius:

"But Doctor, you haven't explained how you got me out so featly."

The learned man chuckled. "I have a cousin named Rodaus, a usurer by trade. This cousin owed me a favor for giving his mediocrity of a son a passing grade in one of my courses at the Academy. The Grand Bastard seeks a loan from Rodaus, and they have disputed the rate of interest."

"To finance his armored horse, belike?" said Jorian. In Othomae, the Grand Duke ran civil affairs, while the Grand Bastard, the eldest illegitimate son of the previous Grand Duke, commanded the army.

"No doubt. Anyway, I passed the word to Rodaus, assuring him that, knowing you from yore, I was sure your release were no injustice. So Rodaus, in return for a promise to drop all charges, let the noble Daunus have his loan for half a percentum point less than he had demanded."

Nodding toward Karadur, Jorian smiled. "My dear old preceptor insists that all decisions be made on a basis of abstract, impersonal right and wrong. But I note that in sore straits, he lets expediency rule his course, even as we common clods." He counted the money in his purse. "By Imbal's brazen arse, they forgot to deduct the cost of my food in jail!"

"They forgot not," said Gwiderius. " 'Twas part of the bargain."

Jorian was volubly thanking the savant when the door opened, and in came the wizardess Goania, a tall, middle-aged woman with graying hair. After her came her bodyguard, a big, gross, porcine man. Following him, a tall, black-haired young woman in a grass-green gown came in. She was not beautiful, but striking-looking, with the lines of a hard life graven on her irregular features. She bore a black eye.

Jorian rose. "Hail, Mistress Goania!" he called. "Ah there, Boso and Vanora! How wag your worlds?"

The stout man growled something in a surly tone. The young woman cried: "Jorian! How good to see you again!" She hurried over to embrace Jorian, who showed no great eagerness to respond. Two years before, just after his escape from Xylar, he had engaged in a brief and stormy love affair with Vanora, who then became the companion of the piggy-eyed Boso son of Triis. She and Boso sat down by themselves at a small table across the common room.

"Now, Jorian," said Goania Aristor's daughter, in the tone of an aunt setting a wayward nephew to rights, "sit down and tell all. What's this wild tale of your rolling into the ducal park in a tub on wheels, and there slaying the Grand Duke's prize unicorn?"

Jorian laughed. "It wasn't like that, albeit what truly befell us was quite as strange." He plunged into the story of his escape from Iraz in the demon-borne tub, his failure to abduct Estrildis, and his unwitting landing in the park. When he told of his imprisonment, Gwiderius said:

"I am shocked, Jorian! Prison management was supposed to have been reformed; I was on the committee to make recommendations to the Grand Duke. But I see things have slipped back into their usual rut. True, persons like this bailiff are not always of highest character, but we cannot permit such persecution of one who is not even tried! I shall get word of this to His Grace."

Jorian thought a moment and said: "Thanks, but you had better let the matter lie, Doctor. If I meet Malgo alone, I may take him on at fisticuffs; but meanwhile the less I'm involved with the ducal court the better. Someone might get the idea of selling me to the Xylarian Regency for enough to equip another squadron of lancers."

Rhuys served their dinners. Later, Jorian said: "Let's talk of how I shall get my darling Estrildis out of her gilded cage. I cannot raise an army to besiege the city, and our flying bathtub is out of service. What else can be had in flying spells?"

"Well," said Karadur, "there is Sir Fendix's flying broom, and Antonerius' tame wyvern, and Coel's spell, whereby he changes himself into a vulture. But all have shortcomings. Fendix has twice been nearly slain when his broom went out of control; it is subject to something he terms a 'tailspin.' The wyvern is but half domesticated and may yet devour Antonerius at one gulp. And Coel is said to have sold his soul into a thousand years' bondage on the Third Plane in return for his shape-changing power. Nay, I see no good prospect for another aerial assault. Besides, the Xylarians will have posted guards on the roof."

"Then we should need more than just me," said Jorian. "I wonder—"

Goania spoke up: "Meseems the Xylarians, fearing

another raid from the air, would have moved your queen to some less-exposed place."

Jorian grunted. "You make sense as usual, my dear aunt. How shall we find out?"

"Leave it to me," said the wizardess. "Is this tabletop clean? Good. I shall probe the Xylarian palace. You!" she spoke to a pot boy. "Fetch me a clean towel, pray."

With the towel she wiped the inside of her empty wine glass. Then she dropped a pinch of green powder into the glass. She muttered an incantation, whereupon the powder smoldered and sent up a thread of purple smoke.

"Break not one of Rhuys's best glasses!" said Jorian.

"Hush, boy!" She leaned over the glass and inhaled. For some moments she sat with her eyes closed. Then she muttered:

"It is dark . . . nay, there is a light, a yellow light . . . the light of an oil lamp. . . . I am in an underground chamber . . . there is a door with iron bars. The walls are of rough stone, as in a cell or dungeon . . . but there are hangings on the walls and a carpet on the floor, as if the place had been made more comfortable . . . I see a small, blond woman, seated at what appears to be a dressing table . . . she seems to be sewing. The scene blurs, as if some force were pushing my second sight away. All over!"

She took deep breaths and opened her eyes. Jorian said: "Me-thinks I know where she is, in the largest cell of our dungeon. But how shall I gain access thereto?"

"Has the palace no secret tunnels?" asked Gwiderius. "Palaces and castles ofttimes possess them, to let the chief man escape if the stronghold falls to a foe."

"Nay," said Jorian. "I investigated when I was king, since such an exit would have let me flee their beheading ceremony. But though I prowled the lower parts of the palace, tapped the walls, and consulted the oldest plans of the edifice, no trace of an escape tunnel could I find. It had been futile to ask the Xylarians to dig me one, since their efforts were devoted to thwarting my escape."

"Could one dig such a tunnel from the outside and bore through the cell wall with miner's tools?" asked Goania.

"Conceivable but not likely. One would have either to start outside the city, or take a house inside and bore down through the floor and then on a level until one reached the palace. Such a task would take months, and I doubt if I could remain undetected so long. For example, one would have to dispose of the dirt dug from the tunnel without arousing suspicion. Since Xylar City is built on soft, alluvial soil, one must bring in timber to line one's tunnel and shore it up, lest it collapse on one.

"Then how could one be sure of reaching the right underground chamber? With but a slight error in deduced reckoning, one might break into the armory or the treasury instead of Estrildis' chamber. And wherever one broke in, it would be a noisy process, which would alert the guards.

"Finally, unless the Xylarian spy system have deteriorated since my day, any such doings would soon come to the ears of the Regency Council. And then. . . ." Jorian brought the edge of his hand sharply against his neck.

"What then?" said Karadur.

"Since the Xylarians have blocked the avenues to direct assault, I suppose we must resort to magic. What can our professionals of the occult offer?"

Goania and Karadur exchanged glances. The wizardess said: "Alas, I am more a seer than a thaumaturge or sorcerer. I have no means of getting your lass out of an underground cell."

"Couldn't you," Jorian asked Karadur, "somehow recall Gorax from the Fifth Plane?"

"Nay, my son. My sorcerous powers are straitly limited. I obtained control of Gorax through a colleague,

Doctor Valdonius, whom you remember from Tarxia. I saved him from a magical predicament, and in gratitude he transferred Gorax, whom he had evoked, to me and imprisoned the demon in this ring."

"How about other demons?"

Karadur shrugged. "Nay; 'tis not my specialty."

Jorian growled: "My two great magical experts seem to have proven a rope of sand. Know you one whom you would trust for such an operation?"

Gwiderius spoke: "One of my fellow pedants at the Academy, Doctor Abacarus, might help."

"What is his line of work?"

"He is professor of occult philosophy, and I believe he performs sorcerous experiments on the side. If you wish, I will present you to him."

"I do wish, thank you," said Jorian. "The sooner the better."

Karadur yawned. "Forgive me, gentles, for interrupting this congenial evening; but an old man wearies fast. I shall withdraw, leaving the rest to enjoy—"

"Karadur!" said Goania. "You shan't remain here tonight. I would fain discuss a new method of astral projection with you; so you shall pass the night at my house."

Jorian spoke up: "Well, Mistress Goania, if you are taking Doctor Karadur—"

"I cannot also accommodate you, young sir," she said sharply. "For one, there is not enough room; for two, the doctor threatens not my repute, whereas a lusty, young springald like you indubitably would. Come along, Karadur. Come, Boso and Vanora. Good night all!"

She swept out, followed by the others. Gwiderius soon excused himself also.

Jorian had just gotten his boots off when there came a knock. "Who is it?" he asked.

"I, Vanora. Pray let me in!"

Jorian unbarred the door. She entered, saying: "Oh, Jorian, how good it is to see you again! What a fool I was not to have kept my grip on you when I had you!"

"Whence got you that black eye?" asked Jorian.

"Boso gave it. We had a dispute this morn."

"The bastard! Do you want me to give him one?"

"Nay. So long as I'm his leman, I must betimes endure his fist."

"What caused it?"

"Forsooth, 'twas not wholly his fault, for I had sorely provoked the lout."

Having received some of Vanora's provocations in the past, Jorian understood this. He even felt a twinge of sympathy for Boso. "How did you get away?"

"Oh, Boso's asleep, and my mistress and your Mulvanian spooker are so deep in magical converse that they never noticed as I slipped out." She put on the pleading look that Jorian had seen before. "Know you what night this is?"

Jorian frowned. "It is the last day of the Bear, is it not?"

"Aye. But does it mean aught to you?"

Jorian looked puzzled. "Nought special. Should it?"

"It was just two years ago that we parted in Othomae, when I took up with that brute Boso."

"So it is; but what of that?"

She moved closer. "Wilt not let a poor drabby correct her error?" She grasped Jorian's hand and drew it inside her gown, so that he grasped her right breast, while looking up at him with slightly parted lips.

Jorian felt a familiar stirring in his tissues. But he said: "My dear Vanora, that is over and done with." Although his pulse quickened, he withdrew his hand. "I'll have no more of those games until I get my own wife back."

"Now, forsooth! Since when have you become a holy anchorite? You were lusty enough two years ago, and at your age you cannot blame senility. Sit down!"

She gave him a sudden push, so that he sat down on the edge of the bed. She undid a clasp, dropped the emerald-green gown around her feet, sat down in Jorian's lap, and began to kiss and fondle him, murmuring: "Then you were the most satisfying of all my lovers, stiff as a sword blade and hardy as Mount Aravia. Oh, my true love, take me back! For two years I have yearned for the feel of your love, penetrating—"

"Get off!" he said sharply. In another moment, he knew, he would cast good resolutions to the winds, although he knew that Vanora would bring him nothing but trouble. As Goania had told him once, Vanora had the unfortunate talent of not only being chronically unhappy herself but of making those around her unhappy as well. "If you get not to your feet, I'll stand up and dump you on the floor!"

Pouting, she stood up but remained swaying nakedly before him. "What has changed, Jorian? Are you having one of your sudden attacks of virtue? You know it will pass."

Jorian looked up at her, secretly happy that he had not been compelled to stand up. This would, under the circumstances, have been difficult, "Nay; I merely resolved to do what I promised myself. Call it exercising my strength of character, if you wish; like lifting weights to enlarge one's thews."

"Why all that pain and trouble? Since the wizard Aello discovered a really effective contraceptive spell, nobody—well, hardy anybody—heeds all those old rules about who may bed whom any more."

"A philosopher at the Academy told me that our present promiscuity is but a fad that comes and goes, like fashions in hats or cloaks. Anyway, I remember you as careless with your contraceptive spells."

"Well, I've never gotten pregnant yet. Of course, were you the father, I might not mind. . . ."

Jorian was of several minds: to lay her on the bed and have at her; to push her out of the room and throw her dress after her. . . . Each course had its perils. If he treated her roughly, she might make trouble between him and Goania; he did not underestimate her capacity for stirring up quarrels. Or she might incite Boso to assault him. While he did not fear Boso, he did not want either complication, for such hostilities would interrupt his quest for Estrildis.

He fumbled for an excuse that would send her away disappointed perhaps, but not bent on revenge. At last his storytelling talent rescued him. He said:

"Sit on yonder chair, my dear, and I'll tell you what has changed. You remember my adventure on Rennum Kezymar, when I saved those twelve slave girls from the retired executioners of Ax Castle?"

"Aye. That was a noble deed, worthy of my Jorian."

"Thank you; but I have not told you half the story. As the *Talaris* sailed toward Janareth, the girls were naturally grateful at not being used to demonstrate those fellows' skills at flaying, blinding, beheading, and other quaint specialties of the executioner's art. The first night out from the island, one of the girls—I think her name was Wenna—came to my berth to show her gratitude, and I did not deny her.

"Next day, about noon, this Wenna was seized by horrible pains and convulsions. Within an hour, for all that Doctor Karadur could do, she was dead. We buried the poor little thing at sea.

"The following night, another girl came to me, and again I sought to pleasure her. And again, the following day, she was seized by cramps and convulsions and died. We wept as her body was committed to the deep.

"These sad events aroused a lively suspicion that there was a connection betwixt their carnal congress with me and their untimely fates. So Doctor Karadur performed a great conjuration. When he came out of his trance, he had located the source of the trouble. The executioners, such as were left after their free-for-all battle, were naturally incensed when they found I had carried off the slaves whereon they meant to monstrate their skills at the banquet. The wife of one, Karadur discovered, was a witch. At her husband's behest, she put a curse upon me, so that any dame with whom I copulated would die within twelve hours.

"Now, Vanora dear, if you wish to take a chance that the curse have lost its potency, let's have at it. But say not that I failed to warn you!"

She looked at him slantwise. "That flapping tongue of yours was always fertile in expedients," she said, "I know not whether to believe you. At Metouro you were ready enough."

"I was a little drunk and had forgotten the curse. Besides, your beauty had driven all other thoughts out of my head."

"Hm; I see you're still as smooth-tongued a flatterer as any courtier. Well, how about Estrildis? If the curse be true, her demise will soon follow your reunion."

"Oh, I won't touch Estrildis, even if I can get her out of Xylar, until the curse be lifted. Karadur is sure that he and Goania can devise an effective counterspell."

"I still think you're lying your head off."

"There's an easy way to find out," said Jorian, standing up and unlacing his shirt. "If that is what you want. . . ." He pulled off his breeches.

"I see that not all of you has turned ascetic," she said.

"Who said it had? If you're fain to take a chance, lie down and spread out."

She hesitated, then stooped and picked up her dress. "Nay, you're as hard to grasp as a greased eel. What befell the remaining girls?"

"I sent them home from Janareth. Well, wilt chance it nor not? I cannot maintain this stance all night."

With a sigh she slipped on her dress. "Nay, I will not. I had but thought. . . . But never mind. Boso may be a brute, but all his members are in working order, without curses save that of stupidity. Good night."

Jorian watched her go with a wry smile and a mixture of relief and regret. It took all his strength not to call her back and confess that the story was a lie. Actually, he had not carnally known any of the twelve slave girls until the night before they parted in Trimandilam. Then Mnevis, the leader, had insinuated herself into his bed without encouragement from him.

He had not told Vanora of his passing off Mnevis and the others at the court of Trimandilam as the Queen of Algarth and her ladies-in-waiting. He was already on the Mulvanians' grudge list for his theft of the Kist of Avlen. He did not wish to give Vanora information that she might, in a fit of malevolence, use against him. Naturally a frank, open, cheerful soul, with a tendency to talk too much and indiscreetly, he was learning caution the hard way.

Doctor Abacarus proved a bald, fat, clean-shaven, red-faced man with a high voice. He reminded Jorian of the eunuchs he had encountered in Iraz; but Gwiderius had told Jorian that Abacarus had children of his own.

Sitting at a desk in the Academy, the philosopher made a steeple of his fingers, saying: "You wish me to evoke a demon and compel it to bring your wife forth from an underground cell in Xylar?"

"Aye, sir. Canst do it?"

"I believe so."

"What would that cost?"

Abacarus made notes on a waxed tablet with a stylus. After calculating, he said: "I'll undertake the task for fifteen hundred Othomaean nobles. I cannot guarantee success; I can only promise to do my best."

Jorian suppressed a temptation to whistle. "Let me borrow your tablet, Doctor. Let's see; in Penembian royals that would be. . . ." He calculated and looked glumly at Karadur. "Had I but known, I'd have fetched a whole tubful of gold from Iraz."

"Gorax could not have borne the weight," Karadur protested.

"Can you pay?" asked Abacarus.

"Aye, though 'twill leave me nigh penniless. Why so much?"

"The spell requires rare ingredients, which will take at least a month to collect. Moreover, it is fraught with no small risk. Fifth Plane demons are formidable bondservants."

Jorian made a half-hearted effort to bargain Abacarus down, but the philosopher-sorcerer was adamant. At last Jorian said: "Shall we agree, half now and half when my wife is delivered to me unharmed?"

"That seems fair," said Gwiderius.

Abacarus cast a sour look at his colleague but grunted assent. Jorian counted out the money. Back at the Silver Dragon, he told Karadur:

"We'd better find ourselves livelihoods whilst waiting for Abacarus. Else we shall run out and be cast into the street. You can read palms or the like, whilst I seek work I can do."

Three days later, Jorian, having canvassed the city in vain for jobs in clock making and surveying, reported to Karadur that he had obtained a job in a windmill. Karadur had a new tale of woe.

"I found a booth for rent and made ready to hang out my sign," he said, "when a man of the local seers' guild appeared, with three bully boys. He told me, politely, that I needs must join the guild, at twice the regular rate because of being a foreigner. Since his escort looked eager for a pretext to set upon me with fists and feet, I forwent argument, promising to pay ere I began practice."

"How much did they want?"

"Fifty nobles for the initiation fee, plus dues of one noble a quarter."

"At that rate, we shan't be able to pay Abacarus his second installment, unless the goddess Elidora suddenly smile upon us."

"You could sell your sword. Whilst I know little of weaponry, meseems it would fetch a substantial price."

"And then what should I do the next time a dragon or a band of rogues assail me? I have a better thought. Let's appeal to Goania. Surely she has influence with this seers' guild."

The next day, while Karadur went to see Goania, Jorian departed for his first day's work at the mill. The miller, an elderly Othomaean named Lodegar, explained that he was taking on Jorian because hitherto he and his wife had run the mill together. He trimmed the sails while the wife sat at the spout from the millstones and caught the flour in bags as it poured out. Now he was getting old for such gymnastics. His son, a soldier, could not help; so he would collect the flour while Jorian manned the sails.

Jorian had a vague idea that running a windmill was easy. One dumped the grain into the hopper, made a few adjustments for wind speed and direction, and waited for the flour to pour out.

The reality proved different. The wind was ever veering and backing, so that the turret bearing the sails had to be turned to face it. A circle of thick wooden pegs arose around the circular top of the tower, and the circumference of the turret bore a series of equally spaced holes on its inner surface. By thrusting a crowbar between the pegs and into one of the holes and heaving, one turned the turret a few degrees.

Outside, the main shaft of the turret bore four booms, crossing at the axis of the main shaft and thus providing spars to bear eight triangular sails, like a ship's jib. The clew of each sail was tied by a rope to the end of the adjacent boom. To shorten sail, one stopped the rotation of the booms by snubbing with a rope, unhitched the sail, wound it several times around its boom to lessen the area exposed to the wind, and tied the clew again to the end of the next boom in the circle. To spread sail, one reversed the operation.

Jorian was kept on the run all day. When the wind shifted direction, he had to man the crowbar to turn the turret. When it freshened, he scrambled down the ladder to stop the booms' rotation and shorten several of the jibs, lest the millstones, by spinning too fast, scorch the grain. When the wind died, he had to go down again to fly more sail, lest the machine grind to a halt. Between times, the miller directed him to lubricate the wooden shafting and gears with liquid soap, kept in a bucket and applied with a large paint brush.

During the morning, Jorian, bustling about in response to Lodegar's commands, tripped on the bucket and knocked it over. Liquid soap ran out over the floor and trickled between the boards into the base of the mill. Lodegar exploded:

"Vaisus smite you with emerods, ye clumsy oaf! Therius stiffen your joints and soften your prick! Go now to my house, get a bucket of water and some rags from my wife, and clean up this mess, or 'twill be too slippery to walk upon!"

The cleanup took hours, because Jorian had to leave it every few minutes to shift the bearing of the turret, or to descend the ladder to spread or shorten sail.

As night fell, Jorian returned to the Silver Dragon, barely able to put one foot before the other. He slumped down on a bench in the common room, too tired to climb the stair to his and Karadur's room. "Beer, Master Rhuys!" he croaked.

Karadur appeared. "Why Jorian, you look fatigued! Was the work at the mill exacting?"

"Nay, 'twas as light as tossing a feather from hand to hand. How fared you?"

"Goania summoned Nennio, the chief of the seers' guild. She persuaded him to agree that I pay my initiation fee in installments over a year. Further he would not abate his demands. She told me privily that the fifty nobles are mainly a bribe to the officers of the guild. No more than a tenth of the sum reaches the guild's coffers, the rest disappearing into the purses of Master Nennio and his henchmen."

"Why does not some disgruntled guild member bring an action against these larceners?"

Karadur glanced about and lowered his voice. "Because, she whispered, they turn over a portion to the Grand Duke, who therefore protects them in their peculations. But say it not aloud in Lord Gwitlac's demesne, an you value your health."

Jorian sighed. "No wonder the romancers write tales of imaginary commonwealths, where all are honest, industrious, sober, and chaste, since such a thing seems not to exist in the real world. Is the afterworld any more virtuous?"

Karadur shrugged. "We shall doubtless ascertain soon enough; or sooner yet, if you permit that restless tongue to betray us."

"I guard my utterances. If such a land of universal virtue existed, I fear 'twere somewhat dull to dwell in."

"We need not fear, Jorian, that such a reign of tedium will ever afflict us. Betimes some simple dullness were welcome!"

# IV

# The Demon Ruakh

Jorian became hardened to mill work, since he was a powerful man, albeit somewhat softened by his life in Iraz. To one who had repaired clocks for a living, the mechanism was simple. Whenever the machine stopped, Jorian located the trouble before Lodegar did. One of the wooden gear teeth on the main shaft had come loose and jammed the gear, and Jorian quickly repaired it.

The Month of the Eagle was well along when Abacarus sent word that he was ready to call up a demon from the Fifth Plane. The next evening, trudging through a light dusting of snow, Jorian and Karadur gathered in Abacarus' oratory. This was a small, circular room in one of the ornamental towers of the Philosophy Building of the Academy. They found the sorcerer marking a pentacle with chalk on the center of the floor, all the furniture having been moved aside. Holding the other end of the measuring string was Abaracus' apprentice, a weasel-like young man named Octamon.

"Keep back!" said Abacarus. "If you step on a line, you will break the pentacle and release the demon ere he have accepted my commands. That might be the end of all of us."

They crowded back against the wall while the diagram was completed. The sorcerers inscribed a pentagram, or five-pointed star in the pentacle, a small circle inside the pentagram, and many symbols in the angles of these figures.

Octamon lit five thick black candles and placed them

at the points of the star, where they burned with a weird green flame. Then he extinguished the suspended lamp that had illuminated the chamber. He lit a thuribulum and stood against the wall, swinging the vessel on its chain. Pungent odors arose, which called to Jorian's mind, simultaneously, a flowery spring meadow, the fish market at Vindium, and the tannery at Xylar. Glancing furtively at his companions' faces, Jorian saw that all were tinged green from the candle flames.

Abacarus began moving his hands while intoning, in a deep voice unlike his normal high, thin tenor, words unknown to Jorian: "*Thomatos benesset flianter, litan izer osnas nanther, soutram i ubarsinens rabiam! Siras etar besanar, nades suradis a. . . .* "He went on and on until Jorian uneasily shifted his weight.

The flames of the candles wavered, shrank to points, and changed to an angry red. ". . . maniner o sader prostas. . . ." droned Abacarus.

In the near-darkness, Jorian felt movement of the air. Something was flickering into view in the center of the pentacle; something anthropomorphic but bulkier than a human being. A heavy, musky odor pervaded the room. Abacarus finished his conjuration: ". . . *mammes i enaim perantes ra sonastos!* What is your name?"

The answer came in a voice like bubbling swamp gas: "If it be any of your business, I am called Ruakh. What is this outrage—"

"Hold your tongue!" said Abacarus. "I have called you from the Fifth Plane to perform a service. Until you swear by the oath that binds you to perform this task featly, and to harm no inhabitant of this plane whilst sojourning therein, and then to return forthwith to your own plane, you shall remain prisoner in this pentacle."

The dim form moved as if it were trying to break through an invisible barrier surrounding it. The barrier seemed to be elastic, so that when the being threw itself against the invisible wall, it rebounded. At last it ceased its struggles, saying:

"This is most unjust of you! On my plane we have long abolished slavery, yet you savages still keep up this barbarous custom. Some day we demons shall find a way—"

"Never mind all that," growled Abacarus, "Will you do as you are told, or must I leave you here to await the coming of day?"

"You beast!" said the demon. "You know we Fifth Planers be allergic to the sun of your plane. If ever I get you on my plane—"

"Vaisus damn it, will you stop arguing! I have never faced so contentious a demon! It will avail you nought, so you might as well get down to business."

"I have a right to remind you of what is right and wrong, since you seem to have no conscience—"

"*Shut up!*" screamed Abacarus.

"—and no manners, either," continued Ruakh. "Ah, well, as you Prime Planers would say, you have me by the balls, or would, if I had those repulsive organs of reproduction you creatures hide beneath your clothing. What is this service?"

"First you must swear the oath!"

"I will swear nought until I know what service you have in mind, lest you send me to find frog feathers or dry water."

Abacarus said: "The large young man with the black beard has a wife imprisoned in the dungeon of the royal palace of Xylar. He wishes you to fetch her out of her cell and bring her here."

"How far is Xylar?"

"Eighty leagues, more or less, east of here."

"How shall I accomplish this task? I can materialize in the lady's cell, but I cannot dematerialize her to carry her through stone walls or an iron-barred door."

"If the door be locked, you must get the key from the head jailer, or whoever has it. If you can find who has it, you can easily frighten him into giving it up. Then you can fly back hither with the lady. The time is not yet midnight, so you should arrive here well before dawn. You must not fly at such a height that lack of air will suffocate her; and you should wrap her warmly, for the winter air aloft will be far below the freezing point."

Ruakh grunted. "I like not the prospect; but as we say on the Fifth Plane, mendicants cannot be optants. Can the young man draw me a plan of the dungeon, lest I go astray in the bowels of this building?"

"Nay, oath first! You hope he will break the circle and loose you to wreak your vengeance upon us."

"I had no such thought in mind!" cried the demon in its bubbly, thickly accented voice. "You Prime Planers are the most suspicious lot in the multiple worlds. You assume all others to be as evil and treacherous as you."

"Forget the rhetoric, my good Ruakh, and let us get to the oath."

"Oh, very well," grumbled the demon.

There followed a long dialogue between the two, in a language unknown to Jorian. At last Abacarus said: "That is done, then. Octamon, you may light the lamp and break the circle. You. realize, Ruakh, what will befall you if you violate the terms of our compact, do you not?"

"Aye, I realize; albeit it is a monstrous injustice. Forcing me to do risky, unpaid labor, forsooth! When I get home, I shall have somewhat to say to my fellow demons."

As the lamp flared up, Jorian had his first clear view of Ruakh. The demon was a being of human size and shape, but from its back grew a huge pair of batlike wings, now folded. Its clawed feet resembled those of a huge bird of prey. The whole creature was covered with what at first Jorian took to be a skintight suit of scarlet silk. As the demon moved, he saw that this was

Ruakh's own skin. As the being had said, it was innocent of visible sexual organs; the skin of its crotch was smooth.

"Pardon me, Master Ruakh," said Jorian, "but how *do* your kind reproduce themselves?"

"It is a long story," began the demon. "At the proper season, we grow—"

Abacarus interrupted. "Do not take time for such discussion, Master Jorian. Ruakh must get to Xylar and back ere dawn. So here is a piece of chalk; pray indicate where he shall find your lady."

Jorian squatted and drew a diagram of the dungeon of Xylar. He was a little startled when Ruakh, leaning over his shoulder to look at the drawing, placed a clawed hand on Jorian's back to steady itself. Jorian pointed to the largest rectangle in the diagram.

"I think she's in there," he said. "They seem to have fixed the place up for her comfort, not like an ordinary prison cell. She is small and light-haired."

The demon, peering, said: "Methinks I grasp the nub. Stand back, all, so that I can dematerialize."

When the men had crowded back to the wall, the demon began to spin round and round. Faster and faster it went, until it became a blur. The blur became translucent, then transparent, and then vanished with a *whoosh* of air.

"Open the doors, Octamon," said Abacarus, "to rid us of this stench."

Cold winter air spilled into the oratory. "Now what?" asked Jorian.

"It will be hours ere Ruakh can return," said Abacarus. "It can hie to Xylar in its immaterial form in the blink of an eye; it should arrive there any minute. But to return, it must remain material. So its flight will consume hours, swift of wing though it be. If you people wish to await its return here, there are couches below."

Jorian and Karadur remained in the Philosophy

Building. As Abacarus was showing them to the lounge where they would pass the rest of the night, Jorian asked:

"Pray tell me something, Doctor Abacarus. In Iraz, a savant of the House of Learning explained that a flying being the size of a man were impossible. Something about the relation of is weight to the area of its wings and the power of its thews. How, then, can Ruakh fly in his material form on this plane?"

Abacarus shrugged. "It has compensating advantages. Its muscles are not made of the same stuff as ours. They are stronger in proportion to their bulk."

"What's this," said Jorian, "about the demons complaining of being enslaved by us Prime Planers? I thought the Novarian nations had agreed to end slavery."

Abacarus chuckled. "The Treaty of Metouro, which will not become effective until all twelve governments sign it, refers only to the enslavement of human beings. Demons, from whatever other plane, are not human and hence do not qualify, any more than would your horse."

"How about the ape-men of Komilakh? Will they count as human beings?"

"That depends on which of the twelve nations you are in. The courts of some have held them human; of others, not. The Novarian nations should establish a supreme court over all twelve systems to reconcile these discrepancies. I belong to a society devoted to this ideal; I must give you one of our broadsheets. But to return to the Treaty of Metouro, only five of the nations have signed it, and do not try to hold your breath whilst awaiting the signatures of the rest."

"What about the demons' threat to organize against exploitation by Prime Planers?"

"Never fear. They will make a start and then fall into internal bickering as they always have. Now I am going home. I shall return an hour before dawn. By then, if all go well, our demon should be well on its way hither. Good night!"

It seemed to Jorian that he had barely fallen asleep on his couch, when he felt his shoulder shaken. "It is time," said Abacarus.

Jorian stood yawning in the oratory for half an hour. Then, just as the east began to lighten, something moved against the star-strewn western sky. Abacarus threw open the doors that unfolded on the small balcony encircling the tower, letting in a wave of frigid air. The flying object took shape, growing from the likeness of a bat to the demon Ruakh with a bulky burden in its arms.

With a muffled thunder of wings, the demon settled upon the railing of the balcony, grasping it with clawed feet as a bird does a branch. Then, wings folded, it hopped down to the balcony and walked into the oratory, bearing a blanket-wrapped body. Octamon shut the door.

"Here you are!" growled the demon. The musky smell returned.

"Had you trouble getting in?" asked Jorian.

"Nay. I materialized outside the dungeon, thinking to get the keys. But I found the barred door at the head of the stair open, and a guard sitting beside it. I frightened him away, descended the stair, and found the cell whereof you told me, also unlocked. So I discovered this woman therein. When I approached her to explain my mission, she fainted. I wrapped her as you see and bore her out. The palace folk scattered shrieking before me, so I had no difficulty in leaving the building and taking to the air."

"Well done!" said Abacarus. "You are dismissed, Master Ruakh."

Ruakh gave a bubbling growl. "Ere I return to my own plane, let me tell you Prime Planers, we demons will not forever submit to being kidnapped and forced to run your errands for you! We shall unite to end this injustice! We shall overcome!"

"For now, be satisfied with your dismissal," said Abacarus. "Begone; we do not find your odor pleasing."

Standing in the center of the floor, Ruakh went into its spin. The towering scarlet form whirled, blurred, and vanished with a rush of displaced air.

Jorian drew a long breath. "I confess that Ruakh's proximity gave me some uneasy moments."

"It is all in knowing how to handle them," said Abacarus. "My last apprentice got himself slain by a demon whom he improperly evoked."

"Jorian is forever deprecating himself," said Karadur. "I have sought to break him of the habit, since modesty is a poor weapon for making one's way in this sinful world; but I fear I have not utterly succeeded."

Jorian was kneeling by the blanket-wrapped form on the floor. As he began unwrapping it, he was struck by the horrible thought that his Estrildis might have perished from mountain sickness at the altitude to which Ruakh had borne her.

Then the form began to wriggle, and it threw off the blanket and sat up.

"By Imbal's brazen balls!" cried Jorian. "You're not Estrildis!"

"Whoever said I was?" said the woman, rising. "I am Queen Estrildis's lady-in-waiting, Lady Margalit of Totens. And you, an I mistake not, are the fugitive King Jorian. Where am I, and why have I been brought on this horrible journey?"

The woman was of about the same age as Estrildis; but there the resemblance ended. Where Estrildis was short and blond, Margalit of Totens was almost as tall as Jorian and dark, with a mop of curly hair tumbling over her forehead. Jorian would not quite have called her beautiful, as he would have said of some of the five wives he had enjoyed as king. But she was handsome in a bold, sharp-featured way, and strongly built. She was fast recovering from the shock of her experience.

Jorian bowed. "I am honored, Lady Margalit. You are in Othomae City, and it was not intended that you be brought hither. I sent Ruakh—that's the demon— to fetch my wife, but he seems to have caught you by mistake. How did it happen?"

"My Queen had gone up to the battlements to walk and look at the heavens, leaving me in our dungeon apartment."

"They don't keep her locked in that cell, then?"

"Nay, though they make sure she leaves not the palace. She may issue from the cell when she pleases, but they send an armed escort with her, lest you have another try at abducting her."

"Was it you who gave the alarm, when I fell over that chair and roused the watchdog?"

"Aye. How was I to know it was you?"

"Why told you not the demon who you were?"

"How could I? I was tidying up the apartment in Estrildis' absence—as you doubtless know, neatness was never her strong point—and the first thing I knew, there was the demon in the doorway, crouching to get his wings through, and mumbling something in that gargly voice with its unintelligible accent. 'Twas then that I fainted for the only time in my life. The next I knew, I was borne aloft, wrapped in this blanket, notwithstanding which I well-nigh froze to death. When I struggled, the demon warned me to lie still, lest he drop me from a height. What an experience!"

Jorian turned to Abacarus. "How could Ruakh have made such a stupid mistake? I told him to look for a small, blond woman."

The sorcerer spread his hands. "By and large, demons are not very intelligent. Belike it forgot your instructions, or got them confused, and when it saw one woman alone in the chamber reasoned that this must be she whom it sought."

"Can you call Ruakh back to rectify his error?" asked Jorian.

"Nay. A demon once dismissed is exempt for years thereafter."

"Why did you dismiss him so hastily?"

"Because it stank, and you did not object."

"I had no time to object; but let's not start apportioning blame. Could you invoke another demon in Ruakh's place?"

Abacarus frowned. "Not for months. Imprimus, these evocations are exhausting, and I must be able to meet my classes. I also find the odor of Fifth Plane demons unbearable. Secundus, it would cost you an additional fifteen hundred nobles. And tertius, you have not yet paid all you owe me for evoking Ruakh."

"What!" cried Jorian. "I owe you not a copper penny! We agreed that your demon should fetch my wife, Estrildis the Kortolian; and that he has not done."

"Young man, you had better watch your tongue. I say you owe me seven hundred and fifty. My expenses have been just as heavy as if the demon had succeeded, and I warned you that I did not guarantee success."

"But you did agree to my paying the rest when and only when you succeeded. I'll not pay for a bungled job!"

"You were as responsible for the bungle as anyone, and you had better pay. I can take you to law; and I also have other means of causing you trouble."

"Try it!" said Jorian. "Come on, Karadur. An I ever resort to sorcery again, I'll try to find a sorcerer who is at least both competent and honest."

"What of me?" cried Margalit. "Am I expected to walk back to Xylar? By Zevatas' whiskers, my Lord Jorian, were we both in Xylar, I'd sue you within a digit of your life."

"I beg your pardon, my lady. Come to our hostelry, and we'll discuss your future."

\* \* \*

Back at the Silver Dragon, Jorian engaged a private room for Margalit, whose initial anger had cooled. He told her:

"Certes, I am obligated to get you back to Xylar. But you cannot travel thither alone, especially at this time of year, when packs of wolves and bands of robbers are desperate for food. I cannot afford to hire a proper escort and procure animals to carry you. And I cannot accompany you into Xylar myself if I wish to keep my head attached to the rest of me."

"I cannot blame you for that," she said. "Like my Queen, I have turned against this custom, venerable though it be."

Jorian continued: "So I will pay your keep here as long as my money holds out. When spring comes, some means of conveying you, such as a diligencia or a merchants' caravan, will surely turn up. Now you'd better get some sleep."

"What next, Your Majesty?" said Margalit.

"I pray, do *not* call me that, even in sarcasm! I never wanted to be king of your preposterous country, and ever since my escape I've been trying to divest myself of the honor. But to answer your question: I must away to my job at the mill. Tonight at dinner, we'll consider what to do. I'll summon the wizardess Goania, who has more sense than most."

Margalit looked down at her gown. "I am no glass of fashion, but I shall really need at least one change of clothing. Without washing, this garment will become as odorous as your demon, and I cannot run about naked whilst it is being cleansed."

"In winter, anyway," said Jorian. "I suppose your abductor gave you no time to snatch up a purse?"

"You suppose rightly, Your M—Master Jorian."

Jorian sighed and took two pieces of gold from his purse. "I know nought of the cost of ladies' garments, but see what you can do with this. Get Karadur to go with you."

\* \* \*

That evening, as they sat at table waiting for Goania, Margalit said: "You certainly seem determined, Master Jorian. You've vainly tried a direct attack, and then sorcery, in your efforts to obtain my Queen; but you still have not given up."

"That's true love," said Jorian. "I'm not ashamed of it. She's the one I chose for myself, not picked for me by the Council to give the leading magnates a stake in my rule. And she's the one I want."

"When and if you recover her, what then?"

"Why, we'll find some safe place, whence the Xylarians cannot snatch me, and settle down as a proper tradesman and wife to earn a living."

"You may find her changed."

Jorian dismissed the idea with a wave. "Were she old, wrinkled, and gray, she would still be my true love."

Karadur chuckled. "My boy is a sentimental romanticist," he said, wagging his vast, white beard. "Do not try to change him, Lady Margalit; for it is one of his attractive qualities. Ah, here comes my eminent colleague!"

The wizardess Goania, followed by her bodyguard Boso, entered. Jorian, relieved to see that Vanora was not with them, made introductions. Goania said:

"Welcome, Lady Margalit. When I saw you, I wondered what magic could have changed you from a short blonde, as Jorian has described his Estrildis, into a tall brunet. What befell?"

When Jorian and Margalit had told their stories, Goania said: "Never underestimate the stupidity of demons. Those from most of the other planes have powers that on this plane appear preternatural. Are you familiar with the theory that every life form is descended from others, all going back to some little blob of primordial slime?"

"Aye," said Jorian. "When I studied here under Gwiderius, a professor was dismissed from the Academy for such ungodly speculations."

"Well, this theory explains the stupidity of most demons. Having these powers, the stress of competition on their own respective planes has not forced them to develop their mental powers to the degree that we, who can neither fly, nor make ourselves invisible, nor dematerialize, have been forced to do.

"I can give an example from my own experience. When I was a mere girl—stare not, Master Jorian; I was once young and quite as pretty as your Estrildis."

"Very well, Aunt Goania. I believe you."

"When I was, as I say, a maiden, I had a suitor named Uriano, who dabbled, unbeknownst to me, in sorcery. This was ere I myself decided to make occult pursuits my life's work. I expected to wed, keep house, and bear brats like most women; and I was sore bessotted with Uriano, for he was a handsome devil.

"My father, a building contractor, had no use for Uriano, terming him a lecher, a wastrel, a dabbler, and generally worthless. Anon I learned that Uriano was all those things; but then my eyes, blinded by love, were closed to them. My sire barred my sweet swain from the house and forbade me to have aught to do with him.

"I wept, carried on, and made a great to-do; for I deemed myself the victim of a monstrous injustice, inflicted by one grown so old as to have forgotten the joys of youthful love and filled with blind prejudice against the newer and more enlightened views of the younger generation. But relent my father would not.

"Uriano, howsomever, discovered that, by skulking through some shrubbery that grew nigh our house, he could approach within twenty paces of the edifice unseen, on the side of my bedchamber. So we presently began communicating by his shooting headless arrows from a child's toy bow, with messages wrapped around them, through my open window, I wrote replies, tied them to the arrows, and threw them back.

"Then Uriano proposed that we elope. I, foolish girl, assumed he meant to hale me to the Temple of Therius and make me his lawful wife. From what I heard later, I'm sure he meant only to enjoy my body until he tired of me and cast me adrift.

"On a certain night, he said, he would appear with a ladder, down which I should descend into his arms, and away we should fly. What he did not tell me was that, in his sorcerous experiments, he had evoked a demon from the Seventh Plane to help him. Seventh Plane demons are fiery beings, particularly dangerous for a tyronic, unskilled sorcerer to handle.

"On the appointed night, Uriano came with his ladder, accompanied by his demon. He placed the ladder against the wall and charged the demon to cover our retreat when, as he thought, we should flee from the house together. He posted the demon at the back door, with orders to incinerate with his fiery breath anyone who came through that door ere we were out of sight of the house. Then the demon should rejoin his master.

"All might have gone as planned but for two things. Imprimus, so crazed with lust was Uriano from thinking of his future leman that he could not wait until we left the house to slake it. Instead of signaling and waiting for me to descend the ladder, which I could easily have done, he climbed the ladder himself to enter my bedchamber through the window, hoping to take me featly then and there before departure.

"Secundus, in emplacing the ladder, he did not set the base far enough from the wall. So as he climbed from the topmost rung through the window, he unwittingly kicked the ladder over.

"When he heard the ladder strike the ground, all thought of carnal congress fled his mind, unhoused by fears for his own safety. He whispered: 'Be quiet, dear one, and I'll soon set this picklement to rights.' Then he leaned out the window and softly called: 'Vrix! O Vrix!'

" 'Aye, Master?' said the demon from below.

" 'Pick up that ladder and set it against the house, as it was.'

" 'Eh?' said the demon. 'What sayst?'

"Uriano repeated his command, but the demon could not seem to understand this simple act. First it set the ladder on edge along the ground. Then it raised the ladder and set it on end, away from the house and unsupported. When it released its hold, the ladder naturally fell over.

"After more blunders, Vrix finally seemed to understand. But as I said, these demons are fiery beings. As it came anigh the house with the ladder, the ladder caught fire from the heat of the demon's grasp. As the demon set it in place, it blazed up merrily, and Uriano had to push it over again to keep it from firing the house.

" 'Gods!' quotha. 'That stupid oaf—but now we must needs go out through the house. Does your sire sleep?'

" 'I think so,' I said. I opened my bedroom door and looked down the hall, hearing nought. I beckoned Uriano, and together we tiptoed to the head of the stair.

"Just then the door of my parents' room opened, and there stood my father in his nightshirt, blinking, with a candle in one hand and a sword in the other. 'What's all this infernal noise—' he began. Then, recognizing Uriano, he rushed roaring at him.

"Uriano let go my hand and bounded down the stairs two at a time, with my sire after him. The speed of my father's motion extinguished the candle, but there was still enough moonlight to see one's way.

"Uriano dashed through the dining room into the kitchen and out the back door. Vrix stood there, waiting for someone to come out that door. When Uriano appeared, Vrix gave him a blast of fiery breath that washed over him like a jet of water from a fountain in the Grand Duke's gardens, for it had been straitly commanded to burn the first person coming out. Uriano gave one shriek as his hair and clothing blazed up, and then there was nought left of him but a black, cindery mass on the garden path. Uriano's death released Vrix from servitude on this plane, and it vanished. So now I hope you appreciate the limitations of employing demons to do your work for you."

"I realize the difficulty," said Jorian. "But what interests me most is the question of what would have happened, had your lover not knocked over the ladder?"

"Oft have I asked myself that question," said Goania. "Things would in time have gone ill, I am certain." She sighed, with a faraway look. "But I should have had one interesting night to remember."

Jorian said: "But still, can you think of a better way to get my darling out of her luxurious lockup?"

"Not at the moment."

"Could you send your second sight to Xylar, to see what they are doing there?"

"I could, if someone will clean this table and fetch me a clean glass."

Goania repeated her previous trance, the one she had employed after Jorian and Karadur had just emerged from jail. When she spoke, she muttered:

"I cannot see inside the palace . . . there seems to be a barrier. . . . It is like a wall of glass, shutting me out. . . . I see the palace dimly and wavering, as things appear to ripple when seen above a paved road on a hot day. . . . Nay, I cannot get in."

After a while she opened her eyes and said: "The

Xylarians have thrown a magical barrier around their palace, like a dome, which keeps out my occult vision. From what I know of such things, I am sure it would also keep out any demon who tried to enter in dematerialized form."

"I suppose," said Jorian, "that after Ruakh's visit they hired a spooker to set up this barrier against further intrusions. What shall I do now?"

"I would start looking for another wife, if you must have one," said Goania.

"Aye," Karadur chimed in. "Relinquish this hopeless quest, my son, ere you bring destruction not only on yourself but also on others, like me."

"You may go your way any time," snapped Jorian. "You are not my bondservant."

"Oh, my dear Jorian! I have become dependent upon you. I am too old and creaky to get about much by myself. Cast me not off like an old shoe! You take the place of the son I never had."

"Very well then, you must needs put up with my vagaries. The single life may suit you and Goania, but it pleases me not."

"If you must have a wife, then, follow Goania's rede. Wed—let me see—why not take Lady Margalit here?"

"Come!" said Margalit sharply. "I am not a prize to be raffled off. Master Jorian may be a fine fellow in his way—"

"But obstinate as a mule when he gets an idea in his mazard," Karadur put in.

"—but there is nought like that betwixt us."

"Do you expect to wed someday?" Goania asked.

"Certes. That's why I took the post of lady-in-waiting. My family, though of good lineage, is poor; so by saving up the allowance the Regency pays me, I hoped to gather enough dowry to lure some reasonably whole, sane, and solvent husband. But my peculum lies still in Estrildis' dungeon apartment."

"Well, then—" said Karadur.

"I must know and like the fellow far better than I do Jorian ere I'd consider such a thing. Besides, he is already bespoken."

"Good for you!" said Jorian. "But as the doctor says, I can be very stubborn. You two spookers are ever talking of the wisdom your years have brought you. So let's have evidence, in the form of a plausible scheme for recovering my wife!"

All four sat in silence. Rhuys brought their dinners. As they were digging in, Karadur said:

"I once told you of a Mulvanian colleague, called Greatsoul Shenderu or Shenderu the Wise. He dwells on Mount Aravia in the Lograms, and such is his name for wisdom that folk come hundreds of leagues to consult him on their affairs. Belike you could seek him out, come spring."

"A splendid suggestion!" cried Jorian, his normal enthusiasm returning. "Why thought you not of that sooner? I'll set out forthwith!"

"Oh, Jorian!" said Goania. "Rush not into needless peril, or your Estrildis may have no husband to rejoin. It's still the Month of the Eagle, and the snows lie heavy on the mountains."

"Methinks we've seen the last of the snow down here," said Jorian.

"Down here is not up there. There you'll find drifts as deep as you are tall, with crevasses and precipices."

"I know; we flew over the Lograms coming from Iraz. But I'll chance that. Doctor Karadur, how does this Shenderu live?"

"People who come with questions are expected to recompense him with the things he requires: food, firewood, and betimes a garment or some knicknack such as a cooking pot. Since he is a vegetarian, his alimentary requirements are bulky."

"I'll buy a mule and load it with firewood, bread,

and turnips," said Jorian. "I'll persuade Gwiderius to gain me access to the Grand Ducal library, where they'll have maps of the region. I shall be off ere the month be out!"

As often happens, it took Jorian much longer to get his expedition ready to go than he had thought. He had to buy a horse and a pack mule with the remains of King Ishbahar's privy purse. He needed a load of grain for the animals, since there would be little natural forage for them at that season.

Then a minor epidemic swept Othomae City with coughs, sneezes, and fevers. All the people in the Silver Dragon, including Jorian, were out of effective action for a sennight.

As the month of the Boar wore on, Lady Margalit became impatient with idleness. One night over dinner, Jorian was counting out his remaining coin.

"At this rate," he said, "I shall be a pauper by summer. It's only right that I should pay Margalit's room and board, since I brought her hither. But with the pittance Lodegar pays me, I cannot save, scrimp though I try."

Margalit said: "Jorian, it is good of you to pay my board; but I should earn something on my own. Could I not find a paying place in Othomae until arrangements are made for my return?"

Jorian raised his eyebrows. "Lady Margalit! One of your kind could hardly be a housemaid or a washerwoman."

"What mean you, my kind? I've known poverty, and I'm not too proud to do what must be done. Besides, much of what I did for Estrildis would elsewhere be housemaid's work."

"I'll ask Goania," said Jorian.

When Lodegar fell sick of the same phthisic, Jorian persuaded him to hire Margalit to take his place in the mill, bagging the flour as it came from the mill-stones. A few days later, as they returned to the Silver Dragon after work, still patting flour from each other's garments, Goania greeted them.

"I have a post for you, Lady Margalit," she said. "My friend Aeda, wife of Councilor Arvirag, needs a maid-of-all-work, hers having left. What say you?"

"I will certainly try it," said Margalit.

"Good girl!" said Jorian. "I admire anyone willing to turn his hand to what needs doing. I hope we can find you a position which shall make better use of that excellent brain of yours. Meanwhile, let's celebrate with a bottle of Rhuys's best!"

They were halfway through the bottle, and Rhuys had served their dinners, when a man entered the common room and strode up to Jorian. The man, wearing a uniform without a sword, said: "You are Jorian of Ardamai, alias Nikko of Kortoli?"

"Aye," said Jorian. "What about it?"

"Here is a summons to appear before the examining magistrate one hour after sunrise on the morrow."

"Eh? What?" said Jorian. "What have I done?"

"You are the defendant in an action brought by Doctor Abacarus of the Academy, for recovery of a debt."

"That bastard!" muttered Jorian.

"Since you are a foreigner; you must either get a local citizen and property owner to vouch for you, or you must come with me to the jail, to assure your appearance tomorrow."

"I will vouch for him," said Goania.

"So? Then kindly sign here, Mistress Goania."

The process server departed, leaving the summons on the table before Jorian. Goania said: "I trust you know, Jorian, that if you lose your case, it's debtor's prison."

"Do they still have that here? When I was King of

Xylar, I got them to abolish it, on the ground that a man in jail cannot earn the wherewithal to satisfy his debt."

"It is a pity that you are not the Grand Duke here. But you are not, so govern your acts accordingly."

The examining magistrate was the same Judge Flollo who had incarcerated Jorian and Karadur. He said: "Master Jorian, methinks that, having gotten out of trouble once, you would have sense enough to stay out. But let me hear your stories. You first, Doctor Abacarus."

Abacarus gave a long, voluble speech affirming his claim that Jorian still owed him 750 nobles. Jorian explained why he did not consider himself so obligated.

"Therefore," he said, "I ask that this suit be dismissed with prejudice. In fact, I ought to sue the learned doctor for my first seven hundred and fifty, since his effort was a complete failure."

"Nonsense!" said Abacarus. "I did not guarantee success, and I warned this upstart. . . ."

Both the doctor and Jorian began shouting, until the magistrate banged his gavel and yelled: "Silence, you two, on pain of imprisonment! This is a hard case, the more so since neither of you has a written contract. One would think that men of your age would have sense enough to put such things in writing, with competent legal advice.

"Now, our calendar is crowded. The earliest trial date I can set is—let me see. . . ." He ruffled through documents. "'Twill be the fourteenth of the Dragon."

"By Heryx's brazen balls, that's half a year away!" exclaimed Jorian.

Judge Flollo shrugged. "It is the best we can do. Time, as the philosophers at the Academy are wont to say, is incompressible. Of course, if you two should settle out of court, no trial would be needed. Master

Jorian, Mistress Goania's avouchment will suffice to leave you at liberty pending the trial. But you must understand that, if you fail to appear and we cannot catch you, the penalty will fall upon her."

Jorian and Abacarus exchanged glares. The sorcerer said: "My resources are not yet exhausted, Master Jorian."

"Nor mine," said Jorian.

Two nights later, Jorian had snuffed the candle in the room he shared with Karadur and stretched himself out beneath the blankets, when he became aware of something else in the room. Out of the darkness a luminous form was taking shape. At first it was so faint that he thought it a mere photism—one of the lights one sees with one's eyes closed. It wavered and shimmered with a faint bluish radiance, resembling a cowled figure. Nothing but blackness could be seen beneath the cowl where its face should be. Then came a moaning voice: "Pay your debts! Pay your debts!"

"Karadur!" said Jorian. "Wake up! Do you see what I see?"

"Unh?" The aged Mulvanian sat up and yawned. "Oh, ah, aye, I see it. This is termed a dunning specter, sent by Abacarus to plague us. 'Tis patent that he is not fain to wait till the Month of the Dragon for the decision on his case."

"Pay your debts! Pay your debts!" wailed the figure.

"What should I do about it?" asked Jorian.

"There is naught much that you can do, short of paying Abacarus his claim."

"That I will not do. Even if I wished, I do not have seven hundred and fifty nobles left. What about these specters? What can they do?"

"These entities inhabit the Second Plane. They are easy to invoke and harmless, since they do not

achieve substantial materialization on this plane.
Whilst not intelligent, they are obedient to the sorcerer's commands, like a well-trained dog. The thing
is immaterial, so your sword would pass through it
without resistance. A project at the House of Learning in Iraz was to ascertain how, without forming
solid vocal organs, these specters could natheless agi-
tate the air of this plane to form articulate sounds—"

"Pay your debts! Pay your debts!"

"Well," said Jorian, "'tis damned inconvenient. The
thing I most look forward to in the world is my first
night after Estrildis and I are again united. But imagine how it would be if, just as she and I prepared to
enjoy our mutual passion, this thing appeared with
its croak!"

"At least," said Karadur, "this entity will assist you
to adhere to the continence on which you have virtu-
ously resolved."

"Oh, bugger my continence! Will it go on like this
all night?"

"Pay your debts! Pay your debts!" groaned the
specter.

"Nay," said Karadur. "After a few hours it will
become fatigued and fade away—until the next
night."

"Pay your debts! Pay your debts!"

"You are a great bore, spook!" growled Jorian.
"Now shut your gob and go away!"

He pulled the covers over his head; but for the
next hour or two, moans and wails of "pay your
debts!" kept him awake.

The next day, since Lodegar's mill was idle for
want of grain, Jorian went to Goania. He said: "I am
no light-hearted manslayer, but I have punctured a
few knaves in my time. If I could get within a sword's
length of Abacarus—" He gripped his hilt, secured
to the scabbard by peace wires.

"Do not even think of it, boy!" snapped Goania.

Jorian smiled. "I like to think of you as my favorite aunt. And why should I not let some of the stuffing out of this great child's doll?"

"Because the Grand Duke's police keep a sharp eye on you, even if you are not aware thereof. You would only end up on the headsman's block, not to mention the trouble you would cause your friends."

"Well then, have you any sort of counter-sorcery against him?"

She pondered. "Aye, I can call up a similar specter from the Second Plane to harass Abacarus. But think twice! First, 'twill cost you money, albeit I am willing to let that debt ride until you can afford to pay. Secondly, Abacarus is an able wizard. He can throw a protective shield about his abode, like that which the Xylarians put up against my second sight."

"Does it bother Abacarus to erect and maintain these shields?"

"To some degree. They consume psychic energy."

"Then by all means send a dunning specter against him. Tell it to say: 'Cease your extortions!'"

Goania promised. Next day she told Jorian: "As I said, my specter had barely begun to harass Abacarus when he threw a shield about his chambers in the Academy. When he went home in the even, it followed him, intoning its message; but when he reached his house, he soon erected another shield against it."

"Can he make a private shield around himself, that shall move with him?"

"Nay. These shields must needs be anchored in soil or in a fixed abode."

"Well then, keep it after him when he goes betwixt his home and his oratory."

The next evening, Jorian idled in the cold, crisp air, along the path outside the Philosophy Building of the Academy. Weird blue lights flickered in the

windows of Doctor Abacarus' tower, so Jorian knew
the sorcerer was still at work. At length the lights
went out, and soon Abacarus issued from the
building.

Behind a tree, Jorian watched as the wizard strode
along the campus path, his vast belly bobbing. Presently a dunning specter like that which harassed
Jorian appeared close behind Abacarus and began to
howl: "Cease your extortions! Cease your extortions!"

Abacarus turned. Jorian could not see his expression, since the near-darkness was relieved only by
starlight and the feeble glow of an oil lamp on a
bracket beside the main door of the building. But
the sorcerer made gestures, and Jovian's own dunning specter appeared, wailing: "Pay your debts!"

A clutch of undergraduates came along the path.
They halted, and Jorian heard one say: "Great Zevatas, here's a duel of wizards! This should be fun to
watch!"

"If they do not blow up the whole Academy in
their strife," said another.

"I fear no spooks!" said still another. "I'll show
you!" The youth picked up a stone and hurled it at
Jorian's phantom. The stone passed through the specter without resistance and struck Jorian in the chest.

"Ho!" roared Jorian, grabbing his unusable sword.
He started toward the group, who scampered away
and disappeared. When Jorian turned back, Abacarus
had also vanished. Jorian set out for the Silver
Dragon, with the specter hovering over his shoulder
and moaning: "Pay your debts!"

During the next fortnight, Jorian continued to be
haunted by Abacarus' sending, while Goania's dunning specter harassed Abacarus as opportunity
offered. The sorcerer, Jorian learned, found it necessary to change his habits. A night worker, he took to
keeping farmer's hours, up with the dawn and home

ere sunset, so as not to be caught abroad at night away from the protection of his shields.

Jorian found other resources in the campaign of mutual harassment. He hired urchins to paint ABACARUS IS AN EXTORTIONIST on the walls of the Philosophy Building. He hired a beggar to stroll about the campus bearing a sign reading ABACARUS IS AN EXTORTIONIST. When the campus police tried to arrest the beggar, a gang of undergraduates took the oldster's side and started a small riot, under cover of which the beggar slipped away.

When Abacarus filed a suit for damages against Jorian for harassment, Jorian filed a countersuit alleging the same tort. Judge Flollo looked sourly at the two litigants, saying:

"We cannot schedule these trials until next year. Why do not you two go to some barbarous land where dueling is legal, or trial by combat, and have it out?"

As the Month of the Bull came on, Doctor Gwiderius told Jorian: "My colleague Abacarus wishes me to tell you that he is willing to discuss a compromise."

So Jorian found himself again in Abacarus' office in the Academy, facing the stout sorcerer across a huge desk. Abacarus said:

"Come, my good Jorian, this is no way for mature men to behave. Let us find a *modus vivendi*, ere the lawyers suck us dry. Otherwise we shall spend more on legal and court fees than the sum at issue."

"Well, sir?" said Jorian.

"Would you consider settling for half?"

"Never. Methinks it's plain, by all Novarian laws—the which I have studied—that I owe you not a copper penny more than I've paid. In fact, a clever lawyer could make a good case for the return of the seven hundred fifty I paid you erstwhile."

"If that idea pleases you not, have you a proposal to offer?"

Jorian thought. "How about submitting our dispute to an impartial arbitrator? Loser to pay the arbitrator's fee."

Abacarus pursed his lips and twiddled his fat fingers. "Not bad. We have some retired judges in Othomae, who could be counted upon to render a just verdict."

"Oh, no!" said Jorian. "An Othomaean judge would be prejudiced in your favor, since I am a foreigner. I should prefer a Kortolian judge; I am sure—"

"Rubbish! With our Othomaean judges, at least I have some notion of their fairness. But I know nought of Kortolian justice. For aught I know, any of your people were willing and eager to take a bribe to find for you."

"Kortolian justice is every bit as just as yours!"

"Belike, but how shall you prove it? Must we fight it out, as Flollo suggested? If you challenge me, I will naturally choose magical spells as the weapons."

"How about this?" said Jorian. "If I can find a jurist of high repute from a third Novarian state, will you accept him?"

"I would consider it with a favoring mind. I should have to make inquiries ere deciding. And this time, let us put our undertaking in writing!"

Jorian rose. "I agree. Let's leave it at that. Meanwhile, if you will banish your dunning specter, I will call off mine, as well as my other partisans. Whilst I fear not your phantom, it does make a good night's sleep hard to come by!"

# V

# The Snows of Aravia

Not till the second of the Bull was Jorian ready to go.
In the evening, he was packing his gear when a knock
announced Vanora.

"Jorian," she said, "you are a fool to undertake this
journey alone. You need at least one extra pair of eyes
to watch for dangers, and an extra pair of hands to pull
you out of quicksands and other traps."

"You may be right," said Jorian. "But, alas, I know
no one here suitable. Doctor Karadur is too old and
feeble. Your friend Boso has barely brain enough to tie
his own shoe laces, besides which he loves me not."

"I could go," she said. "I'm strong, and as you well
know, I've roughed it ere this."

Jorian shook his head. "Nay, my dear; I've been all
through that. Your body may be up to the task, but I
fear that your temper be too stormy and uncertain for
me. I thank you for the offer."

"Be not a fool, Jorian! You need someone, and I'm
the only one to hand. Your tale of a curse on your
prick was but a farrago to frighten me; Goania says
such a spell were impossible."

"I am trying to tell you, I don't wish a female companion save my wife!"

"Oh, that little farm bitch! Forget her. When you
win to her, you'll find one of the local lads has been
tupping your prize ewe. After all, you and she have
been apart now for over two years—"

"You had better go back to Boso and let me get on
with my packing," growled Jorian.

"Look, Jorian darling, you need not bed me along the way if you're not fain to do so—"

"Curse it, Vanora, get out! Will you go, or must I throw you out?"

"You mangy scrowle!" she yelled. Jorian ducked as a shoe came flying at his head. "I'll teach you to cast off an honest woman!" A second shoe followed.

The door opened, and Boso's broad face looked in. "What in the nine hells goes on here?"

"He tried to rape me!" screamed Vanora, looking about for something more to throw.

"What!" roared Boso. "You lure my woman up here, and when she won't go with you, you ravish her? I'll teach you to steal honest men's women!"

"She lies!" shouted Jorian. "It was not—" Then he had to defend himself against Boso's bull-like rush. In an instant, they were floundering about, punching and kicking. A chair went over with a crash.

Feet pounded on the stair, and Rhuys looked in. "Here, here!" he said. "Stop that! If you're fain to fight, take your quarrel outside!"

When they paid no heed, Rhuys vanished but soon reappeared, armed with a bung starter and followed by his two sons and the stable boy. Boso had Jorian's head in the crook of his arm and was striving to punch Jorian's face with his free fist, while Jorian tried to block Boso's blows and to kick his shins.

"Seize them!" cried Rhuys.

The four newcomers grabbed the combatants and tried to pull them apart. They failed, because Jorian and Boso were both large, strong men. Suddenly Boso released Jorian's head and turned to throw a wild swing at the stable boy. The blow hurled the youth back against the wall. Rhuys and his sons pounced upon Boso. While the sons clung to Boso's arms, Rhuys whacked him over the head with the bung starter. Boso subsided. Jorian stood back, breathing hard, with bruises on his face and blood running from a cut lip.

"What befell?" asked Rhuys.

Sitting on the floor, Boso wagged his head and mumbled. Jorian began: "Mistress Vanora came up to have words with me, and Boso thought—"

"He lies!" screeched Vanora. "Jorian tried to rape me, and Boso came to my aid!"

"It was just the opposite!" shouted Jorian. "She besought me—"

"Quiet, both of you!" said Rhuys. To one of the sons he said: "Baltho, run and fetch Mistress Goania. She'll soon find out by her arcane arts who's lying." To Vanora he added: "I shan't be stonished if Master Jorian has the right of it. We've had trouble with you two before."

"Come on, Boso," said Vanora, taking the stout man by the arm. "They're all against us. Everyone hates us." She hauled him to his feet, and the pair went unsteadily out. As she left, she spat at Jorian: "I hate you!"

"Come back, Baltho!" Rhuys called after his son. "The wizardess will not be needed."

"There's your answer," said Jorian to Rhuys. "Now may I get on with my packing? God den, Lady Margalit!"

The lady-in-waiting appeared in the doorway. "What's all this direful noise?"

"Master Rhuys will explain," said Jorian. "As for me, I must be off ere daylight; so pray excuse me." Rhuys and his young men filed out.

Margalit shrugged. "I merely wished to ask if you would mind my sending a letter to my Queen, telling her I am well and will return when I can? A courier departs on the morrow for Xylar, and I can send it by him."

"Hm," murmured Jorian. "I mind not your reassuring her; but I crave not to have my present roost revealed. Else we shall have a squad of Shvenic lariat men come to drag me off for an over-close haircut."

"I could say I wrote from Vindium or Govannian."

"Ah, but if anyone question the courier, he'll tell whence he brought the letter." Jorian frowned. "I have it! Write your letter, without saying whence it comes. I'll inclose it in a letter to my mother in Kortoli, wherein I shall ask her to send the inclosed epistle to Xylar by the next courier."

Margalit sighed. "At that rate, with postal service in its present parlous plight, my letter will not be delivered until summer. By then my position may have gone to another. But I feel responsible to my Queen for you. She'd not thank me for getting her a headless husband."

"Neither should I," said Jorian. "Not that a head ever has much to say after it has been sundered from its body. The operation impairs clear thinking."

"If you are leaving early," said Margalit, "I must write my letter forthwith."

Three days after leaving Othomae, Jorian arrived at the inn recommended to him, the Golden Ibex. This inn stood on a secondary road in the foothills of the Lograms. Over the nearer hills could be seen the snow-clad peak of Aravia.

Jorian rode the horse he had bought. This was a middle-aged gelding, useless for mounted combat or desperate chases; but Jorian hoped he would not need a mount for such purposes, and this animal had been for sale cheap. Jorian named the horse Fimbri, after a carpenter to whom he had once been apprenticed. He led the mule, which he called Filoman, after a notably foolish former King of Kortoli.

"The trail to Aravia leaves the road here," said the taverner, Turonus. "I would not try to ride a horse up to old Shenderu's cave, for the latter part of the journey is too steep and rocky, and the snow too deep. If ye walk leading your pack mule, ye should do all right, an ye fear not the ghost of Captain Oswic."

"What's that tale?"

"In my grandsire's time, they say, Oswic led a band of brigands in these parts, terrorizing the land for leagues around. At last the Grand Bastard, that was then, sent a company of soldiery against Oswic. They trailed him and his band up the slopes of Mount Aravia, until they reached a level place overlooking a steep slope. Here Oswic and his men chose to make a stand; for they outnumbered the soldiers. Moreover, beyond that point the slope became too steep for riding, and they would have had to abandon their horses and struggle up the slope afoot, belike to be picked off by archers in the open.

"Oswic made a fiery speech, that 'twere better to die on their feet than to live on their knees; and that whereas death in battle was a possibility, it was a certainty if the soldiers laid hands upon them. Then he flourished his sword and led a charge down upon the soldiers.

"The banditti were well armed, and after the first shock the soldiers began to give way. But then Oswic raised his sword on high in an inspiriting gesture and began a shout of victory. So intent was he upon harkening on his men that he failed to guard himself. A soldier rode up behind him and smote off Captain Oswic's head, which went rolling down the slope, bumping the bases of trees and rolling on. Some of the soldiers swore that the severed head continued to shout exhortations to the robbers; but I misdoubt this. Without lungs to blow air through the vocal organs, how could a head cry out?

"So fell a fighter, howsomever, was Captain Oswic that the headless body continued to wave its sword to encourage the brigands and to strive to smite the troopers. But, lacking eyes to see, its blows went wild. Some robbers, seeing their leader in such parlous plight, turned away and rode off into the forest, and no amount of frantic gestures by the now headless body served to rally them. And presently, three troopers got the body amongst them and hacked it to pieces, whilst all the robbers who had not fled were likewise slain. And the folk hereabouts claim that at certain times, especially on nights of the full moon, they see Oswic's headless body, still riding about on the slopes of Aravia and brandishing a sword."

"Quite a story," said Jorian. "Does Oswic's ghost ride the ghost of his horse?"

Turonus chuckled. "None hitherto has brought up that point."

"Do you tell this tale to all your guests?"

"Oh, aye, it makes a good one to pass a long even, and primes some to tell me stories in their turn."

Jorian had been alerted by the taverner's name, the same as that of the Chancellor of Xylar at the time of Jorian's aborted execution. Cautious questioning, however, indicated that this Turonus had never even heard of his namesake, let alone admit to kinship. Still, Jorian thought it prudent to go under one of his pseudonyms, Nikko of Kortoli. He asked:

"Could one ride a horse up to the timberline, stake it out there, and walk the rest of the way? I do not anticipate being with Shenderu more than an hour or two."

Turonus frowned. "Ye could, but there's a tiger in these forests, having wandered over from the Mulvanian side. Leaving your steed tethered were a sure way of losing him."

"Then could I board my horse with you until my return?"

"Certes; 'tis usual. Now, an ye would, I'll see ye have needfuls for a call upon the Greatsoul. Many pilgrims, coming to consult the wise one, pass through here in summer, but few at this time of year. And speaking of snow, ye will need a pair of these."

Turonus stepped behind his bar and brought up two

oval wooden frames on which had been stretched a netting of rawhide thongs.

"What are those?" asked Jorian.

"Snowshoes. I can rent you a pair for ten pence a day. On the trail up Aravia, ye'll need them for certain."

Jorian chaffered the man down to five pence a day. He did not altogether believe the story of the tiger, suspecting his host of making it up in order to profit from boarding the horse Fimbri. On the other hand, he could not be sure; so, lacking time to investigate the matter, he acceded to Turonus' recommendation. When Turonus also tried to sell him firewood, Jorian declined, saying: "I brought an ax and a saw to cut my own."

"Well then, belike you'd like a guide. With snow on the ground, the trail's easily lost, and ye could wander for days amongst the peaks ere finding it again. My nephew Kynoc's to be had, for he knows the lay of the land."

Further bargaining enlisted the services of Turonus' nephew, a slender, smooth-faced, small-featured youth. "How long to reach Shenderu?" asked Jorian.

"Ye must needs camp out one night, at least going up. Methinks ye'd better camp below the snow line."

When time came to go, Kynoc saw the crossbow that Jorian had strapped to the back of the pack mule. The youth asked: "Plan ye to hunt on the way, Master Nikko?"

"Maybe," said Jorian. "You'd better bring one, too."

Actually, Jorian was not interested in hunting. He wanted to get to Shenderu, resolve his problems, and hurry back to Othomae. But, having been pursued before by Xylarians intent upon dragging him back to complete their ceremony of royal succession, he thought it well to be prepared. He wore sword and dagger and a vest of light mesh mail beneath his jacket.

\*     \*     \*

"Ho!" said Jorian sharply, halting. He was towing the pack mule Filoman, while Kynoc trudged ahead up the slope. The forest had begun to thin out with altitude. A light snow covered the ground between the black boles of the leafless trees. Here and there rose stands of evergreens, dark green in the light and black in the shadow.

"Eh?" said Kynoc, turning.

"Look at that!" Jorian pointed to a large paw print in the snow. "Is that the tiger your uncle spoke of?"

The youth bent down. "Aye, that's old Ardyman the Terrible. Hold the mule straitly lest it bolt. We think Ardyman has been chased from his former range by a younger cat, and that with age he's like to turn man-eater. We've tried to hunt him down in parties with hounds, but the crafty villain gives us the slip."

The mule seemed to have caught a whiff of tiger, for it jerked its head and rolled its eyes.

Since dark was falling, Jorian decided to camp here. He tethered Filoman securely, put a nosebag over its head, and got the ax and saw from his gear. He chopped down and trimmed four small dead trees, while Kynoc sawed them into billets. Jorian kept raising his head to peer into the gathering darkness for signs of the tiger.

"Best we make a goodly fire," said Kynoc.

"No doubt; but let's not burn up all the wood we've cut. We shall need some for Shenderu."

Jorian passed an uneasy night, alternately dozing and waking to listen for the grunt of a hunting tiger. Once he awoke to find Kynoc, whose turn it was to watch, asleep with his back against a tree. He angrily shook the youth awake.

"Be not so much atwitter, lowlander," drawled the youth. "The tiger won't come nigh whilst the fire burns bright; at least, not unless he starves."

"Well, for aught we know he may be starving," grumbled Jorian. "Come along; it's nearly dawn."

"Best do on your snowshoes," said Kynoc, strapping on his own. "Deep snow begins soon."

Jorian found that walking with snowshoes took practice. If one tried to walk in the normal manner, one stepped on one's own feet. Jorian did this once and sat down in the snow. He got up cursing, to see Kynoc's face agrin.

"Ye must learn to waddle, like this," said the youth, demonstrating a spraddle-legged gait.

When Jorian had mastered snowshoes, he found that the mule had turned balky, either because of the weight of the firewood, or the increasing steepness of the trail. The rest of the journey was made with Jorian hauling on the lead rope, while Kynoc beat Filoman's rump with a switch that Jorian had cut from a branch.

"Master Nikko," said Kynoc, "ye come from the lowlands and have seen more of the world than I. Tell me, is it true that down there any woman will lie down for you an ye but ask her?"

Jorian stared. His breath was becoming labored with the climb, but the spindly mountaineer youth seemed to mind the grade no more than a stroll on level ground. When he had taken a couple of deep breaths, Jorian answered: "Some. Not all by any means."

"Tell me more about it, pray. I have never done it or seen it done. I do but hear tales from other lads, of their adventures with women and sheep and other things. Many stories I am sure are lies. So tell me: how do ye do it? How long does it take?"

When Jorian paused for a breather, he gave Kynoc a lecture on elementary sex. The youth hung on his words with an intentness that Jorian found embarrassing.

"I thank you, sir," said Kynoc, with more respect than he had hitherto shown. "My parents are dead, and my uncle and his goodwife think it a subject not to be talked on by decent folk."

\* \* \*

The sun was well up when the two men and the mule plodded up the path to Shenderu's cave. Below, the foothills of the Lograms spread out, the taller peaks covered with snow on which the bright morning sun glittered.

They found Shenderu, bundled in shapeless brown woolens, sweeping snow from the terrace before his cave. He proved a burly, dark-skinned man of middle age, with a gray-streaked beard. Jorian said:

"Hail, reverend sir! I am Nikko of Kortoli, here on the recommendation of your friend Karadur."

"Ah, yes, dear old Karadur!" said Shenderu, in Novarian with a strong Mulvani accent. "Is that load on the mule for me?"

"Aye, save for our blankets and other personals. I seek advice."

Shenderu sat down on the rocky surface of the space he had cleared of snow. "Say on, my son."

Jorian said: "Kynoc, unload and feed Filoman. Now, Father Shenderu, my problem is this. . . ."

The sun was halfway to noon when Jorian finished his tale. He had let his bent for storytelling run away with him; but the wise man seemed amused. Jorian finished:

". . . so you see, I have tried direct assault on the palace to rescue my darling, and that failed. I tried sorcery, to no avail. What recourse remains?"

Shenderu remained sunk in thought with his eyes closed. At last he looked up, saying: "Have you tried simple bribery?"

Jorian clapped a hand to his forehead. "Good gods! I never thought of that."

Shenderu smiled. "Every large enterprise, be it a merchant company, an army, a ship, or a government, requires a multiplicity of people, organized with lines of command and a hierarchy of ranks. Wherever such a multiplicity exists, there is at least one wight open to bribes."

"How can I find a suitable bribee?"

"You have a brother who visits the palace, have you not?"

Jorian started. "Aye, but how knew you? You must know who I really am."

"I have heard much about you, Jo—What said you your nonce name was?"

"Nikko of Kortoli. For obvious reasons, neither my brother nor I wishes to disclose his kinship to me."

"I understand, Master Nikko. I know somewhat more of you than you would think. Never fear, I wag not an indiscreet tongue, as you have been known to do. My livelihood depends upon my name for reticence. Is your brother discreet?"

"Reasonably so."

"Very well. Set him to learning who is corruptible amongst the clerks and flunkeys that infest the palace. Inveterate gamblers make the best prospects, since they are usually up to their eyebrows in debt. And now perchance you'll join me in a light repast ere returning to the mundane world."

As they ate, clouds drifted athwart the sun. Kynoc said: "Master Nikko, methinks we'd best take our leave; an we'd make our return journey without camping out. Besides, it looks like rain or snow. Unless, that is, ye'd liefer ask the Greatsoul for shelter."

Jorian shook his head. "I'm hot to get back to the Golden Ibex. Let's forth! Thanks and farewell, Doctor Shenderu!"

Going down was much faster than going up. The mule was readier to move without its load of food and firewood, or perhaps it visualized the comfort of Turonus' warm stable.

While they were still above the timberline, rain began. It grew swiftly heavier; the wind rose to a howl and blew the rain into their faces. Jorian tried backing down the slope, but tripped on a rock and sat down again.

"I shall have a black-and-blue arse tomorrow," he growled as he got up.

After an hour of plodding through slush and staggering on slopes where rain made the snow slippery, they reached the shelter of the trees, as much as these leafless trunks could provide shelter. Then the rain gradually dwindled to a drizzle and ceased. They removed their snowshoes.

Kynoc sneezed. "Master Nikko, methinks we'd best halt long enough to eat a bite and dry out."

"Can we still reach the inn without an overnight stop?"

"I am sure of it, sir. By dark we shall be down to familiar country, which I know like the palm of my hand."

"Very good. Tether Filoman whilst I cut firewood, if my tinder hasn't gotten wet."

The tinder was dry, but the brushwood was not, so that it took an hour for Jorian to get a brisk fire going. He and Kynoc draped their outer clothing on nearby branches. They also wrung out their sodden blankets and hung them likewise.

Then they stood as close to the fire as they dared, turning slowly to heat all sides. The afternoon sun broke briefly through the clouds, sending golden spears of light aslant among the trees. All was quiet save for the crackle of the fire and the drip of rainwater from branches.

"I am as dry as I am likely to get," said Jorian. "Kynoc, in my bag on Filoman you will find an oil flask and a rag. Pray fetch them and help me to oil this mail shirt, ere it rust."

The youth was rubbing the mail with the oily rag when Jorian cocked his head. He said: "Didst hear someone call?"

"Aye; but so faintly methought I was hearing things."

As Kynoc finished annointing the links, the call came again, more clearly but still distant: "Oh, Jo-o-oria-a-an!"

"Halloo!" Jorian shouted, peering over the edge of the fell.

"Where are you?" came the call.

"Right here."

"Is that your fire?" The voice, vaguely familiar, came louder.

"Aye. Who are you?"

Movement among the tree trunks, down the slope, sorted itself out into a human figure scrambling up the trail. Jorian pulled on his trews, donned his damp jacket, and got his crossbow and bolts from the mule's back.

As the figure came closer, it appeared to be that of a youth in hunting gear, unarmed save for a sheath knife at his belt.

Closer yet, the figure took on a maddening familiarity that Jorian could not quite place. As it scrambled up over the lip of the fell, Jorian said: "Great Zevatas, are you the twin brother of a lady I know?"

The figure stood panting. When it got its breath, it spoke: "Nay, I'm the lady herself." Margalit swept off her forester's felt hat, so that her curly hair sprang out from her head.

"Good gods! I'm glad to see you; but what brings you hither, and in man's clothing?"

"I came to warn you. The Xylarians are on your track. 'Tis not unlikely they're already ascending the trail below us."

"How—what—how learned you this?"

"I'll tell. 'Twas Goania's wench Vanora. I gather that she besought you to take her on this journey as your leman, and you denied her?"

"Aye. So what befell?"

"The night after you left, I was dining with the old Mulvanian and with Mistress Goania and her two domestics. Vanora got drunk and had a rush of conscience. With tears and sobs she told us that, the very morn you departed, she gave a letter to the courier to Xylar, telling the government there whither you had gone. At that time, she said, so filled with hatred and rancor was she that she looked forward with glee to attending your execution and cheering with the rest as the ax fell. Now she was shamed and abashed. She wept and wailed and called on the gods to chastise her; she bemoaned her thwart nature, which forced her to do such horrid things."

"But you—how did you—"

"Someone had to warn you, and I was the only one young and active enough of our little circle. So I borrowed these garments from Rhuys's younger son, since my gowns are unsuited to riding and mountain climbing. I also borrowed Rhuys's best horse, without his knowledge I'm sorry to say, and followed your track.

"Last night I stayed at the Golden Ibex. Being weary, I retired early; but I was awakened by sounds of revelry below. This morn I arose ere daybreak. At breakfast, Turonus' daughter told me that one Judge Grallon, a Xylarian Official, had come in with six attendants. These she described as tall, light-haired men of wild, barbaric aspect. That sounded like Shvenish lariat-men; so, tarrying no longer, I set out in search of you."

"Were the Shvenites abroad when you left?"

"Nay; the maid said they were all in drunken stupor. But they'll have set forth by now, I ween."

Jorian bit his lip. "Kynoc!" he said. "Canst guide us back to the inn by another route, one that would take us around these pursuers?"

"Not with the mule, sir. This trail's the only way down for beasts, until ye come anigh the inn, where the ground's flatter. I could take you by another where ye'd need but to lower yourselves down banks by gripping the roots of trees."

"Much as I hate to leave Filoman as booty, I mislike

the thought of Uthar's ax even more," said Jorian. "Put out the fire, Kynoc. I'll take my saddlebags—"

"Too late!" cried Margalit.

Cries came from down the slope, and figures appeared among the trees in the distance. Jorian recognized Judge Grallon's voice, commanding: "There they are, where you see the smoke of their fire! Spread out! Moruvikh, farther over to the right! Ingund, to the left!"

"We cannot easily lose them in the forest," said Kynoc, "with the leaves off the trees. Would ye flee back up the trail?" The youth shook with nervousness.

"Nay; they'd catch us more easily with their ropes and nets in the open. Get your crossbow! This little fell's a good place to make a stand. The squad does not usually bear missile weapons. Watch our flanks whilst I defend our front. Margalit, help Kynoc to watch for rogues stealing upon us."

Jorian cocked his crossbow, lay prone in the leaf mold at the edge of the fell, and sighted. The movements among the trees resolved into three or four men—he could not judge their exact number—plodding up the slope. As one on the trail came into plain view, Jorian called: "Stand, varlet!"

The man, a tall, light-haired Shvenite, paused. Judge Grallon's voice boomed from back in the trees: "Go on, faintheart! He cannot hurt you!"

Jorian waited until he got a clear view of the man. He squinted along the groove of his crossbow, adjusted its angle for distance, and allowed a hair for windage. Then he squeezed the trigger.

The bow snapped; the quarrel thrummed away, rising and falling, to strike home in the Shvenite's body. Kynoc discharged his own weapon; but his bolt grazed a branch and glanced off at an angle.

The man who had been struck cried out and folded up on the ground. Grallon called: "Get down, all of you!" Thereupon the other Shvenites dropped to hands and knees, crawling forward. Most of the time they were out of sight behind dead ground.

Kynoc started to rise to recock his weapon, but Jorian barked: "Keep down!"

Plaintively Kynoc asked: "How then shall I reload?"

"Watch me," said Jorian. He rolled over on his back, put his toe in the stirrup at the muzzle of the crossbow, and pulled back on the string with both hands until it caught on the sear. Then he rolled back on his belly and put a bolt in the groove.

"I never thought of that," said Kynoc.

"You're used to shooting at deer and hares, which do not shoot back. Next time, shoot not until I tell you. We have no bolts to waste."

"Go on! Go on!" called Grallon's voice. "Creep up and surround them; then rush upon them from all sides. They cannot number more than two or three."

Jorian bellowed: "Promus, take these javelins off that way. See if you can spear one of these knaves. Clotharo, take the spare bolts off that way; try to hit one in the flank. Nors, get the covers off our shields. Physo, did you remember to sharpen our steel?"

Kynoc looked about in a bewildered way at hearing these commands addressed to nonexistent warriors. Margalit, catching on at once, lowered her voice to sound mannish, calling: "Here you are, sir. Which sword do you wish? Let me lace on your cuirass!"

The creeping Shvenites seemed to have halted their advance. Jorian whispered: "Kynoc, steal off amongst the trees on either side and tell me what you see."

"Go on!" came Judge Grallon's voice. "Keep advancing! It is all a pretence, his having an army. Get in close and rush them!"

A guttural voice spoke in the Shvenish language: "Why does he not lead his grand charge himself?" Jorian understood the words but supposed that Grallon did not.

From the trees on one side came the thud of Kynoc's

arbalest, followed by a yell of pain. The young man came loping back, grinning.

"I got one!" he chortled. "Methinks I did but wound his leg; but he'll molest us no more."

"That will hold them up for a while," said Jorian. "But in a couple of hours, darkness will fall, and we shan't be able to hit the side of Mount Aravia."

"Belike we can then give them the slip," said Kynoc.

Jorian fidgeted, trying to get another clear shot. But the Shvenites hugged the hollows in the earth, offering no targets save an occasional glimpse of a buckskin-clad arse as they wormed their way forward, Jorian shot at one such target but missed.

At last Jorian, unwilling further to prolong the stalemate, crawled back from his edge. "Kynoc!" he said. "I'll try a cavalry charge. Take off the rest of Filoman's load."

"How shall ye guide the beast without a bridle?"

"I'll make one." Jorian began experimenting with the lead rope, threading it through the mule's unwilling mouth and twisting it around the animal's muzzle. The mule jerked its head uneasily.

"Be it trained to riding?" asked Kynoc.

"We shall soon find out. There, that should serve to guide the beast, if he does not chew the rope through. Wilt give me a hand up?"

Since the mule had no saddle, Kynoc made a cradle of his hands, into which Jorian put one booted foot, and then he swung aboard the mule's bare back. Jorian had not ridden bareback in years and hoped his riding muscles were still hard enough to keep him on Filoman's back.

"Here goes!" he said, drawing his sword and thumping the mule's ribs with his heels.

Filoman refused to move. When Jorian whacked its rump with the flat of his sword, it shook its head and bucked. Jorian caught its mane to avoid a fall.

"Get my spurs out of the baggage," said Jorian. Margalit, again anticipating his needs, was already burrowing into his gear. Soon she had strapped the spurs to his feet.

"Here goes again," said Jorian, digging in his spurs. The mule snorted and bounded forward, almost precipitating Jorian back over its rump. When he recovered his seat, he tried to guide the animal by his improvised bridle. But Filoman paid no heed to Jorian's rope. Instead, it ran around in a circle, bowling over Kynoc. Then it galloped off into the woods at random.

In front of it hung Jorian's blanket, which Jorian had suspended from a convenient branch to dry. The mule plunged ahead, ducking its head beneath the lower edge of the blanket. Jorian ducked, too, so as not to be swept off the mule's back by the branch. Hence he struck the blanket squarely, so that it was whisked from the branch and settled down over his head and body, completely blinding him. He yelled: "Halt! Stop! Whoa!" and pulled on the rope, to no effect.

From somewhere before him he heard a shout of terror and, in Shvenic, cries of "Oswic's ghost!" "The headless horseman!" "All is lost!" "Flee for your lives!"

Then came the sound of men running away. One tripped and fell, got up cursing, and ran on. The mule continued galloping, turning this way and that, trying to shake Jorian off. Jorian dropped the rope, caught the mane, and clung to the animal's back.

The mule stopped so suddenly that Jorian was thrown forward over its head. He landed in a patch of brush, while the blanket flew off over his head. Scratched and bruised, he scrambled up and made a flying dive to seize the mule's rope before the beast ran away.

Then he saw a curious sight. Gray-bearded Judge Grallon was kneeling on the forest floor and praying with his eyes closed. Of the Shvenish lariat-men there was no sight save a glimpse of one buckskin-clad back receding in the distance. The man limped, and Jorian guessed that he was the one Kynoc had shot in the leg, left behind by his speedier fellows. Up the trail, half a bowshot away, lay the body of the man whom Jorian had shot.

Jorian gathered up his sword, which he had dropped, and approached the justice, sword in one hand and lead rope in the other. "Get up!" he said.

Grallon opened his eyes. "King Jorian!" he cried. "Methought 'twas the true headless ghost whereof the innkeeper told us. Being too old to flee with that squad of superstitious cowards, I was confessing my sins to Imbal, expecting each instant to be my last. What would you of me? My life?"

"Not yet," said Jorian. "I need you as a hostage. Get up, pick up that blanket, and walk ahead of me. At the first untoward move, you shall be a headless ghost, too!"

Grallon grumbled: "But, Your Majesty, I do but my duty. I wish you well in every way, so long as you in turn perform your duty, which is to attend the ceremony of succession."

"Never mind that. Pick up that blanket!"

Jorian saw that the judge was looking past him with an expression of alarm. Quickly turning, Jorian saw a patch of striped orange and black among the trees. The tiger padded to where lay the Shvenite whom Jorian had shot. The cat lowered its head to sniff at the corpse, then raised it to stare at the two men on the path below. It blinked its big yellow eyes, then lowered its head again. Silently, it sank its fangs into the body.

The Shvenite gave a faint cry. But the tiger raised its head, so that the wounded man's arms and legs dangled. It walked calmly off into the forest, the man's limbs flopping where they were dragged over roots. Grallon said:

"Your Majesty is a villain, if you will excuse my saying so. Odovald was the best man of the squad, and

you slew him. Were we in Xylar, you should answer
for your crime!"

"Horse apples!" snorted Jorian. "I warned him to let
me alone. When he would not, I defended myself.
Besides, I did not slay him; the tiger did. But enough
legalistics; march!"

Soon after dusk, Judge Grallon, his wrists tied by a
strip of cloth cut from Jorian's blanket, stumbled up to
the front door of the Golden Ibex. Behind him came
Jorian, covering him with a cocked crossbow; then Margalit and Kynoc, the last leading the mule.

At Jorian's command, Kynoc went into the inn and
brought out his uncle Turonus, who whistled at the
sight. "What is this, Master Nikko? Some quarrel or
feud? Not in my inn—"

"Never mind your inn," said Jorian. "Your other
guests were after my head. Give me the reckoning,
pray."

Turonus felt in the pocket of his apron and brought
out a stack of thin wooden tablets threaded on a thong.
He leafed through these until he came to Jorian's and
presented it.

"Hers, too," said Jorian. He handed Margalit his
purse, not wishing to have to juggle his weapon and
the money at the same time. While Margalit counted
out the money, the Shvenites appeared in the doorway.

"Your Honor!" cried one, starting to draw his sword.
"What betides?"

"Back inside!" said the judge. "Quickly, ere this des-
perado puts a bolt through my brisket!"

Jorian smiled. "Now, your Honor, you shall come for
a ride. Kynoc, saddle the judge's horse and boost him
up on its back. Then saddle the lady's and mine."

Minutes later, Jorian and Margalit rode off on the
road to Othomae. Jorian led the mule. The judge, gripping the mane with his bound hands, unhappily

bounced on the back of his own horse, like him old and fat.

"I am in your eternal debt, Lady Margalit," said Jorian. "Why did you go to such effort and risk to save my unworthy neck?"

"I told you, I felt responsible to Estrildis for you. As it was, I did not truly save you, since the Shvenites were close upon my trail. Your own valor did that."

Jorian chuckled. "If you but knew the horror with which I felt myself borne along willy-nilly on that cursed mule, blinded by the blanket—but there, Karadur is ever at me not to let my modesty show. At least you gave me a few moments' warning. You are a splendid person. When you get a husband, you deserve the best. If I were not a devoted family man. . . ." Feeling that his unruly tongue was about to run away with him, Jorian ceased talking and concentrated on the road ahead.

# VI

# The Water Wife

After riding through the dark for hours, Judge Grallon called: "Your Majesty, how much farther wilt drag me? 'Twill take all the morrow to get back."

"You shan't get back," said Jorian. "I am taking you to Othomae."

"By Imbal's iron pizzle, what for? Mean you to slay me there?"

"Not at all, your Honor. I have a task, wherefor you are uniquely qualified."

"Task? Art mad? What task could I possibly perform for you?"

"Service as arbitrator in a dispute. You will receive the standard fee and be sent back to Xylar no worse for wear."

"That is the strangest proposal I have ever heard!" exclaimed Grallon. "Why should you trust me to deliver a just verdict, after you have treated me so wrongfully?"

"Because I knew you of old, when I was King. Will you do it?"

Grallon hesitated. "Only if I can discharge my office honorably, without prior conditions or constraint."

"That's my wish, too. I ask not that you incline to my cause because of my connection with Xylar, and even less that you incline against it because of the strong measures I have taken to protect myself."

"Very well, then," said Grallon. "Meanwhile I am half dead from bouncing on the back of this cursed beast. At least unbind me. Do you mean to camp out?"

"Nay. We shall soon reach another inn."

"And who is this young person?"

"You shall know in good time."

"At least tell me whether it be male or female."

"Not just yet. Ah, methinks I see a light through the trees! When we go in, I shall be Nikko of Kortoli, and you Master Grallon. Think not to raise an outcry of kidnapping, for we are now well within Othomaean territory. You know the love between Othomaeans and Xylarians! They'd say, give him an extra kick for me!"

At the inn, Jorian took a room for two. He offered no explanation of Margalit in her young man's garb. If anyone noticed the unmasculine bulges beneath her jacket, they forebore to comment in the presence of one so formidable-looking as Jorian.

Leaving the taverner to warm up leftovers for their supper, Jorian shepherded his two companions into the room. As he set down their baggage, Margalit took off her forester's hat, so that her curly hair sprang out.

"I know you now!" said Judge Grallon. "You are the Queen's lady-in-waiting, Margalit of Totens. I heard of your disappearance from the palace. What do you here? What of these wild tales of a scarlet demon's snatching you from the Queen's apartments?"

"Just a little sorcery gone awry," said Jorian.

"But—but that does not explain her being with you on Mount Aravia! And in men's garb, forsooth! She evanished from the palace in the Month of the Eagle, and here it is almost springtime! What have you twain been up to in the meantime?"

"That's enough questions," said Jorian. "You forget you are my prisoner and not the other way round."

The judge turned to Margalit. "But you, Lady Margalit? What do you here? Are you in some plot with this runaway king?"

Margalit began: "Why, as to that—" Then she saw that Jorian, standing behind the judge, was making motions of clapping his hand over his mouth. "You must needs ask Master Jorian," she said.

"Hah! Were this Xylar, you'd soon be behind bars as a fautor of King Jorian's felonies!"

"Felonies?" said Jorian.

"Certes! For the king to escape the doom assigned him by our divinely inspired laws were a heinous offense. Should we ever win you back to complete your part in the blasphemously interrupted ceremony, you will be scourged, ere you are beheaded, for your irreligious contumaciousness."

"Thanks for the warning," said Jorian. "I'll take good care not to be caught."

The judge clenched his fists, stamped his feet, and sputtered with righteous indignation; but so wrought up was he that no words came forth. At last he dropped his arms and dropped his shoulders, muttering: "Shameless! Shameless! You are lost to all considerations of morality!"

"Lost or not," said Jorian, "the innkeeper should have something for us to eat. Belike a full belly will help you bear my iniquities."

After supper, Jorian chivvied his companions back to the room. "Margalit," he said, "the judge shall have the bed, whilst you and I take turns sleeping beside him and watching him."

Grallon groaned. "If the word gets out that I have passed the night in bed with this young woman, my repute on the bench will be ruined, not to mention what my wife will say."

"When I said 'sleeping,' I meant just 'sleeping,'" said Jorian. "Anyway, if you keep silent about it, we will do likewise. Eh, Margalit?"

She laughed. "I have already been compromised to the point where one more scandal matters not. I promise, your Honor, to make no lascivious advances."

"Now," said Jorian, "I'll trouble your Honor for your shoes, knife, and purse."

"Aha, so Your Majesty has turned robber as well as abductor?"

"Not at all. They shall be returned to you in due course. I merely wish to make sure that, if the one of us on watch fall asleep, you do not stab us in our sleep and flee. Margalit, whilst you are on watch, sit on the judge's things."

The return to Othomae took Jorian half a day longer than had his journey to the Golden Ibex. Two companions, he found, inevitably slowed him down, the more so since one was elderly and Jorian's own horse was showing fatigue. They arrived on the afternoon of the fourth day out of the Golden Ibex, too weary to take up Jorian's business with Abacarus. Jorian did, however, hire one of Rhuys's sons to carry messages to Abacarus and to Goania and Karadur.

At dinner time, Goania and Karadur came to the Silver Dragon. Boso hulked in and gave Jorian a surly greeting. Jorian asked: "Where is Vanora?"

Goania said: "I suppose Margalit has told you of her confession. I served her notice that one more such buffoonery and she was through. She hung around for another few days. But when, by my second sight, I told her that you had escaped the lariat squad and were on your way back to Othomae, she packed up her scanty gear and vanished. Belike she thought you would slay her on your return."

"I do not kill women," said Jorian. "But I might have been tempted to stripe her backside."

Once convinced of Judge Grallon's identity, Doctor Abacarus accepted the learned jurist as arbitrator. He and Jorian drew up a stipulation of facts not in dispute and handed the sheet to Grallon. Then each set forth his argument over the debt, and each had a chance to rebut the other's statements.

When they had finished, Grallon retired to think. While they waited, Abacarus and Jorian killed time with a game of draughts. Jorian thought himself a competent player, but the sorcerer beat him so easily that Jorian suspected magical assistance.

Grallon returned, saying: "On due consideration, I must find for Master Jorian. Doctor Abacarus, your arbitration agreement states that I collect my fee from the loser. Ten nobles, please."

Abacarus counted out the money with the expression of one who has bitten into a lemon. "Not bad pay for a morning's work," he grumbled.

"It is the going rate, sir. Your agreement also forbids either party to attempt future harassments, by dunning specters or otherwise, does it not?"

Abacarus nodded tight-lipped. Jorian saw the judge out. He said: "The first diligencia of the season leaves for Xylar on the morrow. I have reserved a place for you. Permit me to thank you for your just verdict."

"No thanks are due," grumped Grallon. "I did but call the hit as I saw it. I will confess that I was not entirely regardless of the fact that, if Abacarus clapped you in debtor's prison, our chances of getting you back to Xylar were lessened. On the other hand, the rascal richly deserved to lose. He whispered to me that, if I decided for him, he would split his takings with me."

At the inn that evening, Jorian told Margalit of the judge's impending departure. She said: "I suppose I ought to return to Xylar with him."

"Better not," said Jorian. "Remember what he said about your being an accessory to my crimes? If he got you to Xylar, he'd denounce you to the law instanter.

"He is a fanatic in his way. When I was King, he made a fine chief justice, absolutely incorruptible and fearless. You saw how he stood up to me when I held his life in my hand. But these virtues become awkward when one is on the other side of the law from him, no matter how absurd the law. And I like your head much better attached to the rest of you."

Jorian told her of his interview with Shenderu, adding: "Know you anyone around the court susceptible to a bribe? Shenderu said gambling men were the easiest targets for golden arrows."

She frowned. "Let me think. Aha! There's a proxenary clerk, Thevatas, in charge of Estrildis' expenses. I do not know of any defalcations by him, but he is addicted to horse races. He would come to our apartment from one, volubly praising the beauty and speed of the beast he had wagered on if he had won, or berating the animal as bait for crows when he had lost."

"If I know such gentry," said Jorian, "he will have skimmed a little here and there off my darling's income to make up for his losses. We'll see what can be done with him."

"How?"

"Better that you know not. Suffice it to say that I shall depart next month. Meanwhile I must find another means of livelihood. The windmill is shut down until the spring wheat begins to come in."

When he saw the judge off, Jorian said: "Your Honor, you had better warn the Regency Council not to send any more squads of kidnappers after me. I have small influence with the Grand Duke, and he assures me that he would regard another such incursion as cause for instant war with Xylar."

This was a bluff; Jorian had never met the Grand Duke. He delayed his warning until he was sure that Judge Grallon would not have time to make inquiries to confirm or refute Jorian's story.

Grallon grunted: "I hear Your Majesty!" and climbed into the coach, which rattled away on the road to Xylar.

Jorian would like to have left for his native Ardamai right after seeing Grallon off to Xylar. But he had already missed the first diligencia of the season to Vindium, and the next would not depart for three sennights. He could not fare on horseback, because the horse Fimbri, which he had ridden to Mount Aravia, had fallen ill of some equine ailment of the lungs, rendering it useless for hard riding. Jorian was too softhearted to sell the beast to a knacker, so he continued to maintain the animal until one day he found it dead in its stall. The knacker got the carcass at the bottom price.

Jorian decided against buying another horse for the time being. A good one would cost more than he thought he could afford. Besides, he had had enough rides over hundreds of leagues, in all weathers, to last him a lifetime.

Jorian picked up a few nobles as assistant to Tremorin, a fencing master in Othomae City. He even thought of setting himself up as a fencing master on his own; but inquiry convinced him that this was impractical. First, the city's three fencing masters would combine to suppress competition, if need be by hiring thugs to assault or kill him. Second, even if he became established, the Grand Duke would levy not only the usual tax on his earnings but also would add a surtax because he was a foreigner.

One day, Jorian saw, pinned to the bulletin board in the square, a placard reading:

## MERLOIS SON OF GAUS PRESENTS

his superlative, matchless, unexcelled theatrical troupe, the Nonesuchers, performing two new plays by Pselles of Aussar, THE INNOCENT VAMPIRE and THE WRONG BEDROOM, as well as a revival of Physo's classic, THE TINSEL CROWN.

The placard bore further information about time, place, and price of admission. Jorian learned that the sheet had been tacked up by Merlois' advance man. This one told him that Merlois and his troupe would arrive that afternoon.

When Merlois lighted down from his carriage, he found Jorian awaiting him. With a yell of joy, the elderly actor and Jorian seized each other in bear hugs. Merlois whispered: "What name go you by now?"

"Nikko of Kortoli," said Jorian. "So you have your own troupe at last?"

"Aye. I wax a little old for leaping from balconies, slaying dragons, and whacking a fellow actor with a wooden sword, as my profession doth tyrannously demand. Oh, I still take small parts; I shall be the good wizard in *The Innocent Vampire*. You must attend, on pain of my august displeasure! Let me give you these passes."

"Could I beg an extra set for a companion?" asked Jorian.

"Oho, aha, so thither blows the wind! Certes; here you be. Bring a whole harem if such be your desire."

"Nay; this is merely a brotherly friendship. My heart still belongs to Estrildis, mewed up in durance vile in Xylar. I take it *The Innocent Vampire* is a horror show?"

"Aye, verily! 'Twill freeze the blood in thy veins to the consistency of cold tar, bring thy fluttersome heart to an ominous halt, and make thine eyes protrude on stalks, like unto those of the dilatory snail."

"And *The Wrong Bedroom,* I suppose, is a farce?"

"Doth the sun rise in the east? Doth the tiger devour flesh? Doth water run downhill? Indeed, sirrah, 'tis the cynosure, the acme, the epitome of farces! 'Twill shake thy belly with mirth until thy very ribs do ache, as if thou hadst been beaten by the roughhewn clubs of a regiment of Ellornian savages. I shall warn persons with weak hearts against attendance, lest they laugh themselves to death. But one thing worries me."

"And that is?"

"It is a short play, in two acts. I need something wherewith to flesh it out, lest my fickle audience deem themselves cozened. We got some bad notices on this score in Vindium."

"Hmm," said Jorian. "Since my escape from Xylar, I have betimes eked out a living as a storyteller. Thanks to the coaching you gave me in preparation for my flight, I have, I flatter myself, a fair stage presence."

Merlois clapped Jorian on the back. "Just the thing! Zevatas must have sent you in answer to my prayer, or he would have if I had thought to pray to him. You shall come on between the acts and tell one of your enthralling, fascinating, spellbinding, gripping, absorbing tales. I recall hearing some of them when I was teaching King Jorian to act."

"Am I to be paid?"

"Oh, aye, the going rate, as set by the Actor's Guild, minus your initiation fee into that cabal of graspers. When I was but a player, methought producers the world's worst tyrants, oppressors, cheats, and skinflints. Now that I am a producer, meseems that actors are the most grasping, vain, arrogant, capricious, unreasonable, untrustworthy, dissolute, and generally worthless rogues in Zevatas' world."

When the curtain fell at the end of the first act of *The Wrong Bedroom,* Jorian excused himself from Margalit and went around to the stage entrance. Presently Merlois stepped out on the stage and introduced that "celebrated, cultivated, renowned, charming, versatile, entertaining, and altogether irresistible storyteller, Nikko of Kortoli."

Jorian took a bow and said: "I shall tell the tale of a onetime king of Kortoli named Forbonian, who loved a mermaid. Know that all the kings of Kortoli since the days of Ardyman the Terrible have had names beginning with 'F.' This Forbonian was a good-to-middling king, not so brilliant as Fusinian the Fox, but far superior to that ass Forimar the Aesthete. Forbonian went about amongst the people, learning how they practiced their skills and betimes taking a hand at the plow or the loom or the hammer himself. Thus he found himself in the fishing village of Storum, helping the fishermen to haul in a net they had cast.

"The net seemed unwontedly heavy, and when with many royal grunts and heaves it was hauled ashore, it transpired that caught in its meshes was a veritable, palpable mermaid. She was not at all pleased at being snatched from her native element, and she screamed threats at the fishermen in her own language, which none understood.

"One old fisherman said: 'Your Majesty, here's a picklement. Whilst I know not her speech, I had it from my grandsire that mermaids threaten those who capture them with storms and shipwrecks, and that such calamities invariably come to pass. Let us, therefore, slay her and bury her well inland, ere she return to the sea to raise her fishy tribe against us.'

" 'That seems unduly drastic,' said the king. 'I cannot overmuch blame the sea-wench. I should be wroth if the mer-folk were to net me and draw me down into their liquid element. Let me bear her back to the palace. I will essay to turn her hostility to friendship by kind treatment.'

"So Forbonian whistled up his bodyguard. They made a litter of poles and lashed the mermaid to it, notwithstanding that she struggled and gave one guardsman a nasty bite with her needle-sharp, fish-catching teeth. Back at Kortoli City, the king commanded the guards to drop the mermaid into the royal swimming pool, which stood in a small courtyard in the palace, open to the sky. The return to the water seemed to calm her, albeit she still muttered threats and maledictions.

"That very day, Forbonian began to train the mermaid. His first task was to establish communication. This he did by offering her a reward of a small fish every time she learned a new word of Novarian. At the end of a fortnight, the mermaid actually smiled when the hour of instruction came round. She said: 'You good man, King. I love you.'

"Forbonian spent more and more time with the mermaid, to the neglect of his royal business. Since none could pronounce her name in her own tongue, Forbonian bestowed upon her the name of Lelia.

"Let me say that real mermaids are not much like the beings depicted by artists. If you imagine the lower half as the after end of a porpoise, and the upper half as a hybrid of human being and seal, you will have an idea. True, the mermaid had arms much like those of a human being, save for the webbing betwixt the fingers. Her face was more or less human, but the forehead and chin sloped smoothly back. When she swam, she cocked her head up to swim nose first, like a seal, and her head, neck, and body merged smoothly into one another. Under water, her nostrils closed tightly, like those of a seal or an otter.

"Furthermore, real mermaids do not sit on bulging buttocks on the sea rocks, combing their long hair over protrusile breasts. They have no buttocks, their breasts are small and hardly break the piscine smoothness of their shape, and their hair is but a patch of seal-like fur on their scalps. I do not think many of us would find such a creature surpassingly beautiful by human standards, although they doubtless have their own kind of beauty, just as a horse or a tiger may have.

"Natheless, a mutual sympathy sprang up between Lelia and the king, so that his greatest pleasure came to be the hours he spent beside her pool, instructing her. He took to stripping and swimming with her, claiming that she was teaching him new strokes.

"Now, King Forbonian's queen was Dionota, the daughter of the Hereditary Usurper of Govannian. Dionota was a comely female but, alas, not a sweet or companionable one. Her voice had become permanently toughened from screeching at the king, or anyone else within earshot, during her frequent tantrums.

Now she became jealous of Lelia, notwithstanding Forbonian's assurances that the mermaid meant no more to him than a good horse or dog.

"At length, one day when the king was elsewhere, Dionota entered the courtyard of the pool and dumped a bucket of lye into the water. Either she mistakenly thought that the lye would instantly slay Lelia, or she did not realize how fluent in Novarian the mermaid had become, so that she would inevitably tell the king what had been done to her.

"Lelia's shrieks brought the king running, to find his mermaid writhing on the flags beside the pool, her skin blistered and inflamed. He fetched the royal physician, who used several jars of salve in coating Lelia's injured skin, and he had the pool drained and refilled.

"Lelia told Forbonian about the bucket of lye—not that she knew what lye was, but the cause and effect of her distress were plain enough. In a fury, the king went to Dionota and said: 'This is the end, you stupid bitch! Pack your gauds and get out. I am dissolving our marriage and sending you back to your father.'

"And so it was done. A month later, Forbonian got a letter from the Hereditary Usurper of Govannian, saying: 'Curse it, I thought I had got rid of this peevish baggage when I palmed her off on you, but no such luck. I shall have to wed her to the Tyrant of Boaktis, whose wife has lately died.'

"Forbonian chuckled, for he knew there was bad blood between the Usurper and the Tyrant. In this way, in the guise of cementing eternal friendship, the Usurper was playing a scurvy trick on his enemy.

"Now there was no one to come between the king and his mermaid. One day he told her: 'Lelia, I truly love you. Will you marry me?'

"Lelia said: 'But Lord King, how can that be? We are of different kinds, you and I.'

"'Oh,' quoth Forbonian, 'we shall manage. What is

the use of being a king if one cannot put over things impossible to common men?'

"Forbonian went to the high priest of Zevatas to ask him to sanctify the union, but the priest recoiled in horror. So did the priests of Heryx and the other gods. At length Forbonian simply issued a royal decree, making Lelia his lawful wife.

"Then arose the problem of consummating this unconventional marriage. The doors of the courtyard had all been shut, and the only light was that from the twilit sky overhead and some candles that the king had caused to be set on the flagstones about the pool. Forbonian said to his bride:

" 'Lelia dearest, if you will hoist yourself out on the stones, we will have at it.' Lelia did not much like being out of water, claiming that the dry air made her skin itch. But she heaved herself out.

"Assured of his privacy, the king, a man of about my size, doffed his garments and set to fondle and caress Lelia. When he thought her properly receptive, he essayed to mount her; but try as he would, he could not effect an entry. At last he said: 'Devils take it, Lelia, how do they do it amongst your folk?'

" 'I am sorry,' she said, 'but my vent closes up tightly when I am out of water. I cannot relax it even if I would; besides which, I find it painful to be squashed between your weight and the stones. We mer-folk always copulate in the water.'

" 'Then let us try it in the water,' said the king. Both slipped into the pool. Lelia explained: 'We mer-folk approach each other side by side. We turn to face each other and, when the juncture has been made, the pair roll slowly from side to side, so that first one and then the other has its nostrils out of water. We are not fishes with gills, you know, and must needs breathe even as you do.'

"During this explanation, the cold water had robbed Forbonian of his royal rigidity; but by embracing and cosseting Lelia, he managed to restore it. When he attempted to play the part of a mer-bridegroom, however, he found that he could not time his breathing with the alternate surfacing and submersion, since Lelia expected him to stay under much longer than he could hold his breath. At every attempt, he would take a breath at the wrong time and emerge coughing and gasping, all thoughts of love banished by the urgent need to get the water out of his lungs.

"On his third try, after a long period of recuperation from the last one, Forbonian did succeed in penetrating his love. Lelia was by now in a highly excited state. In a transport of amorous passion, she seized him in her finny arms and dragged him beneath the surface. To her it was naught to submerge for a quarter-hour or more between breaths, but the poor king had no such amphibious talent.

"Soon Lelia realized that, instead of marching on to his climax, Forbonian had gone limp all over. In panic she hauled him to the surface, boosted him out on the flagstones, and heaved herself out, meanwhile shouting for help.

"The guardsmen burst in to find Lelia leaning on the prone and naked body of Forbonian, repeatedly pressing his rib cage down and releasing it. A couple of guards seized her arms, while their officer shouted: 'Drown our king, will you? Water witch, you shall beg for death ere the headsman gives the final stroke!'"

"Lelia tried to explain about artificial respiration; but in her excitement she lost command of her Novarian and spoke the language of the mer-folk. They were dragging her away when the king groaned and raised himself on his elbows, gasping: 'What do you?'

"When they told him, between coughs he said: 'Release her! I risked my life by my own folly, and she saved it.'

"Forbonian issued another decree, annulling the mer-marriage. He caused Lelia to be put back into the

sea, and shortly thereafter he wedded the daughter of
a merchant of Kortoli City and begat heirs. But for
years, they say, on moonlit nights he would go down
to the sea and climb out on an old pier at Storum, and
there converse with someone or something in the water
below. The lesson, if you wish me to point one out,
is that marriage is a chancy enough business without
wantonly adding to its problems.

"And now I think the scenery has been shifted, and
my old friend Merlois is ready to announce his second
act. Thank you, ladies and gentlemen."

Jorian's storytelling proved so popular that Merlois
kept him as an adjunct to his shows as long as the
troupe played in Othomae. He insisted on taking Jorian
to a costumer's shop to buy him an outfit more theatrical than his everyday jacket and trews. The costumer,
Henvin, ordinarily furnished materials for the costume
balls by which the gentry and nobility amused themselves. He clad Jorian in a black jacket with spangled
lapels, which glittered when Jorian moved.

"Were these any wider, I could fly with them," said
Jorian, looking doubtfully at the lapels.

Merlois said: "It makes you look like a proper hero
of romance. How would you like a permanent post, to
travel with my troupe and take acting parts as well as
tell tales between acts?"

"I am flattered and grateful, but I cannot accept just
now. When I get my wife back, if you still feel thus,
we shall see. I am a good second-rater at several occupations, including clockmaker, farmer, carpenter,
accountant, surveyor, soldier, sailor, fencing master,
storyteller, poet, and I daresay actor. Which I shall
finally settle into remains to be seen."

Between his storytelling for Merlois and his work at
Tremorin's *salle d'armes*, Jorian managed to save some
money. Hearing that the registrar at the Academy had

died, he went to Doctor Gwiderius and persuaded him to give Margalit a try at the job.

"I never saw such confused records!" she told Jorian after her first day. "The old registrar must have long since discarded his trump cards. I will try to bring order out of this chaos, but 'twill be a struggle."

"How do you get on with the faculty?" asked Jorian.

"Not so different from other men. Some take me for a kind of monster, being the first woman to hold the post. As for the others—well, I can count on at least one attempted seduction a day."

"That's not surprising. You are a spectacularly attractive person."

"Thank you, Jorian. These solicitations are a compliment of sorts, even though I reject them."

In the Month of the Ram, Jorian boarded the diligencia for Vindium, riding through a countryside lashed by spring rains and soon ablaze with spring flowers. At Vindium he took another coach to Kortoli. After the death of his father Evor, his brothers had moved the clock-making business from tiny Ardamai to Kortoli City. His mother remained in Ardamai, living with his sister and her family.

"Country practice is all very well, if you want to take life easily and have little ambition," said his elder brother Sillius when the greetings were over. "It is costlier here, of course, but the wealth of street trade more than makes up for it."

A couple of Sillius' children were climbing over their uncle, whom they had long heard of but never seen. "Kerin," said Jorian to his younger brother, "do you think you could get the Regency Council of Xylar to let you clean and regulate their clocks again?"

"They are about due," said Kerin, who was not only younger then Jorian but also slenderer and handsomer. "You surely provided a market for the clockmaker's skills when you reigned there, gathering all those clocks."

"It was my hobby. Some day we must try to build a clock like one I saw in the House of Learning in Iraz, powered by descending weights instead of trickling water. The engineers had not gotten it to work, but the idea looked promising."

Sillius sighed. "There you go again, Jorian! Always pushing some goose-brained newfangled idea, even though you were never able to master delicate clockwork."

"My hands may be clumsy, but it does not follow that my brain is lame," retorted Jorian. "I'll work with a large model and, when it succeeds, let you copy it in a small size, with gear wheels no larger than fish scales. Kerin, could you set out soon for Xylar, to solicit another contract to clean and repair the clocks in the palace? When I left there were twenty-six of them."

"Aye. I have bethought me of just such a venture."

"Then here is what I want you to do. . . ."

When Jorian had explained his plans for Thevatas the proxenary clerk, Sillius said: "I wish you would not draw Kerin into your wild schemes. Some day it will come out that he is your brother, and the Xylarians will take his head in lieu of yours."

"Oh, rubbish!" said Kerin. "I have no family, as you have, and I know how to keep my mouth shut. The feast of Selind comes up soon. Why don't we all make a holiday of it, go to Ardamai, and surprise our people there? You left seven years ago—or is it eight?—and you've never even seen your niece and nephew there. And Mother would never forgive us. . . ."

# VII

# The Sophi's Tower

In the Month of the Lion, Jorian returned by coach to Othomae. Since it was a holiday, the Feast of Narzes, Goania invited Jorian and Margalit to her house for dinner.

"You must needs take your chances on the victuals," she said. "Since Vanora disappeared, I have been trying to teach Boso to cook; but it is like teaching a horse to play the lute."

Aside from the fact that the beef was overdone, the repast did not turn out so badly as the wizardess had warned. Jorian said: "That was splendid, Boso! I see a lucrative future for you as cook in one of the big city inns, where the nobility come to eat, drink, dance, and ogle one another."

Boso dropped his usual surliness to scuff his foot on the floor. "Oh, I do try, Master Jorian," he simpered.

"But what of your plans for Estrildis?" said Goania.

"You go right to the point, my dear aunt," said Jorian. "I spent hours in Ardamai plotting with Kerin. He should be in Xylar, tending the clocks in the palace. When I get a letter saying 'The fish is hooked,' I shall set out with Karadur."

"Hai!" said Karadur. "You said not that you intended to entrain me with you, my son. I am verily too aged and fragile for another of these temerarious excursions—"

"Can't be helped," said Jorian. "Amongst other things, I shall need your help to locate that cursed crown for the bribe. It's been nearly three years since we buried it, and I am not sure I could find it by memory alone.

"But I am not capable of another long ride, in all weathers, on the back of some fractious quadruped!"

Jorian thought and said: "How if we went as a pair of Mulvanian mountebanks? You've seen these little groups, traveling about in wagons, telling fortunes and stealing farmers' chickens. I could buy a cart, which we can decorate like one of those gaudy Mulvanian vehicles. You can ride in it."

"Well, that would be—"

"Wait!" said Margalit. "I shall go, too."

"What?" cried Jorian. "This will be a rough, risky trip, my lady. Much as I esteem you, why should you—"

"Because my first duty is to my Queen, and I should be with you when you meet her again."

"I really see no good reason—"

"You will. The shock of seeing you may put her into a state where she needs my care. Besides, if you are disguised as a Mulvanian, she may not believe you to be her husband. You will need me to vouch for you."

They argued some more. But Jorian, though he thought Margalit's reasons flimsy, gave in. He was not really sorry to have her as a fellow traveler. He liked her immensely and admired her good sense and ability to cope with contingencies.

"Three would crowd one of those little carts," he said. "My sumpter mule can pull the cart, if I train him in. But I shall have to buy another horse." He looked worried. "I know not if my remaining funds will stretch so far."

"Fear not," said Goania. "I can always lend you enough to tide you over, provided you stop calling me aunt! I am no kin of yours."

"Very well, Au—Mistress Goania. It is good of you. And now, what parts shall we play in Xylar? Father Karadur can tell fortunes. I have some small skill at juggling and the sort of games of chance they play in traveling carnivals. That swindler Rudops, among the shady characters I hired to teach me their skills when I was planning escape, instructed me. And Margalit—why, 'tis plain you shall be a Mulvanian dancer!"

"But I do not know Mulvanian dances—"

"No matter. I have seen them in Mulvan, and Karadur and I can teach you."

"Think you not I am too tall to pass as a Mulvanian woman?"

"Not really; at least in Xylar, whither few Mulvanians go. The folk will have no standard of comparison."

"But stay! That is not all. A couple of years ago, a traveling troupe of Mulvanian dancers and singers passed through Xylar, and Estrildis and I attended a performance. As you might guess, they surrounded us with palace guards the whole time we were out of the palace. But the dancers, male and female, all danced bare to the waist."

"That's how they do it in Mulvan," said Jorian. "Even the dames of the highest caste go to parties thus, with designs painted on their torsos."

I will not slither around thus indecently exposed! There was a to-do in Xylar; the priests of Imbal would have closed the show, or at least compelled the dancers to cover themselves. They were still disputing the matter in the courts when the troupe departed."

"My lady," said Jorian sternly, "you're the one who wishes to accompany us on this journey. Either prepare to dance with bare breasts or stay behind!"

She sighed. "If the priests of Imbal make trouble again, 'twill be on your head! But how shall we get skins as brown as Karadur's?"

"There's a fellow in the city, Henvin the Costumer, who sells wigs, dyes, and everything else to change one's appearance. Merlois took me to him," Jorian answered.

"Must one paint one's skin over every time one washes one's face?"

"Nay; I am told that these dyes do not begin to fade for a fortnight."

"You, my son," said Karadur, "must needs learn to wind a turban. Wait!" The Mulvanian shuffled out and returned with a long strip of white cloth. "Hold still!"

Karadur dexterously wound the cloth round and round, so that Jorian's short-cut black hair was almost hidden. Goania held up a mirror.

"I look quite the Mulvanian potentate," said Jorian. "All I need is a brown skin."

"Now," said Karadur, "let me see you do it!"

Jorian spent the next hour learning to wind the turban. The first few times, the headgear fell apart as soon as he moved, slumping into loops and folds on his shoulders. The others rolled in their seats with laughter. At last Jorian wound a turban that stayed in place even when he shook his head.

"You must also shave your countenance," said Karadur.

"What, again? But I like my whiskers!"

"In Mulvan, as you should know, only philosophers, holy men, and men of the poorest caste wear them. Moreover, you will recall that at the time of your escape from Xylar, you wore a large black mustache over a shaven chin; so the Xylarians would recognize you with that adornment."

"But a full beard like mine—"

"Ah, but recently Judge Grallon saw you with your present hirsute decoration, so it were unwise to appear thus bedight. We might encounter the judge."

Jorian sighed. "Just when I think I have achieved the acme of masculine beauty, you come along and spoil it. Margalit, think you not we should be returning innward?" He rose.

Goania said: "Better not enter the Silver Dragon with that thing on your head. We do not wish folk to know that Jorian and that great Mulvanian mystic, Doctor Humbugula, are one and the same."

"I'll do it off ere we go in. Ready, Margalit?"

Jorian bid a ceremonious farewell, bowing and practicing the gestures he had seen in Mulvan. Out they went. The night was dark and foggy, and there were no public street lamps near Goania's modest house. A lamp in the wizardess's hands, as she stood in the open door, pushed back the dark a little. When she closed the door, the darkness rushed back.

"Hold my arm, Margalit," said Jorian. "One can easily turn an ankle on these cobblestones. Damn, it's blacker than the pits of the ninth Mulvanian hell."

They felt their way slowly along. Jorian peered into the murk, thinking that he would feel very silly if they got lost on a simple walk of eight or ten blocks.

Then Jorian heard quick, soft footsteps behind him. As he started to turn, a terrific blow struck his head. The ground sprang up. Dimly he heard a shriek from Margalit.

Collecting his scattered wits, Jorian rolled over to bring his attacker into view. Against the dark overcast, he made out an even darker form swinging an ax in both hands. He thought he saw the ax rise above the form's head.

He knew he should have instantly thrown himself to the side to avoid the blow. But so weak and dazed was he that he could only blink stupidly as the ax started down.

A second form—that of Margalit, from its silhouette—gave the first one a push. He heard a low snarl of "Bitch!" and saw the attacker turn toward the woman. She sprang back to avoid a sweep of the ax, but slipped on the wet cobblestones and fell. The attacker turned back to Jorian, hoisting the ax for another blow.

Then another form loomed out of the dark. The

intended blow went awry. Jorian climbed shakily to his feet to see two bulky bodies grappling, grunting, and cursing. One combatant caught the other's arm and twisted. The ax fell with a clang.

"I got him, Master Jorian!" panted Boso's grating voice. "Kill the bastard!"

Jorian felt about and gathered up the ax. For an instant he hovered about the struggling pair, peering to make sure he should not strike the wrong man. Both were stocky, burly men in rough, nondescript clothes, but in the fog-shrouded darkness he could not discern faces.

"What are you waiting for?" rasped Boso.

The direction of the voice at last told Jorian which was which. He brought the flat of the ax down hard on the head of his assailant; at the third blow, the stranger collapsed.

"Why'n't you slay him?" said Boso.

"I want to know who he is and what he's up to first," said Jorian. He turned to see how Margalit fared, but she had already regained her feet.

"Are you hurt?" Jorian asked.

"Nay, save for a bruised fundament. Who is this footpad?"

"That's what I mean to learn. Take one leg, Boso, and I will take the other. How did you arrive so opportunely?"

"I heard the lady cry out and rushed into the street," said Boso.

Halfway down the block, a golden rectangle appeared in the fog as Goania's door opened again and the wizardess stood in it with a light. Jorian and Boso hauled the body in and laid it out on Goania's floor, while she leaned over it with a lamp. The man was heavyset, with a strip of cloth covering his face below the eyes. Jorian set down the ax, an ordinary workman's tool, and jerked off the mask.

"Malgo the bailiff!" he exclaimed. "I owed him a few knocks, but wherefore should he strive to murder me?"

Goania poured a dipper of cold water on the man's face. Choking and coughing, Malgo returned to consciousness.

"We should tie him up," said Jorian. "He's a strong rascal."

"I'll see to that," said Goania. She went out and returned with a couple of lengths of rope. She spoke to these and, like tame serpents, one of them wrapped itself around Malgo's wrists and the other around his ankles.

"A couple of minor spirits, whom I have enlisted in my service," she said.

Jorian peeled off the turban. The cloth was slit in several places, where the edge of the ax had penetrated, and stained crimson, where blood had seeped from a scalp wound.

"My best turban cloth!" lamented Karadur.

"I'll get you another," said Jorian. "Henvin the Costumer probably carries them. I owe it to you, since those layers of cloth saved my worthless life." He turned to Malgo, now sitting on the floor with his back to the settee, glaring. "Now then, you, speak!"

"Screw you!" snarled Malgo.

"Why did you try to kill me?"

"That's my affair."

"Oh, is it?" Jorian smiled unpleasantly. "Mistress Goania, may I trouble you for assistance in opening up this mangy scrowle? I am sure you have some ingenious methods in your magical repertory."

"Let me think," she said. "There is a small Seventh Plane demon who is madly in love with me and will do aught I ask. Naturally I cannot accede to his wishes, not wishing to be burnt to a crisp. But if I loose him on Master Malgo, he will do some interesting things, beginning with the man's private parts."

"Oh, I'll talk," growled Malgo with fear in his eyes. "I wanted to slay you because you lost me my job."

"What?" said Jorian. "I had naught to do with that! I never even knew you had been dismissed."

"Well, I was, and I know you did it, by complaining to the Grand Duke."

"You're dreaming! I have not seen the Grand Duke, nor have I complained to his officers, though the gods know I had cause to. Who told you this?"

"I won't tell."

"Goania, how about that fiery imp of yours?"

"Oh, I'll tell, I'll tell. Just let not that witch set her spooks on me. 'Twas Doctor Abacarus at the Academy. I paid him a pretty penny to divine the cause of my dismissal, and he named you."

"You wasted your money," said Jorian. "Abacarus merely sought revenge on me for besting him in a dispute over a debt."

"I can tell you why Malgo was dismissed," said Goania. "I know the Grand Duchess Ninuis—we serve on the same committee to succor the poor—and she is a great gossip. She told me the examining magistrate caught Malgo buggering a young prisoner in his cell. For some legal reason they could not pin a criminal charge on Malgo, but they could toss him out of his post."

"There you are," said Jorian. "Now, what shall we do with this scum?"

"If it was me, I'd kill him," said Boso.

"A pious idea; but then we should have a body to dispose of. And perhaps the swine has friends, who would ask after him. I suppose he is an Othomaean citizen, but I am not."

"I'd still kill him," said Boso. "If any man tried to slay me—"

"I agree with your sentiments, friend Boso; but we must be practical. Any other suggestions?"

"We could surrender him to the law," said Karadur.

"Nay," said Goania. "Jorian has the right of it. Malgo has friends in high places, little though you might expect it. There is a nest of his kind, headed by Lord— but I will not name names. This lord has power, and doubtless his intervention set Malgo free. If we have him arrested, the legal mills will grind on forever whilst Master Malgo is out on bail to make another try."

Margalit said: "We hear a lot about the corruption in high places of Vindium; but from what I hear, 'tis just as rife here."

"True," said Goania. "The difference is that the Grand Duchy has more effective means of covering its corruption in high places."

Jorian asked: "What's the source of Lord Nameless's power? Is Gwitlac the Fat one of Malgo's brother-hood—"

"Hush!" hissed Goania, looking nervously around. "Do not say things like that within the bourne of the Grand Duchy, unless you would destroy us all! But to answer your question: nay, the Grand Duke is nor-mal in that respect. It is purely political; this lord is one of his strongest supporters. Ninuis loathes the man, but she has not been able to turn Gwitlac against him."

"We'll forget arresting Malgo, then," said Jorian. "It were more to the point to set the law on Abacarus; Malgo is but his tool."

"Aye, but the same objections apply. Abacarus would deny the whole thing, and what were Malgo's word against his?"

Margalit asked: "Could you feed Malgo a love potion or something, so that he would do whatever Jorian commanded?"

"I fear," said Goania, "that Malgo would not make a satisfactory servant, no matter what geases we put upon him. He might be made to obey Jorian, but that would not stop him from stealing Jorian's possessions, or holding a sodomitical orgy in Jorian's room in his master's absence. If we compelled him to love Jorian, his manner of expressing his love might not meet with Jorian's approval."

"You ought to make him suffer somehow," said Boso. "It's only right. If it was me, I wouldn't be a man if I let him off free."

"True," Jorian said. "But I am less interested in revenge than in getting him out of the way. We can't have him running loose here, and Goania does not think he can be reduced to useful magical slavery. Goania, can you put a spell on him to make him obey one command from me? Implicitly?"

"Aye, within limits."

"Going to make him kill himself?" asked Boso with a grin.

"Nay, though the idea has merit."

"That would not work anyway," said Goania. "The spell cannot make him contravene his basic instincts."

"How," asked Jorian, "would it be to command him to kill Abacarus? That would be a fair turnabout."

Goania said: "Be not hasty. Abacarus is a clever rogue. If I know him, he will have taken precautions. Let me send out my second sight."

She sat still, breathing deeply with her eyes closed. At last she said: "It is as I thought. He has set up a barrier that will dissolve your command when Malgo passes through it. Abacarus will then aim Malgo back at you, as in a game of paddle ball."

"Bouncing Malgo back and forth at each other could become tedious," said Jorian. He thought a moment. "I have something equally useful. Goania, how long will such a command obtain?"

"One to three months, depending on many factors."

"Then pray put it on him."

"Very well. The rest of you, leave me alone with Malgo. I will call when I have finished."

\* \* \*

They trooped out to the kitchen. From the living room came sounds of chants and incantations in Goania's voice, and then a harsh, crackling voice that was neither Goania's nor Malgo's. Jorian killed time by telling a story. "I am sure," he said, "you have heard some of my tales of King Forimar the Aesthete. He nearly ruined Kortoli by neglecting statecraft to pursue the arts, such as music, painting, and verse, in all of which he made signal contributions.

"Then Kortoli was overrun by the armies of Aussar under Doubri the Faultless, a fanatical priest who wished to foist on other nations the puritanical austerity he had imposed upon his own land. The siege of Kortoli City was broken by the return of the naval squadron under Forimar's brother Fusonio.

"Forimar had sent Fusonio to Salimor in the Far East, ostensibly to establish trade relations, but actually to get rid of his brother, whose carping at Forimar's extravagance and neglect of public affairs vexed the king. But as the price for saving Kortoli, Fusonio forced his brother to abdicate in his favor.

"Anon, Fusonio thwarted a conspiracy by his brother to regain the throne. To prevent further attempts, Fusonio sent the ex-king to distant Salimor as ambassador. Fusonio would normally have dispatched his brother on a warship. But he had heard that the barbarians of Shven were assembling a fleet in the Bay of Norli to ravage the Novarian coasts. So he felt he had to keep the fleet at home.

"The conveyance of Forimar he trusted to a privateer, Captain Joelid, with orders to take Forimar to Salimor. Joelid bore letters of marque from Fusonio; but since Kortoli was then at peace, he was compelled to fill the rôle of peaceful trader.

"Fusonio sent a bodyguard of ten soldiers to act as Forimar's escort and, moreover, to see that he did not slip away at some intermediate port. The soldiers were young single men who had volunteered because they had heard tales of the beauty and availability of the Salimorese girls, who went about clad like those Mulvanian dancers whom Margalit saw. Fusonio also gave the officer of this detachment, Lieutenant Locrinus, a letter to the Sophi, asking that potentate to hold Forimar in genteel confinement all his life.

"So off went Captain Joelid, and off with him went Lieutenant Locrinus and the former King Forimar. Unable to find an adequate cargo in Kortoli, Joelid dropped down the coast to Vindium.

"At Vindium, Lieutenant Locrinus saw to it that the ex-king had no chance to slip ashore and escape. But he had no authority over Captain Joelid, who went ashore on his own business. After an unsuccessful day of cargo seeking, the privateer sought a tavern, where he fell in with a fellow sea captain from Salimor, one Dimbakan.

"Now, in visiting merchants and warehouses, Captain Joelid had heard of a deal very profitable to a skipper who could take immediate advantage of it. It involved a triangular trade amongst Vindium, Janareth, and Tarxia. The thought of these profits made Joelid's mouth water; but he could not sail to Janareth, to Tarxia, and back to Vindium and also carry Forimar to Salimor.

"So, when both Joelid and Dimbakan were well plied with the liquors of Vindium, they struck a deal. Joelid would turn over Forimar and his escort to Dimbakan, who was to leave for home in a few days. He would pay Dimbakan a part of the fee that Fusonio had paid him to take his brother to Salimor. He opened by offering one tenth; but Dimbakan, no stranger to chaffering, laughed in his face. After much haggling, they settled on two-thirds of the fee for Dimbakan.

"Next day, Joelid told Forimar and his men that they were going to Salimor, not on Joelid's privateering vessel, but on Dimbakan's ship, the *Itunkar*. Lieutenant Locrinus vehemently objected. But Joelid said he could make his choice: go ashore, sail with the *Itunkar*, or remain on Joelid's ship, about to leave for Janareth and Tarxia.

"As a privateer, Joelid carried a large crew for the size of his ship. These seemed a hard-bitten lot of rogues, who could easily turn to piracy if lawful occupations failed them. Lacking the force to overawe Captain Joelid, Locrinus grudgingly accepted the new plan. He and his men marched ashore, surrounding Forimar, and adown the waterfront until they came to the *Itunkar*. Two days later, Captain Dimbakan sailed.

"Forimar found himself aboard a long, narrow vessel, with outriggers to keep it upright in all weathers and two lugsails of curious shape. The voyage took a good part of a year, and Forimar was happy to disembark at the capital, Kwatna. He had learned enough of the language to get along with the Salimorese and now dressed as they did, in a simple length of cloth wrapped skirtwise about his loins.

"Since Fusonio's departure from Salimor, the Sophi who had reigned at that time had died and been succeeded by his son Mynang. The new Sophi received Forimar graciously and showed a lively interest in Novarian customs and technics.

"Forimar made a serious effort to discharge the office of ambassador in a creditable way. But he soon became moody and discontented, because there was little for him to do. Kortoli and Salimor were too far asunder to be concerned with each other's military alliances and adventures, and trading ships, selling metalware and glassware and buying tea and spices, arrived from Novaria only at intervals of months.

"So Forimar returned to his old love, art. He studied the Salimorian arts of painting, sculpture, and music. He was especially captivated by the Salimorian dance. A dancer of the royal troupe caught his eye, and he divined that neither was she indifferent to his regard. He persuaded the dancing master to present the girl,

Wakti, to him. When he hesitantly said something about seeing her alone later, she replied:

" 'Oh, that is no matter, my lord. I shall come to your house tonight.' Sure enough, when Forimar returned to his bedchamber after supper, he found a nude Wakti smiling invitingly.

"Although nearly forty, Forimar had never bedded a woman in his life. When he hesitated, Wakti asked him what was the matter. He confessed to being a complete tyro at love, whereupon she was convulsed with laughter, as if it were the funniest thing she had ever heard. But she said: 'That is no matter, dear Ambassador Porimar.' For so the Salimorians called him, having no F in their language. 'Come hither and I will show you how.'

"Wakti's laughter had caused Forimar to lose some of his readiness; but Wakti revived it. Afterward Forimar said: 'Great Zevatas, what have I been missing all this time! But tell me, Wakti darling, what would happen if you should conceive?'

" 'Oh,' she said, 'that is no matter. We have an herb to prevent that. Now sleep for a while, and we will at it again.'

"So Forimar and Wakti became official lovers, a state on which all the Salimorese, from the Sophi down, smiled benignly. Forimar was deliriously happy. But since he could not make love to Wakti all the time, and his official duties were negligible, he took more intense interest in the Salimorian arts.

"In Kortoli he had dabbled in architecture, bankrupting the nation by building costly temples and other structures. To Mynang he suggested erecting a lighthouse like that of Iraz, of which he had heard and seen pictures, but even taller and more splendid. The Sophi, spellbound by Forimar's exotic ideas, asked Forimar to draw up a plan.

"Forimar did so, and Mynang commanded his ministers to assemble workmen and materials forthwith. He also ordained a special tax to pay for this enterprise.

This tax caused much grumbling amongst the common folk, on whom it bore heavily. But Forimar, in an ecstasy of watching his tower go up day by day and at night practicing Salimorian dances with Wakti in both the vertical and the horizontal positions, knew naught of this.

"Months passed and the tower, in a square on the waterfront, soared into the heavens. So impatient was the Sophi to see it that he caused the workmen to be speeded with whips. A little over a year after the laying of the first stone, the tower was complete but for the interior furnishings. Mynang decreed a holiday for the dedication of his tower.

"A platform was erected before the tower, whence the Sophi would make a speech. The square was decorated with flowers and colored cloth. Forimar took his place in the parade behind Mynang, who was borne in a gilded litter. The band stepped out, tooting and tweedling and banging. After them came the royal guard, and then the litter.

"The procession was approaching the square of the tower, where thousands of Salimorese had already assembled, when the earth gave a slight quiver. Forimar had been so busy with his arts and with making love to Wakti that he had never learned that Salimor was a land of frequent earthquakes. Most dwelling houses were therefore low, flimsy affairs of bamboo and palm-frond matting, which would whip back and forth when shaken but remain largely intact. A few of the nobility and the Sophi, only, dwelt in buildings of masonry.

"The earth lurched again, and the tower groaned and swayed. At once, the thousands in the square began to run away in all directions. The first fugitives who raced up the street on which the parade was marching collided with the band and swept the bandsmen along with them.

"Then came the main shock. The tower groaned

louder and swayed wider. Then it crumbled into thousands of separate stones, pouring down from its height like drops in a waterfall, to strike the earth with a roar heard leagues away, smashing and rebounding and shaking the city of Kwatna almost as severely as the earthquake itself. Soon there was naught left of the tower but a huge pile of broken masonry, half hidden in a vast cloud of dust.

"Thanks to the warning shocks, the square had been pretty well cleared of spectators. Natheless, several score were killed, some by rebounding stones and some trampled to death in the rush. Many more suffered lesser injuries. Some other houses in Kwatna, including part of the palace, were shaken down with loss of life and property.

"The crowd that rushed through the street of the parade had knocked down Mynang's litter bearers, so that the Sophi was thrown out on the street. He tried to restore order, but none heeded him. A rumor ran through the crowds, that Sophi Mynang had displeased the gods and thus brought about the earthquake. Some blamed the Sophi, while others blamed his fiendish foreign crony, meaning Forimar. Mynang was recognized as he tried to get back to the palace. A mob, incited by a holy man, set upon him and tore him to pieces.

"Forimar might have suffered a similar fate, but amid the swirling crowds of Salimorese, screaming and foaming with excitement, a brown hand seized his wrist. 'Come quickly!' said a familiar voice, and Wakti dragged him through a doorway. He found himself in the house of friends of Wakti, who let her take him to a back room and hide him.

"Some Salimorese were giving thought to who should succeed Mynang in power. The late Sophi's eldest son was a boy by a concubine, six years old; the eldest by a legitimate wife was four. (The Salimorese did not allow the rule of women.) Each child had partisans, and for a day it looked as if the succession would be settled by civil war.

"Then Wakti reported to Forimar that a new leader had arisen. This was none other than the Captain Dimbakan who had brought Forimar thither from Vindium. Dimbakan harangued the crowds on the form of government he had observed in Vindium, namely a republic, with the chief officers elected at fixed intervals by the people, and no hereditary ranks of nobility. This idea was new to the Salimorese, but they took to it with enthusiasm. Dimbakan promised that, once in power, he would forthwith hold an election to decide whether to abolish the monarchy and whom to choose to run the state.

"In a few days, Dimbakan proclaimed himself regent in the royal palace. Mynang's sons had disappeared; whether slain or smuggled away, Forimar never learned. As time passed, people asked Dimbakan when he would hold that promised election; but he always had some plausible reason for not staging it just yet. Eventually he announced that, albeit reluctantly, he would yield to the unanimous wish of the people and declare himself the new Sophi. As to how unanimous this popular desire was, we have only Dimbakan's words as reported by Forimar.

"On a visit to the hidden Forimar, Wakti said: 'My love, since the royal dance troupe has been disbanded, and you can no longer make me generous gifts, I have decided to marry.'

"Forimar said: 'Do you mean to marry me? Oh, joy! Let us be about it instanter!'

"'What!' cried Wakti, 'Me wed you, a fugitive foreigner? Good gods, what an idea! Nay; I have a good man picked out, a journeyman coppersmith. As for you, you had better take the first ship back to your own land, ere some fanatic recognize you.'

"'But you said you loved me!' bleated Forimar.

" 'True; so I do. But that is no matter. What has love to do with marriage?'

" 'Back in Novaria, they are supposed to go together,' quoth he.

" 'What a barbarous land!' she said. 'Here marriage is the forming of family alliances, the pooling of resources, and the building up of a stable, self-supporting family unit. Such considerations form a much firmer base for happy longtime cohabitation than mere love.'

" 'You make marriage sound like a sordid commercial deal!' he said.

" 'And why not?' she retorted. 'To eat regularly is the most important thing in life—even more so than love, since one can live without love but not without eating—and a well-matched pair can eat better together than separately.

" 'Now, pack your gear, for a ship leaves on the morrow for Vindium. I will fetch a disguise, so you can pass safely through the streets.'

"And so it was done. Some years later, King Fusonio visited Vindium. As usual, he sought a tavern wherein to mingle incognito with the common folk. In this tavern, he found himself seated near a group of fisherman, who could easily be identified by their smell. One slender, middle-aged fellow, with a graying beard, looked familiar. At length this nagging half-memory so irked Fusonio that he went to the other table and touched the man on the shoulder, saying: 'Your pardon, my friend, but do I not know you?'

"The man looked up, replying: 'I am Porimar of Kortoli, a fisherman in the crew of Captain—oh!' the man stared wide-eyed. 'I believe you do know me, and I also know you. Let us go where we can talk freely.'

"They found a secluded corner, and Forimar (or Porimar, as he now called himself) related his adventures. Fusonio brought Forimar up to date on events in Kortoli. The brothers were warily friendly. The king said: 'How do you like your present trade?'

"Forimar shrugged. 'Not bad. There is as much art, I find, in tracking a school of fish and managing a net as there is in painting a portrait or cobbling together a verse.'

" 'Is there aught you would like me to do for you—short of letting you back into Kortoli, that is?'

" 'Aye; give me the money to buy my own fishing smack and hire a crew.'

" 'You shall have it,' said Fusonio, and so it was done. And sometimes, when affairs of state were more than usually vexatious, King Fusonio wondered if, perhaps, his brother did not have the better lot of the twain. But when he thought of the hardships and hazards of a fisherman's life, he put aside such thoughts as sentimental romanticism. And he resolved to get such satisfaction as he could out of the rôle to which the gods had called him."

When Goania called, they came back to find Malgo standing blank-faced. The magical cords that had bound him now dangled harmlessly from the fist of the wizardess.

"Give your command, Jorian," said Goania. "Take not too long about it."

"Malgo!" said Jorian. "Wilt obey my command?"

"Aye, sir," growled Malgo.

"Then you shall leave Othomae City forthwith, travel east to Vindium, and take ship as a deckhand for the Kuromon Empire, or the Gwoling Islands, or Salimor, on whatever ship thither bound has a berth open. Do you understand?"

"Aye, sir. Can I stop back to my room to get supplies for the journey?"

"Aye, but without needless delays. Now go!"

Like a walking corpse, Malgo shambled out the door and into the night. Jorian said: "By the time the command loses power, he'll be well on his way to the Far East. Once aboard ship, 'twill avail him naught to change his mind. If he survive the voyage, he could not get back in a year, by which time I hope to be elsewhere."

"Can I dress your wound?" said Goania.

"Nay, it is but a scratch. Betwixt my thick skull and Doctor Karadur's best turban, I have nought worse than a slight headache. And thanks for saving my life, Boso."

Boso scuffed his shoe. "Oh, that was nought. You once saved mine, when we fell into Lake Volkina. Besides, you said you liked my cooking."

On the way back to the inn for the second time, Jorian told Margalit: "It is strange. I've fought with Boso thrice—not mere words, but twice with fists and once with swords. It started when he learned I was the son of the man who built Othomae's chiming municipal water clock, thus ending his job as the city's gong ringer.

"Either of us might have killed the other, for he has the thews of an ox. I thought he hated me. At the same time, I did drag him out of that lake when the Goblin Tower fell; and now he saves me from being chopped up like kindling."

Limping from her fall, Margalit said: "I once read in the *Aphorisms* of Achaemo that one should treat every friend as if he might some day become an enemy, and every foe as if he might some day become a friend."

Jorian grinned in the darkness. "Good worldly advice. But I don't think I could imagine you as my enemy, Margalit."

# VIII

# The Marshes of Moru

In the Month of the Dragon, Jorian received an unsigned letter, in Kerin's hand, reading: THE FISH HAS SWALLOWED THE HOOK. As soon as they could gather their gear, Jorian, Karadur, and Margalit set out. Karadur and the girl, the latter in the masculine attire she had worn to Mount Aravia, rode in a cart with a canvas top and two large wheels, drawn by Filoman the mule. Jorian had spent many weary days in training the balky animal to obey the reins and was not altogether satisfied with the results.

Jorian himself rode a new horse, Cadwil, of better quality than the late Fimbri. When a storm blew up, Jorian crowded into the cart and led the horse behind the vehicle.

Short of the Xylarian border, Jorian took a side road that led southwesterly through the forest, clad in the dense green foliage of late summer, toward the Marshes of Moru. When the road petered out to a mere track, he halted, tethered the animals, and left Margalit in charge. He also left her his crossbow with instructions for its use. He was pleased to find that she, unlike most women, was strong enough to cock it.

Jorian and Karadur set out afoot. They followed a copy of a map from the Grand Ducal archives and Jorian's memory of the country from his flight through it nearly three years before: Flies buzzed round their heads; Jorian slapped one that bit him in the neck. The woods resounded with the metallic song of cicadas.

At the time of Jorian's previous visit to this area,

Rhithos the Smith had laid a confusion spell on the forest around his house. He did this as a favor to the Silvans, the aboriginal inhabitants, to keep hunters and woodcutters out of their woods. In return, the Silvans furnished Rhithos and Vanora, who was then his slave, with food. But when Rhithos had tried to kill Jorian in order to put a spell on a magical sword he was making, Jorian killed him instead. So the spell was broken.

They had been walking the trail for an hour, going slowly because of Karadur's age, when Jorian jerked his head back as something whispered past him. The sound ended in a sharp *tick*. Jorian saw a dart sticking in a tree beside the trail; he pulled it out. The point had been smeared with some sticky stuff.

"That must be the doing of the Silvans," said the Mulvanian. "It is doubtless poisoned."

"I thought they dwelt leagues farther east, in the vicin_ty of Rhithos' house?"

"Nay, they range widely through the forest belt north of the Lograms."

"But why should they shoot at me?"

"You slew their ally the smith. We had better get back to the wagon—"

Another whisper, and another dart struck another tree, this time behind them.

"Get down!" said Jorian, throwing himself flat on the trail. "Are they warning us, or are they merely bad shots?"

"I know not," said Karadur, lowering himself more slowly.

Jorian had already started to crawl back along the trail. Another dart struck his leather jacket; he snatched it out.

"They seek to slay us, forsooth!" he said. "There goes one of the losels!" A small, hairy, naked form with pointed ears and a tail flitted among the trees. "And me without my trusty crossbow! Canst work a spell to get us out of this?"

"If they would stop shooting blowguns at us, I could effect another confusion spell. It is a simple magical operation."

"O Silvans!" roared Jorian, rising on his elbows. "We are friends! Come out and let us talk!" He ducked as another dart whizzed past.

"Crawl faster!" he growled, wriggling along the trail past his companion.

"I cannot keep up with you!" panted Karadur.

"If I could get close enough to seize one. . . . Look you," Jorian whispered. "I'll pretend to be hit and dying. Do you likewise."

A dart flew at Jorian's face, but a twig deflected it at the last istant. "*Ai!*" screamed Jorian, thrashing about as if in his death throes. Behind him, Karadur made similar noises and motions. Then both lay still.

After what seemed a long wait, a rustle in the greenery announced the forest folk. Three appeared on the path, with blowguns made from canes. When they stepped closer, Jorian bounded to his feet and threw himself on the nearest one. Since the little fellow was only waist-high to Jorian, he was easily overcome.

The other two leaped back, squeaking in their own tongue. As they raised their blowguns, Jorian put the blade of his knife against the captive's neck.

"Don't shoot, if you want your friend alive!" he shouted.

Whether or not they understood the words, the two hesitated. Karadur came up behind Jorian and spoke in the twittering tongue of the Silvans, who answered. Then they lowered their weapons.

"What say they?" asked Jorian.

"They say they shoot all 'big folk' who trespass here. Since their friend the smith was slain, their woods are overrun with our kind."

"Tell them you will put another confusion spell if they will leave us alone."

"I was about to do so." Karadur and the Silvans conferred further.

The Mulvanian gathered twigs and started a small fire on the trail. From one of the many internal compartments of his wallet he took a pinch of powder and sprinkled it on the blaze, intoning words. The vapors made Jorian, holding his captive, sneeze.

"They say," said Karadur, "that you may release their fellow now without fear."

"I know not how far to trust these creatures."

"Oh, I am sure—"

"Aye, I have accepted your assurances to my sorrow ere this. What's their most binding oath?"

"By Thio's soul, I believe."

"Very well, tell them to swear peace with us by Thio's soul. I must release this fellow sooner or later, since I cannot dig for the crown and hold him hostage at the same time."

More twittering, and Jorian released his captive. The three Silvans faded into the vegetation. Jorian asked:

"How did you come to know so much about them?"

"I had to pass examinations in those subjects when studying wizardry at Trimandilam."

"If you knew their language, why didn't you speak to them sooner?"

"I was too frightened and out of breath."

They plodded on. Jorian sweated, swatted flies, and cast anxious looks through the aisles of the greenwood. The day wore on.

In the afternoon, they came out on the shore of a branch of the Marshes of Moru. One of the small crocodiles of the marsh slipped into the water, sending ripples out across the still, black mere, over which glittering, glassy dragonflies hovered and darted.

"This is odd," said Jorian, frowning at his map. "It looks like the middle finger of the north branch of Kadvan's Marsh. But we should be much farther south, around here." He pointed. "I thought I knew this country like the palm—great Zevatas! I know what's the matter! Your confusion spell has confused me, too!"

Karadur spread his hands. "What expected you, my son? I had no means of immunizing you from its effects."

"Does it affect you, also?"

"Not really, since I never did learn my way about this lieu so well as you did when you were King; so I have little knowledge to be twisted by the spell.

"Jorian shrugged. "Then there is naught for it but to keep on trying. Come on!"

He started off on a vast circumambulation of the marshes, plowing through thickets of shrubbery and sinking into boggy patches. Karadur's fatigue forced them to stop to rest more and more often. Time and again, Jorian would set his course by the sun and start off in what he meant as a straight line, only to find soon after that he had somehow gotten turned around and was heading in the opposite direction. At sunset they were still struggling.

"I thought we should be back at the cart with the crown by now," grumbled Jorian. "I can testify that this spell of yours, at least, works fine. Had I known, I should have brought food and blankets. No use blundering on without light to see our way."

"Must we spend a night on the ground?" asked Karadur.

"So it seems. Let's hope that tiger I saw at Mount Aravia wander not down this way. 'Twere not an impossible distance for it."

Jorian built a small fire and spent an uncomfortable night, sleeping in snatches with his back to a tree and wondering whether the sounds he heard were those of some prowling predator or the rumbling of his empty stomach. Karadur seemed to manage better, settling into a cross-legged position, putting himself into a mystical trance, and awakening with dawn apparently none the worse.

They plodded on through the morning, as the cool of the night gave way to the steamy heat of midday. At last Jorian said: "We should be near our goal. The lay of this land looks familiar, unless your spell has addled what memory I have. Have you a short-range divination spell that will tell us where lies the crown?"

"Nay; that is Goania's specialty. Let me see; we buried the bauble beneath a log, did we not?"

"Aye. Yonder lies a log; could that be the one?"

It was not; nor were the next six logs they investigated. Jorian said: "I shall have nightmares of digging under one fallen trunk after another through all eternity—ah, that one looks familiar!"

A few minutes later, Jorian gave a whoop as they dragged out a mass of rotted rags wrapped around a heavy object. The rags were the remains of the clothing from which Jorian had changed when he made a rendezvous with Karadur here on his flight from Xylar. Inside the tatters, bright and gleaming, was the crown of Xylar.

Jorian held it up to admire the glitter of the morning sun on the jewels around the rim, which flashed scarlet and azure and green. "At least, 'tis some satisfaction to have guessed right for once. . . . What's that?"

A sound of a heavy body moving came to his ears. He sprang to his feet, peering about. The swish of displaced branches and the thud of heavy footfalls came closer. Jorian cried:

"It's a Paaluan dragon! Up a tree, and yarely!"

Through the brush came a monstrous lizard, over thirty cubits long. Jorian sprang to the nearest large tree, an old silver-gray beech, with enough low branches for easy climbing. As he swarmed up the trunk, he turned to see how his companion fared.

Instead of climbing a tree, Karadur had loosed the

rope from around his waist and laid it in a coil before him. He was chanting a spell over it. The upper end of the rope reared up, like the head of an angry cobra. As it rose to man-height, Karadur seized the tip in both hands and wrapped his scrawny legs around it lower down. The rope continued to rise until it almost stood on its tip, raising the wizard three fathoms above the ground.

The dragon came briskly to the foot of the tree that Jorian had climbed. It placed its foreclaws against the trunk and reared up, maneuvering its head among the branches and shooting out a long forked tongue. Jorian climbed higher to keep out of its reach.

The dragon backed down the trunk and turned its attention to Karadur, bunched at the top of his rope. It cocked its head to one side and then to the other; it approached the rope and gingerly touched it with the tip of its tongue.

Jorian foresaw that even its small reptilian brain might have the wit to seize the rope in its fanged jaws and shake Karadur off his precarious perch. Without stopping to ponder, Jorian descended with reckless speed, ran to where the lizard was still scrutinizing the rope, and drew his sword as he ran. He aimed a cut at the dragon's tail, opening a small gash in the thick, scaly hide.

With a hoarse bellow, the dragon swung its ponderous head about to see what had stung it. Prepared for this, Jorian sheathed his sword and ran, the dragon lumbering after.

Jorian did not run so fast as he could have, knowing that if he tripped and fell, the dragon might gobble him up before he regained his feet. So he ran cautiously, watching for roots and fallen branches. Behind him came the dragon. From the sounds it made, Jorian thought it was gaining; but he held to his course.

Jorian ran and ran. His heart pounded and his breath

came in gasps. At least the sounds of pursuit seemed to be getting no closer.

Then, despite his care, he put his foot into a hole in the turf, masked by dead leaves, and fell sprawling. He scrambled up, expecting the fanged jaws to slam shut on him. A glance showed him still several fathoms ahead of his pursuer. He ran on.

When his laboring lungs seemed ready to burst, Jorian became aware that the dragon, too, had slowed. He risked a glance back. The monster was still coming, but more and more slowly, like a clockwork toy running down.

Jorian slackened his own pace, taking care not to gain so much on the dragon as to lose sight of it altogether. A savant in Iraz had explained that cold-blooded organisms like lizards had less efficient hearts than birds and mammals and hence could not sustain such strenuous efforts so long. And so it had proved.

The dragon stopped altogether, lowering its huge barrel to the forest floor and lying still, save for the movements of its tongue and rib cage. Breathing great gulps of air, Jorian watched from a distance. After a while the lizard rose to its stumpy legs and ambled off. Jorian feared it might head back toward Karadur; but instead it set out at right angles to its former direction. When it was out of sight and hearing, Jorian returned to the place where he had buried the crown.

Karadur still clung to his perch. "Is it safe to come down?" he quavered.

"Aye, at least for the moment. Didn't you realize it could seize your rope in its jaws and jerk you back to earth?"

"Oh, I thought of that. But whereas I find tree climbing impossible at my age, and we had no ladders as in the Grand Duke's park, I knew the rope would carry me up on the strength of the spell." Karadur slid to the ground. At his command, the rope fell in a limp heap at his feet. He picked it up and wound it round and round his waist. "My thanks for saving my life at the risk of your own. Whatever your faults, my son, you are a true hero."

"Oh, rubbish!" said Jorian, looking embarrassed. "Had I stopped to think, I should have been too fearful to do aught."

"Jorian!" said Karadur sternly. "What have I told you about deprecating yourself?"

"Sorry. I haven't run so hard since Estrildis' father chased me with a scythe, the first time I came over to his farmstead to spark his daughter." Jorian picked up the crown. "I feared lest the dragon swallow this. Then I should have had to slay the beast, cut it open, and dig out the crown, and I have no idea of how to do that. Let's be off, ere another come along."

"I saw none when I met you in Moru before. Whence come they?"

"That was a dragon of Paalua, from across the Western Ocean. The Paaluans used to raid the coasts of other lands to seize the folk to eat; for, albeit civilized in some ways, they retained this unneighborly habit. Several generations past, they landed on the coast of Ir, hoping to replenish their larders with Novarian captives. They brought a number of these lizards as mounts for cavalry, each dragon bearing half a dozen soldiers. When the Paaluans were crushed, some dragons found their way south to the Marshes, where they survived and bred. There have been rumors of them, but this is the first one I have seen."

By paying close heed to the map and the terrain, they finally found their way back to the wagon despite the confusion spell, which several times sent them astray. Jorian wore the crown of Xylar as the easiest way to carry it.

As they neared the glade where Jorian had left the cart, the sound of voices jerked him alert. He stole forward, motioning Karadur to keep behind him and be quiet.

As the cart came into view, Jorian saw figures moving. Coming closer, he perceived that they comprised two raggedly-clad men holding a struggling Margalit by the arms. A third was pulling things out of the cart; only his lower half could be seen. The horse and the mule placidly grazed.

Jorian slipped behind a tree as he eased his sword out of its scabbard, lest a flash of sunlight on the steel alert the brigands. Behind him, Karadur whispered an incantation.

Jorian gathered his legs beneath him and hurled himself toward the cart in a swift, silent charge. He had covered half the distance when a robber saw him and shouted: "Ho! Aldol, beware!"

The third robber, who was stripping the cart, whirled around. He was smaller than Jorian but lithe and quick. Before Jorian, his sword extended before him, could get home, Aldol had drawn his own sword, a double-curved hunting falchion.

Going too fast to stop to fence, Jorian bore in. His point plunged into Aldol's chest halfway to the hilt. At the same time, the robber brought his short sword down on Jorian's head in an overhand cut. The blade struck the crown of Xylar with a clank.

A little staggered, Jorian tried to withdraw his own blade, but it seemed to have become wedged in Aldol's spine. As Jorian pulled, the man struck again, forehand at the side of Jorian's head. Jorian threw up his left arm. He felt the blade bite through leather and cloth into the flesh. Then Aldol sagged as his knees gave way, dragging Jorian's sword down with him.

The robbers holding Margalit released her to reach for their weapons. Still trying to free his sword, Jorian thought: this is the end; they will make ground steak of me ere I can get my hanger free.

But to Jorian's surprise, a look of terror flickered in

the surviving robbers' faces, even as they drew. Instead of attacking, the pair turned and ran down the track toward the main road until lost to sight.

Jorian got his sword loose at last. The robber he had skewered moved and groaned. Jorian put his point over the man's heart and, with a vigorous thrust, quieted him.

"Jorian!" cried Margalit, throwing her arms around him. "You came just in time! They were boasting of how often they would rape me ere cutting my throat."

"Take care; you'll get yourself bloody."

"Art wounded?"

"Just a scratch. What befell?"

He peeled off his jacket and shirt. Aldol's falchion had been stopped by the ulna, but there was a freshly bleeding cut on his forearm, a finger's breadth long. As Margalit washed and bandaged the wound, she told her tale:

"I was washing my face in the stream, when these stinkards pounced upon me. The crossbow was in the wain, so I had no chance to use it. Methinks I gave one a black eye." She glanced down and saw that her shirt had been widely torn open. She pulled the edges together. "What was that I saw, as you rushed upon the chief robber? It looked like three or four Jorians, all running toward us with bared blades and all wearing golden crowns. 'Twas a daunting sight."

"Just a little illusion spell," said Karadur. "It sufficed to put the other twain to flight. Lady Margalit, if you keep much company with Jorian, one thing is sure: you will never suffer boredom. Life in his vicinage is one dire endangerment after another."

"I know not why," said Jorian in plaintive tones. "I am a peaceable man, who asks for nought but to be suffered to make an honest living."

"Perhaps," said Karadur, "you were born on the day sacred to your Novarian war god—what is his name?"

"Heryx; but I was not born on his feast day." Jorian took off the crown, in which Aldol's sword had made a deep nick. "This thing saved my brainpan, just as your turban did. I do not think the cleft will much impair its value."

Margalit exclaimed over the crown's beauty, saying: "Jorian, are you sure you wish to give it up to get your Estrildis back?"

"Of course I'm sure!" snorted Jorian: "That's what I said, is it not?" He looked down at the dead robber. "It behooves me to carry this rogue afar off, lest the corpse draw beasts of prey. He will soon stink in this heat anyway."

"Jorian!" said Karadur. "Ere you remove the body, should we not report this manslaying to someone in authority?"

"To whom?" said Jorian.

"Are we in Othomae or in Xylar?"

Jorian shrugged. "The boundary has never been surveyed so far south. When I was King of Xylar, I tried to persuade the Othomaeans to set up a joint boundary commission. But they suspected some swindle and made so many difficulties that I gave up. In sooth this lieu has no government and hence no law."

He relieved the body of its purse and weapons, hoisted it to his shoulders, and carried it back up the trail for a tenth of a league before dropping it and returning to the wagon.

During the rest of the day and all of the next, the cart was bedizened with bright paint and astrological symbols. Jorian shaved his face, and he and Margalit were turned a deep brown all over.

When it came Margalit's turn to be dyed, she said: "Jorian, I pray you, go off and hunt something. I care not to have you staring whilst I stand nude before Father Karadur to be painted."

Jorian grinned. "If you insist; although he is a man, too."

"At his age, I do not feel the same as I should about you. You know wizards; he is probably centuries old."

"Folk exaggerate so!" said Karadur. "True, I may have somewhat lengthened my span by austerities and occult arts; but I have not yet reached a hundred."

"A wizard's life may or may not be centuries long," said Jorian. "But with so few amusements, it doubtless seems so in any case. Congratulations, Doctor. Here you are, at ninety-odd, looking like a limber lad of seventy!"

"Mock me not, saucy boy!" said Karadur. "Now take your crossbow and shoot us a hare or something, whilst I transform the lady."

The next morning they set out on the main road from Othomae to Xylar. Karadur took the name of Mabahandula, which he had used before. He wanted to give Jorian an equally polysyllabic Mulvanian name; but Jorian balked, saying: "It is all I can do to remember yours. Should we not feel silly if, when asked my own name, I had forgotten it?"

So Jorian became Sutru, while on Margalit was bestowed the name of Akshmi. Jorian wore a turban, a crimson jacket with many glass buttons, and baggy trousers gathered at the ankles, all bought from Henvin the Costumer. Margalit's Mulvanian garment was a broad, twenty-cubit length of thin material, wound round and round and over in a complicated way.

At a leisurely pace, they traveled through Xylar, stopping to pick up a few pence by fortune telling, juggling, and dancing. Margalit performed the dances that Jorian and Karadur had taught her, clattering finger cymbals while Karadur tapped a little drum and Jorian tweedled on a flute. His wound had become inflamed, making use of his left arm painful.

Jorian played such musical phrases as he could remember from Mulvan, repeating them over and over.

Although Karadur muttered that generations of Mulvanian musicians would rise from their graves in fury at Jorian's treatment of their art, the villagers found nothing amiss. As Jorian pointed out, they had no standards of comparison. With practice the trio improved. The result, if not authentic Mulvanian art, was at least a good show.

On a day of heavy overcast, Karadur asked: "How far to the next village, my son?"

Jorian frowned. "That should be Ganaref, as I remember. By my reckoning, 'twill take us till after dark. I could get there sooner by spurring Cadwil, but Filoman shows signs of lameness. He needs a new offfront shoe; the smith in Othomae botched the job."

"Must we camp out again?" said Margalit.

"Belike not. The road to Castle Lorc branches off near here, and the castle would afford some shelter." He glanced up. "An I mistake not, we may have rain."

Karadur said: "Didst tell me, Jorian, that Baron Lorc's castle was haunted?"

"So it was reputed; I never looked into the matter. I pay little heed to such legends."

"Betimes you pay too little," said Karadur. Thunder rumbled.

Margalit and Karadur broke into speech at the same time. The Mulvanian urged that they turn off the road at once and rig their tent; the girl demanded that they press on to Ganaref. They were still arguing when Jorian said:

"Here, methinks, is the road to Castle Lorc."

Margalit peered from the cart. "It is half overgrown. Does none use it?"

"I suppose not. Here comes the rain!" A few large drops struck the canvas top of the cart. "That settles it; we spend the night in the castle. Hand me my cloak, somebody." Cloaked, he turned his horse on to the weedy track.

"I lust not to meet my ancestor's ghost," said Margalit.

"Are you a descendant of Baron Lorc?"

"Aye."

"Then, if ghost there be, it should be friendly. Come along!"

Trotting through the weeds and avoiding occasional small trees that had grown up in the road, they clopped through the forest up a long, easy slope. The rain began in earnest. Jorian was soon so wet that he decided it would serve no useful purpose to crawl into the cart.

At the top of the hill, the forest opened out into an area of low, thin second growth, where a wide greensward around the castle had been abandoned. Over the spindly little trees, black against the clouds, loomed the broken walls of the castle.

The front gate, fallen to pieces, admitted them to the courtyard. The yard was not only overgrown with weeds and a few saplings, which in their growth had pried up the cobblestones, but was also dotted with man-made pits, which the travelers had much ado to avoid.

"Treasure hunters have been here," said Jorian. "The folk of Ganaref have been here, too. They have taken the portcullis and a lot of the loose stones for their own uses. Let's see if enough roof is intact to keep off the rain. Wait whilst I search."

Jorian dismounted, handed the reins to Margalit, and strode into the castle, whose doors sagged on broken hinges. Inside, he had to climb over heaps of rubble where parts of the roof had fallen in. He moved warily.

At last he emerged, saying: "I've found a chamber that seems tight enough. Tie the animals to the statues around the fountain and come on in."

Jorian pulled the blankets and other gear out of the cart and carried the heaviest items in on his shoulders. He and his companions were no sooner settled than the rain stopped. The setting sun turned the undersides of the breaking clouds to crimson and purple.

"Damn it!" said Jorian, sneezing. "I wish I could get dry. Belike one of these fireplaces still draws. Luckily for us, the chimney had been invented in Lorc's time."

Jorian returned to the cart, got out the ax, and as twilight fell reappeared with an armful of slender logs. "This stuff is green and wet," he said. "You may have to use your fire spell again, Doctor."

They were still trying to light the fire when sounds from outside brought Jorian up. "Visitors," he muttered, rising and tiptoeing to the door. Returning, he whispered:

"Seven or eight, with horses; either robbers or treasure hunters. I could not be sure in this light, but two looked like those who ran from us near Moru. Margalit, would you get my sword? It is in the chamber with the rest of our gear."

"What good is one sword against eight rogues?" said Karadur. "You might earn a hero's death, but what would that avail us?"

"We must do something! They are standing about the wain and the beasts. Soon they'll come seeking us. Even if they fail to find us, they will take the cart and the animals."

"Here is your sword," said Margalit.

Karadur said: "Methinks we shall do better to afright them. Lady Margalit, pray fetch a blanket. . . . Here!" He draped the blanket over Jorian's shoulders. "When they enter, do you impersonate the baron's ghost. Come back to the chamber, Margalit."

Soon, several armed men crowded into the crumbling hall. They glanced nervously about, looking up at the broken ceiling and the gallery that ran around the second story.

Draped in his blanket, Jorian stepped down the bottom steps of the stairway. As he emerged, he became barely visible in the deepening dark. In a sepulchrally deep voice, he said: "Who disturbeth the rest of Baron Lorc?"

As he spoke, he gripped the hilt of his sword beneath the blanket. If they saw through his disguise, they would not find him helpless. On the stair, they could not come at him more than two at a time.

The seven looked around with a hiss of sudden breaths. One uttered a low cry.

"Who violateth the demesne of Baron Lorec?" moaned Jorian, advancing a step.

The foremost man gave back. Another, turned and ran for the door, crying "Fly!" He stumbled over a loose stone, falling and scrambling up again.

In a trice, the other six also ran, tripping and stumbling. Jorian advanced by slow steps, in case one should look back in. From without came sounds of men hastily mounting, and a dwindling clatter of hooves. When Jorian got to the door, the courtyard was empty but for his horse, mule, and cart.

Jorian shrugged off the blanket and drew his forearm across his sweat-pearled forehead. "Come on out! They have fled!"

"I congratulate thee, young sir," said a voice behind Jorian. Jorian's hair prickled, for the voice was neither Karadur's high, nasal whine nor Margalit's clear contralto. Though faint and whispery, its tone was as deep as Jorian's own. He whirled, half drawing his sword.

A few paces away hovered a shadowy, translucent shape. It became the semitransparent figure of a short, stout, elderly man, clad in garments as antiquated as his speech.

Jorian started violently; his tongue seemed stuck to the roof of his mouth. At last he croaked: "Are—are you Baron Lorc? I m-mean, his ghost?"

"Aye, aye; in good sooth I am both. Thou hast most featly put to flight yon gang of scroyles and saved thy possessions. Had I not—"

The ghost broke off as Karadur and Margalit emerged from the stair passage. Jorian heard Margalit's catch of breath. Having somewhat regained his composure, Jorian remembered his current persona. Assuming his Mulvanian accent, he said:

"Exalted sir, these are traveling friends of me, dancer Akshmi and Doctor Maha—Mabahandula of Mulvan. I Sutru of Mulvan are. This Baron Lorc is."

Staring in the gloom, Margalit managed a wordless curtsey. The ghost smiled. "Thou seekest to cozen me to believe ye be Mulvanians. But I have harkened to you since ye entered my dilapidated manse, and I wot ye speak Novarian as do those born to the Twelve Nations. So I take it ye be merely Novarians in garb oriental. Now wherefore this imposture?"

Jorian sighed. "Well, I did but try. We are earning our way as entertainers from afar. Permit me to present the Lady Margalit of Totens, who tells me she is a descendant of yours; and Doctor Karadur, who is truly a Mulvanian."

The ghost bowed, saying: "Indeed, it rejoiceth me to meet a kinswoman. I cannot kiss thy hand, for my form is insufficiently material; but I prithee, take the intention for the deed. I thank Zevatas that, after all these years, he hath allowed me visitors who flee not in terror from my aspect. Know that I am a harmless phantom, who findeth the lot of haunter a wearisome sameness. Will ye remain the night, keeping this lonesome wraith company and telling me somewhat of what hath befallen in the world of late? Since my friend Alaunus died, I have had no mortal copemate."

"Who was he?" asked Jorian.

"Alaunus was an aged drunkard, who lived by begging and promiscuous employment in Ganaref. Betimes he came hither to down a bottle and gossip with me. He was the only mortal for leagues hereabouts who feared me not."

"Why must you haunt this ruin, instead of going on to the afterworld?" asked Jorian.

" 'Tis a long and heavy-footed tale. Were it not wiser to ignite your blaze and prepare your even's repast whilst I do speak? I were a poor host, to keep you standing. Take seats, an ye can find any that the tooth of time hath not destroyed."

When Jorian at last got the fire going and Margalit had spread out their modest supper, the baron resumed: "Now, where was I? Ah, yea; I was to relate the tale of my being bound to this place. Know ye that, in the last year of my mortal life, a wonderworker, clept Aurelion, appeared at the castle begging shelter. He was, he said, a wizard and alchemist. My health being bad, with disturbances of the heart, Aurelion said that, for a modest sum of gold, he would transmute lead into gold of ten times the quantity. Moreover, this alchemical gold was of such potency that, reduced to powder, it would cure all my ills and enable me to live on indefinitely.

"When my daughter and her husband came to visit, she warned me that the wight was but a charlatan. But so convincing was Aurelion's presence and so beguiling his mien that I gave him the gold and commanded him to proceed forthwith.

"For the greater part of a twelvemonth, the alchemist dwelt in the castle, making, he said, his preparations. Ever he required more money to procure rare ingredients, some of which he went to Xylar City to obtain. He studied ancient books he had with him. He practiced magical operations in the tower of the castle that I had set aside for his use.

"As time passed, I became impatient with Aurelion's neverending flow of promises. At last I told him plain, either produce his gold or get himself hence, ere he eat me out of house and home. At last he announced that the final operation would take place the following night.

"That he was a true wizard or sorcerer as well as a cheat I have no doubt, the terms not being mutually exclusive. He evoked an authentic demon to assist him. Hath any of you witnessed a sorcerous evocation? Yea? Then I need not recount all the tedious details of the pentacle, the suffumigations, the chants, the gestures, and so forth. Suffice it to say that this fellow did place a hundredweight of bars of lead upon a table and performed a mighty conjuration thereover. When the smoke and flames cleared away, the bars did gleam with the aureate hue of authentic gold.

"Delighted was I with this addition to the familial fortune and even more so with the prospective banishment of the ills the flesh is heir to. Thinking but to test the softness of the gold, I stepped forward as soon as the metal had had time to cool, and thereupon did scratch one of the bars with my dagger. Ye may conceive my dismay when, at the touch of the steel, the bar instantly resumed the glaucous tones of lead. Fearing the worst, I speedily touched the other bars with my blade, and as I did so they in turn did lead once more become.

" 'Hah, sirrah, what is this?' I shouted at Aurelion, who in turn bawled at his demonic assistant: 'What's this, thou noodlehead? Thou hast cheated us!' The demon roared back: 'I did but follow thy commands, as I have done many a time and oft before!' 'Tis not my fault that this mortal detected thy cozening ere we had won clear!'

"Both wizard and demon screamed at each other until the demon vanished with a flash of light and a clap of thunder. I summoned the guards and bade them whip the alchemist from the castle.

"As he was being led, bound with ropes whilst two lusty guardsmen belabored his bare back till the blood flew, he snarled back at me: 'Baron Lorc, I curse thee with the curse of Gwitardus! When thou diest, thy spirit shall be bound to this castle until thou canst persuade a queen to scrub thy castle floor!'

"That was the last I saw of Aurelion. A few months later, my heart worsened, and one morn I arose to find I was looking down upon myself lying stark and still upon the bed. Then I wist that I had died in my sleep. I soon discovered that the alchemist's curse had come to pass, for my shade could not leave the castle.

"My daughter and her husband returned hither to carry out the funeral and the execution of my will. They moved into the castle for a time, since she was my principal heir. But, alas, whenever I sought converse with any person, that one became palsied with fright. My shade cannot be seen by full daylight; but as ye do observe, it becometh visible at night.

"Day or night, howsomever, none would linger to befriend a lonely old phantom. By day, they would hear a disembodied voice and run witlessly hither and yon, like unto a yard of fowls befrighted by the swoop of an eagle. At night they would run at the mere sight of me, whether or no I spake. Little by little the guards and other retainers departed to seek employment elsewhere. At last my daughter and son-in-law followed them forth, leaving me alone.

"At first I was not altogether discontented, for my wife had predeceased me, and I feared to encounter her in the afterworld. This prospect pleased me not a whit, by which hint ye may judge our state of marital felicity whilst she did live."

"You need not worry," said Karadur. "According to our savants, one is born into the afterworld virtually without memory of life in this one. Moreover, I am told that the people in that world number in the thousands of millions, wherefore the chances of your encountering your whilom spouse were too small to consider."

"Thou relievest my mind," said the ghost. "But, lacking a queen to scrub the floor, I know not how I shall ever attain that plane. I am like to spend all eternity here, whilst the castle crumbleth about me. Had I material hands, I would, an all else failed, make the repairs myself to stay the gaunt hand of decay. But as things be, what time doth not disintegrate, the treasure seekers rend asunder."

As the others ate, the ghost launched into a long account of his experiences in life: the year of a famine; his defense of the castle against a free company; and notable hunts in which he had taken part. He seemed a good-natured person of modest intelligence, limited experience, and somewhat narrow interests. He and Margalit got into a long discussion of genealogy, tracing her descent from him. There was talk of "Third Cousin Getion," "Great-Aunt Bria," and other relatives whose names meant nothing to Jorian.

Then the garrulous ghost got off on the revolution in Xylar, several generations back, which had deprived the nobility of its feudal privileges. "A monstrous folly!" said the ghost. The baron spent the next hour fulminating against the injustice done his fellow lords and against the iniquities of the Regency Council, the true ruler of the nation ever since.

Jorian found the baron a nice enough fellow but a terrible bore. It took simultaneous yawns by the three travelers to remind the baron that, unlike him, mortals did from time to time require sleep.

# IX

# The Proxenary Clerk

"To address royalty in Mulvanian," said Karadur to Margalit, "one uses the politest form. Sentences whereof the ruler is subject or object are put in the third person singular subjunctive. For another member of the royal family, or a priest in his official capacity, one uses instead the third person singular indicative with the honorific suffix -*ye*—"

"Doctor," said Jorian, "we need not waste Margalit's time on these distinctions. Imprimus, we shan't perform before royalty; secundus, nobody in Xylar would know the difference anyway. Teach her the form used between equals and let it go at that."

"But, my son, if she is to impersonate a Mulvanian, she must not speak my beautiful mother tongue brokenly!"

"Jorian is right," said Margalit. "I find these lessons hard enough without more complications than are absolutely needed."

Karadur sighed. "Very well. Lady Margalit, suffer me to explain the significance of nasal vowels. . . ."

"You had better compress your lessons," said Jorian. "Tomorrow we shall raise Xylar City. Meseems she already knows the sentences she will most need, such as 'I do not understand Novarian' and 'No thank you; my body is not for sale.'"

"Where are we stopping?" asked Margalit.

"Kerin and I have arranged to meet at the Fox and Rabbit."

\*　　\*　　\*

The taverner, Sovar, looked suspiciously at the three exotic foreigners, but a deposit of a golden Xylarian lion quieted his fears. He gave them two rooms, a single for Margalit and a larger one for the two men. As they settled it, Jorian said to Karadur: "Doctor, pray ask our host if Synelius the Apothecary is still in business."

"Why me?"

"Because I am fain to keep out of sight. I patronized Synelius when I was king. If I ask after him and go to his shop, someone may put two and two together despite the costume and the bogus accent."

"What would you with this Synelius?"

"I wish some salve for this cut. My arm is still sore, and I want you to make the purchase."

"Ah, my old bones!" sighed Karadur, but he went. Later, when Jorian was applying the salve, Sovar knocked, saying: "A gentleman below asks after a party of Mulvanians. Be you they?"

"I will see," said Jorian. Below, he found his brother Kerin. Resisting an impulse to throw himself into a bear hug with his brother, Jorian clasped his hands in the Mulvanian manner and bowed low, murmuring: "Sutru of Mulvan, at your service. What can this unworthy one do for noble sir?" In a whisper he added: "Keep your voice down!"

Kerin, taking in his brother's costume and manner, compressed his lips in an effort not to burst into laughter. He said: "Ah, I understand. How about supper?"

"Nay; a Mulvanian cannot eat with a foreigner without pollution."

"I thought you told me," murmured Kerin, "you attended a party given by the Mulvanian emperor?"

"I did; but that was a dance, not a banquet. All they served was fruit juice, and I suppose that counts not." Raising his voice and resuming his accent, Jorian continued: "But do you chew by noble self, and then we will forgather in my humble quarters."

So Kerin ate by himself, while the pretended Mulvanians, eating their own supper, ostentatiously ignored him. Later, when only a few remained in the common room and those absorbed in their own affairs, Jorian caught Kerin's eye, winked, and gave a slight jerk of his head. After Jorian had disappeared into his room, Kerin rose and followed him up the stairs. In the room, they hugged and pounded each other's backs, grinning.

"Well?" said Jorian. "Can Thevatas deliver her?"

"So he claims. Have you *it*?"

"Aye; 'tis in yon bag atop my soiled garments. You can feel it through the cloth. When could he fetch her?"

Kerin shrugged. "Belike tomorrow even?"

"Make it earlier, at least an hour ere sunset. I am not lief to try to talk my way out of the city after the gates are closed for the night. When the palace finds she is gone, they'll swarm out like hornets."

As the sun approached the horizon, an increasingly nervous Jorian repeatedly stepped out of the Fox and Rabbit to look at the sky, or to walk down the street to glance at the water clock in the window of Vortiper and Jeweller.

At last, a worried-looking Kerin hastened up, murmuring: "Thevatas said he would be delayed."

"Why?"

"I'll tell you. Let us go inside. I'll wait in the common room, drinking beer; you shall return to your chamber. We would not make a public scene of this reunion."

"That's sense," said Jorian. "When did he say he'd be late?"

"I was to meet him in the Square of Psaan and guide him hither, since I had not told him where you were staying. When he appeared not, I cast about the nearby streets, thinking there might have been a misunderstanding. I met him coming out of the apothecary's shop.

When I asked about this, he said *she* had a headache and besought him to fetch her one of Synelius's simples. Hence they would be late."

Heart pounding, Jorian returned to his room, where he found Karadur and Margalit looking questions. "There's been a delay," he said shortly.

"But, my son," said Karadur, "darkness falls without, and the gates will close. How then shall we issue forth?"

"I wish I knew, too. Belike I can persuade or bribe the officer of the gate watch to open for us."

"Could we climb down the Doctor's magical rope from the city wall, as they do in romances?" asked Margalit.

"We could, but that would mean leaving the cart and the animals. Afoot, we should soon be run to earth."

"Were it not wiser to remain the night?" said Karadur. "In the morn, those who pass through the gates are not questioned."

"It would be, could we count upon Estrildis' disappearance to remain undiscovered. But someone is sure to sound the alarum. Then every guard, soldier, spy, and flunkey in Xylar will be out searching. They'll poke into every dog kennel and henhouse."

Karadur muttered, "We had better pray that this proxenary clerk and your Queen are stopped from leaving the palace. An they come hither, we are undone."

Jorian asked: "Could you send us to the afterworld, as you did me three years since?"

"Nay. That spell was one of the mightiest whereof I have command. It required extraordinary preparations, which took months. Ah well, they say beheading is one of the least painful forms of execution."

"Perhaps; but I have never heard a beheadee's side of the story."

"Anyway," said Karadur, "if they come seeking us, I will see what my illusion spells can accomplish."

"I can return to the palace, saying you snatched me

thence, and I have only now escaped your captivity and made my way back to Xylar," Margalit suggested.

"That would not do," said Jorian. "Judge Grallon knows that you and I were on friendly terms in Othomae, not captor and captive. Mark you, if I must lose my head, it does not follow that you should lose yours. I can give the twain of you the names of other inns, not of the highest repute, where you will be taken in without questions. If men from the government question you, say you had no idea of who I really was."

"What about you?" said Margalit. "Why hide you not likewise?"

"I might; but let us first see whether Thevatas come hither, with or without Estrildis. Then we can better decide."

They went down to supper. Although Sovar's food was excellent, Jorian left half his repast uneaten. Kerin had returned to the Square of Psaan to await Thevatas. When one of Sovar's patrons became drunk and offensive, Jorian was tempted to beat the man up and pitch him out. Such was the tension within him that he felt he would burst if he could not discharge it in some violent action. With effort he controlled himself, and Sovar ejected the unruly patron.

Afterward they went back to the large room and sat gloomily, composing plan after plan to save their skins. They tried out various schemes, according to whether Thevatas came, with or without Estrildis, or did not come, or others came to arrest Jorian.

At last came a light tap on the door and Kerin's low voice: "Here they are!"

Jorian leaped up, overturning his chair, and threw open the door. Three stood in the door frame: the tall, handsome, youthful Kerin; a small, paunchy man of middle age; and a short woman in a hooded cloak, which fell to her ankles and hid her features.

"Come in!" whispered Jorian. He closed the door behind them and turned.

"Have you *it*?" said the small man.

"Aye. Is this *she*?" Jorian pulled back the hood. Estrildis' blond hair and round-featured face came into view. She seemed to stare unseeingly.

"Where is it?" demanded Thevatas. "I must begone, to establish my alibi."

Jorian dumped the contents of the bag out on the bed. He extracted the crown from the soiled clothing and handed it to Thevatas, who turned it over, hefted it, and put it back in its bag.

"Good!" muttered the clerk, turning to go.

"One moment!" said Jorian. "What mean you to do? Melt it down for bullion?"

"Nay; I have grander plans." The little man giggled. "Next time you visit Xylar, you shall find me a man of authority, perchance a member of the Regency Council. Meanwhile, keep your mouths shut, and I'll do likewise. Farewell!"

The clerk scuttled out and was gone. Jorian turned to Estrildis. "Darling!"

She turned her head slowly toward him but seemed unable to focus her eyes.

"What ails you, beloved?" Jorian asked.

She did not reply. Karadur said: "Your woman seems under some spell or drug. Smell her breath!"

Jorian sniffed. "There is something strange here. . . How can we bring her round?"

Margalit grasped the girl by the shoulders and gave her a slight shake. "My lady! Your Majesty! Estrildis! Know you me not?"

"I have had some experience," said Karadur. "Suffer me to try."

He went to the washstand and dipped a corner of the towel in the water. Then he faced Estrildis and began slapping her cheeks gently with the wet towel, repeating her name.

Jorian untied the drawstring at Estrildis's throat and took off the enveloping cloak. His first impression was that his favorite wife had gained weight in the three years since they had parted. Then he looked more closely.

"Margalit!" he said. "Tell me honestly. Is she pregnant?"

Margalit stared at the floor. "Aye, she is."

"Did you know of this when the demon bore you off?"

"I had a strong suspicion. She had missed a period."

"When is the child due?"

"Methinks in a month or two."

"I cannot be the father. Who is?"

"I had liefer she told you," said Margalit.

Jorian turned back to Estrildis, who seemed to be coming round. Staring wide-eyed, she looked from one to the other, murmuring: "Where am I?" Then she shrieked: "Margalit! Do I dream?"

"Nay, dear one, it is I," replied Margalit.

"But what has made you so brown, like a nomad of Fedirun? Hast been lying all day in the sun?"

Jorian said: "Estrildis, dear!"

She stared at him in puzzlement. "Are you truly Jorian? And all brown, too?"

Jorian said: "You are at the Fox and Rabbit, in Xylar City. We came to fetch you away. But I see that things have changed."

For a long moment she stared wordlessly. Then she glanced down at her belly. "Oh, Jorian, I am so sorry! I could not help it."

"Who is he?"

"A young man of noble family, attached to the Regency."

"His name?"

"I—I won't tell. You would slay him, and I l-l-love him." She began to weep.

Jorian picked up the chair he had upset and sat down in it, burying his face in his hands. Then he said: "Sit down, the rest of you. We must think what to do."

Karadur said: "It is a shame we let that clerk make off with the crown ere we had looked into this matter."

"Spilt milk," said Jorian. "He'll be back at the palace by now, not to be dug out save by a siege. But he'd better not meet me on a dark night. Estrildis, did you wish to wed this other wight?"

"Aye; but the Regency would never dissolve my marriage to you whilst they had hope of luring you back to cut off your head."

Margalit asked: "Jorian, if you knew the father, would you kill him?"

Jorian heaved a deep sigh. "That was the first thought that entered my mind. But then. . . ."

"And the second?"

"Then reason took hold. If I slew him, what should I have but a wife mourning her slain lover and rearing an infant not mine? I thought this would be the most loving reunion of history, but as things be. . . . Why did you not tell me ere this?"

Margalit spread her hands. "I could not foresee the outcome."

"How mean you?"

"Well, you might have died, or Estrildis might have died, or young Sir—the youth in question might have died. Then what good would it have done to tell you, save to make you unhappier than you need be? Besides, my first loyalty belonged to her. I did drop a hint or two."

"So you did. Did they companion often, those twain?"

"During the past year, he came to visit daily. After a while she asked me to leave them in privacy during these visits."

Jorian turned to Estrildis. "My dear, what has this young man that so turned your head?"

"Oh, he is handsome and brave and gallant, like a knight from feudal times. And he comes of noble family."

"You mean, like a knight as described in romances. We still have knights in Othomae. Some are not bad fellows; but others are mere bullies and lechers, who'll cut a commoner down over a fancied slight. And I am homely and hardworking and practical, and my forebears, like yours, were farmers and tradesmen. But tell me why, when Thevatas brought you hither, you acted drugged?"

"Because I had been. That rascal drugged me."

"How?"

"This afternoon he came, saying he could smuggle me out of the palace so I could rejoin my husband. But I refused. Much as I esteem you, Jorian, my heart belongs to—to the other."

"What then?"

"Thevatas went away. After supper he came back, saying he had obtained a pot of rare tea from the Kuromon Empire. He carried the pot wrapped in a towel to keep it warm and invited me to join him. I thought it tasted strange, and the next thing I knew, I was in such a daze that I knew not what I did. I remember Thevatas's wrapping me in that peasantly cloak and guiding me out, telling the guards I was a light leman of his."

Kerin said: "That explains what Thevatas was doing at the apothecary's."

Jorian sat silently as the others watched. Their expressions mingled curiosity, expectancy, and a trace of fear. At last he said:

"I see no way out of this tangle but to cut our losses and run. Kerin can take Estrildis back to the palace gate and leave her there. She can make up her own taradiddle of having walked out by a ruse, to wander the city unescor—"

A sharp knock interrupted. Jorian picked up his scabbarded sword from where it leaned in a corner, drew the blade, and faced the door, muttering:

"If that's the Regency's bully-rooks, they shan't take

me alive. Stand back, all! Come in, whoever you are! It is not bolted."

A slim, strikingly handsome man, several years younger than Jorian, stood in the doorway. At the sight of Jorian's blade, he said: "Ha!" and reached for his own hilt.

"Corineus!" cried Estrildis.

Jorian backed a step. "Another mystery explained. Well, come on in and close the door! Stand not there like a ninny!"

The young man drew with a *wheep*. He entered, saying: "I perceive you wish to slay me to wipe the stain from your honor. So, have at you!" He took the guard position.

"You mistake me," said Jorian. "I know about you and my wife, but I do not wish to cause unnecessary sorrow or to leave the child fatherless. Neither do I wish the task of rearing it. So take her and it; they are yours."

Sir Corineus frowned in puzzlement. "Did I hear you aright? Methought Jorian was brave, not an arrant coward."

"My bravery has nought to do with it. If we fight, either I shall slay you, or you will kill me. I am not eager to be slain just yet; and as for slaying you, what would that profit me? What could I get for your carcass? Your hide were of little value as leather, and we don't eat our fallen foes as in Paalua."

"You have no knightly sense of honor! You sound like a mere tradesman, a cold, scheming, money-grubber!"

Jorian shrugged. "Suit yourself. If you attack me, I'll give a good account of myself; but I shan't be sorry if you refrain."

"It is plain that you are no gentleman, or you would have demanded instant satisfaction when I implied you were a coward."

"My dear boy, you are living in the past! Those ideas have been obsolete in Xylar for a century."

"To you, belike, but not to me. How much must I insult you ere you fight me?"

"You try my patience, young man, but I'll essay to be reasonable. Wherefore are you so avid to fight?"

"Because, so long as you live, I cannot wed Estrildis. So one of us must die. Have at you again!" And Corineus rushed forward, aiming a slash at Jorian.

In an instant they were furiously hacking and thrusting. Sparks flew from the flickering blades. The others crowded against the far wall to keep out of harm's way.

Jorian found that Corineus was a fair but not a first-class fencer. He beat off the young man's frenzied attacks until Corineus, panting and sweating, began to flag. Then Jorian made a quick feint and a slash at the top of Corineus' head. The blade bit into the youth's scalp, but the blow was not hard enough to disable him. Corineus backed off to wipe from his forehead the trickle of blood that ran down from the scalp wound.

Jorian was not yet breathing hard. Presently Corineus came on again, more slowly and carefully. He got his point into the sleeve of Jorian's shirt, opening a rip.

"Another sewing job, Margalit," said Jorian. Again he feinted, doubled, and brought his blade down on Corineus' pate. Corineus backed off, wiping a fresh flow of blood from his scalp. His face was becoming smeared with blood.

They fenced on indecisively until both simultaneously attempted an advance-thrust and found themselves in a *corps-à-corps*, with blades crossing near the hilts. For an instant they struggled frozen in position, each trying to push the other off balance.

By sheer strength, Jorian forced the other blade up and back, until he could bring his own blade down on Corineus' mangled scalp again. He sawed two more gashes in the flesh. Corineus staggered back and disengaged, frantically wiping his face with his free hand.

It was no use. Blinded by the flow of blood, Corineus stood helplessly, pawing at his face. Jorian whacked his sword hand with the flat of his blade. Corineus' sword clattered to the floor. Jorian put a toe beneath it, tossed it into the air, and caught it.

A knock sounded, and Sovar's voice said: "Is all well within, gentlemen?"

"All's well," replied Jorian. "We did but practice." He turned to the others. "See if you can bandage this poor fellow. Sit down, Corineus."

"Where? I cannot see."

Jorian pushed Corineus into a chair. The youth said: "You have made a mock of me! My honor is in ruins! I must seek an honorable death to atone for my disgrace."

"Oh, for the gods' sake!" snorted Jorian. "Play the man for once and not the silly child!"

"What would you of me?"

"Tell me more of this affair. How did you find us here?"

"I saw Thevatas leaving the palace with Estrildis, whom I knew despite that cloak. The eye of true love sees through all disguises. I followed until the clerk entered the inn. I waited without, trying to decide whether to alert the Regency Council or to cope with the matter myself. After Thevatas emerged and hastened furtively away, I decided it were a more honorable and knightly course to essay the rescue myself. So here I am."

"Lucky for us, young man," said Jorian. "I cannot fight the whole garrison single-handed. Now then, you claim the title of 'Sir.' Why is that?"

Corineus nursed the hand that Jorian had struck, on which an angry bruise was rising. "As you surely know, it is a title accorded sons of a hereditary baron, since we have no true orders of knighthood any longer. My sire, Lord Holdar, is titular baron of Maesbol."

"I know of that family. What do you for a living?"

"I am undersecretary in the foreign department."

"Maesbol is close to the borders of Ir, is it not?"

"Aye."

"Does your father dwell thereabouts?"

"Aye, we still have a small castle and enough land to support it, albeit we are much fallen from our former estate. No longer can we compel hinds to swink in our fields as their feudal duty, but must hire these oafs for real money, like any untitled squire."

"Tsk, tsk," said Jorian. "Having worked as a hind, I sympathize with the oafs. But do you love Estrildis enough to give up your post in the govenment?"

"Aye! What true knight would not—"

Jorian held up a hand. "Has your father influence with the syndics of Ir?"

Corineus looked puzzled. "Aye, now that you mention it. Those money-grubbers buy our surplus crops. Why?"

"Why not take Estrildis to Ir and, with some hidden influence from your father, get your marital status sorted out? When things quiet down and you and she are legally joined—at least under Irian law—you can slip back to your father's estate and work for him. If he makes difficulties, the sight of an infant grandchild should soften him."

"But what of you, King Jorian?"

Jorian grinned. "No titles, pray. As you said, I am a tradesman at heart. I shall manage, albeit differently from your way."

Corineus shook his head, muttering: "I do not understand this modern world. In feudal times, every man knew his place and what he must do to defend his honor. In our bout just now, you could have slain me six times over; I knew it almost as soon as we engaged. Yet you refrained, as though I were nought but a bad-tempered child."

"To slay you once would have been sufficient; and had I been full of your ancient notions of honor, I had done just that. But let us be practical. Have you means of reaching Ir? Estrildis is in no condition to ride horseback."

Corineus pondered. "My friend Vercassus has a gig, which he has lent me in times past. Belike I can borrow it. I keep my horse in Vercassus' stable, and my groom Gwithion sleeps in the servants' quarters there. I can take both with me to Maesbol, and my man can return the gig to Vercassus. If Gwithion have not gone out on a round of the mughouses, we should be ready to fly within the hour."

"How will you get out of the city at night?"

"The captain of the watch at the North Gate owes me a gambling debt. Now, if you will excuse me whilst I return to the palace for my belongings—"

"Better not take time for that. Belongings can be replaced, but your head cannot. And pray take Estrildis to your friend's house forthwith, for our safety here."

Corineus seemed inclined to argue, but Jorian said firmly: "Nay, out you go, the twain of you. As the little clerk said, keep your mouths shut and we'll keep ours likewise. Good-bye, Estrildis."

She began to weep again. "I know not what to say— it is awkward—you are a true gentleman despite what he said—"

"Na, na, forget all that and get tha hence," said Jorian, reverting to the rustic Kortolian dialect of his boyhood. "Partings, like executions, were best done speedily; but a shall remember ma bonny little farm lassie."

Wrapped in the hooded cloak, Estrildis went out sniffling. Corineus shepherded her, treating her as if she were a fragile glass vase.

"Whew!" Jorian drew his sleeve across his forehead. "Let us hope they get safely away ere the palace come looking for them. Think you not that we need a draft of Sovar's best? All but Father Karadur, whose principles forbid."

"I'll fetch the wine," said Kerin.

"Methinks even I could bend my principles a trifle," said Karadur. "This is a change from how you formerly spoke, Jorian, of skewering any villain who so much has made eyes at your lass."

"That's your doing," said Jorian. "I remembered your lecture, when we were flying over the Lograms. So I've tried in accordance therewith to take the long view of what were best for all concerned. Corineus would call that unknightly, but happily I have no knightly code to live up to. The lad may be handsome and brave and gallant, but he is also a damned fool."

Margalit said: "That's the main reason I insisted on coming on this journey."

"How mean you?" said Jorian.

"Methought that, when you learned of her infidelity, you might slay her in your rage; and I thought it my duty to protect her. Thank Zevatas I did not have to throw myself betwixt her and your steel!"

For the next hour they sat in the large bedchamber, drinking from the bottle that Kerin had brought and talking plans. Then, bottle empty, Kerin spoke of returning to his quarters and Margalit, of retiring to her chamber. They were bidding good night when a noise from below caught their attention. There were footfalls of many men, a rumble of speech, and a clank of weapons.

Kerin looked out, then softly closed the door. "It's a squad of the Royals, looking for *her*," he said. "They will search every digit of this place, their officer says. What now ?"

"Let me think," said Jorian. "If we try to run for it—nay; and if they look us over closely, they may see that Margalit and I are disguised. . . . I know one trick that might throw them off. Kerin and Karadur, get under the bed! Margalit, take off your clothes and get into the bed!"

"What!" she cried. "Art mad? Why—"

"Just do it! I'll explain anon." As he spoke, Jorian peeled off his own garments. "Hasten, curse it! Fear not for your virtue; this is but a charade to cozen them. Yare!"

"Every last stitch?" quavered Margalit, unwinding the voluminous Mulvanian garment.

"Every stitch!" Standing naked, Jorian waited until Margalit was under the blanket, while his brother and Mulvanian were out of sight beneath the bed. Then he blew out the lamp and slid under the blanket. Below, Kerin grunted as Jorian's weight pressed the bed down upon him. "Quiet!" whispered Jorian, sliding an arm around Margalit, who stiffened at his touch. "Let me do the talking."

The tramping and voices outside went on and on. At last the door burst open. Turning his head, Jorian made out the silhouette of two Royal Guardsmen in the doorway. Half sitting up, still holding Margalit closely, he roared:

"Heryx smite you with emerods! Cannot a man make love to his own lawful wife in privacy? Have you no decency? Get out!"

"I beg your pardon, sir," said a voice. The door closed, and the trampings died away. When all sounds of the visitations ended, Jorian got out of bed, opened the door a crack to peek out, and relit the lamp.

"They've gone," he said, pulling on his trousers.

Margalit held the Mulvanian garment against her front. "May I go now?"

"Aye, my dear. If any wight besmirch your fair name as a result of this play-acting, Kerin and the Doctor can swear I took no liberties. They'd have known."

"But you thought of those liberties. I could tell." She giggled. "After traveling about with you, Jorian, I misdoubt I have any fair name left to preserve."

# X

# The Haunted Castle

Margalit, handling Filoman's Reins, said: "Jorian, for one whose heart has just been broken by his love's faithlessness, you seem unwontedly cheerful."

Jorian, riding Cadwil beside the cart, had been singing an air from *The Good Ship Petticoat*, by Galliben and Silfero:

> "Oh, I am a pirate captain bold;
> I fill my vessel with jewels and gold
> And slaughter my captives, young and old,
>     To rule the raging sea, oh!"

He gave Margalit a searching look, saying: "You are right, now that I bethink me. It was a shock, of course. But later, when I pondered the matter, along with my grief, disappointment, and resentment, I realized there was an element of relief."

"Meaning you loved her not so desperately as you have been alleging?"

"Well, three years is a long separation for one so young and lusty as Estrildis. True, I loved her—I still do in a way—and had she remained true, I would have tried to be a loving, faithful husband. When she did not, I found the break less painful than I might have expected. Mean you to return to your post at the Academy?"

"Aye; what else? There are few positions as a queen's lady-in-waiting open."

They had been traveling southeasterly, wasting no

time but not moving so hurriedly as to arouse suspicion. Once a squadron of horse caught up with them and searched them. But Jorian's Mulvanian accent, together with the lack of any trace of Estrildis, convinced the troopers that these were merely harmless foreigners. They galloped on.

Jorian said: "We shall soon come to the road to Castle Lorc. Let's spend the night there. Baron Lorc is not a bad sort as ghosts go, and we shall have a roof over our heads."

When neither of his companions objected, Jorian led the cart up the long, overgrown slope to the ruined castle. Margalit called: "Jorian! Had we not better station the cart and the beasts behind the castle, instead of in the courtyard? They were less visible."

"That's my wise woman! How have I managed without you all these years?"

"Welcome, my friends," said Baron Lorc's ghost, as darkness fell and Margalit set out their supper in the main hall. "Let me think. The large man, albeit clad as a Mulvanian, saith he be Nikko of Kortoli. The lady is Margalit of Totens; and—I forget thy name, reverend sir. If thou hast noted a failure of memory with advancing age, thou mayst imagine how much worse it be for me."

"He is Doctor Karadur," said Jorian.

"Now, this doth excite mine interest," said the ghost. "Ye see, yesternight a squadron of cavalry made free with my demesne, and I overheard their talk. Several troopers seemed not to know what their mission portended, having been mere boys when these events began. So their officer related the particulars.

"It transpired that they sought one Estrildis, Queen of Xylar, who hath vanished. The burthen was that she had been abducted by her husband, the fugitive King Jorian, who disappeared three years since. He fled, they said, to escape beheading at the ceremony that taketh place every lustrum—or would, had not Jorian's desertion thrown the calendar into confusion."

"We heard something of that," said Jorian.

"Ah, but that was not all. According to this officer, this Jorian also passeth under the name of Nikko of Kortoli, to which name thou didst admit when I confronted thee with proof thou wert no true Mulvanian. Now, were that not a coincidence singular? And furthermore, this officer spake of one Margalit of Totens, once lady-in-waiting to Queen Estrildis, who vanished last winter—some say carried off by a demon, but the officer believed not that tale and hath not been seen since. One such coincidence of names were within the realm of the possible; but two! That passeth all bounds of rational belief."

Jorian sighed. "Very well, I confess—again. Means this that you will set the next group of searchers on our trail?"

"Nay; why should I? But what in sooth hath befallen the Queen? I see her not with thee."

"She has gone off in another direction, with one who, she hopes, will become her new husband."

The ghost shook its transparent head. "I regret that she came not with thee. Then ye could set me free from this curse."

"You mean, if Estrildis would scrub the floor?"

"Yea, verily. Be ye still wedded, thou and she?"

"Legally, I believe so. She hopes to arrange a divorce in another state, since Xylar won't give her one."

The ghost frowned, chin in hand. "A new thought doth begin to blossom in my brainpan, or whatever phantoms have in lieu thereof. In life I was the local magistrate, and none hath ever canceled my appointment. I can grant thee a divorce. Her refusal to accompany thee maketh her guilty of desertion."

"Is a legal act by a ghost valid?"

"I misdoubt the point hath ever come before thy high courts. But let us assume it so be. Then thou couldst wed the Lady Margalit here. Since thou art King, thy consort is Queen. So if she scrub my floor—not all of it, I do assure thee—I were instanter enlarged from this durance tedious."

Jorian and Margalit stared at each other. "Well!" said Jorian at last. "That's an interesting suggestion. We should need time to consider it."

Margalit said nothing. The baron said: "All the time ye wish, gentles. I would not coerce you into hasty acture. But think: once I am suffered to depart for my next life, ye need no more worry about my betraying you to the Xylarians! A favor meriteth a return favor."

"Let's sleep on it," said Jorian.

Next morning, Jorian said: "Margalit, let's take a walk and see how our beasts fare."

When they had found the horse and the mule thriving, Jorian looked at Margalit. "Well?"

"Well, what?" she replied.

"You know. The baron's proposal that you and I wed."

"Mean you that you do not altogether trust this ghost? That, if we yield not to his urgings, his resolution not to betray us might weaken? He hinted as much."

"That was a consideration; but it is not what I had in mind."

"What had you in mind?"

Jorian kicked a stone from the path. "I had not meant to speak thus but three days after parting from Estrildis. I have been drawn to you ever since the demon fetched you to Abacarus' sanctuary. You have all I should wish for in a life's companion, including the good sense that I, alas, sometimes lack. When I see you dance in your Mulvanian guise, 'tis all I can do not to leap up and bear you off.

"Ere the break with Estrildis, I told myself: Jorian, you are a faithful husband who'll do aught to recover his beloved wife. What you feel for Margalit is mere lust. But now I cannot deny that I am in love with you. I had meant, after a decent interval, to press my suit; but the baron has forced my hand.

"True, this journey has made a beggar of me, since Thevatas got away with the crown. But I have always been able to earn a living in one way or another."

"How legal would such a marriage be?" she asked. "I have heard of taking a ghost's deposition in a lawsuit, but never of one's acting as magistrate. Even if the marriage were legal, a royal divorce might not be, since the Regency claims authority in such matters."

"Well," said Jorian, "if I be King, then by Xylarian law I am entitled to five wives. So I cannot be faulted for bigamy whatever Estrildis' status. At least, that is, in Xylar, whither I hope never to return. How think you?"

"Jorian, promise me one thing."

"Aye?"

"That as soon as we cross into Othomae—assuming they do not catch us—you will file similar actions for divorce and marriage under Othomaean law, so that no awkward questions shall arise."

"Mean you that your answer be 'yea'?"

"Aye, I do so mean. Well?"

"I promise. And back in Kortoli I'll do it again!"

Told of the betrothal, Karadur said: "My felicitations on you twain. But it does seem a pity that all your arduous efforts, over the last three years, to regain your spouse should come to nought."

"Rubbish, old man!" snapped Jorian. "My efforts have given me an infinitude of stories to tell. And without these attempts, I should never have known Margalit. So from adversity has come treasure."

"As to that, we shall judge ten years hence."

"No doubt; but I can't wait until we are all dead ere making up my mind. Let's to it."

Under Baron Lorc's directions, Jorian found some yellowing papers in the desk in the baron's cabinet.

With the ghost invisibly dictating, Jorian wrote legal phrases on them. He signed the first, and both he and Margalit signed the second. The problem was getting the baron to sign, since the ghost was not material enough to grasp Jorian's quill pen. At last, by concentrating his psychic force, the ghost made a small scorch mark on each of the sheets where his signature would have appeared. Jorian, Margalit, and Karadur signed their names around the blackened spots as witnesses to Baron Lorc's mark.

"Hail!" said the disembodied voice. "Now stand ye before me—"

"Where is that?" asked Jorian.

"Oh, pox! Anywhere will do. Stand side by side and clasp hands. Dost thou, Jorian. . . ."

The ceremony was soon over. The ghost said: "Now, sir and madam, I pray you to carry out your side of the bargain. Goodwife Margalit, thou shalt find a bucket in the kitchen, and the well still holdeth water. For a rag, thou must needs employ something from thine own possessions, for the looters have swept the castle clean of aught of that sort."

They made a rag by cutting a piece off the tail of Jorian's older shirt. Margalit got down on her knees and scrubbed. After a few moments, the invisible ghost said:

"That will suffice, my dear. The curse is lifted; I do perceive the walls of the castle fading from view.

"Oh, ere I depart, one small matter. The treasure hunters have poked and pried all over my poor castle. If ye covet the small hoard they sought but never found, pry out a stone to the right of the main fireplace: third course from the bottom, second stone from the left. 'Tis of no use to me. And now fare ye well! I am . . ." The voice faded to silence.

Jorian pried the stone loose, disclosing a hollow containing a bag of coin. When counted, the hoard came to ninety-nine Xylarian lions plus some small change.

"Ha!" said Jorian. "'Tis almost exactly the sum

wherewith I fled from Xylar the first time. 'Twill not
buy an army or a kingdom, but at least we shan't starve
for a while!"

Four days later, riding through broad farmland,
Jorian said: "We should reach the Othomaean border by
nightfall. We could get there sooner by hard driving,
but I like not the look of Filoman's leg."

They were seated beside the road, eating. Karadur
said: "Silence, I pray." His dark eyes took on a glassy,
faraway look.

Jorian whispered: "He is listening for some message
from the astral plane."

At last the old Mulvanian shook his head. "My son,"
he said, "my second sight informs me that we are
again pursued."

"How far? How many?"

Karadur shook his head. "I cannot say at the distance, save that they approach swiftly."

Jorian wolfed down his last mouthful. "Finish up, my
dears, and let us to horse—or to mule."

Soon they were again trotting along the road to
Othomae. An hour later, Karadur said: "I caught
another glimpse. I estimate them as not above two
leagues behind us."

"Jorian," said Margalit, "why do you not gallop on,
leaving us? We can turn into some side road and let
them go past. We must not slow your steed to a trot,
when you can reach the border safely ahead of them."

"And leave you to their mercies? Be not silly, wife!"
snorted Jorian. "Besides, this country is too open for
playing hide-and-seek with pursuers. They'd see you in
no time."

"Then," said Karadur, "why not mount Margalit on
the horse behind you and gallop on? I can drive the
cart, and if they stop me, I am but a poor fortune-
teller who knows naught of Xylar and its fugitive kings.

I can change my appearance by a small illusion spell. What ails that plan?"

"Two things," said Jorian, speeding up his trot while Margalit lashed Filoman to hasten the placid mule. "Imprimis, Margalit's weight would slow Cadwil almost as much as my staying with the cart. She's a big girl. Secundus, we have been seen together enough so that they'll be looking for you as well as me."

"Belike," said Margalit, "they would not punish us severely. Karadur and I could say you deceived us."

"Count not upon the Regency's mercies. At the least, you would likely spend most of your lives in dungeons dank. If anyone shall play fox to their hounds, 'tis I. Karadur is small and slight. You and he together weigh no more than I. You twain could gallop in tandem to the border, trusting me to dodge or cozen the puruers."

"Nay!" said Karadur. "My old bones are too brittle for such a dash. The mere thought of perching precariously atop your great destrier makes me dizzy."

"Well, we had better do something, and speedily," said Jorian. "Try your astral vision again."

Karadur closed his eyes. After a while he said: "They are less than a league behind us. I make ten or twelve."

Margalit: "Perchance they are not concerned with us."

Jorian shook his head. "They would not push their beasts so hard, save in flight or pursuit."

For several minutes they trotted as briskly as the pace of the cart allowed. As they topped a rise, Jorian called out: "Ha! I see woods! I remember now; when I was King, this tract was the subject of a lawsuit betwixt a syndicate of magnates, who wished to cut the timber, and the Xylarian Navy, who wished to preserve the forest for future ship timbers."

"How did you decide?" asked Margalit.

"Grallon decided for the Navy, and I supported him. It was a close thing. He might have ruled the other

way had not one of the magnates made the error of
trying to bribe him, as Abacarus did lately."

"What then? Mean you to hide in the forest?"

"Nay; the tract is not large enough. But—Karadur,
you have your magical rope, do you not?"

"Aye. But its magical charge is nearly exhausted.
After two or three more usages, it will require to be
ensorcelled again."

"Canst use it against our pursuers?"

"I can inflict a painful overthrow upon them, but
that will not necessarily slay them."

"I would not fain kill the poor fools, but I urgently
yearn to get my hands on their commander. Here is
what we shall do. . . ."

Half an hour later, the cart had been pulled well off
the road and concealed behind several saplings. Jorian
had cut these with his sword, trimmed them at the butt
end to points, and thrust them into the ground. Out of
sight behind the cart, the horse and the mule were
tethered.

Karadur unwound the rope from his waist and tossed
it so that it lay athwart the road. He muttered an incantation, and the two ends of the rope groped around
until they found tree trunks. These ends, like questing
serpents, then crept up the trunks and wound around
them. The bulk of the rope still lay limply, hardly visible, in the dust.

They waited for what seemed hours to Jorian but
was in fact less than half an hour. Then the squadron
of horse appeared on the road, coming at a tired gallop.
The panting horses were flecked with foam from hard
riding. Jorian suspected that some would never be good
cavalry mounts again; they had been used up.

On came the soldiers, in scarlet coats under their
mail shirts, the afternoon sun flashing from their silvered helmets. The lieutenant, distinguishable by the
little silver wings on his helm, rode in the lead.

"Now!" breathed Jorian.

Behind him, Karadur muttered another spell. At once the ends of the rope coiled around the tree trunks came to life, like serpents constricting their prey. The bulk of the rope rose from the dust to stand as a rigid horizontal bar at knee height.

The rope snapped into position just as the lieutenant's horse reached it, so the rider had no chance to jump his mount over this not very formidable barrier. The horse did a somersault, throwing the lieutenant ahead of him into the dirt. With a hideous clatter, the following horses piled up in a kicking heap.

Before any of the thrown soldiers had time to rise, Jorian leaped out from behind his tree and sprinted to where the lieutenant had fallen. As he arrived, the man was sitting up with a dazed look. One of the silver wings on his helmet was crumpled.

Jorian seized the lieutenant around the neck from behind and pressed his dagger against the young man's throat. "Order them back!" he roared, "or you're a dead man!"

Those soldiers who had regained their feet paused, taking in the situation. So did the three troopers who had pulled up their mounts in time to keep their saddles. Of the fallen soldiers, one lay still with his neck twisted; another was calling out something about a broken arm. Others nursed lesser injuries.

"Stand back!" wheezed the lieutenant. "Do nought to disturb this man!" He turned his head a little. "Are you King Jorian?"

"Never mind who I am. You shall come with me as hostage. Karadur!"

"Aye, my son?"

"Give your rope that other command."

Karadur muttered another spell. The rope came alive, snaking out from under a fallen horse and slithering to where Jorian held the lieutenant. The rope coiled around the captive's wrists and ankles. In a trice the lieutenant was tied as securely as a hog on the way to market.

"Order them to return to their quarters!" said Jorian. "And tell them that, the instant I see we are again pursued, away goes your tender young throat!"

The lieutenant repeated the command. The soldiers gathered in a group, arguing in low, tense tones. Jorian guessed that they were debating whether to ignore the officer's orders, as given under duress, and try to seize Jorian anyway. Jorian suspected that he had some sympathizers, who would be glad to see him escape.

At last the soldiers mounted and rode off, the dead man draped across his saddle and another with his arm in a sling.

"I regret that young man's death," said Jorian. "One would think you people would learn that seeking to lay violent hands on me entails risks."

"I do my duty," rasped the lieutenant between set teeth.

Margalit led Jorian's horse from the woods, and Karadur followed with the mule and cart. Jorian boosted Lieutenant Annyx, whose horse had gone off with the rest of the troop, into the cart. Margalit said:

"Jorian, do you go through life taking hostages? In the short time I've known you, you have done it thrice already."

Jorian shrugged. "Only when I must. Forsooth, I never took them ere meeting you; that is just how events have fallen out."

The sun was a crimson ball on the horizon when Jorian came in sight of the fence marking the border between Xylar and Othomae. A Xylarian border guard was closing the gate on the Xylarian side but opened it again as Jorian and his party appeared. The guards gave them a bored, perfunctory glance, not inspecting the cart, wherein Lieutenant Annyx lay bound, gagged, and covered by a blanket. The horse and mule proceeded into the neutral strip, three or four fathoms wide, between the two nations. At the far end of this strip stood another fence and gate.

In the neutral strip, Jorian halted, reached into the cart, and hauled out Lieutenant Annyx. "Turn him loose," he told Karadur.

The Mulvanian incanted; the rope fell limply to the ground. Karadur gathered it up and wound it around his waist.

Annyx arose with murder in his eyes and tore the gag loose. As Jorian led his horse to the second gate, the lieutenant shouted:

"Seize that man! He is wanted in Xylar! He is a violent criminal, a kidnapper, a fugitive from justice!"

The officer of the border watch on the Othomaean side said: "Send us a formal request for extradition, laddie, and we'll see what we can do."

The lieutenant looked as if he could cry. "You damned Othomaeans never do aught we ask, no matter how reasonable! This is a flagrant case of hot pursuit, so I am entitled to demand your aid in apprehending him!"

The Othomaean grinned. "That's the first time I ever heard a man who has been carried hog-tied in a cart claim he was in hot pursuit of anyone." He turned to Jorian. "And you, my fine oriental friend, what is your business in the Grand Duchy?"

Pulling Annyx's sword and dagger out of the cart, Jorian tossed them back into the neutral zone. He got out his papers. "Here you are, sir: permit for a foreigner to reside in Othomae; permit to wear a sword; permit to hunt and fish. As for the costume, I had business in Xylar and wished to do it without losing my head."

"Jorian of Ardamai!" exclaimed the guard. "We hear fantastic tales of you. Is it true that you slew a unicorn in the Grand Duke's park with your bare hands?"

"Not quite," said Jorian. "If I remember—"

Lieutenant Annyx had picked up his weapons. He shouted: "I demand—"

"Oh, shut thy gob!" said the Othomaean officer. "This man is well known in Othomae and, from all I hear, is entitled to political asylum. Now go away like a good boy and cease to pester us."

"You shall hear more of this!" said Annyx, turning back to the Xylarian side.

"The first inn," said Jorian, "is a league or so down the road. May we be on our way, to reach it ere dark?"

Two years later, a small party appeared at the entrance to Evor's Sons, Clock-Makers, in Kortoli City. A foppishly dressed young man asked if Jorian were in. Sillius, the senior man of the firm, said:

"My brother is in but busy. May I have your name and business?"

"I am Corineus son of Holdar, and I bring a message from the Provisional Government of Xylard."

Sillius's eyebrows rose. "Wait, good my sir," he said, and disappeared. Soon he returned, saying: "I will show you the way in."

Corineus found himself in a large room used as a workshop. Tables were littered with tools and with sheets of paper bearing diagrams and sketches. In a chair at one end sat a tall, handsome woman nursing a year-old baby. At the other, Jorian, wearing a workman's leather apron over his clothes, puttered with a device of gears and levers.

It took Corineus a few heartbeats to recognize Jorian. When they met in Xylar, Jorian was clean-shaven and turbaned, with a dark-brown skin. Now he was light-skinned, bare-headed, and bearded. Corineus noted that he had put on weight, and that his black hair had receded a little.

"Your Majesty!" cried Corineus at last.

Jorian looked up. "By Imbal's iron yard!" he cried.

"What brings you hither, Corineus? If you think to kidnap me back to Xylar to cut off my head again, forget it. I have taken measures."

"Nay, nought like that," said Corineus. "We have had a revolution and abolished the Regency Council, along with the custom of lustral regicide. We have a new constitution, with a king of limited powers and an elective legislature. And we want you for King!"

"Well, dip me in manure!" After a pause, Jorian smiled. "Tell them I thank them, but nay. I have all I wish right here." He glanced toward Margalit, who smiled back. "Tell them to find some other popinjay, intelligent enough to follow public rituals but not so clever as to plot to seize absolute power."

"But King Jorian! My liege lord!" pleaded Corineus, sinking to one knee. "You are famous! You have become our national hero! The tale of your adventures—slaying the dragon single-handed, overthrowing the Goblin Tower, routing the besiegers of Iraz—is worth an epic by Physo!"

"I see the tales have not shrunk in the telling. Get some poet to make a lay, then, and send me a copy. 'Twere good for business."

"Business!" said Corineus in tones of disgust. "After all your splendid adventures, do you not find a mere tradesman's life dull?"

Jorian laughed. "Not at all, my dear fellow. As you once said, I am a tradesman at heart. We prosper. I have the respect of my workfellows, the love of my dear ones, plenty to eat and drink, and money at usury with my banker. My wife, by doing the bookkeeping, keeps us solvent.

"Furthermore I am engaged in a problem more fascinating to me than how far one must run to tire out a pursuing dragon."

"What's that?"

"To make an accurate clock powered by falling weights instead of falling water. I saw them working on such in Iraz. My little brother Kerin has gone to the Far East to learn the secret of their superior escapement."

Corineus shook his head. "I cannot imagine how one who has survived all your knightly adventures could settle down to so drab a life."

Jorian: "Since I survived those adventures by the skin of my teeth, they make fine fireside talk. But I sought them not; the goddess Elidora forced them upon me. Whilst they were going on, I should have been heartily glad to be elsewhere. Meseems that when one has had as many narrow escapes as have been crowded into the first half of my life, one is happy to spend the second half in a safe, peaceful, humdrum pursuit. At least, that's how I feel."

"Do the honor and glory of the kingship, without the hazard of execution, not beguile you?"

Jorian shook his head. "Had I never experienced it, it might. But for five years I had my fill of donning ornate costumes, and sitting through tedious ceremonies, and hearing the lying arguments of litigants and petitioners, and trying to collect enough taxes to keep the kingdom going without inciting a revolt. So tell your people I am flattered but firm in my refusal."

"But think of all the good you could accomplish!"

Jorian smiled. "That's the excuse every tyrant gives in snatching at total power. But from what I've seen of the world, plans to better the lot of the people seldom turn out as the planners hope, even with the best intentions."

"Will nought persuade you?"

"Nought whatever. Your legislature will have to muddle along without my wisdom."

Corineus stared at the ground. "I—I ought to thank you—I made a bit of an ass of myself on our first meeting. You—you had been justified in slaying me. . . ."

Jorian grinned. "Forget the whole episode. When I

was ten years younger, I did silly things, too. But let me ask you: How did you, an admirer of the old feudal regime, get involved in a popular revolutionary movement?"

Corineus looked embarrassed. "Forsooth, Estrildis talked me into it. She said 'twas the only way our marriage would ever be fully recognized as legal in Xylar. She can be very persuasive."

"I know," said Jorian. "How is she?"

"Fine, and so is the boy. She is getting—well; a trifle plump."

"Give her my brotherly love."

"Where is the old Mulvanian?"

"Karadur is a professor in Othomae, having compassed the ouster of his predecessor Abacarus. I had something—" Jorian was about to say "to do with that," but thought better of it. "He wants me to teach an engineering course at the Academy. What befell that clerk, Thevatas?"

"He was hanged."

"Indeed? My grief overwhelms me not. How fell it?"

"The Regency offered a generous reward for recovering the crown, but he held out for a seat on the Council. Believe it or not, he lusted to command the army. Losing patience, they feigned to agree and then, as soon as they had the royal headpiece, hustled him off to the scaffold with hardly a pretense of legal process."

"So perish overreachers!" said Jorian. "Now join me in a glass of wine, and then be off to tell the Xylarians what I have said. When one has been to as many places, and worked at as many trades, and suffered through as many vicissitudes as I have, if he have learnt nought else, he should at least know when he is well off!"

# HARRY TURTLEDOVE:
## A MIND FOR ALL SEASONS

### EPIC FANTASY

*Werenight* (72209-3 ♦ $4.99) ☐
*Prince of the North* (87606-6 ♦ $5.99) ☐
In the Northlands rules Gerin the Fox. Quaintly, he intends
to rule for the welfare and betterment of his people—but
first he must defeat the gathering forces of chaos, which conspire to tumble his work into a very dark age indeed....

### ALTERNATE FANTASY

*The Case of the Toxic Spell Dump* (72196-8 ♦ $5.99) ☐
Inspector Fisher's world is just a *little* bit different from
ours...Stopping an ancient deity from reinstating human sacrifice in L.A. and destroying Western Civilization is all in a day's
work for David Fisher of the Environmental *Perfection* Agency.

### ALTERNATE HISTORY

*Agent of Byzantium* (87593-0 ♦ $4.99) ☐
In an alternate universe where the Byzantine Empire never fell,
Basil Agyros, the 007 of his spacetime, has his hands full thwarting
un-Byzantine plots and making the world safe for Byzantium.
"Engrossing, entertaining and very cleverly rendered...I recom-
mend it without reservation."            —Roger Zelazny

*A Different Flesh* (87622-8 ♦ $4.99) ☐
An extraordinary novel of an alternate America. "When
Columbus came to the New World, he found, not Indians, but
primitive ape-men.... Unable to learn human speech...[the ape-
men] could still be trained to do reliable work. Could still, in
other words, be made slaves.... After 50 years of science fiction,
Harry Turtledove proves you can come up with something
fresh and original."            —Orson Scott Card

---